# the Warlock's trial

COLLEGE OF WITCHCRAFT BOOK FIVE

## ALICIA RADES

A special thank-you to sensitivity reader Kris Riley of Blissful Services, who is a member of the Cherokee tribe, for her invaluable feedback on smudging and its significance in indigenous culture.

This book features characters with the following medical conditions. The information included is meant to educate readers on disabilities featured within the College of Witchcraft series.

### HEARING LOSS

In the United States, approximately 48 million people are affected by hearing loss. Hearing loss can be caused by a number of factors, including genetics, infections, drugs, and aging. Individuals with hearing loss may use hearing aids or cochlear implants, and may communicate with American Sign Language, or ASL. ASL is a unique language that uses hand gestures to communicate. ASL has its own rules for grammar and syntax, and does not follow the same rules as English. However, all conversations in ASL in this series have been translated to English for ease of reading.

# ONE

T'd rather be in hell right now than stare at this damn whiteboard any longer.

My eyes roamed over the information I'd been compiling for three months. All kinds of clues had been tacked up and connected by strings. The longer I looked at it, the less it made any sense.

I eyed the drawings of the Oaken Wands, along with other clues we'd replicated from memory. Journal entries from Helena's diaries had been ripped out and tacked alongside the photos. We thought we'd find clues that her late husband had left behind, but Nicholas hadn't told her where he'd hidden the Wands. His journal was long gone, so we had nothing to go off of.

My vision blurred the longer I stared. I couldn't remember the last time I slept.

"It was the butler," Nadine muttered. "It's always the butler."

"Huh?" I whirled toward her. She'd been quiet for so long, I'd forgotten she was there.

Nadine sat at a table in the sunroom we'd commandeered for our research purposes. A thick layer of clouds blanketed the September sky, and raindrops trickled down the windows around us. She set aside the thick binder she'd been flipping through, then hit *pause* on the phone in front of her.

"I said the butler did it," she repeated. "Are you listening to the podcast?"

I'd totally forgotten it'd been playing. Nadine had started listening to true crime podcasts a week after our friends left to investigate the Oaken Wands. I'd portaled them to different supernatural societies in order to help us gather clues. They reported back twice a month, but so far, no one had learned anything useful. Even though Helena and our cats stayed at the safe house with us, it could get boring and lonely sometimes. There was only so much Oaken Wand research we could do when we were stuck here. Nadine thought true crime podcasts would help us pass the time, and we'd both gotten really into it. We tried to solve the mysteries together, and it was a lot of fun.

Today, though, I couldn't focus on any mystery that wasn't our own.

"Sorry, I wasn't listening," I said. "I'm trying to find answers before everyone else shows up. I'm portaling them for check-in today. We've got to give them *something*."

Nadine sighed. "I know this is hard, Lucas, but we can tell them the truth."

"The truth is that we're no closer to finding the Oaken Wands than we were three months ago."

"We're *getting* closer," she insisted. "Grant and Talia have made allies in Malovia. They're meeting with their contact as we speak. This contact might know a way inside the Abyss. We're so close to finding an entrance, so that we can find the Mentalist Wand that we lost through the demon's portal."

Hence my point—I'd rather be in hell right now. At least then we'd be closer to the Mentalist Wand. We'd decided three months ago that we'd walk through hell for that Wand. Without it, the other four were useless to us. We needed all five Oaken Wands to end the Waning and win our fight against the priestesses' tyrannical rule.

"*I'm* not any closer to making Abyss portals, though," I pointed out. "If I could make portals to the Abyss like I *should*, we wouldn't have to send Grant and Talia to a warring fae nation who places every witch they come across at the end of a noose. Malovia is in the middle of a civil war. They've got two monarchs competing for the throne. It's dangerous enough as it is for their own people, let alone witches and warlocks. Don't forget what they did to Kenna and her family a few months ago."

Kenna and her parents hadn't even *been* in Malovia when they were captured and hanged. They'd been visiting Paris, and the fae took it as a threat because they were too close to the country's border. I didn't want to think about what would happen to Grant and Talia if the fae found them *inside* their borders. Their sentence would be far worse than hanging, for sure.

"Grant and Talia know the risks," Nadine reminded me, though she sounded worried.

I raked my fingers through my hair. It felt pretty grimy, and I realized I couldn't remember the last time I showered, either. This research had practically consumed me. "I just thought we'd have answers by now."

"You should sit down," Nadine suggested. "The last time you were standing this long, your leg started giving you trouble."

My broken leg had healed, but it still twinged painfully if I was on my feet forever. Still, I couldn't sit down right now, even if I wanted to. I was too on edge.

I began pacing instead. "I don't want to sit down, Nad. I want answers."

"Have you ever considered that maybe that's not your job?" she asked calmly. "Our friends are out there getting answers. Our job is to be a safe place for them to come back to."

I gritted my teeth and pointed to the stacks of textbooks on the table in front of her. "Our *job* is to do our research and draw connections. And I feel like a fucking idiot because I can't see how it all connects!"

"It may be simpler than we think," Nadine pointed out. "Perhaps it isn't this big puzzle that needs solving but just breadcrumbs to follow."

I turned back to the whiteboard and tapped my chin as I surveyed the information we had. "All right... breadcrumbs. Where do we go from here?"

The room went silent, and I was starting to get really freaking pissed. What did I expect? For the whiteboard to answer back?

"Maybe a new perspective will help..." I mused. The whiteboard hung off a frame on wheels, so I spun it ninety degrees. It probably looked like I was crazy, but it was the only thing I hadn't tried yet.

My gaze darted from one string to the next. My eyes began to cross, and it felt like I was looking at the board from under water. Even the sound of raindrops on the window became distant. My hands curled into fists, and my whole body shook in frustration. I shoved my hands into my hair and yanked on the strands. This was fucking pointless. I'd been studying this board for months, and none of it made a damn bit of sense. Three months caught up to me in a single moment, and I snapped.

"These breadcrumbs are useless!" I screamed as I grabbed the strings and yanked them off the board. Papers went flying across the room, and one of the strings tangled around my finger. I grabbed the corners of the whiteboard and threw it at the wall, which was a feat in itself, because the thing was huge. Pain sliced across my hand. The whiteboard hit the wall, then bounced back toward me. It landed on my head pretty dang hard, and I collapsed onto the ground, pinned beneath the massive whiteboard. A piece of paper landed in my mouth, and I sputtered, but it went nowhere.

Nadine rushed to my side and helped lift the whiteboard back onto its wheels. "Lucas, are you okay?"

Truth was, I'd hurt my pride more than anything. I huffed as I got to my feet and spat the paper out of my mouth. "I'm fine," I grumbled.

Nadine placed her hands on her hips. "That was a bit dramatic."

I crossed my arms but didn't meet her gaze as I mumbled, "These breadcrumbs are dry and stale anyway. They taste awful."

Nadine stared at me for a few seconds, before a smile crept across her face. She burst into laughter. I froze, until I looked down at the papers at my feet and began laughing along with her.

It wasn't funny. Not in the slightest. But it was better than the alternative—and that involved wallowing in my own self-pity because I'd somehow tied my worth to solving this mystery. I'd get an earful from Nadine and Helena both, because neither of them were going to stand for my bullshit anymore. They heard enough of it last June. I tried my best to find the joy where I could, and that was pretty damn difficult today. So when Nadine laughed, I allowed myself to laugh along with her.

"Come sit down," she said between laughs. She led me over to a chair, then leaned down to inspect the cut on my hand. It throbbed, but I didn't really give a fuck. Nadine gasped.

"What?" I asked, sitting up straighter.

"You broke a nail!" she said dramatically. She was trying to lighten the mood.

I scowled. "What a tragedy—oh, wow. That's not good."

Nadine stretched my skin a little, and I saw that the cut was deeper than I thought. The corner of the whiteboard had sliced across my whole palm. Blood began pooling in my hand.

Her voice turned serious. "Stay here. I'll get a first-aid kit."

She left me in silence, and I glanced around the room. Papers were scattered everywhere, and the string lay in a tangled mess on the floor. This was going to be a bitch to put back in order.

I got up and knelt beside the closest pile of papers, trying hard not to drip blood everywhere. I started gathering our clues and stacking them together with my good hand.

"Lucas." Nadine stopped me when she returned. "Your clues aren't going anywhere."

She was clearly annoyed by how consumed I'd become with this. I sighed and sat down again. She took my hand and gently wiped the blood away, inspecting it closely. "You're not going to need stitches, but I need to get it cleaned up. Hold still."

Nadine positioned a towel on the table, then placed my hand palm-up on top of it. She poured hydrogen peroxide over the cut, and damn, that stung like a son of a bitch.

She cleaned out the wound, then gently wrapped gauze around my hand. I couldn't help but let my eyes roam over her as her fingers moved over mine softly.

She caught me staring and turned a deep shade of pink. "What is it?"

"You," I said simply. "You're so nice to me."

"That could be because I'm madly in love with you," she teased. She taped the gauze, then placed a gentle kiss on my hand. "All better."

"Thanks," I told her, before drawing her in for a kiss.

After she cleaned up, Nadine plopped herself in front of her thick binder again. "Do you prefer pumpkin spice or apple cider?"

That was an odd question, but I thought she was trying to distract me. "Um… apple cider, I guess."

She scrunched up her nose. "You *guess*? Are you sure?"

I shrugged. "If I was given the choice, I'd choose apple cider. Pumpkin spice isn't a real thing."

Nadine gasped dramatically, like I'd thoroughly offended her. "It is!

How can you not love the impeccable blend of cinnamon and nutmeg and ginger and cloves!?"

"Is that all?" I teased flatly.

"And sometimes allspice," she added proudly.

"It's fine, but have you ever had fresh apple cider straight from the orchard?" I asked.

"Yes. You took me last fall."

"Right, and it was fantastic, wasn't it?"

"Yeah, it was good, but…"

"But you want me to say pumpkin spice," I finished for her.

"No," she answered quickly. "I want your *honest* opinion."

"My honest opinion is apple cider. What's this about?"

Nadine propped up the binder for me to see. She'd pasted all kinds of photos of various cakes and recipes inside. She wore a goofy grin and exclaimed, "It's for our wedding cake!"

I furrowed my brow. "How'd we get from apple cider and pumpkin spice to cake?"

"I'm trying to decide our flavor."

"Apple cider isn't a flavor," I said. "It's its own thing. It's a drink."

"No, but like… you make an apple cake with cream cheese and cinnamon frosting. It's a whole thing. But then there's the pumpkin one, and I was leaning toward that."

"Then go with pumpkin," I offered.

Her shoulders sagged. "But it's *your* wedding, too. I want to make these decisions together."

I reached across the table and took her hand in mind. My fingers trailed over her engagement ring. "As long as I'm married to you by the end of it, I don't care about the details."

I tugged on her arm, and she came around the table to sit on my lap. I curled my arms around her middle and pulled her close to me. I inhaled the rose scent of her hair, which always made my head spin. My fingers trailed down her body.

Nadine wiggled her hips. "Mm… right here?"

I kissed the back of her neck. "I get excited when I think about marrying you. In just a few short weeks, you'll be my wife."

Nadine turned around, until she was straddling me. "October thirty-first can't come soon enough," she whispered, before pressing her lips to mine.

I leaned back in my chair and ran my hands over her backside as she began kissing me. The stress of the whiteboard completely fell from my mind as desire for my fiancé consumed me. Nadine reached down for the button on my jeans…

"*Eh hem.*" Someone cleared their throat in the doorway, and Nadine jumped.

My shoulders slumped. Not again.

I loved Helena as if she was my own grandmother, but god damn it. This woman was always *right there* whenever Nadine and I were about to get it on. Hell, Nadine and I were about to fool around in the master bath the other night. As soon as we filled the jet tub, Helena knocked and wanted to *clean.* Nadine had gotten rid of her, thank the goddess, but it'd really put a damper on the mood.

"I made tea!" Helena said brightly as she came into the room carrying a tray. Isa, Oliver, and Cornelius followed along at her feet, meowing like they were waiting for treats. Helena stopped in her tracks and eyed the mess. "Oh, my."

She set down her tray, then went to start cleaning up the papers.

"That's not necessary," I told her quickly. "I'll get it."

Helena hesitated, like it physically pained her to witness a mess without cleaning it up. I swear, all she'd done in the last three months was clean and cook. She wasn't faring well with the cabin fever any better than we were.

Helena cleared her throat. "You should have some applesauce. It turned out perfect."

Nadine and I had gotten really bored here at the safe house, so we gardened over the summer, then canned fruits and vegetables with Helena whenever we needed a break. Helena had found stacks of empty jars in the basement our first week here and suggested we use them, and we just… never stopped. She'd planted all kinds of vegetables around the property, and we'd found a handful of apple and pear trees near the house we'd been harvesting. I didn't know how many batches of applesauce we'd made, but we'd started storing food in the basement because the pantry was too full. We certainly weren't going hungry anytime soon.

Nadine climbed off of me and returned to her seat. "Thanks, Grammy."

I tried the applesauce, and all kinds of flavors burst in my mouth. "This is our best batch yet. What'd we do differently?"

Nadine snickered. "I snuck in a pumpkin spice blend."

I frowned. "You're trying to convert me."

"I am not!" she insisted with a giggle.

At Helena's feet, the cats continued to yowl.

"All right, all right," she said impatiently. "But only one for each of you."

Helena reached into the pocket of her apron and tossed three cat treats on the ground. Isa gobbled hers gone, then shoved Oliver out of the way and ate his, too. Oliver just licked her ears, like he didn't care. What a doormat.

Helena turned back to us. "I brought something for you two as well. Picked it up on my last supply run."

She reached into her apron and set several large boxes on the table. All I saw was the big bold letters reading *Value Pack!* Then I realized in horror what it was.

"Condoms!" Nadine gasped. "Grammy, what makes you think we need that many? Wait... how much sex were you having when you were our age?"

Helena scowled. All it took was one sharp look to know she wasn't about to answer that question. For someone who walked in on us every freaking time we tried to get it on, she seemed pretty encouraging of our physical relationship. I must've turned the brightest shade of red.

"They're not just for you," Helena said. "Your friends are coming back today. We all know Chloe and Miles will need a whole pack to themselves. I want *everyone* to be safe."

I laughed. "You're not wrong."

"Now finish up," Helena pressed. "You're scheduled to portal everyone in soon."

Helena left the room, and Nadine and I quickly finished our tea before heading out into the living room. The room was large, with a ceiling that reached two stories and a balcony from the second level. A sectional sofa faced the fireplace, along with a large TV mounted above the mantle.

Helena was already sitting on the couch, and the cats surrounded her, purring in her lap.

"Are we ready?" Helena asked.

I checked the clock on the wall, then nodded. "Ready."

I lifted my hands, and magic surged down my arms as a portal bloomed in front of me. It was like a hole had been punched straight through reality. The fireplace was replaced with the image of a forest lit by the rising sun. A warm breeze rustled my hair, and it smelled like pine trees. A couple holding hands stepped through the portal. Their cats followed, and they hopped onto the couch beside the others, looking excited to see them. I closed the portal behind them.

"Chloe. Miles," I said, nodding to them. "How's life in *Hok'evale?*"

"It's a lovely town," Miles said. "Last week, we rode a dragon!"

My face fell. His enthusiasm really rubbed me the wrong way. "This isn't a theme park, Miles. You're supposed to be out there hunting down clues for the Oaken Wands, or did you forget about that while you were on *vacation?*"

Chloe's jaw dropped. "Whoa! *Someone's* in a mood. It's better to be on vacation than to hang out here, where you're either moping around or hounding us for answers."

"That's not all I do," I shot back. "We canned a batch of pears yesterday."

Chloe scoffed. "Forgive me if I'd rather be sipping mimosas on the beach."

"*Mimosas on the beach—*" I nearly choked on the words. "Dear Goddess, we're never going to find answers."

"Actually, the mimosas paid off," Chloe said proudly.

"Yeah, I'm sure the afterparty was a blast," I replied flatly. "Hopefully someone else found something."

I turned, then lifted my hands again, forming another portal. The air was cold, and I smelled a fresh sea breeze. A girl with purple hair stepped through the portal, along with her cat.

"Welcome back, Onyx," I said. "Learn anything from the merfolk?"

"Let's bring everyone back before we start sharing our discoveries," Miles pressed, sounding annoyed. Clearly, I was a bit too harsh.

A light dusting of snow had covered the ground when I portaled Verla through from the Midnighter's society. The vampires were spread all over the world, but Verla had been trying to get information from a group in Canada. The headmistress shivered when she stepped through the portal.

"Come," Helena said quickly. "I made tea."

"That's so kind of you," Verla said as Helena ushered her to the kitchen.

I couldn't see what Celestial City looked like when I portaled Professor Warren back to the safe house. He was holed up in a nice hotel room, with white sheets and a golden bed frame. He seemed the coziest out of everyone. The angels weren't the nicest supernatural race on the planet, but they'd pretty much do anything for you as long as they thought they could convert you to their religion, and Professor Warren was good at placating people.

"Good to see you, Lucas," he said kindly.

I nodded back, then turned to Nadine. "Nad, I'll need your help with this one."

She stood at my side, and we combined our powers together to create a portal. It wasn't easy, because we were fighting against wards to get inside the fae's borders, but we managed. A forest appeared in front of us, but it was different from the last. The coniferous trees were smaller here, and it smelled of damp mountain air. The sky was overcast, and the ground was wet, as if it had just rained. Wind whistled through the portal, but everything else was silent. I didn't see Grant or Talia anywhere.

I hesitated. "They're supposed to be at the meeting point."

"Give it a minute." Nadine's voice trembled. "They should be on their way."

I held my breath, waiting to hear the sound of their footsteps through the mud. But there was nothing.

"Something's wrong!" I insisted. "Grant and Talia have never missed a portal."

"Are we sure about the coordinates?" Chloe asked. "This doesn't look like where we've picked them up before."

"I'm certain," I stated. "Grant and Talia were meeting with a contact inside Malovia's borders earlier today. We moved the meeting point so they didn't have as far to travel."

"Maybe they got lost?" Onyx suggested.

Miles crossed his arms. "Or they were betrayed. We shouldn't have trusted the fae!"

The portal faltered around the edges, and my hands shook as I tried to steady it. "I can't hold it much longer."

"We have to go after them!" Nadine decided immediately. She ran toward the front door and grabbed our shoes and coats. She tossed mine at my feet, then slid hers on.

"You can't go alone," Professor Warren protested.

"The fewer witches we bring to Malovia, the better," Nadine said. "We don't want to draw attention, and Lucas and I can get in and out using portals. We'll be back soon. I promise."

Helena and Verla heard the commotion, and they raced into the living room. "What do you think you're—?" Helena started, but I didn't hear the end of it. I grabbed Nadine's hand, and we leapt through the portal together.

My stomach dropped from my abdomen, and my body seemed to stretch and distort as we tumbled through the portal. We landed firmly on our feet on the other side, still holding hands. The air was chill and damp, and a shiver traveled down my spine as I glanced around. We stood on the side of a mountain, but we couldn't see much through the pine forest except the darkened clouds covering the afternoon sky.

"We've got to find a vantage point," Nadine said, tugging on my arm.

We traipsed through the forest, our feet squishing through the mud. The trees broke ahead, and when we stepped out of them, my stomach turned to a rock in my belly. Nadine drew a sharp gasp.

We stood on the highest point of a hill, looking out over a large battlefield. The battle had already been lost, judging by the bodies strewn across the muddy landscape. There had to be at least a hundred fae shifters and sorceresses lying down there. Fresh blood seeped into the ground as wolf, dragon, alicorn, and griffin shifters lay still beside their mates, who'd perished trying to save them.

Below us, a makeshift camp had been set up with large tents. Someone cried out in agony, their voice carrying up the hillside. On the other side of the battlefield, far out in the distance, we could make out the shadows of a small town.

Nadine covered her mouth. "What happened here? You don't think Grant and Talia got caught up in it? The fae are known for taking hostages!"

I shook my head. I refused to believe that unless I saw it with my own eyes. "No. They wouldn't involve themselves in fae affairs. Though this could certainly be why they were held up."

Nadine's eyes glistened. "So how do we find them?"

"We're here!" a ragged voice came from behind us.

We turned to see two figures climbing the hill. They wore large backpacks and were covered in mud from head to toe.

"Talia! Grant!" Nadine cried. She rushed over to them and threw her arms around them, not caring about the mud. "Thank the Goddess you're okay."

Grant blew a breath. "No kidding. We were nearly ambushed, but we managed to slip into the trees until the battle was over. The fae king attempted to take the city of Pruska, which you can see over there, because the rival queen captured it for herself. He ended up losing, though, and it's pretty clear his forces were demolished."

He sounded really winded, and Talia hadn't said a thing. They were both in pretty rough shape. They must've been on their feet for days.

"Are you alone?" I asked. "Where's your contact? Don't tell me he led you into this battle on purpose!"

"No," Talia promised. "Oakley never showed up. He was a member of the king's army, and…"

Grant dropped his gaze. "He fought in the battle. He didn't make it."

My stomach clenched. "He was supposed to show us the way into the Abyss! We don't have time to scour Malovia for entrances. We'll never find an opening on our own."

Grant scowled. "I'm sorry our friend was too preoccupied with *dying* to show us the way to hell!"

My shoulders fell. "I'm sorry, Grant. I didn't mean it like that."

"We've been gone for three months," Grant reminded me. "Forgive us for making friends while we were away. *You* might not trust the fae, but Oakley was one of the good ones. He was fighting with the king's army to end persecution of dark magic wielders in Malovia. He sympathized with us and really wanted to help. I just… can't believe he's gone."

The hill went quiet for a few beats, before Nadine broke the silence. "If the king's army is sympathetic to dark magic users, then maybe we can go straight to the king himself."

Talia scoffed. "There's the kicker. You'll never believe who's on the throne. Remember those fae you helped last year, the one who needed

Hattie to help them out with a demon problem? You said their names were Ethan and Emma."

I nodded. "Yeah, that's them."

"Ethan's the king now," Talia said. "Emma's his queen."

Excitement rushed through me. "This is great!" I cried. "They owe us a debt for helping them. We can go to them and—"

Grant held up a hand. "Not so fast. We've tried to get in contact with the king and queen, but we can't touch them. Even Oakley couldn't get a message. They're guarded more than ever, with the state of the Malovian Revolution. And I don't blame them."

Grant gestured out over the remnants of the battlefield.

Movement caught my eye in the camp below. A man and a woman stepped out of a tent, surrounded by uniformed men. Whoever they were, they looked important. The woman turned, and her red hair flowed around her. It hit me then that I recognized her.

"That's Ethan and Emma!" I realized. "We can talk to them!"

I was already on the move, but Grant grabbed my arm. "Lucas, we can't. Look at their security detail."

"Emma will recognize us," I insisted. "We helped save her mate."

"Emma and Ethan will want to help us, but the rest of those soldiers will kill us on sight for being witches," Grant pointed out. "You can't just waltz up to royalty and expect a meeting. We'll never get close enough before their guards kill us first. They just lost a battle. They're not going to ask questions."

Fuck, he was right. We were so close, but they were untouchable.

"All right," I said reluctantly. "Let's get moving."

My friends and I hurried into the trees, where we couldn't be seen, and Nadine helped me form a portal strong enough to hold against Malovia's wards. Shouts came through the portal, and we hurried through as quickly as we could.

The shouting stopped abruptly as the portal slammed shut behind us. "Thank the goddess!" Helena cried.

"We're fine," Nadine assured her. "Grant and Talia… are alive."

Talia shivered a little. "We're just glad to be back."

"What *happened* to you?" Verla demanded, eyeing their dirty clothes.

"We, um, got a front row seat to the Malovian Revolution," Grant admitted.

"You're not going back," Verla insisted. "This is too dangerous!"

Grant sighed. "Well, our luck has run out anyway. Our fae contact is dead. We're not finding a portal to the Abyss anytime soon."

"Good," Helena said firmly. She'd never been a big fan of us walking through hell to retrieve an Oaken Wand, but it wasn't like we had any choice. We couldn't exactly send someone else after it. All eyes turned to her, and she quickly added, "I mean, it's good that you're alive. You're safe now. Let's get you a warm bath and a hot meal."

Helena took their backpacks and helped them to their rooms.

"What are we going to do now?" Onyx asked. "Malovia is the only place we know of with portals to the Abyss. It's our only way to get to the Mentalist Wand."

"Technically, not the *only* way," Nadine pointed out.

I scowled. "You're *not* talking about making a demon deal. That's worse than going in alone."

There were all kinds of reasons that was true. Demons could turn on you or trick you into faulty contracts. For a task this big, they'd want something major in return, something none of us were willing to give up. The last demon we'd dealt with had killed dozens of people before we were able to kill him, and it hadn't been easy. I wasn't putting my friends in danger by entering into a demon deal.

"If we can't find another way in, we may have to consider it as a last resort," Nadine said.

"You have no idea the cost you'd have to pay!" Verla protested. "You can't, Nadine."

"I don't *want* to," Nadine replied. "I'm only saying it's an option, even if it's a bad one."

"It's off the table," I stated. "If I have to kill myself making Abyss portals, that's better than working with a demon."

"There has to be a way to get the Wands without people dying," Professor Warren demanded. "No one's making deals with demons."

"Perhaps we should focus more on the other two Wands," Verla suggested. "Let's take some time to think about pursuing the Mentalist Wand. We can't afford any mistakes."

"We may be closer than you think," Chloe stated.

Everyone turned to look at her. She stood with her arms crossed and lips pursed.

"What do you mean?" Nadine asked.

Chloe drew herself upright. "As I was *trying* to say before, our mimosas paid off. Miles and I had a drink with someone we deem to be a credible source… and we learned something big."

My heart leapt. "How big?"

Miles hesitated, like he wasn't sure where to start. Finally, he sighed and said, "You need to come with us. This could change everything."

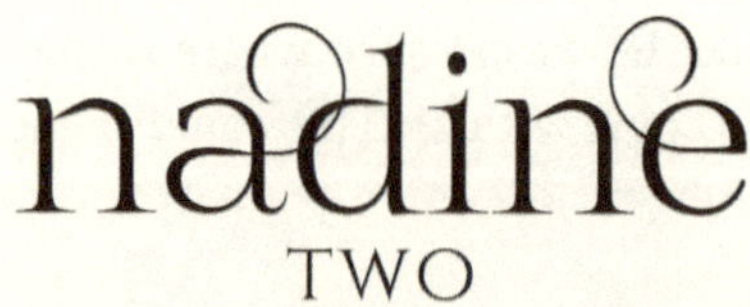

TWO

Excitement rushed through me at the possibility of finding another Oaken Wand. We hadn't made progress in three months, and now it sounded like we were close to a breakthrough. We'd already found several Oaken Wands, but they'd fallen through our grasp each time. We weren't going to let that happen again.

We knew the priestesses had possession of the Seer and Alchemy Wands. We'd obtained the Alchemy Wand from the Crock of Death, and I'd given it up to save my friends. Last semester, we found the Seer Wand in a pocket universe within the Vanishing Stairwell, and the priestesses had forced us to give it up in exchange for my kidney transplant. Then we witnessed the Mentalist Wand fall into the pit to the Abyss when we fought the demon, Professor Leto. We hadn't found any leads on the Mortana or the Curse Breaker Wands yet, but it sounded like this could be it.

Obtaining all the Wands before the priestesses was imperative to stop them from gaining control over the coven's magic. Once we had the Wands, we could work to heal the coven and bring an end to the Waning.

"Tell us everything," I insisted.

"It will be easier if you speak to our source directly," Chloe said.

"Who exactly *is* your source?" Lucas asked.

"He's a wandmaker named Beau Blankard," Miles stated.

"You met Beau?" Grammy cut in, sounding shocked.

"Yeah. You know him?" Miles asked.

"Beau and I were friends when we were young," Grammy said. "He's half-witch, half-fae."

I didn't know much about the fae, but I knew they hated the witches. We'd been on opposite sides in the Great Supernatural War. From my understanding, the fae came to Earth hundreds of years ago from another realm and settled in Europe. They were made up of four Factions, categorized by their shifting abilities. The male of their species could shift into dragons, wolvens, alicorns, or griffins. Each shifter was mated to a female fae sorceress, whose specialty was the power of illusions and portals. It was odd, to say the least, that a witch and a fae would ever mate.

"Beau's the man who made Nadine's wand," Grammy added.

I pulled my wand from my pocket and twisted it in my hands, eyeing the swirls and the moonstone crystal embedded into the handle. "I remember you telling me about him. He used hair from his faekin companion in my wand."

"Yes," Grammy confirmed. "I haven't been in contact with him for ages. I didn't know he was still alive."

"He is, and he's living in *Hok'evale*," Chloe said. "As a wandmaker, he's studied wand lore, including legends of the Oaken Wands. Nadine and Lucas need to meet with him as soon as possible."

Lucas took my hand. "Then let's get going. Chloe and Miles, you're with us. We'll call the rest of you if anything goes wrong."

We'd all purchased new phones when we came to the safe house, and we'd protected them with magic so the priestesses couldn't track them.

Lucas lifted his hand, and a portal bloomed in front of us. A pine forest appeared—the same forest that Chloe and Miles had been standing in when we portaled them to the safe house earlier. Our cats stayed behind as the four of us stepped through. The morning California air felt nice, and the scent of saltwater drifted through the trees.

"How far is it into town?" Lucas asked.

"It's a hike, but we know a faster way." Chloe gestured for us to follow her.

The trees here were taller than the pines back home. I couldn't see much through the forest, until we stepped into a clearing at the edge of a mountain. Back home, our mountains were more like rolling hills, but here, the peaks were much higher. Far off in the distance, I could make out the ocean.

Lucas and I both paused to take in the beautiful landscape.

"Gorgeous, isn't it?" Miles asked.

"It's beautiful," I agreed. "I might be a bit jealous of the Elementai tribe."

"Their tribe's name is Hawkei," Chloe clarified. "Elementai is their supernatural name. It's like how supernaturals refer to us as witches, but we belong to the Miriamic Coven. They're Elementai belonging to the Hawkei tribe."

"I don't know that much about them," I admitted.

"I'll tell you on the way." Chloe cocked her head, and we followed her down a narrow footpath. "From what I know of the Elementai, they're a fairly young supernatural race. Their people are indigenous to the Americas, and they were driven from their homes when the European colonizers arrived. They came together here in Northern California to protect themselves from further threats. Their ancestors gifted them powers of the elements, as well as made them protectors of magical creatures. The Hawkei tribe is made up of five smaller tribes, also known as Houses, one for each element."

"Kind of like our Casts?" I wondered.

Miles nodded. "Sort of, but their magic is inherited, where ours is chosen. There's Toaqua, who control water. And Koigni, who control fire. Then Yapluma for air, Nivita for earth, and Anichi for spirit. They believe that each Elementai's soul resides within a magical creature. When an Elementai comes of age, they bond with their special creature, which they call a Familiar."

"That's really cool," I said. "Are the Hawkei the only tribe of elementals?"

"Yes, they mostly stick together," Chloe replied. "But just like in our coven, some of them travel, and there are locations all around the world where people of all supernatural races are welcome."

"*Hok'evale* is one of those places," Miles added. "The Hawkei's main city, Kinpago, isn't too far from here. Technically, *Hok'evale* is outside the reservation's protective borders. It was a place of refuge during the Hawkei Civil War, which only ended a few months ago. *Hok'evale* has been around for a while, taking in people from all supernatural races who don't have anywhere else to go."

"I've heard the Hawkei are very diverse," Lucas said thoughtfully. "Is that true?"

Chloe nodded. "Absolutely. We visited Kinpago a few weeks ago, and their city is full of influences from around the world. When the Hawkei tribe formed, they sent their people all over the world to form alliances and grow their numbers. They brought back people of all races, and they've continued to honor global cultures to this day. We ate at this really good restaurant in Kinpago's Chinatown, and we went shopping in the Italian district. Their college, Orenda Academy, is at this beautiful castle built by a friend of the Hawkei who came over from Scotland."

"It sounds like a wonderful place," I said. "Have you guys seen many magical creatures in *Hok'evale?*"

Miles gave a cunning smirk. "Buckle up, Nadine, because you're about to experience the magical world like you've never seen it before."

Miles pulled back branches and thick brush, and I stopped in my tracks. I could hardly believe what I was seeing. Ahead of us stood a large clearing filled with magical creatures I could only ever picture in my wildest dreams. I knew that dragons and unicorns existed, but it hadn't ever quite felt *real* until I saw it with my own eyes.

Unicorns with fire manes and shimmering horns grazed in the clearing. Among the Fire unicorns was a unicorn with white fur that shimmered blue in the sunlight. Its horn looked like an icicle, and it blew snowflakes out of its nose.

Dragons of all sizes frolicked through the clearing. A mother dragon with black scales and red spines spread her wings and launched into the sky, and three baby dragons flew behind her, blowing fire at each other as they navigated around other flying creatures. I spotted flying sheep and birds of all different colors. Some of them looked small enough to fit into the palm of my hand, and others had wingspans as long as a school bus. Watching them fly through the sky was like witnessing a rainbow dance. The birds sang a song together that sounded coordinated and calmed my nerves.

Tiny rodent-like creatures chased each other around and scampered up trees, before swinging like monkeys to the next branches. They were all different colors, with big eyes, tiny noses, and big bushy tails. Their ears looked like that of a fennec fox, and the creatures reminded me of bush babies with bigger bellies.

Something I thought was a pile of rocks moved, and I realized it was a goat with granite for skin. I spun around to take it all in, but I wasn't sure what to marvel at first. It was all so amazing.

Lucas gasped and pointed. "It's a real chimera and a hippogriff!"

A winged creature with three heads—a lion, a dragon, and a goat—tackled an animal with the body of a horse and the head of an eagle. The hippogriff clacked its beak. The three-headed creature Lucas had called a chimera rolled onto the ground, like they were playing a game.

Felines of all sizes and colors lazed in the sun, but they were unlike any cats I'd seen before. One of them had feathers that shimmered blue and purple, and another white and pink-speckled feline had horns on its head and wings on its back. One of the cats didn't even look solid, and it gleamed an ethereal blue as it played with a baby dragon. The creature looked like it was made of air.

Nearby, a stream cut through the clearing, and water creatures of all sorts splashed in the brook. I witnessed a small sea serpent with blue fins slither up to a green horse-like creature with the tail of a fish. There was so much to take in, and it was like all of the magic of the Elementai permeated this clearing.

"This is incredible!" Lucas exclaimed.

Chloe beamed. "Wait until you ride one."

"Are we allowed to do that?" I asked.

Chloe shrugged. "All you have to do is ask."

She gestured to a group of people surrounding the dragons. They scrubbed down the dragons' scales and fed them snacks. The dragons had their eyes closed and faces pointed to the sun, like they were enjoying every second of being pampered.

"Come on." Chloe gestured for us to follow, and we made our way across the clearing to the group of people.

"Chloe, Miles," a guy greeted. He looked about our age, and a black alicorn followed behind him. "It's good to see you again. I see you brought some friends."

"Hi, Sam," Chloe said. "These are the friends we told you about; Lucas and Nadine."

"Oh, my Goddess!" A woman emerged from behind one of the dragons, followed by a gray cat. I saw her black hair first, and my heart leapt in recognition.

"Monica!" I cried.

"Lucas! Nadine! It's so great to see you both." Monica rushed over to us and squeezed us into a tight hug. "I can't thank you two enough for saving my life after I was framed for The Hearse Tragedy."

Monica had been playing piano on The Hearse the night the demon caused the crash that killed seventeen people. The priestesses had blamed Monica's mentalist abilities for manipulating the driver, even though they knew the demon had been behind it. The priestesses had intended to poison Monica as execution for the crime, so the coven would have someone to blame. We slipped her a fake potion that mimicked death, then revived her body after the funeral. She left for *Hok'evale* to seek refuge that same night.

"It's good to know you made it safely," I said as I drew away. "We had no way to contact you."

"It's better that way," she promised. "As long as the priestesses believe I'm dead, I can live my life in peace."

"So you like it here?" Lucas asked.

"Yes, very much," Monica replied. "I've met so many wonderful people. My best friend here is a Nivita woman who named her little girl after me! I'm splitting my time between teaching music lessons and caring for magical creatures. How are things in Octavia Falls?"

Lucas and I exchanged a glance. "Tense…" I admitted.

Monica sighed, appearing sad. "I assume you aren't in *Hok'evale* for a vacation."

I frowned. "Unfortunately, no."

"In that case, I won't keep you. Good luck to you both." Monica waved, then returned to the dragon she was caring for.

Sam dropped his gaze. "Chloe and Miles say you've been looking for information to help your coven. Ancestors know how brutal a civil war can be."

Something dark flashed in his eyes, and it was obvious he'd seen a lot over the last few years. The Hawkei Civil War might be over, but it'd take ages for their people to recover.

Sam extended his arm to show a tattoo of a broken arrow surrounded by a partial circle. "Ours was a genocide, and they marked people like me as weak and inferior. I do hope your coven treats its people better."

"We're doing our best to prevent the coven from taking it that far," Miles told Sam. "We might've found information that can help us, but we need to speak to someone in town named Beau Blankard. Can you get us there?"

Sam patted one of the dragons on the shoulder. "Leslie's all ready for a flight, but she's the only dragon I've got at the moment."

Leslie was a smaller dragon compared to the others, but she was still the size of a small car, with shimmering purple scales and blue spines running down her back.

"Leslie can only carry two riders at a time," Sam said.

"Then she should take Nadine and Lucas," Chloe offered. "It's important that they hear what Beau has to say."

Leslie bowed her head to me, nudging her nose against my shoulder. I ran my fingers over her scales, and I was surprised by how smooth they were. The dragon licked me, as if to say she liked me. I saw she had a forked blue tongue that glittered in the sunlight.

"How will we find Beau?" I asked.

"He should be at the library right now, working a fundraiser for foster kids," Sam said.

It seemed so positively normal. A witch couldn't host a fundraiser in Octavia Falls these days, and it's not like the priestesses would care about the foster care system, anyway.

"A lot of kids lost their parents in the war," Sam added. "We're doing what we can. The community's really come together to help them, but it's been a tough road so far."

My stomach sank. "I'm sorry things have been hard for your people."

"It gets easier every day," Sam assured us. "Take it as a sign of hope. If our people can end their civil war and become one tribe again, then so can your coven."

"Thank you," I told him.

"It's nothing," Sam replied with a shrug. "Are you two ready for a ride?"

I bounced on my toes, and Lucas looked thrilled. I hadn't seen him that excited in a long time.

"We're ready," Lucas said brightly.

"All you have to do is grab her spines, hoist yourself up, and she'll take care of the rest," Sam instructed. "She knows where she's going, and when you're done, just hop back on her and she'll bring you back here."

"Thanks for all your help," Lucas said. "If there's any way we can repay you, let us know."

Sam waved his hand. "Don't worry about it. Go help your people."

Lucas grabbed one of Leslie's spines and jumped. He settled into a smooth area on her back, then reached down to help me up. I sat in front of him and was surprised to find I felt secure in the curve of Leslie's back. I held one of her spines to steady myself, and Lucas wrapped his arms around me to keep me even more secure.

"See you soon!" Chloe waved goodbye.

Leslie spread her wings, and my heart plummeted to my abdomen as she leapt into the sky. Lucas and I both screamed as we rose high into the air, until Chloe, Miles, and Sam looked like mere ants beneath us. My legs tightened on the dragon's sides, and wind whipped through my hair as she pumped her wings.

I squeezed my eyes shut tightly as my heart pummeled against my rib cage. I thought this would be fun, but now that I was doing it, I realized I wasn't at all prepared. One wrong move, and Lucas and I would plummet to our deaths.

Lucas's screams turned to laughter. He let go of me, and I instantly curled over the dragon, clutching her neck for dear life.

"Lucas!" I screamed.

He tapped me on the shoulder. "Nad, it's okay. Open your eyes."

The ride seemed to even out, and the wind seemed calmer. Slowly, I peeled my eyes open and looked around. Clouds surrounded us at all angles, and Leslie had stopped flapping her wings. She soared through the air, her wings slicing through the clouds like butter. I glanced at Lucas to see he had his arms straight out to the sides. His fingers grazed the moisture around us.

"Woohoo!" Lucas screamed like he was having the time of his life.

And he was; I could tell. We'd been cooped up in that cabin for so long, and we'd been living in survival mode for even longer. Riding on the back of a dragon felt like freedom.

Gingerly, I reached a hand outward, while holding firmly to one of

Leslie's spines with the other. My fingers cut through the clouds, and tiny water droplets swirled around us.

"I've got you," Lucas said as he laced his fingers in mine. He gently took my hand off the dragon's spine and stretched my arms outward.

I expected to freak out, but I leaned my back against him, and I found that I felt confident up here in the clouds. My heart rate began to slow, and for a moment, I let myself take it all in—the warmth of Lucas's body on mine, the strength of the dragon beneath us, and the cool air blowing my hair back. It felt like we had no care in the world.

My shoulders sagged against Lucas, and he kissed my cheek. In an instant, the scene around us changed as we broke out of the clouds. I gasped and grabbed Leslie's spines again as the ground came into view. We must've been hundreds of feet up, but I only had a moment to process it before the most incredible sight stole my attention.

All around us, flocks of magical winged creatures flew through the air. A herd of hippogriffs flapped their wings beside us, and I looked up to see a group of winged serpents spinning through the sky. Below us soared a massive bird with six wings, leaves in place of feathers, and horns that looked like tree branches.

I spotted a break in the landscape ahead. It ran like a line through the mountains, all the way down to the ocean. I thought for certain it was a river, until we got closer and I realized the land below us was dry. It was a narrow canyon, and it was bursting with life.

There had been no signs of human life since we left the clearing, and it occurred to me why. *Hok'evale* was designed to be hidden, and it'd been built deep within the canyon. Unless you knew what you were looking for, the city was difficult to find. You wouldn't know there were people living here until you were right on top of them.

Leslie flew downward so I was able to get a good look at the town below. People milled up and down the canyon, riding in carriages or on the backs of magical creatures. Parts of the canyon were narrow, with thatched-roof houses lining the canyon walls and a street running between them. I spotted holes in the sides of the rock face, as if doorways had been carved out for living quarters.

The canyon widened, and we saw a market below us where vendors sold hand-made items and dancers spun to the sound of drums and flutes. In a nearby alcove, a copper-haired woman in a long, flowing skirt and bangles played a singing bowl, while others moved in a slow, coordinated motion around her. She looked to be guiding a group meditation. As they waved their hands, elements rose up around them. Vines grew out of the earth at Nivita's command, and Toaqua controlled water droplets in the air. Yapluma controlled the breeze and sent leaves spinning around the alcove, and Koigni lit flames in their palms. It was all very calm and controlled.

As we flew closer to the ocean, I noticed a tall structure in the widest area of the canyon. I realized it was a pyramid built of stone, in the style of an ancient Central American temple. Far in the distance, I could see the beach with houses built on stilts. A sea serpent a hundred feet long broke the surface of the water, before splashing down again and causing a huge wave.

Leslie let out a loud cry.

"I think she wants us to hang on," Lucas said.

I clutched tight to her spines, and my stomach leapt to my throat as the dragon dove downward. Lucas squeezed me close, and I let out an exhilarated scream as we dove into the canyon. The wind blew back my hair, and my body was buffeted by the plummet. I had to hold on tight to keep from being torn off.

Leslie made a soft landing, and my heartbeat began to slow. I looked at the people walking around, but barely anyone glanced our way. It was like dragons landing in the middle of the streets was an everyday occurrence, and I supposed it was here.

Lucas slipped off Leslie's back, then helped me down. I held on to him to steady myself, because I still wasn't sure my feet were on solid ground. It felt like we were still flying, and I wasn't sure how long it'd take me to come down from the high.

"Did you have fun?" Lucas asked.

I beamed. "We can definitely do that again."

Lucas patted Leslie's neck. "Good girl."

Leslie gave a coo, then licked Lucas' face affectionately.

I giggled. "I think she likes you."

"I would hope so," Lucas replied as he stroked her scales. "She could've bucked us off her back at any moment. But you wouldn't do that, would you, girl?"

Leslie cooed again.

"Wait for us here," I instructed her. "We'll be back soon."

Leslie had dropped us off next to the edge of the canyon, where the rock face stretched up taller than a six-story building. Above a large wooden doorway hung a sign that read *Hok'evale Public Library.* The doors were propped open, and a banner outside advertised a fundraiser.

Lucas took my hand. "It looks like we found the right place. Let's see if we can locate our guy."

Inside, the library was air-conditioned, and bookshelves stretched to the back wall. People gathered around fundraiser tables, which were filled with items for sale or set up for raffles. Most people were accompanied by magical creatures. I expected someone to notice the cauldron tattoo on my arm and tell us witches to leave, but people just passed by and nodded kindly.

Lucas and I approached a girl our age sitting behind the raffle ticket table. She had long white hair, and a luna month sat on her shoulder.

"Excuse me," I said. "We're looking for a man named Beau Blankard."

The girl didn't look me in the eyes. Instead, she kept her gaze on my lips. She didn't say anything as she made a motion with her hands. She was deaf and communicating in American Sign Language.

"I'm sorry," I said, signing one of the few words I knew in ASL by making a circle over my chest with my fist.

The girl smiled and signed something else. I didn't know what it was, but she had this look on her face that told me I shouldn't worry. She made a gesture that told us to follow her.

She guided us behind a row of shelves, where an older man was walking toward the fundraiser tables. A white jaguar bigger than a grizzly bear prowled beside him. The creature had glowing blue lines running through his fur and shimmering blue eyes. The man stopped when he saw her approaching, and she signed something to him.

The man looked a lot like the girl, but he had long black braids with white feathers twisted into the ends. He had the kindest eyes, but I also saw wisdom in them. It wasn't hard to believe we could trust him.

The man nodded kindly to the two of us. "My daughter tells me you are looking for someone."

Lucas kept his voice low. "Yes. We're looking for a man named Beau Blankard. We believe he might have information that will help the Miriamic people."

"We have heard of the conflict within your coven," the man said. "I'm Chief Cauac, leader of the Anichi House, and this is my daughter Luana. I've spoken with other witches who have come to *Hok'evale*."

"Then you must know Chloe and Miles," I said. "They sent us. I'm Nadine, and this is Lucas."

"Yes, they mentioned you," Chief Cauac said brightly. "You certainly understand that given the nature of your conflict, I must ask what you wish to speak to Mister Blankard about."

Lucas and I exchanged a glance. I nodded to him to let him know we could trust these people. We had to if we were going to get any information.

"Our priestesses are searching for antique relics known as the Oaken Wands that could control all witch magic if they get their hands on them," Lucas explained. "We intend to find the Wands before they do, so that we can unite our people before the priestesses divide them completely."

I lifted the hem of my shirt and showed Chief Cauac my crescent moon tattoo. "I'm the only Curse Breaker of my coven. I served on the Imperium Council before they stripped me of my title, because I opposed their tyrannical methods. If it helps… Beau made my wand."

I showed Chief Cauac my wand, and his contemplative gaze roamed over the craftsmanship.

"All we want is to help our coven," I told him. "Beau may have information that will stop our priestesses from hurting our people."

Chief Cauac looked sympathetic. He signed something to his daughter, and she walked away.

"Although we do not wish to involve ourselves in other supernatural affairs, we cannot witness the downfall of another people," Chief Cauac said. "We will help in any way we can."

"Thank you," Lucas replied kindly.

Luana returned with an elderly man who seemed to have years of wisdom in his eyes. He had salt-and-pepper hair and wrinkles around his eyes, and he walked with a cane. A miniature cat-like creature with the wings of a dragonfly fluttered onto the front of the green wool suit he wore. The animal reminded me of some of the other Familiars in *Hok'e-vale*, but this man was part-witch, part-fae, so he couldn't have one.

It hit me then that the animal on his shoulder wasn't a Familiar. It was his faekin companion. I didn't know what I expected faekin to look like, but Grammy had said they were companions to the fae and shared some of their blood. It was my understanding that there were many types, but this faekin appeared to be part of a group of tiny animals with fairy wings that could fit into the palm of your hand.

"These witches wish to speak with you, Mister Blankard," Chief Cauac told him.

"I believe you might recognize this," I said, holding out my wand. "It contains hair from your faekin."

The faekin locked its feline eyes on me and gave a low growl.

"Settle down, Bitsy," Beau scolded the small creature. "I apologize. Faekin are very protective. May I?"

Beau reached for the wand, and I handed it to him. He turned it over curiously.

"Yes… I remember this," he said thoughtfully. "But I didn't design it for you."

"You made it for my mother, Faith Evers—her maiden name is Tucker," I told him. "I inherited it."

"Yes, I recall making it for Helena Tucker's daughter," he recalled. "I heard what happened to her. It was awful she was driven out of the coven by a family curse."

"I broke the curse. But not before…" I choked up.

Beau dropped his gaze. I didn't have to say it out loud for him to understand. "I'm deeply sorry for your loss."

"Thank you," I replied. "Our friends Chloe and Miles say you may be able to help us."

Beau's demeanor brightened. "Yes, I spoke with them. Lovely couple. You must be the friends they mentioned."

"Nadine is a Curse Breaker—the only member of her Cast—and I'm the Reaper's Apprentice," Lucas said. "I will become a reaper when I die and ferry the souls of our coven members to Alora."

"I'm honored to meet you!" Beau grabbed Lucas's hand and shook it enthusiastically. "Boy, do I have a story for you."

"Why don't we go somewhere private to talk?" Chief Cauac suggested. "Luana and I can escort you to the Hall of Records."

"A good idea," Beau agreed. "There is much to discuss about your Wands."

Beau handed my wand back. We followed Chief Cauac through the library, until we came to an elevator. We stepped inside, and we rode the elevator to the next level. We came to a hallway, and Chief Cauac guided us to the doors at the end.

We entered a small room lined with bookshelves on all sides, with sconces hung between them. Arching stained glass windows let in sunlight, and two tables sat in the center of the room. Sculptures of magical creatures filled the shelves beside the books. There was no one else here, so we could talk freely.

Luana signed something to her father, and Chief Cauac said, "My daughter and I would like to stay and help in any way we can."

"Yes, of course," Lucas agreed. "We could use all the help we can get."

Chief Cauac gestured to one of the study tables. "Please, have a seat."

The five of us gathered around the table, and Chief Cauac interpreted for Luana as Beau began speaking.

"If you wish to learn more about wands, then you've come to the right place," Beau began. "Wands are my specialty, as I am a wandmaker myself. I've been studying them most of my life, even before I moved to Octavia Falls."

"You weren't born there?" I wondered. "My grandma said she knew you when you were both young."

Beau chuckled. "*Young* can mean many things to a person my age. It's true I lived in Octavia Falls in early adulthood, but I was born in Malovia to a sorceress mother and a warlock father."

"How's that possible?" Lucas asked. "The witches and fae despise each other."

"My mother was Unseelie fae, which means she can draw magic from sources outside herself," Beau explained. "It is a rare classification, as the Unseelie were all but wiped out by the Seelie fae long ago. Unseelie fae have kept their magic secret for a long time, as the Seelie deem their magic *dark*, and will criminalize anyone who uses magic they don't like. The Seelie fae consider wands to be black magic, and they are banned in fae culture. However, as I am half-warlock, I could never resist the call to wands myself."

"That's why the fae don't like witches, isn't it?" I asked. "We use wands and crystals, and they don't approve of that."

"Yes," Beau confirmed. "But my mother did not see it the same way, as she wielded dark magic as well. She met my father at a supernatural hub located in Paris while researching Unseelie magic, and they fell in love. They settled in Malovia, because my mother was hired to do important work for the monarchy, though they had to remain in hiding. When I came of age, my father performed my Evoking Ceremony, and I received the mark of Mortana. I came into my dragon-shifter powers at the same time, and I attended Arcanea University to learn my shifter magic. It was there that I began studying wand making in secret. My unique warlock gift is to work with gems to amplify their powers for other members of my Cast, and I found these gems worked well when embedded in wands."

"So you put your magic inside of them, like transference?" I asked.

Beau shook his head. "No. I work with the natural magical qualities in the stone. I don't give my power to others. Rather, I pull that power out of the stone, so that the gem's power to amplify a Mortana's ability is even stronger. I was able to keep those powers a secret, but before I graduated, I found my mate. The fae did not approve of my mating bond, and my mate and I were forced to flee."

I couldn't believe they'd do that. Witches didn't bond magically the way the fae did, but just thinking of someone trying to break Lucas and me apart made my blood boil.

"How could they do that to you?" Lucas asked. "From what I've heard of the fae, the bond between a shifter and his sorceress mate is the most powerful type of magic they have."

"That, precisely, was their objection," Beau said. "I did not mate with a sorceress. I mated with another dragon shifter. Same-sex relationships were considered blasphemous in my day. I have much respect for the current reigning Malovia monarchs, because they are fighting for the rights I never had as a gay man with Unseelie magic. I hope they succeed in their endeavor, because I don't want anyone to go through what I did. My mate Sebastian and I kept our relationship secret for a time while we finished up our studies at the university, but we had no choice but to leave when my parents were discovered. Their intersupernatural relationship was outed, and they were hanged for it."

"That's terrible," I said sadly. "I hope Octavia Falls was kinder to you."

"For a time," Beau admitted. "We found a home in Octavia Falls. I opened a wand shop, while Sebastian worked at one of the cider mills in town. He posed as an Alchemist, as fae are able to brew potions. We were able to conceal our true nature using fae magic and went undetected for over twenty years. But it took only a moment for the magic to falter, and Sebastian was discovered as a dragon shifter living within Octavia Falls. He was poisoned by yarrow, which is deadly to fae. It was my parents' execution all over again, though even worse, because he was my mate."

Beau dropped his gaze. "To lose a mate you're magically bound to… it can make a man go mad. And that's exactly what it did. I left Octavia Falls and began researching the Oaken Wands profusely, with a keen interest in the Mortana Wand. I thought if I could find it, I could use its power to bring him back from the dead."

"Is that even possible?" I wondered. "The coven can't bring people back to life, so it stands to reason that the Wand can't, either."

"The Wand has power over death, but nobody knows for sure how far that magic extends," Beau admitted. "I wish I had the answer, but I stopped asking that question long ago. I pursued the Mortana Wand because I was so in love that I didn't know who I was without my mate. I was in denial that he was gone from this life for good, and I'd bargain anything to get him back. But my grief stretched into decades, all while the world was changing around me—and I with it. I came to realize that even if I was able to bring Sebastian back today, I couldn't go back to who I was and have what we had again. I spent all that time mourning the life we'd lost, that I forgot to continue living myself. I abandoned my search for the Mortana Wand several years ago, and I came to *Hok'evale* to heal."

"So you never found the Wand?" Lucas asked softly.

"No, but I got close," Beau admitted. "Your friends tell me the Oaken Wands were hidden from the Imperium Council decades ago, in order to protect the relics. However, what your friends mistakenly assumed was that *all* the Wands were in the council's possession."

"Nicholas didn't take them all?" Lucas wondered. "Which ones was he missing?"

I could see Lucas calculating it in his head, and I did the same. We knew that my grandfather had the Mentalist Wand four decades ago. At that time, the demon, Professor Leto, took it and gave it to Chloe's grandfather, Jebediah Olson, which resulted in the feud that got my grandfather killed. The demon had taken possession of the Mentalist Wand again before he was banished all those years ago. It remained in his possession until he returned to Octavia Falls last spring and posed as a professor to kill people for power. We battled him, and the Mentalist Wand fell into the pit to the Abyss.

As for the others, my grandfather had used the Curse Breaker Wand during the feud. Grammy had kept it for years after his death, until it was stolen from her. We didn't know where it ended up. Before he died, my grandfather hid the Seer Wand in the vanishing stairwell, and he'd placed the Alchemy Wand in the Crock of Death. Now the priestesses had both of those Wands in their possession, along with the Crock. Which meant there was only one Wand my grandfather had never touched.

"The Mortana Wand," I said. "If that Wand was never with the priestesses to begin with… where has it been all this time?"

Beau leaned forward and lowered his voice, even though we were alone. "My research indicates the Mortana Wand resides with the Reaper Order."

Lucas's jaw dropped, and my heart stalled. When Miles said this information could change everything, he wasn't exaggerating. This information was enough to lead us straight to the Mortana Wand. I'd bet the priestesses didn't even know where to start, or they'd have pursued it by now.

I grabbed Lucas's shoulder, nearly bouncing out of my seat. "Lucas, you can get it! As the Reaper's Apprentice, you can contact the reapers and get the Wand from them."

Lucas stared straight forward, like he was still trying to process this information. Finally, he turned to look at me. "I'm not sure that I can, Nad. I can only summon them on the Reaper Moon, and our chance to do that has passed. There's not going to be another Reaper Moon for a hundred years."

"That can't be our only option," I insisted. "We hold séances and converse with the dead all the time. Reapers are just people. There must be another ritual we can use to summon them."

"They *aren't* just people, though," Lucas said. "Reapers aren't like any old spirit. They have power over the realms, to move between them at will. A normal ghost can't do that. That's why our people need reapers to lead them to the other side, or why other cultures have their ancestors to greet them at death. Not just anyone can hop realms at any time—not without a powerful portal."

"If reapers can come here willingly, then we must be able to summon them," I theorized.

Lucas shook his head. "Even though reapers are powerful, you know how touchy Mortana magic can be. Summoning a reaper before we're ready to cross over could have deadly consequences. They could reap our soul unintentionally, and with our souls tethered to living bodies, the results could be worse than death. It could damage our souls permanently. I know we said we're willing to risk death for these Wands, but what I'm talking about is far worse than that. The only reason summoning them on the Reaper Moon even works is because the magic of the stars is just right to allow it."

"There is another way," Beau said. "I researched much about the Reaper Order and what it takes to join them in my attempt to get my hands on the Mortana Wand, but I came to learn it is far out of my reach, as I don't have the power to become a reaper. But it is possible for you. You are the Reaper's Apprentice, which means that once you master your powers, you will join the Reaper Order."

Lucas furrowed his brow. "I'll join the Reaper Order when I die. That's the only way I can get in."

Beau's shoulders fell. "My dear boy, where is your reaper master?"

Lucas chuckled nervously. "Well, I *sort of* shoved the last reaper I met into a portal to the Abyss. I suppose perhaps I was meant to learn something from him. There's not much record for me to go off of, since there's only one Reaper's Apprentice per generation."

Beau sighed, like he really felt for Lucas. "Then let me share with you what I know. A reaper does not gain the full height of his power upon a death. The apprentice must master his power to move beyond his apprenticeship and become a full member of the Reaper Order. This is something that can be done before or after death, once his training is complete."

"I haven't *been* trained, though," Lucas said. "I've been learning on my own. I don't even know what powers I need to master."

"To master your powers, you must undergo the Warlock's Trial," Beau said.

Lucas and I both leaned forward, but it was Lucas who spoke. "What's the Warlock's Trial?"

"As I'm not a reaper myself, I can't speak to all the details, but what I do know is that the trial is a demonstration of your reaper power," Beau explained.

"So it's a bit like an Evoking Ceremony?" I asked.

Beau tilted his head. "In a way, I suppose, but less on the ritual side and more on the practical application side. It is a trial of death."

"So… that sounds like I need to die," Lucas mused.

Beau sucked a breath, like he was struggling to explain. "It's more about your magic—your comprehension of your power. Once you demonstrate that you've mastered your abilities, the reapers will appear to welcome you into the Reaper Order. It's one of the few ways that they appear to the living."

"So once they come to me, I can ask them about the Wand," Lucas said.

Beau gave a cunning smile. "Better than that—they'll give it to you. The Mortana Wand passes down between reapers, from the master to his successor. When you are ready, the Mortana Wand will be yours."

"I'll do whatever I need to do," Lucas decided. "What steps do I have to take?"

"That information lies solely with the reapers," Beau said regrettably. "I searched for many years for more information on this trial, but it's like someone took all that information for themselves. I wasn't able to learn more."

I furrowed my brow. "Who could be hoarding all this reaper information, and why would they? Lucas is the only living reaper, and the Reaper Order hasn't offered up any information to him. There must be someone alive who knows more."

Lucas leaned his chin on his fist, looking thoughtful. "Or maybe there's a ceremony I'm supposed to do that I'm unaware of. If the Reaper's Apprentice is meant to have a master, there's got to be another way to get in touch with the reapers. Maybe it's not about summoning them fully, but communicating with them in another way. The reaper I fought the night of your Evoking Ceremony was the last one to live before me, which means Edgar Nowak must be my master. He's gotta have the Mortana Wand."

"There must be a reason you've been left on your own," I theorized. "I never received priestess training, but that was because the priestesses didn't want me on the council, and they just wanted to get rid of me. Intuitively, I don't feel like that's the case with the reapers. If we can't summon Edgar, we'll have to go to him."

"How?" Lucas pondered. "He's got to be somewhere in the afterlife when he isn't reaping. I can't portal to other realms myself yet. Astral traveling isn't going to get us between realms, and we're not sure of the consequences if we could. The only thing I can think is that I could hitch a ride while I'm reaping, but reaping is more than just creating portals. It severs a tether between your soul and this earthly plane. I could risk destroying my soul in the process. What I need to do is figure out how to portal between realms in my physical form. I've got the power—I just need to learn how to isolate it."

I tapped my fingers on the tabletop. "Let's say you figured out how to do that. Portaling between realms isn't enough if we don't know where to find Edgar Nowak. He could be in Alora, or the Abyss, or anywhere in between. I don't know much about the afterlife, but I bet each of these places are huge. How do we track him down?"

"A tracking spell might work," Lucas suggested. "We'll track Edgar down and find a way to communicate with him, then I'll complete my training and pass the trial to get the Wand."

He conjured a bundle of white sage. "Let's smudge the room with some sage, cast a spell, and see what we find."

Chief Cauac had been interpreting the entire conversation to Luana, but for the first time, she signed back.

Chief Cauac turned to us. "We'd kindly like to remind you that witches can't *smudge*. Smudging is a religious ceremony done by indigenous cultures. As you are not indigenous, you cannot smudge."

Lucas furrowed his brow and addressed Chief Cauac. "We've been doing it for ages. Is there a better cleansing ritual we should be using?"

"You may address my daughter directly, and I will interpret in first-person," Chief Cauac offered.

Luana continued to explain, and Chief Cauac spoke aloud. "What your culture does by burning herbs for cleansing is a suitable ritual, but it is not *smudging*. What you do is called *smoke cleansing*. Smoke cleansing can be performed by anyone by burning herbs to cleanse your spirit, altar, or home. It looks a lot like smudging, but they are not one and the same. Using words that describe our rituals and herbs from a closed practice is harmful to our people, as it erases the significance it has on our culture."

Lucas and I exchanged a glance. Neither of us knew any of this, and I was horrified that we'd participated in something damaging like this.

"We're sorry," I told Luana genuinely. "We had no idea there was a difference."

Chief Cauac signed to Luana, and she responded back. "We do not tell you this to assign blame—only to educate. Smudging is very sacred to us, and it's something that only certain members or spiritual leaders of our culture can do. People of other cultures can't do it, because they simply aren't qualified. Adopting this ritual into your culture is like blessing water and calling it Holy Water. Blessed water is not Holy Water unless it is blessed by Catholic clergy members. Similarly, smoke cleansing is not smudging because it lacks the cultural significance to carry out the ceremony properly. You are free to continue smoke cleansing as you wish— we simply ask that you do not use our religious terminology in your practice. Continuing to do so contributes to the erasure of our culture. We have already been stripped of our land due to colonization, and we wish to preserve as much of our culture and spirituality as we can."

"Absolutely. We'll stop using that term immediately," Lucas told Luana. "Our coven should have educated us on this. It's not fair to you, nor your job, to educate us, but thank you for doing so."

Luana looked down at the white sage bundle in Lucas's hand. Chief Cauac interpreted. "White sage is sacred to our religious practice, as it is native to our lands. Due to overharvesting of white sage, it can be difficult for our people to find access to white sage. Because of that, we do ask that you find an herb significant to your ancestry that may contribute more ethically to your smoke cleansing rituals."

"Yes, we can do that," Lucas agreed. "I'm sure there are plenty of other cleansing herbs we can use. I'm just confused why the coven would care to use sage when there isn't enough for you."

"The Elementai used to trade with the witches, so some of our herbs got traded as well. However, herbs alone do not invite others into our spiritual practices. Our lands are not the only thing your ancestors took," Cauac responded.

Lucas looked horrified. "I thought our land was cleared before the coven settled. I hate to think we had anything to do with harming your people."

"Regardless, you are still on stolen land," Chief Cauac interpreted.

"That's awful." I felt sick to my stomach.

I knew American history, but I knew little about the coven's involvement. From what I learned in my history class, witches settled all across New England when they arrived in the Americas. They came over here to escape the witch trials in Europe. But the trials continued here, and it harmed so many humans who had no magical blood. The coven formed Octavia Falls to go into hiding and stop the witch trials.

"Even if we weren't a complete people when the land was cleared, it's naive to think members of our coven had nothing to do with it," I said. "Our coven needs to take responsibility for the hand our ancestors played in the atrocities."

Luana wore a sympathetic expression as her father said, "We cannot change the past, but I urge you to do better in the future."

"We will," I promised. "It's clear we have a lot to learn, and we will work with the Hawkei to do better. What can we do to mend the harm done?"

Luana signed, and Chief Cauac said, "Acknowledging harm caused and choosing to change your actions in the future is the first step—as you've acknowledged you will use the term smoke cleansing from now on. We greatly appreciate your willingness to learn."

"The last thing we want is to cause harm to anyone," Lucas replied. "We'll stop using sage, too."

"There are many different types of sage—it's specifically white sage we ask that you stop using," Luana explained, while her father spoke. "White sage is native to the Americas, but common sage is found elsewhere in the world. I would encourage you to look into your roots and use herbs tied to your ancestry."

"The Miriamic people came from Europe, so you may want to explore herbs similar to what the fae use," Beau suggested. "The fae priestesses use Siberian cedar to smoke cleanse, and it's what I use when I need to clear my energy. You could use that, as well as cedar oil. You can also use rosemary, thyme, spruce, or fir. Most witches lived in what's now Germany in the 1500s, so ancestrally, the proper plants to use for smoke cleansing for witches would be those that naturally grow in that area."

"I didn't know that," I remarked. "I don't understand why the coven would ignore their own history and cultural practices."

"We lost much of our culture due to the witch trials," Beau explained.

"The Imperium Council forced their people to assimilate to American culture so they wouldn't be hunted. They outlawed mass-produced information about our heritage so that other people wouldn't be able to identify them as witches, and so they could hide easier. Family grimoires were allowed, but sharing information among other witches was outlawed. I only know this much because I have been researching our history for decades, and I had to search outside the coven to obtain this information."

I tensed in my chair. "The Imperium Council chose to control the way we worshiped, in order to control our people. They've been playing this card for a long time, convincing the coven they're doing this for our benefit. We thought the Imperium Council we're facing now was the worst, but they've been doing this for all of history."

Beau frowned. "I do not put my trust in the Imperium Council of our modern day, but I do believe the council did what they had to back then in order to keep our people safe, even at the cost of our culture. You must understand the extent of the witch trials back then. Mother Miriam settled in what is now Germany with her children in the 1300s. The coven grew their numbers there, and witch families spread across Europe until the 1600s, when the worst of the Würzburg witch trials were taking place in what is now Germany. It was one of the biggest mass extinction of witches in known history. Over nine-hundred people died as a result of these trials. The Miriamic people were forced to gather anyone they could and migrate to America. Anyone who stayed in Europe was killed at the stake."

Lucas's hands curled into fists. "Regardless of their intentions, it's still wrong, because it wiped out our cultural identity. Our cultural practices and knowledge were stolen from us."

"That's why we adopted our ceremonies from ancient open practices, like Samhain and Yule, that pre-date the coven," I realized. "We were never able to develop a unique culture, because it would be stripped from us if we did. It's a miracle we managed to hold on to these pagan rituals at all, even if they aren't completely ours."

"It is wrong," Beau agreed. "But sometimes, people are not given a choice. Tension grew when the witches petitioned to join the first iteration of the United Supernatural Union, before the Great Supernatural War eighty years ago. The angels and the fae objected, and the witches had to water down their culture further so the angels wouldn't slaughter them. The angels had already stolen pieces of our culture to get us to convert. They made Santos out to be a devil in their lore, in order to demonize him and make us abandon our god. Ultimately, we were able to hold on to our deities, and a few pagan rituals, but many of our other cultural practices died."

"It's clear there's much that needs to change," I stated. "We will win our war against the priestesses, and we will make sure the coven knows of this history. We will bring back the old practices we lost."

Lucas held up his white sage bundle. "In the meantime, should I return this bundle to the Hawkei?"

"That won't be necessary," Chief Cauac interpreted for Luana. "As long as you commit to sourcing your herbs ethically, that is all we ask. We have traded sage with your people in the past, but our war is over, and things are changing. The witches must be more careful about their religious practices if they hope to mend relations with the Elementai—especially after the witches sold us the Omnimotus curse that infected our Familiars, started a pandemic in the tribe and killed many people several years ago."

"We've heard of the curse, but what was it exactly?" Lucas asked.

"The Omnimotus curse was a horrific spell from the Miriamic Coven purchased by members of a Hawkei resistance party, intended to target the Familiars of powerful Elders to overthrow them," Luana explained, while her father interpreted aloud. "It is a spell used in war that doesn't affect other witches but can harm other magical races. It takes a strong witch or warlock to cast the curse—not just anyone can do it. If cast properly, it causes another's magic to turn inward and become deadly. It acts as a viral disease and can spread to members of the same magical species. Since Elementai magic is drawn from our Familiars, the curse was designed to target our magical creatures, which in turn killed the Elementai they were bonded with when the creatures perished. Luckily, we were able to eradicate the plague, though not before it claimed many lives."

My heart sank deeper the more she explained. "Who would sell you such an awful thing?"

I was horrified that anyone from my coven would harm another community like this, only I could think of several people who would sell a curse in a heartbeat and not think twice about it.

"Priestess Stella was trading with the Hawkei—nightshade for unicorn hair," Lucas pointed out. "I wouldn't put it past her or any of the priestesses to strike a bargain for a curse like this. If it takes a powerful witch or warlock to cast, then Priestess Stella fits the bill. That must be how she got her hands on the unicorn hair in the first place to start nightshade production. Then once she had enough product, she turned to trading the nightshade itself."

"This is wrong," I insisted. "How many other people has our coven hurt? This needs to end."

Luana looked at me when she signed. "You need to heal your people first, because you can't do this alone," Chief Cauac said.

Lucas shook his head in disbelief. "We have so much to learn, and we won't let our coven continue to sit in the dark and act as if our actions don't impact other people. Once this is over, we're going to learn all we can about other cultures and share that knowledge with our people so we don't harm them again."

"I agree," I said. "We aren't our ancestors. We can't undo the harm they've done. But we need to do better."

Chief Cauac interpreted everything we said, and Luana signed back to me. "You can make reparations once your own people are united, because a divided tribe cannot help anyone, only cause harm. When the witches have come together as one, we can all contribute to the path of peace. Go to them. Find your Wands, and bring your coven back together."

"We will," I promised. "We don't know how to thank any of you enough—Beau for your information about the Mortana Wand, Chief Cauac for welcoming us into this wonderful place, and you, Luana, for educating us. You've all been so kind."

"We only want to help," Chief Cauac interpreted for Luana.

Beau stood and reached out to shake my hand. "I'm glad all my research has finally culminated in something useful. I no longer wish to use the Mortana Wand for myself, so I've been more than happy to pass this information along to the two of you, as I trust you will use it for good. I hope that one day peace is restored and I can return to Octavia Falls to open my wand shop again."

"We'll do everything in our power to make that happen," Lucas promised. He reached out to shake Beau's hand, but Beau hesitated and reached into his pants pocket.

"Take this," Beau offered, drawing out a clear cushion-cut gem. "I keep gemstones on my person at all times, as is the nature of a dragon shifter. It's nothing valuable—just a simple quartz—but I've used my power on it, and the gem will help amplify your Mortana abilities."

Lucas took the gemstone and couldn't tear his gaze away from it. "Wow. Thank you so much."

"It's nothing," Beau said with a wave of his hand. "I'm only happy to help."

"I speak for myself now when I say that if we can be of any help, please let us know," Chief Cauac offered as he stood. Luana signed something to him, and he added, "My daughter is a certified healer and a medicine woman. She works at the hospital in *Hok'evale* as a midwife. If you or any witch needs medical attention and can't get it inside your coven, she is more than willing to help you get it here."

"That's very kind of you," I told her. "We don't currently have medical resources, so we'll let you know if we have an emergency."

"Nad..." Lucas gave me a pointed expression. "We have medical needs outside of emergencies."

It felt like too much to ask. Ever since the kidney transplant, I'd been feeling much better, but I still had a host of meds I had to take—namely, immunosuppressants to prevent my body from rejecting Lucas's kidney. I'd be on them the rest of my life.

My friends had been paying off a shady fae pharmacist in France near the borders of Malovia all summer to get my meds. It was cheaper than dialysis for sure, but my medication was eating into Grammy's savings. I had a problem asking anyone for help with my health, but I promised Lucas I'd be more honest about it.

"I suppose I should see a doctor about some medications," I admitted. "As long as we're here, we might as well see what it costs."

"You don't need to worry about that," Chief Cauac promised. "Our health institutions run independently and have programs to cover refugee healthcare. Now that our war is over, we pay for everyone's healthcare now, including refugees in *Hok'evale*."

It sounded too good to be true. "I'm technically not a *Hok'evale* resident, though," I pointed out.

"It doesn't matter to us," Chief Cauac said gently. "You are on the run from your people, and we want to help. Let me give you directions to the clinic, and you should have your prescriptions filled before you leave today."

I couldn't express how touched I was by his offer. This place was so unlike the coven. The priestesses didn't give two shits about whether I had my meds or not. Part of me wanted to run away to *Hok'evale*, but then Lucas squeezed my hand, and I remembered the rest of the coven. The priestesses would continue hurting people until there was no one left to go against them. We had to keep fighting until our last breath, because we could not let them win.

Chief Cauac drew a rough layout of *Hok'evale* on a scrap piece of paper, then showed us where to find the walk-in clinic next to the hospital. We said goodbye, and Lucas and I left the Hall of Records with a new spring to our step.

"I can't believe what we learned today!" Lucas exclaimed once we got outside. "All we have to do is track Edgar down and get the Mortana Wand."

"You make it sound so simple," I said.

"Well, it isn't simple because I still have to learn how to portal between realms, but we have more answers than before," Lucas admitted. "At least we have a direction. And we have resources and allies. For the first time in months, it feels like we're making progress."

"We're definitely on to something," I told him. "I can feel it in my bones."

We approached Leslie. The dragon was right where we left her, and Lucas showed her the drawing. "Can you take us to the hospital?"

She gave an affirming coo, and we climbed on her back. Leslie walked through the streets of *Hok'evale*, since the hospital wasn't far enough to warrant flying. From the ground, we got a better view of the town. Children ran through the streets laughing, and a woman pushed a cart handing out ice cream. She must've been fae, because her ice cream cones shimmered with illusions that looked like fireworks.

We passed by a café with a sign that read *The Falcon's Nest*. I caught sight of a man dining outside beneath an umbrella that blocked out the sun. He brought a glass of thick red liquid to his lips. At first, I thought it must be a Bloody Mary, until I saw the flash of his fangs. I realized it was *real blood*, and the man was a vampire. A waitress approached his table. I noticed a string of stars tattooed over her arm. She had to be an Astromancer, an enchantress who got her magic from the stars.

Nearby, a teenage girl laughed as a guy her age chased after her playfully. "Race you to the beach!" she called. She jumped into the air, and brown feathery wings as tall as she was burst out of her back. She flapped them and flew high above the town.

"Not fair!" the guy shouted. One moment he was running along on two feet, and the next his body had morphed into that of a griffin. He had the haunches of a lion and the head of an eagle. He pumped his wings and followed close behind the angel girl, nipping playfully at her ankles with his beak.

Here in *Hok'evale*, people of all different supernatural races interacted. It was odd to see, considering members of our own coven avoided each other if they weren't part of the same Cast.

We arrived at a large building near an entrance marked *Walk-In Clinic*. We left Leslie outside, then entered and spoke to the receptionist. She asked us to sit and wait, but it wasn't long before a woman came to get me. She was accompanied by a hamster-like creature with purple eyes and white tufts of fur on its ears. The woman had to be an Elementai, and this was her Familiar.

I was surprised by how short the wait was. It struck me how similar it felt to the first time I'd visited Dr. Yonker in Octavia Falls. When I first came to the coven, my quality of health care was better than I could've ever hoped for. That had quickly declined once the priestesses started shoving their bullshit policies where they didn't belong. Dr. Yonker had really cared about me, and Dr. Mack had cared deeply for Lucas, but once the priestesses decided we didn't deserve care, it didn't matter. In the midst of it all, I hadn't realized how quickly things had shifted, because I was used to being discriminated against when it came to my health. Now looking back, I was more appalled than ever.

Lucas stayed in the waiting room while I followed the woman into a long hall.

"This must be your first time in *Hok'evale*," she said kindly.

"Did I make it that obvious?" I joked.

"First-time visitors are sort of my thing." She gestured me into an exam room, then shut the door behind us. "Let me start by saying welcome to *Hok'evale*, Nadine. I'm Dr. Metzi, and I'm a specialist who meets with patients their first time at the clinic. As you know, *Hok'evale* is full of refugees, so it can be difficult to obtain their medical records without alerting the society they're fleeing from. That's where I come in. Using my healing magic, I can assess your medical history as well as diagnose certain things we may not see through traditional tests. I'll also work with you to develop a treatment plan."

"Healing magic? So you're Anichi?" I asked.

"Yes, I'm a member of the Spirit House. Spirit magic can be used in many ways, but one of greatest strengths is healing."

"Can you use magic to treat me?" I wondered. I'd asked Dr. Yonker the same thing when I first met him, but he'd told me that witches didn't have powerful healing magic like other supernatural races. Our Alchemists could brew potent medications, but they couldn't heal in an instant.

"Treatment through healing magic is possible," Dr. Metzi told me. "But our healing magic is limited by your body's own capabilities. My magic works by speeding up the healing process, rather than replacing it. Something like cuts and broken bones could heal very quickly, but my magic is already sensing that you've come for something much more complex. I can administer a healing treatment today that should help you feel better for a while, but again, it's going to be limited by your body's own capacity."

"Do you know why I'm here?" I asked, trying not to give anything away. This whole idea of healing magic had me intrigued.

She reached out a hand. "May I?"

I placed my hand in hers, and her hands began to glow a bright white. I felt warm magic enter my body, and I found it incredibly soothing.

Dr. Metzi closed her eyes. Her brow furrowed as she explored my body with her magic. Something told me I was a bit more complicated than her typical cases.

Finally, she drew away, and I spotted a look of intrigue in her eyes. "You have three kidneys. It's standard to leave the old kidneys in the body when a kidney transplant takes place. I'm guessing you had the transplant less than a year ago?"

"Yes," I told her.

"You needed the transplant because of your lupus," she stated. It wasn't a question. Her magic had told her everything that was wrong with me. Dr. Metzi turned to her computer and began typing. I couldn't wrap my head around how quickly she had diagnosed me. If I'd had access to healers years ago, I wouldn't have waited two years to get my diagnosis.

"I noticed some scars on your leg," Dr. Metzi said. She glanced downward, like she could see the scars even though they were covered by my pants.

I shrugged casually. "I had a bit of a run in with monsters from hell."

Her eyes lit up, looking intrigued. "Can I see?"

I lifted the hem of my pants to show her the twisted scars. Grammy's herbs had helped after I'd fought off the monsters that crawled out of the demon's pit a few months ago, but the wounds had been very deep. The herbs kept the injuries from getting infected, but the scars were still red and dimpled.

Dr. Metzi looked over my legs. "Since the injuries have already healed over, I can't completely get rid of the scars, but we can heal some of the redness to reduce their appearance."

"I would love that," I said.

Dr. Metzi was gentle with me as she rolled my pant leg up further. She propped my foot up on her knee, and her soft hands curled around my leg. That warm white magic began to glow again. There was a dull ache in my leg I'd become so accustomed to that I hadn't even realized was there until her magic made it feel better. Before my very eyes, the twisted red scars on my leg began to smooth out, and the redness subsided. They weren't completely gone, but they blended in with my skin better.

My eyebrows shot up. "Wow, that's amazing! You said you can heal broken bones, too? My fiancé has been having problems with his leg since he broke it a few months ago. Can your magic help with that?"

"Yes, absolutely," she replied brightly. "I can see him after I'm done here with you."

Another idea struck me, though I was nervous to ask. I drew a deep breath. "Can you also heal mental illness?"

Dr. Metzi frowned. "Mental health is one of the few things healing magic can't fix. The brain is so complicated. It's difficult to fix chemical imbalances with medicine, let alone using magic to fix it. We can help clear the mind and take a bit of the edge off, but we can't cure it."

"Oh," I said flatly. That was disappointing to hear.

"We have mental health specialists on staff if you need to talk to someone," she offered.

"I was asking for my fiancé," I said. "I'll let him know."

She nodded kindly. "Of course. Let me know if you have any other questions. We're here to help. For now, let's get you a treatment plan."

Dr. Metzi asked me a lot of questions about my lupus and my kidney transplant—like when I was diagnosed, if I had any complications with the transplant, if I had allergies to any medications, and more. We talked for a long time about my health, and it felt like she really cared and wasn't just trying to rush me out the door so she could see her next patient.

"What medications are you currently taking?" she asked.

I told her, but quickly added, "I get headaches from my meds, though."

She frowned as she typed something into the computer. "Although the brand you take for your immunosuppressants is common, headaches are a well-known side effect. However, there are alternatives. I'm going to put you on something new. I'm sending the prescription to the pharmacy now. You'll be able to pick it up down the hall before you leave."

"Thank you," I told her.

"Of course," she said. "That's what I'm here for. If you're all right with it, I'm going to give you a full-body healing treatment that should make you feel better for a couple of weeks. We'll get rid of some aches and pains, and get some of your energy back. Then I'll walk you down to the pharmacy to show you where to get your prescriptions. Obviously, healing magic isn't a replacement for your pills, so you'll have to keep taking them daily."

"I understand," I told her.

When I walked out of that exam room, it felt like walking out of a day at the spa. Dr. Metzi's treatment made me feel refreshed and focused.

She showed me where the pharmacy was, then left to talk to Lucas while I waited for my prescriptions to be filled. When I returned to the waiting room, Dr. Metzi was gone, and Lucas was right where I left him, flexing his foot like he'd just gotten a new leg.

"I take it Dr. Metzi worked her magic?" I asked as I approached.

"Literally. The ache in my bones is gone." Lucas raised the hand that he'd sliced earlier and wiggled his fingers. The bandage was gone, and the skin looked like it'd never been cut at all. "Good as new."

I lifted my bag from the pharmacy. "And I got my meds. This place is like a dream."

Lucas stood and wrapped an arm around me as we left the clinic. "It's certainly amazing."

"The coven needs a clinic like this in Octavia Falls," I remarked.

"Maybe when the Miriamic Conflict is over, we can open one," Lucas suggested. "We'll have free check-ups, testing, prescriptions, and mental health resources."

"I love that idea."

We approached Leslie, but I didn't reach up to climb onto the dragon right away. Instead, I looked around to take in the town one last time. Nearby, a man helped a woman with a broken spoke on her carriage. Beyond them near a small cluster of houses, I spotted neighbors harvesting a garden of beans together. Someone played a flute from their porch swing, while a drum matched the beat several houses down.

I turned to Lucas. "The town here is so vibrant. Don't get me wrong, I love the dark vibes we get in Octavia Falls, but it's more than just the colors and the sunshine. The people here seem so connected. Back home, we're divided."

Lucas looked thoughtful as he glanced around. "The Miriamic Coven can be vibrant again. There's community in our hearts, and our people are going to come together. We just have to stop letting ourselves be ruled by fear, so that we can love each other again."

"You're right," I agreed. "And Luana was right when she said we can't do this alone. For so long, it's felt like the coven *needs* us to save them, but I don't think that's the case. I think in some ways we've fueled our own fire and witch hunts by trying to fight back, but maybe fighting isn't the answer. Maybe we just need to be our authentic selves, lead with love, and people will unite."

Lucas nodded. "I think that's accurate. We've fought so long for people to believe in us, when maybe we don't need them to believe us. We just need to do the right thing."

I wanted to believe that was true. But I also feared that this conflict wouldn't be over until more blood was shed.

Some of it by my own hands.

# LUCAS

## THREE

Visiting *Hok'evale* was a welcome reprieve to the darkness surrounding Octavia Falls. The people there seemed so happy and carefree. I wanted that for our coven, too.

We flew on Leslie's back high above the trees. I still couldn't take my eyes off the magical creatures. I'd heard so many stories about them, but I'd never seen them with my own eyes. *Hok'evale* was certainly a place I'd like to return to one day, when this was all over.

We returned to the clearing, where Miles and Chloe were playing with the magical creatures. Miles slowly tip-toed toward a creature with a lion's body, the tail of a scorpion, and long, leathery wings. "Here, kitty kitty."

"Leave the manticore alone," Chloe called as she stroked the head of a large feline. "He's going to bite you."

"I'm sure he's—" Miles cut off as the manticore let out a loud roar. He quickly scurried back across the clearing in our direction. Chloe laughed.

We slid off Leslie's back, and Sam fed her a few treats.

"You two look like you're having fun," Nadine remarked as we approached Chloe. "It seems you made a friend."

Chloe sat cross-legged in the grass, and the feline she was petting rolled over as she scratched it under the chin. The cat was nearly as big as she was, but it didn't look like anything I'd seen before. It had the backend of a dog, and its long tail thumped against the ground happily. Although it had a mane like a lion and the pointed ears of a feline, its snout was blunt like a bear. Brown fur covered its body, and its eyes were a strange light gray with no irises or pupils. Two small horns protruded above its eyes. The creature kept its head low, never locking eyes with anyone.

"She's beautiful, isn't she?" Chloe asked. "I want to take her home with me."

Sam chuckled. "I'm sure she'd *love* it if you took her home, but magical creatures aren't allowed outside our borders. A glawackus like her snuck past the borders back in the late 1800s. It made it all the way to Connecticut and caused quite a ruckus with the lumberjacks. Killed a lot of livestock, too."

Chloe scratched the creature behind the ears. "She must like the habitat by us."

"I'm sure she'd be happy there," Sam said. "But it'd be too dangerous. These creatures may be blind, but if you look them straight in the eyes, they'll completely wipe your memory."

Chloe looked up at him. "She seems so docile."

Sam laughed. "Until she gets mad. You're lucky she likes you."

The glawackus sniffed Chloe, then put its head in her hand, like it wanted to give her something. Chloe gasped as she pulled her hand away, and a single whisker remained. "Look what she gave me!"

Sam furrowed his brow. "Is that... significant?"

Chloe nodded. "In witch culture, it's a good omen when cats give you a whisker. They're offering it up to use in your spells of protection and good luck. She's giving me some of her magic."

Sam's eyebrows shot up. "You better hold tight to that whisker. She's a very powerful creature."

Chloe subconjured the whisker, so she wouldn't lose it. "I will."

"Thank you for everything, Sam," I said. "We can't stay long, but we appreciate all your help."

"Anytime." Sam waved, and we said our goodbyes.

The glawackus let out a strange bark—almost like the sound of a hyena. The creature bowed its head to Chloe, before I opened a portal to the safe house. We stepped through it and into the hallway. Voices came from the home library a few doors down.

"They've been gone too long!" Helena insisted.

"It's only been a few hours," Verla assured her. "I'm sure your grand-daughter is fine."

"Nadine and Lucas can handle themselves," Professor Warren added. "*Hok'evale* is a safe place."

We approached the open doorway. The library was one of the largest rooms in the house, apart from the main living area. The walls were lined with bookcases, and a narrow staircase led to a second-level balcony. A big mahogany desk stood in front of a large, ornate window. A couch and matching armchair sat in the center of the room next to a coffee table.

Grant, Talia, and Onyx sat on the couch, and I noticed another guest had arrived while we were gone. Hattie sat in the chairs, stroking her wolf Familiar's head. Usually, Hattie stayed within the borders of Octavia Falls. She kept us updated on what was happening in town, and the priestesses didn't know she was working with us. It was dangerous for her to come here, but Verla must've called her in. This was important.

Helena paced the room, while Verla and Warren tried to comfort her. She heard the sound of our footsteps and whirled around. Her eyes lit up when she spotted her granddaughter. "Nadine, you're all right!"

"We're fine, Grammy," Nadine promised.

Helena frowned. "What took you so long? We were worried sick!"

"You might want to sit down," Nadine suggested. "We have a lot to tell you."

Everyone gathered around, and we told them what we'd learned while in *Hok'evale*. There was a lot of information to go over, and it took nearly an hour to come to a conclusion.

"If I'm to obtain the Mortana Wand, I need to pass the Warlock's Trial," I said. "That's how I will become a member of the Reaper Order. Once that happens, the reapers will pass the Mortana Wand on to me. We don't know what this trial entails, though. Every apprentice needs a master, but mine hasn't appeared—for whatever reason. Since there isn't magic we can do to summon a reaper, we'll have to go to Edgar Nowak so I can complete my training."

"How are you going to get to him?" Talia asked.

"That's a problem, because I can't portal between realms yet," I said. "Our first step is to track Edgar down, then find a way to him. There's no point in discussing our options until we know where we're going."

"Then let's find him," Grant said. "How exactly do we do that?"

"I have an idea for a tracking spell that should work, if we all combine our magic," Nadine announced. "The priestesses and I used something similar before. I don't think it would normally work, except that Lucas is the Reaper's Apprentice, so he has a connection to Edgar. With Lucas's reaper magic in the spell, we should be able to learn where Edgar is."

"Then let's get to work," Verla said. "What do we need?"

"A crystal ball, for starters," Nadine requested.

"I've got you covered." Talia conjured a crystal ball and set it on the coffee table.

"Everyone join hands," Nadine instructed. I took her hand on one side and Hattie's on the other.

Verla stepped out of the circle we were forming. "I won't be of any help. I had to use magic to cover my tracks when I went to meet up with Hattie earlier today, and I haven't been able to cast any spells since. I took every precaution to prevent being followed, and it drained my reserves."

"It's got to be the Waning," Nadine theorized. "It's like the closer you get to town, the more it affects you."

It was the Waning for sure, because Verla was a powerful witch, and though her spell was complicated, it shouldn't drain her completely. I sighed heavily. "Damn the Waning."

Chloe chuckled. "If we succeed, we may do just that. Let's give the Waning hell."

"All we need now is an incantation," Nadine said. She thought about it for a moment, but I'd already quickly formed an incantation in my mind.

*"Through this crystal ball we'll see where he's been. Show us the realm we'll find Edgar Nowak in,"* I suggested.

Nadine nodded, then addressed the others. "Lend me your power and repeat the incantation. I'll do the rest."

We began to recite the incantation. Magic surged through me, and it was so powerful I nearly lost my grip on Nadine's hand. I held on tighter. My friends' magic pulsed throughout our circle as we combined our power into a single spell. Above us, the lights flickered, and then went out.

Onyx gasped, and Grant gave a start. Talia shot nervous glances around the room, and Miles looked a bit shaken. Helena didn't take her eyes off Nadine. Chloe, Hattie, and Professor Warren remained relatively calm.

I watched Nadine as I continued speaking the incantation with the others. She had her eyes closed, looking deep in concentration. Slowly, the magic pulsing through me evened out, and it flowed effortlessly.

Nadine opened her eyes and stared into the crystal ball. Smoke swirled within the glass, and all gazes turned to watch the images taking shape. It was like watching a movie. We saw a cloaked figure with bones for hands and a skull for a head appear. A bright light shone behind him— so bright I had to squint to see anything. I couldn't make out any shapes except for the reaper. I assumed this to be a depiction of Alora.

Then the scene shifted, and it showed him stepping through a portal. His surroundings turned dark, though I could make out the shadows of gravestones in front of him. He approached a figure in the cemetery and spoke with them for a moment, before the scene shifted again and he appeared inside a home. I recognized Helena's living room, and I saw Nadine as the reaper took her soul from her body.

The incantation had asked us to show us where he'd been, and it was playing out the night we'd encountered him—the night of Nadine's Evoking Ceremony when I'd sent him to the Abyss so that he couldn't take Nadine there.

The scene sped up, until it depicted three figures in the woods— Edgar, Nadine, and me. Edgar and I fought, until I kicked his skull off his body and sent it sailing through the portal. Edgar's headless form approached me, and he blasted off another spell that ricocheted off my shield. The spell hit him, shooting him through the portal. Thunder cracked, like it had that night when the portal slammed closed.

Nadine and I disappeared from view as the scene followed Edgar's perspective. He tumbled downward into a dark, fiery landscape. He landed on black, crusted ground that looked like the remnants of cooled lava. His bony fingers felt around until he found his skull and positioned it back on his head. Though his eye sockets were empty, Edgar shifted his head from side to side, taking in the fires of hell. His jaw hung slack, and he quickly lifted his hands like he was going to create another portal.

Nothing happened. Edgar drew a wand from his cloak. The end glowed a bright red, and sparks flew out of the end of it…

But the portal never came. Edgar was stuck in the Abyss.

The smoke inside the crystal ball faded, until the glass became clear again. The lights overhead turned on, and our magic dissipated. The whole room remained silent for several beats.

Nadine was the first to speak. "Edgar is in the Abyss, and he has been since Lucas sent him there. Lucas, you said that reaping is different from portal magic. Even though reaping uses portals, it also affects the soul. Edgar was in the middle of reaping me, but he fell through the portal and reaped himself. Your powers could've amplified the reaping, too. It must've damaged his soul, so he can't escape. Edgar's been stuck there all this time."

"I never meant to hurt him like that," I admitted. "I only wanted to protect you."

"You couldn't have known," Nadine insisted.

I furrowed my brow thoughtfully. "This actually makes a lot of sense. This must be why he hasn't come to mentor me. Maybe he wants to contact me but can't because of something I did that night."

"At least we know where to find him, and he isn't going anywhere," Professor Warren said. "We know we need to get to the Abyss to get the Mentalist Wand. Now we know the Mortana Wand is there, too. We can get them both in one journey and bring them back together."

Verla stepped forward. "We have to go to Malovia as soon as possible, so we can find a portal to the Abyss and get those Wands."

"This is dangerous," Helena insisted.

"But necessary," Nadine argued.

Helena placed her hands on her hips. "And once you get to the Abyss, how are you getting out?"

"The same way we got in," Nadine stated. "Monsters slip through portals to Malovia all the time. If they can get out of the Abyss, so can we."

We'd gone over this before, and Helena never liked the answer. Helena sighed. "I'm merely stating that you must be prepared."

"We've been infusing crystals with magic all summer, so we'll have extra power to make our spells stronger," I reminded her. "The crystals will give us an edge if the Waning affects us while we're down there, but I don't believe that'll be a problem. The Waning has barely touched us all summer. It's like the further we are from Octavia Falls, the better our magic performs."

Talia looked thoughtful. "Maybe it's not about distance, but about *uniting*. The divide in the coven is causing the Waning. Perhaps our magic is working because our group is united."

"I think you're on to something," I mused. "But there has to be a connection to town, too. Verla said her magic has been affected since she approached town earlier, when she met up with Hattie."

"Either way, if division is causing the Waning, then uniting is the solution," Miles said. "If we can convince everyone else to unite, the Waning will go away, right? If that's the answer, then why aren't we focusing on uniting the coven instead of finding these Wands?"

"If we don't get them, the priestesses will, and then we'll be powerless to stop them," I explained. "They've already summoned a demon. They can do it again and use it to locate the Wands in the Abyss. All it takes is for them to make a deal with a demon to give them the Wands, and if they offer a demon the right bargain, he'll get the Wands for them. We need to get them first."

"Who cares if the priestesses have the Wands?" Miles argued. "If the coven unites, everyone can defeat them together. Besides, even if they get the two Wands in the Abyss, they still don't have the Curse Breaker Wand. The priestesses are powerless without Nadine."

"That's not true," Nadine cut in. "With four Wands, they would have the power of four Casts at their fingertips. They could take magic from everyone except me, and then they could kill me in an instant. The only reason they didn't kill me earlier is to prevent an uprising, but we're past that now. We have enough wards that the priestesses can't curse us or track us down right now, but if they have the power of all four Casts, they can overpower all the coven. No one is going to be able to revolt if the priestesses are controlling their magic. Even if we unite the coven and bring an end to the Waning, none of it will matter if the priestesses have the Wands. They'll create a Waning of their own to control people. Then the priestesses will use the Oaken Wands to divide us further."

"It's imperative we keep the Wands out of the priestesses' hands, because they've shown they'll only use the Wands to control people," I added. "We can use the Oaken Wands to restore the magic we've lost and end the Waning. Once the Waning is over, the priestesses will no longer have control over the coven, and our people can make choices for themselves again. They can choose to unite on their own, instead of this false union the priestesses are forcing that's only dividing us further. This divide will get worse with the more Wands the priestesses obtain. They're ruling by fear, and if we eliminate the threat by ending the Waning, people's hope will be restored, and we can work together again. The coven can choose who to put on the council, to build a better future. The only way to stop the priestesses' tyranny is to give the coven's power back to its people."

"So how do we get to the Abyss?" Grant asked. "Our Malovian contact is dead, and that was our ticket to hell. We can't just waltz into the fae capital and ask them where to find a portal to the underworld."

"Nadine and Lucas have been working on getting past Malovia's wards with portals all summer," Miles pointed out. "Why can't they just portal us to one of these entrances?"

"Nadine and I can combine our powers to get into Malovia, but we don't know where we're going from there," I replied. "Roaming around Malovia is dangerous, because if we stay too long there's a big chance we'll be spotted and killed. Not to mention Malovia is crawling with monsters, and we aren't familiar with the terrain. We have to know exactly where one of these entrances are before we show up, and we need someone to show us the way. Entrances to the Abyss aren't exactly tourist destinations. We need a guide."

"Lucas is right," Verla agreed. "We can't spend more than twenty-four hours in Malovia, or we'll surely be found out and executed. Even just getting in to deliver a message could prove deadly. It's not the same as Grant and Talia meeting their contact at a remote location. We can't simply portal into their capital city of Dolinska. Even if our portals didn't set off alarms, our presence would. They'll smell that we're witches and hang us before we make it a block. We need a powerful ally on our side who has authority in the city, so they can help us if we get into trouble. If we're going to do this, we need protection. To outsmart the fae, we need a fae on our side."

"Establishing new contacts could take months," Onyx pointed out. "The priestesses could summon a demon and get the Wands before we're ready."

"They will not," Hattie spoke up. "Rumor has it, the priestesses do not wish to summon another demon, as their last attempt failed. Professor Leto did not deliver an Oaken Wand to the priestesses as promised, and they'll want a sure thing before they take such a risk again. The priestesses need to be in control to maintain their power, and demons aren't controllable."

"Then they must not know there are Wands in the Abyss," Chloe said. "If they did, they would've already made a deal."

"As far as I understand, they do not know where to look for the other Oaken Wands, but that doesn't mean they won't be able to track them down," Hattie said. "I do not know the means in which they will do this, but I do know they won't stop until they have all the power of the coven in their hands. Octavia Falls has changed in just a few short months. You would be surprised to see how quickly people have converted to the priestesses' side. The religious group they call Miriam's Chosen was only the beginning. The members are following them blindly, going so far as to hand over their businesses and their properties to the Imperium Council in exchange for false promises. The Chosen believe that this is the road to salvation."

Nadine grimaced. "That's horrible. The priestesses can't keep taking without giving anything back."

"That's exactly what they'll continue to do, unless we stop them," Verla stated.

Grant cracked his knuckles. "I say we curse them."

"If we could, we'd have done that by now," Verla said. "Their wards are as strong as ours, if not stronger. To curse the priestesses, our powers would have to outperform theirs, and that takes energy away from us that we need to use for other purposes. Our focus needs to be on the Wands. If we're going to establish new connections in Malovia and get to the Abyss before the priestesses, we need to act quickly."

"There's a fae couple on the throne who we've met before—Ethan and Emma," I pointed out. "If we can get close enough to speak with them, they can help. I believe you know them, Hattie."

The fae had come looking for Hattie the night we ran into them outside Octavia Falls' border last November. Emma said Ethan had been possessed by a forest demon, and Hattie had since exorcized the demon.

Hattie gave a light nod. "It's true that I have met Emma and Ethan, but things are different now in Malovia than they were a year ago. It will be impossible to get in contact with the monarchs. However, their court may prove useful. I know someone connected to them who will help. She's a dark magic sympathizer. I haven't attempted to contact her yet because her enemies already have eyes on her, but we've run out of options. If I can get her a message, I'm confident she'll help us, but it will take time to make contact from the outside. The Malovian Revolution has taken over the country, and slipping a message past the fae's borders won't be easy. The messages will have to be coded, because if discovered by the wrong people, she'll be killed for speaking with witches. It will require several messages so that even if these notes are intercepted and decoded, the full message remains unread. I have to be extremely careful."

"Then let's get her a message, whatever it takes," Nadine said. "In the meantime, we need to develop a spell that will disguise our scent once we're in Malovia. Like Verla said, the shifters will smell us the second we arrive. We'll have to blend in, even if it's only for a short time."

Grant conjured a bundle of herbs. "I have just the thing. It's wolfsbane. Talia and I got it while we were traveling. Some shifters are allergic to it, so we brewed it into a tea to help cover our scent when we crossed the border."

"Wolfsbane, as in monkshood?" Chloe asked. "That plant is poisonous."

Grant shook his head. "It's a different herb called wolfsbane—a fae plant. It affects shifters, but it's safe for witches. There are no side effects. But it only affects the wolven Faction, and there are three other Factions of fae shifters—dragons, griffins, and alicorns. If we're to cross through the city, we'll need something stronger. Onyx and I can research how wolfsbane affects wolvens and locate similar herbs for the other Factions. It will take time, but we can brew a potion that will help disguise our scent."

"We'll need to disguise our outer appearance, too," Talia added. "The fae dress differently than we do, in regal dresses and elaborate, colorful cloaks. Helena's got a sewing machine in her room, and there are extra blankets and curtains in the linen closet that we can repurpose into cloaks."

"What about weapons?" Miles asked. "Iron is deadly to the fae. We might want iron weapons on hand in case we're discovered."

"No," Verla said. "They'll sense the iron, and it will give us away immediately. Our own magic shall suffice as a weapon. A scent-concealing potion and physical disguises is all we need, and we must be ready with them once it's time to move."

I nodded firmly. "Then let's get to work."

I knew what I was asking my friends to do, and it was risky. If anyone wanted to back out, I wouldn't blame them, but nobody did. We were all on the same page. It didn't matter the risk, because there were two Wands in the Abyss.

We couldn't afford to lose them.

# nadine

## FOUR

*I stood in a damp room shrouded in darkness. I could feel the floor beneath me and sense the walls boxing me in, but I saw nothing. An eerie silence sent a shiver down my spine. Immediately, panic swelled within me, though I wasn't sure where it had come from. It didn't feel like my own.*

*I cast a witch light, and I found myself standing in a long hall with a concrete floor and stone walls. Several doorways stood in front of me, and I wasn't sure which to investigate first. I didn't know what it all meant.*

*As I took a step to the closest doorway, I heard a whimpered cry come from down the hall. It was almost indiscernible, but it was hard to miss in the silence. My gaze locked on the door at the end of the hall, where I thought the sound had come from.*

*Slowly, I tiptoed toward the door. My heart beat wildly in my chest, and my hand shook as I reached out for the doorknob. I hesitated before my fingers connected with the handle.*

*I eyed the door, then slowly pressed my ear to the wood. My heart leapt into my throat as a shrill cry tore through the darkness.*

*Then everything disappeared.*

☾

I STARTLED AWAKE, and Isa mewed as I nearly kicked her off the bed. Lucas stirred beside me, and the details of the dream began to slip away as my

59

heart rate slowed. I tried to grasp on to the fading memory, but the dream eluded me more and more each moment.

It wasn't unusual for any of us to face bad dreams these days. Weeks had passed since we'd visited *Hok'evale*, and Hattie was still working out details with her contact in Malovia. Things were quiet here, and life had been peaceful the last six weeks. But far into the depths of my subconscious, I knew our time here was temporary, and I feared what we might face to obtain the Oaken Wands. My dreams merely reflected that unsettling worry I couldn't quite shake.

Lucas groaned as he reached for me, and I rolled over to snuggle into his arms. His lips brushed the skin beneath my ear. "Everything all right?"

I sank deeper into the mattress. "Everything's perfect."

It wasn't a lie, but it wasn't exactly the truth, either. We knew where to find the Mortana and Mentalist Wands, but we were no closer to finding a way into the Abyss, not until Hattie got a message through the Malovian borders. The fae were more cautious than ever, and Hattie's messenger had died before she was able to get her last message through. Her letter was intercepted, so we had to keep trying. There was nothing any of the rest of us could do to speed the process along, so we'd busied ourselves with wedding planning as a way to distract ourselves.

Our wedding was only two weeks away now. I prayed that we could hold on to these perfect moments for just a few weeks longer, at least until the wedding was over. I wasn't going to let the priestesses—or anyone else for that matter—ruin our special day.

Lucas placed a tender kiss on my lips, and my heart fluttered. *That's* what was perfect about all this. It was these little moments that nobody could take away from us. The priestesses could show up tomorrow and slaughter us on our own front steps, but they couldn't take away this moment in time when I woke in the arms of the man I loved.

I ran my fingers down the side of his face, taking in every detail of his features. "I wish I could freeze this moment, so we never had to leave this bed."

Lucas smirked. "If we were frozen, how would I ever do this?"

He rolled me over, then climbed on top of me to trail kisses down my neck. I could feel the hardness of his erection through the thin layers of fabric between us, and my thighs grew hot in wanting.

I snickered, and my hands slid down his body. "Keep kissing me, and you're going to get lucky."

He pressed a passionate kiss to my lips, then drew away with a smile. "I'm counting on it."

Just then, we heard footsteps outside the room, and Lucas and I both held our breath to listen. Grammy had walked in on us one too many times over the last few months that we were extra cautious about it. Our room had a lock, but still…

The footsteps faded down the hall, but the moment between us had already ended. I wanted to curse whoever had been out there.

Lucas sighed as he crawled off of me. "If we start now, your grandma's bound to interrupt. I can smell bacon. Whatever your grandma's up to, she wants us down for breakfast."

He wasn't wrong. The scents wafting up from the kitchen smelled delicious.

"She's just trying to put people in good spirits," I said. Hope was a good thing, because spirits hadn't been high around here lately. It's why we were still having the wedding despite being driven out of town. We needed hope, and there was no better way to foster it than bringing our friends together.

I dressed in a purple maxi dress with a warm black cardigan, then secured the old key Grammy had given me around my neck. I'd gifted it to Lucas, but he'd tried to give it back, and we'd resolved to share it.

We left our bedroom but stopped in the doorway when we saw a small package sitting outside our door. The box was a deep purple to match our wedding colors, and it was held closed by a teal ribbon. A note in Onyx's handwriting said, *Open Me!*

I exchanged a curious glance with Lucas. "What's this?"

"No idea, but I guess we're about to find out." He opened the package, and inside sat a piece of paper that had been rolled up like a scroll. I reached inside and unfurled it, then began reading.

*You'll have plenty of time for just you two,*
*but you haven't yet said I do.*
*You're ours until that special day.*
*Your friends are just a few clues away.*

*One goes left, and one goes right.*
*You'll meet back up late tonight.*
*For the bride taking the groom's last name,*
*Don't peek outside or you've lost the game.*

I smiled. "It's a scavenger hunt!"

"They're stealing you from me!" Lucas protested playfully.

"You'll get me back tonight," I teased.

"They better bring you back in one piece," he joked.

I sucked a breath. "I don't know. We're walking into danger here."

Lucas tapped his chin. "I guess we're just going to have to take a risk."

"I'm the one with rules," I said, waving the paper at him. "The only question is, which one of us goes where?"

Isa and Oliver pushed past us, and Isa turned the hall to the right. She started meowing, while Oliver went for the stairs.

"I guess that answers that question," Lucas said. "Have fun." He placed a kiss on my lips, and we went our separate ways.

I followed Isa and found another box sitting at the end of the hall. I opened the box and jumped when a spell like fireworks erupted out of the box. White sparkling lights exploded above my head and rained down on me. A magical tune of celebration sang from somewhere inside the box. I laughed as I pulled the scroll out and began to read it.

*Congratulations, Nadine. You found your first clue.*
*The second one may be a challenge for you.*
*Downstairs and through a door is another clue,*
*If you want to have your cake and eat it, too!*

I thought about it for a few moments, but I wasn't sure what door Onyx was talking about. I figured the cake had to mean something, so I went downstairs to the kitchen. I noticed all the windows in the house were covered by curtains. They were really serious about me not peeking outside.

In the kitchen, I started opening the cabinet doors, but I didn't find any clue box. I checked the pantry, but still nothing.

I read over the clue again, tapping my foot. "Mm, Isa. You'd think the cake would be a clue to the kitchen, right? Or maybe the dining room…"

I trailed off as my eyes landed on the oven. "I've got it!"

I opened the oven door, and victory surged through me when I found a cupcake sitting inside. It was decorated in purple frosting with teal sprinkles. I withdrew it from the oven and turned it around, looking for clues, but I didn't find any writing on it. I peeled back the cupcake liner, thinking I'd find a clue inside, but there was nothing there, either. It was obvious what I had to do.

I bit into the cupcake, and the most glorious spell overtook my whole body. Joy filled my chest, and a tingling sensation made me feel as if I was floating several inches off the ground. The euphoria made me giddy. I closed my eyes to take it in.

The spell lasted only a few seconds, before I felt my feet against the solid ground again. I opened my eyes to see a piece of paper sticking out of the cupcake. I pulled it out and cleaned it off, then unfurled the paper.

> *We knew you could do it.*
> *You're so very clever.*
> *The third clue is hidden*
> *Where you'd feel better.*

I had to think about this one for a minute, until I realized it could only mean the medicine cabinet in the bathroom. I went to the bathroom, where I found a cauldron sitting on the counter. A shimmering purple liquid swirled inside the pot, and a teal vial sat beside it.

I clicked my tongue. "Oh, Onyx, you're making this too easy."

I poured the teal liquid into the purple potion, and a message in a small bottle floated to the top, bobbing along the surface. I pulled the bottle from the cauldron and tipped the scroll into my hands.

> *You're getting so close!*
> *Just one clue more.*
> *You'll find it on blades—*
> *not one, but four.*

I furrowed my brow. "Four blades. That's oddly specific."

I went back into the kitchen and looked around the knife block, but there were no clues hidden anywhere near it. I checked the silverware drawer, but still nothing.

"Blades..." I said thoughtfully. "It must be talking about knives, right, Isa?"

I looked down at my cat, but she looked as clueless as I was. "Except there are twelve knives in the knife block, and more than four in the drawer. Where else do we keep knives...? Unless it isn't about knives at all. It says *on* blades, rather than near them. What else has blades? A wand, maybe..."

Then it hit me. I went into the den, where a fan with four blades hung from the ceiling. I flipped the switch on the wall, and the fan started to spin. To my surprise, feathers exploded out of the ceiling, as if from out of nowhere, raining down on me. I laughed as the feathers tickled my skin. I looked upward, and my eyes caught sight of a piece of paper fluttering downward with the feathers. I reached out to grab it and caught the clue in my fingertips.

"Damn, Onyx," I said with a smirk. "That was a good one."

*You figured it out!*
*Just one step more.*
*The final surprise*
*is through the glass door.*

"Come on, Isa." I cocked my head. There was only one glass door the clue could be referring to, and now it made sense why all the windows were covered by curtains. Isa followed me to the patio door, and we stepped outside.

"Surprise!" a chorus of female voices shouted.

The girls all sat around the patio table, where a full breakfast had been laid out for us. It was a warm autumn morning, and the trees surrounding us were all shades of oranges, reds, and yellows. Purple and teal streamers hung from the furniture and danced in the breeze.

Talia checked her phone. "Three minutes and fifty-two seconds," she announced. "Who was closest without going over?"

Grammy raised her hand. "I bet three forty-five."

"That makes Helena the first prize-winner of the day," Talia said. She conjured a gift bag and gave it to Grammy. Grammy pulled out a small bottle of maple syrup.

I placed my hands on my hips. "What's going on here?"

"Your bridal shower, of course." Chloe rolled her eyes, but she wore a playful smile.

"Did you guys place bets on how fast I could find the clues?" I asked.

"Yes, and I underestimated you," Talia admitted. "I said four-fifteen."

"I wasn't sure how long it'd take you on that last one," Onyx added.

"It was a good one," I told her as I took the empty seat at the head of the table. "You did a great job setting it up."

"We have a whole day of fun planned," Chloe raved. "But first, I'm starving."

Grammy had prepared a feast. I started with two pancakes and passed them around the table. Talia kept shoving more and more plates of food at me until my own plate was so full I couldn't find room for any more. Along with the pancakes, Grammy had prepared French toast, bacon, three types of eggs, hash browns, sausage, fruit salad, and muffins. It was like every breakfast food imaginable had been placed on this table.

"Wow, Grammy," I said. "You really went all-out."

"I wanted to give you options," she replied. "When you were a kid, you were a *very* picky eater. I remember Christmas Eve when you were seven years old, and you wouldn't eat anything except for peppermint candy canes."

I laughed. "That can't be true."

"It is!" Grammy cried. "Your mom begged me to pull off some culinary alchemy magic. I turned those mashed potatoes into peppermint candy canes—all the taste of candy but the nutrition of vegetables. You wouldn't believe how fast you ate those up."

"You did not!" I chuckled.

"I swear it," Grammy promised.

"It's true," Verla added. "I remember your mother telling me about it."

Grammy kept telling stories about my childhood, and everyone was laughing. They all seemed to be having a really good time, and I couldn't remember the last time I laughed this much.

Even the cats seemed to be in good spirits. They ate, then started chasing each other around the patio.

I was stuffed by the time Grammy finally stood and said, "Well, these plates aren't going to clean themselves."

"I don't know about you, but mine has no problems," Chloe joked as her plate rose into the air. She used her telekinesis to open the patio door and float her plate inside.

"Then you can help me wash the dishes," Grammy suggested.

Everyone helped clean up, and within a few minutes, the dishes were clean and the table was washed down. We gathered in the living room, where a warm fire flickered in the fireplace.

Chloe stood in front of everyone with a stack of papers in her hands. "Helena has given us the run-down of Nadine's childhood, but this wouldn't be a bridal shower if we left the groom out of it. So we're going to play some games—"

*Kaboom!*

I startled, and Isa jumped into my lap. "What the hell was that!?"

Verla waved her hand. "The boys. Jonathan warned us it might get a little loud."

"Professor Warren is *blowing stuff up*?" I demanded.

Verla shrugged, like she expected this from him. "He calls it target practice."

"We're not going to let some boys ruin our relaxing day." Chloe stomped over to the patio door and leaned out to shout, "HEY! WOULD YOU KEEP IT DOWN OUT THERE!?"

"Sorry!" I heard Miles shout in the distance, before another explosion went off.

Chloe rolled her eyes, then proceeded to pass out cards. It was a game that asked questions about the bride and groom, and the guests were supposed to guess the answers. I filled out my sheet with the real answers so that Chloe had an answer key.

Apparently, Chloe had filmed Lucas giving his answers beforehand, and she put the video up on the TV for us all to watch.

*"Who said I love you first?"* Chloe asked in the video.

*"I did,"* Lucas answered.

"Wait, no!" I protested. "That's not true. *I* said I love you first."

Chloe paused the video. "Now I *have* to hear this story."

"It was the night of my Evoking Ceremony, after Lucas saved me from that reaper. He's like, *Why'd you do that?* And I'm like, *Don't you get it, you fool? I love you.*"

"That's not the story *he* told me," Chloe said. "Look."

She played the video again, and Lucas kept talking. "*It was the night of her Evoking Ceremony, after I saved her from a reaper. Right before I put her soul back in her body, I told her I loved her.*"

"That doesn't count," I insisted with a laugh. "I wasn't conscious."

We all had a good laugh, and I recounted other stories about our relationship as we went through the questions. It was a lot of fun.

Talia had brought a wedding-themed tarot deck, and we all took turns giving each other readings. Talia drew for my future with Lucas, and it was no surprise that she pulled The Lovers card, which depicted a bride and groom at the altar. The Lovers was a card of harmony and meaningful relationships. It was certainly a good sign for our relationship.

Finally, Chloe wheeled out a cart full of liquor and fruit juices, and we broke into teams to compete on who could brew the best wedding cocktail. Verla and I teamed up, and since I didn't drink alcohol, we used a shot of Grant's Fizzy Bubbly he brewed last week. It was a potion he'd come up with designed to keep his blood sugar from spiking. It was alcohol-free, but whatever spell he'd put on it still made a person tipsy. Verla and I won by mixing it with cranberry and orange juice.

We lounged on the couches in the living room, sipping our cocktails and laughing.

"If you'll all turn your attention to our cats, I believe they have prepared some entertainment," Chloe announced.

Verla stood, and when she cleared her throat, the cats came running. "Places everyone."

Verla pressed a button on the TV remote, and a slow wedding song came over the speakers. The cats began to spin around each other in a coordinated motion, like they were ballroom dancing. Then the beat changed, becoming more upbeat. The cats joined in a center circle, then jumped outward in sync. They spun around like they were chasing their tails, then rolled over on their bellies. It was beautifully in sync and fun to watch. We all applauded when they finished.

"Good kitties!" Verla praised as she tossed them all treats.

"I think it's time for presents!" Onyx exclaimed.

All around the room, people conjured their gifts. I was overwhelmed by how many packages there were.

"Open mine first!" Chloe said, shoving a package in my direction.

I sat straighter on the couch and set my drink on the end table. I tore open the wrapping paper and found a white candle inside. Mine and Lucas's name were etched on the candle, along with our wedding date.

"It's a wedding candle for relationship rituals," Chloe said. "You and Lucas can use it in your spellwork. Miles and I made it at a shop in *Hok'evale.*"

"That's really thoughtful," I told her. "Thank you, Chloe."

I unwrapped Onyx's present next and found a box full of all kinds of amethyst crystals. Some of them were raw stone, while others were cut to points. I could feel the alchemy magic pulsing off of them.

I laughed. "You know me too well."

Onyx chucked. "I figured you could have fun brewing potions."

Onyx knew I'd been using Alchemy crystals in class when I was pretending to be an Alchemist. She charged up the crystals with her magic so I could use them to brew potions.

"I love it, Onyx." I set the crystals aside and started opening her next present. I stilled when I saw the next gift she'd given me. It was a leather-bound book, and when I opened it, I found handwritten instructions for love potions. It was incredible. It came in a box with a few herbs to accompany some of the potions.

"These are the best potions I could find for relationships," Onyx said. "The first one is an aphrodisiac brew for your wedding night."

"Ooh, I'm making that for sure. Is it safe for my body?" I asked.

"It's totally safe for everyone," she confirmed. "It's even approved for pregnant women."

"Thank you, Onyx." I leaned over to give her a hug.

Verla went next, and she handed me a small box wrapped in blue foil. Inside sat a beautiful hairpin with blue stones in it.

"It's your something old, something borrowed, *and* something blue—symbols of good luck for a bride on her wedding day," Verla told me. "It was my grandmother's. I lent it to your mother when she got married."

I went speechless. "My *mom* wore this to her wedding?"

Verla nodded. "Yes. And I think she'd want you to wear it, too."

I couldn't help it when I started tearing up. I didn't have a lot left of my mom. Most of my mementos had been destroyed in the fire at Grammy's house. I still had a small box I'd rescued from my dorm room that I kept in my stash, but that was it. I knew *technically* this hair pin didn't belong to my mom, but she had a connection to it, and that made it really special. I couldn't believe I'd get to wear the same hair pin on my wedding day as my mother did.

"Thank you so much," I told Verla, before crossing the room to pull her into a hug. I choked up and couldn't find the words to tell her just how much this meant to me. My own mother wasn't here, but Verla had brought a piece of her to this party, and I couldn't be more grateful. I knew my parents were gone, and they weren't coming back in the same way they'd been here before. I'd said goodbye to them long ago, but I still wished they could've made it to this wedding. I didn't think Verla realized it, but she was the family I needed when my own wasn't here.

I pulled away and sniffled, then bent to show Isa. "Hear that, Isa? It's the hairpin you wore in your last life."

Isa sniffed it, then rubbed her head against my hand. She wouldn't remember, because even though she was my mother reincarnated, she didn't keep her memories from her past life.

I returned to my spot on the couch, and Grammy handed me her present. Inside the box was a crocheted blanket made of purple and teal yarn. I pulled it out and held it up. "Grammy, this is gorgeous! Hold on, this looks familiar... You said you were making this for the nursing home!"

"Well, I made *some* blankets for the nursing home, but you seemed to like this one so well," Grammy said. "Did you know that in the Miriamic Coven, purple symbolizes spiritual connection and teal symbolizes peace?"

"I knew about purple, but not about the teal. I love the colors together." I pulled the blanket close and inhaled the scent. It smelled just like Grammy. "This is perfect. I love it."

Talia was last, and she had two large packages for me. I opened the first one, and it was filled with all kinds of spa treatments—Epsom salts, face masks, lotion, teas, and more.

"This is for the morning of the wedding," Talia said. "We're treating you to a whole spa day before you walk down the aisle."

"That's so thoughtful," I told her.

"And this one is for *after* the ceremony," she said, handing me the next box.

I furrowed my brow, because I wasn't quite sure what she meant. When I opened the box, I slammed it shut immediately.

"Holy fuck, Talia!" I cried. "My grandmother is here!"

Talia snickered. "Hey, I didn't pull this off alone. Helena made a few suggestions."

"We all pitched in," Chloe added, practically bouncing in her seat.

"What is it?" Verla asked curiously. Verla clearly hadn't been in on the joke, because she genuinely had no idea.

I blushed and sheepishly opened the box again. I pulled out a vibrator, still in the package, and held it up for everyone to see. "Sex toys. A *lot* of them."

"Oh..." Verla's eyebrows shot up, and she took a long sip of her cocktail.

I pulled toys out of the box and set them aside. There were so many—nipple clamps, a butt plug, and a feather on the end of a stick. Talia had even included a white lace one-piece with a slit in the crotch for easy access.

There was something that looked like a large flashlight. I didn't realize what it was at first, until I accidentally pressed a button on the side and it started vibrating.

"You guys!" I cried.

"What's the problem?" Talia asked. "Toys are really fun!"

"Lucas doesn't *not* need one of these," I said. "That's what I'm here for."

Chloe just about died laughing.

That wasn't all of it, either. There were all kinds of massage oils and lubricants for different parts of the body. I didn't want to know how much they spent on all this.

I set the box aside. "You guys *really* went all out on the gag gift."

"Someone had to!" Talia nearly died laughing. "It was totally worth it to see the look on your face."

"I have no shame," I told her, but it *was* a little weird with Grammy and Verla in the room. Neither of them showed any indication of what they thought of this, but my cheeks still flamed.

"Now that presents are over, it's time for our final game..." Talia conjured a basket and handed it to me. "We wrote down some memories we have with you and put them into the basket. You read them out loud, and we'll guess who wrote them!"

"This is a neat idea. Let's see…" I picked out one of the sheets of paper and began reading. *"I remember the first day I met Nadine. Helena must've shoved a hundred condoms into her hands and told her to stay safe in college."*

I burst into laughter.

"That one is Talia's!" Grammy cried, pointing to my best friend.

"Hey, you're the one who tainted her first impression," Talia laughed.

"I just wanted her to be safe!" Grammy defended.

"You know the school supplied those for free, right?" Verla told her.

"What if the health services center ran out?" Grammy asked.

"Believe me, Grammy, I did not run out," I said, before picking up another piece of paper. *"I remember finding a box of condoms in Nadine's room—*you guys! Is this all you think about?"

"Apparently," Talia snickered. "That one has to be Chloe. She broke into our room Freshman year."

Chloe cringed. "Sorry about that. But it makes for a good story, right?"

"Yeah, because you're my excuse when I say I didn't run out, because my condom box was sabotaged!" I joked. "You're forgiven, Chloe."

I kept pulling memories from the basket. A lot of them were funny, but most of them were really sweet. My heart felt full the more I read.

*"I remember Nadine decorated an ice cream cake for my birthday. She accidentally left it next to the stove, and it melted."* I read the last paper aloud, smiling lightly.

"That's got to be Talia's," Onyx guessed.

"It wasn't me," Talia said. "I'm guessing Helena."

Grammy smiled proudly. "Yep. It was my sixtieth birthday, and she was only ten years old. I don't blame her for leaving the cake out. She gets points for effort."

I stood. "I think I might be able to make it up to you, Grammy. Hold on."

I'd had this planned for a while. I knew it was my special day, but Grammy was turning seventy tomorrow. She insisted she didn't want a party when we'd celebrated Grant's birthday last weekend, but I wanted to do something special for her regardless.

I opened the freezer and pulled out an ice cream cake, then grabbed two candles I'd stashed in the back of a cupboard. I found a box of matches and lit them, then returned to the living room.

"Happy birthday!" I exclaimed.

The room burst into song, and Grammy threw her hands over her mouth. "Oh, Nadine! You didn't have to."

"No, I didn't, but I *wanted* to," I said. Lucas and I made a run to *Hok'e-vale* a few days ago to refill my prescriptions, and we'd picked up the cake while we were gone.

I set the cake on the coffee table in front of Grammy. She grabbed my hand and squeezed it. "That's so sweet of you. Thank you."

Grammy blew out her candles, and we all cheered.

I had the best time laughing and chatting with my friends. We spent the rest of the day playing games, doing puzzles, and snacking on leftovers from breakfast. It was the most fun I'd had in a long time.

I joined Grammy in the kitchen that night to help her wash dishes. The other women were still chatting in the living room, and the guys hadn't come in from outside yet. I listened to my friends' laughter as I scrubbed cocktail glasses in the sink.

"Is everything all right, Nadine?" Grammy asked. "You're awfully quiet."

I wasn't quite aware of the thoughts going through my head until Grammy brought attention to them. I noticed the rocks settling in my gut. I wasn't ready for this day to end.

I set a glass on the drying rack and sighed. "I had the best day with you, but I feel like I'm waiting for the other shoe to drop. It seems that any time something good happens, something bad has to come along to even out the scales."

"I don't believe in that nonsense," Grammy said as she dried the dishes.

"I don't *want* to believe it, but it feels true," I admitted. "Lucas and I won our trial, but Everly died. This kind of stuff happens to us all the time."

"That doesn't mean the events are tied together by cosmic forces," Grammy stated. "Perhaps good and bad things just *happen*, and one doesn't depend on the other. It's okay for good things to exist independently."

Verla's laughter rang from the other room, and I looked over to see her clutching her stomach.

Grammy noticed me watching her. "Clarice has changed since your mother died. There's a light that has left her eyes, but she's still able to find the good in things. Trauma changes people, but we can still find joy after the fact."

I nodded along, but I didn't say anything as I thought about what she said.

"The last thing I want is for you to get hurt, but I can't go back and change the past," Grammy said. "I wish I could have protected you, but all we can do is look toward the future."

"You tried," I told her as I reached for the key around my neck. "You gave me this key to protect us, but I don't think it has. We've all been through so much. What is this key, really?"

She shook her head. "I don't really know, to be honest. Your grandfather gave it to me before he died, and he said it was very important. Perhaps it was never meant for me or you."

"Then who's it for?" I wondered.

"I'm not sure, but we best hold on to it for now," Grammy said. "In the meantime, enjoy what you have. You are surrounded by friends and family who love you very much, and we will *always* be there for you."

I set the last glass in the drying rack. "Thank you, Grammy."

The patio door opened, and the guys' laughter filled the house. I dried my hands and returned to the living room. Lucas was laughing so hard that his eyes crinkled at the corners, and it made me forget what Grammy and I had been talking about. He looked so happy and carefree.

"Looks like you ladies had a blast," Grant said as he stood in front of the pile of presents. "What'd Nadine get?"

He reached for the box of sex toys, and I nearly jumped out of my skin as I raced across the room to slam the top shut. "Nothing!"

"Ooh," Grant sang. "It's *that* kind of gift."

"Lucas," I said quickly. "Could you help me carry all this up to our room?"

It was funny when the girls made me open the gag gift, but I did *not* need to be showing off sex toys to Professor Warren. I think I'd die.

"Sure." Lucas approached me nonchalantly. I didn't think he'd realized what was in the box.

Talia nudged me as I passed her. "Have fun."

I shot her a nervous smile. I'd been in the mood this morning, but now my friends' teasing had ruined that for sure. Lucas and I went up to our room, and I locked the door behind us.

"What was all that about?" he asked as he set the box on the bed. "You were acting like—oh."

Lucas opened the box, and his eyebrows shot up. *"Oh.* Wow, that's uh… a big dildo."

"It wasn't my idea," I said quickly, wringing my hands together.

Lucas eyed me curiously. "You're acting strange. What's going on?"

I shot a glance toward the door, even though everyone else was downstairs. "I know the toys are a gag gift and I'm supposed to laugh at it, but I don't get why they'd spend all this money on this stuff if they didn't expect us to actually *use* them. But don't toys seem… a bit much? I'm happy with our sex as it is."

Lucas wrapped me in his arms and held me close. "Nad, we don't have to use them if you don't want to—not now or ever. I don't want you to feel like you have to just because they're there."

"It's just… I would never want you to think you aren't enough for me," I told him. "We don't need the toys."

"Fair enough." Lucas drew away, then he closed up the box and slid it under the bed. "It's like they were never here to begin with."

"Thanks," I told him as we curled up together on the bed. Lucas took me in his arms, and though neither of us made a move to take things further, I felt intimately connected with him anyway. All the tension in my body melted away. "This feels really good."

"I'm glad you're happy," Lucas whispered.

"I am. I had a really good day." I rolled onto my side to look at him. "How was your day?"

Lucas roamed his hands over my body, but he was gentle about it, admiring me more than anything. "It was good. Hardly anyone died."

I rolled my eyes. "You say that very nonchalantly."

Lucas shrugged. "I listen to people die every day. Some days are darker than others. Today was better—natural deaths only."

"That's good," I said. "How was your bachelor party?"

"It was fun. We drank beer and blew shit up. Professor Warren used containers from the recycling to make targets in the yard, and we shot them with our magic. Grant helped make some potions that made soda bottles explode like rockets. I think we got one to fly at least a hundred feet in the air."

Lucas's hands traveled over the scars on my legs, and his lips turned down at the corners.

I stiffened. "What's wrong?"

He traced my scars with his finger. They were lighter in color now, but still discernible up close. "We've been through so much. I wish we could be this happy forever."

"We will be," I said, but I think we both felt the hollowness of the promise. We couldn't be sure, not until this conflict was over. I quickly added, "At least for now, we have a wedding to look forward to. I want to make the most of it."

"I do, too," Lucas agreed, before placing a kiss on my forehead. "No matter what's happening in the world around us, you never fail to make me happy. And that, Nad, is exactly why I asked you to marry me."

I could tell his words were honest, but I sensed uncertainty, too. I didn't think he was afraid to marry me, but it was more like something was missing. I'd felt it all day and knew exactly how he felt. We were about to join ourselves in marriage, and that was a commitment great enough to rearrange the cosmos. It was something everyone we loved should be here for, but they wouldn't get the chance. My mother should've been here today to celebrate my bridal shower, and my dad should be preparing to walk me down the aisle, but they were both gone. Lucas's brother and his parents wouldn't be here, either. It was the melancholy side of an otherwise perfect union.

I was prepared to move forward with this wedding no matter what, because I'd been forced to keep going even when my loved ones could no longer walk beside me. I didn't know if Lucas was willing to do the same, but by the goddess, I hoped so.

I wanted to move forward, even if the family I'd once had wouldn't be here beside me to watch me do it. I wasn't sure if Lucas was ready to do the same.

# FIVE

"This isn't working," I complained.

I slumped to the ground and kicked my feet off the outcropping of rock Professor Warren had brought me to, swinging them over the edge. The rock face wasn't very tall; I could easily jump down. The safe house wasn't far, and I could hear Nadine's laughter carrying across the yard. She'd picked apples with the girls, and they sat at a picnic table to cut them up for apple pies. It looked like it'd turned into a food fight. Meanwhile, I was supposed to be working on my powers.

Professor Warren wanted me to try summoning a ghost. He figured if I could help spirits move on to the afterlife, I must be able to see them. Otherwise, I couldn't harness my gift.

"Perhaps we're too far away from any spirits who will hear your call," he suggested. "Or maybe it's our wards."

"Or maybe I can't see spirits until I've crossed over myself," I theorized. Oliver gave a trill and came to sit beside me. "I'm not a Seer. I've only ever helped spirits cross over under specific circumstances. Either Miles helped bring them onto the physical plane so I could interact with them, or I saw them while astral traveling."

"You can't rely on Miles to be there every time you wish to help a spirit cross over," Warren said. "I know there isn't a handbook for reapers, but there *has* to be more to your powers."

I scoffed. "There *should* be a handbook."

"With a gift as rare as yours, the stories get lost over time," Professor Warren pointed out. "We can figure this out. I know we can."

My shoulders fell, but I didn't respond. I kept my gaze on Nadine as she dodged another piece of apple Talia had thrown at her. Isa licked the apple slice, then batted it around with her paw.

Professor Warren came to sit beside me. He wore jeans and a black t-shirt, which seemed in casual contrast against the suits I was so used to seeing him in. "It's not your powers that you're upset about."

It wasn't a question. I shook my head in confirmation.

"You're not getting cold feet, are you?" he asked.

"What? No." *Nothing* could stop me from marrying Nadine. "I just wish it were happening under better circumstances."

I'd been thinking about this for a while now. I tried not to let it get under my skin, but as the wedding approached, it weighed heavier on my mind. I was certain Nadine had picked up on it the other night, but she didn't ask about it. The last thing I wanted was for her to think I didn't want to get married to her, because that was the exact *opposite* of how I felt.

"Tell me more," Professor Warren encouraged. "It's best to get it off your chest before the wedding."

I sighed heavily, because I knew he was right. I knew Dr. Mack would say the same thing, and her therapy sessions had helped so much. I'd been able to work through a lot of my issues, but I'd resolved long ago that there was one wound I may never heal from.

I didn't like to talk about it, but I knew I could open up to Professor Warren. He was supportive in ways my own family never had been. I never quite understood how Professor Warren had so much wisdom, yet my father completely lacked emotional intelligence at all. They were the same age—both in their forties—and they'd both been through some rough shit. My father had taken all that crap out on me, whereas Professor Warren used his experience to help. They were complete opposites.

"I want to give Nadine the world," I told Warren. "And this is… okay for now. But this place is also a reminder of everything we've lost—and everyone who won't be here. I made a choice to leave Octavia Falls and leave my family behind. I don't regret it, but part of me wishes my parents had cared enough. They never would've approved of this wedding. Hell, they'd try to stop it, if they were here."

"I understand," Warren said. "I'm proud of you for walking away from your parents, because most people don't have the strength to do that. It's hard living with parents who don't respect your choices. Nobody cuts off contact from their mom and dad unless they truly feel like they have no other choice. And even then, some kids prefer to die before they'll choose to walk away."

I immediately thought of Eric. A chill breeze passed over my skin, and I gave a shudder. His words hit a bit too close to home. "I just don't know why I can't forget about them."

"No matter how long it's been, you aren't going to get over how horrible your family is. Even if you've decided that you no longer want them in your life, that decision is still going to hurt. It rarely gets easier with time, even if it's the healthiest thing for you." Professor Warren had told me before about his absent father, and I knew he understood.

"I'm used to the way my parents are, and I'm okay with that. It's more that I wish I had family here at all. No one is here to support me."

"That's not true," Professor Warren said, gesturing toward the house. "*We're* here for you."

"I know that, but it isn't the same," I admitted. "Parents are supposed to be there for their children, but mine never were. I've held on to hope for so long that my parents would change, but they've shown me that's never going to happen."

I could never forget the last time I saw them. They'd invited Nadine and me over for dinner before we fled Octavia Falls, and I'd been naive enough to accept their request, thinking we could finally make up after all this time. Instead, my father had gone into a rage and almost hurt Nadine. I'd fought back and knocked him out. My mother had the chance to come with us, but she made the choice to stay with *him*.

I didn't want to see my parents again, that was for sure. I only wished they'd cared, and maybe things would be different.

"It's scary trying to find my place in the world," I continued. "I know my place is with Nadine, but there's this other voice in my head that says if the family I came from didn't want me, why would anyone else? Parents are supposed to love their kids unconditionally, and mine despise me. I'd be lying if I said it didn't make me feel unlovable."

"No one can replace the love your parents were meant to provide you with, but it does not mean you cannot be loved by others," Warren said softly. "Your parents were incapable of showing you the love you deserved, and that's a reflection of them, not you."

"I know that logically, but my heart tells me a different story," I said. "My parents were never there, and so I was alone in this world from the start. I had my brother, but Eric's gone now, too. Sometimes it makes me feel like I really am alone in this world. After all, if your own mom and dad can't love you or treat you right, what's going to happen with your chosen family, who isn't obligated to stick around because of blood? They'll eventually get sick of you too and leave. Friends come and go, and Nadine could choose to leave at any time. If she really wanted that, I wouldn't make her stay, because I'd want her to be happy no matter what."

"Nadine chose to love you, because *you* make her happy." Warren gestured toward Nadine and the others across the lawn. "All of these people love you, and their love means more than the love you receive from the people who gave birth to you, because your friends chose you. Nadine loves you for who you are, not because she's related to you. You've been trying to prove yourself to your parents your whole life, and you've never been good enough for them. Here with your friends, you don't have to prove yourself, because they already accept you for who you are."

"I know I'm worthy of love, and I believe these people love me, but it's also scary to think they could take that back at any time," I said. "My parents' love was always conditional, if I ever received it at all, so it's hard getting used to someone loving me in a different way. It's even harder believing the people in my life now aren't going to cut and run at any time, because that's what my parents did to me, over and over whenever I didn't do what they wanted… and even if I did, they still abandoned me at times, even if I was the perfect kid. You only get one family, and if your family is broken, you don't get a chance at a new one. I was born to fucked-up parents, and I'm not going to get new ones. I think that's the hardest part of all this. I know I can be loved, but I'll never be loved in that way… like a son should. I wanted my family to show up for me, and they won't be here. They wouldn't come to my wedding even if I asked, and I won't ask, because it's not safe for Nadine and me to have them here. And not just because of the priestesses."

"Perhaps your real family is closer than you think," Professor Warren mused. "Family isn't who you're born to. Helena has taken on the role of your mother, and Grant is your brother. You're making a new family here. After the wedding, Nadine will be your family—your *wife*."

I liked the sound of that. Marrying Nadine was all I'd ever dreamed of, but it couldn't replace what I never had in the first place.

"I want to, but I don't know if I can believe that," I said. "I just keep waiting for the moment when Grant, Nadine... *everybody* just gets tired of me, and leaves."

"The only way around that is to trust that they won't," Professor Warren said. "After all, waiting around to get hurt is a self-fulfilling prophecy you put upon yourself. If you think the ones you love will always leave you, they're going to have a hell of a hard time convincing you they want to be here. But if you trust that you're the person they truly want and value... well, it gets a lot easier from that point out to convince yourself you're where you ought to be."

His words had a profound impact on me. I didn't want my family back, but I was still grieving losing them. No matter how much love my friends gave me, hell, how much love Nadine gave me, I always felt alone. There was a big hole in my heart that told me I was so empty inside that everyone I loved would end up leaving eventually, because if my blood didn't want me, who else would? For fuck's sake, Eric had died to get away from it all, even if it meant leaving me behind. So with where I was at now, what did it all mean for me?

I wasn't sure, but I at least had to give it a shot. Marrying Nadine meant choosing to believe that I could be loved and believing that I could start over. I wasn't sure if she and my friends could be the family I so desperately wanted... but maybe if they couldn't replace my parents, at least they could become something better. I definitely didn't want the kind of *love* that I'd had before.

I wanted something new. And maybe this could be the fresh start that I needed. I only had to hold on to the hope that what I was fighting for would always choose to stay.

SIX

The wedding couldn't come soon enough, yet somehow, the following two weeks passed in the blink of an eye. Before I knew it, I was waking in Talia's bed. For a moment, I forgot where I was, and then I remembered that I'd slept in her room the previous night. She said it was bad luck to sleep with the groom the night before the wedding, and I wasn't about to ignore superstition.

Talia jumped onto the bed and squealed, "You're up! Do you know what day it is!?"

For fun, I answered, "Halloween?"

Talia swatted me. "Yes, but it's also *your wedding day!*"

A huge smile spread across my face. "Is that today?"

"Today's the day!" She hopped off the bed and went over to the window to pull back the curtains. "The birds are chirping; the sun is shining… Well, the sun isn't really shining, but that's all right."

I sat up to see that it was drizzly outside. The bright oranges and reds of autumn seemed dull under the overcast sky.

My face fell. "That's not good. We're supposed to have the ceremony outside."

"No, this is perfect," Talia said. "Rain on your wedding day symbolizes cleansing and fertility. It's like nature is washing everything clean for you. This is a good omen."

I brightened up. "Oh! In that case, bring on the rain."

81

"It should let up before sundown," Talia promised. "In the meantime, we have an entire day of pampering planned to get you ready for the ceremony."

"That sounds like fun. Where do we start?" I asked.

"Right in here." Talia gestured to her attached bath.

I got out of bed—careful not to disturb Isa, who was sleeping at my feet—and went into the bathroom. The scent of lavender filled my nose, and I noticed that Talia had already filled the bath. Beside the tub sat a neat pile of pampering supplies from the gift basket she'd given me at my bridal shower. There was a face mask, moisturizer, a loofah, and more. The lights were off, and candles had been lit all around the room. Soft music played through a speaker on the counter.

"I already put in the Epsom salts, and there's a robe for you on the back of the door," Talia said. "The girls will be here at ten to start on hair and makeup, which should give us plenty of time until the ceremony at sunset. Enjoy!"

Talia left me in the bathroom, and I stripped down and sank into the water. It was so warm, and the bath salts made my skin feel silky and smooth. I put the face mask on and rested my head back, enjoying the calmness surrounding me.

I didn't know how long I sat there, but I nearly fell asleep again. I washed my hair and shaved, but I didn't get out until the water had turned cold. I dried off and wrapped the robe around myself, then returned to the bedroom. Talia had made the bed, and I noticed a new collection of oils and lotions on the nightstand.

"Next up on our day of pampering is a massage!" Talia exclaimed.

"I was not expecting the five-star treatment," I said with a smile.

"Girl, it's your wedding day. I'm not giving you a free moment to worry. Today's all about you."

"And Lucas," I added.

"Well, this morning, it's about *you*," she said. "Lay face-down on the bed and relax. You leave the rest up to me."

Talia left the room for a minute while I stripped off my robe and lay down, pulling the blanket up around my waist. She returned and dimmed the lights, before turning on calming music. Talia rubbed lotions and oils over my back, and I found myself relaxing deep into the mattress.

Talia finished an hour later and announced breakfast was on its way. I dressed back into my robe, and the rest of my bridesmaids arrived several minutes later. Talia, Chloe, and Onyx wore robes that matched mine, but Verla and Grammy were dressed casually.

"I hope you're hungry!" Chloe exclaimed. She stepped aside, and plates of food floated into the room behind her.

"Starving," I said.

The girls all gathered around to nibble on pastries and fancy cheeses, and Chloe called Talia over to the mirror to start working on her hair. We listened to music and joked around while I helped steam the bridesmaid dresses. Hours passed, and everyone seemed to be having a great time.

"All right, Nadine. It's your turn," Chloe announced.

I sat in the chair in front of the mirror. Chloe curled my hair, then twisted the strands into an intricate bun at the base of my neck. It took her over half an hour to pin my hair back, taking extra care with each strand. She finished the look by curling several loose pieces in front to frame my face.

"What do you think?" she asked when she finished.

I turned my head to view it from all angles. "I really love it. Thank you."

Chloe picked up a brush. "Now, for your makeup."

"I've got that covered." I waved a hand in front of my face, and the color in my cheeks brightened. My eyebrows darkened, along with my lashes, and my lips turned mauve.

She stepped back to take a look at me. "Mm... let's go a little wider with the eyeliner."

I waved my hand again, and the line above my eye thickened.

"Add some contour here..." Chloe ran her finger below my cheekbone.

I followed her instructions, and she gasped. "I think that's perfect!"

I stared at myself in the mirror, loving the way my eyes seemed brighter than normal. "Wow, I look *really* good."

"Everyone gather around," Grammy instructed. "I want to take some pictures!"

We spent another few hours snacking, laughing, and getting ourselves perfect for the ceremony. Grammy and Verla moved in and out of the room as they helped set up for the ceremony and reception elsewhere.

Soon, it was time to get our dresses on. All of the girls wore long purple gowns. Each was a different shape, as I'd let them pick out the dresses that they liked best when we went shopping in *Hok'evale*.

Grammy and I went into the bathroom so that I could change into my wedding dress in private. Grammy and I had picked it out over the summer, when everyone else was off researching the Wands. We'd called the bridal shop in *Hok'evale* to order it and picked it up with the bridesmaid dresses, but no one else had seen it yet.

Grammy helped me into it, and she buttoned up back. "How are we feeling?"

"I don't have cold feet, if that's what you mean," I said.

"You're confident this is the right thing to do?" she asked.

I noticed she didn't ask if I was nervous, like so many other people would. It helped shift the focus to the *good* I was feeling, and I could honestly say I had no second thoughts about marrying Lucas.

"I know Lucas and I are meant to be together," I told her. "I can't wait to marry him. I'm also really excited to be attending my first witch wedding!"

"I guarantee it won't disappoint," Grammy said with a chuckle. "We're going to show you how fun a witch wedding can be."

Grammy finished with the buttons, and I spun to look at myself in the mirror. My gown was a sleeveless A-line dress with a plunging neckline and beads all over the bodice. The beading was both subtle and intricate, and I felt like I sparkled with every motion. The skirt was made of tulle, and the dress had a simple sweep train that flowed behind me. I hadn't liked any of the white dresses we looked at, so I'd opted for silver, and I couldn't be happier.

Grammy gazed at me in the mirror. "You look beautiful, Nadine. Lucas is going to faint when he sees you."

"I hope not! He needs to say his vows."

Grammy chuckled. "Let's show the girls."

She opened the door a crack and announced, "We're coming out!"

The chatter died, and I stepped into the bedroom to see four beautiful faces smiling back at me.

"Oh, my Goddess!" Talia cried. "You look gorgeous."

Chloe's jaw dropped, and Onyx threw her hands over her mouth. Verla's eyes watered as she placed her hands over her heart.

"The dress is beautiful," Verla said. "It's just missing one thing."

Verla took the blue hair pin from the vanity, and I watched in the mirror as she placed it in my hair. It looked perfect.

"It's almost time to head down for the ceremony," Verla said. "But before we go, we must prepare your Blessing Brew."

Grammy had told me this was a tradition for all women in the Miriamic Coven. It was a ceremony that the bridesmaids performed to bless the union before the ceremony. I was really excited to see what it was like.

The girls stepped aside to reveal an altar they'd set up while I was in the bathroom. Atop a small table was a bubbling cauldron surrounded by candles and crystals. Five vials of herbs stood in a neat line in front of the potion.

Grammy gestured everyone forward. "Gather around!"

We stood in a circle around the altar. Our cats came running, too, and they hopped onto the tabletop and began circling the potion.

"As the maid of honor, Talia will act as Mother Miriam's proxy, in which she stands in place of our goddess to bless the bride," Grammy explained.

Talia stood opposite me and raised her hands above the cauldron. "Mother Miriam, we call upon you to bless this union so that we may celebrate the love between Nadine and Lucas, and bring the coven closer together."

Talia wasn't an Alchemist, but the brew began to bubble more rapidly.

"Speak the incantation with me," Talia instructed.

The five women surrounding me spoke in unison.

*On this night,*
*this bride becomes a wife.*
*Through this potion,*
*take our blessings into a new life.*
*So shall it be.*

Talia nodded to Chloe, and she picked up one of the herb vials. "Nadine, I gift you red clover, to symbolize fertility. May you be fertile in mind and spirit, to conceive new ideas and produce solutions in your marriage."

I smiled at Chloe as she dumped the vial of clover into the potion. "I will be fertile."

Onyx went next. "I gift you lavender, to symbolize devotion, that you may be devoted to your spouse and seek strength in one another."

I nodded as she tossed the herbs into the potion. "I will be devoted."

"I gift you thyme, to symbolize courage," Verla said. "Find courage through your spouse, and you two will be able to face anything together."

"I will be courageous."

"Nadine," Grammy said, tearing up. "I gift you sage, to symbolize wisdom. May you be wise to know which battles to fight, and which solutions to seek out."

"I will be wise," I promised. My voice cracked as I accepted my grandmother's blessing.

Talia took the last herb vial and held it over the cauldron, but she never took her eyes off me. "Nadine, I gift you mint, to symbolize virtue. May you always do what is right for your spouse, your community, and yourself."

"I will have virtue," I told her.

Talia sprinkled the mint into the potion, then lifted her hands again. "Join me."

The women all grabbed the handle of a long wooden spoon and stirred the potion together. Magic of various colors swirled down their hands and into the potion. The cats stopped circling the potion, and all five of them placed their paws on the edge of the cauldron to peer inside. The cats' eyes shimmered blue, and the potion began to glow a bright white.

"The Goddess has accepted our blessings, and now Nadine must accept them as well," Talia announced. She dipped a cup into the potion and scooped a small amount into it, then handed it to me.

"So shall it be," I said, before tipping my head back and drinking the potion. It was sweet like honey and went down easily.

I set the cup on the altar and thought that was the end of it, until I felt a strange buzzing all throughout my body. It felt *really* good, like I was floating several inches off the ground.

"Finally, we will don the veil," Talia announced. "This long-standing tradition will ward off evil spirits so that they can't see the bride and curse her before the wedding."

The girls went to a box on the bed, and they pulled out a long silver veil that matched my dress. Together, they fitted it into my hair and over my face. The veil was so long that it nearly touched my toes. I could just barely see through it.

Something tickled my arm, and I thought it was the veil, but when I looked down, I saw a spider crawling over me.

"You can't walk down the aisle with me, little guy," I said as I pulled the spider off of me.

"A spider!" Verla exclaimed in excitement. "This is a good omen."

"A spider and rain on my wedding day?" I asked. "I guess that makes for extra good luck."

"Very good luck, indeed," Grammy said. "Just in time, too. The sun has set, and it's time to make our way to the ceremony. As is tradition, your bridesmaids will go first. We will meet you down there. We love you, Nadine."

The girls each gave me a hug, then left the room. Verla was the only one to stay behind. All the weddings I'd been to had the bridesmaids walk in with the bride, but witch weddings were different.

"I'm sorry your mother couldn't be here to see this," Verla said softly while we waited.

I gazed down at Isa. "She is, sort of."

"Her soul is here in a way," Verla agreed. "But it's not the same. She should've been here to walk you down the aisle. I'm honored that you asked me to take her place, but this was your mother's right."

"If my mother can't be here, I'm glad it's you. You've done so much to help me with my powers, and you've supported me every step of the way the same way my mother would have if she was still alive. You advocated for me against the school board, and you saved mine and Lucas's lives in our trial. I owe you so much, Clarice. I'm happy you're guiding me down the aisle."

Verla furrowed her brow. "You called me by my first name."

I shrugged. "You're not Headmistress Verla. You're family."

"I'm not family, Nadine," she said gently. "I'm honored you would say that, but I can't take your mother's place."

"You aren't taking her place, and you never could, but you're honoring her by stepping in when she can't be here. You've been here for me since I arrived at Miriam College, teaching me everything you know and guiding me every step of the way. I can't have my mom here, because she's gone now, but I can have *you*. You're my mother, Clarice, and you have been ever since I came to Octavia Falls. Even before that, you were looking out for me, when I didn't even know it. I want you to be my mom, and I hope you'll believe me when I say I love you. I just wish it didn't take so long to say it."

Tears beaded in the corners of Verla's eyes. "If this is the way you feel, then I will accept you as my own. I've always seen you as my daughter, Nadine, though I was terrified to say such a thing out loud. I hope you can forgive me for holding back."

I fell into Verla's arms and began to sob. Tears streaked my cheeks, and one of her tears fell onto my shoulder.

Verla held me close. "Family is the most important thing, Nadine. I'm honored to be considered part of your family, and I'm happy to witness you starting a new family with Lucas. You must protect this union, because your family will always be there for you."

I sniffled. "I don't mean to get emotional."

"Do it!" she cried. "Get emotional. It's your wedding day!"

I laughed, but the laughter came with tears of joy. Verla hugged me tighter, and the strong emotions overcoming me eased.

I gently wiped my eyes and drew away. "How's my makeup?"

"It's perfect." Verla took my hand. "Come. It's time to tell that boy you love him."

I looped my hand through Verla's elbow, and she guided me downstairs and through the front door. The rain had let up, just as Talia had promised. Although the sun had set, I could still make out the beautiful oranges and yellows of the leaves on the ground and in the trees.

Verla led me into the forest beside the house, and Isa and Odin followed at our feet. She guided me down a narrow trail that twisted through the trees. In the distance, I heard an owl hoot, then caught the sound of a stream trickling nearby. As we neared the ceremony site, I heard voices singing a traditional Miriamic wedding song in a minor key.

Verla and I stepped into a clearing beside the stream, and my jaw dropped in wonder. Glowing orbs danced above our heads, and red autumn leaves swirled beneath a large oak tree. In the center of the clearing, Grant, Talia, Chloe, Miles, Onyx, and Professor Warren were cloaked in black, dancing in a circle to the rhythm of their song. There were no drum beats or instruments to accompany their voices—just a beautiful a capella tune sung in perfect harmony.

*Hush, now*
*The time for vows*
*Is coming all so soon*

*Tonight we seek*
*Our mother's blessing*
*Underneath the moon*

*Protect this space*
*And hear our prayers*
*To bless this sacred union*

A large white orb hovered between each of their hands, creating a beautiful lights display as they danced. Their cats made a circle around them, and Isa and Odin rushed forward to join the cats in the dance. I spotted movement across the clearing, and I saw Oliver and Cornelius rushing to join them as well.

That's when I noticed Grammy leading Lucas into the clearing opposite me. Lucas was dressed in a black tux with a purple tie, and his hair had been slicked back in a really sexy way. He looked as starstruck as I did at the beautiful setting.

Then his gaze focused past the dancers, and a smile spread across his face when he saw me. Everything around us seemed to fade as our eyes locked. Time seemed to stand still for a moment, and my knees locked up as I took him in. I couldn't believe our time was finally here. Grammy nudged Lucas, and he started forward.

Verla leaned over to whisper, "It's time."

My heart pitter-pattered in my chest as I walked forward. The circle of dancers expanded, until Lucas and I met in the middle. I wanted to reach out for him—I couldn't wait—but my veil was in the way.

I noticed something about Lucas I hadn't seen before. His form almost *glowed*, but the magical glow was dark, barely discernible in the fading light.

As the song began to fade into the last chord, my bridesmaids approached and gently pulled back my veil. Bright white light shimmered off my form and lit up the clearing. Grammy had told me this would happen, but I was still surprised to see it. It was a product of the potion they'd given me, and Lucas's glow came from the potion his groomsmen had brewed for him. I represented light, and Lucas represented darkness. Together, we represented the union of the entire spectrum. The darkness and the light, finally united as one.

Our friends dropped the hoods of their cloaks as the forest became quiet. I heard Verla and Grammy approach and join us, but I couldn't take my eyes off Lucas. He wore a huge grin, like he couldn't wait to take me in his arms.

Talia stepped forward, and everyone else joined hands to lock us into the circle. They began swaying from side to side in unison. Witch weddings were seen as a community event, to bless the couple and bring them into the coven as a singular unit. Traditionally, the bride and groom's closest friends formed an inner circle to help officiate the ceremony, while the rest of the guests sat in chairs in a secondary circle outlining the ceremony space. Tonight, however, only our closest friends and family were in attendance, so everyone participated in the inner circle.

"Nadine, Lucas," Talia said. "You have chosen me to act as Mother Miriam's proxy, to facilitate this ceremony so that you may be wed in the eyes of the Goddess. Join hands."

I beamed as I reached out for Lucas. His hands were warm when they met mine, and the tingles throughout my body grew in intensity as our glows merged together. I had to physically hold myself back from throwing my arms around him. Tendrils of magic swirled around our hands, locking them together. The light emanating from my skin dimmed, while his glow grew brighter.

Grammy had called this part of the ceremony *handfasting*, in which our hands were magically tied together to represent the binding of our lives.

*I love you*, Lucas mouthed to me.

*I love you, too*, I mouthed back.

"Nadine, Lucas," Talia continued. "We are gathered here tonight because you have asked your family and friends to bless your union, so that you may be bound together in this life and become one amongst the coven. We will begin by inviting the community to give their blessings."

Talia turned to Grammy. "Do you accept this union?"

Grammy stepped forward. "I accept this union and bless the couple with the sign of the owl, to offer you wisdom when all seems hopeless. So shall it be."

"*So shall it be*," everyone repeated.

The women had already offered blessings in the bridal ceremony, but when they had brewed the potion, they had blessed *me*. Here, they were proclaiming their approval of our union and blessing our marriage. Grammy had chosen the same blessing of wisdom at both ceremonies, though the guests could choose anything they wanted.

Chloe went next with the sign of the cat, a blessing for us to remain independent beings while still thriving as a couple. Onyx followed with the mark of the potion, to brew a new beginning between the two of us. Verla blessed us with the power of the oak tree, symbolizing strength, stability, and courage. Miles chose the mark of the wand, to cast our dreams into reality, and Grant chose the sign of the toad, to bring abundance.

Professor Warren stepped forward. "I accept this union and bless this couple with the power of the oak tree, to give them strength, a stable marriage, and courage for the path ahead. So shall it be."

I found it interesting that Professor Warren and Verla had chosen the same blessing, but they *were* both our mentors, and I was certain they believed we needed courage for the path ahead of us. Goddess knew we did.

Talia went last. "I accept this union and bless this couple with the sign of the raven, to transform from two people into one. So shall it be."

My hands shook in anticipation as I spoke, "So shall it be."

"Goddess, gods, ancestors, and guides," Talia called out into the forest. "Descend upon us to bless this union between this witch and warlock through sacred matrimony."

Silvery lights appeared in the trees above us. They were unlike the orbs floating there—shinier and more ethereal than any magic I'd seen before. It took me a second to realize they were *spirits*!

The spirits dimmed into wispy features of those that had left us far too soon. I didn't recognize any of them at first. They must've been our ancestors, because they wore all different kinds of dress that dated back hundreds of years. There had to be dozens of spirits, circling us in and bringing us close.

Then I saw the most beautiful faces in the crowd, and I had to squeeze Lucas's hands to keep from falling to my knees. My parents stood before me in spirit. They didn't look a day older than I remembered them. Dad's cheeks still dimpled when he smiled, and Mom's eyes twinkled in that way they always did when she told me she was proud of me.

Grammy had told me our ancestors could appear during the wedding ceremony, but I didn't actually believe it was possible. I knew my religion taught there was a life after death, and I'd seen ghosts before, so I knew it was real, but actually seeing my loved ones waiting for us on the other side was profound. It was one thing to know it in my soul, and something else entirely to experience it first-hand. I didn't think I'd ever see my parents again, not until I joined them in Alora, but the magic here tonight was strong. A piece of me had been broken when they'd died, but seeing them here tonight made that hole inside me disappear for just a brief moment.

"Mom? Dad?" I whispered.

Isa broke away from the circle, and she ran over to my mother. Cornelius followed and bowed his head to a young man who stood beside her.

"Grampy?" I recognized him from photos. Mom and Dad smiled at me, and Grampy gave a kind nod.

Oliver approached a man who looked so much like Lucas. It was his brother, Eric.

Lucas's hands shook in mine, and tears fell from his eyes. He squeezed my hands tighter, like it took everything within him to hold himself together. I squeezed him back to let him know that if he needed to break down, I'd be here to help him pick up the pieces.

But that didn't happen, because a smile stretched across his face then, and he whispered to his brother, "*I love you.*"

Eric placed his hand over his heart to show Lucas he knew exactly how his brother felt.

Beside the others, I noticed a girl with the kindest eyes. Amy smiled brightly, opening her arms wide to me, and tears began streaming from my eyes. All these people had moved on. I never thought I'd see them again.

I wanted to run over to them, to say goodbye one last time, but they were there one moment and gone the next. The faces I so desperately missed faded into the forest. The cats looked upward, meowing as pieces of their souls faded away.

Lucas reached out a hand into the empty forest, as if begging his brother to come back. I shared his sentiment; we hadn't had enough time with them.

"Your ancestors have appeared, and given their blessing," Talia said. "And with it, they will bless you with a message."

Talia pulled a deck of tarot cards from her cloak. They were unlike any deck I'd seen before, with beautiful silver foil on the backs that shimmered under the orbs.

"You will select a card for your union, to guide you into your marriage," Talia announced.

She spread the cards out, and Lucas and I reached for the same one. Together, we pulled the card from the deck and flipped it over.

The card depicted a warrior on a chariot being led by a white sphynx and a black sphynx. The warrior appeared to be driving the chariot, but there were no reigns. In his hand, he simply held a wand.

"You have chosen The Chariot," Talia announced. "Together, you are strong and courageous. Though you may be pulled in two directions, you two hold the power to lead your relationship in any direction you choose, and you will find strength in navigating those opposing forces together. Rely not on what others expect from you, but know that you are in control of your relationship, and through determination, you two can achieve anything together."

I knew relationships required work, and that effort didn't end when we got married, but I knew whatever we faced, Lucas and I could do it together.

"Finally, you will receive a blessing from the Earth," Talia said.

Lucas kept hold of my hand as he led me to the base of the oak tree at the edge of the clearing. Grammy had told me about this part of the ceremony, and I'd memorized the incantation by heart.

Lucas shot me a glance, and I nodded. We spoke in unison.

*Heart of oak and love's pure light*
*We seek your blessing on this wedding night.*

Together, we pressed our palms to the base of the tree. Something shifted beneath our hands. My fingers curled around a long stick, and we pulled it from the trunk together. A wand appeared in our hands, and we held it up for our friends to see. The wand was eleven inches long with a twisted blade and engravings of roses on the handle.

It was a Wedding Wand—a special wand that could only be forged during a Miriamic wedding ceremony. Lucas and I could use it together in relationship rituals, in order to strengthen our marriage.

"Now for the rings," Talia said.

Grant pulled the rings from the breast pocket of his suit, and he handed them to us.

"Do you, Lucas Taylor, choose Nadine Evers to be your one and only, for as long as this incarnation lasts?" Talia asked.

Lucas beamed and spoke with firm conviction. "I do."

He slipped the ring on my finger, and my heart filled with so much joy I thought it might explode. The light glowing around our forms began to twist together, glowing brighter as they merged as one.

"Do you, Nadine Evers, choose Lucas Taylor to be your one and only, for as long as this incarnation lasts?"

"I do!" I could hardly get the words out fast enough. We'd been waiting for this moment for so long, and now, it was finally here. I beamed as I placed a white gold ring on his finger. I'd never been happier.

"Your word is your intention," Talia said. "I now pronounce you warlock and wife. You may now seal this union with the show of your love."

Lucas let go of my hands to take my whole body in his arms. I threw my arms around his neck, and we fell into a deep, passionate kiss.

Our friends cheered so loud it echoed through the trees. A white light shone so bright I could see it through my lids. I opened my eyes to see our forms glowing brighter, then all at once, the light exploded upwards. I watched in awe as the magic burst like fireworks, then turned into a million tiny bits of starlight that rained down upon us like confetti.

Warm magic tickled my skin, and I laughed happily. "Grammy didn't tell me about this part!"

Lucas grinned as he drew me closer. "It's the best part—it means our marriage is complete."

Words couldn't do it justice just how passionately in love I was with him. I took his face in my hands and kissed him again.

"Witches and warlocks, I present to you Mister and Mrs. Taylor!" Talia announced.

Their cheers faded into the background as I kissed Lucas over and over again. I could hardly believe we'd made it. After everything we'd been through, I wasn't sure we'd ever get this far. Lucas and I had defied death, survived the Burning, fought a demon, and won our trial. I wasn't sure we'd live long enough to make it to the altar.

Furthermore, we defeated the Reaper's Shadow curse. When Lucas and I first started dating, we'd agreed we wouldn't marry because of the curse that had been placed on all reapers. If a reaper like Lucas fell in love, his lover—known as the Reaper's Shadow—was destined to suffer. According to the curse, if the couple had sex, the woman would experience a great illness. If they married, she would suffer a tragedy. Once they had children, the child would be destined to kill their mother.

But that was all over now. Lucas and I had tracked down the graves of the women who had been affected by the Reaper's Shadow curse, and I'd broken the curse in the cemetery. We didn't know back then if we'd ever be able to get married, but goddess damn it, we did it.

I was surrounded by my family and friends, and I felt healthier than ever. More than that, Lucas and I were together, and it was everything I ever wanted.

Nothing could ruin this day. It was an absolute dream come true… and no force in hell or otherwise could shatter this beautiful dream. Lucas and I were forever tied. Whatever the future held, we could handle it side by side.

Come what may, this fantasy of ours would last forever.

# SEVEN

My heart soared in my chest as I kissed Nadine. I felt like I was flying a mile above the ceremony. She was my wife now, and despite everything that nearly tore us apart up until this point, we had made it.

I finally drew away from Nadine, though I didn't want to. "I can't believe we're married."

I had to say it out loud again, because it didn't quite feel real. This had to be a dream, because it was already the best night of my life.

"We are, so you better start believing it," Nadine joked.

Grant cupped his hands around his mouth. "Let's get this party started!"

Everyone cheered, and we danced happily as we made our way back through the trees to the house. Nadine and I led the way, and the others followed. Witch lights floated above the patio like twinkling Christmas lights, and a feast surrounded by candles had been set out on a long table. In the center of the table, a punch bowl had been enchanted to spray upward like a fountain. Nearby, a self-serve cocktail bar had been set up. Grant had made a poster that said *Pick Your Poison* with various mixed drink suggestions he'd made up himself.

There was also a table for gifts and another for cake. Nadine and I had opted for a multi-layer cake—one layer pumpkin spice, and the second layer apple cider. The cake was violet, with dark purple roses set into the frosting. Talia placed The Chariot card on top of the cake, which served as our wedding topper. After tonight, we would frame the card to hang in our home someday.

Everyone had worked really hard to make this night perfect. It was everything I imagined—except for one table set near the cake that I didn't recognize. It held a large poster with all kinds of photos, and various items scattered across the tabletop.

I shot Nadine a glance. "What's this?"

"I wanted to surprise you," she said as we approached the table. "It's everything of ours that I kept."

We stopped beside the table, and I could finally make it all out. My jaw dropped as I took it all in. There were tons of photos of us and our friends. In one of them, Nadine and I were slow dancing at the Midnight Formal, and in another, we were twirling around the bonfire at the Halloween festival. There were photos of us playing games in her dorm room the night before the kidney transplant, and a picture of us with Grant and Talia after we won The Haunted Tournament at school my sophomore year. I laughed, remembering how we'd signed up for the magical competition out of pure spite and ended up winning the challenge against upperclassmen.

Photographs weren't the only thing tacked to the board. There was also a ticket from The Hearse dated for Valentine's Day over a year ago, along with a voided massage gift certificate I'd given Nadine that night. Next to that sat another gift certificate we received after Nadine and I had solved a mock mystery at a haunted mansion last Halloween. I also noticed a flier for corn mazes at Blossom Orchards that Nadine must've picked up when we went. I reached out to touch our medical bracelets that she'd saved from the transplant.

"I had no idea you'd kept all this," I said.

Nadine placed the Wedding Wand on the table with the other items, as if adding it to her collection. "I keep all my memories of you. They're the best ones."

I smiled wider. "They are, and tonight is one for the books."

"Look here!" Talia called.

We turned, and a flash went off in our faces. Talia snapped a few photos, then said, "We need to get everyone in. Come on!"

Talia set the camera on a tripod, and we all gathered around to take a few pictures.

"Everyone say *cheese!*" Talia cried.

I was too happy to be serious, so as the timer was counting down, I grabbed Nadine and swept her into my arms. Nadine wrapped her arms around my neck, and laughter rang around us as the flash went off.

Nadine didn't let go of me even when I set her down. She pulled me into a tight hug and whispered, "I haven't been this happy in a long time."

I kissed the side of her head. "I haven't been this happy *ever*."

We all gathered around the table and took our seats. The food smelled divine. Helena's famous brisket had been set on platters in front of us, along with homemade dinner rolls, veggies from the garden, applesauce Nadine and I helped make, and various salads that looked delicious. Mugs of hot apple cider steamed in front of our plates.

We chatted and laughed as we ate. I noticed Nadine kept her eyes on Isa, who was eating with the other cats nearby. She looked thoughtful.

"Something on your mind?" I asked lowly. Everyone else was talking and didn't hear us.

She turned her gaze to me. "I'm trying to understand. Isa is my mom reincarnated, but my mom's spirit still showed up at our ceremony. It's the same with Eric and Oliver. How can they exist in two forms at once?"

"The concept of souls can be complicated. I'm not sure I entirely understand the mechanics myself," I admitted. "From what I know, when a soul reincarnates, that soul energy brings about new life, but a piece of it stays behind in Alora. So even though you're born to experience new things, there's a version of you that still remembers your past life, imprinted as a sort of memory. She *is* Isa in this lifetime, but she's also still your mom, in the afterlife."

"Could I ever summon her and speak to her, as the mother I remember?" Nadine asked.

"In theory, when you die you'll be able to speak with her, but it's hard enough as it is to speak to crossed spirits, and even harder when they reincarnate," I explained. "Her soul energy is here now in Isa, so if you were to summon her, you'd be speaking more closely to Isa's energy."

"What about my father?" Nadine wondered. "He wasn't Miriamic, but he showed up at our ceremony."

"Regardless of someone's religion, their spirit still exists in the afterlife," I told her. "People can change religions once they get there, too. It's possible your father is living in Alora, if he chose to do so. He could reincarnate as a witch or warlock in his next life—that's up to him. As long as he chose to participate in the wedding ceremony, he showed up because you invited him to be there."

She sipped on her apple cider. "I'm glad my parents got to be there, even if it was only for a moment."

The sound of silverware tinkling against glasses rang throughout the reception, distracting us.

"Kiss!" Miles cheered.

Nadine and I smiled, and I pulled her into a deep kiss.

Grant cleared his throat next to me and stood. "Now that we have everyone's attention, I'd like to say a few words. I've been thinking for a long time about what I would like to say in this speech. I know if Lucas was the one giving this speech, he'd find all the right words to say— maybe write a poem or two. So I thought I'd try my hand at it and keep it short and sweet."

Grant pulled a piece of paper from his coat pocket and began reading.

*Nadine and Lucas, what can I say?*
*It's finally here—your wedding day.*
*I've seen you together through dark and through light,*
*and I'm honored to be here on this special night.*

*You've been through it all.*
*Through the highs and the lows.*
*Honestly, it seemed forever*
*Until Lucas proposed.*

*He's crazy about you, Nadine.*
*I won't lie.*
*I've never seen a man*
*As madly in love as this guy.*

*Nadine won't admit,*
*But she's wild, too,*
*About one guy named Lucas.*

*I swear that it's true.*

*Our friendship is special,*
*But what's even more,*
*I haven't seen a love like yours*
*Ever before.*

*There are rings on your fingers*
*Our tummies are fed.*
*All I have left to say is:*
*Cheers to the newlyweds.*

Everyone clapped and took a drink. Grant looked nervous as he sat back down, and I placed a hand on his shoulder. "That was great."

Grant adjusted his tie. "Was it really?"

"Absolutely. The greatest best man speech ever," I said honestly. He'd stumbled a few times, and the lines didn't always have a smooth cadence, but he'd put in a lot of effort, and that's what mattered.

Talia stood next. "I guess that means it's my turn. I'm not very good at this, so I thought instead of a speech, I'd play you a song."

Talia took a seat at a keyboard that had been set up on the patio, and she started playing a beautiful tune she had written herself. The witch lights above us twinkled in time with the soft melody. The song was beautiful, and Talia had obviously put a lot of thought into it. It was clear she really admired our relationship. Nadine had tears rolling down her cheeks by the end of it.

Soon, we were ushered to the cake table to cut the cake. Nadine and I had promised not to shove the cake in each other's faces, and we held true on that promise. Flavors burst across my tongue when Nadine placed the cake in my mouth, and I realized she'd made the perfect choice with pumpkin spice.

Miles put on some music, and we all started dancing in the grass. I held Nadine the whole time through fast and slow songs as the celebration continued around us.

An upbeat tune came on. Onyx, Chloe, Miles, Grant, and Talia broke out into a coordinated dance routine they'd practiced to surprise us with.

Nadine and I hollered in celebration. Even Professor Warren hit the dancefloor, and I was surprised to see he actually had some moves.

We must've been dancing for over an hour before Nadine and I sat back down to rest. She beamed from ear to ear before popping an olive in her mouth. "Our friends are the best."

"*You're* the best." I drew her closer, pulling her into my lap. I nuzzled my nose into her neck, inhaling her captivating floral scent. I wanted to take in every sensation this night had to offer, because I didn't want to forget a single moment.

Nadine laughed as I tickled her with my breath. "Are you drunk?"

"Drunk on you," I teased. "I've only had one drink, and that was during dinner."

Nadine turned until she could take my face in her hands. "Mm... I could get used to this happy, carefree Lucas."

My fingers trailed across the beads of her dress. "You're enjoying it?"

"Very much." She leaned in to place a kiss on my lips, and excitement stirred in my chest.

"You should *enjoy* me more," I teased when she drew away. I placed a hand on the side of her face to draw her back to me. Nadine's tongue slid inside my mouth, and my dick hardened.

"You're going to have to get this dress off me first," she whispered.

Fervent yearning for her ignited throughout my body. I threw a glance at the others dancing in the yard. Our cats were gathered near them, looking to be having the time of their lives. "I bet no one will notice if we slip away for a second."

"Only a second?" Nadine joked. "I thought it'd take longer than that."

I pretended to think about it. "All right, eleven seconds. We'll make it a quickie. Our guests will hardly notice us gone."

Nadine snickered. "If you're serious, so am I."

"Hell yeah, I'm serious. It's our party."

Eagerly, Nadine hopped off my lap and took my hand. Talia and Grant noticed us heading for the door, and I caught Grant's eyes just in time to see his eyebrows shoot up. I winked, and Nadine made a crude gesture to Talia. Talia burst into laughter.

Nadine covered her mouth to laugh. "Now *everyone's* going to know what we're up to."

I shrugged. "Let them. We're *married* now. We're allowed to do whatever we want."

Nadine reached for the door, but I stopped her.

"Allow me." I swooped her up into my arms and carried her through the doorway. "It's tradition. Brides are considered vulnerable on their wedding night, because unity in any form—including marriage—makes the coven stronger. It's a threat to evil spirits. It's said that evil spirits lurk at the threshold of the home and can influence the bride through the soles of her feet."

"So *that's* why you have to carry me over the threshold. I never understood that tradition."

I held her close. "You're safe now with me."

She laid her head on my shoulder. "I've *always* felt safe with you."

I carried Nadine up the stairs and into the bedroom. We could still hear the music from outside. It seemed no one was at all bothered that we ditched our own party.

I set Nadine on the bed, but her veil got caught underneath her. She stood. I helped her unpin it from her hair, then gently set the veil aside. Nadine turned her back to me, and I worked on unbuttoning her dress. My trembling fingers moved slowly, drawing out the anticipation, even though my hammering heart wanted her *now*. There wasn't a single part of me that didn't ache for her—mind, body, and soul.

The dress fell from her shoulders, and I was surprised to see she was wearing white lace lingerie underneath. My gaze roamed up and down her body.

"Damn, wifey, you look good," I said, enjoying the way the word *wifey* felt on my tongue.

"You like it?" She turned one way then the other to model it for me.

"I like it *a lot*." My dick was rock hard and ready for her. I could hardly get her body against mine fast enough. I looped my hand around her waist, and our bodies crashed together as our lips collided.

Nadine couldn't contain her desperation. She yanked on my tie to draw me closer, and wanting flared through my veins as she made her desire very clear. She clung tightly to me as her tongue slid inside my mouth. I cupped her ass and lifted her, until her legs locked around my middle. I took a few steps, until her ass hit the top of the vanity. Contents crashed to the floor, but we barely noticed. Her hands tangled in my hair, while mine ran up and down her curves, down her legs, and back up to her breasts.

The urgent *need* to be inside of her called to me, and I forced myself to pull away from her. Nadine leaned back on the vanity, her legs parted and waiting for me. Infatuation filled her eyes as she watched me kick off my shoes and strip down.

I slipped on a condom, then resituated her on the vanity to make sure she wouldn't slip off. Slowly, I ran my hands over Nadine's body, and I trailed kisses down her neck. She shivered under my touch, until she began fisting her hands in my hair. She didn't have to say a word to tell me she wanted more. I dipped my hands between her legs, and the warmth of her arousal was welcoming.

"I've been waiting for this all day," she whispered breathlessly.

Hell, so had I. I moved her lace panties aside and slid my cock inside of her. Nadine gasped as our bodies moved in sync. I worked slowly at first, making love to her in a calculated, deliberate fashion. Nadine looked downward, watching my cock pleasure her. I observed the craving in her features grow, until something inside of her snapped.

She grabbed my hair and yanked on the strands, begging me for more. I couldn't help myself. I thrust my hips upward, burying myself deeper inside of her. Waves of pleasure surged up and down my body, and the passionate moans escaping her lips sent my head reeling. I *needed* her closer to me—as close as we could possibly get.

I grabbed her ass and lifted her from the vanity. Her legs wrapped around me in desperate wanting. I held her leg with one hand and wrapped the other around the back of her head, keeping her lips on mine as I took a few steps across the room. I pinned her against the wall, and my knees nearly buckled beneath me as intense desire swelled between us. It took everything in me to keep us both upright. I thrust upward over and over again with a blazing passion that couldn't be rivaled by any sex we'd had before.

She was my *wife* now, and nothing was hotter than that.

"Lucas!" Nadine gasped as she clung to me harder.

Her cry nearly undid me. I pulled her away from the wall, and this time, I *did* fall to my knees, as if I were a subject bowing to his goddess.

Gently, I laid her on the floor, but Nadine had other ideas. She grabbed me and rolled me over, then gently slid down onto my erection. I beamed as she rode me hard, every movement she made sending another thrill through my dick. The floorboards squeaked as she rolled her hips over me faster and faster. I couldn't help but grab her hips and bury myself deeper inside of her—inside *my wife*.

That thought sent me over the edge. Magical tingles spread over my skin, until the glorious sensation exploded. I thrust upward as I reached my peak, and Nadine gasped as she came with me. Together, it felt as if we had become one with the cosmos itself, reaching a place where time and space held no meaning. I could feel *her* as if we had become one... until the matter that made up our bodies slowly knitted itself back together again.

The moment seemed to stretch for several wonderful minutes, but it must've only been seconds. I had never imagined that making love to Nadine for the first time as a married couple could be this incredible.

Nadine collapsed onto the floor beside me, panting to catch her breath. I took her in my arms. Light shone from behind my lids, and I opened my eyes to see witch lights dancing above us. Tiny little orbs swirled around us like a kaleidoscope.

"Was that me, or you?" Nadine asked, looking up at the magical lights that twinkled like stars.

"I think it was both of us."

Nadine snuggled into me. "I like being your wife."

I let out a blissful sigh. "I love being your husband."

"Those are beautiful words—wife and husband," Nadine said dreamily. "I want to marry you all over again already."

"The night isn't over," I reminded her.

"That's right. We should probably get back to the party," she said.

I kissed the top of her head. "I suppose we should."

We cleaned up, and I put my suit back on. I helped Nadine back into her wedding dress before we left the room.

Nadine paused at the top of the stairs. "That's weird. The music stopped."

I hadn't noticed until now, because we'd been so wrapped up in each other. Now that I noticed the silence, it was very eerie.

We quickly hurried down the stairs. Through the glass door, we could see our friends sitting around the table. They looked to be talking in hushed whispers. I caught sight of concern etched on Chloe's face.

The moment we stepped out onto the patio, their entire demeanor changed. "Who's ready for another round of shots?" Miles asked loudly, before grabbing a drink from the cocktail bar.

Everyone cheered, but Onyx threw a worried look our way. They were trying to act like everything was fine, but Nadine and I could both sense something was up. Isa and Oliver circled our feet, like they were trying to tell us something.

Nadine looked around. "Where's Grammy? And Verla, and Professor Warren?"

"They, uh, went to get ice," Miles lied.

Everything went dead silent, and a shiver traveled down my spine.

"Tell us the truth," I demanded, feeling panic rising in my throat. Something wasn't right.

"Everything's fine." Talia rose from her chair and bounced over to us. "We took a break, and now we're ready to get back to dancing!"

Nadine placed her hands on her hips. "You all are terrible liars. Where. Is. Grammy?"

Onyx sighed. "We have to tell them—wedding or not."

Chloe turned to us. "We don't want you to worry. But Professor Warren was doing a routine perimeter check, and he spotted Executors not far from here."

"Executors!" I shouted. "How did they find us? They've never come this close to the safe house."

"We're not sure they *have* found us, or if they're just scouting the area," Chloe said. "They weren't headed straight for us, but if they reach the wards, they'll know we're here. Helena, Verla, and Warren went to deal with them before they could get close enough to discover us."

"How many Executors?" Nadine asked.

"Warren saw five," Chloe said.

Nadine started around the side of the house, and the rest of us followed. We had a high vantage point up here on the mountain, but it was difficult to see anything through the trees—let alone in the dark of night.

"Nadine!" Chloe called after her. "They told us to stay!"

She whirled toward Chloe. "We're stronger together! I'm not letting my grandmother—or anyone else I love—face our enemy alone."

"They're not alone," Grant said. "Helena, Verla, and Warren have each other. They didn't want us getting involved."

"There's three of them and five Executors," Nadine cried. "They're outnumbered, and we need to help."

"It's your wedding night, and we're not letting some stupid Executors ruin it," Chloe said. "If you want to send someone after them, let *us* go. You two shouldn't have to deal with this tonight."

"I'm not going to stand here when my grandmother is in trouble," Nadine argued. "Where are they?"

Talia pointed across the landscape, not far from the border of our ward. "Warren spotted the Executors on that outcropping of rock."

The Executors were gone now, and Nadine frantically searched the landscape. "There!" she cried, pointing to a dim light through the trees. It was close to the border of our ward. That had to be Helena, Verla, and Warren. They were using witch lights to guide themselves through the darkness. I spotted another cluster of lights moving through the trees, guiding the Executors up the mountain.

"The Executors can't see them from that distance. Your grandma will turn her light off when they reach the border." I tried to assure Nadine, though I couldn't be sure. "The Executors won't know they're coming."

Nadine held her breath as her grandmother's light faded at the edge of the border, then she gasped and pointed in another direction. "There's movement over there! The Executors are coming in two groups. They're going to corner them, and Grammy doesn't know!"

Horror tangled in my gut as the Executors began closing in.

Nadine gathered her skirt in her hands and tossed her heels into the grass. "We have to go after them! They can't be out there alone. I'm going to help. Anyone who doesn't want to come is welcome to stay behind, but I'm going after my family."

I was with Nadine. She was my wife now, and we'd come together as one. Her family was now my family, and I'd do whatever it took to protect it.

"Let's go," I said. "These Executors aren't getting away without bloodshed tonight."

# EIGHT

A terrible sensation tangled in my gut, telling me to get to Grammy right the fuck *now*. I hiked my skirt up and ran down the mountain in my bare feet. My friends raced behind me, and our cats scurried ahead of us.

My pulse grew loud in my ears, and sweat dripped from my brow. My dress caught on underbrush and tore, and rocks sliced my feet. It barely registered, because all I could think about was getting to my grandmother and the others before the Executors cornered them.

My magic tingled, indicating I'd crossed the ward boundary. Ahead loomed a steep hill covered in loose rock. I grabbed trees to help me steady my balance as I ran down the hill. I kept running, but then came the sound of tumbling rock behind me.

I whirled around to see Lucas's silhouette sliding down the steep incline, loose rock tumbling down with him. A loud *crack* sounded—as if a rock had hit him aside the head—followed by a pained grunt. Lucas caught himself at the bottom of the hill.

I turned to go back for him, but then the sound of screaming voices came in the distance. A loud explosion rocked the forest, and streams of lights shone through the trees up ahead.

"Get their shields down!" Verla shouted.

I hesitated. Lucas was on his feet and conscious, and right now, the others needed magic. I turned away from my husband and sprinted through the trees toward the sound of exploding battle magic. Ahead, the trees cleared enough that I could see Grammy, Verla, and Warren facing off against a dozen Executors. Magic blasted off in every direction, illuminating the scene. Our cats had already reached them, and they were fighting the Executors' cats. High-pitched meows and low growls filled the air.

A spell caught Professor Warren in the shoulder, but it barely fazed him as he shot a spell back at the Executor who'd hit him. The spell hit the Executor in the chest, and he slumped to the ground.

A shield shimmered around Grammy and Verla. It looked like they were working together to defend Professor Warren as he went in for the kill. Verla lifted her hands to the Executors, but she hesitated, like she didn't want to hurt the cats who were in the middle of it all. If she cast a spell at the wrong time, it would kill all of them. Odin screeched as one of the other cats slashed its claws across his face. Blood trickled down his black fur.

An Executor aimed a spell at Grammy, but I reached out with my Curse Breaker powers and siphoned his spell for my own. The spell died in his hands, and I used the power to throw a deadly battle orb in his direction. The spell hit him square in the back, and his whole body went limp.

I had almost reached Grammy and had to be less than fifteen yards away when I heard the *whizz* of a rogue spell flying out of the forest. I only had a split-second warning. I didn't get a chance to react before the spell hit my ankles and swept my feet out from under me. My body was yanked to the side, and my head smashed against a nearby tree. I landed with a hard *thud* on the ground. I thought I felt the warmth of blood trickling down the side of my face, but I could hardly process it. The forest seemed to spin around me as I staggered to my feet. Grammy spun to the side to block a spell, but I spotted an Executor behind a tree raise their wand to her.

My voice rang through the forest. "Grammy, behind you!"

Grammy whirled around just in time to deflect the incoming spell. Her eyes turned in the direction of my voice. Her gaze locked on mine, and the color drained from her face. "Nadine, run!"

Grammy threw out her arm, and the shimmering protective shield that had encompassed her projected in my direction. In the blink of an eye, an Executor raised their wand, and a sizzling red battle orb shot toward me. I barely had a moment to process it before it bounced off Grammy's shield—which protected me—and back in her direction. Verla saw the spell, and she swung her hand out to deflect it, but her shield was cast too late.

The red battle orb hit Grammy in the chest, blasting her off her feet. The power of the spell was so intense that it tore a wound through her skin. Blood sprayed across the forest, splattering against my face and over the front of my dress. Grammy's body hit the ground hard several feet away from where she'd been standing.

I stumbled to the side and caught myself on a tree. The sounds of magic whizzing through the forest grew distant. I waited for Grammy to stand. She was fine… she just had to *get up*.

Out of the corner of my eye, I was vaguely aware of the rage marring Verla's features. The sound of her furious scream cut through my bleary daze. Verla raised her hands, and over a dozen streams of battle magic shot from her fingertips all at once. The spell was so powerful that it tore straight through the Executors' shield and burned through their chests all at once. Screams echoed across the mountain range, along with screeches from the Executors' cats. Abrupt silence followed immediately as the Executors' bodies dropped to the ground in unison.

The light faded, until blackness consumed the forest once again. All I could hear was the sound of Verla's ragged breathing.

I stumbled forward and dropped to my knees beside Grammy's unmoving body. Blood soaked down the front of her dress, but the wound wasn't as deep as I thought it'd be. I pushed her white hair out of her face, but her eyes remained closed.

My voice became a broken whisper as I said, "Grammy, wake up. The Executors are gone now."

I turned my gaze up to Verla, who stood several feet away. I thought she appeared to be in shock, but it was hard to see much of anything behind the tears forming in my eyes. "Help her," I pleaded.

"Nadine…" she started softly, but anything she was going to say in that tone of voice wasn't something I wanted to hear. Verla knelt beside me and placed a hand on my shoulder. It was supposed to be comforting, but it was anything but. I shoved her off of me. Verla had already given up, but I wouldn't.

"YOU NEED TO HELP HER!" I screamed. "Why aren't you doing anything!?"

I shook my grandmother and tried to call out her name, but my throat had completely closed up. All that came out was a heart-wrenching whimper. I waited for Grammy to open her eyes… but she never did.

A twig snapped behind me. I whirled around, a spell crackling in my palm. Lucas stared back at me with wide eyes. The heartbreak in his features told me everything I needed to know.

He'd heard someone's last thought. And I knew exactly who had spoken it.

I dropped the spell. "Lucas…"

He knelt beside me and took me in his arms. I couldn't muster the energy to push him away. He stroked his hand over the top of my head, and his voice cracked as he whispered, "I know."

I couldn't bear to hear those two simple words, because it confirmed everything I didn't want to believe. He'd heard her last thought, and that meant she was already gone. Sobs racked my body, and tears streamed down my cheeks to soak into his tux. Inside of me, something snapped, and I could swear the sound of my breaking heart filled the forest.

Footsteps approached us from both sides, and Talia's choked sob came through the darkness. "Nadine, I'm so sorry."

Arms encompassed me from all angles as my friends wrapped me in a group hug. Nobody said anything else, because they all knew there were no words that could mend my heart in the wake of the devastation.

Grammy was dead… The last of my family was gone.

I didn't know how long I sobbed. Eventually, I pulled away from Lucas and turned back toward Grammy. Someone must've lit a witch light above me, because I could see Grammy's lifeless features clear as day. I ran my fingers over the side of her face. She was still warm, but no breath escaped her lips. Hushed voices reached me, but I couldn't be entirely sure of what they were saying.

"Nadine needs to see her one last time," Onyx said.

"I can't help," Miles replied. "Her spirit isn't here."

"She already moved on," Lucas cut in, his voice rough. "I can feel it. Her reaper's already been here."

His words seemed to echo in my mind. *Her reaper's already been here.*

Grammy wasn't just gone in the flesh; her spirit was gone, too. I didn't get a chance to say goodbye.

I curled over my grandmother's lifeless form, sobbing for what could've been hours until I couldn't cry anymore. I couldn't be sure how much time passed, but it felt like decades all crammed into one single moment.

Eventually, Verla cleared her throat, though her voice came out sounding broken. "Lucas, take Nadine back to the house. Jonathan and I will remove all traces of what happened here—magical or otherwise."

Nobody moved for a beat, until Professor Warren added, "If we don't act soon, the priestesses will be able to track the Executors to our location. We must cast our spells now."

Gentle hands helped me to stand. My feet moved under me as Lucas supported my weight, but my spirit seemed to exist somewhere outside my body, like I was watching the scene from above.

Somehow, we made it back to the house, though I didn't remember walking that far. Lucas helped me sit on the couch, and someone draped a blanket around my shoulders. My friends spoke in broken whispers, but all I could do was stare into the crackling fireplace that seemed nothing more than a blur. I couldn't process any of their words.

It had all happened so fast. One moment, I was living in euphoric bliss… and the next, my entire world had been shattered to pieces.

It didn't feel real.

Worst of all, I realized it was still my wedding day.

Hours must've passed, or maybe it was minutes. I couldn't be sure, but even time couldn't convince me of what I'd seen. My eyes had become raw with tears, and they burned when I blinked. Isa had curled up in my lap. Her weight could usually comfort me unlike anything else, but tonight, it felt like a boulder crushing me.

Voices came from another room. Verla and Warren must've returned by now.

"Are we confident the perimeter is safe?" Chloe asked.

"Yes," Verla said. "Our wards are strong, and we've expanded them to conceal what happened here tonight. The priestesses would need all the Oaken Wands to break through them."

It didn't matter if my body was safe, because the priestesses proved tonight that they could take everything from me that mattered. What was the point of staying here and being in hiding if my body was safe but my soul was in pieces?

I'd sworn they wouldn't take anyone else from me, but they had. They'd driven us from Octavia Falls. They'd taken our home. Now they'd taken my family.

I should want to burn the priestesses and everything they cared about to the ground—to raid Octavia Falls right now and make them suffer for what they'd done in the worst ways possible. But all I wanted to do was curl into a ball and drift off to a place where none of this was happening. Grammy couldn't be gone… she just *couldn't*.

"The Executors got too close to the safe house tonight," Grant said.

"They're narrowing their search, but we don't believe they know exactly where we're hiding," Professor Warren replied. "We bought us some time with the wards."

"What if it isn't enough?" Miles asked. "We may need to leave the safe house."

Verla cleared her throat. "We can't. Our wards are concealing us in more ways than one. If we leave, we're vulnerable to the priestesses' magic. Even if we find some place to stay and cast more wards, the priestesses will continue looking until they find us. We're safest here, and we need to stay for as long as possible. Let's all get some rest."

I wasn't sure if they said anything else, because I couldn't bring myself to focus on anything right now. Eventually, I heard footsteps approach.

"You should get her to bed," I heard someone say. I thought it was Verla, but her voice sounded distorted through the fog clouding my mind. "She needs to rest. We all do. We'll hold a funeral tomorrow."

Isa moved off my lap, and Lucas helped me stand. It was the first time I noticed I'd been holding a cup of tea, only the tea had gone cold. I didn't know who had given it to me. The mug was still full, and I hadn't taken a sip.

Talia took the teacup from my hands, and Lucas helped me upstairs. Cornelius lay at the bottom of the stairs. He looked up at me with shining eyes, like he could feel my heartbreak as his own.

Lucas led me to our bedroom. This room had been so full of love and passion earlier tonight, but all that magnificence had been replaced by anguish. Lucas helped me out of my dress, but the motion felt nothing like it had before.

He wrapped a robe around my body, then lowered me onto the bed and pulled the covers up around me. I lay on my side, staring into the darkness that seemed all-consuming. I feared that if I closed my eyes, I would see the spell impacting Grammy all over again—or hear her scream telling me to run.

I couldn't help but think this was my fault. Grammy had cast a shield to protect me, and it caused the Executor's spell to ricochet and hurt her instead. If she'd just kept her shield around herself instead of trying to save me, she'd still be here.

Isa curled in my arms, and Lucas snuggled close to me, but I could hardly feel them. All I could feel was the agonizing tightness in my chest that no amount of tears could alleviate. It was bizarre to think that Grammy wasn't just down the hall, sleeping two doors down.

At some point, I fell asleep, but it was a restless sleep. I didn't have any dreams—or at the very least, they were so harrowing that my mind couldn't bear to remember them.

I woke to an all-consuming ache curling around every muscle and joint. I lay in bed for a long time, unable to process how much time had passed. Rain pelted the window, and thunder cracked over the house. It was very unlike the drizzle that had been a good omen the morning of our wedding. This was a symbol of turmoil.

I didn't understand how the good omens of our wedding day had led to *this*. Either the omens meant nothing, or I couldn't trust them. Grammy's death was anything but a *blessing* the rain and spider had promised me. That, or there were larger forces at play. The thought terrified me to the very core. I refused to believe there was a larger meaning to Grammy's passing, because nothing could justify this kind of loss. I didn't care if there was a reason for her leaving, because I needed her right now. She was gone because of me.

I had to get out of bed to prepare for the funeral. We were supposed to bring an offering to Grammy's grave, which she would be buried with, and I couldn't imagine her being buried with anything other than the flowers from the garden she loved so much. I dug a lily bulb out from one of her potted plants and returned to my room to get dressed.

I couldn't, though. I sat on the bed and stared across the room, unable to move.

By mid-afternoon, the rain had let up. Voices came from downstairs, but I couldn't be sure whose they were. I kept expecting to hear Grammy, but her voice never came.

Lucas sat beside me on the bed. I lifted my heavy eyes and noticed he wore a black suit. A long black dress hung from the back of the door. I wasn't sure who put it there, though it looked like something that had come from Chloe's closet.

"Is it time for the funeral already?" I asked, my voice cracking.

Lucas pushed my hair back. "Not until you're ready. Take all the time you need."

Funerals in the coven often happened quickly after someone died—usually the following day. Grammy's spirit had already moved on, and we had to put her body to rest, too. Witches had a strange way of embracing death, and I was still learning how to view it like the rest of them. I wasn't used to it yet.

"It feels too soon," I admitted.

"We have to perform the funeral ceremony to release her," Lucas stated softly.

"I thought she'd already moved on."

"Her spirit has crossed over, but the coven must let her go, too," Lucas explained. "We still have some time, though. We can wait."

I shook my head. "I don't want Grammy to have to wait for me. She chose to move on, so I have to let her."

It felt like a lie on my tongue. I didn't want to let her go, and I knew that it'd take a hell of a lot more than a funeral to do it. I was still grieving my parents' death, and this only made all that grief and loss come rushing back. I had to go through it all over again—but this time without *her*.

She'd been at my parents' funeral to hold me together when I was breaking down... quite literally. Grammy's hugs were all that had gotten me through that day. She'd held my hand when their caskets were lowered into the ground, and she helped me walk across the cemetery when we placed flowers on their graves, because my knees were so unsteady I didn't think I could do it myself. I felt like I was unraveling at the seams now, and Grammy wasn't here to knit me back together.

Lucas helped me into the black dress, and I sat at the vanity while he brushed my hair back. Isa purred on my lap, trying to comfort me, but nothing could help right now. The lily bulb sat on the vanity, and I picked it up. There was still dirt under my nails from when I'd dug it up this morning.

We went downstairs, where the others were dressed in funeral attire. Everyone remained eerily quiet, and it was obvious they'd all been crying. I noticed my friends weren't the only ones there, though. Hattie had arrived with her wolf Familiar.

She stepped forward and placed a bundle of blue flowers into my hands. "They're forget-me-nots, because we will always remember her."

I wiped my nose. "Thank you for being here."

Hattie placed a gentle hand on mine. "I wouldn't miss it. Let's lay your grandmother to rest."

We followed her outside in our bare feet, to connect us to the earth, which was Grammy's final resting place. The grass was wet, and the sky overcast, but there were no raindrops. I noticed the decorations from the wedding from the night before had been cleaned up. It already felt like weeks ago. It was ironic and heartbreaking that we'd had a wedding and a funeral in the span of less than twenty-four hours.

Hattie led us through the trees and to a flat clearing that seemed so removed from the house. Lucas had said we needed to bury her far away so her body didn't contaminate our water supply, but I hated that. I wanted Grammy close to me, but now she was going to be all alone out here in the woods.

A large stone stood at the head of her grave. Hattie had used her powers to etch Grammy's name into the grave marker. The earth had been upheaved, and Grammy's body lay four feet below us. We were giving her a natural burial, because even though the coven used caskets and held traditional funerals now, this was the way we used to do things. It's what Grammy would've wanted, being in nature and surrounded by her flowers. It was a shallow grave, so Grammy's body could return to the earth quicker and nourish the plants she so loved.

Grammy's features were pale, and her arms were crossed over her chest. She wore a white gown and was laid on a thin cotton shroud to symbolize Mother Miriam's skirt surrounding her, like it would if she was a child embracing her mother's legs.

When I saw her corpse lying there, the crushing reality hit me all over again. She was *really* gone.

I was never going to hear her laugh again, or taste another one of her delicious homemade dinners. Her warm embrace would never envelop me again. She'd never bring me another cup of tea, and the garden she'd planted here at the safe house would wither away without her.

Cornelius stood beside the grave. He took one look at Grammy's corpse, then turned his face to the sky and yowled. The other cats joined in the song of mourning.

Beside the grave stood a small table, which served as an altar and held a white, unlit candle and a silver goblet filled with a dark liquid. Verla approached the altar and lit a match. "We will begin by lighting a candle, to symbolize the light that Helena brought into this world while she was with us, and to guide her way home to Alora."

Verla lit the candle. The wick instantly ignited, burning at least three inches high. Grammy was with us, all right. She had to be, because there was no light in this world brighter than hers, and this flame knew it.

Verla lifted the goblet. "You have all brought an item with you, which will serve as an offering to Mother Miriam. We pray that our offerings will be accepted as a symbol of our love for Helena, so that Mother Miriam may grant her a peaceful rest in Alora alongside her family, friends, and community. When you are ready, take a sip of the bitter funeral wine, which has been brewed by the Alchemists in attendance today. Drink the wine as a symbol of your acceptance of the bitterness of death, then place your offering within the grave and speak your parting words."

Verla took a sip of wine, then placed it back on the altar. "Helena, you were a mother to us all. I've known you since I was a child and spent so many nights at your house when Faith, Nicole, and I had sleepovers. You helped me study through law school, and you came to all my graduations. When I was named headmistress, you brought me flowers you had grown from your own garden, and you told me you were so proud, when my own parents couldn't even bother to show up. When Nicole died, you came to her funeral, and you stood next to me when I gave her eulogy."

Tears streamed down Verla's face. She never talked about her sister. Everything I knew about Nicole Verla was based on what others had told me. Grammy must've meant more to Verla than I ever thought, because she wouldn't bring up her sister if Grammy didn't mean the world to her.

Verla conjured a thin yellow shawl. "You bought me my dress to the Midnight Formal my freshman year of college when I couldn't afford one myself. I've kept the shawl all these years, to remind me to show kindness to others the way you showed it to me. I offer this shawl as a symbol of your empathy and caring nature. I give you all my love, and I pray this love brings you peace in Alora."

Verla gently folded the shawl and knelt down, lowering it into the grave beside Grammy.

"You told me when Faith died that Nadine would need someone to look up to, someone to help her and protect her," Verla continued. "I promise to be that for her and look after her. Rest in peace, Helena."

Verla finished by tossing her forget-me-nots into the grave, then stepped back for others to approach. Tears streaked my cheeks.

Professor Warren came forward next, holding a throw blanket in his hands. He took a sip of wine, then began to speak. "Helena, you made this house a home for all of us when we were cast out of our own. We cannot thank you enough. I offer this blanket that kept me warm for many nights here in this house, as a symbol of the home you built and the love we all shared."

He placed the blanket over her legs, then sprinkled his flowers over her body. More tears leaked from my eyes. Grammy's body was so cold down there in the grave, and Warren's blanket would keep her warm.

Hattie stroked her Familiar's head and came forward to partake in the wine. She held a potion bottle in her hands. "We knew each other for a brief time, and in that time, we became great friends. I offer this potion that you brewed me, meant to bring strength and vitality to the body. Now, I return it as a symbol of the strength and vitality you showed. You will be dearly missed."

Professor Warren helped Hattie to her knees, so that she could place her offering and flowers inside the grave. She lingered there a moment as several tears leaked from her eyes, then Warren helped her stand again.

Onyx drank the wine and knelt beside the grave with a bundle of herbs in her hand. "I offer this herb bundle of chamomile and peppermint to symbolize your wisdom. You taught me many healing potions, and I will take that knowledge with me and continue to heal through the wisdom you passed on."

Miles stepped up next. He held something that looked like a large gold coin in his hands, and when he shifted, I realized it hung from a ribbon. It was a gold medal. "I offer this medal I won in a Skee-Ball tournament last school year. It was the only thing I got to take with me when we fled Octavia Falls, and I wouldn't have it without you. I didn't know who you were at the time, but you found me in the halls of Miriam College when you were visiting Nadine one day. You asked me what was wrong, and I told you I was considering entering the tournament, but wasn't sure, because I thought I'd lose. You asked if I was going to have fun, and I told you I would. You said as long as I loved what I was doing, I'd already won. You convinced me to join the tournament, and I won, just like you'd said. I offer this medal as a symbol of your ability to uplift us all."

I'd never heard this story before. It made me cry harder.

Grant knelt beside the grave with a container of cookies. "I offer you these gingersnap cookies I baked. It's the same recipe you made a month ago. When I asked you for the recipe, you took me to the kitchen and showed me how to bake them right away, like it was the only thing that mattered. You always saw me, even if it was for the smallest things. I offer these as a symbol of your generosity."

Talia wiped her tears and pulled out a sheet of paper when she approached the grave. "When I was in a bad relationship, you found me crying at the park, and you sat there with me for over an hour as I contemplated breaking up with my ex or not. You were so kind and gentle, even though you told me to leave him. I never told anyone about that day, but I went home that night and wrote this song about what you said. I've held on to it because these words became a part of me, and I couldn't bear to let them go. But I'm ready now. I offer this sheet music, as a symbol of the compassion you showed. I'm never going to play this song again, and that's okay, because I don't need to anymore."

I didn't know what Grammy had said to Talia, but it must've been profound. Cody had been so horrible to Talia, and as friends, we'd all done everything we could to help her ditch that awful relationship. I never realized that it was Grammy's words that had given Talia the courage to leave.

Chloe went next. "Helena, you showed me kindness I didn't deserve. I am descended from the man who killed your husband, and I was cursed to keep your granddaughter out of town. I made bad choices and treated people poorly. I came to Nadine and joined her cause to create a better coven, and it is because of you that I have the chance to be here at all. You could have cast me out and refused to welcome me as one of your own, but you didn't. You welcomed me with open arms, without any hatred or bad blood. That says everything about who you are as a person, and as a witch. You showed me the power of forgiveness, and I will carry that with me forever."

I barely concealed a sob. Chloe and I had been through a lot to get to where we were today, and breaking our curse together had been a catalyst for the friendship we shared now. But I'd never thought about what Grammy must've thought of her, because it was so natural for Grammy to be kind to *everyone*. Chloe was right, and Grammy's kindness toward her made the coven—and the world—a better place. It wasn't fair that Grammy had to die when people like the priestesses got to live and continue ruling the coven through fear. We needed more people like Grammy in the world, who were willing to forgive.

Chloe conjured a can of olives, and I didn't understand what it meant until she started speaking. "I wanted to offer an olive branch, as a symbol of the peace and reconciliation you offered me. Since I do not have an olive branch, I offer these olives to symbolize my gratitude for the forgiveness you have shown, and to give my love back in these final moments."

Lucas approached the grave with a jar of applesauce in his hands. It was the applesauce we'd made with Grammy over the summer, and it hurt to even look at it. It was all the moments we shared with her, and everything she taught us, all condensed into a single glass container. I feared the jar may shatter, because I was certainly falling to pieces on the inside.

Lucas drank the wine, then paused for a few beats to collect his thoughts. "Helena, I met you in my darkest time. I had lost my brother, and I thought that the only person who'd ever care for me was gone. I came to you seeking healing through herbs and potions, but you saw I needed so much more when I didn't know it myself. You gave me a safe space to speak about what I'd been through, and you offered advice when I didn't know how to ask for it. Your love saved my life. Without you, I wouldn't be here, and I hate that I didn't get a chance to tell you that. I offer you this applesauce as a symbol of the memories we created together. I love you deeply, and your memory will live on."

Lucas placed his offering and flowers into the grave, then took a step back. It was my turn, but the words felt stuck in my throat.

"It's okay if you don't say anything," he whispered.

"I want to." I approached the altar and lifted the goblet to my lips. A horrible bitter scent filled my nose, and I already knew what it would taste like on my tongue. Still, I wasn't prepared for how awful it would be. The bitterness of the wine flowed over my tastebuds, and I wanted to spit it back out. I forced myself to choke it down, because I didn't want to ruin the ceremony.

I rushed to set the goblet back on the altar, but in my haste, the goblet fell over, spilling the remaining wine across the grass. I stared as the bitter liquid seeped into the ground.

"It's okay," Verla quickly assured me. "You may speak whenever you're ready, Nadine."

I tore my gaze from the wine and turned to the grave. I drew a deep breath, though my voice cracked. "Grammy, I thought I had more time with you. You've been there for me through everything, from the moment I was born, through my therapy sessions, and during my time in the hospital. It didn't matter how long the drive was—you'd always make it. Then Mom and Dad died, and you gave me a home again. You taught me some of the hardest lessons in life and guided me when I felt lost. You may be gone from this life, but you'll always be in my heart. The world was a better place with you in it."

I knelt at the edge of the grave. "I offer this lily bulb as a symbol of your love. I know how much your garden meant to you, and how much you loved us all. My love for you is like this lily. It will survive throughout the changing seasons, and it never needs replacing. I've loved you since the day I was born, and I will love you long after I die. Rest in peace, Grammy."

I tossed the forget-me-nots into her grave, then gently placed the lily bulb beside her. I stepped back and began to sob.

We joined hands in a circle, and a low funeral tune filled the air as my friends began to sing a witch's song. Though I mouthed the words, I couldn't bring enough air through my lungs to make it audible.

*You were the crystal on my altar*
*And the wand that I had conjured*
*You were the potion in the cauldron*
*The incantation I once pondered*

*You were all that gave me power*
*You lifted me so high*
*Now at this final hour*
*I bless you with goodbye*

*We had a life together*
*But if it's right with fate*
*I'll meet you in my spirit*
*Right at Alora's gate*

As the funeral song continued, Cornelius jumped into the grave. He nudged Grammy's hands a few times, as if he could get her to wake, but she didn't move. Then he curled up on her chest and laid his head down. His whole body sagged as the breath left his lungs.

I looked around to see if anyone else was as shocked as I was, but they all seemed to take it surprisingly well. I guess it made sense. Cornelius had incarnated in this life to serve as Grammy's companion. Now that she was gone, his purpose had been fulfilled, and his soul energy could return to Alora with her.

The song concluded, and Hattie lifted her hands to control the earth. Her elemental powers shifted the dirt to cover Grammy's body, until the grave was completely covered. Hattie commanded the grass to grow over the grave, until it looked as if the ground had been left undisturbed entirely. My breath caught in my throat as I witnessed a lily spring from the grave, growing before my very eyes.

It should have been a beautiful moment, but it was difficult to watch. This wasn't right, and I hated the priestesses even more now. Grammy didn't get to be buried in the cemetery next to Grampy back in Octavia Falls. It was too dangerous for us to go back to town and bury her there, a place that had always been her home. The priestesses had torn her community from her, and now she'd been laid to rest here all alone. It wasn't fair.

Verla blew out the candle, and I couldn't believe it was over already. It all happened so quickly, which was all too symbolic of the way she died. Twenty-four hours ago, Grammy was helping me into my wedding dress, and now, she was buried in the ground.

Lucas reached for me, but I couldn't take his hand. The walk back to the house felt hollow. I should be walking inside to ask Grammy for a cup of tea, not retreating from her grave. I didn't know if everyone else felt like they'd said a proper goodbye, but I certainly didn't.

"I'll put on some coffee," Verla offered, and Onyx followed her into the kitchen to help.

I didn't want coffee. I wanted tea—Grammy's tea, specifically. Something I'd never get to have again.

"Nad," Lucas whispered. He gestured me down the hall away from the others. I appreciated the moment alone, because I desperately needed it. Isa and Oliver followed, but they stood at the end of the hall, making sure no one interrupted. Lucas didn't say anything—just wrapped me tight in his arms and rocked me back and forth. This time, I didn't pull away.

"I didn't say enough," I cried into his chest.

He stroked my hair back. "Everything you said was perfect."

"But there's *so much more* I want to say to her," I sobbed. "I never got to say goodbye. Why didn't she stay, Lucas? I wish she'd just stayed one more minute so I could let her know how I feel."

"I don't know what it's like to die, but I know that if someone's ready to go, they're not going to hang back," he stated gently. "Your grandmother knew her time was coming."

"It was too soon," I argued. "She was only seventy. She could've had another twenty or thirty years left."

"I'm not sure she wanted those extra years for herself," he said hollowly.

I wasn't sure what he meant. When I glanced up, he couldn't quite look me in the eye. "What do you mean… What was her last thought?"

Lucas swallowed, like he was hearing it all over again. "*I died protecting what I love most.*"

My face grew hotter, and my lips trembled. "She died thinking of me?"

He nodded. "I think she's been prepared for this for a long time. She always knew there'd be a chance she'd die protecting you."

I drew away from him without thinking about it. "I didn't want her to!"

"But *she* was okay with it. I think that's why she went with her reaper so quickly. She was already prepared to go."

A lump rose in my throat. I tried to swallow it down, but it didn't budge. My words squeaked past the lump. "I just wanted to save her."

"She *needed* to save you," Lucas said in a small voice.

I looked into his eyes—*really* looked at him this time. Tears brimmed his bottom lids, and the corners of his lips twitched like he was trying to hold back a pained cry. I realized he was trying to hold it together for me.

Grammy was as much of a grandmother to him as she was to me. She had been a safe place to come to after his brother had died. She had been a mentor to him.

She hadn't just moved on without saying goodbye to me. Lucas had been standing *right there*, and yet Grammy had gone with another reaper. I saw the pain in my husband's eyes. He wanted to be there for her, and he didn't get there soon enough. She'd chosen not to have him help her into the next life, and he didn't understand why.

"I'm sorry, Lucas," I whispered. "I know this is hard for you, too."

His gaze became distant. "She moved on before I even got to the clearing. I could've helped her cross over. We could've all said goodbye. I don't know why I couldn't help her, and why I wasn't enough."

"There has to be a reason," I said. "Perhaps she thought it'd be too much for you, or that we wouldn't let her go. She may understand things in death that we don't yet, and it has nothing to do with you."

"I could've helped her, though, and maybe this wouldn't feel so heavy if I did," he admitted. "I'm so sick of losing the people I love. I didn't want to lose her, too. Not so soon. I have to accept that she was ready, and we must honor her wishes."

"We could hold a séance," I offered.

Lucas shook his head. "It's not going to work. Miles and I tried what we could last night, to make sure she'd really crossed over, and she's already gone. Even if we could summon her, a séance wouldn't help heal our hearts. Once someone dies, that's it. They don't get to come back."

I missed Grammy so much already, but I was angry at her, too. She knew what power we had, and she could've chosen to stay another minute and let us say goodbye. Grammy's spirit may be gone, but I wasn't ready to let her go.

Lucas led me back into the living room, where the others were quietly sipping on coffee. He went into the kitchen to prepare us each a cup, but I was magnetized to the patio door. I stared out across the damp lawn, at the entrance to the trail that led to where we'd buried my grandmother.

Quiet whispers filled the room, but I didn't hear what anyone said as I slid the patio door open and walked across the grass and into the trees. It was drizzling now. My hair was getting wet, and my feet squished in the mud, but I barely noticed. My chest ached as I approached the grave, Isa following at my feet. A crushing weight on my shoulders forced me to my knees, and Isa snuggled against my leg. I wanted to say something, but nothing came out.

I sat in silence for several long minutes, until I heard the sound of light footsteps approaching. Talia knelt in the wet grass at my side, and she wrapped a gentle arm around me. Tears streamed down my cheeks, and I rested my head on her shoulder.

"The first day I met Helena, she couldn't stop talking about you," Talia said gently. "You were her shining light, Nadine. You're the reason that woman's heart kept beating, until the very end."

I sniffled and wiped my eyes. "Is that why she died for me? I caused this, Tal."

"That's not true, Nadine. Your grandmother loved you very much, and she chose to fight for you. The Executors killed your grandmother, and they're the only ones to blame."

"Their spell hit the shield she'd used to protect me," I insisted. "She wouldn't have died if I hadn't gone after her."

"You don't know that," Talia said.

I clutched my stomach, because it felt as if my insides might come spilling out. "I wish I could believe you."

My conversation with Grammy from the night of my bridal shower weighed heavy on my mind. I'd told her I was waiting for the other shoe to drop, and it had—only that shoe had been a massive fucking boulder, barreling through my life to destroy everything I held dear.

I despised the Executors for casting that spell. They'd taken my grandmother from me, under order from the priestesses. I swore right then and there that the priestesses would pay for what they'd done. I didn't know how or when, but I was going to destroy every last Executor to get to the priestesses if I had to.

"Grammy died because things were going *too* well," I said. "Every time something goes *right* in my life, something bad has to happen to even the scales."

Talia shook her head. "Witches don't believe in that."

"Don't they?" I lifted my gaze to hers. "Do we not believe in karma?"

"In a way, but balance isn't about weighing good and bad. It's about creating our own energy and guiding the outcome."

"So if this happened to us, that means we created it," I reasoned. "When things get good, I'm expecting something bad to happen, so I caused it. Tal, I'm…"

I couldn't believe I was going to say this out loud. I couldn't admit it to myself, really, but I couldn't ignore the ache in my chest telling me this is how I truly felt.

"I'm worried that marrying Lucas was a mistake," I spat out.

"Your wedding didn't cause this," Talia pressed. She seemed so desperate to help, but I was so convinced that I'd gotten Grammy killed, and she couldn't tell me otherwise.

"How can you be sure?" I asked. "Lucas and I were cursed when we got together. I may have broken the Reaper's Shadow curse, but being with him feels too good to be true. I'm afraid I never should've pursued a relationship with him at all."

Talia furrowed her brow. "What are you saying? Are you going to annul the marriage?"

"No!" I said quickly. "I love Lucas so much. I would never want to leave him. I'm terrified of the future because time is going to keep moving forward, and I'm not ready to lose another one of you. Things were *really* good for a moment, and now it feels like there isn't any point in putting myself back together, because if this is the price I have to pay for happiness, I don't think I want it."

Talia pulled me closer. "I know what it's like to feel that things are too good to be true, and to seek out the *bad* because that's what you're used to. When things are going *good*, it feels uncomfortable. What's important is that you embrace the good and detach it from the bad. They aren't two sides of a scale where one has to influence the other. I know we need the bad to see the good in things, but sometimes the good can exist on its own."

"How can you be sure of this?" I asked.

"Because I've been through it," she answered. "I was never good at relationships. It didn't occur to me that someone could actually *want* me the way Grant does. I pushed him away and dated Cody because that's what felt normal. Cody really messed with the way I viewed myself and how relationships could work. Hell, he taught me sex was bad and uncomfortable. When Grant and I started fooling around, it was really hard, because I couldn't completely open up to him at first. Everything we did just made me feel *dirty*."

"I'm sorry you went through that," I whispered. "Lucas and I have a great time together, but sometimes when I'm with him, I feel like we're breaking the rules, because we were never supposed to get this far in the first place. If I'd never broken the Reaper's Shadow curse, we never wouldn't have gotten married."

"Sex should feel freeing and empowering for both of you," Talia said. "It shouldn't feel restrictive, like you're breaking the rules. Have you tried the toys yet?"

I shook my head. "I don't know if we're that kind of couple. They make me nervous."

"I felt that way at first, too, but they really helped," Talia said. "I found them therapeutic."

I furrowed my brow. "In what way?"

"It was something new for Grant and me to connect over—something I'd never done with anyone else," she explained. "We got to experiment together, and it became a meditation for us. I could just *be* with him and trust that he would take care of me. When I was focused on all the *good* with Grant, I forgot about the bad with Cody. I won't ever forget, but it also doesn't weigh on me anymore. In order to change the way I felt, I had to involve my mind *and* body."

"So when I'm with Lucas, I should focus just on him, and not all the bad that will come as a result?"

Talia nodded. "I understand you're looking for an explanation for what happened, but you and Lucas are not responsible just because you shared a moment of happiness. Putting the blame on yourself isn't going to save you from your grief."

I turned back to Grammy's grave, and my stomach clenched tighter. I understood what Talia was saying, but I couldn't quite accept it.

"The people we love in life make choices," Talia added. "Helena made the choice to defend you no matter what price she had to pay. One day, you're going to understand why."

I drew her into a hug. "I miss her so much already, Tal."

My best friend sniffled and squeezed me tightly. Then she gave a little chuckle and said, "Look at us talking about sex toys in front of your grandmother. She'd be so proud. I bet she's shouting down from Alora right now, *Stay safe, girls!*"

I wiped my tears. "I know she is. She certainly always wanted to protect me. Who's going to buy us condoms now?"

Talia snickered. "I'll take one for the team. It'll be my job from now on."

I forced a hint of a smile and laid my head on Talia's shoulder. I drew a deep breath, though the air felt thick as syrup in my lungs. "Grammy, I'm really going to miss you. I love you so much."

I placed a hand on her grave, and though there was no magic pulsing through it, I could swear I felt her love flowing into me. Grammy may not be *here* with me, but she would always be watching over me.

It was a comforting thought for now, but something told me it'd take me a lot longer before I was all right again. If I ever would be.

☽

ONE MELANCHOLY DAY faded into the next. A numbness had taken over my entire spirit. I didn't feel much of anything.

Lucas found a scrapbook Grammy had left in her room and brought it to me, and that helped a lot. They were all old pictures, from back when Mom was a kid. It reminded me of how much life they lived—even if they had left too soon.

By the afternoon following the funeral, I noticed the ache in my belly twisting tighter, and I realized I hadn't eaten anything. I didn't *want* to eat, but I knew I needed *something*. The house was quiet as I found my way downstairs to the kitchen. Leftovers from our wedding reception were packed into the fridge, and I pulled out a container of brisket to heat up.

If anything could break me from my stupor, it was Grammy's food. Flavor burst in my mouth as the tender meat crumbled on my tongue. It made me believe that for just a moment she was right in front of me. The taste of her brisket was like the warmth of her hugs. I shoveled more food into my mouth, as if that would help me reclaim her memory. She had made *this* brisket. It was the last meal I'd ever have from her—

My thoughts came to a screeching halt, and my chewing slowed. This was the last thing she'd ever made… if I ate it all, it'd be gone for good. I'd never have one of Grammy's home-cooked meals again.

The thought made me want to hurl up every bite I'd just eaten. I slowly choked down the food in my mouth. I took the rest of my plate back into the kitchen and wrapped up the leftovers, then placed them in the freezer. I wanted to keep that last piece I had of her with me for as long as I could. Grammy's recipes were a part of her.

It occurred to me that maybe she had left behind more than just this brisket. If I could find her recipes and recreate them, maybe I could keep her with me longer.

Isa followed me into Grammy's bedroom. The room was neat, and the bed had been made. I walked over to the vanity, and my fingers grazed across her jewelry. I picked up a bottle of perfume and smelled it. Goddess, the sweet floral scent smelled like her, and sadness tangled in my gut all over again.

I set the perfume down and went over to the closet. All kinds of skirts in different colors hung from a rod, and I reached out to touch the soft fabrics. I noticed a stack of scrapbooks on the top shelf, as well as a few shoe boxes. This must've been where Lucas found the scrapbook he'd brought me earlier.

This was all that was left of what Grammy had rescued from her house the night we'd escaped Octavia Falls. I had to preserve it, so I could keep what was left of her.

I pulled the shoe boxes down from the shelves and set them on the bed. The first box was filled with keepsakes that didn't make much sense. I picked up an old watch, a button, and a small seashell. I didn't know why Grammy had bothered saving all these things, but I realized they must've been important to her. It broke my heart that the meaning and stories behind these items would die with her.

Inside, I found an old picture of Grammy and Mom. Mom must've been a teenager in the photo. It would've been taken before she had her magic, but the two were stirring a cauldron together like my grandma was teaching her Alchemy secrets.

They looked really happy. I wanted to keep the photo, so I conjured my own keepsake box. My fingers shook as I shifted through the contents inside. I'd kept pictures of my parents, along with one of Mom's old aprons and a candle that smelled like her. I'd also kept used score cards from *Clue* games I'd played with my father, and an old collector's license plate from one of his cars. I placed the photo of Mom and Grammy inside, then went over to Grammy's dresser and added a necklace of a cat she often wore into the box.

I opened another one of Grammy's shoe boxes, and I found a small wooden box inside. I lifted the top to reveal a stack of recipe cards—exactly what I was looking for.

I pulled out the first index card and smiled. It was Grammy's brisket recipe. The next several cards were tea blends, and I found more for cookies, cakes, and pies. My heart lifted as I pulled out more and more recipes I recognized.

Grammy had always been very organized, but I noticed the recipes weren't placed in any particular order. She must've had them all memorized by now and hadn't opened this box in a long time.

I pulled out the recipe cards and started organizing them into stacks, separating them between dinner items, desserts, appetizers, and tea blends.

As I reached the end of the recipes, I realized the last one was thicker than the others—folded up like it had been added to the box as an afterthought. I unfurled the paper and nearly fell off the bed when I recognized my mother's handwriting.

Isa jumped onto my lap and nudged my hands. I scratched her behind the ears while I began reading.

*Mom,*

*Thank you for your last package. The spira cacti worked like you said and made the protection potion ten times stronger. I'm sending a sample along so you can test it and let me know if I need to make any adjustments for the next batch. Nathan and I sold what stock we had to the vampire woman you told us about. Don't worry—we were careful about our meeting spot. We have enough money to get us through next month, but we're almost out of ingredients and will need more before we meet with her again the Friday after next. We hope to see you soon. Nadine misses you.*

*Much love,*
*Faith*

My hands shook as I read over the letter. What did all this mean?

Mom was brewing potions and selling them on the black market—and *Dad* was involved? Did she realize how much danger this could put her in, working with other supernatural races she couldn't trust?

I had the horrifying realization that perhaps my mother understood the danger and did it anyway. I quickly checked the date at the top of the letter, and my stomach dropped. It was dated two weeks before my parents' death. They had died on a Friday…

I shot to my feet, ready to go find Grammy and demand she explain, until I stumbled against the side of the bed when I realized I couldn't ask her a damn thing anymore. Still, my heart pounded fiercely, demanding I find answers about what happened.

I stomped down the hall, toward the sound of voices in the den. I entered to find Verla, Professor Warren, and Hattie. They all wore serious looks on their faces, but their conversation died when I entered the room.

Verla's features fell. "Nadine, what can we help you with?"

"I need to talk to you," I stated firmly. "Now."

Verla shot the others a worried look. "Yes, of course. Let's go somewhere private."

Verla led me to her bedroom. The moment the door closed behind us, I handed her the letter.

"Do you know anything about this?" I demanded.

Verla's eyes scanned the words, and her shoulders dropped. "I'm afraid I do. Your mother came to me for help years ago."

"She was selling potions? Verla, look at the date! Mom was going to meet a *vampire* the night she and Dad died. The police told me the brakes on their car failed! Tell me the truth. Was Mom killed by vampires?"

"No," Verla assured me. "It's true—your parents died in a car accident. It was an unfortunate accident."

"But that's where they were driving that night, wasn't it?" I asked.

Verla dropped her gaze. "Yes."

I began pacing around the room. "I don't get it. What did Mom need the money for? Were my parents involved in something illegal, besides selling magical potions?"

"It's not like that," Verla insisted. "Your parents were honorable. They were only trying to pay the bills."

I shook my head. "I didn't know we were struggling. Mom never said anything."

"She didn't want you to know. Bills added up over the years. She didn't want you to feel responsible."

"You mean my therapy and medical bills?" An invisible force constricted my stomach, like someone was trying to suffocate me by tying a ribbon around my ribs. I felt responsible all over again. I'd spent years in talk therapy, which I'd come to learn later I needed because I was fighting the curse inside of me. That was before I was diagnosed with lupus, and then the insane medical bills just kept coming after that.

"Yes. I'm sorry you have to find out this way, but your parents took out loans to pay off your medical bills, and they couldn't afford the interest," Verla explained. "Your mother saw a way to use her powers for good, to help your family. I promise you she only brewed potions that would *help* people. Your mother was a good person—to a fault at times, even."

"I didn't realize Dad knew she had magic."

"He'd known for years."

"Why didn't they just ask Grammy for money?"

"They did. They asked your grandmother; they asked me. We all helped. But eventually, your mother wanted to manage on her own. She was fiercely independent, much like yourself. She didn't want to burden us."

"If you knew all this, why didn't you tell me?" I demanded.

"Your mother didn't want you to think it was your fault, and neither do I." Verla reached out for me, but I yanked away from her.

"I don't want to believe it's my fault, either, but that doesn't change the fact that it feels that way," I said bitterly. "My parents were trying to make money to cover my medical care, and they ended up dying for it."

"Nadine, this is not your fault. All this means is that they cared. Your parents and your grandmother died to keep you alive, so you can honor them by doing what you came here to do."

"Everyone's dying for me all the time, and I'm sick of it!" I yelled. "I wish I would've just died, because everyone else would be alive. My lupus should've killed me. Then the people I love would still be alive."

Verla gasped. I'd never admitted something like that to anyone before, but it was true, because that's exactly how I felt.

"Nadine, you can't think that way," Verla warned.

Angry tears sprang to my eyes. "I can't help it. There's always been this side of me that believes it. I don't get it... I already got rid of Dark Nadine, but it's like there are still shadow aspects outside my family curse that have hung with me."

Verla's shoulders fell, and her voice was soft and understanding. "We can't fix our grief with Curse Breaking."

"Why not? It fixes a hell of a lot of other things."

"Of all the things we can fix with magic, grief is not one of them—hard as we may try," Verla assured me. "Even healers from other supernatural societies can't heal grief. There are no potions or spells for this. The only thing we can do is take the time to process it. It's okay if you don't feel better today or next week, or even years from now. We all handle our grief differently, and it is perfectly normal to take our time on it."

I crossed my arms. "How much time is reasonable?"

"As long as it takes."

"That's not good enough!" I snapped. "How can you sit here and act so calm? You said Grammy was like a mother to you, too, yet you want to just sit around and do nothing and hope that *time* is going to fix things? Bullshit!"

I stormed out of Verla's bedroom, and she didn't follow. I wanted to cry alone in peace, so I returned to Grammy's room. I needed to do something with my hands, or I was going to break something just to give my anger somewhere to go. I packed Grammy's belongings away, then threw the skeleton key around my neck into my memento box. I was angry that Grammy had given it to me for protection, and it had failed to protect her at all. I slipped the recipe cards back into their box, then carried it all up to my room. I slid the boxes under the bed, where they could easily be retrieved again, but just as easily be forgotten.

I cried for hours. By the time I left my room, it was already close to dinner time. I heard voices coming from the living room. It sounded like everyone was there. I followed the sound of conversation and found everyone gathered around the fireplace. All eyes turned to me, and Lucas approached to take my hand.

"What's going on?" I asked.

"I finally have word from Siona—our contact in Malovia," Hattie said. "She has a safe place to meet, but we have to move fast. The revolution in Malovia is unpredictable, and we don't know how long we have to sneak through the borders."

Good. I needed something to do right now, because I couldn't change that Grammy was gone. Sitting around here wasn't going to help me deal with it, either. We were one step closer to walking through hell—though it felt like I was already there.

I stepped forward. "Tell us where to go."

"You're not going anywhere," Verla stated firmly. "Malovia is dangerous for anyone right now, but especially for members of the Miriamic Coven. Jonathan and I will go to make first contact, and the rest of you will come once we know it's safe. We'll be in touch as soon as possible."

"We should all go!" I argued. "I may not be strong enough to break all their wards, but with mine and Lucas's magic combined, we can portal directly into Malovia."

"We don't know where we're going from there," Verla said. "We can't bring nine witches across the Malovian border without a solid plan in place. Let *us* go and talk to Siona, so we can bring the rest of you through safely. We don't know this person. We need to make sure she's a trustworthy guide before we allow her to take us to an entrance to the Abyss. You're safe here for now. Give us a day or two, and we'll be able to bring the rest of you safely into Malovia. We'll see each other again soon."

Professor Warren placed a hand on Lucas's shoulders, the look in his eyes very serious. "Take care while we're gone."

Warren wasn't just telling Lucas to keep himself safe, but to take care of all of us.

"Take this." Grant conjured a potion bottle and pressed it into Warren's hands. "It's a tincture I've been working on that will conceal your scent from shifters so you can blend in. Place three drops under the tongue every twenty-four hours. Be careful not to waste it, because I don't have much more of it."

"Take these, too." Talia conjured two cloaks she'd made with Grammy's help. One was a pretty gold velvet, which she handed to Verla, and the other was a silver satin with Celtic knots embroidered across the front. "They will help you blend in."

"Find Siona at Enchanting Whispers," Hattie instructed. "There will be a sign for her shop in the merchant district in their capital city of Dolinska. Turn down the alley next to the sign and follow the winding path until you get to the stone gargoyle. *Griffin dick* will get you through."

Verla nodded, but my brow furrowed. Now wasn't the time for jokes.

Only, I realized maybe that it wasn't a joke. I didn't know much about the fae, and I wondered what strange offerings they required there. Maybe it was the name of an herb.

Lucas and I joined hands, and a portal bloomed. The Malovian mountains appeared in front of us. Verla and Warren stepped through, and then the portal vanished.

They were gone so fast, and the house felt wholly empty, even though we were surrounded by our friends.

Hattie stepped forward, stroking her Familiar's head. "Everest and I must return to Octavia Falls. I will not see you for some time. Whenever I come here, it puts us all at risk. However, if you need anything, you can call me."

I hugged her. "Thank you, Hattie."

Hattie left, and our friends dispersed.

Lucas turned to me, his hands rubbing up and down my arms. "I want to help."

He couldn't give me what I wanted, which was to have Grammy back. "I just need some sleep."

He wrapped an arm around me. "Then let's get you to bed."

It was still early in the evening, but I just wanted to sleep and forget about everything. Lucas and I got ready for bed, and he wrapped his arms around me as I drifted off.

☾

*I* OPENED *my eyes to find myself surrounded by blackness. I cast a witch light to see I was in the same hallway I'd seen once before, with its damp air and stone walls. I turned toward the door at the end of the hall, sensing something important was behind it.*

*Something* thumped *from behind the door, followed by a whimper. It sounded like someone was in trouble!*

*I scrambled down the hall and yanked the door open. A small, dark room stood beyond me. The walls were made of stone, and a tiny window at the top of the room let in the smallest bit of light. All I could see out the window was a stone archway with ivy twisting around it.*

*Through the darkness, I spotted the shadows of two women huddled together* in the corner. *Their hands had been bound, and their mouths were covered in tape. I rushed over to them, and their familiar features became clearer.*

*"Mandy! Tate!" I cried as I ripped the tape from Mandy's mouth. Talia's sister trembled from beside my friend.*

*"Nadine!" Mandy shook as she reached out for me. Her terror permeated the room, and I felt her horror deep within my bones. She gripped tight to my shirt as she begged, "The priestesses have imprisoned us. You have to save us!"*

*"Where is this place—?" I started to say, but I never finished. Darkness closed in on me abruptly, and the scene disappeared from view.*

☾

I SHOT UPRIGHT IN BED, rasping for breath. Lucas startled awake beside me, and he reached for my hand. "Nadine, what's wrong?"

I placed a hand over my racing heart. "Mandy can project herself into other people's dreams, and she sent me a message. She and Tate are being held captive by the priestesses, and they need us. Lucas, we need to go back to Octavia Falls and get our friends back."

# LUCAS

## NINE

"Tell them what you told me." I tried to keep my voice calm, but my pulse raced as everyone gathered in the dining room. Although there were seven of us sitting around the table, the room felt empty without Warren and Verla.

Nadine sat at the head of the table. "Mandy came to me in a dream to tell me she and Tate are in trouble. I think she's been trying to get into my dreams for a while now. The priestesses have locked them up."

Talia's hands smacked against the table as a gasp traveled around the room. "What the hell are the priestesses doing with my sister!?"

Nadine shook her head. "I don't know much—just that we need to get them out."

Talia's fingers trembled. "I told Mom and Dad to leave and take Tyler and Tate with them, but they didn't want to go. Tyler said if they left, the priestesses had already won. My whole family wanted to stay to fight for us."

"Either Tate did something to piss them off, or the priestesses are targeting her for being our friend," I stated. "Either way, we need to get them out before the priestesses determine they aren't of any use and hang them for treason."

Miles drummed his fingers on the tabletop. "This could be a trap."

Nadine's eyes narrowed. "It isn't. Mandy's the only person I know who can enter someone else's dreams. She was *begging* for our help.

When she touched me, I could *feel* her terror. You can't fake that kind of fear."

"She betrayed you," Miles reminded us harshly. "Mandy led the priestesses to the Gravestone, where we kept all our evidence of our plan to go up against the Imperium Council. If she hadn't ratted out our hideout, the priestesses would have nothing on you. It's her fault you were put on trial."

"I know that," Nadine bit. "But it doesn't matter what she did to us in the past. If we leave her at the hands of the priestesses, she will die. She doesn't deserve this."

Miles dropped his head. It didn't matter what he said. Nadine was determined to save our friends, no matter what, and I was with her.

"Do we know where they're being held?" Chloe asked.

"I saw them tied up in a basement somewhere," Nadine explained. "The walls were made of stone, and there was an archway outside a window covered by ivy. I know it's not much to go off."

Chloe's eyebrows pinched together as she processed the information. "Would you be able to draw this archway?"

Nadine nodded, and Chloe conjured a pen and paper. She set them in front of Nadine, who began sketching

"It was arched like this, with two protruding stones on either side and a keystone in the center here…" Nadine drew the keystone at the top of the arch bigger than all the other stones around it. "There was ivy growing up the sides, but I'm not sure what kind. The leaves were really big."

"I know this arch," Chloe stated matter-of-factly. All eyes turned to her. "It's the entrance to my grandmother's garden."

"The priestesses are keeping prisoners in your grandmother's *basement?*" I asked, though I couldn't say I was surprised.

Chloe nodded. "It appears that way."

Grant crossed his arms. "How do we get in? We can't just waltz up to your grandmother's front door and ask her to hand over two prisoners."

"We'll have to break in, of course," Chloe said.

"If someone sees us, we're dead," Grant pointed out. "No one's going to stop to ask questions."

"We need to disguise ourselves," Onyx agreed.

"Hold on." Talia hurried out of the room. She shuffled around in the laundry room down the hall for a minute, then came back carrying a pile of hooded cloaks. "We still have these from the wedding."

Nadine picked up a cloak and wrapped it around herself. "It's a start, but it's not going to do us much good if someone recognizes us."

Talia passed out a cloak to each of us. I put mine on, but I agreed with Nadine. We needed more.

"Is there a potion we can use?" I asked.

Onyx bit her lower lip. "There's transformation potions. We could make ourselves look and sound like someone else… but you need the best Alchemists to brew it."

"Perfect. We've got two great Alchemists right here." I gestured to Grant and Onyx.

Grant shook his head. "It's not going to work without the right ingredients, and those are pretty damn expensive and hard to come by. It takes powerful fae herbs to pull off, and even if we *could* get into Malovia right now, you don't walk into any shop and find that stuff."

"We could turn ourselves into animals," Chloe suggested. "A potion to turn ourselves into toads shouldn't be too hard."

Grant frowned. "And we're just going to *hop* into Octavia Falls? We can't break Mandy and Tate out if we're toads."

"We need to do *something*… hold on! This might work!" Chloe conjured something, but it was so tiny and nearly invisible that I couldn't tell what it was at first. "We don't need to disguise ourselves. We just need to make people forget we were ever there in the first place!"

"Is that the whisker the glawackus gave you?" I asked.

"Yes." Chloe nodded proudly, before turning to the others to explain. "While we were in *Hok'evale*, a glawackus gifted me her powers with this whisker. As legend says, you'll lose your memory if you look into the eyes of a glawackus."

"How do we use it?" Nadine wondered.

"I'm a Mentalist, and even though my power lies in telekinesis, my Cast specialty is mind manipulation," Chloe said. "The Elementai have a word for harnessing magic from sources outside your own body. It's called *intrafusion*. Perhaps we can perform a similar magic. As long as I can overpower the magic in the whisker, I can combine it with my own. I can cast a spell over all of us so that when anyone looks at us, they immediately forget they saw us in the first place."

"That sounds like our best bet," I agreed. "Let's give it a shot."

Red magic swirled out of Chloe's fingers, and the tip of the whisker burned to ash. She didn't look any different.

"I don't think—" I glanced around the room and cut off.

"You don't think… what?" Miles asked.

I desperately tried to grasp at the memory of what I was saying, but I had no clue. "I'm not sure."

"That means it's working," Chloe said from beside me. I turned toward the sound of her voice and remembered she was there. It was definitely a jarring experience.

"You can see me and hear me, but once you look away, you forget I'm there, which is exactly what we need," Chloe said. "Even if we're spotted, the magic in the whisker will wipe the memory of us from whoever sees us once we're gone from their sight."

I offered her an approving nod, careful not to take my eyes off her, or I'd forget again. "Good job, Chloe. There is one catch, though. I still remember what you said when I wasn't looking, which means people will be able to hear us and remember what we said, so we'll have to keep our voices down."

She held up what remained of the whisker. "If I do the spell right, we won't forget each other, because we'll all be under the spell. Everyone ready?"

Magic swirled up her fingers, encompassing the whisker until it turned to ash in her palm. Her magic swelled throughout the room and gently settled over each of us, including the cats. The cats shook their heads, like the spell made them feel funny. My skin tingled, then returned to normal.

"The spell should get us through the night," Chloe said.

I flipped my hood up, then I lifted my hands. "I'm going to portal us a few blocks from Lilian's mansion. We'll have to survey the area first. Her house is likely warded, and we don't know how many Executors might be on the property."

Nadine nodded in approval. "Good idea."

A portal appeared at my command, and a dark forest came into view. Everyone followed me through, and my stomach flipped before my feet landed on solid ground. The portal shut behind us, leaving us in the quiet of the forest.

"I portaled us to the woods bordering Coven Park," I told them. "Lilian's house isn't far. Come on."

I started through the forest, but the cats stopped dead in front of me, their ears perking up.

"Hold on." Nadine grabbed my arm, and I paused to listen. The sound of distant drum beats broke through the silence… or was it footsteps? I could make out the sound of voices—a lot of them.

Onyx peered through the trees. "Something's going on in the park."

Chloe strolled forward, like she had no care in the world. "We have to cross the park anyway. Might as well see what's going on while we're at it."

A huge crowd had gathered. It was impossible to get to the main road without wading through a horde of people. It seemed as if the whole town was here. People looked our way, but no one seemed to recognize us thanks to Chloe's spell. I spotted a few other people in cloaks, so we blended in easily. Still, I kept my hood low as my eyes scanned the area.

Food vendors were scattered throughout the park, and people snacked on popcorn as they moved toward a large stage. Executors paced around in their black uniforms, but they didn't seem to be patrolling for trouble. Instead, they were laughing and eating candy apples like they were celebrating something. Several of them had painted their faces blood red.

On second thought… I didn't think that was paint.

A group of people passed in front of us, and I peeked from under my hood to step around them, but what I saw stalled my heart. Goat skulls had replaced their human features, and huge ram horns grew out of their heads. For a second, I thought I was seeing creatures of lore, until I realized they were masks. The horns were reminiscent of Santos in his godly form—as if these people had donned the masks to honor him.

We continued moving through the crowd, but I took cautious steps. This was all very strange, to say the least. There shouldn't be a festival going on right now, because the Halloween festival was only days ago. It had never been part of our customs to paint our faces with blood or wear ram horns like our god. It was like these people were trying to make a statement, though I didn't know what it was.

"Is anyone else majorly creeped out?" Onyx asked, shooting glances around the crowd.

"I wouldn't be lying if I said the hair on the back of my neck is standing up," Miles agreed.

Oliver rubbed against my leg and meowed. I turned in the direction he was looking, toward a long line of vendors. The closest was a tattoo booth with a big sign showing a five-pointed star. It was the mark of Miriam's Chosen—the priestess's cult they were trying to convert everyone to. A few months ago, they'd announced Miriam's Chosen as an elite group of witches and warlocks, and they'd advertised it as a revelation from Mother Miriam. Anyone who joined Miriam's Chosen had to follow strict rules, including leaving any intercast relationships. In return, members were promised more power and a place in Alora. Anyone who didn't join was subject to fines and ridicule. The priestesses were intent on separating those who would follow them blindly from those who would question them.

It seemed that things had only gotten worse since we'd left. People lined up to get their tattoos. It looked like a few people even had multiples.

Nausea swirled in my gut as we passed by more vendors. Professor Clarke and Professor Lewis handed out flyers at a booth with the school's crest. Professor Clarke was a Seer who taught Miriamic Law, and Professor Lewis was an Alchemist who taught Magical Plants and Herbs. I snagged a flyer and began reading it.

Across the top in big bold letters were the words *School Reopened!* It looked like it was meant to be hopeful, but this was the furthest thing from that. *Due to limited space, enrollment is now open to elite members of Miriam's Chosen, to train the next generation of Executors.*

I wanted to hurl. "It looks like the school has reopened to test people's loyalties."

Nadine scanned the page. "Tuition rates have gone up, too. And look at the fine print. *Tuition must be paid in full by the first day of term. Scholarships will not be accepted.*"

"So only the people with money can afford to go?" Chloe asked rhetorically.

"Why do they say the *next generation* of Executors, as if we've ever had them before?" Grant spat. "It's like they're selling it as some prestigious tradition."

"They want it to seem *honorable*," Talia said sarcastically.

We slowly moved through the crowd. The next booth was a land development company. Big posters showed upcoming projects, and I noticed each new apartment complex was named for its Cast. It was an obvious ploy by the priestesses to divide the coven even further, by making each Cast live apart from each other.

We passed by another booth, where the bank had a big sign that read, *Apply For a Relief Loan Here!*

Ever since the priestesses turned the Casts against one another, businesses had begun failing, and a lot of people had lost their jobs. People were desperate for money just to put food on the table. A lot of families didn't have options other than to take out loans to cover their basic costs of living. I overheard the man behind the booth tell a woman the interest rates, and my soul just about left my body. It was like the priestesses were intentionally putting their people into debt. It was just another way to control them.

A line had formed near a booth advertising some new employment program. Oliver ducked through the crowd and came back with a pamphlet in his mouth. I took it from him and began reading.

At first glance, the employment program sounded like a good deal. The coven was promising that factory workers would be provided housing, food, healthcare, and all other essentials in addition to a salary. Then I got to the part where it outlined their *mission*, which spewed all kinds of nonsense about how the coven needed to manufacture magical objects so they could sell them and use the money to build their army.

*The fae are knocking on our door, and we must heed the call!*

The whole thing seemed targeted toward students who couldn't afford to attend Miriam College. The priestesses were going to make them work at their factories, or they'd be left on the streets. I caught sight of the fine print at the bottom, saying that all these perks would be immediately rescinded if you stopped working. People weren't allowed to change jobs, and they had no security if they fell ill or were injured.

My hands curled into fists, crushing the pamphlet between my fingers. I wasn't sure how much more of this I could stomach.

The next booth had a big banner that read *Miriam's Chosen*. I didn't want to hear what bullshit they were trying to sell, until I spotted a student I recognized speaking to an elderly woman behind the booth. It was Samantha Stone, a girl who'd been in most of my Mortana classes. She was always at the top of the class and usually kept to herself.

"I've been thinking about joining Miriam's Chosen," Samantha admitted to the older woman.

*No, not Samantha*, I thought. She had been against the priestesses' methods and had spoken up during the Burning. It didn't seem right that she would be swayed toward their side. Things were clearly worse than I could've ever imagined.

"Can you tell me more about the organization?" Samantha asked.

"Miriam's Chosen is not an organization in which you join, but a choice to devote yourself to our deity," the elderly woman said.

Her voice sounded familiar, and as I peered closer through the crowd, I realized I recognized her, too. It was Miss Leanne, my old kindergarten teacher. She'd long since retired, and she'd aged nearly twenty years since I last saw her, but she spoke with the same soft, kind voice I remembered. That was dangerous, because Miss Leanne's kindness was the type that made anyone feel welcome, no matter what rhetoric she was pushing. I didn't think she was trying to manipulate people on purpose, but I *did* believe the priestesses put her behind that booth for a reason.

"You are already a member of the coven, and therefore have already agreed to follow Mother Miriam," Miss Leanne continued. "Joining Miriam's Chosen is simply a declaration of your decision, one which will elevate you to your highest potential."

"That's why I haven't joined yet," Samantha said. "I've been struggling with my faith, because I don't understand why Mother Miriam would make this declaration now, when we've already devoted ourselves to her. We've all undergone our Evoking Ceremony to join the coven, so why do we need another ceremony?"

"We do not need to wonder why Mother Miriam asks this of us. We must simply hold to our faith and trust our mother, for we are merely her children, and there is much we cannot understand in our earthly forms. I implore you to cast out your doubt, for faith is all you need. It is not the nature of a good witch to question her goddess, but the nature of an apostate to doubt her will. Each of us must choose which path we will follow."

"I don't wish to be an apostate. I know where they go." Samantha apprehensively pointed downward, like speaking the word aloud was a sin itself.

*Oh, for fuck's sake!* The priestesses couldn't really be telling people that they'd be tortured in the Abyss if they didn't join the Chosen. Except… that's exactly what it sounded like.

"I wish to follow the Goddess," Samantha said. "I'm just struggling to understand all of this. We used to be able to marry within our Cast, but members of Miriam's Chosen aren't allowed to do that anymore."

"Times are changing, but the Goddess will always protect us," Miss Leanne said. "Mother Miriam has provided the priestesses with revelation that will restore our magic and lead us into a new age. The priestesses will protect us and never lead us astray."

Samantha shifted uncomfortably. "Some people say Mother Miriam is punishing us by taking away our magic, and that Miriam's Chosen is her plan to bring it to an end and lead us to salvation. But why would she cause suffering if we were already devoted to her?"

"The Waning is a test of our faith," Miss Leanne answered. "Many of us have lost our way, and Miriam's Chosen is the path that leads back to our Goddess."

"But those who join Miriam's Chosen are still affected by the Waning," Samantha pointed out.

"Mother Miriam will continue to test our faith, to ensure we are true believers. When we declare our devotion to the Goddess, she bestows her love upon us in ways we can't understand before undergoing this spiritual transition. It is through a simple ritual of prayer and marking ourselves with the Chosen tattoo that we become closer to our goddess, for those who are closest to her will receive answers. Miriam's Chosen will bring us together as one. We are not just a coven, but a family."

Samantha dropped her gaze. "I could really use a family. I feel like I've always struggled to find where I belong, and I think Miriam's Chosen could be it."

Miss Leanne gave Samantha a kind smile. "When you are ready, we will pray with you, and you will receive the mark of the Chosen. Pray, my dear, and the Goddess will show you the way."

Samantha pushed a strand of hair behind her ear. "Thank you for the information. I'll be praying to the Goddess about my decision."

Samantha turned away from the booth and started toward another that was looking for volunteers to do work around the community. It was obvious the priestesses were trying to get free labor out of these people.

It broke my heart to hear Samantha's confession, because I hadn't realized how alone she felt. I recalled that she'd tried out for the dance team one year and didn't make it, then shortly after, she'd become addicted to nightshade and had to go into therapy after battling with the withdrawals. I realized now she was pressured into drugs because she'd been trying to make friends and find where she belonged. It didn't work then, and I feared she'd join Miriam's Chosen for the same reason. She'd only get hurt all over again.

I couldn't let that happen. I stepped toward her, but Nadine caught my arm. "Lucas, we can't interfere," she protested. "We came to rescue Mandy and Tate, and if we're caught before we get to them, we put them in even more danger."

"We came to rescue our *friends*," I emphasized. "I may not be able to get Samantha out of Octavia Falls, but I can't stand around and do nothing. I have to speak up, even if she doesn't remember."

I hurried in front of Samantha, and her eyes grew wide in shock when she saw me. I didn't give her a chance to react before I began speaking in a low voice. "You won't remember seeing me here, Samantha, but I need you to know you *cannot* join Miriam's Chosen. You're smarter than this, and you know better. That's why you asked all those questions. Your intuition is telling you that this is not the way."

Tears beaded at the corners of her eyes, like she knew I was right but wouldn't admit it to herself. Her voice wavered as she said, "I don't have a choice."

The crowd near the stage cheered loudly. The noise caught her attention, and she looked away from me. Her brow furrowed in confusion, but she shrugged it off. She'd forgotten I was standing there and didn't remember a thing I said.

I returned to my friends, feeling hopeless. "I want to help her, but I don't know how."

"The best way to help her is to find the rest of the Oaken Wands and bring an end to the priestesses' control," Nadine said, and I knew she was right.

The cheering near the stage grew louder, and we left the vendor area to see what was going on. We hung toward the back of the crowd.

Five women in black cloaks step onto the stage. Priestess Margaret and Priestess Lilian stood in the middle, their shoulders thrown back and their noses turned up to the crowd. Claudia—the latest Seer priestess—stood beside them, along with a tall woman I didn't recognize at first. When she turned, I realized it was Professor Hernandez, who taught Enchanting.

I'd never had much opinion on Professor Hernandez before. She was a good teacher, but I didn't know much about her outside of class. It appeared she had taken the priestesses' side and had stepped up to become the next Mortana priestess. I liked to think she'd joined them out of fear, but something told me otherwise.

The final priestess was Mira, who was pretending to be a Curse Breaker. Before Priestess Charlotte had fallen into the demon's pit, she'd told us Mira was really Mortana, but she'd lied so that the priestesses could throw Nadine off the council. Rage flared in my bones just looking at her. All I could think about was the night of the trial, when Nadine and I had lain in the mud, beaten and bruised while Mira proudly announced she was a Curse Breaker.

I wanted to throw a battle orb at the stage right now and end them all, but we were surrounded. Our magic may conceal us for now, but it wouldn't stop a spell from searing straight through us and ending our lives on the spot. We had to be careful, and I'd already risked being caught by speaking to Samantha.

Priestess Margaret gestured to a couple near the stage. "You have been chosen by the Goddess. Come. Proclaim your devotion to Mother Miriam, and join her elite children. We will speak our prayer to the Goddess, and you will be blessed with the mark of the Chosen."

The couple stepped onto the stage, and I realized I recognized the woman. It was Monica's sister, Meredith, who we'd met at Monica's fake funeral. She appeared confident as she approached the center of the stage. A tall man with a beard followed beside her, and I noticed they had matching Mentalist tattoos on the backs of their hands.

Priestess Margaret placed a white shawl across the couple's shoulders. My stomach tightened, because it reminded me all too much of the shroud we'd buried Helena in, which was meant to symbolize Mother Miriam's skirt and the love of a mother. It was twisted of them to use such symbolism in this initiation ceremony, because it indicated the end of one life and beginning of another, whether the participants realized it or not.

Priestess Lilian handed the couple each a daffodil, then turned to the crowd. "With this shawl, we encompass these coven members with our love, and we gift them each a daffodil to symbolize a new beginning. We praise Meredith and Max's unwavering and everlasting faith, as they join our ranks as elite members of Miriam's Chosen!"

Cheers rang out in the crowd, and Meredith looked near tears as the coven showered her and her husband with praise.

Or, at least, I thought it was her husband, until I heard someone call out from the crowd.

"Meredith, you can't do this!" a man shouted. "We've been married over fifteen years!"

Executors dragged the man on stage. He had an average build with blond hair and glasses. He shoved the Executors off and hurried over to Meredith. The eye tattoo near his elbow marked him as a Seer.

He fell to his knees and reached out for Meredith. "Please reconsider."

She pulled away. "I cannot return to this marriage, Scott. This is what Mother Miriam wants, and I must listen to my Goddess, even if it breaks my heart. If my goddess wishes me to marry Max, then I will. Max is a member of my own Cast, as well as one of the Chosen, as am I. You and I must go our separate ways now, Scott. I have faith you will find your perfect match within your Cast, if you choose to follow the Goddess and join Miriam's Chosen."

"How can I put my faith into a deity who would have us torn apart?" Scott demanded. "You are the love of my life, Meredith. What Mother Miriam is asking us to do is not love!"

"We cannot question our Goddess, or apostates we become," Meredith insisted. The words didn't seem like her own. It sounded like she was repeating a phrase she'd heard many times before. "Join us, Scott, for you cannot understand the true nature of Mother Miriam's love until you choose to surrender to her will. I see it all so clearly now, and you will gain insight once you join us."

"You know I can't do that," Scott insisted.

"Meredith has made her choice," Lilian sneered. "Give up your wedding ring and join her."

"You can't do this!" Scott raged. "Our marriage is legal in the state of Connecticut."

"Your marriage is not recognized in Octavia Falls," Margaret bit back.

"Miriam's Chosen will find you a new wife, one whose magic is compatible with your own. Mother Miriam gave us a revelation. Our magic is dying, and we must preserve what we have by making new matches."

Grant lowered his voice and growled, "Cast magic isn't inherited. What do they think they're protecting? This is nonsensical."

I swallowed the lump forming in my throat. "I think that's the point. If they can control people on this, they can control them on anything."

"Intimacy brings us closer to our Goddess," Margaret announced. "To strengthen your magic, you must copulate only with members of your own Cast."

Chloe rolled her eyes. "They can't be serious."

"They're punishing Scott because he hasn't joined Miriam's Chosen with his wife. They're making him an example," Nadine said hollowly.

Priestess Margaret raised her hands. "Let us pray for those with little faith."

*"Mother Miriam,"* the crowd spoke at the same time, making me jump. This prayer had obviously been spoken many times, because the entire coven knew it by heart. Their voices came together as one. *"We pray to you to bestow faith upon the non-believers. May their hearts be softened, and their love abound, as they surrender their doubts and embrace your blessings. So shall it be."*

Scott took a step back, obviously not wanting to be a part of this.

"We must multiply our numbers to defeat the fae!" Margaret added. "Show your devotion to Mother Miriam, and disavow your marriage."

Scott stood tall. "I will not. Meredith, please…"

He reached for his wife again, but she took several steps back. She took Max's hand, driving in the knife of betrayal. "You could have been happy, Scott, but you chose the path of an apostate instead," Meredith said. "I will pray that Mother Miriam grants you mercy in the Abyss."

Lilian wore a mask of indifference. "If Scott chooses the path of an apostate, then he deserves his fate."

I wasn't sure what *fate* she was talking about.

"He doesn't deserve this!" a man in the crowd shouted. "He's only acting on love!"

A chorus of agreements rang throughout the crowd, though it wasn't as loud as the opposing protests. I didn't understand what the priestesses had in store for Scott, but the rest of the crowd seemed to understand. They'd certainly seen it before.

The Executors quickly found the person who'd spoken up and forced him onto the stage. He had the same blond hair as Scott and similar features. They looked like they were brothers.

"You shouldn't have spoken up, Simon," Scott insisted. "I will accept my fate, but I will not have my brother suffer the same."

Simon turned toward the priestesses. "Let my brother live and take me instead. I proclaim myself to be an apostate, and I will suffer the consequences in my brother's place."

"You have brought this on yourself," Lillian accused.

The Executors locked Simon's arms behind his back as the priestesses came forward. Margaret withdrew a potion vial out of her cloak and forced the liquid down Simon's throat. He gurgled and tried to spit the liquid out, but the poison had already taken hold. His body started to convulse as red veins spiderwebbed across his skin. The Executors dropped him, and his body slumped to the ground, yet a ghostly imprint of his features remained standing.

There was no life in those ghostly eyes, no indication that the soul of the man remained at all. The ghost moved forward like he was being controlled. He grabbed Scott and held him firmly in place. The potion was obviously very powerful, because his ghostly form was able to materialize to solid form.

Simon raised his voice to the crowd. "My brother will see the truth, or he shall join me in the Abyss."

"What's happening?" Talia's voice squeaked.

"It must be the potion the priestesses forced Hector to make with the Alchemy Wand before he died," Nadine said in horror. "It has the power for the priestesses to control whomever they administer it to, even in death. When I first heard about it, they said it was slow acting, but they must've modified it to make it even worse. The priestesses are controlling Simon's ghost."

"My brother shall receive the punishment he deserves for his lack of faith," Simon announced.

"Simon, no!" Scott protested, but the words halted on his tongue.

All at once, projectiles flew from the crowd and hit Scott from every angle. I realized with horror that they were stones. The coven was *participating* in this atrocity!

"Confess and beg the Goddess for forgiveness!" someone in the crowd shouted.

"This is what the non-believers deserve!" another person yelled.

So many people were on the priestesses' side, though I witnessed others hesitate to throw stones. Nobody dared utter another protest, though, or they would be killed the way Simon was.

Scott screamed as the stones hit him. Bruises bloomed over his skin, and blood trickled down the side of his face. Meredith simply watched. She was so deep into this cult mindset that she didn't even react when her husband of fifteen years was tortured in front of her. He hadn't joined Miriam's Chosen, and therefore, in her eyes, he *deserved* it.

I wanted to rush forward and stop this, but this wasn't the same as talking to Samantha. The second I got up on that stage I'd be executed for objecting, just as Simon had.

"We have to do something!" Talia hissed.

"If we do, we're dead," Chloe warned. "Our spell may cause people to forget we're here, but we're not invisible—nor invincible."

All we could do was stand there and let this take place. My stomach twisted, and I turned my gaze away from the stage. This was difficult to watch. I couldn't imagine agreeing to void my marriage with Nadine just because our magic differed, no matter the consequences.

Claudia pointed a wand at Scott. "Only members of Miriam's Chosen are afforded the privilege of their magic."

She was going to strip him of his powers! Except the Wand she held didn't *look* like the Seer Wand—it was too short and twisted on the end. Claudia couldn't even *use* the Seer Wand. It had rejected her before, but it didn't matter. The coven knew the Priestesses had at least two of the Oaken Wands. It'd been revealed during our trial. But the crowd didn't know whether it was the real Wand or not, and the threat was enough to force Scott to back down.

"All right! I was wrong!" he shouted.

Priestess Margaret raised a hand, and the sound of stones raining down on the stage stopped. A stillness settled over the park.

Scott staggered to his feet, though he could barely stand. He limped forward, leaving a trail of blood behind him. "You have shown me the error of my ways. It was wrong of me to question the Goddess. I put my faith in her, and I devote myself to her will."

Scott pulled his wedding ring from his finger and shakily handed it over to the priestesses. He shot one last longing glance at his wife, but she kept her eyes on the crowd.

Lilian wore a proud smirk. "Welcome to Miriam's Chosen!"

The crowd erupted into cheers. Simon's spirit walked off stage, only to return a moment later, escorting a woman with the mark of a Seer on her neck. Simon forced her beside Scott, and the priestesses draped another white shawl around their shoulders. Scott barely looked at the woman. All he could do was stare at his wife desperately, though she wouldn't return his gaze. He looked absolutely miserable.

Lilian raised her hands. "We will now recite the blessing for these new members of Miriam's Chosen!"

Together, the crowd began to speak in unison, and the couples on stage were forced to speak it as well. *"Blessed be the Chosen, for we are Mother Miriam's true children. She is the single voice of truth, who speaks through the priestesses revelation. We devote our lives to her, in this life and the next. So shall it be."*

A tattoo artist came on stage carrying an enchanted quill. Meredith and Max held out their arms willingly, to be marked with the symbol of the Chosen.

Onyx shook her head in disbelief. "All of this, just to fight the fae?"

Nadine's jaw tightened. "They aren't afraid of the fae. They're just using them as scapegoats to control the people. The priestesses are more afraid of coven members turning on them—afraid someone might take their place. They have to control their people to maintain their power. All this—dividing people into Cast neighborhoods, driving them into debt, and forcing them to work the factories—it isn't about money. It's about taking the power from the people. Taking their money and their magic away means they can't fight back. Worse, if they can't associate with members of other Casts, then they can't work together to make their magic stronger and revolt."

"I don't get it," Miles said. "Why harm your own people like this?"

"The priestesses believe they're on a holy mission, and they'll do anything to achieve it," I growled. "Once the Waning started, they lost control of the coven. If their magic could be taken away, so could their influence. They can't control the Waning, so they have to control the people."

"And they know exactly how to do it," Nadine stated bitterly. "I've watched enough cult documentaries to know this is exactly how they work. Cults always have charismatic leaders, who people are easily influenced by and willing to follow. The priestesses were already in the perfect position to lead a cult, because they already have the coven's trust and don't answer to any earthly authority. They're able to gain control over people's finances, living situations, and relationships, because people believe the priestesses alone have the single answer to salvation. Even if you wanted to question them, you can't, because you'll be labeled an apostate, and therefore deserving of whatever punishment the priestesses deem appropriate."

"Why would anyone join them?" Grant asked in disgust.

"Because when you aren't allowed to question them, you're easily convinced that the ends justify the means," Nadine answered. "Even if you *did* question it, the priestesses are tying people's lives to the Chosen by providing housing, food, and healthcare through them. It would take more than a question of faith to leave. Furthermore, the priestesses have made promises the people can't resist—the answer to salvation, as well as the promise of praise, love, and belonging. People think they will find purpose and meaning by being a part of this, and to truly be a part of this, they can't question what they're participating in, or they risk being cast out themselves. They believe anyone who does not join merely lacks understanding. Make no mistake, the priestesses didn't force Meredith to leave her husband because they are of different Casts. They forced her to leave him because she joined the Chosen and he didn't."

"The priestesses have taken their power too far and removed any and all autonomy from their people," Onyx said sadly.

"They may have this crowd convinced, but they're not going to get away with controlling our friends," Nadine insisted. "We can't save these people right now, but we have to get Mandy and Tate out while the priestesses are still distracted. Come on."

We left the park, and the sound of cheers faded behind us. Lilian's house was located on a wide street full of gothic mansions with large yards. We approached from the back and slowed before we reached her house. I expected Executors to be patrolling the property, but I didn't see a soul. The entire street was dead silent.

"We should send the cats to scout the perimeter," I suggested. At my word, the cats took off running, slinking through the darkness like shadows.

"I can feel a ward around the house," Nadine observed. "I can break it, but if I do, Lilian will know immediately. I'm not sure we can get in and out before we're caught."

"I know how we can get through without alerting her," Chloe said. "Wards like this work to protect families, and I'm still blood. My grandmother has probably warded the house against me already, so I can't get through myself. But if Nadine and I work together, she can manipulate the magic and we can trick the ward into letting us through safely. My grandmother will never know."

Nadine nodded. "We should be able to pull that off."

The cats returned. Oliver gave a confident nod, indicating it was safe to approach the house. We crept closer, until Nadine threw a hand out to stop us.

"Right here," she said. "I can feel the ward boundary."

Chloe stopped at her side. "Let's get to work."

The girls grabbed hands, then lifted their opposite palms to thin air. Magic swirled down their arms, becoming one at their joined hands. The ward began to shimmer beneath their fingers, appearing as a bubble surrounding the house.

Chloe suggested an incantation, and the girls spoke it together. *"I am family; this is my home, too. Drop this ward and let us through."*

A slit appeared in the ward, pulling back like a curtain to reveal an opening.

Chloe smiled proudly. "My grandmother messed with the wrong bitch."

"Quickly!" Nadine gestured everyone through, and we slipped past the ward with our cats. "This should stay open until we get out. Let's hurry."

We rushed across the lawn and through Lilian's gardens. The archway Nadine had seen in her dream stood before us, and we had to pass under it to reach the back door. It was unlocked, and we slipped inside. I bet Lilian thought the ward was enough to keep us out. Darkness blanketed the house. The smallest bit of light from town entered the windows, casting shadows across the mahogany.

The cats scurried down the hall, barely making a noise. They stopped at a door near the kitchen and pawed at it. The hair on the back of my neck stood up, but I saw no threats as I glanced around the house.

Chloe approached the door. "The basement is this way."

We descended a dark stairwell that creaked under our weight. I listened closely, as if expecting someone to hear us and come running. I was only met by silence. The air dropped a few degrees, making me shiver.

Chloe led us down a long hallway. The whole basement was made of stone and had various archways and doors leading in different directions. It reminded me of a dungeon, even though the rooms were probably just meant for food storage.

"Nadine saw the garden arch through the window in her dream. That means they must be in a room near the back of the house, which puts them… right here." Chloe stopped at a heavy wooden door.

Nadine ran her fingers over the frame, assessing it for magic.

Miles's eyes darted down the hall. "This is weird, isn't it? There aren't any guards. It's too easy."

"I'm certain my grandmother didn't expect us to get through the ward," Chloe said. "Even if Executors are normally around, the event in the park is too big for them to miss."

Nadine stepped back. "Your grandmother must've been very confident in the ward around the house, because there aren't any wards on this room."

A muffled sound came from behind the door. I grabbed the handle, but it was locked. Magic drifted out from my fingers, and the lock disengaged. I threw the door open.

What I saw made my stomach twist. Mandy and Tate were huddled in the corner, their hands bound together by ropes. Duct tape covered their mouths. Their hair was matted on the top of their heads, and bruises and cuts marred their faces. Their eyes were sunken in, and they'd both dropped a considerable amount of weight.

It looked like Tate had received the worst of the torture. Burn marks scarred her arms, and her fingers bled from where the priestesses had removed fingernails.

Tears of relief sprang to the girls' eyes when they saw us. I ran over to them and knelt down. I pulled the tape off their mouths, then got to work on the ropes.

"Thank the Goddess!" Mandy cried. "We've been down here for—"

She cut off as she looked down at the rope. Her mouth bobbed open, and she blinked rapidly. Tate glanced at her, and confusion settled over her face, too.

"They're confused," Grant said. "The second they look away, they forget we're here."

"Fuck," I growled. I took Mandy's chin and guided her face back toward mine. "I need you to turn toward the wall. I'll explain everything."

Tears beaded in Mandy's eyes, but both girls turned away from me.

I started speaking quickly before they could look back. "Close your eyes. It's me, Lucas. We got Mandy's message, and we're all here, but we're under a spell to conceal us. If you look at us, you'll forget us the moment you look away. Focus on my voice so you don't forget."

Tate whimpered and nodded.

"I've been trying to contact you for weeks, but I can hardly access my magic," Mandy sobbed. "I overheard the priestesses talking about the festival, and I knew tonight was our best shot. I used everything I had to send you a message."

Nadine and Talia knelt beside me. Talia rubbed her sister's back, while Nadine took Mandy's hand.

"We're here," Nadine assured them. "All of us."

"Tal, is that you?" Tate asked, keeping her eyes shut tightly. Her hand shook as she reached out for her sister.

"It's me." Talia took Tate's hand.

"Thank the goddess you're alive!" Tate cried. "I didn't know if you were still out there, but the priestesses didn't believe me. They tortured me to get me to give up your location, but I didn't know where you'd gone. I never would have told them even if I knew. I swear it."

"We're here now, and the priestesses won't touch you again," Talia vowed. "How long have you been here?"

"It's hard to make sense of time down here," Tate admitted. "I feel like I've been here for a month, at least."

My stomach twisted into a ball of knots. I wished we'd gotten here sooner. We may have been able to spare these girls from the priestesses' torture.

"Things have gotten really bad in the coven," Mandy said. "The priestesses have bought up a bunch of businesses and are making people work for them. If you don't agree to work—or if you weren't selected to go to school—they strip you of your powers."

Which they could do, at least to Alchemists and Seers, because they had the Alchemy and Seer Wands. Last I knew, the Oaken Wands hadn't worked for the priestesses, though. They must be torturing others to use the Wands for them, whenever they saw fit.

Sobs broke from Tate's chest. "No one can afford anything anymore. They've raised rent and food prices. Independent businesses are shutting down. There's hardly any food in the grocery store. Mom has to buy potions from Alchemists that trick you into feeling full but don't nourish you, just to get to the next meal. Dad's sick from the factory work. They've got him making iron weapons to use against the fae. It's been nothing but hell since I got out of rehab."

"We're going to get you out, but we'll have to get outside the ward before I can cast a portal. If I cast a portal within the ward, they might be able to trace it, and we can't risk them locating our safe house." I finished untying the last knot. The ropes fell away, and both girls breathed a sigh of relief. "Let's get you back to the safe house."

I helped Mandy to her feet and supported her weight as we left the room. Her whole body quivered. Nadine and Talia draped Tate's arms over their shoulders and followed behind us. We helped the girls up the stairs and were almost to the door when my eyes landed upon a book sitting on a table in the hall. A symbol on the front caught my eye, and I stopped in my tracks.

"What is it?" Miles asked.

I couldn't take my eyes off the book. The symbol was in the shape of a teardrop with swirls inside of it. It was so familiar, yet it didn't belong in a witch's house. My pulse quickened.

"Help Mandy," I told Miles. "Something about this isn't right."

He supported her weight, and I took a step forward. I grabbed the book off the table and flipped the leather binding open to reveal hand-writing on the inside. "It's a journal," I realized.

Nadine observed the journal, and her eyes went wide. "Lucas, this symbol belongs to an Elementai. A Toaqua elemental, a caster of Water."

"I know," I said. "Lilian wouldn't have kept this journal if it didn't contain something important."

I quickly flipped through the pages, and my heart stalled when I saw the words sprawled at the bottom of the page. *Wands with Miriamic religious symbols carved into them...*

This entry could only be referring to the Oaken Wands. I quickly scanned the entry, and I knew that's exactly what I was looking at. I wasn't about to spend a second longer in Lilian's house than I had to, though. I had to get my friends out, and then we could investigate what this all meant.

"We may have more investigating to do tonight than we thought," I said. "Onyx, Miles, I need you to take Mandy and Tate back to the safe house. Then the rest of us are going to investigate what's in this journal."

I didn't give anyone a chance to ask questions. I tucked the journal under my arm and hurried out of the house, gesturing to the others to follow. We passed the ward, and I waited until we were concealed in the trees behind Lilian's house before I cast a portal. The forest near the safe house appeared in front of us.

"We'll be back as soon as we can," I promised Onyx and Miles.

"Wait!" Chloe called. She grabbed Miles and pulled him into her arms, planting a passionate kiss on his lips. The two started making out, putting on quite the show, before they finally drew away from each other.

"Stay safe," Miles said.

Miles and Onyx led Mandy and Tate through the portal, their cats following behind them.

As soon as the portal closed, Chloe whirled on me. "All right, smart guy. Why'd you send my boyfriend away? You better have a damn good excuse why we aren't all returning to the safe house with them."

"Mandy and Tate need help, and I figured Miles and Onyx were the best equipped to care for them right now," I said. "What we've just found is going to require at least one member of each Cast."

"What exactly do you think you've found?" Talia asked.

I held up the journal. "This Elementai ran across something he shouldn't have, and the priestesses were going to execute him for it. I believe he found where the priestesses have hidden the Alchemy and Seer Wands, and using this journal, we're going to get them back."

"How do you know this guy?" Grant asked.

I swallowed the lump rising in my throat. "Because Nadine and I saved his life."

## TEN



*Five Months Earlier*

The air was warm, and the stars twinkled above us as Lucas and I snuck through the trees. The safe house was far behind us, and I wondered how long it'd take Grammy to notice we were missing. We'd left a note, but I didn't think that'd stop her from worrying.

It was mid-June, and our friends had left over a week ago to visit other supernatural societies. We hoped they might learn something about the Oaken Wands, but so far, we'd received no word from them.

I breathed a sigh of relief as I took in the crisp night air. "It's nice to get out of the house."

Lucas squeezed my hand as he led me through the forest. "I love your grandmother, but I just want one night where she isn't breathing down our necks."

"Agreed!" I laughed. "She was following me everywhere yesterday. I can't believe she walked in on us when she did. Can you imagine if it was a minute later? I don't know why she wanted to vacuum our room anyway. She already vacuumed earlier this week."

"And the way she asked us what we were doing, like she didn't already know," Lucas added.

I snickered. "Grammy can handle a few hours alone without us. I told Isa to distract her. Where are you taking me?"

Lucas gestured down the mountain. "There's a waterfall not far from here. I

159

*wanted to take you there, if you're okay with it. It's outside the boundary of the wards."*

*I listened to the forest intently, but I heard nothing except crickets and the distant hoot of an owl. "No one knows we're here. We can cast our own ward around the waterfall once we get there, so we'll be safe."*

*We walked for another fifteen minutes, until we came upon a beautiful waterfall with a calm pool beneath it. The sound of trickling water was soothing, and a woodsy scent surrounded us. The light from the quarter moon glistened off the water.*

*We cast our ward, then turned to each other. My heart hammered as Lucas wrapped an arm around my waist and pulled me in closer. We hadn't been intimate in a while now, since Grammy was always right there.*

*My fingers roamed up his arms, and my eyes danced around his body, savoring his presence.*

*His hand came up to cradle my face. "I want to make love to you in this pool."*

*My breath caught. "Lucas, if you get me out of these clothes, you can do whatever the hell you want to me."*

*His lips were on mine a second later, and my fingers tangled in his hair as our bodies crashed together. He grabbed my ass, pulling me close to his erection. One hand slid under my shirt to cup my breast, and heat pooled between my thighs. He reached for the hem of my shirt to take it off.*

*A stick broke in the trees, startling us both. We whirled toward the sound, instinctually conjuring battle orbs at the same time. The light from our sizzling orbs reflected off a pair of eyes. The rest of the creature was cast in shadow. Whatever it was must've been within the boundary of our ward when we cast it.*

*A low growl emitted from the creature's throat, and it stepped forward until I could make out the features of a large feline. Lucas immediately threw himself in front of me.*

*"Is that a mountain lion!?" I cried, my heart hammering. I might have battle orbs to protect myself, but this creature was huge, with claws that looked razor-sharp. One mistake, and that creature could tear us both to shreds.*

*"Mountain lions don't live here," Lucas panicked. "That's way bigger."*

*It looked like an African lion, though it had no mane, so it must've been female. What the hell was a lion doing in the mountains of Connecticut?*

*"It looks hungry," I said warily as the lion began to pace in front of us.*

*"It's not getting anywhere near us," Lucas promised. The battle orb in his*

*hand grew brighter. His voice became stern as he spoke directly to the lion. "Walk away now, or you'll be sorry."*

*"Lucas, it doesn't understand you," I insisted.*

*The lion bared its teeth, and for a moment, I thought I caught recognition in its eyes... like it* did *understand us.*

*Then the lion lunged. Lucas threw his battle orb, but it bounced off the lion's fur. She flew through the air, her claws aimed straight for his throat. Lucas created a shield around us, and the lion slammed straight into it. She stumbled back, shaking her head.*

*"That battle orb should've killed her!" I cried. "That's not normal."*

*The lion bared her teeth again, and a loud, terrifying roar erupted from her lungs. Flames burst across her fur, lighting up the night like a bonfire.*

*"That's because that's no normal lion!" Lucas cried.*

*The creature jumped at us, but I created a shield that guarded us from all angles. The lion slammed against it, unable to get through. She swiped her claws out, and red-hot fire seared the shield from all angles. It felt like the flames were covering my entire body. I cried out, and my shield fell. The pain dissipated, but the lion readied for another attack.*

*Lucas shoved me. "Run!"*

*The ward we'd created shattered, and we took off running. Lucas threw battle orbs behind us to slow the creature down.*

*"Maybe I can... siphon her powers," I suggested through ragged breaths.*

*"You're never going to get your hands on her—" Lucas's words cut off, and I whirled around to see the lion latch her jaws around his pant leg. Her fur bristled as her eyes locked on mine for a second.*

*"Lucas!" I screamed.*

*The lion dragged him backward. Lucas clawed at the ground, but he couldn't escape her hold. I shot magic at the lion, but nothing I did fazed her. She dragged Lucas through the forest, leading me onward until coming to an abrupt halt.*

*"Get off, you fucking—" Lucas's insult died on his tongue as the lion leapt on top of him and pressed a paw to his mouth.*

*I caught up with them, though I was winded. Their eyes locked. I feared if I moved, the lion would attack him again. "Lucas...?"*

*Slowly, the lion backed away, and Lucas got to his feet.*

*"She didn't hurt me," he said in astonishment. "I think she wants us to follow her."*

*The lion ducked her head, and I realized that I saw fear in her eyes for the first time. She hadn't come to attack us. She'd come to ask for help.*

*"She's a Fire lion, which means she belongs to the Elementai. Her bonded companion must be nearby," Lucas pointed out.*

*"All right," I said warily. "Lead the way."*

*The lion looked to Lucas again and nodded.*

*"I think she's telling us to be quiet," he said.*

*The lion slunk through the trees, and we followed closely behind. The sound of voices came from up ahead.*

*A man cruelly laughed. "The priestesses said we should take you outside the town boundaries and kill you, but there's no reason why we shouldn't have a little fun with it first. We dragged you all the way out here so that no one would hear you scream."*

*"You don't understand," an older man begged. "I have a research license granted to me by the United Supernatural Union. We were welcomed into Octavia Falls—"*

*"No Elementai is welcome here!" another voice raged. "You should've stayed within your own borders, savage!"*

*"How dare you talk to my husband like that!" a woman snarled. "Now get out of our way, you withered old witches!"*

*We came close enough that I could finally see what was going on. A dozen Executors had surrounded a man and a woman in the woods. The woman looked to be in her forties, and the man had to be at least ten years older than her. The woman was beautiful, with long red hair, but the man wore a wrinkled shirt, and his hair was disheveled. He wore glasses and carried a large backpack.*

*"Who are you calling withered?" an Executor growled.*

*The woman threw back her head and laughed. "You have no idea who you're dealing with."*

*She threw her hands out, and I expected magic to blast from her palms, but only a tiny flame came out. The man next to her aimed his hands at a puddle on the ground. Water droplets rose into the air, but that was it.*

*"What did you do to us!?" the woman seethed.*

*A big, burly Executor laughed maniacally. "Did the priestesses forget to mention the tea at your hotel was laced with noxite? It's a precautionary measure provided to all visitors who are not of our kind. You should've kept your nose where it belonged, and we wouldn't have to kill you."*

*"You wouldn't dare," the woman sneered. "Doing so would be a declaration of war against the Elementai!"*

*"As if they'll ever know what happened to you two," an Executor said.*

*I lowered my voice and whispered to Lucas. "What do we do? These are Elementai. If they're killed by witches and the tribe finds out, they'll start a war with the coven for sure."*

*"We have to help them. But if we kill the Executors, the priestesses will find evidence we were here," he replied.*

*The lion looked up at us with a desperate plea in her eyes. She'd come to find us to ask for help, which meant she didn't think she could take on this many witches at once.*

*The woman opened her mouth again, but her husband stopped her. "Eleanor, please. Let me handle this. Whatever the priestesses think they can charge us with, they are sorely mistaken."*

*The woman blew a breath. "Elliot, you're making it worse."*

*Her husband continued. "There must be a way we can work this out."*

*The burly Executor glanced at the others, then shrugged. "Yeah... I think we can work something out—at the end of a noose."*

*The Executors threw ropes around the couple's necks. Within a moment, they'd tossed the ends of the ropes over a tree branch and yanked, pulling the couple's feet off the ground. The sound of their strangled rasps filled the forest.*

*Our cover be damned. These innocent people would die if we didn't help them.*

*We leapt from our hiding place in the trees, and battle orbs shot from our palms in all directions. Lucas dropped two Executors at once. My orb hit one Executor in the chest, while the other missed the Executor I was aiming at.*

*The lion leapt from the trees and aimed her razor-sharp claws at the nearest Executor. His dying screams turned to silence as she swiped her claws across his throat.*

*Four down. Eight to go.*

*Lucas threw up a shield around us, and battle orbs ricocheted off of it. I sent deadly orbs soaring through the shield, and Lucas defended all of my attacks. My orbs bounced off the Executors' shields, spinning off into the forest.*

*The Executors dropped their ropes, and the couple landed hard on the ground. All together, the Executors turned their attention to the lion. Battle orbs assaulted her from all angles, and the power was too much. Magic knocked the lion off her feet, sending her flying into the base of a tree nearby.*

"Naomi!" Eleanor shouted. Her cries were cut off as one of the Executors yanked back on the ropes.

The lion whimpered, before limping to her feet. Fire burst across her body again, but the Executors didn't back down. One of them walked straight up to her. He threw his hands upward as he tossed her into the sky with his telekinesis. She landed on the ground so hard that the ground sank in where she lay.

"Step aside," the burly Executor growled. He shoved the others away, and I noticed the mark of a Mortana on the back of his hand. "I'm going to rip this bitch's soul from her body and send it straight to the Abyss."

"Um... actually, it's Aiya Nocshun in Elementai culture," Elliot choked out past the noose.

His wife gasped for breath. "This isn't the time for a religious lesson. Do something, Elliot!"

"Lucas, hold the shield," I told him. "I have an idea."

I closed my eyes and focused on the magic around us. I could feel all kinds of energy signatures—the smooth energy of a Seer standing behind us, the electric sizzle of several Mentalists, the high-frequency buzz of an Alchemist, and the chaos of Mortana. I could even sense the heat coming off the lion, though I couldn't quite tap into her energy. I honed in on the Mortana and pulled his magic into me.

"What the hell?" the burly man shouted. I opened my eyes to see sparks shooting from his fingers, but the Death magic he expected never came.

"It's the Waning!" one of the others panicked.

I smirked. Not the Waning. Just a Curse Breaker.

The magic rattled around inside of me, until I couldn't contain it any longer.

"Duck on three," I warned Lucas. I shot a glance at the Elementai, but they were already on their knees. "One... two... three..."

Lucas dropped his shield, and the magic I had siphoned burst out of me all at once. A blast of energy soared over Lucas's head as he ducked, and it slammed into all the Executors at once. Their bodies fell to the ground.

"Hurry!" I shouted, racing over to help loosen the nooses around the couple's necks. "His magic was weak. I only knocked them out."

I pulled the noose over Eleanor's head, and she shrugged me off. She got to her feet and glared down at the Executors sprawled across the forest floor. "We'll take care of them."

Lucas helped Elliot stand, then stepped aside. "Be our guest."

Eleanor held her head high. "Naomi—attack!"

*Naomi found her footing, and rage marred her features. She curled her lips back, then sank her fangs into the throat of the burly Executor. Blood sprayed the underbrush, and Lucas shuddered as death filled the forest.*

*Naomi quickly moved to the next Executor, until she had slaughtered each and every one of them. The priestesses would find their bodies, but their deaths would be attributed to an animal attack. They'd never know Lucas and I were here in the first place.*

*Naomi returned to Eleanor's side, licking her lips proudly. The woman patted the lion affectionately, paying no attention to the blood staining her hand.*

*"Thank you," Elliot said as he rubbed the bruises on his neck. "You are much kinder than the other witches we met. We could have never gained the upper hand without you."*

*Eleanor crossed her arms. "We wouldn't have to be thanking them if you hadn't wandered off, Elliot! I had to walk the whole town looking for you."*

*"I told you I was going to do research. I'm a professor. That's my job," Elliot insisted innocently, before turning to us. "I am Professor Elliot Baine, of the Hawkei tribe, and my wife is Madame Eleanor Doya. We are doing research on supernatural societies, and dare I say, I didn't realize witches took their hangings so seriously! This cultural experience was wonderful research for my book."*

*"Research—" Eleanor sputtered. "Ancestors' cock, Elliot, we were nearly strangled!"*

*"All part of the risk of being an anthropologist, my dear," Elliot said cheerfully. "What is exploration without the threat of an unavoidable, treacherous fate?"*

*Eleanor's chest heaved. Her fingers twitched, like she wanted to strangle him herself, but was resisting with all her might.*

*"By the way, I have to say that your people have a lovely museum," Elliot added. "You witches have a variety of wonderful magical artifacts on display."*

*I shot Lucas a questioning glance. I wasn't aware we had a museum in Octavia Falls. Lucas shrugged, like he didn't know what they were talking about.*

*Eleanor's lips pressed into a thin line. "You shouldn't have been able to get into the museum in the first place. The priestesses said the room was warded."*

*"It was warded against witches, not Elementai," Elliot said. "How was I to know? After all, the ward didn't affect me!"*

*"You still should have known better," Eleanor replied curtly.*

*Elliot turned back to us and slipped off his backpack. I noticed a blue symbol on the flap—a tear-drop shape with swirling designs in the center. He began digging through his bag. "There must be some way we can repay you."*

*"We have nothing to give them, Elliot," Eleanor pressed. "All you have in there is stale bread, dirty socks, and a journal I daresay is of little use to them."*

*Elliot gave a nervous chuckle. "About that... uh, we'll have to pick up another on our way to Malovia."*

*Eleanor huffed, like it was typical of her husband to misplace something so important. "We can* thank *them by getting as far away from Octavia Falls as possible. We'll contact the* Hozho *for an early pick-up and get the hell out of Connecticut. After all this, I'm sure Malovia will be much kinder."*

*"We can help—" Lucas started, but Eleanor cut in.*

*"You've helped enough. We don't wish to bother you further." She'd clearly made up her mind. "Unless you have a car that can take us far away from here, so we can meet our transport ship at a safer location."*

*Grammy's car was back at the house, but it didn't matter if these people were innocent—we weren't leading them back there.*

*Lucas shook his head. "I'm sorry, we don't. We've been hiking all night."*

*It was a small lie, but one that ensured our safety.*

*I stepped forward. "If you ever find yourself back in the area, we'll help in any way we can. I'm Nadine, and this is Lucas."*

*Eleanor held her chin high. "Believe me, we will not be back. Come now, Elliot. We must begin the trek to the nearest town."*

*Eleanor strode off with her Familiar at her side. Her husband scrambled behind them, though he turned back to bow his head and thank us again.*

*They disappeared into the trees.*

*I turned to Lucas as my heart rate finally settled. "Grammy's going to kill us."*

*Lucas took my hand, and we started back up the mountain. "Not if we don't tell her. I can hear the lecture now.* You could've been caught!*"*

*I chuckled. "Yeah, by you, Grammy. For the millionth time."*

*Lucas smirked, though he looked more relieved than anything. "I think we better keep this to ourselves for now."*

*"Right," I agreed. "It'll be our little secret."*

☾

I RECOUNTED the story to the others, and Chloe's jaw hung open as she listened.

"Why didn't you tell us?" she demanded.

"We didn't tell *anyone*," I said. "Grammy would've killed us for going past the ward boundaries. We never left the safe house after that. Everyone was safe at the time."

Lucas thumbed through the journal. "The priestesses ordered the Executors to kill the Elementai couple after they'd already been guaranteed security in Octavia Falls by the United Supernatural Union. It's not unusual for us to get visiting professors now and then. I didn't think much of it at the time, but the professor's wife said he'd wandered off, and an Executor mentioned he'd been sticking his nose in places it didn't belong. He must've stumbled across something he wasn't supposed to."

"Lilian must've taken his journal before she ordered the Executors to kill them," I noted. "What does it say?"

Lucas turned to a page dated the middle of June. "*We have reached Octavia Falls and settled into our hotel room. The staff here is lovely and even offered us tea at check-in brewed by the best Alchemists in town! I feel relaxed already. I can't wait to try the witches' famous maple syrup at breakfast. First, I hope to make a visit to their college campus. I hear their library is wonderful.*"

Lucas flipped to the next page. "*The school is smaller than I anticipated. It appears to be in need of some serious renovations, but I suppose the cracks in the walls lend themselves to the centuries-old charm. I was unable to find my way to the library, but I did find a lovely museum—or perhaps an archives room? The double doors leading me here are carved beautifully with Miriamic symbols, though there was no label on the door. Either way, I have found myself among antique Miriamic artifacts I would love to study further. Items I see from where I sit include books on various supernatural races, potions vials, wands with Miriamic religious symbols carved into them, a large cauldron, and...*"

"And... what?" Chloe asked.

Lucas shook his head. "That's it. It just cuts off here."

He showed us the page. I saw that there was a long line of ink stretched across the paper, as if someone had yanked the journal from his hands before he could finish writing.

"He's referring to the Oaken Wands," Lucas stated. "I know it."

Chloe looked thoughtful. "That makes sense. It's too obvious to keep them at the Imperium headquarters, and the school is always going to have Executors defending it."

Talia furrowed her brow. "But where in the school? That doesn't sound like the archives room at school. I've been in the archives, and it's just a bunch of shelves of books and old newspapers."

"He describes double doors with Miriamic symbols," I pointed out. "It's Headmistress Verla's old office. Elliot didn't walk into a museum at all. He just thought he did."

"Then we have enough information to take a shot at this," Grant said. "We could get the Oaken Wands while the Executors are still at the festival. Tonight's our best shot."

"Let's go before our spell wears off," Chloe stated.

Lucas lifted his hands to create a portal to take us to the school. A beat passed, but nothing happened.

"The school is warded against portals," he said. "We can't portal directly in or out of the school. Nadine and I can try to work together to get past the wards, but they're strong, and that's going to take time we don't have. It took us weeks to work through the Malovian wards before we could open a portal to get Grant and Talia through the last time."

"Get us as close as you can," I decided. "The second Lilian returns and finds Mandy and Tate missing, the Executors will swarm town looking for us. We have to move quickly."

Lucas formed a portal leading into the trees surrounding Miriam College. We stepped through, and the portal shut behind us. Slowly, I crept through the trees, keeping my eyes on the school. A chill breeze swept through the trees, but other than that, the grounds were quiet.

"Looks safe," I remarked. "Come on."

We crept across the grass and snuck into the school. The outside of the mansion looked the same as it always had, apart from some construction material near the ballroom entrance. Inside, everything was different.

The last time we were here, the school was under attack. The space-bending spell that expanded the dorms and classrooms had been collapsing, and we'd barely gotten out. The room we entered wasn't at all what I remembered the Main Foyer looking like. It had the same red carpet and black walls, and the painting of Mother Miriam still hung above the mantle, but the stairs were closer to the door, and there were fewer sconces.

Grant spun around to take it all in. "This looks like a smaller version of the Main Foyer."

Chloe rolled her eyes at him. "That's because it is."

"We don't have time to marvel at it." I gestured for them to follow me. "Come on."

We started down the hall, and I counted turns until we reached where I thought Verla's office was—except the hall that was supposed to be there wasn't.

"It should be right here." I ran my hands over the flush wall, as if expecting the doorway to be concealed by magic.

"We can't expect the school to be laid out the same way we're used to," Lucas said. "Not since the space-bending spell collapsed. They had to change things in order to rebuild. I think her office is probably back the way we came."

Footsteps sounded down a nearby hall, and we quickly ducked into an alcove. The cats scurried behind us, and Isa hid beneath my cloak. I held my breath as I peeked around the corner. Two Executors walked past the end of the hall.

"I hate patrol duty," one of them complained. "We should be down at the Festival of Chosen."

"Don't say that," the other sneered. "This job is an honor."

Their voices faded down the hall, and my heart rate slowed.

"Looks like we aren't alone," I whispered. "We have to be careful."

I cocked a finger, and the others followed. I threw glances up and down the halls, but we didn't see anyone else.

Navigating the school wasn't as easy as I thought, because things weren't in the same places I was used to. The halls were narrower, and there were fewer doorways than I remembered. We got turned around a few times until we reached a hall that looked familiar.

"I think this is it," I said. We turned once more, and the double doors of Verla's office came into view. My heart lifted. We were *so* close.

We took a step closer, until my magic slammed into something dangerous. Instinct took over and I threw my arms out to protect my friends. "Stop!"

They all jumped back.

Slowly, I approached the doors, but I didn't touch them. Magic pulsed through the hall, and a high-pitched note rang in my ears. "There's a strong ward here, a hell of a lot stronger than the one at Lilian's house. Several witches cast this."

"Can you break it?" Talia asked.

"It's going to be tough," I admitted. As I reached out, my magic recoiled on instinct. "The ward is strong, so transforming that magic into something else like a battle orb could bring the whole school down on us. Not to mention breaking it would alert the priestesses. I'll have to try something else."

Lucas eyed me warily. "What did you have in mind?"

"In theory, Curse Breakers can absorb magic," I said. "I'm going to do *that*."

Lucas grabbed my hand before I could move. "You've never done that before. You don't even know if it will work."

"I know it's our only option," I insisted. "If I can hold on to the ward without breaking it until we get out of here, we can escape without alerting the priestesses. We *need* those Wands, Lucas. You have to at least let me try."

"How confident are you in this?" he asked.

"Enough to give it a shot," I pressed.

Lucas stepped back. "All right. Do what you need to do."

"We should all work together," I suggested. "Lend me your powers, and I'll use it to get past the ward, then take that power inside of me. The stronger our magic, the easier it will be to overpower the ward."

We all grabbed hands, and my brows knitted in concentration. I gathered my friends' magic together and manipulated it, directing it at the ward. The ward resisted, pushing against me. My magic recoiled, and my body shook as I fought harder. Every muscle in my body tensed, and a whirlwind swept through the hall as magic clashed together.

The doors began to glow an angry red. My dark blue magic pushed against it, and it took everything in me to keep the spell alive. My arms grew weak, and my breaths became shallow. It was like trying to push over a brick wall. The cats approached the door and began scratching at it.

"Get back!" I warned them.

"Maybe we should stop," Lucas said nervously.

"No. I've got this," I insisted.

I searched the ward for weaknesses, until my magic brushed up against an unsteady edge. Something within me snapped, and I managed to find my way inside the ward. The door began to glow a bright blue. My magic entangled with the ward, and I drew backward, dragging the magic toward me.

The magic was heavy, like a dark sludge swirling in my gut. All magic felt different to me, and I could tell the priestesses hadn't cast this ward with the intent to protect what was inside. Their ill intentions were designed to hurt anyone who tried to get past. This spell wasn't cast out of love, but out of hate.

A sharp pain twisted my stomach, and I gagged.

"Nadine!" Lucas cried.

I squeezed his hand tighter. "I've almost got it."

I gritted my teeth. The pain in my gut spread to my extremities, feeling like tiny blades slicing into my muscles. I tried not to let it show. I couldn't let Lucas stop me—not when we were this close. We had one shot at this, and I wasn't leaving Octavia Falls without the Oaken Wands in hand.

I yanked harder, and the blue magic lighting up the door funneled into me, until the glow subsided completely. "I did it!"

Chloe stepped in front of the doors. "We don't know how long Nadine can hold that magic. We need to move our asses and get out of here, because right now Nadine's a ticking bomb."

Chloe placed her hands on the door handles and flung the doors open. Inside, shelves were filled with all kinds of books, and potion vials shimmered around the room. On Verla's desk next to a large cauldron stood two display cases that housed none other than the Oaken Wands.

I leaned against Lucas, and together, the five of us stepped into the room.

A high-pitched squeal assaulted my ears, so loud that it brought me to my knees. My hands clapped over my ears, and I looked to my friends to see them doing the same. Lucas's eyes went wide, and his lips moved, though I couldn't hear what he was saying.

The priestesses' ward wasn't the only thing keeping other witches out. They'd cast some sort of alarm spell over the room. Of fucking course. The priestesses wouldn't cast just one spell over this door. They'd make multiple in case someone managed to break their ward, and I should've realized it sooner. The noise rattled my bones, and the whole building seemed to shake. I couldn't get to my feet even if I wanted to.

The pain permeating my body turned to absolute horror as a darkness crept over the walls, enveloping the room. For a moment, I saw nothing but the shadows, and I felt nothing except an icy-cold chill. Ghostly moans could be heard over the alarm, and that's when I realized this wasn't an alarm system at all.

It was a *curse*.

My friends shot spells across the room, but it did no good. A window shattered and the wind from outside quickly swept in, swirling around us.

The eerie shadows closed in on us. They weren't anything like spirits I'd seen before. These shadows crept across the walls, as if they could only stalk their prey in obscurity.

Long, spindly fingers slithered from the wall to the carpet, then slowly up my leg. I tried to scream, but my voice couldn't be heard over the ringing in my ears. The spirit's frigid touch turned my skin to ice. The shadowy hand inched up my body, curling around my throat.

My scream died on my tongue as my airways constricted. Darkness entered the corners of my vision, and I tilted my head to see that my friends were suffering the same fate. Each of us had been rendered immobile, and in moments, the curse would strangle us. Dark energy turned my friends' blood black, and inky veins spider-webbed across their skin. The cats tried to fight back, clawing at the walls, but more shadowy figures emerged and held them down.

I had to stop this. The ward I held within me was dark—cast with the intention to harm. And that's exactly what it would do.

I released the magic, and the sound of shattering glass filled the room. We were blasted backward. The ward turned solid as it broke, sending shards of glass raining down on us. I threw my hands up, but it was too late. The glass sliced into my face, and my friends cried out as the remnants of the ward cut into their skin.

I landed hard on my back and gasped as I tried to get to my feet. I could hardly find my fingers, let alone my legs. I lifted my gaze to the shadowy figures to see they had grown bigger than before. The temperature in the room had dropped even more as they continued to descend upon us. I glanced around at my friends to see them lying on the floor, blood dripping down their faces. The spell hadn't hurt the ghostly figures, but it had harmed my friends.

The shadows were back on us in a mere moment. I seemed to freeze beneath their touch as the shadows surrounded me. They felt even stronger than before.

I realized then that the shadows only fed on the dark energy of the ward. Trying to harm them with the priestesses' magic had only made them stronger. There was only one way to cast out the darkness—and that was to outshine it.

Protection magic swirled out of me, appearing as a glowing orb that lit the entire room. The orb expanded, splitting into five beams of light that I aimed at the shadowed figures. The spirit's hold on me tightened. I clawed at my neck, but my fingers met nothing but air. I gripped the shadowy magic with my Curse Breaker powers, but it quickly slipped from my grasp.

I couldn't do this alone.

My fingers trembled as I reached out for Lucas on one side of me and Chloe on the other. They saw what I was doing and desperately reached back, until the five of us were holding hands.

Protection magic poured into me, causing my whole body to glow like the light of the sun. The screeching of the ghosts intensified, until the magic came bursting out of me. Like a shield exploding, our magic swept across the room, blasting the spirits back. Pained screams filled the air… then faded.

I slumped to my hands and knees, gulping in greedy breaths. My friends were on their knees panting, but they were still here, thank the Goddess.

Lucas crawled over to me and placed a hand on my back. "We did it," he rasped.

Isa ran over, rubbing her head on my chin. At first, I thought she was trying to comfort me, until she pushed again, then let out a low growl.

"We have to get moving," I said. "I broke the priestesses' ward, which means they know we're here. They could be here at any moment."

Grant and Talia scrambled to their feet and hurried over to the desk at the center of the room. Grant picked up the cauldron and lifted it above the displays that held the Seer and Alchemy Wands. Something made him pause.

"Uh… anyone else recognize this?" Grant asked.

We'd been in such a hurry, I hadn't had a chance to look at it closely.

Now that I did, I realized the handles were twisted into the shape of branches.

"It's the Crock of Death," I realized.

"We should take that with us, too," Lucas suggested.

Grant nodded, then brought the cauldron down to smash the Wand displays open. He quickly subconjured the crock, then reached through the broken glass. Talia took the Seer Wand, while Grant snatched up the Alchemy Wand. The wands glowed at the ends, and magic swirled up their arms. Matching tunes filled the room.

"They're the real thing," Grant said. "I can feel it."

Relief flooded through me. We had worked so hard for those Wands, only for the priestesses to manipulate them out of our grasp. Now that we had them again, they couldn't use them to hurt our people.

We quickly turned to leave, but Chloe stopped us.

"Hang on. There might be other things here we can use against the priestesses." Chloe lifted a scroll she found lying on a table. "Look at these. They're some sort of decree records... They're making new laws. *The following laws are set forth by the Imperium Council, led by revelation from Mother Miriam. It is imperative the coven follow her guidance to protect the town from outside threats.*"

"They're liars," I growled. "I doubt they've talked to her, because I *have*, and this isn't what she'd want."

Chloe curled up her nose. "These scrolls talk as if the coven can't be trusted to know what's best for themselves. *Compliance is the only way to fulfill Mother Miriam's will.* This document details the next stages of their plan. They're going to implement a law that says if you're not teaching your children the ways of the Chosen, you will be charged with religious abuse. People who haven't joined the Chosen will have their children removed from their home, so that the priestesses can raise the kids under their own religious doctrine."

"That's sick!" Lucas raged. "They can't take innocent children from good homes."

"What is this?" Grant sneered. "Some sort of genocide?"

I shook my head. "During genocides, the leaders mark the oppressed, like they did in the Hawkei Civil War. The priestesses are marking themselves and their followers, because we're fighting a different force here. The marking of the Chosen is a ritual initiation, which means all those people willing to go through with it will agree with and support the priestesses. They aren't going to bother questioning the priestesses removing children from good homes, because they're so far into the ideology that they'll be the ones to do it for them. They'll turn in their neighbors, not because they're afraid of what will happen if they don't, but because they actually believe they're doing the right thing."

"This is wrong and evil," Lucas snarled.

"That's not the worst of it…" Talia's features turned paper white as she picked up another stack of papers. "It's drawings of the Mentalist Wand… and pictures of the Abyss."

Talia turned the drawings toward us, and my stomach plummeted to my toes. The sketches showed the Mentalist Wand, the twisted tree symbol carved onto the handle. It appeared to be falling into a glowing red pit, with shadowed creatures lurking in the background.

Lucas snatched the drawing from her hands, terror filling his wide eyes. "This looks like the Wand falling into the demon's pit. It's got to be a recreation of a Seer's vision, which means the priestesses know where to find the Wand. I don't understand how they managed to get this information when the Wands can't be tracked."

"A Seer could've been looking into our past, or Professor Leto's, and seen what played out that night," I pointed out. "The Mentalist Wand could've appeared in the vision, even if it can't be tracked on its own."

"Do you think they've been to the Abyss yet?" Grant wondered.

Talia flipped through more pages. "According to these notes, they've tried summoning demons for answers, but no one is willing to strike a deal with them after what happened to Professor Leto."

"I'm surprised they're willing to work with demons at all after what he did," Chloe said. "He was uncontrollable. These women don't take kindly to being out of control."

"Which means they're going to be looking for other options, just like we are," I pointed out. "We have to get to the Abyss before the priestesses do. With all the coven's power of mind manipulation in their hands, they could do more harm to the coven than ever before."

Lucas crushed the drawing in his hands. "Then let's get moving."

We hurried out of the room and down the hall. We were met with nothing but empty halls as we turned the corners—

Until we came to a screeching halt in the Main Foyer. Our cats hissed and backed away. Ten Executors stood in a row, blocking the doors. Several of them held wands, while others had battle orbs at the ready.

Lucas grabbed the back of my cloak and yanked me in the opposite direction. We ducked down the hallway a moment before the battle orbs exploded right where I'd been standing.

Lucas put an index finger to his lips. "Shh… they'll forget they ever saw us."

"Come out, come out, wherever you are," an Executor taunted.

Chloe's voice trembled, which was so unlike her. "I gave everything I had to that last spell. When we cast out those spirits, our disguise broke."

"We can run, but we don't know where the exits are anymore," Grant pointed out. "The Executors won't hesitate to hurt us."

Lucas shook his head. "We don't have to run. We have two Oaken Wands. What do they have? An over-inflated sense of ego?"

"If we face them, they'll die," Talia stated. She wasn't protesting, more or less stating a fact. She wanted to make sure we were okay with that.

"We're in the middle of a war," Chloe said. "We can't keep pretending that we can spare the people who want us dead. Let's kill these fuckers."

Footsteps approached slowly. "Come out and face us," an Executor sneered. "Unless you're too scared."

The others laughed, as if they actually believed we'd be scared of *them*.

I exchanged a glance with Lucas, and he nodded, like he knew exactly what I was thinking. "We won't kill innocent people," I said. "So we'll give them a choice."

Lucas's voice remained steady as he shouted around the corner. "You don't know what you're getting yourselves into. Fight us, and you'll die. We're giving you the option to walk away now."

"Or what?" one of them laughed. "You'll cast a little curse on us? We'll kill each of your friends one by one, saving the Curse Breaker for last, so she can watch. There will be no trial this time."

Lucas had heard enough. He grabbed his wand and leapt around the corner. I barely blinked before a powerful battle spell erupted out of the end of his wand. It connected with an Executor's stomach and blasted him off his feet and straight through the front doors of the mansion. The wood crumbled, and I was certain the Executor had to be dead from the blow.

My friends and I quickly followed, and our cats hissed as spells shot all throughout the room. Battle orbs smashed into the front of Lucas's shield and ricocheted back at the Executors. Chloe threw her hands apart, and her telekinesis sent the Executors flying into the walls.

We ran for the door. We were barely two paces away when one of the Executors on the ground reached out and grabbed the hem of my cloak. I tripped and caught myself on my palms, then promptly spun around and slammed my foot into his face. He reeled back the same time a female Executor lunged for me.

She landed on the ground beside me. I caught sight of an eye tattooed on her skin as her arm curled around my neck, pinning my back to her front. Physically, she was strong, like the kind of girl who'd been on the wrestling team. She certainly knew how to put someone into a headlock.

"Tell me where you and your little friends have been hiding!" she sneered.

I gasped for breath, and past my panic, my Curse Breaker powers sensed her magic invading my mind. She was trying to read my thoughts, and terror rocked through me. I tried to push her out of my mind, but she only pressed further. If this was how I died, I wasn't taking any of my friends with me. I thought of anything but the safe house, but I felt her creeping past each wall I tried to throw up to block her.

"Get off her, you bitch!" Talia cried. She leapt in front of me, and the end of the Seer Wand began to glow. Slowly, I felt the Seer's magic leave my mind. Talia kicked the girl in the face as hard as she could, and she loosened her hold on me.

The other Executor was already back on his feet, and a spell crackled in his palm, aimed at me. I barely had a moment to process it before Lucas jumped on him. He tackled the Executor, and they stumbled into the wall near the fireplace. The Executor lifted his crackling hand to deliver the deadly blow, but Lucas was faster than he was. My husband grabbed the Executor by the head and smashed his face into the mantle.

Blood spurted everywhere, spraying across Mother Miriam's painting and down Lucas's cloak. The Executor slumped to the ground, and blood trickled onto the floor.

Lucas heaved a breath as he stared down at the man's unmoving form. He glanced to his hands for a beat, before turning his gaze to the painting of Mother Miriam. I didn't think he could believe what he'd done—he'd just killed a man with his bare hands.

The painting began to glow white around the edges, and I swore to the Goddess I saw the painting of Mother Miriam *move*. Her eyes turned down toward Lucas, and she gave the slightest of nods.

I got to my feet and reached out for Lucas, but he barely noticed my touch. "She chose me as an agent of death," he said hollowly. "She wanted me to protect you."

"You did the right thing," I told him.

"You killed him!" an Executor shouted. He had to be an Alchemist, because he conjured a potion vial and threw it at our friends. I caught sight of a shimmering green liquid inside, which I'd seen before. It was a potion meant to explode when the vial was shattered, and it was headed straight toward Grant.

"Grant!" I cried.

He'd already seen it. Grant raised the Alchemy Wand, and the magic siphoned out of the potion a second before it hit the ground. The potion sizzled and smoked as the liquid seeped into the floor, but it failed to explode as intended.

I quickly assessed the other Executors and realized there was only one Seer and one Alchemist in the group. Grant and Talia siphoned their powers, but the others aimed deadly spells at us.

We ducked, then shot back spells of our own. One of my spells caught an Executor in the leg, and I heard the snap of bone. His scream echoed off the walls of the Main Foyer as he fell to the ground.

A spell hit Grant in the chest, and he was blasted off his feet. Talia and I rushed to help him stand. Before we could get anywhere, an Executor jumped in front of us, separating us from Chloe and Lucas.

"Nadine!" Lucas cried. He aimed a spell at the Executor. It hit him, and he went down, but several more had closed in.

I cast a shield around myself, Grant, and Talia. Spells slammed into my shield from all angles. Grant and Talia quickly took my hands, and we fortified the shield with our collective power. It held, but Chloe and Lucas were cornered on the other side of the foyer.

"What do you say?" one of the Executors laughed maniacally. "Shall we have a bit of fun with them before they die?"

The ghostly figure of the man Lucas had blasted through the front doors appeared in front of us. An Executor with a skull tattoo on his arm flicked his wrist, and the ghost swept forward at his command, flying straight into Lucas. The ghost disappeared, as if Lucas's body had absorbed him.

At the same time, Chloe halted mid-step. At first, I thought it was because she was shocked by what she'd seen. Then I noticed her eyes had gone glossy. She didn't appear as herself as she took a step toward Lucas. He turned toward her slowly with a twisted smirk on his face. It wasn't his own; I knew that for certain.

A woman with the mark of a Mentalist on her hand laughed. "A possessed reaper versus my puppet. Which will win?"

I realized then that the woman had invaded Chloe's mind, and she was controlling her now. In the same moment, the Mortana had ordered the ghost of the dead Executor to possess my husband's body.

Chloe gritted her teeth, though she continued to approach Lucas. "Get out of my head, bitch."

"Ooh," the Executor laughed. "She's a fighter. Let's see how well you fight our friend."

Chloe and Lucas lunged at each other. The Executors' laughter filled the air as the two engaged in a fistfight created for the Executors' sick entertainment. Purple bruises broke out across their faces, and Chloe was forced to curl her fingers around Lucas's neck.

Rage filled my entire body, and I didn't even have to form a spell in my hand to cast a curse. I set my gaze on the Mentalist who was controlling Chloe and aimed all my anger at her. I wanted her to stop hurting my friends. I wanted her to *die*.

Dark magic crept over the Mentalist's skin, turning her features an ashen gray. The veins in her neck turned to black as my killing curse overtook her body. She let out a pained cry and stumbled back a few steps. Executors threw their hands over their ears as her piercing scream filled the air.

I felt it when my curse overtook her form entirely, because the magic reached a peak. The curse exploded and took her body with it. Her form turned to ash, and her screams died out as the curse reduced her to nothing but dust where she'd been standing.

Chloe gasped as she gained control of her body once again. She let go of Lucas's throat, and she took several steps back.

Lucas pursued her with that twisted smirk. He still wasn't himself. I turned to the Mortana who had cast the spell that possessed my husband. I intended to cast a curse on him as well, but I never got the chance.

"Lucas, you can fight this," Chloe said.

The smirk wiped from Lucas's face, and he gritted his teeth instead. A spectral form appeared around him, like he was forcing the ghost out of his body. The ghost fought against him, until Lucas let out a primal scream, and the apparition separated from him entirely.

The ghost swept across the room, aimed straight for the Mortana who cast the spell. The ghost screeched and slammed into him, knocking the Executor off his feet. He went flying into the wall and hit his head so hard he was knocked out.

"Lucas, how did you do that!?" Chloe cried.

Lucas gasped for breath, and sweat dripped down his brow. "Don't know. Something to do with my death powers, I guess. Let's go!"

I ran toward Lucas, and Talia and Grant followed. Executors pursued us, but Lucas conjured a shield that held as we fled toward the front doors. A powerful spell landed against his shield and bounced off. Magic exploded against the wall, shattering one of the windows. Another spell blasted through the doorway. I saw a flash of light out of the corner of my eye, then heard the sound of Lucas's shield shattering.

I whirled around to see four Executors standing in the doorway, their wands raised and ready for another attack. I didn't take a moment to think about it. Something within me snapped, and I siphoned their magic for my own before they could cast a spell. Power burst out of me.

Magic swept up the stairway in the blink of an eye, encompassing the entire foyer in the blast. Windows shattered, and walls crumbled. Everything happened so quickly that the Executors didn't get the chance to scream. They were killed instantly, their bloody bodies falling into a heap at the front of the school.

Building materials rained down over the front steps, and the earth beneath us rumbled. I sank to my knees as my head spun. Lucas's features swam in front of me.

"Nad, are you okay?" He grabbed my shoulders and shook me. I was relieved to see him on his feet.

My hands shook. "I wasn't going to let them hurt my family."

"Never," Lucas promised as he wrapped me in his arms.

"Time to go!" Grant said in a rush.

My vision steadied, and I looked toward the front gates to find Executors pouring onto the school grounds. There had to be over a hundred Executors, all coming for our heads.

"Run!" Lucas shouted. He grabbed my hand and helped me to my feet, and we took off running.

Spells rained down on us. Lucas threw up a shield, but it was only enough to deflect battle spells. My feet swept out from under me, and I felt the magic of a Mentalist lift me off the ground until I was dangling upside down.

Chloe grabbed my hands, and I felt her magic fight against my attacker. The magic levitating me snapped as Chloe overpowered the spell. I landed hard on my stomach and scrambled to my feet before I could catch my breath. I took off running beside my friends.

The Oaken Wands glowed as Grant and Talia siphoned magic from the Executors. We skirted around the side of the building and sprinted toward the trees.

"Keep running!" Lucas shouted. "We aren't outside the ward yet."

We ran through the trees. Spells whizzed by our heads and hit tree trunks beside us. They were closing in on us—and fast.

"Get ready for the portal," Lucas warned

Talia shot a panicked glance behind her shoulder. "They can't follow us through, can they?"

Lucas dodged around a tree, and his feet faltered beneath him. "Not if I take us to the one place they can't go."

The heaviness of the ward surrounding the school passed through me, and I felt lighter as we broke through the other side of the ward. "Now, Lucas!" I cried.

Grant and Talia aimed their wands behind us. Powerful magic blasted out of the ends of the Oaken Wands, causing an explosion on the other side of the forest. Screams filled the air.

Lucas grabbed my hand and lifted the other palm. Magic surged through us both, and a portal bloomed in front of us. I paid no attention to what was on the other side. I trusted my husband whole-heartedly, so when he told me to jump, I did.

The cats yowled as we tumbled through the portal. I landed on solid ground and rolled across the dirt. When I came to a stop, I saw pine trees towering above me. The sound of a stream trickled nearby. We had landed in a coniferous forest that appeared to be thousands of years old. It had been the dead of night when we left, but now I could see the first of the morning sun rays peeking over the horizon.

I shivered as a cold chill spread across my skin. Snow dusted the ground, and through a bit of sparse trees, I spotted mountains in the distance. Magic pulsed through the air around me, but it felt different from the witch magic I was used to—though I couldn't quite put my finger on the strange sensation.

I pushed myself to my elbows and glanced around. Remnants of giant shells from hatched eggs scattered the area, along with bones that were so large they could've belonged to dinosaurs. I dropped my gaze to the dirt, where I saw wolf paw prints that were larger across than my hand. Large feathers that could've belonged to a griffin were spread everywhere. In the distance, I heard the sound of a dragon's roar.

I took a moment to catch my breath. The silence filling the air told me we were safe, though my pulse still pounded in my ears. Lucas immediately cast a shield around us, and his gaze darted around the forest to check if we were safe.

"Where are we?" Chloe asked.

"The one place the priestesses and the Executors are scared to go," Lucas said in a dark tone. "Malovia… the home of the fae."

## ELEVEN

I had to make a quick decision. If Talia had been right and the Executors saw through the portal to where we were going, I couldn't risk taking us back to the safe house. The priestesses would find us, and then rescuing Mandy and Tate would all be for nothing.

I had to take us to the one place they'd never come. We had to face the enemy of our enemy if we hoped to survive.

"Good call," Chloe said in approval as she got to her feet. "The priestesses won't follow us because it's dangerous for them to be here. But don't forget that it's just as dangerous for us. Verla and Warren came here to find a way to the Abyss, but they don't know we're here, and we have no way to reach them. If we're discovered by the fae, we'll be killed."

"Then we're going to have to exercise extreme caution," I said. "We can't go back to Octavia Falls right now. The priestesses are hunting us, and if we return to the safe house, we're putting everyone at risk."

"Lucas is right," Nadine agreed. "We weren't expecting to come here so soon, but we're here now. We need to find Verla and Warren and gain passage to the Abyss, so we can obtain the Mentalist and Mortana Wands."

Grant's eyes darted around the forest. "I recognize these woods. We can't be far from Pruska, where we witnessed that deadly battle. This isn't a safe place for us to be. We have to get out of this area."

"We need to find a vantage point first to get our bearings." I looked upward, to see if there was a tree I could climb, but all the lowest limbs were high above our heads. Instead, I conjured the enchanted broom I kept in my stash ever since we found it at Wicked Alchemy a year ago. I hadn't used it since the night of the Burning. Nadine, Grant, and Talia all had one just like it.

"Be careful!" Nadine warned. "If the fae see a witch flying a broom, we'll be dead."

"I'll keep near the tree line," I promised. I mounted my broom, then kicked off. The broom was enchanted with a Mentalist's telekinesis magic and followed my command. I used the broom to fly me high into the trees, until I could see far across the landscape. Mountains rose along the horizon, and a large city loomed ahead of us. Behind me, I spotted a small town that had to be Pruska.

Miles away, large creatures looped through the skies, and their bird-like cries and dragon roars could be heard from here. My stomach dropped at the sight of the shifters, though they looked like mere pinpricks in the distance. Nonetheless, Nadine was right—we couldn't fly, or we'd be spotted.

I lowered myself back to the ground and subconjured the broom. "Pruska's behind us, and there's a large city a few miles ahead."

"That's their capital city of Dolinska," Grant said. "That's where we'll find Verla and Warren."

"We need to get moving," I stated firmly. "Nadine and I are powerful enough to portal past the Malovian wards, but getting around safely is going to be a challenge. We're lucky I portaled us somewhere secluded. I can't portal us any closer to the city, or we risk being spotted, but we also can't stay in one place for too long."

"We need to don our disguises," Talia said.

She conjured a pile of cloaks she'd made for this very purpose and handed them out. They looked nothing like the black cloaks we were wearing. These were colorful, with pretty embroidered designs all over the fabric and fur stitched along the hoods.

We ditched our black cloaks and subconjured them in favor of the robes Talia had designed. The one she handed me was a silky regal purple, with golden knots embroidered into the fabric. Nadine's was a navy blue with snowflake designs all over it. Grant draped a velvety green cloak around his shoulders, and I recognized the fabric from the curtains in our den. Chloe's cloak was red with a silver trim, and Talia's was a plush pink with white fur outlining the edges. My friends and I certainly looked like fae.

As I observed my coat, I noticed a large pocket inside. "What's this for?" I asked.

"The pockets are for our cats," Talia said. She picked up Gus and tucked him inside her pocket to demonstrate. He poked his paws out the top of the pocket, looking particularly pleased. When she curled the ends of her cloak around her, I couldn't even tell he was there.

We certainly couldn't walk into Dolinska with our cats at our feet. Disguises or not, our cats would be a dead giveaway.

"Good idea," I told her. I picked up Oliver and tucked him inside my cloak, and the others did the same with their cats. Oliver tucked close to my belly and remained quiet.

Grant conjured a small vial with a dropper. "This is the tincture I've been working on. Three drops under the tongue should disguise our scent for the next twenty-four hours. It's powerful, but it was difficult to brew, so there's only enough for one dose each. We can't waste any time finding Verla and Warren."

He passed the tincture around, and we all placed a few drops under our tongue. The cats took the tincture too, because if our scent didn't give us away, the smell of our cats would. Magic tingled over my skin, and I could feel the tincture working.

"I can feel the magic in all of us," Nadine said. "We should be safe now. Let's get moving."

We started toward Dolinska, which was at least a two-mile hike from where we started. We only made it a quarter of a mile when I spotted dark shadows through the trees. Three figures appeared to be walking in our direction, until I realized that they weren't moving forward at all. Instead, they appeared to be swaying in the wind.

That's when I noticed the ropes hanging from the trees, and I shuddered.

Talia's features paled. "Are those… *people?*"

"Dear Goddess," Nadine breathed, and her eyes widened in horror.

Grant stopped in his tracks, as if he didn't dare take another step.

I swallowed down the lump in my throat as I crept closer. I could feel death permeating the air. The bodies were in our direct path to Dolinska, so we couldn't go around them. "They must be traitors, left hanging as a warning."

"Uh… I don't think those are traitors," Chloe said in a chilling voice.

As we came upon the bodies, my stomach plummeted to my toes. Oliver must've felt the melancholy in the air, because he poked his head out of my cloak. I gently guided him back inside, but I couldn't take my eyes off the figures.

Two women and one man hung from the trees. I realized the black cloaks they wore were all too reminiscent of our own in our stashes. Then I spotted the skull tattoo on the back of the man's hand. I didn't want to look at their faces, but I forced myself to anyway. I didn't recognize them—thank the Goddess—but there was no doubt about it. These three people were from the Miriamic Coven. They'd been hanged as a warning, all right.

A warning to people like us.

Grant's voice wavered. "I don't get it. I thought the king and queen were sympathetic to dark magic wielders."

My stomach felt hollow as I answered, "This wasn't Emma and Ethan's doing. An execution by the monarchs would be a public spectacle. Someone else hanged these people and then left them here to rot."

"Who would do that?" Talia questioned in disbelief.

"I'm sure most fae would love to see us hang," I said.

"We need to cut them down and bury them." Nadine's hands shook as she moved forward, but Chloe grabbed her wrist to stop her.

"No!" Chloe insisted. "We don't have time."

"They need a proper burial," Nadine shot back.

"We're disguised, but if the fae find us tampering with these bodies, we'll be buried alongside them," Chloe argued. "What happened to these members of the coven is unfortunate, but it is already done. I don't wish to join them."

I didn't want to admit it, but Chloe was right. "I don't feel lingering spirits," I admitted. "They must've already moved on to Alora."

I was still uneasy from the hollowness of death filling the forest, but my confession was enough to get the others to agree with Chloe.

Nadine dropped her gaze, like she couldn't bear to glance back at the bodies. "All right. Let's keep moving."

As we approached Dolinska, I could make out a large stone wall surrounding the city's borders. A road led into town, where caravans of merchants traveled on their way into the city. They rode in wagons pulled by alicorn shifters to bring their goods into town. The gated entrance was guarded by two big men in full suits of armor. I guessed they had to be dragon shifters. It wasn't going to be simple to slip inside unnoticed.

We ducked in the cover of the trees next to the edge of the road.

"There's a ward surrounding the city," Nadine whispered. "I can feel it from here."

Grant grimaced. "I didn't know the city was warded. Our disguises will work on the people, but I don't think we can trick the wards."

Nadine closed her eyes, as if concentrating on the magic. "I can move the magic aside long enough to create a hole in the ward to get us through. Fae magic is different from ours, but it's close enough that I can still manipulate it."

My wife never ceased to amaze me. I loved that about her.

"Nadine can get us past the wards, but we still need to get past the guards." I pointed to a large group of approaching merchants. The group was full of carts, carriages, and other supplies, with a group of people following behind one of the wagons on foot. "To get through the gates, we'll need to slip into the crowd unnoticed and act as if we're with the other merchants."

"Then we need to move quickly," Chloe said. "They're almost here."

The group of merchants passed our hiding spot, and we quickly ducked out of the trees and into the back of the group. A woman in a golden cloak shot a glance back at me, and I could've sworn her eyes flashed red, but she turned away and didn't say anything. My heart pounded, and I prayed she wouldn't rat us out.

We approached the gates, and I noticed Nadine's eyes lock straight forward. She was concentrating deeply to shift the ward magic aside to let us through. The guards' eyes roamed over the crowd and gestured each carriage through. I held my breath as the final wagon we stood behind approached the gates. The guards took a quick look in the back to inspect the merchandise, then waved the merchant team through.

We followed behind the others as if we belonged, though I noticed the woman in the golden cloak shift closer to us. She came so close to me that we were nearly touching.

"Hold up!" one of the guards ordered in a gruff voice. He had a thick Malovian accent, which sounded similar to Russian.

He stepped in front of me, and my heart stopped. He was huge—at least six inches taller than me, with big, broad shoulders. Magic tingled in my fingers, ready to retaliate if necessary.

The guard sniffed the air. "Something isn't right here."

I began to panic, and I shot a quick glance at Grant. His eyes went wide, and his expression was easy to read. His potion *should* work. It was the strongest thing we had.

Before I could think of a lie to give the guard to explain our strange scent, he reached toward me—except his hands moved right past me. Instead of grabbing me like I thought he would, his hands curled around the golden cloak of the woman beside me.

He yanked her forward and pulled her hood down. "You're no fae!"

"P-please, sir," the woman stammered, and that's when I noticed her fangs for the first time. "I am half-fae. I'm seeking refuge—"

"*Half-fae!*" the guard spat. He inhaled her scent deeper. "You're part vampire. Our treaty with the vampires just ended. You aren't allowed here anymore."

"I have family in the city—" the woman started, but the man was already dragging her away by her hair.

"I don't care who your family is. Your vampire blood isn't welcome here," he growled. "You'll be escorted by the Arcanea Alliance to the palace dungeons, where the Circle will decide your sentence."

She tripped and cried out, but he continued dragging her along even as she lost her footing. It was cruel the way he treated her. All I could do was stand and watch. I knew if I fought back and tried to save her, my magic would be revealed, and they'd do far worse to us than lock us in a dungeon.

"Move along!" the second guard shouted cruelly to the rest of us. "Or you'll be next!"

We didn't have to be told twice. We hurried along inside the city with the other merchants, and I didn't take a breath until we were at least two blocks away from the guards.

Nadine dropped her shoulders in relief. "That hole in the ward wasn't easy to hold, but we made it inside."

"Thank the Goddess," Talia added. "If that's how they treat vampires, I don't want to see what they'll do to a witch. We'll be hung on the spot."

Chloe glanced around the street, which was beginning to bustle with morning traffic. "We're not out of the woods just yet. We still have to follow Hattie's instructions to reach Enchanting Whispers, which is where Verla and Warren should be."

"The sooner we get there, the better," I said. "Let's get moving."

We followed behind the merchant carts, which were headed into the center of the city. Thank the Goddess we had others to follow, because most of the signage here was written in Malovian. The fae spoke English, but it wasn't their mother tongue, and it was clear we were out of our element here.

We walked along cobblestone streets and passed by large family estates, before reaching buildings that must've been standing for hundreds of years. People emerged from homes and followed us deeper into the city to open their shops or start their morning shift.

Pubs and cafés stood on every street corner, and the most delicious scent of crepes and kielbasa skillets wafted through the air. We passed by a tiny café with outdoor seating. I witnessed a woman sip her tea, before heart-shaped bubbles formed around her head and popped once the illusion wore off. We passed by bakeries that had tiny faekin in the windows who dusted glitter over powdered sugar donuts, tempting us to come inside.

The city grew louder and more boisterous the further we walked. Large Gothic buildings and beautiful cathedrals rose above us. The clang of metal could be heard from blacksmith shops as the fae forged swords and other weapons. We passed by a shop selling shimmering armor and weapons of all kinds, including intricately crafted daggers and axes. Another shop on the corner sold lances designed for jousting, and the sign in the window read in English: *Jousting Tournament Today! Place Your Bets Here.*

As we turned the corner, the crowd thickened. Shops lined the entire street, and dozens of traveling merchants had already set up temporary shops for the day. We had reached the merchant district, where Hattie had said we would find her contact, Siona.

Soldiers prowled up and down the streets, waving Malovian flags and singing what sounded like a patriotic song. Posters hung from shop windows, encouraging people to defend the Malovian Revolution. Nearby, a group of protestors held signs that said things like, *Unseelie Fae Don't Belong* and *Dark Magic is a Crime!*

The sound of swords clanging caught my attention, and I turned to see two burly men sword fighting in the middle of the street. One of them had a beard, and the other was clean shaven. Both the men were laughing, and it was obvious it wasn't a vicious battle, but a cordial match between friends. A group had formed around them, and the city folk cheered them on. The men moved with grace, like they'd been training for this all their lives. The bearded man knocked the sword out of the other man's hand.

"Well done," his opponent said, giving a bow.

They congratulated each other on their fight, then the bearded man turned to the crowd. "Come! Who will fight me next?"

Someone grabbed me by the shoulder and started dragging me forward. "You look like a healthy young chap! Won't you join us?"

I hesitated. "I—uh… don't have my sword with me."

The guy lost all interest. He must've seen a friend, because he called someone's name and quickly wandered off.

I barely took a step before someone else cut in front of us. A woman shoved a potion vial toward Nadine and spoke in words I didn't recognize. It had to be Malovian.

"Um…" Nadine hesitated.

The woman quickly switched to English, but she spoke in a Malovian accent. "Did you hear me, or are you stupid? I *asked* if you wanted to buy a love potion, to find your mate?"

Nadine took a step to the side and spoke kindly. "No, thank you."

The woman eyed her curiously, like her refusal was strange—she had clearly expected Nadine to be rude back, and because she wasn't, she didn't know how to respond. "Are you sure? Best not to take chances. Don't want to end up alone."

Chloe stepped in front of us. "She's mated already. Now bugger off."

"*Him?*" The shopkeeper glanced at me and huffed. "She could do better than that scrawny thing."

"Let's see *your* mate, then. If you're such a great matchmaker, he must be a real stud. Bring out Prince Charming!" Chloe demanded.

The woman turned up her nose at Chloe. "You are a ruthless fae, girl. You would do well as a merchant. Would you like to have a job?"

"Not here," Chloe replied shortly.

The shopkeeper rolled her eyes. "Very well. Can't convince anyone what's good for them."

That's all the woman said before scampering off to harass someone else. She got into an argument with a nearby shifter, and seemed absolutely delighted about it, like the conflict was the one thing that had made her happy all day.

Chloe held her head high. "You have to be direct with the fae. They don't respect you unless you're a rude asshole just like them. Acting nice is suspicious around here."

"Well, at least one of us can handle them," I said.

I turned to continue onward, but a small child blocked my path. "The royal wedding is approaching!"

The child shoved a newspaper toward me. He had to have at least a hundred more in the messenger bag he carried. The top of the paper read *The Annual Arcanea*, and the front page showed a photograph of a red-haired woman in a regal dress. I realized it was Emma, the queen, and the girl we'd helped long ago.

"Get the inside scoop on what the queen will be wearing on her big day!" the child pressed.

"Sorry, kid," I told him. "We don't have any money."

"You *must* stay informed!" he insisted, really trying to sell me on it. "Enemy forces remain close to Dolinska. Don't you want to know what the king and queen plan to do about it? You can read all about it on page three!"

"He said we're broke, kid," Chloe snapped. "Now scram."

The boy gave a huff, but he hurried away and proceeded to shove his paper into someone else's face. Jeez, everyone was really pushy here.

We kept our heads down and walked quickly, so that no one else would bother us. My heart pounded faster than our footsteps. If anyone saw through our ruse, we were dead.

I caught sight of a sign in English. *Enchanting Whispers*, it read, with an arrow pointing down an abandoned alleyway.

"This is it," I told the others, recalling the instructions Hattie had given to Headmistress Verla and Professor Warren.

We ducked out of the busy merchant district and followed a twisted alleyway until we reached a stone gargoyle shaped like a griffin. The sculpture had the head and wings of an eagle and the body of a lion, with talons on its front legs and heavy paws on the back. A doorway stood behind the gargoyle, which had to be the entrance to Enchanting Whispers.

Grant went to step around the gargoyle, but the statue *moved*. The griffin jumped in front of him, blocking his path.

Grant placed his hands on his hips. "What's this? Some sort of illusion. Ooh, I'm so scared."

He wiggled his fingers at the gargoyle sarcastically, then went to step around it again. The gargoyle snapped its stone beak at him, then swiped out its talons. Grant yelped and jumped back. The sharp stone caught the edge of his cloak, tearing it. Bella yelped and jumped out of Grant's cloak. She landed on her feet and hissed at the stone statue. The gargoyle paid the cat no mind and swiftly spun around, smacking Grant in the side of the head with its tail. It kicked out its back leg and hit Grant square in the chest. He went flying and landed flat on his back.

"Grant!" Talia rushed to his side.

Bella quickly followed and licked his face. Grant coughed to catch his breath, then wheezed, "I'm okay."

The griffin statue went still again, as if it hadn't come to life at all.

"This is where Hattie said to go, isn't it?" Talia asked as she helped Grant to his feet. He picked up Bella and tucked her back inside his cloak. *"Follow the winding path until you get to the stone gargoyle."*

"We're in the right place, but I don't think brute force is going to work," I said. "There has to be another way through that won't get our asses kicked."

Nadine approached the griffin statue, eyeing it from multiple angles. "What else did Hattie say? Something about griffin private parts? It certainly seemed strange coming from her at the time, but there's got to be something to it."

Chloe approached the statue and peered between its legs. "You think she meant it literally? Like, maybe we need to… stroke it."

Nadine crossed her arms. "If that's the case, the fae are sicker than I thought. I figured Hattie meant we need some sort of herb to give up as an offering."

"I don't know any herbs referring to griffins," Grant said.

"Then what could Hattie have meant by it?" Nadine wondered. "Unless… it's a password!"

Nadine walked straight up to the gargoyle and simply stated, "Griffin dick."

The gargoyle stepped aside, revealing the door behind it.

Chloe smirked. "Siona apparently has a sense of humor. I like her already."

I opened the door to reveal a small coffee shop that doubled as a bookstore. The smell of sweet pastries hit my nose, mixed with the scent of old books and cinnamon. Patrons sat at tables sipping coffee and nibbling on baked goods. A couple by the door met our eyes when we entered, and they quickly scrambled outside, like the sight of strangers terrified them.

A counter stood in the corner, and shelves of books lined the opposite wall. One of the shelves housed wands and crystals, which was strange, because the fae classified tools like that as dark magic. I couldn't imagine any of that was *legal* here.

We approached the counter, where a barista was handing a patron their order. The sign next to her read *Flavor of the Day: Spiced Chai.*

The barista had dark skin, long black hair, and a green crystal hanging around her neck. The woman wore a kind smile and called the patron by name as she told him to have a nice day.

She turned to us as we approached. "Welcome to Enchanting Whispers. How can I help you?"

"We're looking for Siona," I said lowly.

"I am Siona," she replied. "Someone must have sent you, or you wouldn't have made it past my spell."

"Who are you exactly?" Chloe demanded. "We need to know we can trust you."

"I'm a griffin sorceress who helps supernaturals seeking refuge in Dolinska," Siona explained. "I own this undercover shop and sell contraband magical items to people who need them, most specifically, dark fae. I'm not a dark fae myself, but my parents taught me that this world is better when everyone can coexist and find strength in our differences, so I do what I can to help. How can I be of service?"

I glanced around, and though no one was watching us, I lowered my voice anyway. "Hattie sent us."

Siona's features brightened. "I've been expecting you, though not for another few days."

"Plans changed," I admitted. "How can we be sure it's really you, and that you want to help us? I know the fae can trick us using illusions."

"I assure you I will help anyone, even witches," she said. "This is a safe place for all dark magic users, including the Unseelie fae who are attempting to gain their rights back in Malovia. I'm afraid they are still persecuted here."

I had the thought that maybe the fae weren't all bad like we thought, but that some of them were just as desperate as we were.

"I understand, however, that my word is not enough," Siona added, lowering her voice so only we could hear. "Therefore, I offer you this… Hattie's Familiar is a gray wolf, and her name is Everest."

I nearly reeled back in shock. This wasn't just any random bit of information. The fae took names very seriously, and Hattie wouldn't give her Familiar's name to just anyone. For Siona to know Everest's name was confirmation enough that we were speaking to the right person.

I glanced to my friends, and they shared a look of approval.

"We believe you," I said. "Perhaps we could speak in private?"

Siona gestured to another barista behind the counter. "Can you handle the register? I'll be back soon."

Then she turned to us and said, "Follow me."

Siona turned on her heel, and we followed her down a hallway behind the counter. She stopped in front of a bookcase and waved her hand. The sound of a lock disengaged, and the bookcase swung open like a door, revealing a narrow, twisted stairway behind it.

We ascended the dark stairwell to a small room above the shop. Shelves full of boxes and books lined the walls, and the ceiling was short. There were no windows—just a small lightbulb above us that barely lit the whole room. Labels on the boxes read things like *Highly Dangerous* and *Extremely Rare*. It was some sort of hidden attic where Siona must've kept the most illegal items in her shop.

A narrow doorway stood in front of us, and I heard unfamiliar voices beyond it.

"Our soldiers are on high alert," a man said. "They're looking to infiltrate Pruska, and anyone who is found to be disloyal to the king and queen will be eliminated. It's going to be difficult to get your friends past the border."

"We're already here," I stated as we entered the room.

This room was larger than the last, with a table in the center. Verla and Warren stood over it, looking at a map. Verla's cat, Odin, sat on the table and peered down at the map beside them.

A guy our age stood beside them, and his gaze snapped upward as we entered, like he sensed us there before we stepped into the room. He wore an expression of worry, and I didn't think it had anything to do with us. A girl who looked a lot like Siona stood next to him—his mate, I presumed. She had long hair and dark skin like Siona, with lighter patches of skin across her face and arms. The guy wore a military uniform, though the couple looked young enough to still be attending Arcanea University.

Verla looked shocked to see us. "What in the Goddess's name are you doing here? We were going to send for you when it was safe!"

"We didn't have a choice," I explained. "The priestesses captured Mandy and Tate, and we were almost caught escaping their rescue. I portaled us here, because right now Malovia is safer for us than Octavia Falls."

Professor Warren stood from his seat, alarmed. "Thank Alora you're all right."

Verla relaxed, but she still asked, "Nobody's hurt, are they?"

"We're all right," Nadine promised.

"Then our first objective is complete," the man said, nodding politely. "If it is a portal to the Underworld you seek, then we must get you there as soon as possible, before our troops move again."

Nadine stepped forward, eyeing the couple curiously. "You both look very familiar."

"You do, too," the girl said. "I believe we met you once, outside Octavia Falls about a year ago. Our friend needed help."

I recalled the group of fae that had passed through Octavia Falls the night Professor Daniels was hanged. There'd been eight of them, though most of my attention had been on their friend Ethan, who'd been in the final stages of a demon possession and couldn't stand on his own two feet. They'd asked us to help them through the protection spell to get to Hattie. Ethan would've died without her help.

"I'm Kiara, a sorceress of the griffin Faction," the girl said, before gesturing to the man beside her. "This is my griffin mate, Alexei. My sister Siona asked us to help you find a way to the Underworld. She said the fate of your coven relies on it."

We had to be careful, because the fae didn't typically do anything out of the kindness of their hearts. Even if they really did want to help us, we could be tricked into owing them back later, whether any of us intended that or not.

I recalled what Nadine had said the night we first crossed paths with Alexei and Kiara. *Pay us back later*, she'd said after we helped them pass into Octavia Falls. She had no idea an agreement like that could magically bind one to a fae. I wouldn't make the same mistake twice.

"We appreciate your help," I stated honestly. "But you must understand that we are wary to accept help from the fae simply out of generosity. Fae require an exchange, and in order to avoid entering into any magical contracts, I suggest we trade something for your help."

Alexei nodded. "Fair enough. What did you have in mind?"

I turned to Grant. "We should give them the Crock. It belongs to the fae. They're friends with the monarchs, so they can return it to them."

"I agree," Grant said. "The Crock of Death was never ours to begin with."

"You have the Crock?" Verla asked in astonishment.

I quickly recounted the events of the night, and how we'd stolen the Crock from the office where the priestesses had kept it. Verla's astonishment turned to horror, as if she wished she could've been there to protect us.

"Thank the Goddess you all made it out alive," Professor Warren said.

Verla wore an expression of warning. I didn't think she trusted the fae any more than I did. "Are you sure you want to do this, Lucas?"

"We've already retrieved the treasure inside," I said. "This was their goddess's cauldron, and we need to return it. I'd expect them to do the same for us. I'd rather fulfill a deal now than owe them later."

Verla must've agreed with me, because she stepped aside. "Very well. If it will get us closer to the Oaken Wands, then we'll do what we must."

Grant conjured the Crock and set it on the table.

Kiara's eyes went wide as she looked over the Crock. "I thought Milonna's Cauldron was merely a legend! Our people will be pleased to have it back. This gesture is quite a sufficient exchange. We'll keep it in the royal treasury, where it belongs."

"So how do we get to the Abyss?" Chloe wondered.

"Portals to the Underworld are difficult to locate," Alexei said. "They can open and close at random as monsters slip through. However, there is a dark pit our friends found a while ago. We haven't been down there to investigate it, but we know there's dark magic there. The pit is guarded by a terrible beast. If you have any hope of finding what you're looking for, this is the place to start. We've been discussing how to best get you there without being spotted."

"Why not ask the king and queen?" Chloe asked. "They seem sympathetic, and they surely have resources."

"Ethan and Emma *are* sympathetic, but their rule is already insecure with the rival monarch opposing them," Siona explained. "If the people knew they were making alliances with witches, they'd certainly be overthrown."

Kiara wore an apologetic expression. "We want to help you, but not at the cost of our own monarchy. You must understand—my mate and I have agreed to help you, but you must swear that the king and queen can't know about this, nor can any others who aren't inside this room. Emma and Ethan know that my mate and I are helping witches who may be stuck inside Malovia, but they do not know who or why, and I believe it's better that way. We are unable to lie to them, so keeping quiet is the only way."

"Why can't you lie to them?" Nadine asked. "I mean, you shouldn't lie to your king and queen, but why can't they know anyway?"

"Our goddess set us on a very important quest, to find items of great power," Alexei explained. "Kiara and I once swore a powerful magical oath not to keep secrets from our friends, so we are unable to lie to them about anything pertaining to this quest. But aiding you has nothing to do with finding these items, and the king and queen can't be distracted with trying to help witches when the country is on the line."

"What about the Crock? They're going to ask questions when it shows up in the royal treasury," Chloe said sarcastically.

"We will tell them that a witch who stole the Crock from her priestesses gave it to us in exchange for directions through Malovia. It is the truth, after all. Once the revolution has come to an end, we will explain everything to them. Otherwise, this secret will die with us," Kiara insisted.

"There's a merchant trade route that goes through here," Siona said, running her finger along the map. "We can take my wagon and hide the witches in the back. You have disguised your scent, but taking this many people out of the city at once when the revolution is in full swing will raise suspicion. The problem will be getting past the checkpoint here. Most fae aren't allowed out of the city, for their own protection."

Alexei pressed his lips together. "I'm certain I can persuade the officers on duty, but we should wait until nightfall. We'll have a better chance of getting out of the city when most fae are sleeping."

"In the meantime, you should all rest, as you have a long journey ahead of you," Siona suggested.

I was grateful for the suggestion, because we'd had a *long* night. Siona was kind enough to provide us with a meal after we cleaned up in the bathroom. She fed us breaded pork cutlets and some sort of potato dumplings called *pierogi*, which were absolutely delicious. I really didn't like the fae, but I had to admit, they had some damn good food.

Once our bellies were full, Siona led us to another small room, where it was obvious Verla and Warren had been staying. Two twin beds covered in warm blankets stood on opposite sides of the room. Siona cast an illusion, and several more beds appeared. I reached for the closest mattress and was shocked to find it was solid. I thought for sure my hand would go straight through it.

"The illusions will remain solid until you wake," Siona explained. "Now get some shut eye. You're going to need it."

Nadine and I snuggled up in one of the beds, and Isa and Oliver curled at our feet. It felt like we were out in moments. We must've all been really tired, because we didn't wake until after sunset. Just as Siona said, the beds disappeared before my eyes once we climbed out of them.

Siona fed us another meal, then led us downstairs and through a door at the back of her shop, which was empty now. We entered a private stable, and I stopped in my tracks when I spotted a white alicorn with a golden horn. Nadine came to a halt beside me, unable to take her eyes off the magnificent creature. His horn glowed a sunny yellow hue, and his white mane sparkled.

"Is something wrong?" Siona asked.

I shook my head. "It's just… I've seen magical creatures in *Hok'evale*, but I don't think I'll ever get used to it."

"This is not just any alicorn, but an alicorn shifter," Siona said as she stroked the alicorn's nose. "He is a dear Unseelie friend, but you will understand if I do not give you his name."

I couldn't say I understood why the fae were so particular about names, but I respected that it was a big deal to them. To them, names were power, so it made sense why she didn't want to share his name.

"Into the back—all of you." Siona ushered us into the back of a large horse-drawn cart, while Alexei and Kiara readied the reins. We had to lay down, and it was a tight fit. Siona draped a large canvas tarp over us and our cats to conceal us, then hopped onto the seat in front beside her sister.

Soon, the wagon began moving beneath us. We rode through the streets of Dolinska, to the opposite side of the city than we'd entered. It seemed to take longer than it had to walk to Enchanting Whispers. Dolinska was huge, and crossing it was no easy matter.

"We're almost to the edge of the city," Alexei whispered. "It's just past Arcanea University."

I'd never seen the fae college, and I was too tempted to pass up the opportunity. I lifted my head to peek past the corner of the tarp. Arcanea University was absolutely massive. Behind a golden gate resided a massive stone palace, with an elaborate garden, tall towers, and intimidating statues of shifters and sorceresses. It was the most expensive and grand building that I'd ever seen, and it made Miriam College appear small.

Voices came from up ahead, and the carriage slowed. "State your business and uncover your merchandise for inspection," an officer ordered as we came upon the exit point of the city. Footsteps approached us, coming far too close for my liking. I held my breath, and Nadine stilled beside me.

Alexei hopped down from the front of the carriage and spoke in a strong tone. "That won't be necessary. This shipment contains important military supplies for our troops stationed around the city and has been ordered by the king."

"All shipments are subject to inspection," the officer argued. The tarp rustled as he reached out for it, but Alexei jumped in front of him.

"Do you really think you know the king's wishes better than I do?" Alexei sneered. "I am a general of the king's royal guard."

He must've flashed one of his military badges, because the officer quickly stepped away from the wagon, "No, sir. You may pass."

I let out my breath, and the carriage began moving beneath us again. After a few minutes, the terrain turned bumpy, as if Siona had led us off the normal path. Darkness enveloped us from all angles, until we finally came to a halt. The fae hopped off the carriage, then yanked the tarp off from us.

We all sat up, breathing a collective sigh of relief. The air under that tarp had been hot, and I was starting to feel claustrophobic. I jumped over the side of the carriage, then helped Nadine down. Our cats hopped out of the wagon and followed at our feet. Verla cast a witch light and tossed it into the air to illuminate the forest ahead.

We stood at the edge of a steep hole in the ground, and a dark forest surrounded us at all angles. I could hear the sound of a stream nearby, but otherwise the forest seemed dark and foreboding. We couldn't see far into the cave entrance, and it seemed like the darkness lasted forever. The pit appeared to swallow light completely, as if it were a black hole waiting to suck *us* inside, too. All I could make out under Verla's witch light was the piles of boulders and rocks surrounding the hole opening, which was big enough for a small dragon to fit through.

It certainly looked like an entrance to the Abyss—or at the very least, a monster's lair. It wasn't the kind of place you wanted to explore. Just looking into its depths gave me the chills.

Kiara pointed into the massive hole. "What you seek is within the pit."

Nadine started for the opening. She'd already braced herself against the rocks before any of us could move. "Well, are you coming?"

"My mate and I cannot accompany you," Kiara stated. "We are important people in Malovia, and our absence will be noticed. We can't risk alerting anyone of your location or what you might be doing, so we must go. We'll come back for you at sunrise."

"I'll wait for you here in case something goes wrong," Siona offered. "But I can't stay long, so please hurry."

"One more thing," Alexei added. "These woods are full of monsters, some of which have made that cavern their home. Beware of the questing beast."

"The questing beast?" Nadine asked warily.

"You will know it if you see it," Alexei said. "Good luck."

That was all he said before he turned and shifted into a griffin before our very eyes. One second a man was standing before us, and then feathers were everywhere, drifting down slowly to the forest floor. A massive bird stood before us, and I swore when he spread his wings, they were wider than The Hearse was long.

Alexei was an impressive creature, and he looked incredibly strong. No wonder the king had assigned him as a general in the royal army.

Kiara swung her leg over Alexei's back and waved goodbye. Alexei then pumped his wings and took off toward the skies.

Nadine's gaze followed them upward, but she looked skeptical, like she was trying to decide if they were leading us into a trap. She must've made up her mind to take that chance, because she turned her gaze back toward the rocks and continued her descent into the pit.

Grant leaned over to me. "It's quite big; a dragon could fit through there. You don't think this questing beast is that big, do you?"

"It doesn't matter how big it is," Nadine called up to him. "Do you really think it can take on seven witches?"

"The fae train their whole lives to hunt these monsters," Grant argued, his voice rising several pitches. "If the fae haven't killed the beast yet, what makes you think we can?"

Nadine shrugged. "Call it a hunch. We need to get to those Wands before the priestesses do, and nothing—not even a questing beast—is going to stand in our way."

I started following Nadine downward. The incline was so steep I had to lower myself to my ass to shimmy down the rocks. "We can either stay out here talking about it, or we can enter the pit and see what we find. Besides, I don't see any beast guarding the opening. Maybe it's already dead."

"Or out on a lunch break, hunting for its next meal," Grant squeaked, shooting a glance around the forest.

Chloe smirked. "Then let's get going before it comes back… unless you're too chicken."

Grant hurried to follow us. "No way."

"Then we better get moving," Professor Warren said as he helped Verla down the rocks.

The cats moved with agility, jumping from rock to rock until they were the ones leading the way. Verla guided her witch light in front of us, illuminating the rocky sides of the cave. I could've sworn her witch light looked dimmer than it should have, as if the darkness inside the pit fed at it.

Nadine and I helped each other down the slope. The rocks were loose, and I nearly lost my footing more than once. Pebbles tumbled around us as we gently maneuvered onward, the sound echoing off the rock around us. The temperature dropped several degrees as we traveled deeper underground.

Eventually, the tunnel floor evened out, until we could walk upright without using our hands to steady ourselves. We must've been walking for half an hour, and we'd seen nothing but rocks and dirt. There weren't any other tunnels branching off from this one. The tunnel ahead seemed never-ending.

"This has to be some sort of joke," Grant said, his voice echoing off the cave walls. "I bet the fae are laughing at us right now. There's nothing here."

"I'm sure if journeying to the Abyss was quick and simple, the fae would've found a way to utilize the realm to their advantage," Chloe said. "We just have to keep walking."

"Hang on, what was that?" Talia asked, pointing ahead.

Verla narrowed her gaze ahead. "It looks like the tunnel widens."

"Not that," Talia said. "I thought I saw something… sparkle?"

Verla shifted her witch light, and I caught sight of something in the distance, as if reflecting off water…

Or eyes.

I pulled Nadine closer to me, and she shivered. I lifted my hand, and a shield bloomed in front of us. We waited for a beat but heard nothing. Slowly, we crept forward.

As we approached the area where the tunnel widened, more shimmering objects came into view. They weren't the eyes of mysterious cave-dwelling creatures. They were *jewels*.

The cavern widened to reveal the lair of some sort of jewel-hoarding beast—a dragon, perhaps, or the questing beast Alexei had mentioned. There was no beast in sight, just treasures the monster had stored for safekeeping.

Piles of coins scattered the cavern, along with various pieces of jewelry. A sword lay on the ground, though it seemed it'd been down here so long it barely had any shine left to it. Grant picked up a twisted silver crown with blue gemstones and inspected it.

"Don't touch anything," Professor Warren warned cautiously. "We don't know what kind of magic or curses may be on these objects."

Grant quickly tossed the crown aside.

Our cats slunk forward, sniffing the cave floor. They surrounded three large pits in the ground. At first, I thought they were new tunnels opening below us, but when I gazed into them, I found that these pits were bowl-shaped, like they were once pools that no longer held any water. They weren't very deep—six feet max. The cats circled the pits to nowhere, seeming particularly interested in them.

"I don't see any entrance to the Abyss," Grant said. "This is it—there's no way forward. The only way out of here is back the way we came. We've literally hit a dead end."

"Perhaps that's a clue that things aren't quite what they seem here," Verla said thoughtfully. She circled one of the dry pools, following the cats' lead. "There are words carved into the edge of these pools. It's written in Unseelie runes."

"Can you read it?" Nadine asked.

Verla shook her head. "No, but I may know a spell that will translate it for us. Everyone stand back."

Verla raised her hand. Magic swirled out of her palms, shimmering off the riches surrounding us. "*Verbis revelare!*" she shouted, bringing her hands down in one swift motion.

A loud *poof* sounded, and a gust of wind whooshed through the tunnel. The cats jumped in unison, and Oliver ducked behind my leg. Magic erupted inside the pools, billowing smoke upward toward the cavern ceiling. As the smoke cleared, I saw that the runes had rearranged themselves into letters.

Professor Warren's eyebrows shot up, and he gazed at Verla in admiration. "I might say, that was quite an impressive spell. I have yet to learn it."

"How did you do that?" Nadine wondered.

"Witches can do many things with enough power," Verla replied. "You didn't think we could just cast shields and unlock doors, did you?"

"You're going to have to teach me that," Chloe said.

I peered into the empty pool and began reading the carving aloud. *"Beware those who enter the Pits of Despair, for your worst fears lie along the path to the Underworld. Speak now your Unseelie intention.* What does that mean?"

I took a step back, waiting for someone to answer, but they all shared a puzzled expression.

Nadine tapped her chin. "These must be the Pits of Despair. I'm assuming the Underworld is another term for hell? Alexei kept calling it that."

Talia nodded. "It's the fae's term for it."

"So the pits are a path to the Underworld," Nadine determined. "So… could these pits be an entrance to the Abyss? Maybe they aren't pits at all, but an illusion."

Nadine bent to pick a coin off the ground, then tossed into the pit like she was throwing a coin into a wishing well. The coin clanked against the stone, then settled at the bottom of the pit. It obviously wasn't an illusion.

*"Speak now your Unseelie intention,"* Professor Warren repeated. "It's asking us to perform a spell, perhaps to open a portal."

"But the Unseelie are a type of fae, which means our witch magic won't work," Chloe pointed out.

"Actually, it might be just the magic we need," Talia said thoughtfully. "There are two classifications of fae—Seelie and Unseelie. Seelie draw magic from within themselves, while the Unseelie take magic from outside energy sources, or utilize tools like crystals and wands. The fae would consider Unseelie magic *dark*, just as they would classify witch magic. The translation may not mean Unseelie magic literally, but *dark* magic. By technicality, what the fae believe to be dark magic is the kind of magic witches use, so we should be able to do something here."

Chloe placed her hands on her hips. "Okay, say we could cast a spell to open a portal to the Abyss. How can we be sure the portals will stay open so we can return?"

"We will have to sustain the spell," Verla said.

"So someone has to stay behind?" Chloe wondered. "We have a better chance in the Abyss if we go together."

"Someone *has* to stay behind to sustain the spell and keep the portals open, but it does not have to be one of us." Verla's gaze turned toward the cats circled around the pits. "Cats have one foot in the spirit realm at all times, and therefore can assist in spellwork. If we succeed at casting this spell and a portal appears, the cats must stay behind to keep the gateway open."

"Then let's get to work," I stated.

The seven of us circled the largest pit and conjured our wands, before joining hands. Each of our cats sat at their respective person's feet.

"We need a simple incantation," Verla suggested. *"Our dark intention is simply this: We seek passage to the Abyss."*

We repeated her words in unison, and tendrils of magic surrounded our circle, blowing Nadine's hair back beside me. I could feel the magic growing, pulsing through the cavern as we spoke the incantation a second time. The cats peered into the center of the pit, until their forms began to glow with the power of our magic.

We spoke the incantation a third time, and I witnessed movement from deep within the pit. A dark, slimy liquid bubbled up from the center, rushing into the pit as if spilling out of hell itself. I shot a glance to the pit behind me and saw that the sludge was filling that one as well. Each second that passed, the pits filled another inch, bubbling and snapping with a tar-like substance.

"Uh… that doesn't look like a portal," Grant said warily.

"You must trust the process," Verla stated calmly.

The sludge continued to rise to the lip of the pit, and several of us took cautious steps backward.

"I'm trying to be calm, but if that stuff keeps rising that fast, this place is going to be flooded," Grant pressed.

Just as the sludge was about to tip over the edge of the pit, it stopped rising. Several tense beats passed as we waited to see if the sludge would do anything else, but nothing happened.

"So… now what?" Talia started, but she was cut off as the sludge in the largest pit blasted upward toward the ceiling.

We leapt back, and black liquid splashed down on us. A clump landed on the ground with a heavy *splat,* and then the entire pit of sludge began to bulge upward.

The clump moved… and I realized it wasn't a clump of sludge at all. It was the leg of a beast crawling out of the pit!

"Everybody back!" Professor Warren shouted. He grabbed Nadine and me, shoving us behind him. Verla stood at his side, a battle orb at the ready. Grant, Talia, and Chloe ended up on the other side of the pit, their backs against the wall of the cave. Our cats stepped aside, their forms still glowing with the magic of the spell.

Nadine peered over Professor Warren's shoulder. "That must be the questing beast. And it's in our way!"

The creature pressed a hoof to the cave floor and hoisted itself out of the pit. Black sludge dripped off its form, showing patches of leopard spots on its fur. The creature had a serpent's head and a horse-like body, with a long narrow tail that whipped from side to side. It opened its mouth and bared its sharp fangs at us. My hands trembled as I pulled Nadine closer to me.

Professor Warren blasted off a battle orb straight into the creature's mouth. The magic sizzled through the air, but the beast did nothing except shake its head. The questing beast narrowed its eyes at us and let out a loud roar.

"Not helpful!" I cried. "All you did was piss it off."

Professor Warren took another step backward, shoving Nadine and me closer to the wall. "If you have any better ideas, I'm all ears."

"It's got to be magical to withstand your spell, right?" Nadine asked. "If I can touch it, I can withdraw its magic. I've done it before with other monsters. Cover me."

Before I could stop her, Nadine slipped past Professor Warren, aiming her sights straight on the beast. Nadine intended to grab the monster, but before she could, the questing beast kicked out its front leg. Nadine let out a pained *oof* as she landed on her back.

"Nadine, no!" The sound of Verla's cry echoed off the walls of the cavern. She leapt forward the same time the questing beast snapped its fangs at Nadine. Verla lifted her arm protectively, but her shield failed as the beast snapped its jaws forward so fast that he blasted straight through her spell.

The beast's fangs sank into Verla's arm. Its jaws clamped down tightly, even as the rest of us aimed deadly spells at the beast all at once. The spells had no effect on the creature, other than to royally piss it off.

The questing beast wrenched its head to the side, then the other, dragging Verla along the floor. I heard the crunch of bones, and then came her cries of pain. Blood spurted over the cave floor. It all happened so fast that only mere seconds had passed.

A shield blasted from my palms, smacking straight into the beast's nose. He dropped Verla as my spell sent him spiraling over one of the pits. He landed hard against the wall of the cave and slumped to the ground.

"Clarice!" Nadine screamed. Verla collapsed, and Nadine rushed to her side.

The questing beast wasn't done with us yet, though. It shook its head and began to rise from the ground. Its eyes narrowed on Verla, like it'd already had one taste of her blood and wanted to finish the job. The creature jumped, soaring over one of the pits, its fangs aimed straight for Verla's throat.

Professor Warren didn't hesitate for a moment. He caught sight of the sword beside the pile of treasure, and he dove for it. He snatched up the sword then leapt in front of Verla, aiming the blade straight at the questing beast.

The sound of tearing flesh and a pained yelp filled the air. The beast immediately backpedaled a few steps. The sword remained lodged in its flesh, right above its front leg. Professor Warren's aim hadn't been precise enough to kill the creature, but it'd slow it down for sure.

The beast's back legs slipped into one of the pits. It let out a loud cry as it tried to climb its way back out, but with an injured front leg, it couldn't manage. The beast slipped into the pit, and the black sludge swallowed it up as it fell backward into the hole it came from.

We all rushed over to Verla. My stomach bottomed out when I saw the blood dripping down her arm. The beast's fangs had sliced deep twisted cuts through Verla's forearm, leaving chunks of hanging flesh behind. The white of bone poked through the gruesome wounds.

Warren stripped off his coat and wrapped it around Verla's arm as her whole body trembled. Odin lay at Verla's side, meowing loudly.

"Why did you do that? You didn't have to save me!" Nadine shouted. I could see the pain written across her face. She blamed herself for getting Verla hurt. "That thing could've killed you! You should've let it bite me."

"I would've snapped you in half," Verla argued.

"It almost did that to *you*," Nadine shouted.

Verla winced as she pulled her injured arm closer to her chest. "I'm stronger than you think. If it didn't hurt me, it would've hurt you, and I couldn't let that happen. You need to survive, Nadine, for the coven's sake."

Tears leaked from Nadine's eyes. She didn't want to see anyone get hurt, especially for her sake. It was too similar to what had happened to Helena.

Verla's eyes drooped. "We must follow the beast through to the Abyss…"

Her words trailed off, and her head lolled to the side, like she couldn't quite see straight. She'd lost a lot of blood, but this was something else…

"That creature was venomous!" I realized.

Horror filled Professor Warren's features. "We'll need an antidote to counteract the venom."

"Great," I replied sarcastically. "Where are we going to find that?"

"We'll have to turn back and request help from the fae," Warren insisted. "We know nothing of questing beasts and don't know how long it takes for that venom to take hold of her bloodstream. If we don't act now, she could be dead within the hour. We have no choice but to leave."

"No," Nadine said firmly, her mind already made up. "We aren't going to get another chance to return to Malovia, and we aren't leaving here without the Oaken Wands. You can carry Verla back to the entrance, where Siona can provide help, but the five of us must go on."

I didn't have to read her mind to know what she was thinking. Nadine didn't give a shit about the Oaken Wands right now. All she cared about was Verla, but Nadine had told me she didn't want people dying to protect her. If we left now, then Verla suffered for Nadine—and Nadine alone. If we kept going, then Verla's sacrifice would be in the name of the Oaken Wands. Nadine didn't want anyone else getting hurt for her.

"Nadine's the chosen one," I said. "It's up to her."

"It's what has to be done," Nadine insisted. "Any time we sit around talking about it is wasted time."

We all knew what that meant. Professor Warren had to get Verla back to the cave entrance as soon as possible, or it could be too late.

Chloe caught on. "Nadine's right. We don't have a choice."

"All right," Professor Warren agreed reluctantly. "I suppose there is no other option. Clarice and I will be at the entrance when you return."

Warren stood and lifted Verla in his arms. Odin cried out and followed them back up the tunnel.

Nadine stared after them long after the sound of their footsteps faded. I wrapped an arm around her, and she leaned in to me, sniffling. "Verla shouldn't have stepped in front of me. The creature was coming for us. We didn't have time to talk out a plan. I knew what I was doing. I could've weakened it."

"Don't beat yourself up, Nad," Grant told her gently. "Verla's going to be all right."

Nadine scoffed bitterly. "Yeah, so long as I'm not there to kill her, I'm sure she'll be just fine. Can't say the same for the rest of you though, since you're traveling with me. Who else wants to die for me?"

Talia reached out to squeeze her shoulder. "That's not going to happen, because we're all going to walk out of there alive."

"You can't know that," Nadine argued.

Talia conjured the Seer Wand, and the tip began to glow. "Yes, I can. I can't see what we're getting ourselves into down there, but I know we're going to make it."

Talia could've been lying for all any of us knew, but nobody questioned her, because we all wanted to believe she was telling the truth. It was the hope we needed to push onward.

Slowly, Nadine nodded and got to her feet. She approached the largest pit and peered into the dark slime. "We named our movement The Coven's Shield, and the coven needs us now to get those Wands. Let's keep moving."

Grant gazed into the pit beside us. "We're like a band of superheroes. Might I suggest we call ourselves the *Shield Squad*?"

Chloe frowned. "We don't need a dumb squad name. We just need to get this done. To hell and back…"

"Even if it kills us," I added with a heavy sigh.

Talia gingerly approached the pits. "Into the Abyss?"

I nodded, and Nadine and I spoke in unison. "Into the Abyss."

Nadine took my hand, and we leapt into the darkness of the pit.

# nadine

TWELVE

Darkness in every sense of the word enveloped me from every angle, and Lucas's hand slipped from my grasp. Blackness blanketed my vision, and the dark magic of the sludge seemed to permeate through my skin, soaking into my body until it felt like the darkness had filled my lungs and settled deep into my stomach. I sank deeper into the pit, expecting to come out the other side, but I only kept sinking deeper and deeper…

Voices filled my ears.

*You got Verla hurt.*

*You shouldn't have let Grammy leave the house.*

*You should've been quicker.*

*It's your fault she died.*

*You're going to get everyone else killed, too.*

This had to be some sort of trick or curse. I knew I needed to protect myself from the voices saying these awful things, but I found no light within me to outshine them. Everything they said was true.

I had the thought that I didn't want to live with that truth. If I had to die down here, so be it. Maybe I deserved it.

It was a strange thought, because I'd never thought that way before. My survival instinct kicked in, and I tried to swim upward, but the sludge was so heavy I could hardly move my limbs, let alone swim through the viscous material.

My lungs compressed, and it became clear in that moment that the voices were correct. I was going to suffocate, and so were my friends. It was all my fault.

How naive was I to think getting to hell would be so easy? Of course we had to die to get there. And now because of me, my friends would suffer for eternity.

The thought made me want to give up entirely. My limbs stopped thrashing, and all I could do was sink…

Hands landed on me, and I felt myself being dragged through the thick slime. The weight of the darkness seemed unbearable.

Then warm air hit my face, and I gasped a breath. My eyes shot open to see Lucas above me, dragging me out of the pit and onto solid ground. Black sludge covered his body, and his features were illuminated by an ominous red glow. The corners of my vision blurred, and all I could see was him. My whole body trembled as he wrapped me in his arms. I was so grateful to feel him close to me.

"Are you all right?" Lucas asked breathlessly.

Tears streamed down my face as I curled into his chest. "I'm sorry, Lucas! I didn't mean for anyone to get hurt. I thought the pits would lead us to the Abyss."

"Nad," Lucas said gently. "Look around you."

Slowly, I drew myself away from his chest, and my vision cleared. We were no longer in the cavern. A dark, desolate landscape stretched as far as the eye could see. The ground was made of black stone, with cracks between it where glowing red lava flowed. Bubbling pits of black tar scattered the landscape, and steam hissed from geysers nearby. The sky was completely black, with no stars in sight. Against the light of glowing volcanoes erupting in the distance, I could see jagged black rocks rising toward the sky like swords poised to attack an enemy. The howling wind carried the sound of faint tortured screams. My guts clenched as the darkness of hell rocked my soul.

A trail of sludge mixed with droplets of blood led away from one of the pits. The questing beast was long gone, though judging by the blood trail, it was certainly still alive.

Grant and Chloe knelt at the pit next to ours and dragged Talia to the surface. She coughed and sputtered, but relief overtook me when I saw they were all alive.

"Is everyone okay?" I asked.

Talia glanced around at the desolate landscape. "As good as one can be in hell, I suppose."

I turned back to Lucas. "How did you get out of the pit? I couldn't move."

Lucas shrugged, like it'd been all too easy for him. "I gave into it."

Those words held a darker meaning than he would say out loud, and my heart sank for him. He'd been living with these thoughts for so long that he didn't even try fighting them anymore.

"I'm sorry," I told him.

"Don't be." Lucas helped me to my feet. "Let's get moving. The Wands have to be around here somewhere."

"Here, let me help," Chloe offered. She lifted her hand and used her telekinesis to drag the sludge from our bodies, leaving us dry again.

"Where do we start?" Grant asked.

I peered through a cloud of steam, where a shadowed figure took shape in the distance. I pointed. "Maybe we should ask him."

Chloe placed her hands on her hips. "You really want to get tortured on your first day here?"

"We need to start somewhere," I insisted. "Do you have a better idea?"

Chloe eyed me a moment, before she said, "Fine, but you're doing the talking. *I'm* not about to piss off an eternal being who gets off on torture."

As we started the trek across the landscape, I noticed the figure was moving—not walking, but *floating* across the landscape. When we got closer, I realized he was standing on a wooden boat, floating down a stream of lava. I wasn't sure how the boat didn't burst into flames; it had to be a magical boat. He wore a long cloak with a hood that covered his face, and he carried a long staff that he used to push the boat along.

"Excuse me, sir!" I called, flagging him down.

He kept his gaze ahead. I didn't think he'd heard me. "Sir, please! We need your help!"

Again, there was no response.

I quickened my pace, and the others followed until we were running to catch up with the man. We reached the edge of the lava river, and I paused to catch my breath.

Lucas waved his arms at the man. "Hey! Over here! We need your help!"

The man dipped his staff into the lava and continued pushing himself along. I thought he was going to float by us, until I realized he was pushing himself to the bank. He stopped alongside us and lifted his head for the first time.

He appeared old, with wrinkles across his face and hunched shoulders. Beneath his hood, I noticed his ears were pointed.

He was an Elf. The Elves had died out long ago on Earth, so he must've been here a while.

He frowned and spoke flatly. "I heard you the first time."

"We just got here, and we don't know where we are," I said. "Can you help us?"

He gestured around. "This place goes by many names. The Eternal Torment, the Underworld, hell—take your pick."

"Yes, but we don't know what *part* of hell we're in," I stated. "We're witches looking for the Abyss."

"Why didn't you say so?" the man asked. "I am the Ferryman. It's my job, honor, and pleasure to ferry you to where you need to go. The witches' village is downstream, the furthest region from here. It will be a long journey, but not one I'm unable to make. Climb aboard."

"What's the catch?" Chloe asked before any of us could move. "You're a creature of this place. You must have some ulterior motive."

"Not all who reside in this realm are evil," he stated. "I choose to be here, as it is my eternal purpose to escort people to their darkest fears, so that they may conquer them."

"So, you aren't condemned here?" Talia asked curiously.

"Blessed, no," the Ferryman said. "I am here to help souls gain clarity so they can ascend to the next level. Nobody living here is condemned, only visiting temporarily, in order to learn more about themselves. Anyone can move through the spiritual realms if they wish—some go up, some go down. Some who started up may go down, and some who started down may go up."

"So you can still make it to Alora if you start in the Abyss?" Grant asked.

"Yes, and it works the other way around, too," the Ferryman answered. "The spirit realm is always in movement, in a constant state of change."

I turned to Chloe. "I don't think we have a choice but to trust him. We need to get those Wands and bring them back to Octavia Falls, so we can reunite the coven."

The Ferryman laughed. "I'm afraid the Earthly realm doesn't work the same as the others. You cannot go back once you have died…"

He trailed off, eyeing us curiously. "Except… you have not died. How is this possible? You shouldn't be here."

"We came in through a portal, and we're not leaving until we find what we came for," Lucas stated firmly.

The Ferryman looked down at the remnants of sludge on Lucas's shoes. "It is not my job to ferry the living."

"But we need your help!" I begged. "You said the Abyss is the furthest region from here. How far will we have to walk?"

The Ferryman frowned. "You said your purpose here is to help your coven?"

"Yes," I said desperately.

He nodded kindly. "Then I will help you. But since you are living, you will have to pay a fee."

"I knew there was a catch," Chloe protested. "You want a piece of our souls, don't you?"

"A piece of your magic will suffice," the Ferryman stated. "Consider it insurance, to assure me of your intentions."

"Will this work?" I asked, conjuring a small crystal infused with my magic.

The Ferryman nodded. "This is enough to grant you passage, but I will need one from each of you."

Everyone conjured one of their crystals and handed them to the Ferryman. He pocketed each one into his cloak, then stepped aside to welcome us aboard. The boat wasn't very big, but it had two slabs of wood nailed across the top that served as benches. We took our seats, and the Ferryman used his staff to push us away from the bank. Whatever magic this boat was made from kept the heat of the lava from touching us. We began to float down the lava river, past the geysers and volcanoes.

The river flowed into a boiling lake of lava, and the screams around us intensified. I heard the harrowing cry of a baby wailing in the distance, as if crying out for its mother. The mere thought of a child being out here all alone shattered my heart into a million pieces. I looked around for the source of the voices, but I saw no one.

I turned to the Ferryman behind me. "Where are those screams coming from? We can hear people screaming, but we can't see them."

"That is something you wouldn't understand," he said ominously.

"How can a baby be trapped here?" Chloe wondered, shifting uncomfortably at the sound of the child's cries. "Children are innocent. They don't belong here."

"There are many ways to end up in this realm—and not all of them by individual choice," the Ferryman stated. "Some can be condemned here by the evil choices of others."

I shuddered to think of who would condemn a child here. The priestesses were able to make deals with demons for the souls of the coven, because the coven is their kin. I assumed the same could be true of others. It disgusted me that there were people in this supernatural world like the priestesses who would do such a thing.

My heart seemed to shrink, shielding me from the disturbing nature of the realm. I leaned into Lucas, and he pulled me tighter to his chest.

We passed by an island filled with all kinds of monsters. "This is the realm of monsters, where all demons and ghastly beasts are born," the Ferryman explained. "From here, they crawl out from the Pits and venture onto Earth."

From this distance, I could make out various humanoid demons with devilish features, along with animal-like monsters with twisted limbs and leathery skin hanging off their bones. The monsters fought one another, using sharp teeth and deadly claws to slice each other to bits, while other demons cheered for their slaughter.

A man on the back of a horse lifted a canine-like monster and threw it into the boiling lava. The pained screams of the monster echoed across the lake. The lava began to bubble upward, and large, heavy paws clawed at the surface. The canine emerged from the lava larger than before. It was at least a thousand pounds or more, roaring as it climbed back to the island and aimed its razor-sharp teeth at the horse rider.

I looked closer, until I realized the man and the horse were one and the same. The horse's head had only one eye. The entire creature's skin appeared to have been peeled off, revealing the raw flesh underneath and black blood coursing through its veins. The arms of the human half were spindly and long, with knuckles that dragged on the ground when he walked.

The Ferryman shuddered. "A *nuckelavee*. Vile creatures. Should one ever escape this place, they will bring drought with them and destroy crops with a single breath. Keep your cattle away, for the poison in their lungs can also kill living beings. Many epidemics have been attributed to these creatures. They are shapeshifters of the sea and terrified of fresh water, so if you ever cross one's path, it's best to find yourself to the nearest stream."

The canine leapt for the *nuckelavee*, slicing its claws across the face of the horse. Blood spurted across the blackened ground. The human half of the *nuckelavee* caught the canine around the neck. The *nuckelavee* opened its mouth to breathe into the canine's face, and the massive monster fell to the ground, gasping for breath as it was poisoned.

"Let's hope we never run across one," Grant said in a shaky tone.

The Ferryman gestured ahead of us. "We are now entering *Aiya Nocshun.*"

"I heard about this place from the Elementai culture," Chloe said brightly, like we were on some field trip and not being ferried across hell.

Ahead, the sea of lava met a shore of sand. The Ferryman guided the boat to the shore. Just as I thought we were going to hit solid ground, the sand began shifting beneath us. It flowed like a river, guiding us from the lava lake and through a desert.

Here, the landscape was dry as far as the eye could see, and the dirt cracked at the surface. The blazing sun was too bright. People walked around aimlessly, calling out names with heartbreaking cries. The sound of beastly wails filled the air, and I spotted magical creatures searching the landscape, but whatever they sought seemed to be out of reach.

"What are they looking for?" Lucas asked.

"Each other," the Ferryman said. "In Elementai culture, the worst thing that can happen is to lose your loved ones. The elementals trapped here cannot see the ones they love. But if they only opened their eyes, they'd find each other again. Your soul is always right there, if you're willing to look."

"Can't we help them?" Talia asked.

"We could try, but it would do no good if they are not willing to listen. Observe. Hey!" The Ferryman shouted so loud it made me jump. "Your Familiar is right there! Look at him!"

He pointed, but the woman he spoke to didn't acknowledge him. She walked alongside a unicorn, but continued forward like she couldn't see it, stumbling across the landscape as she sobbed. My stomach twisted into knots listening to her tragic screams.

The Ferryman shrugged. "See? It's no use."

"But you said they could get out if they wanted to," Talia pointed out. "Have you ever actually seen someone who's left this place and went to a better realm?"

"Yes. Lots of people make it to the Blessed Haven," the Ferryman said matter-of-factly. "Most, I would say."

"What's that?" Grant asked.

"You would know it as Alora," the Ferryman said. "Alora is one place inside the Blessed Haven, but there are many others—the Great Hunting Grounds of fae lore, and the Ancestral Lands of Elementai culture. The Blessed Haven is a blissful realm, where all people go when they are ready."

"What about humans?" Chloe asked. "Is this place only for supernaturals, or do people without magic come here, too?"

"That would depend on what religion they follow," the Ferryman said. "There are multiple realms within this land, magical and not, and where you end up depends on what you believe. Should you follow no religion, you may pass through any one of these realms, depending on where your soul chooses it belongs. It is a great pleasure to see souls ascend from this realm to the Blessed Haven. People are constantly going up and down, in a cycle after they die. Nobody stays in one place for too long, because even after death, you're always learning, and this is a realm of teaching, not punishment."

He pointed ahead. "We're coming upon the Underworld."

Ahead of us, the desert came to an abrupt halt, where it met up with an oasis surrounding a shining city of gold. Even the river we floated upon changed to a shimmering gold stream. I stared up at the towering structures in awe. Waterfalls cascaded from beautiful towers, and precious gems were embedded into the streets. Lucious trees grew all throughout the city, with the most delicious-looking fruit growing from them. Everywhere we looked, there was abundance and wonder.

"This city looks out of place here," I remarked. "How can a city so beautiful be regarded as the Underworld?"

A fae with a beaming smile approached one of the trees and plucked the fruit from its branches. He took a bite, but immediately began sputtering. A cloud of ash sprayed from his mouth, and the fruit in his hand crumbled into nothing.

The city's central square came into view. In the middle stood a tall fountain, overflowing with gold coins. Men and women reached for piles of gold, but their hands went straight through the riches.

Nearby, a man fell to his knees at the foot of a woman. He wailed as he tried to touch her, but every time he did, it was as if his hand ran into an invisible brick wall.

"My mate!" he cried. "Please, notice me!"

She did not seem to see him there, only kept attempting to drink from the gold fountain, which immediately became sand once it touched her tongue.

We continued down the stream, until we passed a palace. At the top of the stairs sat a pedestal with a plush pillow atop it. A golden crown with precious gems embedded all around it shimmered against the sunlight.

A tall fae man with dark hair and hooded eyes approached the pedestal with confidence. The way he threw his shoulders back and looked at the crown as if it was already his made me think this man must be a monarch. He picked up the crown and placed it on his head, but it merely turned to ash that rained down around him. His eyes darted in every direction, as if searching for the culprit of the trick. His gaze fell upon the pedestal again. The crown had reappeared, looking as solid as it did the first time. He picked up the crown again, and it crumbled into ashes.

"This crown is *mine!*" he roared, before fur exploded across his body. He fell onto all fours in his wolven form—a black wolf with feathery wings. He lunged at the pedestal, tearing the pillow apart with his teeth in rage.

That was all I saw before the palace disappeared behind us, leading to more glorious mansions. Through the windows, we could see the fae reaching for velvet chairs that disappeared when they sat down. They stood before tables of feasts and tried to fill their plates, but the food vanished before their eyes. A woman reached for a violin to begin playing, but it made no sound. She opened her mouth to sing, but her voice died in her throat.

"I guess that answers your question," Lucas said. "The fae here have everything they want, but it's out of their reach."

"Precisely," the Ferryman said. "You can have all your heart's desires, but if you are spiritually bereft, it means nothing. These fae could have what they wish, if only they turned inside themselves, and looked within to see what truly matters."

Ahead, the gold river flowed into a building, but it was unlike the gold buildings surrounding us in the Underworld. This building was made of trees that intertwined, as if the plants themselves had made the building from their roots and branches. We floated inside the building, and the river transformed into a red carpet. The boat hovered above the carpet, floating along as if the river never changed.

We entered a dark room. The floor opened beneath us, plunging down into a massive auditorium filled with people. We floated along the top balcony, staring down into the room. It was some kind of theater, though I wasn't sure this was any theater I wanted to be in. Images played in front of each person on a personalized screen. Nobody seemed to notice the others around them.

"Welcome to the Eternal Torment, believed by the Elves to be the worst place imaginable," the Ferryman said.

I peered at the closest screens, and I could make out stories playing across them. The Elf below us seemed glued to his screen. In moments, I watched the same Elf abandon his family and make a new one, only to lose them both. Sad music played, and the scene ended with the Elf kneeling in the rain at the graves of the people he'd lost. The Elf who observed his life's mistakes playing out before him appeared hollow, as if he was unable to stop witnessing the biggest errors of his existence play out on repeat.

Beside him, an Elf woman sobbed as she watched herself enter a room over and over again, only to hear the words, *"You're too late. He's already passed."* Her greatest mistake in life was that she hadn't gotten there in time to say goodbye to the man she loved, and she was forced to never stop reliving it.

"Here in the Eternal Torment, the Elves must watch their own mistakes in life, and be reminded of every choice they made that turned out to be wrong in the end," the Ferryman said.

What an absolutely horrible fate. The scenes continued to play out in dark tones, accompanied by melancholy music. I observed an Elvish woman sob as she watched herself onscreen, begging her past self not to go to the beach.

The woman on the screen didn't listen. She took her child to the beach, and she turned away for a moment while her child climbed the rocks. The child slipped into the water, and by the time she realized what had happened, her son had already drowned.

Next to her, an Elvish healer clutched at his throat, observing as he administered the wrong medicine by mistake, and his patient died. Another Elf wept as he saw his past self onscreen say the wrong thing, only for his closest friend to take their own life soon after. On and on it went.

It was heart-wrenching to watch, and I had to turn away. To have no other choice but to relive all the most torturous parts of your life for all eternity… there was no worse punishment.

Talia leaned over the side of the boat, watching with interest. "Their greatest fear is to make mistakes?"

"No. Their greatest fear is that they cannot be forgiven once a mistake is made," the Ferryman said. "But these screens show only one perspective. It doesn't show exactly how things played out, but what these Elves *believe* happened. If they changed their internal beliefs, the screen would change, and they could leave this torment behind."

The music on one of the screens changed, and the scene became brighter. It was the woman who hadn't made it in time to say goodbye to the man she loved.

The Elvish woman stood and spoke to herself in a shaking tone. "No. I won't do this. I cannot continue to blame myself for not making it in time. I got there as fast as I could, and no amount of replaying the scenario will change what happened. We had three-hundred wonderful years together. I will not let our love be reduced to this moment, because we were so much more than this."

Images of their life together flashed across the scene, until the scene slowed. This time, it showed her kneeling at his bedside. Though her lover was already gone, she spoke the words she'd intended to say all along. *"I loved you dearly, and I pray to the Goddesses that you find peace in the Blessed Haven. I will meet with you again soon, my love."*

"I belong with my love," she said. "I forgive myself for the mistakes I made, and I will choose a better future."

A bright light appeared behind her, and I had to shield my eyes. The woman stepped into the light, and as it faded, she disappeared.

I gazed around at the other Elves, expecting them to notice and follow her lead, but nobody even stole a glance in her direction.

"Where did she go?" Grant asked.

"She has ascended to the Blessed Haven," the Ferryman answered. "All she needed to do was change her perspective and choose to leave her regret behind. Once she was able to forgive herself, she could enter heavenly bliss."

It was beautiful watching her ascend, but I felt bad for the other Elves. They didn't understand they could go with her, if they only forgave themselves for their mistakes.

We reached the end of the balcony, and a door opened. Ahead, skyscrapers loomed against a black sky, and sirens blared in the distance. We floated from the red carpet into a narrow murky brown river that smelled of sewage. Garbage floated alongside us. I pinched my nose shut as I glanced around the city streets and shadowed alleyways.

"Where are we?" Lucas asked.

"This is a place only known by name to the vampires who reside here," the Ferryman said.

We were in a modern city, but it was as if a warzone had broken out many years ago and we were peering into a dystopian future, at a time when all residents had given up hope. Most of the windows on the tall skyscrapers had been shattered, and the smaller buildings closest to the river were all boarded up. A car had been abandoned in the middle of the road, and it was on fire. Above us, a helicopter whirred loudly, and a spotlight swept through the city in pursuit of criminals. The streets were mostly deserted, but we could see people moving through the shadows. I heard explosions somewhere inside the city, and smoke rose through the air.

Glass shattered as someone threw a liquor bottle at a nearby building. Someone ran out of the building yelling obscenities. The vandal took off down the street, and the sound of tires squealed in the distance.

As we continued down the river, another street came into view. A female in a short, tight dress approached a man in a leather jacket. They barely exchanged words before he wrapped an arm around her waist. His fangs flashed against the light from a flickering streetlamp, and he sank his teeth into her neck. The woman threw her head back, appearing to enjoy the sensation as her own fangs elongated.

In the next alleyway, pained grunts rang out over the street. We witnessed a group of five men kicking and punching another vampire, until the victim stopped moving completely. The five vampires jumped on the man and began to feed.

I turned toward the Ferryman. "Is there no way to help him?"

"You will be slaughtered if you step foot off this boat," the Ferryman said. "These vampires cannot be saved."

One of the vampires feeding lifted his head and sniffed the air. His head jerked in our direction, and his eyes flashed red. I gave a start, but we were already past them a moment later.

Down the street, somebody whistled. Three vampires stood outside a grungy-looking bar, smoking cigarettes. One of them eyed me up and down, and I felt dirty just looking at him.

"Hey, sweet stuff," he sang. "Why don't you come join us and give Daddy some sugar!"

His buddies laughed. "Yeah! You can give us all a ride!"

"Fuck off!" Lucas sneered, flipping the men off. If the Ferryman hadn't warned us to stay inside the boat, Lucas might've gone over there and shoved a stake through their hearts. Just the look the man gave me made my skin crawl. There was no question about the things that vampire was fantasizing about doing to me.

We passed the men—thank the Goddess—and continued through the city.

Talia gave a shudder. "This place is horrible. How can they go on living like this?"

"This is the way of their city," the Ferryman said. "There's a demon god who runs this place. A vampire's worst nightmare is having to follow orders, never moving from their position for the rest of eternity. They're stuck here with no improvement—just monotony and the same thing, day in and day out, for the rest of their lives."

"How can they settle for that?" Chloe wondered. "Don't they understand things could change if they worked to build a better city?"

"They don't believe there's anything better out there for them," the

Ferryman answered. "They've resolved themselves to their fate. They're stuck in the same spot, not doing what they want to do, but doing what other people ask of them. Worse, they attempt to drag other souls into it."

"How do they get out?" Grant asked.

The Ferryman dipped his staff into the polluted river. "That is for the vampires to decide. So many vampires live like this on Earth that they don't see the difference between the life they lived when they were alive and the life they live as the dead, and that's why they can't get out. They're here because they don't know any better. They don't know they can choose differently."

I was grateful to see the streets come to an end up ahead. I didn't want to stay in this place a second longer than we had to. The river spilled out into the ocean, and the skyscrapers disappeared behind us as we floated onto the surface of the sea.

Our boat rocked from side to side, and we had to grab on to the edge so we weren't thrown into the water. Cold saltwater splashed into my face, and I feared the boat might capsize and sink. The sky above us swirled with dark clouds, and choppy waves stretched far to the horizon. The ocean water was gray and murky, with shining pools of oil floating along its surface. Something splashed in the distance, and I swore I saw giant tentacles rising from the ocean's surface.

"We are now at the Deepest Trench of Atlantean lore," the Ferryman announced. "Merfolk reside deep in these polluted waters, hiding from the monsters that lurk within. Their gills cannot breathe or see in the water here, as the oil is too thick, but neither can they die, so they continue to suffer in sickness and pain."

The surface of the water beside us broke. A gigantic sea creature emerged. I could make out jagged scales, barbed, poisoned fins, and razor-sharp teeth, but the majority of the creature was so massive, I couldn't see it all. It looked like it was going to gobble us up!

The Ferryman smacked it with the end of his staff—*hard*, I might add. "Be gone, beast!" he sneered, and the monster ducked back beneath the surface.

The boat rocked violently, making my heart lurch. I tried to hold on to the edge of the boat, but my fingers slipped. My friends and I were thrown into the water. An icy chill enveloped me, and thick liquid surrounded me at all angles. When I moved my arms, I found that the water was so oily and thick that it was difficult to swim through. My head broke the surface, and I glanced around frantically to see my friends gasping for air, too. The boat remained upright several feet away. The Ferryman stood upon it, appearing unbothered.

"Hurry back into the boat," the Ferryman said flatly. "We don't have all day."

We started swimming back, but just as Lucas and I reached out for the boat, Lucas disappeared from my side. He let out a scream before his voice was silenced by something yanking him under water.

"Lucas!" I cried. I ducked my head under water to go after him, but the water burned my eyes. I couldn't see anything.

My hands found his, and I grabbed him tightly and yanked him to the surface. As Lucas broke the surface, another pair of hands came out of the water, clawing up his body to try dragging him under.

A mermaid appeared, but she didn't look like how I envisioned a mermaid would be. She looked like a skeleton, with hollow eye sockets and flesh rotting from her bones. Her long black hair was patchy and covered in oil. She lifted her tail from the water and smacked the surface, and I saw that her scales were rotting off.

"Help me!" the mermaid begged. "Take me out of his dreadful place!"

"I wish we could, but we can't," I told her.

"*You must!*" she screamed. Her voice had changed, taking on a deep, eerie tone. "*Don't leave me here!*"

She lunged for Lucas and me, but the Ferryman's staff came between us as he smacked her away. She hissed and ducked back into the water.

Lucas curled his arm around me, and he grabbed the Ferryman's staff. The Ferryman dragged us out of the water and back onto the boat. Lucas and I lay on the bottom of the boat as we caught our breath. I quickly looked around to see our friends had made it back on while we'd been distracted by the mermaid.

"What the hell was that?" Lucas rasped. "Why is that poor mermaid trapped here?"

"There are many of her kind beneath these waters. The merfolk's flaw is that they are always looking for someone else to save them," the Ferryman said. "They want someone else to be their hero. What they don't realize is that they can save themselves. They could swim out of here and to paradise, if only they believed they could."

We situated ourselves back in our seats, and Grant immediately started to panic. "What's that ahead!?"

At first, I saw nothing. I thought he was simply pointing to the end of the horizon. Then I realized the clouds were missing. He really was pointing at *nothing*. My breath caught, and my heart began to race.

"There's a huge cliff ahead of us!" Lucas yelled at the Ferryman. "We're going to fall off. You're steering us the wrong way!"

The Ferryman said nothing as he continued to dip his staff into the water, steering us toward the edge.

"Hey!" Chloe cried. "Are you going to listen to us, or keep paddling us to the edge of the world!? You said you'd take us to the Abyss."

"That is exactly what I intend to do," the Ferryman said.

"That drop will kill us," I protested.

The Ferryman shrugged. "You never said I had to keep you alive."

Talia gripped tightly to her seat and began to scream as we came closer and closer to the edge of the waterfall. "I want to get off!"

Lucas curled me tight in his arms, and I squeezed my eyes shut. We reached the edge of the ocean, and the boat tumbled off the cliff.

My friends and I screamed as we fell through the air. My stomach leapt into my throat, and I thought we'd never stop falling.

Abruptly, the free-fall ended. My eyes shot open, but I saw nothing. Wherever we were, it was pitch black and eerily silent. I could feel the boat beneath me and Lucas's arms around me, but that was it.

I cast a witch light, and my heart rate began to slow. My friends and I were safe in the boat, and we were dry again. We appeared to be floating—on what, I wasn't sure. We could have been floating on the water or in the deepest parts of space. I couldn't tell, because there was no light and no sound. Beyond this boat, it was as if the light from my spell was entirely consumed by a black hole. It was the kind of place that would make you go mad if you spent any amount of time here. There was nothing, save but your own thoughts to preoccupy you.

The Ferryman began to laugh. "I've been doing this for thousands of years. I know where I'm going."

Chloe gazed around in wonder. "Where are we?"

"The Astromancers call this place the Endless Void," the Ferryman said.

"They get their magic from the stars, don't they?" Grant asked. "But there are no stars here."

"Which is precisely why it is the worst place for them to be," the Ferryman replied.

"But where is everyone?" I wondered.

"They're silent," the Ferryman said. "The Astromancers here don't feel like they can speak up, only that they must endure the darkness alone. But if they just turned on their light, they could get out of here."

Chloe squinted into the distance. "I see something ahead. Is it the angels' hell region?"

The Ferryman shook his head. "The angel hellscape is back where you started. What you see ahead is the Abyss."

The tiny pinprick of light Chloe had seen grew bigger, until I could make out the shadows of twisted, barren trees amongst a dense fog. The river turned black, and a broken sign read *Now Entering the Abyss*.

The Ferryman paddled us to shore, stopping along a muddy path within the dark forest. "Take this trail to the witch village. When you are finished here, follow the river downstream to return to the pits you came here through."

"Downstream?" Grant asked as he stepped out of the boat. "So it's all just an endless loop? If we were so close to the Abyss before, why didn't you just take us here to begin with?"

"The river only flows in one direction," the Ferryman stated. "I wasn't going to paddle you *upstream*."

Lucas held my hand as we stepped off the boat, and my shoes sank into the mud several inches.

"How far is it?" Talia wondered once we were all on shore. "Perhaps you can stay and wait for us."

"That was not part of the agreement," the Ferryman said, sounding annoyed. "I have souls of the dead to ferry."

"But what if we—" Grant started.

The Ferryman cut him off by dropping his hood once more. An illusion of some sort replaced his Elvish features, displaying a ghostly face of twisted bone and sunken eyes. My heart lurched, and we all jumped back as a hiss echoed throughout the forest.

"*I have brought you here like you asked,*" the Ferryman sneered in an ethereal voice. "*Now you are on your own.*"

He threw his hood back up and calmly placed his staff in the water, pushing away from the bank. His laughter faded as he floated downstream, like he thought scaring us was the funniest thing in the world.

Talia placed her hand over her racing heart. "I don't think I like that guy."

Lucas turned to face the path. "He got us to where we need to be. That has to count for something."

I shivered, glancing around the damp forest. I couldn't see much past the thick fog. "I don't like this place."

Chloe started forward, her shoes making a *squishing* sound in the mud. "The sooner we get moving, the sooner we can get out of here."

Lucas took my hand, and he kept me close as we followed behind Chloe. An eerie chill traveled down my back as we made our way through the forest, past swampy puddles and gnarly trees with no leaves on their branches. The sound of screams came from up ahead. Talia hesitated and curled closer to Grant.

"Remember what the Ferryman said," Grant assured her. "These people are torturing themselves. We should be safe."

He sounded uncertain, and I felt that deep within my gut. We didn't *actually* know what we were getting ourselves into here. This was the witches' hell, and that meant it was made for those of our kind. We needed to be more careful here than anywhere else.

The screams became louder the further we walked. Ahead, figures took shape behind the fog. Just off the path, a man with dark hair lay on a wooden table, strapped down by shackles. A small metal cage with no bottom and rats inside had been placed on his abdomen. Another man with a crooked nose shoveled coals from a nearby fire pit and hovered the coals above the top of the cage.

"No, please!" the man on the table begged.

"You did this to me, so now I get to do this to you," the man with the crooked nose sneered.

He placed the coals atop the cage. In a desperate attempt to escape the heat, the rats began burrowing downward, into the captive man's stomach. He screamed, his tortured cries filling the forest.

"Stop!" Lucas and I cried at the same time.

Lucas moved before I could. He sprinted through the trees, tossing the rat cage to the ground. The rats scattered, scampering away. The man's abdomen was torn and bloody, and it made me want to hurl.

"Leave him alone!" Lucas raged.

"Who made *you* king of the Abyss?" the man on the table snapped. "This is what I deserve!"

Lucas stumbled back a step. "You… *want* this?"

"Yes," the man with the coals sneered. "He deserves it. You want to be next?"

"Get out of here," the dark-haired man growled at Lucas, before turning back to his torturer. "Let's get this over with."

The torturer grabbed a piece of wood off a nearby table and began shoving splinters under the other man's fingernails. My stomach twisted, and I willed myself to look away, but I couldn't stop watching the horrible scene. When the man finished with the splinters, he took an ancient pair of pliers and began pulling off the man's fingernails.

Lucas returned to my side, shaking his head hopelessly. "I can't stop it."

"We're not here to change these people's minds," Chloe reminded him. "We're here to get the Oaken Wands, and that's it. We can't stop this torture if they want it to happen."

The sound of shackles clanging together met my ears, and I dared to turn my gaze back to the tortured man. His torturer had let him go. He was in so much pain that he stumbled to the ground, before pulling himself upright and grabbing his torturer by the hair.

"Let's see how you like the pyre!" he roared.

The torturer whimpered, and it became clear in that moment that the two had swapped roles. The dark-haired man dragged the other man through the trees.

"Where's he taking him?" Talia wondered.

We kept to the path, but we eyed the men through the trees. The dark-haired man pulled the man with the crooked nose onto a platform with a stake in the center. Dry branches surrounded him at every angle. The dark-haired man tied him up, then stepped back and watched with a smile as the brush lit aflame on its own. The man with the crooked nose screamed as flesh melted from his skin. Each time the skin fell off, another patch of fresh skin would replace it. He could burn for all eternity like this.

I turned away. I couldn't watch any longer.

Lucas shuddered. "It's just like the reaper Edgar described. I just never thought *we'd* be the ones torturing each other."

"I don't get it," Talia said. "The Ferryman made it sound like all these places came with lessons. What does torturing one another do for us?"

"It's obvious, isn't it?" I asked. "Here in the Abyss, witches are persecuting one another. It's a literal witch hunt. If they stopped accusing each other, and the community worked together, no one would be tortured. All they have to do is come together and agree on something. But here, people can't do that. That's why they're stuck."

Chloe scoffed. "They can't do that back home, either. We've created our own Abyss in Octavia Falls. Come on, let's keep moving."

More screams came from up ahead, and I turned my face away as we passed by others in the forest torturing each other. I couldn't look away fast enough, and I saw a man drop a spoked wooden wheel on top of a woman tied to a stage. I heard the snap of her bones and shuddered, while the crowd forming around her cheered.

The closer we got to town, the more and more torture devices we witnessed. A man sat on a chair while a woman tightened some sort of spiked device over his knee, effectively shattering his knee cap. His cries echoed throughout the whole forest. A similar—but smaller—device was used on another woman to crush the bones in her fingers.

I saw a pair of pincers with teeth on the sides. It glowed red from the heat of sitting upon coals. I didn't want to think about what those were used for.

Chloe sucked a breath between her teeth. "Crocodile shears. *Ouch.*"

Grant shuddered. "Don't tell me that's used to rip off a guy's penis."

"I'd rather not know," Talia insisted.

The trees cleared up ahead, giving way to a small village with cabins reminiscent of the 1600s.

Grant spun around to take it all in. "This looks like Octavia Falls when it was first settled."

Lucas's voice came out hollow. "That's because it is."

Screams filled the town, though they sounded more like screams of protest rather than those of torture. I saw the cages first. High above our heads and hanging from the trees were what looked like large bird cages.

Witches with sunken eyes and skin that seemed to suction to their bones sat in the cages, begging for food. The townspeople ignored them.

A crowd had gathered in a central square, shouting obscenities over one another. As we got closer, I got a better look at what was going on.

A woman stood hunched over, locked between wooden boards with holes cut out for her head and wrists. A putrid scent filled the air, and I realized people were throwing feces and rotten eggs at her.

Not far from the pillory, another crowd had formed. They sat on benches facing a long podium. It looked like a courtroom that had been set up outside. A woman in a red hooded cloak read a list of crimes off a long sheet of paper, and another in a black cloak stood at a pulpit, judging the trial.

A man on the witness stand shouted over the woman in the red cloak. "I didn't do it! I swear it!"

The crowd yelled back. "He's guilty! Take him to the pyre!"

The man didn't have a chance to plead his case before a crowd of people swarmed him and dragged him off into the woods. We heard the crackle of flames, then the sound of his screams growing louder as the fire burned him.

My stomach clenched. "It's the witch trials all over again."

Eyes began to turn in our direction as people noticed our arrival. "You there!" a man called, pointing at us. "It seems like you're new here. Do you want a turn?"

Lucas stepped aside as the crowd began closing in on us. "No, we're just here for a visit."

"That's too bad," a voice cackled from behind me. "You're here just like the rest of us, and that means you deserve to be punished!"

Hands landed on my friends and me all at once, and my heart leapt into my throat. All around us, townspeople laughed mockingly as they dragged us toward the witness stand.

"Get off us!" Lucas shouted.

"Don't touch me!" I screamed. I formed a battle orb in my hands, but it barely flickered before someone slapped shackles onto my wrists. They had to be magical, because I suddenly couldn't access my powers.

"You can't do this!" Talia cried. "We're not even dead—we don't belong here."

Grant struggled against the townspeople, while Chloe whispered beneath her breath, "Just go with it. We get to choose our fate, right?"

The townspeople shoved us into chairs behind the podium. They plopped me down between Lucas and Chloe.

A stack of papers magically appeared in front of the woman in the red cloak. When she turned, her long red hair beneath her hood became apparent, and I realized I recognized her.

"Priestess Charlotte?" I gasped.

She dropped her hood and wore a sad expression on her face. "Yes, it is me. It's nice to see you all again."

The woman behind the pulpit lowered her hood as well, and I saw her dark curls. It was Priestess Stella. I hadn't expected to see her here. The last time we'd seen her had been in the courtroom the day of our trial. She'd appeared as a ghost and spoken out against Lilian and Margaret, but Professor Leto had cast some sort of spell on her that made her disappear. We'd never known what happened to her after that. I didn't realize she'd moved on from Earth.

"Priestesses, what are you doing here?" I asked. "You already acknowledged your mistakes and apologized for them. You helped protect the coven. You should both be in Alora."

"They're not the ones on trial!" someone in the crowd shouted. "Get on with it!"

The crowd cheered in agreement.

"Priestesses, please let us go," Lucas begged. "You were on our side in Octavia Falls. We are only here to find the Oaken Wands. You must find it in yourself to show us mercy."

"We are truly sorry you have to go through this, but this is the way things work here," Charlotte said regrettably. "It's something everyone must do, though we will be as fair as we can be. To avoid the torture the others will put you through, you must prove your innocence."

I didn't want to go through with this, but I trusted Priestess Charlotte. When Professor Leto was in town, Charlotte realized the mistake she'd made in striking a deal with a demon. She came to us to seek a solution. She helped us fight Professor Leto, and she gave herself up so we could defeat him. She had fallen into the demon's pit and died. If she believed this was the way to walk out of here unharmed, then we had to go through with it.

"This court is now in session," Stella said, smacking a gavel on the pulpit.

Charlotte began reading off the papers in front of her. "Lucas Taylor, Nadine Taylor, Grant Bryant, Talia Murphy, and Chloe Olson, you are hereby called upon by Mother Miriam to state your sins and be judged by a jury of your peers."

It was disgusting by how they used Mother Miriam's name as if she approved of this torture. I didn't think Priestess Charlotte liked it either, because she shifted uncomfortably.

"There's nothing you can say to hurt us," Grant insisted. "We're innocent."

"You cannot deny your feelings in front of us," Charlotte said. "There are Seers among us. We know all of your deepest regrets."

Lucas spoke calmly. "We've already been through this on Earth. We aren't afraid. What are our charges?"

The crowd appeared puzzled, and a man in the front row spoke up. "Why aren't you angry? If you're innocent as you say, don't you wish to put *us* on trial for false imprisonment?"

"Why should we be the ones to determine your fate?" I asked rhetorically.

"Because somebody has to," the man sneered. Others spoke up in agreement.

Stella pounded the gavel, and the crowd quieted. "Order in the court! We will be the ones leading this trial. You will all remain quiet until a verdict has been reached."

Charlotte turned on her heel and walked to the end of the podium, where Grant sat. "Grant Bryant, you are hereby accused of breaking the Bro Code."

"What's that supposed to mean?" Grant demanded.

She looked down at her papers. "The Bro Code—it is a series of unspoken rules for male friendship—"

"I know what the Bro Code is," Grant started, but Charlotte continued like she hadn't heard him.

"—Including but not limited to sleeping with your best friend's ex."

"I never slept with Nadine!" Grant cried. "We only went out on one date!"

"And yet you are guilty of breaking the Bro Code, are you not?" She cocked an eyebrow.

"I… may have some regrets," Grant admitted.

Grant and I had been out on one date my sophomore year, while Lucas and I were broken up. Grant and I were both single at the time, and we figured there was no harm in hanging out for the evening. It'd been a complete disaster, though. We'd gone to a restaurant on the lake, and Grant's enchanted crab pinched his ear and then ran off into the trees. Then we'd gone to a lake party, where Grant and I shared a kiss, and he and Lucas had gotten into a fist fight. We all had regrets over that night, but I thought we'd moved on from it. Apparently, we hadn't.

Charlotte strolled up to Lucas. "Isn't it true, Lucas, that you want to get back at Grant for what he did to you?"

Lucas hesitated. "Nadine and I were broken up. That's in the past."

"Nonsense!" she insisted. "Grant doesn't care about you. The moment he had a chance at Nadine, he took it, and he never paid for that crime."

"Look," Grant said. "If Lucas was mad about that, we'd talk it out. We don't need the whole coven's opinion. Lucas and I are tight. He's not mad."

Charlotte raised her eyebrows. "That's not what the Seers have revealed. Lucas, how do you feel about it?"

Lucas kept his jaw tightly shut, but his nostrils flared. "Like Grant said, we're tight."

"See? We're *fine*," Grant insisted.

"Lucas, aren't you angry that Grant asked out your ex-girlfriend without consulting you first?" Charlotte pressed. "Aren't you upset that he kissed Nadine, and he would've continued to date her if she wasn't still hung up on you? Aren't you mad he went behind your back?"

I wanted to stick up for Grant, and say it never would've turned into anything, because neither of us were into each other like that. But Lucas spoke up before I could.

"You know what?" Lucas sat straighter in his chair, facing Grant. "I *am* pissed about that. Nadine and I were broken up—I couldn't tell her who to date, but *you*? You didn't even ask me!"

"The invite wasn't even meant to be a date," Grant defended. "We were just supposed to be two friends hanging out. Nadine's the one who suggested the date."

"No," I defended. "I asked if *you* were asking *me* on a date."

Grant sighed. "It just *happened*, and it's not something that will ever happen again."

"Why are you so insistent on defending yourself?" Lucas demanded. "The fact is you went out with Nadine without asking me!"

"I didn't know I *had* to ask you," Grant replied. "You two were broken up."

"That's not what matters," Lucas pressed. "How can you be so insightful about everything, but *this* is what goes over your head? Of course I wanted to see Nadine happy—no matter who she was with—but if you two had ended up together, I couldn't have hung around to watch that happen. It would've ruined our friendship. Hell, you didn't just hurt *me*. Imagine what this did to Talia."

"I really wanted to be with Talia, but I figured she'd turn me down, so I lost my courage to ask. She didn't even like me back then," Grant said, turning to her for confirmation.

Angry tears beaded in Talia's eyes. "I've been in love with you for a long time, Grant. To be honest, it really stung to see you ask out my best friend."

My heart sank. I never wanted to hurt her. "Tal, you told me you were fine with it."

"Well, I lied," she admitted harshly. "You knew I had a thing for Grant, too. It was kind of bullshit you did that, Nadine."

"We were all in the wrong," Grant said. "Even Nadine only dated me to make Lucas jealous."

My jaw dropped. "Grant, come on. That is not true."

"Sure it is, Nadine. You weren't even into me. It's not a bad thing. I mean, you and Lucas ended up together in the end." Grant gestured between us. "And Lucas, you didn't advocate for yourself—you just let her go."

"I didn't know the date was happening until I saw you two locking lips!" Lucas raged.

Grant sighed. "You know that's not what I meant."

"Why can't you just admit you did something wrong?" Lucas demanded. "You're so busy pointing fingers. Why don't you look in a mirror?"

"You want me to say it?" Grant asked, sounding annoyed. "All right. I did something wrong. What more do you want from me?"

"I want you to be genuine," Lucas insisted. "You can't just say what people want to hear and get over it. That doesn't actually solve any problems."

"You want the truth?" Grant yelled, shooting to his feet. "I wanted you to *be* there that summer. Hell, it'd been years since we lost you. I wanted my best friend back. I watched you torture yourself—just like the people in these woods—all because you thought you deserved it, but you *didn't!*"

Grant's voice cracked, and tears began streaming down his face. "You were suffering needlessly, and nothing I said or did could help you. So if I had to hurt you to snap you out of it, Goddess damn it, I was going to do it. I just wanted to wake you up, Lucas."

We all went quiet for a moment, before Lucas spoke. "That's a really fucked up way to wake someone up."

"I didn't know what I was doing at the time," Grant admitted. "Now that I've grown up and can reflect on it, I can see why I really did it."

"You really hurt Lucas," I said bitterly. "But you know what? That wasn't fair to me, either. It makes me feel used, Grant. I've been carrying Lucas for a long time, and that's fine, because I choose to do that. But it isn't fair of you to choose that for me, and to pull me into your shit. I'm Lucas's wife, and his partner, and I'm happy to shoulder his burdens and help him through life. I will always be a safe place for him, and I will give him the love, kindness, and grace he deserves, but I'm not his therapist. I don't have the training, knowledge, or understanding to be that for him. Other people shouldn't be forcing me into that role, even if it's unintentional. Lucas and I were broken up back then, and even at that point, when I was on a date with *you*, you were having me take on his feelings when I needed space to heal myself."

"I hurt everyone, and for that, I truly apologize," Grant said in a broken tone. "I went too far, and it never should've happened. I'm sorry you were caught in the middle of this, Nadine. Lucas, I'm sorry I ever asked Nadine out in the first place."

He turned to Talia. "If I'd have known you had any interest in me, I never would've hung out with Nadine. I'm sorry. I didn't mean to hurt anyone. I just hope you can all find it in your heart to forgive me."

A silent beat passed before Lucas nodded. "There's no reason to let this hurt any of us anymore. I believe that you're truly sorry, and that's all I need. I'm sorry for scaring you and making you feel as if you had to go through these lengths to save me from myself."

"Apology accepted," Grant said.

"This is unacceptable!" someone in the crowd shouted as they leapt from their seat and shook a fist. The townspeople followed suit, shouting protests so loud I couldn't understand what anyone said.

"It matters not!" Stella shouted over the others. "Their sins are far greater than broken friendships. You five have killed members of your own coven. You've lied to your own people. You sat and watched as others were burned, hanged, and poisoned. You all will do anything to get your way. What have you say?"

"It doesn't matter what we say, because you won't believe us, anyway," Talia growled.

Charlotte turned to her. "It's interesting that you would be the one to speak up. Your sin, Talia Murphy, is silence. You let people walk all over you, and you've never done anything about it. People needed you, and you were too timid to help them."

"How do you know all that?" Talia demanded through gritted teeth. She lunged across the podium, reaching for Charlotte's papers, but the priestess yanked them away.

"Things got bad in the coven, and instead of speaking up, you stayed quiet," Charlotte accused. "You didn't say anything until people started coming for you and your friends."

"And I've learned from my mistakes!" Talia insisted.

Lucas quickly cut in. "She hasn't done anything wrong."

Charlotte turned on him. "Lucas, you should've been there for your brother. You were too self-absorbed to see his cries for help."

"That's not true!" Grant shouted. "She's making things up."

I whirled toward my husband. "Lucas, she's preying on our insecurities."

"I know," Lucas said calmly. "She's saying stuff I believed for a long time, but I understand Eric better now. It's nobody's fault that he's gone—not his, and not mine."

Charlotte continued. "You've used your depression as an excuse not to deal with your shit and make decisions. You hide away in your room, so you don't have to face real-world problems."

"I've learned to take my time to process, and then I find solutions," Lucas stated.

"Leave him alone," I snarled. She couldn't get to him anymore, because she was trying to guilt-trip him, and he had nothing to feel sorry for.

Charlotte didn't even lift her gaze as she continued reading. "Nadine, you let your grandmother die. Worse, you sacrificed the coven for your own benefit. You gave up an Oaken Wand to the priestesses in order to get a kidney. You're selfish."

"She didn't want to," Talia argued. "We told her to do it."

Chloe scoffed. "You can list off our sins all day, but you can't make us feel bad for what we had to do to save each other."

"Why are you defending her?" Charlotte asked Chloe curiously. "Not long ago, you wanted Nadine dead. You would have considered her death a necessity, the same way you have justified the deaths of other people you have killed. Who are you to decide who lives and who dies?"

"We're nobody," Chloe said. "Nobody gets to justify those deaths, because they *can't* be justified. Octavia Falls isn't much different from this place. Up there, it's kill or be killed, but we shouldn't have to make that choice in the first place. There is a third path—just as Nadine and I came together to end our curse, the coven must come together to end their conflict. Here in the Abyss, you could stop the torture, if you all just agreed to get along."

The crowd around us laughed, like the suggestion was impossible.

Charlotte paced in front of the podium. "You don't believe any of that. Isn't that correct, Chloe? Our Seers do not lie. You have slipped potions into people's drinks without their knowledge, called them the worst of slurs, gossiped behind their backs and made up lies, broke into their rooms to destroy their belongings, cast hexes and threw punches, humiliated them—"

"I know what I've done!" Chloe shouted, cutting her off. "I did what I thought I had to do at the time to protect myself, and I went too far. I thought when Nadine came to town, she was going to get me killed, so I had to stand up for myself. I may have started it, but Nadine kept it going. Every time I did something bad, Nadine came back with something worse."

I gaped. "How can you say that? You literally tried to hang me."

"You put me in the hospital!" Chloe shot back as tears rose to her eyes.

I shuddered at the reminder, because I hated what I'd done. Our second semester, Chloe and I had gotten into a fight so bad that she'd been sent to the infirmary.

"Don't act like such a saint—you tried to kill me, too," Chloe continued. "Maybe I deserve to be on this stand, or tied to the pyre, but you deserve to be right there with me, Nadine. I wasn't the only mean girl at Miriam College. You were a closet bully hiding behind a mask, trying to play the part of the good girl who was sweet and kind, but really, you wanted to be in control and act like you knew it all. You had to make me pay, and you damn well made sure I did. You didn't have to take things that far, but you wanted to. You hurt me, too."

Her words sliced into me like a knife. Back then, I only thought I was defending myself, when really, I was just hurting her.

"I'm sorry, Chloe," I said honestly. "You're right. I was a mean girl, even if I didn't intend to be. I take full accountability for what I did, and I wish I could take it back."

Chloe placed a hand over her mouth as her shoulders began to shake. Tears streamed down her face. If it had been any other moment. I'd have thought Chloe was crying to manipulate the court. But it was clear that these were honest-to-Goddess uncontrollable tears that she couldn't hold back.

"It doesn't matter what you did, because Charlotte's right," Chloe sobbed. "I've done so many bad things—terrible things that are unforgivable. Maybe I should just stay here in the Abyss. This is where I belong, being tortured like all these other people. It's what I deserve."

"No, Chloe," I insisted. "If you think that way, then your sentence is already determined. But we don't have to sit here defending ourselves. We need to be working together, just like you and I did when we broke our curse."

"Let's face it," Chloe said. "The night you broke our curse, you won. You're the one who's going to stay in the coven, because you actually have a place there. My friends hate me. I've cut off my family, and I have nothing left to go back to."

"That's not true," I told her gently. "Chloe, you have *us*. We may not have gotten along in the past, but you and I know how to work together to get shit done. You belong with us, searching for the Oaken Wands so we can restore the coven's magic. And when that's all over, we want you to stay, because you're our friend."

Chloe sniffled. "You don't *want* to be my friend. You've kept me close and used me to get the Oaken Wands, because you need a Mentalist on your side and I'm your only option. Once we get the Wands and save the coven, you're going to toss me aside and abandon me, because you won't need me anymore."

"That's not true," I insisted. "I want to be your friend, and you know why? Because I admire you, and I look up to you. You're strong and confident in a way that I want to be. I'm sorry I was mean to you. There's no excuse. Neither of us needed to do that to each other, but you showed me that we can choose to change, and I want to be there to see who you become."

I turned to Charlotte. "You said your Seers know all our regrets?"

She nodded, like she wasn't sure where I was going with this.

I looked back at Chloe. "That's how I know you've changed. They wouldn't know all these things about you if you didn't regret it. It doesn't matter who's in the right and who's in the wrong if the behavior on both sides is hurting everyone. We need to take action to benefit the community and not just defend ourselves. So please, Chloe. Stay with us and help us make that change."

Chloe wiped her eyes. "Do you really think people can change, Nadine?"

"I *know* they can," I told her gently.

Chloe shook her head. "But I haven't paid for what I've done."

I stood and reached for Chloe's hand. "I think you've suffered enough."

Chloe hesitated, then took my outstretched hand and stood.

The crowd erupted into protests. "They can't do this! Lock 'em up!"

Chloe turned to the crowd. "Nobody here needs to be locked up, or burned, or tortured. You can all return to Alora—"

A rotten cabbage smacked Chloe in the face, cutting her off. "Nobody who comes here is getting out!" a villager yelled.

Lucas stood, and Grant and Talia followed suit. Lucas lifted his chin. "We are. Because we might not be innocent, and we did make mistakes, but we are willing to forgive each other."

The shackles around our wrists rattled as they sprang open and clanged to the ground. The townspeople gasped, like they'd never seen such a thing happen.

A smile crept across Stella's face. "I believe this case is closed. You are free to go."

She smacked her gavel, marking the end of the trial.

"Pft," one of the townspeople scoffed, waving his hand. "They aren't worth it. This trial was boring, anyway."

The townspeople quickly lost interest in us and dispersed. Stella and Charlotte approached us as soon as the townspeople were gone.

"I'm deeply sorry we had to treat you that way," Stella apologized.

Charlotte shared a look of regret. "I had to push you in order for you to proclaim your innocence."

"It worked out, as we are free to go," I said.

"How are things in Octavia Falls?" Charlotte asked.

I shook my head. "Not well. Margaret and Lilian have only made things worse. They're taking away people's resources so they'll obey the priestesses."

"They're splitting up families, and they're forcing people to work for them," Chloe added. "People are going hungry."

"You have not yet died," Charlotte remarked. "How have you come here?"

"We came through a portal in Malovia," Chloe explained. "We've come to find the missing Oaken Wands. Do you know what happened to the Mentalist Wand after it fell into the demon's pit?"

Charlotte nodded and reached into her cloak. "I retrieved it when I fell into the demon's pit. I landed here in the Abyss. The Mentalist Wand was lying in the forest beside me, as it too fell into the pit. I have been holding on to it until it could be passed into the proper hands. You have proven that you are worthy of wielding it by forgiving each other. The Wand trusts you and is willing to come back to Earth with you."

Charlotte withdrew the Mentalist Wand and placed it in Chloe's hands. The end of the Wand began to glow, and it sang a beautiful note.

"You've earned this," Charlotte said. "What you did on that witness stand proves that when the time comes, you will all come together to do right by the coven. I know you will use this Wand for good."

"Come with us," Talia offered. "You fell into the demon's pit and were portaled here. You don't belong here, either."

Charlotte frowned. "I'm afraid I do."

"You died on the way down," Lucas stated matter-of-factly. He wasn't guessing. It was clear there was a part of his Death magic that *knew*.

Charlotte nodded.

Lucas shook his head, like he refused to accept this answer. "That doesn't mean you belong here."

Charlotte didn't appear convinced. "You know what I've done. I started the Miriamic Conflict with the other priestesses."

"And you chose better," Lucas pressed. "It's not what we've done in the past that defines us, but what we choose to do now—in the present. You saved us from the demon, Charlotte. You sacrificed yourself to break the contract and kill him."

"One good deed does not outweigh my sins," Charlotte said.

"No, but you can choose not to let it weigh you down anymore," Lucas replied. "I know what it's like to punish yourself—to feel like you deserve it, yet feel out of control at the same time. But we can make a new decision at any moment. We might slip up, but what matters is that we keep trying to do better. The only question is… do you *want* to do better?"

Charlotte nodded. "I do."

"Then this isn't where you belong," Lucas told her. "Lessons can't be learned by torturing yourself. It's a symptom, not a solution. If you're ready to break that cycle, then you belong in Alora, where you can shed light on your wrongdoings and heal from them."

Tears rose to Charlotte's eyes. "I'd very much like to heal."

A bright light appeared behind Charlotte, outlining her form. It was so blinding I had to shield my eyes.

"Thank you all," Charlotte said. "I will move onward toward Alora. I pray that whatever happens, the rest of you will be able to lead the coven into the light."

Charlotte began walking toward the portal, until it engulfed her entirely, before she was gone for good. The light dimmed, and we were left standing in the mud without her.

It was a profound moment, seeing one of our own coven members ascend. Charlotte had been on the Imperium Council when the Miriamic Conflict began. She'd ordered witches and warlocks to hang, and she'd burned our friends on the pyre the night of the Burning. She'd been among the priestesses who summoned the demon that killed over a dozen coven members. By all accounts, it appeared that she belonged here in the Abyss.

But she'd owned up to her mistakes and stood accountable for them. She'd chosen a different path, one that led her home to Mother Miriam. If she of all people could do that, then each one of us could follow her lead. Because of people like her, the coven could change for the better.

If we accomplished nothing else in the Abyss, coming down to help Charlotte was worth it.

The light that guided Priestess Charlotte into Alora was so beautiful that I wished I had conjured the portal on my own. But I hadn't. Charlotte had done that all by herself.

My gaze lingered on the area where Charlotte had disappeared, before I turned toward Stella. "You can move on, too."

She shook her head. "I'm afraid the demon banished me here."

I recalled how her spirit disappeared during our trial, and we suspected Professor Leto had cast a spell to force her out of the courtroom. I never imagined his spell had forced her *here*.

"The demon is dead," I told her. "He holds no power over you now. You can choose to leave."

"I can, but make no mistake, the demon may have banished me here, but I have stayed by my own volition," Stella said. "I understand now what I must do, but I'm not there yet. I have much to sort out before I ascend to Alora, but I will go when I am ready."

"Is there anything we can do to help?" Grant asked.

Stella shook her head. "Only I can make the decision to ascend, but perhaps I can give something back to the coven the way Charlotte has given you that Wand. If there is anything you need here in the Abyss, I will do my best to help you."

"Actually, there is one thing," I said. "You can provide us with information. We're looking for a reaper named Edgar Nowak."

"Yes, I know Edgar." Stella pointed down a muddy path. "He lives in a cabin just down there. If that is all the information you require, then this is where we must part. I must prepare for another trial."

It was sad to see she wasn't ready to move on, but I had faith she would get there soon.

"Thank you for your help, Priestess," I said. "We wish you the very best."

"Good luck on your journey." Stella waved us goodbye as the towns-people started gathering for the next trial. We weren't about to stick around for it, so we hurried off.

We followed the path in the direction Stella had pointed us, until we came upon a small cabin with a scythe leaning against the front of the building. This had to be Edgar's house. My friends stayed behind me as I nervously approached the cabin and knocked.

The door creaked open, revealing a dark figure behind it. The cabin was so dim that the man appeared as nothing more than a shadow. He wore a black cloak that concealed his features.

I peered inside cautiously. "Edgar Nowak?"

"Oh, it's *you*," he sneered. "I knew you'd be back."

"Then you know who I am," I replied.

"You are Lucas Taylor—the Reaper's Apprentice. I could never forget the man who sent me here."

My bones seemed to rattle at the accusation, though it was not a false one. Edgar was here because of me.

Edgar took a step forward and stopped in the doorway. He dropped his hood, and I noticed he looked vastly different from the last time I'd seen him. The night of the Reaper Moon, he appeared to me as a skeleton in long robes, with nothing but bony fingers and empty eye sockets. Here in the Abyss, pale skin covered his body, and dark eyes stared back at me. He looked old, with wrinkles across his skin, as if evidence of the wisdom he'd collected over the years. It shocked me at first, and I took a step back.

Edgar crossed his arms and narrowed his eyes. He wore a bitter expression, like that of a cat that had just gotten wet. "Am I not what you expected?"

"You look different than the last time we met," I remarked.

"I take the form that you expect of me," Edgar explained. "On Earth, my skeletal form is an omen of death, a confirmation to confused spirits that they have passed. Here, the people are already dead, and so I look like them."

"You're not able to leave, are you?" I wondered.

Edgar shook his head. "Recall that reapers can take other reapers' powers. It is why you summoned me at the Reaper Moon. When we fought that night, you overpowered me. You took control over my sentence and sent me through that reaping portal. The magic bound my soul to this realm, and I'm unable to escape the Abyss. I am a reaper—a master of death. Reapers are not meant to be reaped."

"I never intended to trap you here. There has to be a way we can get you out," I insisted.

"The only one who can free me of this place is the one who sent me here, and that's you, Lucas. You must be the one to lead me out of the Abyss." Edgar glanced at my friends behind me. "But you didn't come all the way to the Abyss to save me. You are still living. You've come here for a purpose greater than my soul."

"We've come for the Oaken Wands," I admitted. "The coven is breaking apart, and the Wands are powerful enough to restore our magic—and our hope. We know that you possess the Mortana Wand, and that it's passed down among members of the Reaper Order. I know about the Warlock's Trial. It's a trial of death, so I have to demonstrate to you my Death magic."

Edgar frowned. "I cannot give you the Mortana Wand as you wish."

I certainly didn't like that answer, and I was desperate. I didn't come all this way to the Abyss just for him to tell me he wasn't going to hand it over. We needed those Wands to save the coven. This was bigger than any resentment we may hold towards one another.

"Then perhaps we can make an exchange," I offered. "If I get you out of the Abyss, then you will hand over the Mortana Wand."

"That isn't how it works," Edgar grumbled. "I cannot hand over the Wand because you are not yet a member of the Reaper Order. You must pass the Warlock's Trial before I could even think of giving it to you."

"If I have to earn it, then so be it," I said. "Let me show you what I can do, and when I join the Reaper Order, you can give me the Wand so I can help the coven."

I gestured for my friends to back up as I faced the forest. "My magic is strong."

I lifted my hands, and a shimmering shield bloomed around us, expanding to encompass Edgar's cabin, the woods, then all of the village. Edgar turned his gaze upward, but my shield had disappeared into the clouds. He barely blinked, and I could tell he wasn't impressed, but I was only getting started.

Battle orbs formed in my palms, and I placed my hands together, melding the orbs into a singular weapon. I aimed the high-powered orb at the forest, and the magic erupted from my hands. A deafening explosion sounded, uprooting trees in an instant and sending clods of dirt raining down on us. I quickly formed a shield, and obliterated bits of tree trunks bounced off it and went flying in the other direction. My friends flinched, but my shield protected them. In the distance, I heard the townspeople scream as the explosion rocked the forest.

The dust settled, revealing a huge crater in the ground where hundreds of trees once stood.

Edgar appeared unfazed. "Your magic is powerful, but this is not Death magic."

"I'm a reaper," I pointed out. "All the souls here are already dead. My powers of death are limited."

Edgar frowned. "You don't understand the power of death if you think it is limited here."

It was clear I had to pull off something big if I was going to convince him. It had to go beyond anything I'd ever done before—Death magic that exceeded all my perceived limitations. I wasn't entirely sure what that entailed. There was so much I didn't know about my powers, but I couldn't wait around to learn these things when I needed the Mortana Wand *now*.

I glanced around for inspiration and noticed townspeople sticking their heads out of their cabins or peering through the trees. Their ghostly faces stared back at me, as if cautiously anticipating another explosion.

A big explosion wasn't going to cut it. Any witch or warlock could make a shield or cast a battle orb. I had to show Edgar that I wasn't just any warlock. I was a reaper, and to become that, I had to become a master of death like he was.

I recalled the day Professor Warren tried to get me to summon spirits, because he thought I must be able to interact with them in order to help them cross over. I was going to take it one step further. I needed to not just become a master of death, but a master of the dead themselves.

I conjured all the Mortana crystals I had, every last one that I'd spent months infusing with my magic. They were like batteries charged with more Death magic than I could ever conjure up on my own in one go. With them, I withdrew the stone Beau Blankard had given me from my pocket. He'd enchanted it to amplify a Mortana's power, and I had to use everything in my arsenal to convince Edgar of my power.

I curled the crystals in my fists. Magic surged through me, filling me with power unlike ever before. I let it permeate every cell of my body until I couldn't hold it back any longer. I reached a tipping point, and Death magic blasted out of me. I heard my friends gasp in surprise, but I was too focused on my magic to turn and see their reaction.

Black tendrils of magic twisted through the streets of the village, aimed at the spirits of the dead surrounding us. There had to be over a hundred of them within sight. The magic seeped into their forms, until the spirits and my power were one and the same.

I swayed on my feet, but I willed myself to remain standing. I ordered the dead forward with nothing more than a simple thought. They followed my command and marched down the path to line up behind me like an army of soldiers.

The brief wave of dizziness passed, and I turned to Edgar with my head held high. His features hadn't changed, though. If anything, he appeared bored.

"You can't deny the power I have over death," I stated.

Edgar frowned, like I was merely wasting his time. "You think you are a master reaper, but a mistake you made bound me here, and I can see that you've only slightly grown in maturity since then."

"Slightly grown?" I balked. The day I met him was the first time I'd cast a shield. My powers were hundreds of times stronger now.

"I have conquered death!" I protested. "Look at all these spirits I can control. I am a reaper through and through."

"And yet you have still not mastered death," Edgar replied calmly.

My teeth gritted. I'd just pulled off the greatest feat of magic I'd ever done, and it wasn't good enough for him? "I'm in the Abyss. That's close enough to death."

"And still death eludes you," Edgar said flatly.

Frustration didn't even cover the rage brewing inside of me. Edgar was so calm and collected, when he should be doing everything in his power to help me pass this trial. It was like he didn't want to hand over the Mortana Wand and help the coven. I bet he wanted to keep all that power to himself.

"What do you want from me?" I demanded. "To die? I don't have to die to know death. I've seen death. I've felt the life drain from people's bodies. I've suffered with the grief of dead family members. I've watched the people I love pass away without me being able to do anything to stop it. Every day, I hear more and more voices as the coven takes its last breath. I've crossed over spirits, and I've brought them back to life. I'm here in the Abyss, controlling the spirits of the dead, and you still want to stand there and tell me I don't understand death?"

The rage building up inside of me snapped, and the spirits I controlled spoke my final words in unison. *"Death is final, as am I."*

I lifted my hands, and the dead followed my command. Our power combined, until a glowing column of magic rose to the sky behind us. Power pulsed through the village, so much that a hum fell over the town, and the magic lit up the forest like the sun. The column stretched far into the clouds and must've been at least a mile long, stretching so far we couldn't see the end of it. It was the kind of magic that could level the whole town in an instant if I commanded it to.

"Lucas..." I heard Nadine's voice in the distance, warning me not to take things too far. It was too late.

I ignored my friends and aimed my gaze on Edgar. I would command this spell to destroy him if I had to. Surely it wouldn't kill him here in the Abyss, but if the torture I saw in the woods was any indication, it would hurt like a son of a bitch. This kind of power could blast him apart, until there was nothing left to knit back together.

"I need that Wand, and I'm not leaving here without it," I growled. "If you won't give it to me, then I'll take it from you."

"You came here asking for my help, and now you want to hurt me?" Edgar sneered.

"If that's what I have to do," I stated. "Are you going to hand over the Wand, or not?"

He shook his head. "I will not."

"You just want the Wand for yourself!" I accused.

I couldn't say I hadn't warned him. The magic I'd summoned via the dead exploded forward, following my command. It slammed into Edgar's chest, and he was sent reeling off his feet, soaring backward over his cottage. Magic blasted straight through the walls of his home, reducing the house to mere splinters. Edgar landed hard on the ground behind the obliterated cottage. He didn't move.

I thought I might've killed him—*again*. I carefully stepped forward, but I only got a few paces before Edgar sat up, shaking leaves out of his hair like the blast had merely tickled. I stopped in my tracks.

Edgar stood and reached into his robes. He withdrew a white wand painted to look like bone, with the shape of a rib cage carved into the end of it. My heart leapt at the sight of the Mortana Wand.

"You want this Wand?" Edgar asked. "Come and get it."

I hesitated. "What kind of trick is this?"

"It is not a trick," he stated. "You have shown how desperate you are, and the lengths you are willing to go through to get it. If you want it, take it from me."

I wasn't sure what he was playing at, because this was the last thing I expected of him. But he seemed dead serious.

I cautiously stepped toward him. My fingers curled around the end of the Mortana Wand, and I could feel its power pulsing through it. But when I tried to take it out of his open palm, the Wand wouldn't budge.

"You see?" Edgar asked. "You can try, but even so, it will not work. The Reaper Order cast a spell long ago to protect this Mortana Wand, and the Wand accepts the protection spell. You could try to pry this Wand off of my soul, but my soul won't give it to you until you become a member of the Reaper Order. I was never your enemy, Lucas, nor am I now."

All my rage melted away, and I saw how ridiculous I'd acted. Edgar wasn't trying to keep the Wand for himself. He was only being reasonable, because there was magic here at play I clearly didn't comprehend.

My shoulders dropped hopelessly. "I attempted to hurt you and destroyed your home, all for nothing. You tried to tell me, and I didn't listen."

"I will find a new home," Edgar assured me as he placed the Wand back in his cloak. "Your intentions are noble, Lucas, but your methods are foolish."

"I've done everything I can. What more power do you want to see from me?"

"I don't need to see any of this." Edgar gestured around. "All this has shown me is that you are not ready yet. However, when the time comes, you will see me again."

I wasn't sure I believed him. "How will you find me?"

"You can put an end to my sentence and give me back control of my power," he said. "If you can get me out of here, I will be able to cross the spiritual realms once again. I want to go home, but I need your help."

"Will that earn me the Mortana Wand?" I asked.

Edgar placed his hands on my shoulders. I couldn't explain it, but something deep in his eyes calmed me. There was caring nature there, like he really wanted to help, but he couldn't. "There is no bargain you can make to obtain the Wand. The Warlock's Trial is not for me to judge. I have no choice. I cannot physically give you the Wand until you've earned it."

"We *need* the Oaken Wands," I stated desperately. "The coven is dividing, and we're losing access to our magic. If this continues, the coven will be destroyed. Then death itself means nothing, because our magic is what unifies us. If we don't have our magic, we will have no religion anymore. Our descendants will stop believing. We either live together, or we die alone. The Wands will give us our power back, and our people will come together once again. Please, Edgar. I'll do anything."

"Perhaps that is the problem," Edgar stated. "You will do anything, but all you need to do is the *right* thing. The Warlock's Trial is not by my design, and therefore I cannot tell you what needs to be done."

"You had to pass it in order to join the Reaper Order. What did you do?" I questioned.

He shook his head, like I still didn't get it. "My trial will not be like your own. You must search inside yourself for the answers. Dig deeper, Lucas, because power over death is more than just magic."

There had to be more to it than that. "I've done the inner work," I pressed. "I know it's not my job to carry other people's burdens, but obtaining these Wands is up to me. If I don't bring home the Mortana Wand, then I'm letting my people down. I can't do that. The coven's fate can't rest on me figuring out who I am or some bullshit like that. There are people counting on me to save them."

"You don't have to save the coven alone," Edgar assured me, shooting a glance toward my friends. "One man can't change the world, Lucas. He can only change himself, and then the world changes around him."

My breath wavered. "What if I'm too late?"

Edgar took a step back, releasing his hands from my shoulders. "I believe in you. Now, you must believe in yourself."

The weight of the magic I'd been holding on to crashed down on me, and I sank to my knees in the mud. The power I'd used to control the dead dispersed, freeing them from my control. Behind me, the townspeople muttered words of confusion, but I barely registered it.

I gazed up at Edgar. "Tell me what to do next."

"I cannot. That answer alone lies with you," he replied.

I didn't understand why he couldn't simply name me part of the Reaper Order and pass over the Wand. Surely he had power over such a process, and once I joined the Order, the spell binding the Wand to Edgar would release, until the Wand was bound to me.

Unless… it didn't matter one way or another. I could become part of the Reaper Order, but if the Mortana Wand didn't want to work with me, I couldn't wield its power. Edgar had no control over the Wand's decision. My friends had undergone their own trials to obtain their Wands, and none of them had been acquired by force.

I already knew what I had to do. I got back to my feet and stood tall. I hadn't realized until then that my friends had approached and were standing beside me. "If I am to wield the Mortana Wand, then I must earn it properly, or it will not honor me as its master. I must return to Earth and continue my work to pass the Warlock's Trial, as that is the only way I will rightly earn the Wand. I will guide you out of the Abyss, Edgar, if you are willing to trust me."

I reached out a hand, and Edgar took it. "I trust you, Lucas. I pray that you will trust me to return when you are ready. We will see each other again. That, I can promise you."

Edgar and I shook on it, sealing our promises to one another.

Nadine came to my side. "You're not giving up."

I wasn't sure if it was a question or not.

I glanced toward my other friends. Grant and Talia shared a crestfallen expression, and Chloe appeared disappointed. My gaze traveled to the Mentalist Wand in her hand. We got one Wand today, and that was worth walking through hell for.

"No, I'm not giving up," I said. "One way or another, we'll get that Wand, but not today. Let's go home."

I took Nadine's hand, and the others followed as we trudged through the swampy forest, the sounds of tortured screams fading behind us. We found the black river the Ferryman had brought us here on and followed its bank downstream.

The forest thinned, until the landscape ahead turned black with volcanic rock. The river became a stream of lava. We stood upon a tall hill, overlooking the hellscape. From here, we could see the lake of lava far in the distance, and the sound of monsters echoed across the realm.

We continued following the river of lava, until we came upon geysers I recognized. We passed by them, until we found the bubbling pits of sludge we'd come through. Grant squeezed Talia's hand, and Chloe approached one of the pits with cautious steps.

I stood at the edge, staring into the dark liquid. Getting through those pits hadn't been fun the first time, and I certainly didn't *want* to go through them again. But I also didn't want to remain in this hellscape any longer.

"This is the way out," I told Edgar, and he replied with an understanding nod.

Nadine squeezed my hand. "You ready?"

I shuddered to think what the sludge might have in store for me this time. I drew Nadine close. "Hold on to me, okay?"

"I won't let you go," she promised.

I reached out for Edgar's hand, and together, the three of us jumped into the pit. The darkness of the sludge surrounded us once more. I held my breath, but the thick tarry substance still filled my nose. Nadine's arms tightened around my neck as we sank deeper.

*You failed the trial, and you've failed your people.*

*Death follows you wherever you go.*

*Everyone leaves you. Even Helena didn't say goodbye.*

*You're better off dead.*

*You should end it right now.*

It wasn't like I hadn't already said all this to myself. The words barely seemed to faze me now.

Edgar's fingers slipped out of mine. The weight of the sludge pushed down on me, carrying me away from Nadine. She began to slip out of my hold, my hands trailing along her arms. I found the ends of her fingers and squeezed her hands tightly. My lungs burned…

Then I felt nothing.

For a brief moment, I was completely unaware. Then my head broke the surface, and I inhaled a deep breath.

I wiped sludge from my eyes with the back of my hand. I saw that I was back in the cave, surrounded by our cats. A witch light still hovered near the ceiling, illuminating the cavern. Oliver's shimmering form raced over to me, meowing in relief.

Nadine gasped from beside me as her head broke the surface. I quickly reached for the edge of the pit and climbed out. I grabbed Nadine's arm, fighting against hell to drag my wife out of its depths.

She emerged from the sludge, heaving heavy breaths. Edgar reached the surface after her and dragged himself over to the edge. Nadine and I fell onto our backs, panting.

She rolled over and placed her hand on the side of my face. "Lucas, are you okay?"

I closed my eyes, enjoying the feel of her touch on my skin. "Fine, Nad," I rasped.

"No, Lucas," she pressed. "Are. You. *Okay?*"

Her words held a deeper meaning. I was alive, but she wasn't asking if I was physically fine. She wanted to know how I'd handled the pits.

I opened my eyes to stare up at her. "The darkness of the pit is familiar, but I'm not going back to that dark place," I promised. "I'll be okay."

Coughing and sputtering came from the pits, and Nadine and I rushed over to help pull our friends from the sludge. We pulled Grant out, and he helped Nadine yank Talia and Chloe into the cave.

The cats gave a collective *meow*, and the glow from the spell faded. The cats laid down beside each other, appearing exhausted. The sludge drained from the pits until they were dry once more.

"We made it," Grant said in relief.

Chloe glanced around frantically. "Where's Edgar?"

"He's right here…" I trailed off as I turned back to him.

Edgar was nothing more than bones covered in a dark robe, though his form wasn't completely solid. I could see right through him—like he wasn't on the same plane as me. I realized I was the only one who could see him.

Edgar offered a kind nod. "Now that you have pulled me from the Abyss, I am free to journey back to Alora. It takes a powerful warlock to see a reaper on Earth, which means your magic is getting stronger. It shouldn't be long until we meet again. Goodbye for now, Lucas."

Edgar waved his hand, and a portal emitting a bright light appeared beside him. I'd felt the encompassing warmth of that light before, and I knew it was Alora.

"Edgar, wait," I called. "There's so much about my powers I have yet to learn. I don't understand how I'm going to pass the Warlock's Trial. I'm merely an apprentice, but I have no master. Is there no way you can help me?"

He turned to me. "I am a master of death, but I am not *your* master, Lucas. But I will leave you with this. Continue your fight, and you will join the Reaper Order sooner than you think. You will know when you have passed."

His words were ominous, as if warning me of something yet to come. It felt so final, as if he spoke of death itself—as if our fight with the priestesses was sure to end me.

"What does that mean?" I asked, but Edgar had already stepped into the light. His ethereal form faded, until my friends and I were alone in the cave.

"What did he say?" Nadine asked. Nobody else had heard him, and they all watched me curiously.

I couldn't answer for a beat, as if I was waiting for him to appear again and give more answers. All I was met with was silence. I took Nadine's hand. "He said I'm going to join the Reaper Order soon, but from what it sounds like, it's not going to be anything like what I've faced before."

"That means we're closer to the Mortana Wand," Nadine noted.

I swallowed the lump rising in my throat. "Let's hope so."

Talia shivered. "At least we got one of the Wands."

"Well worth it," Chloe agreed. She flicked the Mentalist Wand, and the remaining sludge dripped off our bodies effortlessly.

"Verla and Warren are waiting for us," Grant said. "Let's get out of here."

The cats led the way down the tunnel. Everyone remained quiet on the way back. I must've been walking slowly, because Grant, Talia, and Chloe went on ahead of us.

Nadine nudged me lightly. "Are you sure you're okay?"

"Seeing the Abyss got me thinking," I admitted. "The night of your Evoking Ceremony, Mother Miriam asked you to go to the Abyss for me. She told you later it was a demonstration, didn't she? To show her where your heart lies. When you told me that, I thought maybe she never intended to send either of us to the Abyss at all, but maybe she had intended to send us there, knowing we wouldn't be there long. Because the thing is, it wouldn't have mattered anyway, because we could've gotten ourselves out."

Nadine pressed her lips together thoughtfully. "Do you think we could've gotten out at the time? We've learned so much since then, about ourselves and how this all works. Could we have learned those lessons in the Abyss?"

"I think so," I said. "I think that's why Mother Miriam asked you to take my place—because she knew you'd get out."

"I think *you* would've, too," she argued. "It may have taken you time to learn the lessons, but you're strong, Lucas. You would've figured it out."

Nadine had faith in me I couldn't always understand, but I was starting to.

The trek didn't seem so long on the way out, and soon we emerged into daylight. I inhaled a deep breath of fresh air. We climbed the rocky slope of the cave entrance to find our fae allies waiting for us. Verla sat on the back of the wagon, leaning against Professor Warren. Her arm was in a sling, and her skin appeared ashen, but she was alive—thank Alora. A bundle of crushed herbs lay beside her, and Siona looked to be cleaning up from brewing an antidote. Kiara had returned and was helping Siona, but I didn't see Alexei anywhere.

Verla's eyes lit up when she saw us, and Warren sat up straighter.

"Did you get the Wands?" Professor Warren asked.

"One of them," Chloe said.

Verla glanced between us, looking worried. "And the other?"

"Not yet," I admitted.

"But we *need* that Wand!" Verla rasped. She tried to sit up, but Professor Warren insisted she lay back down.

"We still have a chance to obtain it," I said. "We'll tell you everything once we return home."

"Wait!" a voice called through the trees, and we turned to find Alexei racing in our direction. He slowed to catch his breath and survey the scene. His somber gaze roamed over Verla, settling on her injured arm. "Thank the gods you're all alive, though I see you haven't all made it out unharmed."

"We ran across the questing beast in the cave, and it harmed Clarice before we injured it and ran off," Nadine explained. "I suggest your people continue to keep an eye out for the monster, because it's bound to return to protect its lair."

I wanted to thank Alexei, Kiara, and Siona for their help, but I knew better than to thank the fae. It was a good way to get yourself into a bad bargain. Instead, I said, "It's time for us to portal home now."

"You can't," Alexei warned. "That is why I've come so quickly—to advise you to heed caution. I have received word that your last portal raised alarms. The enemy monarch knows that there are witches in the country. Her people are looking for you so they can kill you."

"The one who seized the city of Pruska a few months ago?" Grant asked.

"Yes," Alexei confirmed. "She's opposing Ethan and Emma in the revolution, and she's not kind to our people, let alone to any other supernaturals. Any witches found within her territory are immediately made an example of, and we are farther away from the protection of Dolinska than I would like. Her own army isn't stationed too far from here. She's been hanging any witches she finds, and leaving their bodies in the woods as a threat to any witches that might stray into the country."

"That explains the bodies we ran across earlier," Chloe mumbled.

"Then we should portal out of here as soon as we can," I insisted.

"If any one of us make a portal and a witch crosses through, her forces will be alerted, and they'll be here before all of you can portal out," Alexei said. "They won't hesitate. Our enemies are looking to recruit followers, and the rival queen knows the more witches she hangs, the more fae will join her. It's best we all avoid portals altogether, because they're already looking for you."

"How are we getting out of here?" Nadine asked.

The sound of flapping wings came from overhead, and a large shadow passed over us. I looked up to see a group of massive reptiles with large wings descending upon us. Talia screamed, and I grabbed Nadine as we scrambled backward. Branches snapped, and the trees groaned as the creatures landed in the forest around us.

"It's okay!" Alexei quickly assured us. "They're windfarers—friendly faekin."

Only when the creatures landed did I get a good look at them. The windfarers were over a dozen feet tall, with long necks, round heads, and colorful bodies covered in both fur and feathers. Their tails were skinny and long, and their wings appeared delicate and transparent, like those of a butterfly's. Five of them stood before us, all in different pastel colors.

"I thought faekin were supposed to be small," Nadine remarked, staring up at the marvelous creatures.

"There are many species of faekin, all related to our kind," Alexei explained. "The windfarers are friends with the fae, and they will take care of you as well. Take the windfarers to Malovia's border. You can portal back home once you're out of the country."

Cautiously, I approached one of the windfarers. He was light blue and the largest of the group. I reached out a hand, and he gently brought his velvety nose downward. I stroked his head a few times, and he cooed. Oliver followed along at my feet, and the windfarer bent down to lick him. Oliver meowed happily.

"They appear to be safe," I told the others. "We should get moving."

"I hope you found what you were looking for," Alexei said. "It's best if you don't return. It's not safe here even for our own people, but certainly not for your kind."

"We won't be back," I promised.

Professor Warren helped Verla to her feet, and they approached a lavender windfarer. He guided her onto the windfarer, then situated himself behind her to help her hold on. Grant climbed onto a pale green creature, while Talia took the pink one. Chloe rode a tangerine one, and Nadine and I settled onto the back of the large blue windfarer. Isa and Oliver jumped up beside us, then climbed into the hoods of our cloaks to hang on. The other cats settled in alongside their respective owners.

"Use the clouds as cover," Alexei instructed, before pointing in front of us. "Head straight that way. The border is miles off, but it's a short flight. There's a wide river that marks it. Dismount the windfarers before you reach it, then cross the river to portal home. Keep a lookout for potential threats. There's an enemy fae general who scouts the area nearby. His name's General Davor—big red dragon. He works for the rival queen and has given us plenty of problems. You'll know if you run into him. If you do, fly as fast and far as you can, and pray to your goddess you make it out alive."

It sounded ominous, but I was sure we'd make it. "Take care."

"We will," Alexei replied. "And good luck."

The windfarer spread its wings and kicked off the ground. Alexei, Kiara, and Siona waved goodbye as we departed.

My stomach flip-flopped as we took off, and my arms tightened around Nadine. She leaned against me as if to assure me she was okay. This was different from riding the dragon, because the windfarer's fur was softer, and the beat of its wings quieter. The flight was steady and felt like floating upon an insect, instead of being on the jostling back of a dragon. I felt secure up here on a creature's back.

The windfarers flew us high above the trees. The Malovian landscape stretched for miles, the woodland giving way to the mountains. Wind whipped through our hair, and I felt free in the air.

I didn't get much of a chance to view the landscape before we flew into the clouds. The cloud cover concealed us, but every now and then, I caught glimpses of the landscape below. The ruins of an old battlefield appeared through a break in the clouds. I figured we had to be getting close to the border by now.

I caught sight of Talia on the back of a pink windfarer beside us. She clutched tightly to the Seer Wand, which was glowing at the tip. Her eyes were squeezed tightly shut, and I knew she must be having a vision.

"Tal!" I cried. "What's happening?"

Talia winced, before her eyes shot open and she called out to us. "We've got company! Follow me. I know where we need to go!"

Talia leaned to the right, and her windfarer turned in another direction. The rest of us immediately picked up speed and followed behind her.

The sound of a terrifying roar rocked the skies. Nadine whirled her head around the same time the windfarer dove downward. Our cats squealed, and Oliver's claws clung to the fabric of my cloak. I had to grab tightly to the windfarer's feathers to keep us on his back. My heart hammered so hard I was sure Nadine could feel it against her back. She curled closer to me as we dipped downward.

Just as we broke out of the clouds, a large pair of jaws with razor-sharp teeth appeared above us. They snapped in our direction, and the windfarer banked left to avoid the monster.

"Dragon shifters!" Professor Warren's voice called through the sky.

I looked up to see the shadow of a massive beast closing in, its talons headed straight for us. The dragon was over twice the size of the windfarer, with long leathery wings and hard red scales covering his body. He had his eyes set on Nadine.

The need to protect overcame me, but a protection spell wasn't enough. This dragon shifter would die before it laid a talon on my wife.

The dragon snapped its jaws again, and the windfarer dodged its attack. The dragon flapped its leathery wings and rose above us once more. I raised my hand, and a high-powered death spell erupted from my palm, shooting straight toward the sky like a rocket. It slammed into the dragon's chest, and a cry of pain filled the air. The spell sizzled outward like lightning bolts consuming the shifter. He went spiraling out of the sky, and I watched as he hit the ground head-first. His chest continued to rise and fall, but he didn't get back up. My spell had been strong, but not enough to kill the shifter; I'd merely knocked him out. This wasn't going to be as easy as I thought.

I frantically looked around for signs of my friends, and I saw their windfarers emerging from the clouds.

"There's more!" Grant screamed, pointing behind us.

My stomach plummeted when I saw a horde of shifters rising into the sky. Men morphed into dragons, griffins, alicorns, and wolves with wings, and female sorceresses mounted the shifters backs before they took to the skies to pursue us. Despite our best efforts to not raise any alarms, we had been spotted, and the shifters were closing in *fast*.

"Faster!" I ordered the windfarer. He beat his wings harder, but the shifters were still catching up.

"Lucas, you have to portal us out of here!" Nadine demanded.

I looked to our friends, who blasted spells back at the shifters. The windfarers swooped and twisted through the sky, avoiding dragon fire-balls and illusion spells from the other shifters. There was no way to get us all through a portal up here. If I tried and didn't aim the portal just right, any one of us could be killed.

"I can't!" I shouted over the roar of the wind. "We have to get on solid ground!"

Off in the distance, I could see the river that Alexei had mentioned, but there was nothing between us and the river except a barren landscape. There was nothing to conceal us long enough to dismount our windfarers and cast a portal. The shifters would have us slaughtered before we made it that far.

Chloe flew up beside us. She whirled around and shot a spell behind herself. It hit a griffin shifter in the face, and he tumbled out of the sky. Several spells blasted in her direction, and I instinctually cast a shield around her. The spells slammed into my shield, unable to penetrate it, but my magic recoiled. Their spells were *strong*.

We had to be stronger.

Grant conjured the Alchemy Wand and aimed it toward the clouds above us. The clouds darkened, until the sound of heavy rain followed behind us. I wasn't sure what that was supposed to do, until I heard the pained cries of shifters as the rain hit their bodies. I twisted around to see the rain sizzling off feathers, fur, and scales. Roars of pain ricocheted through the sky as the acid rain burned holes through their bodies. Grant had used the Alchemy Wand to poison the clouds.

It wasn't enough to kill them all, though. Hundreds more were in pursuit.

Professor Warren lifted his hands, and at least a dozen bodies of dead shifters flapped their wings, following the command of his necromancy magic. He ordered the bodies to take flight and fight off the incoming shifters. Griffin talons tore at dragon's eyes, and wolvens gnashed their teeth at alicorns. Several more shifters fell from the sky, but it barely slowed the others down. It was an impressive feat to manipulate so many corpses at the same time, but there were far more shifters than Professor Warren could fight off at once. He slumped against his windfarer as he summoned more magic that continued to drain his energy.

Our windfarers climbed higher in the sky, traversing the clouds, until we broke through on the other side. Spells whizzed through the sky at random as the fae shifters tried to guess where we had gone. I shot a glance over my shoulder to see shifters rising above the clouds, closer than before. I wasn't sure we could outrun them.

Shifters with sorceresses on their backs broke through the clouds ahead of us. The windfarers nearly toppled out of the sky as they quickly shifted course.

"Emma and Ethan have let witches into our country!" a fae sorceresses yelled. "We must kill every last dark magic user."

A chorus of cheers filled the air, and a split second later, my vision went completely black. I blinked several times, looking one way and then the other, but I saw nothing.

"Lucas!" Nadine shrieked. "I can't see!"

I gritted my teeth. "Neither can I."

"It's a fae illusion!" Verla's voice came from far off.

Chloe gave a maniacal laugh. "Oh, no you don't!"

Magic crackled from beside me. My vision returned the same time screams filled the air. Ahead of us, shifters had turned on one another. Dragons lunged out for griffin shifters, tearing their wings off their bodies. Alicorns rammed their sharp horns into the bellies of the wolven men.

I was shocked, until I looked over at Chloe and saw her holding up the Mentalist Wand. She'd gotten into their minds and was forcing them to kill one another!

"I've distracted them!" Chloe yelled. "Let's keep moving."

I kicked the sides of the windfarer's body, and he flew above the shifters. Their dying cries grew distant, but flapping wings still followed. The original group of shifters were still in pursuit, and they'd nearly caught up to us.

"What do we do!?" Grant cried.

"We've always been told witches can break fae magic," I shouted to my friends. "One on one, they're stronger than us, but together we're stronger than they are! Let's see if the stories are true. We need to combine our magic."

We all lifted our hands in unison, and magic of all colors began to swirl through the sky. Nadine gathered the power of all five Casts into one central core at her heart. Then it expanded outward, encompassing us all in a protective shield. Spells slammed into the shield. Nadine gave a shudder with each one, but our magic held.

Then Nadine did the most incredible thing. She commanded the spell to grow, until our magic touched the fae. One by one, Nadine broke the fae spells and the shifters turned back into men. Screams tore through the air as the fae fell through the skies. Women tried to conjure their fae wings, but it was to no avail. Our enemies spiraled out of the sky, plummeting to their deaths.

Talia maneuvered her windfarer in the direction the Seer Wand had shown her, and we all followed. We banked to the right, avoiding the open space ahead. Instead, the windfarers landed in a cluster of trees, and we quickly made our way across the river. Our shoes squished with mud as we came out on the other side. The second we were across the river and outside the boundary of Malovia, I created a portal, and we leapt through.

The air shifted around us, and we stood in the forest just outside the safe house. I quickly glanced around to see if everyone and their cats had made it, and I breathed a sigh of relief when I saw we were all here.

"Thank the Goddess," Talia cried, before falling into Grant's arms.

Verla sagged against Professor Warren. "We made it," she breathed.

Warren got a worried look on his face, then turned to me. "The venom did a number on her. I'm going to get her to her room right away. You should all rest, too. It's been a long night."

The morning sun peeked through the overcast sky. It was only then that I realized how tired I was. The others looked exhausted. Warren led Verla inside ahead of us, and we followed behind them.

When we stepped into the living room, my stomach dropped. Tate and Mandy sat on the couch, curled under blankets. Tate was sleeping, though Mandy was wide awake, watching the door. Tate stirred when we arrived.

Miles and Onyx were both pacing the room, looking worried. It'd been over a day since I portaled them to the safe house, promising to return as soon as possible. It'd been a long time to make them wait. When we walked in, both of them gave a start.

"You're back!" Onyx cried.

"Finally," Miles added. "Is everyone okay? We thought maybe…"

He winced, like he couldn't bear to finish.

"We made it," Chloe said. "And we brought three Wands with us."

Mandy sat up straighter. "You found all the other missing Oaken Wands, the ones the priestesses don't have?"

"We found *one* of the missing Wands," Grant explained. "We stole the Alchemy Wand and the Seer Wand from the school where the priestesses were keeping them. Then we took a detour to Malovia, hitched a ride to the Abyss, and we came back with the Mentalist Wand."

Grant had a strange way of making it sound easy.

"The priestesses aren't going to be happy," Mandy said, sounding worried. "They'll come looking for the Wands. We should keep them in a safe place."

"The safest place is on our person, so they're readily available if we have to use them," Chloe suggested.

"Then the priestesses will come after *you*," Mandy insisted. "They should be kept together, somewhere the priestesses can't get to."

"Isn't it better to split them up?" Grant asked. "That way if the priestesses get one of the Wands, they don't get them all."

"I'm with Grant and Chloe," Talia agreed. "As long as the Wands are on us, we can use them. Then if the priestesses come after us, we're stronger with the Wands."

"Maybe each Cast should agree on what to do with their respective Wand," Nadine offered.

Talia turned to her sister. "All right. Tate, Miles? What do you want to do with the Seer Wand?"

Tate drew a deep breath. "I don't think that's something you should be asking me."

Talia tilted her head. "But you're a Seer—and my sister. I care about your opinion."

Tate stood. "That's sweet of you, but I don't think I can continue to be a part of this fight. I'm not in a good place mentally, and I'm at risk of a relapse if I don't get help. My time in rehab helped after I overdosed on nightshade, but I'm still not stable enough to stay and fight. Believe me, Talia, I *want* to help, but I know my limits, and I don't want to hold the team back."

"You're not going to hold us back," Talia pressed.

"Tal, be real," Tate insisted. "I know you want me around because I'm your sister, but I don't belong here. If I stay, I'm going to end up hurting people, and I don't want that for anyone."

Tears welled in Talia's eyes. "Where will you go?"

"I don't know, but I can't stay here," Tate replied. "All I know is that if I continue to be a part of this war, I'm going to relapse. I need to get out of here as soon as I can."

"I can portal her to *Hok'evale*," I offered. "She'll be safe there, and the healers can reverse the worst of her injuries. There's a rehab clinic. I saw fliers for it when we visited. She can stay there until she gets better."

Tate nodded. "I think that's where I need to go. And maybe when I'm in a better place, I can help others like me."

Talia reached out for her sister. "Are you sure you have to go?"

"Positive." Tate's voice cracked. "I *need* you to let me go, or I'm going to end up staying for you, and that's not going to turn out well for anyone."

"Okay," Talia said gently. "Once the Miriamic Conflict is over, we'll come back and get you, and we'll bring you home."

Tate shook her head. "You don't understand. Octavia Falls is too triggering for me. Being there reminds me of everything that happened and all I went through. It makes me want to start using again, so I need to start over in a completely new place. I can't come back home ever again, even if the priestesses fall. I need to start over and make a new life somewhere else, because Octavia Falls isn't my home anymore. I love you, Tal, but this is what's best for me."

"*Hok'evale* is a good place to start over," Nadine said. "They'll welcome you with open arms."

Talia teared up. "I'm sorry for everything you went through, Tate, but I'm proud of you for knowing your limits and setting boundaries. If this is what you believe you need, then I'll support you."

Tate sniffled, like it was hard to admit all this. "It is what I need."

Talia drew her sister into a tight hug. "I'll come visit, all right?"

Tate squeezed her back. "I was hoping you'd say that. You and Miles can decide what to do with the Seer Wand together."

"You should keep the Seer Wand, Tal," Miles voted. "It chose you—you deserve it. And I agree we should have access to the Wands' powers at all times, in case something bad happens…"

He trailed off and glanced toward Onyx, like the two of them knew something we didn't. Something was definitely up. We could all feel it.

"What's going on?" Talia asked slowly.

Onyx twisted her hands together. "There's something you guys need to see."

Footsteps came from down the hall. Professor Warren stopped in his tracks when he saw the worried looks on our faces.

"Clarice is in bed," he said. "Is everything okay?"

Miles shifted his weight between his feet. "Not really, Professor. We ran across bodies on our way back, after Lucas portaled us home. We didn't want to touch them or move them until you guys returned. You should all come see."

Onyx and Miles led us out the front door. Mandy followed, but Tate stayed back, like she knew whatever they had to show us was awful.

They led us through the trees. Miles was silent for several minutes, until we got closer to the border of our ward. "Onyx cast some spells to see if she could figure out what happened to them. What'd you call it? A magical autopsy."

"Yes. I made a potion I learned in my nursing classes," Onyx said. "I sprinkled it around the scene. It's supposed to show the areas of injury, but we didn't find any injuries. We don't know how they died."

They hadn't exactly said what *kind* of bodies they found. I thought maybe they'd found dead animals or something. Then I saw where they were leading us. Ahead of us in the forest, not far beyond the boundary of our ward, two corpses lay motionless on the ground. The two men were dressed in identical black uniforms.

"Executors?" Nadine stopped in her tracks. She steadied herself against a tree, while Professor Warren stepped forward cautiously.

"We figure the priestesses sent more Executors looking for us, after the others we killed didn't report back," Onyx said.

"But they were dead by the time we got here," Miles added. "We don't know what killed them. It looks like they just collapsed."

Talia stepped closer. "We're at the border of our ward. If they came much closer, they would've found it. Nadine, can our ward *kill* them?"

Nadine shook her head. "No. Our ward keeps us concealed, but it isn't deadly."

I stepped closer to inspect the bodies. Something about this was very strange. Usually I could feel the emptiness of death permeating the air, but this was different. I felt less than empty.

I felt... nothing.

"Lucas, what did you hear when they died?" Nadine asked. "It might give us clues as to what happened."

I shook my head. "I can't be sure. I hear multiple thoughts every day. I can't identify whose thoughts they are if I don't know them personally. I've learned how to handle it so it's more like background noise. We were fighting Executors and then escaped to Malovia when this all happened. I wasn't paying attention, so I'm not sure what they said."

"Any idea how long they've been out here?" Chloe asked Professor Warren.

He waved his hand over the bodies, using his Death magic to assess the scene. "They haven't been here long. They must've died right before Miles and Onyx found them."

I looked at Miles. "Were you able to sense their ghosts when you found them?"

He shook his head. "No. I tried, but they must've already moved on by the time we got here."

Chloe turned to Talia. "Can you see into the past and find out what happened here?"

"I can try." Talia held up the Seer Wand, which began to glow at the end. She closed her eyes, and her lids began to flicker.

The Wand glowed brighter until Talia's knees gave out. Grant rushed to catch her, then gently lowered her to the ground.

Talia shook her head as she came to. "That was intense, but the details are fuzzy."

Mandy narrowed her eyes. "You have all the power of the Seer Cast with that Wand. Can't you see everything?"

"No," Talia explained. "The coven's visions are often hazy and left up to interpretation. We aren't as powerful as prophets. I can't tell you who killed these people, but I can tell you they were murdered."

"What did you see?" Professor Warren asked.

"I saw a person in a black cloak, but it was dark outside. I couldn't see their face," Talia said. "I saw them watching the two Executors from the tree line. Then there was a flash, and the Executors were on the ground."

"A flash like a battle orb?" Miles asked.

Talia shook her head. "More like a flash in my mind, like the vision can't read what killed them. Whatever the spell was, it was powerful, and it didn't leave any traces. Then I heard Miles's voice, and the person in the cloak fled."

Miles's features fell. "So we stumbled upon them right after they were killed. The killer didn't even get a chance to hide the bodies."

"Or they wanted us to find them," Chloe pointed out. "Like they want us to know they're here watching us."

A shiver traveled down my spine. "The killer can't be with the priestesses. They wouldn't have slaughtered their own people."

"Well, if the murderer isn't on the priestesses' side, and they aren't on our side, what does it mean?" Mandy wondered.

"I don't know…" I said, eyeing the bodies curiously. "Something about this isn't right."

"You think maybe it's some sort of trap?" Nadine wondered.

I glanced around the quiet forest. "If that were the case, the priestesses would've been here by now."

Nadine turned to Talia. "Can you use the Seer Wand to track down the killer?"

Talia closed her eyes again, but a confused expression crossed her face. "I'm getting images of a forest… *this* forest, I think. But it doesn't make any sense. I can't tell where the killer's gone."

"Either way, now we've got two more missing Executors the priestesses are going to come looking for," I remarked. "They're going to send more until they find something."

"Then let's give them bodies to find," Professor Warren suggested.

I nodded, understanding his intent. "We need to move them far away from the safe house. It will throw the priestesses off for a while, get them looking for us elsewhere."

"Let me cast a spell. I'll block any visions that might lead the priestesses back here." Talia waved the Seer Wand, and tendrils of magic settled over the bodies, then faded.

Professor Warren lifted his hand, and the bodies moved to his command like puppets. They started walking like zombies. I cast a portal leading several miles from here, along the river bend at the base of the mountain. Professor Warren puppeteered the bodies through the portal, until they were out of sight. The portal closed behind them.

"This doesn't change that someone still knows where we are," Chloe pointed out. "That black-cloaked murderer in Talia's vision is trying to tell us something."

"Well, he didn't get past our wards, so we're still safe here," I stated. "We should get back inside."

I started back toward the house, and the others followed.

"What do we do now?" Talia asked once we were back inside.

"We keep investigating the Wands," I decided. "We have three, so we're over halfway there. We still need to find the Curse Breaker Wand and obtain the Mortana Wand. We know where the Mortana Wand is, and we have a rough idea of how to get it. We need to put everything we've got into learning more about reaper powers, so that I can pass the Warlock's Trial and get the Mortana Wand."

"Where do we start?" Nadine wondered. "You've tried researching reapers before, and it didn't get anywhere."

"Then we need to ask for help," I said. "Maybe Hattie will have connections we haven't thought of. In the meantime, we can work on reinforcing our wards. Onyx and Miles can work with Talia on her visions to see if they can get more clues about this mysterious cloaked figure. That's all we can do for now. We all need to get some rest."

People started heading off to the respective bedrooms, but Nadine and Chloe hung back. I watched curiously as Nadine made her way over to Mandy.

"I'm really glad you're back," Nadine told her. "I know being friends with me hasn't been easy, and I'm sorry you were ever caught in the middle of it."

That was an understatement. Mandy had been in love with Amy, and Amy had died in the Burning because she'd helped *us* decipher nightshade ingredients to track down the manufacturer. Mandy had been stabbed by a ghost in Pinewood Manor because we'd asked her to help uncover the mystery of the haunting. Then Mandy had led the priestesses to our hideout in the school, which resulted in our trial. She'd come to us to apologize for turning us in before our trial, but it hadn't ended well. That was the last time we'd seen Mandy.

Tears beaded in Mandy's eyes. "You have no idea how much it means to hear you say that. I worried you wouldn't want me around, after I turned you into the priestesses."

"Not at all," Nadine said gently. "I want to be friends again. You're the first person I met on my first day at Miriam College. Our friendship means a lot to me. I understand if things got too intense for you, and I'm sorry we ever had to put you in that position. I want to move forward with a better understanding of each other so that no one gets hurt again."

"I want that, too," Mandy said. "I agree that things got hard, but if I could do it over again, I'd never turn you in to the priestesses. I never wanted to stop being friends, even when I couldn't handle the pressure. All I wanted was your forgiveness."

"And you have it," Nadine promised.

Tears streamed down their faces as the girls hugged.

"I owe you an apology, too," I told her. "The last time we spoke before our trial, I was very harsh with you. I should've put myself in your shoes. Maybe I would've understood better what you were going through."

"If you can forgive me for turning you in, then I can forgive you for what you said that day," Mandy offered.

"Then we have a deal," I told her, reaching out to shake her hand.

Chloe stepped forward. "If you'll accept my apology, I'd like to say sorry as well. I treated you awful, especially after you dated Ryan right after we broke up. I mean, the guy's not even worth it. There's no excuse for how mean I was, and I never should've treated you that way."

Mandy chuckled, like Chloe was already long forgiven. "Don't worry about it. I'm totally over him."

"So… we're good?" Chloe asked.

"Yeah, we're good," Mandy said, glancing between the three of us. "We're all good. I've been through a lot since you've been gone. I used to think we couldn't go up against the priestesses, but I was wrong. I've never been more ready to face them. I want to keep working with you to find the Oaken Wands and do right by the coven."

I didn't think we'd ever be friends with Mandy again after she turned us into the priestesses, but I'd been wrong. If we could mend our relationship with Mandy and unite our friends, then we could certainly heal the coven, too.

We just had to keep trying.

# nadine

## FOURTEEN

Two weeks passed since we returned from the Abyss, and I'd slept through most of it. We'd been through so much, and sometimes, it all felt like a dream I hadn't fully processed.

When we'd returned home, it hit me all over again that Grammy was gone, and that sent me to a dark place. It didn't help that we weren't getting new leads on the Warlock's Trial, and it didn't feel like we were making any progress at all. I felt out of control to change anything.

I cried every day, so I slept a lot just to block out the world, because there was nothing else for me to do. I napped for hours at a time, curled under the blanket Grammy had crocheted—the one she'd gifted to me during my bridal shower. It still smelled like her, and I couldn't decide if that brought me comfort or hurt even more. My friends kept trying to push on without me and gain answers, but I couldn't find it in me to join them.

I'd gone to the Abyss and seen what the witches were willing to do to each other, even in death. If we were that hellbent on torturing one another in the afterlife, what was the point? There were witches in the Abyss who'd been tormenting themselves and others for centuries, and they were happy doing it, so why bother interceding? Why was I even trying to stop any of this, when most of the coven was going to keep persecuting those among us even in death?

That's how I thought sometimes, though the thoughts didn't feel like my own. I knew we had to push on and find the rest of the Oaken Wands, but it was hard when I felt empty inside.

It was like Lucas and I had swapped places. He cooked me meals and convinced me to get out of bed at least once a day to take a walk. He'd gotten really good at taking care of me.

When Lucas wasn't sleeping next to me, he was going through old books Hattie had given us shortly after we returned. She couldn't find anything on reapers, so she'd sent along books about the afterlife from other supernatural societies and suggested we start there. She thought there may be some similarities between the lore. So far it didn't sound like Lucas had found anything new.

We couldn't go up against the priestesses until Lucas had the Mortana Wand. We could use the Mentalist, Seer, and Alchemy Wand against the priestesses, but with an army of Mortana Executors on their side, we'd be slaughtered by Death magic the second we showed our faces in Octavia Falls.

I witnessed Talia's tearful goodbye with her sister before Lucas portaled Tate to *Hok'evale*. Talia had baked her cookies and sent Tate with one of her sweaters and a care package. Tate seemed relieved to be leaving Octavia Falls for good. I really thought *Hok'evale* was going to be good for her.

Talia hadn't learned much else from her visions about the mystery man who was lurking our ward borders. No one had disturbed us since, so I figured Lucas was right and that we were safe here. With the three Oaken Wands we'd obtained, our wards were stronger than ever.

Talia was using the Seer Wand to keep an eye on the priestesses. We'd thrown them off our location by moving the Executors' bodies, and they'd been searching for us miles away. The priestesses were so preoccupied with searching for us that they weren't doing much else inside the coven right now, according to Hattie's report. They were obviously preoccupied with finding out where we'd taken the Wands, but they hadn't been able to track us down.

Miles suggested we use the Wands to read the priestesses' minds to get more information, but neither Chloe nor Talia could get their Wands to work that way. There were witches from both the Mentalist and Seer Casts who could read minds to some degree, but it required skill that neither Chloe nor Talia had mastered. The Wands were powerful, but they were still limited by the confines of witch magic, and by the caster themselves. Though some witches could read minds, most couldn't do it at a distance, and it was especially difficult to read someone's mind without their consent. Most witches' mind-reading abilities only captured fragments of thoughts anyway. It was a skill that might prove useful, but Talia and Chloe were still working on it. Even with the Wands, they weren't all-powerful. They needed to find, then teach themselves, a way to get around all these constraints, and it wasn't an easy process.

Things were getting worse inside the coven. It was obvious because the Waning had hit all of us harder over these last few weeks than it had all summer. We had three Wands to combat it, but they weren't much help with mine or Lucas's powers. He'd gone days unable to use his portal magic, and we needed to make a supply run soon.

I woke one morning to find Lucas was already out of bed. My joints protested as I rolled over to check the clock. It was almost noon already. I sat up in bed and yawned. All I wanted to do was curl up and go back to sleep.

It took everything in me to haul my ass out of bed. My legs felt like noodles, and I had to lean against the nightstand for support. Dread sank in my stomach.

"Fucking hell," I growled. "Not again."

I was no stranger to fatigue, but my health had been *so good* these last few months. I wasn't about to let my lupus take over my life again. It was only a matter of time before one of my friends found a lead, and we were going to act fast to obtain another Wand. Furthermore, the priestesses could show up on our doorstep at any time, and I'd have to be ready to fight them.

I didn't have the time or ability to continue lying in bed anymore. I needed to be proactive.

It was one hell of a wake-up call.

I sank back down onto the bed. I waited several minutes, like the fatigue might pass, but I knew this feeling all too well. Chronic illnesses were unpredictable, and an episode like this could last for months before I got my energy back.

I became increasingly angry the longer I lay there. My doctors had predicted a three-to-five-percent chance my lupus would ever return after the kidney transplant. What's more, Dr. Yonker had told me my lupus would go into remission a year or two after I got my magic. He'd obviously lied.

Either way, the chances of symptoms returning was so low. Why was this happening now of all times?

The possibilities terrified me. If my lupus was back… did that mean my kidney was failing?

Was it too much to ask for my symptoms to just be over and done with?

The mattress shook beneath me, and I gave a start. I looked over to see Isa jumping onto the bed. She nudged her nose into my hand, as if to ask if I was okay.

I wiped my eyes and stroked her head. "I'll be all right."

I didn't think Isa believed me, because she snuggled up on my belly and began purring. I could hear chatter from downstairs. I wanted to go join everyone else, but I couldn't muster the energy to talk to a single person, let alone a whole group. At the same time, the bed was so uncomfortable when I felt like this, and I didn't want to go back to it, but I had to do *something* with my body, because otherwise, I'd just sit here and suffer.

I hated it.

This was not the life I wanted. I didn't want to spend my life wasting away. I'd done enough of that these last two weeks. It'd been my choice, but if my illness flared, I couldn't get up and live my life when I wanted— no, when I *needed* to. I had to get ahead of this before my lupus flare gained control over my life again.

"Isa," I whispered as I stroked her fur. "I've got to ask for help."

Isa gave a light meow, like she agreed with me.

Taking a deep breath, I swung my legs off the corner of the bed. Down the hall, Onyx's door was wide open, and she was organizing Alchemy supplies inside. A cauldron sat on the dresser, surrounded by various crystals and herbs. Charms hung from the ceiling fan, and incantations scribbled on sticky notes stuck to her mirror. A haunting melody played from her phone.

"Onyx, do you have a minute?" I asked.

She looked up from the herbs she was arranging on her dresser. "Sure, Nadine. Come in."

I stepped into the room, and Isa followed behind me. I closed the door, because I didn't want anyone to overhear, then sat on her bed. Onyx shot a curious glance at the closed door, like she knew whatever I had to say was serious.

"You worked at the hospital," I started. "What do you know about lupus?"

Onyx spoke slowly, like she was worried where I might be going with this. "I have my nursing license, but I'm not a doctor. I only know what I've gathered from reading up on it. Is everything okay?"

I tried to keep the worry from my features, but I wasn't sure it worked. "No," I admitted in a broken voice. "I woke up really fatigued. I'm afraid my lupus is coming back, and I wouldn't normally ask for help, but we're fighting a war. I can't deal with the unpredictability of my illness, so I need to get on the front end of this before it gets worse, because I know it inevitably will."

Onyx dropped her herbs immediately and came to sit beside me. "Nadine, I'm so sorry. I thought the kidney transplant was supposed to help."

"It did. For a while, at least," I said. "I've been feeling *really* good. I've been off antibiotics for a while, and my immunosuppressants have been keeping everything in check. The doctors said I was good. And now... I'm scared that I'm not."

"We'll figure it out," Onyx promised. "I can brew something to help with the fatigue."

I swallowed the lump rising in my throat. "I'm worried it's more than that. What if my body's rejecting the kidney?"

Onyx's features paled. "I can help you manage symptoms, but if you think your kidney's failing, you need to see a doctor immediately."

I sighed heavily. "I thought I was done with all that."

"We won't know anything for sure until you see a doctor," Onyx said.

"You don't have any potions that will help?" I asked hopefully.

Onyx frowned. "Nadine, you just told me your kidney could be failing. I can't mess with something as severe as that."

"I know. It's just... the last thing I want is to end up in the hospital again."

"Then we have to get you treatment right away." Onyx stood and reached out a hand. "Come on, let's go talk to Lucas."

"No," I said quickly. "I don't want to worry him if it's nothing. I know I agreed to open up about my health more, and I'll tell him everything, but I need to talk to the doctors alone first. Then if it's bad news, I can find a way to tell him myself."

There was no use in worrying anyone until I knew what was going on. I could be overreacting. But if it was as bad as I was thinking, I needed time alone to cry.

Onyx eyed me for a few moments, before nodding in understanding. "All right. You can talk to your doctors first, but we still need to get Lucas to portal you to *Hok'evale*. He's downstairs planning a supply run."

"I need to refill my prescriptions anyway, and I'm due for a pharmacy visit," I said.

Onyx led me out of the room, and we found the others gathered in the living room.

Lucas held up a list. "The tub in the downstairs bathroom is having some plumbing issues, so Grant and I are going to pick up some supplies to fix that. The pantry's running short on essentials. Warren has made strong allies with various charities in Celestial City, so we can get those essentials there for a good price. He's convinced the angels he's interested in converting to their religion, so they'll continue to provide him with supplies so long as he keeps up the ruse. They'll do anything to get him baptized. Unfortunately, the angels don't carry some of the herbs we're running low on for spellwork."

"The vampires are willing to trade for the right price," Verla offered. Her arm was out of the sling, but the questing beast's attack had left a permanent twisted scar even the healers in *Hok'evale* couldn't fix. It would forever serve as a reminder how much she cared—that she was willing to sacrifice herself to save me.

Lucas nodded. "Then I'll send you to negotiate with them. Let's see... what else?"

"My meds are running low." My tone came out sounding even, but my heart was in my throat. "I need to go to the pharmacy in *Hok'evale*."

Lucas made a mark on his list. "All right, Nadine will pick up meds. I think we're all set then. Text me when you're done so I can portal you all home."

Lucas started portaling the others to their respective locations, and I slipped on my shoes. I was still in my pajama pants and sweatshirt, but I didn't really care. I didn't think I could bring myself to get dressed now, anyway. I was too worried.

"Do you want someone to come with you?" Lucas asked before he opened my portal.

"No," I said almost too quickly. *"Hok'evale's* a safe place. I'll text you once I'm done at the clinic."

Lucas gave me a kiss, then portaled me right outside the walk-in clinic. A few people looked my way when I stepped through the portal, but I ignored them and headed straight for the doors.

"How can I help you?" the receptionist behind the counter asked.

"I need to see a doctor. How soon can I get in?"

She typed a few things on her computer. "Dr. Malach is available. He's a world-renowned doctor and will take good care of you."

"That sounds perfect. Thank you."

"Yes, of course. What's your name?" the receptionist asked.

"Nadine Taylor," I told her. "You might have me in the system as Nadine Evers—I recently got married."

The receptionist gave a kind smile. "You can have a seat. Dr. Malach will be right with you."

I turned to the waiting room, and I was shocked to see two familiar faces. A guy with dark hair sat beside a woman in a wheelchair. They saw me at the same time, and their faces lit up.

"Nadine!" Quentin cried. "What are you doing here? Good news, I hope."

I sat across from them. "That's what I'm here to find out. I'm glad to see you made it here safely."

Quentin and Lydia had tried to stay in Octavia Falls after surviving The Hearse Tragedy, but after Quentin stood up for us in the town square, it wasn't safe for them anymore. They'd fled Octavia Falls to find refuge here in *Hok'evale*.

Lydia pushed her purple-framed glasses up her nose. "Safe and sound. Life has been good in *Hok'evale*. We got married!"

"Congratulations. So did I." I held out my hand to show them the ring.

Quentin's eyebrows shot up. "Wow. Who's the lucky guy?"

I smirked and rolled my eyes. "I'll give you one guess."

Quentin grinned in a teasing manner. "Congrats to you and Lucas."

"Sorry we couldn't be there," Lydia said. "Travel isn't very easy for us at the moment."

I waved my hand. "Don't worry about it. We had to keep the ceremony small and private."

Quentin nodded. "Understandable. Last we heard, things have only gotten worse back home. We want to come back to Octavia Falls eventually, but we can't come back until things settle down. We're taking classes again, and Lydia's got her physical therapy and treatments."

"The Anichi doctors have been amazing," Lydia raved. "Their healing powers have sped up my recovery significantly."

"What kind of prognosis did they give you?" I wondered. I knew they couldn't heal *everything*, but I wondered just how far the Anichi's healing magic went.

"The damage to my spine the night of The Hearse Tragedy was too severe to fix," Lydia told me. "Besides that, I'd already been healing by the time we came here, so they couldn't undo what my body had already done. I'm not going to be able to walk again, but I've been able to manage my pain better. Months of recovery were condensed into weeks, but we're not finished. Every spinal cord injury is different, so we've just been taking it one day at a time."

"So you come here often for physical therapy?" I wondered.

"Actually, my physical therapy is in another building," Lydia replied, before glancing toward Quentin.

He replied with a goofy grin. "We're actually here because we just found out we're pregnant!"

"Wow…" I trailed off. I couldn't imagine having a baby in the midst of everything going on in our coven, but Quentin and Lydia seemed safe and happy here in *Hok'evale*.

Lydia noticed my hesitation, and she laughed. "We're very excited."

"Well in that case, congratulations!" I cried.

"It was a bit unexpected," Quentin admitted. "But we can't wait to meet our little one."

He placed his hand on Lydia's belly, and she rested hers over the top of his. I didn't notice a bump, so she couldn't be very far along.

"I guess the Anichi treatments made me extra fertile," Lydia said with a laugh. "My legs may not work, but my reproductive organs are operating just fine."

I forced a smile. I was happy for them, but I wished we were meeting under better circumstances. "I'm glad everything's working out for you two."

Quentin squeezed Lydia's hand. "We're doing great. We really are. I can't wait to be a dad. It's killing me not knowing if it's a boy or a girl. I just want to give the little one a name, you know?"

"Do you have names picked out?" I asked.

"We haven't settled on a girl's name yet," Lydia said. "But if it's a boy, we're naming him Alistair."

"Maybe you won't need a girl's name," I offered. "In less than nine months, we could be meeting little Alistair."

Lydia lit up. "I like the sound of that."

"Nadine Taylor?" a voice came from behind me.

I turned to see a nurse. I waved goodbye to Lydia and Quentin, then stood to follow her. She led me back to an exam room and took my height, weight, and vitals.

"What concerns do we have today?" she asked.

"I have lupus, and I got a kidney transplant a few months ago, but I woke up with some stiffness and fatigue that worry me," I said.

She typed something into the computer, then stood. "All right. Dr. Malach will be right with you."

I waited uneasily for the doctor after she left the room. I hoped to the Goddess this was nothing, but my intuition told me I was about to receive life-altering news. My donor kidney was failing; I was convinced of it. Which meant I'd have to go back on dialysis and wait on the transplant list again. I worried I'd never reach the top of the list, or if I did, my body would reject that kidney, too.

I choked back my worry when the doctor entered the room. He wasn't anything like I expected. I thought I'd be meeting with an Anichi healer, but this man had large white feathery wings growing out of his back. The doctor was tall, with broad shoulders, and although he looked to be twice my age, his skin was perfectly smooth.

I must've been gawking, because he said, "I take it you haven't seen an angel before."

I snapped my mouth shut. "No, sorry. I thought the doctors here were all Anichi."

He eyed me like he thought I might be joking. "Not all of them. Why don't you tell me what's wrong?"

I repeated what I'd told the nurse, then dove into more details about my diagnosis and transplant.

Dr. Malach leaned back in his chair. "And you're here because you're… tired? How much have you been sleeping?"

"I'm sleeping just fine," I replied. "I wouldn't say I'm tired. It's more than that. The fatigue encompasses my whole body. It feels like when I was first diagnosed with lupus. That's why I'm worried."

"When was your last period?" he asked bluntly.

I was taken aback. "Is that relevant?"

"We should rule out hormonal fluctuations first," he stated simply.

What was this guy saying? That I was overreacting because I was a woman?

"I get my period regularly," I bit harshly. "I'm familiar with the effects my hormones have on my body. I'm telling you this is different."

He paused for a beat. "Very well. Let me examine you."

He reached out his hand, and I hesitated.

His tone grew bitter, like he was annoyed with me. "Anichi are not the only ones with healing magic. I can assess you as well, unless you'd like to wait and make an appointment with another doctor."

"No," I said quickly. "I'd like answers today, if possible."

I placed my hand in his, and his magic filled me. Angel magic was very different from Elementai Soul magic. When I'd first come here and met with Dr. Metzi, her magic was warm and inviting, encompassing my whole body in a gentle light. Dr. Malach's magic was harsher, almost piercing as it swirled deep in my gut. It was like he was prodding for something inside of me. I winced, and he dropped my hand.

He quickly typed something into the computer, then turned back to me with a cocked eyebrow. "A regular period, you say?"

"Pretty regular," I replied. "Usually anywhere between twenty-nine to thirty-one days."

"And how late are you this time?" he asked in an accusing tone. He placed his hands on the keyboard, awaiting my answer.

I furrowed my brow. "I'm not late. I should get it today or tomorrow. I'm not fatigued because I'm PMS'ing."

"No, I know," he said with a light, almost mocking chuckle. "You're fatigued because you're pregnant."

I reeled back in my chair. I couldn't have heard him right. I quickly glanced at the computer. "No, you must have the wrong chart pulled up. I'm not pregnant."

He gave a cocky smirk. "You misunderstand, Miss Taylor. I'm not reading your chart. I've just diagnosed you."

"Diagnosed me?" I repeated. "With… pregnancy?"

He said it like I was sick with a parasite, not pregnant with a child. He had to be wrong.

"That's not possible," I insisted as he continued typing things into my chart.

"Are you married, Miss Taylor?"

"Yes," I answered automatically without thinking about why he'd need to know in the first place.

He paused to look at me. "Aren't you fulfilling your marital duties?"

I went speechless for a beat, but quickly scrambled to find my tongue. "Are you asking if I'm sexually active?"

He crinkled his nose, like the phrase was a sin to speak aloud. "I wouldn't put it that way. Are you and your husband having *intercourse?*"

The question felt wholly inappropriate, but he *was* a doctor, and it wasn't the first time I'd been asked the question at a medical appointment. I just didn't like the way he said it. "We are, but—"

"How many sexual partners have you had in the last year?" He stared at me with a pointed expression, like he expected me to answer more than one.

I gaped. I couldn't believe he'd have the gall to even suggest I was cheating on my husband. "One, for the Goddess's sake! But my husband and I use protection—condoms, every time."

"And what about your birth control pills? Are you taking those regularly?"

"I'm not on birth control," I said. "We didn't want it interacting with my other meds."

"Well, if you weren't planning for a child, you should be on the pill," he stated. "Condoms aren't entirely effective. I certainly wouldn't blame your husband if he chose to go without them every now and then."

All I could do was stare at the doctor, because I was so shocked. Was he implying what I thought he was? Lucas would *never* do something like that.

"My husband and I are monogamous," I stated firmly, so he couldn't miss a single word. "We respect each other, and we use protection. Your diagnosis is wrong, and I'd like to speak with a specialist about my condition."

He smiled proudly. "You're in luck, then. I've delivered many babies."

"I'm not pregnant," I insisted. I couldn't be.

"If you'd like, we can take a urine sample and perform a traditional pregnancy test," he offered, though his tone was less than kind. "You said your period is due today, so the test should be accurate."

I crossed my arms. The only reason I'd do the test was to prove this guy wrong. I felt sorry for the women who walked into his office pregnant and had to receive the news from him so bluntly. He was a horrible doctor, and he needed someone to put him in his place.

"Yes. I'd like that," I said.

Dr. Malach stood and went over to a drawer by the sink. He pulled out a urine cup, a disinfectant wipe, and a baggie, then handed them to me. "The bathroom is just down the hall."

I stomped out of the room in malicious compliance. I got my sample, then returned to the exam room. When I stepped inside, Dr. Malach had a testing kit spread across the counter, and he was wearing a pair of latex gloves. The test kit was different from the at-home tests I'd seen before, but the idea was the same.

Dr. Malach snatched the urine cup straight out of my hands. He used a dropper to place a drop of urine on a test strip. I tapped my foot impatiently from behind him, waiting for the test to reveal the truth—that he was *wrong*. He shot a narrowed glance over his shoulder, but he didn't say anything for at least a full minute. The liquid seeped through the test strip until a singular solid line formed…

Followed by a second light pink one.

Dr. Malach grinned smugly. "Pregnant. Just as I said."

The room swayed around me. I couldn't be sure which way was up or down. I stumbled backward and caught myself on the chair behind me, then sank into it. I'd walked through hell and back, and it wasn't nearly as terrifying as this moment.

"How can I be pregnant?" I whispered, more to myself than to the doctor.

"It's quite simple," he started.

"I know *how*," I bit. "Is the baby going to be okay?"

Dr. Malach sat back down at his computer to look over my chart. "We recommend women wait at least a year after a transplant to start trying for a baby. Your medications could harm the baby, so we usually switch women over to pregnancy-safe meds at least six weeks before they start trying."

My pulse quickened. "So the meds I'm taking aren't safe?"

Dr. Malach typed a few things into his computer, and his eyebrows shot up. "Actually, they are. It looks like you started a new prescription recently."

My shoulders relaxed. Thank the Goddess for Dr. Metzi. She'd put me on new meds when I first came to *Hok'evale*. It'd been such a lucky break.

"But you haven't been on the meds long enough," he added. "Besides, women with lupus shouldn't have babies until their disease has been inactive for at least six months."

"It's been six months since my transplant," I stated.

Dr. Malach frowned. "You didn't plan this pregnancy."

I furrowed my brow. "But if my lupus is under control and my meds are safe, then what does it matter? What would we have done differently if we'd planned this?"

"It hasn't been a year since your transplant," he pressed. "Regardless if everything else is in order, it's too soon."

"What happens if I go through with this?" I asked. "Is my kidney going to fail? Is the baby going to be safe?"

"Your donor kidney should perform fine," he assured me. "However, you're at high risk of preeclampsia. It's a serious blood pressure condition that often develops in pregnancies like yours."

He said it like it was a sure thing, but my own health wasn't my main priority right now.

"Is the baby going to be safe?" I repeated again. I couldn't help but notice he'd avoided my question multiple times now.

He leaned back in his chair, sighing heavily. "The truth is your condition puts you in a higher risk category than the average mother. If you continue with this pregnancy, you should expect a miscarriage—or worse. No doubt about it, if you try to have this baby, you'll certainly die."

My stomach clenched, and I thought I was going to throw up.

"I don't see a reason to continue with the pregnancy," Dr. Malach said coldly. "Your best option is to get an abortion while it's still early."

My breath caught. I'm sorry—*what* did he just say?

"I don't want to do that," I stated breathlessly.

He tilted his head to the side like he cared, but it came off looking more like a shrug. "I'm afraid that may be your only option. I don't see why you would continue the pregnancy."

I gaped at him. "I didn't plan for this, but that doesn't mean I don't want this baby. My husband and I wanted to start a family someday."

"That's an irresponsible decision for someone with your illness. It appears you have a habit of being irresponsible." His gaze darted toward my stomach.

What the hell was wrong with him? I was a grown-ass married woman, not some teenager who didn't use protection.

"I want to keep the baby," I stated firmly.

He sighed and sat up straighter. "I understand why you would want to start having children now. Many women start having children young, so they don't end up old and alone."

"Alone?" I balked. What the hell was he talking about?

"Many women try to get pregnant before it's too late. After all, once you're past your prime, your husband is going to find someone younger and leave you," he stated, like it happened to everyone. "Men want to impregnate *young* women, after all, and since sperm remains viable no matter how old a man is, it's understandable you want to do whatever it takes to keep your husband."

I was so shocked; all I could do was gape at him. Nothing had left me this speechless before.

"Regardless, there's too much at stake here," Dr. Malach continued. "Besides losing your life, you could pass on your lupus."

"That doesn't matter," I snarled. "I'll still love this baby, and even if they're sick, I'll take care of them anyway."

The doctor rolled his eyes skeptically. "Everyone thinks they'll love their child no matter what, until the child shows up with a disease. You'll regret it once the child gets here. Are you *sure* you want to live with the guilt of knowingly passing on a chronic illness?"

He spoke as if it would be *my* fault if my baby got sick. Even if it was, did that make my child's life any less valuable?

I knew the answer to that. Yeah, lupus totally sucked, but I still deserved to live. And so did this baby, even if they were sick.

"You'll also have to consider how you'll take care of a sick child," Dr. Malach said. "Your illness will make it difficult to care for even a normal child. You couldn't care for any baby adequately, let alone a disabled one."

"I'll have help," I insisted.

"Do you have a financial plan to help you pay for medical assistance?" he asked. "Where are you going to get the money to pay for this child? What are your employment options?"

"I don't have a job now, but I plan to in the future. My husband and I will figure it out. If my lupus flares and puts me out of work, my husband will always be here to support me. He's not going anywhere," I pressed.

"And what happens if you die during this pregnancy, or in labor?" Dr. Malach asked. "You'll leave the child motherless, and that's not fair to the child, nor to its father. Your husband will be left to take care of a sick child alone. I understand that all women want to be mothers, but it's *unethical* to bring a sick child into this world. Morally, it's wrong and selfish."

Bile rose in my throat. He couldn't be serious. "What are the chances my child will end up with lupus?"

I wanted to hear him say it—to prove to him that he was wrong. Everything he said was disgusting. Sick kids deserved to live, too.

He huffed, like he was annoyed by the question. "It doesn't matter, because even *if* you gave birth to a normal child, you couldn't take care of them. You can't work because of your lupus—it's that simple. I don't understand how you think you can hold down a job and be a parent at the same time, because it isn't realistic for someone with your condition. I'm only trying to prepare you for the inevitable reality."

According to him, sick kids didn't deserve to live, and disabled people couldn't be parents. He was quite the fucking tool. Disabled people could be just as good of parents as anyone—better, even, I bet.

"My baby and I at least deserve a chance," I insisted.

"A chance for what?" he asked, like he actually gave a shit. "To suffer?"

My stomach sank, leaving a gaping hole in the middle of my abdomen. Is that what I'd be doing to this child—bringing it into a world of never-ending suffering? Could I have a baby while we were still fighting the priestesses? Was it better if they didn't exist at all?

"If you're this insistent on getting pregnant, we have the means to do it the *right* way," Dr. Malach offered. "You could abort this unsafe pregnancy, then we can explore the option of in-vitro fertilization. We'll be able to test the embryos to make sure we give your baby the *good* genes, and get rid of the embryos that are abnormal. I can make a referral now."

He turned to his computer. I felt my skin crawl when he said the word *abnormal.* Is that what he thought I was, and what he thought this baby would be if they came out sick?

"I don't want that," I heard myself say. I wasn't even sure I said it at first, because I no longer felt attached to my own body. It felt more like I was hovering above the room, watching this doctor take my future away —a future I'd only just discovered was a possibility for me.

"We can certainly wait on the IVF discussion," Dr. Malach said, before pressing a few keys on his keyboard. "But we should get you in for that abortion soon. There's an opening this afternoon—"

"I said I didn't want an abortion," I snapped.

He backed away from the computer. "You're right. Perhaps we should talk to your husband first, see what he thinks about all of this. Does he have any preexisting conditions?"

"Just depression," I said. It'd become such a normal part of our lives; I didn't think anything of it.

Dr. Malach's lips turned down. "Your husband is likely not a suitable candidate, either. Depression can have genetic components. There's enough mentally ill people in this world. We don't need another one. You don't want to have a child that's messed up, do you?"

"My child won't be *messed up!*" I yelled, shooting to my feet. "My baby could end up with lupus and depression and every other diagnosis in the book, and they'd still be a better person than you. You're cruel to assume this baby doesn't deserve to live, and that mine and my husband's lives are of less value than anyone else's."

Dr. Malach crossed his arms and turned his nose up. "If that's the way you feel, then proceed with the pregnancy. But understand that your body will fail."

"Show me the evidence," I demanded. "I want to see the statistics on how many women with lupus die in pregnancy. What organs are going to fail, and what's the cause of death?"

"That data is difficult to find, Miss Taylor," he said condescendingly. "We don't exactly have specifics, and I can't give you any answers on that, but it's my professional assessment that you *will* die."

"You don't know anything," I sneered. "If you don't have the data, then how can you possibly come to that conclusion? You don't know what's going to happen to me."

He arrogantly leaned back in his chair. "You're misunderstanding what I'm trying to tell you."

"How is it possible for me to misunderstand that you told me it's too dangerous, but you don't have any information to give me on *why?*" I pressed.

He gave an indignant sigh. "Look, you're not only gambling with your life, but you're gambling the life of a child. If you pass away because of this pregnancy, it's on you, not on me. I gave you medical advice, and you chose not to listen to it."

"I guess I'll just die then," I snapped, before turning on my heel and fleeing the room.

I raced down the hall, choking back sobs. It hit me halfway down the hall what a horrible thing I'd just said, because I *had* almost died—more than once. I'd fought so hard to stay alive. Could I really let my body give up if there was something I could do to prevent it?

The truth was, I couldn't make this kind of decision right now. There was a baby inside of me, and I had to weigh the horrible decision of whether to let it live, and put my own life at risk, or terminate the pregnancy, and live with the thought of what could've been for the rest of my life.

I pushed through a doorway that I thought led outside, but instead I found myself standing in a courtyard filled with trees and flowers. Clinic walls boxed me in on four sides, though the sky was open above me.

I had the thought that I couldn't run from this, and I was *so fucking tired* of running.

I sank into a nearby bench and buried my face in my hands. Tears sprang to my eyes. I was alone in the courtyard, and I couldn't hold myself back from breaking down. This was all so much to take in. First, I found out I was pregnant, and before I could even process that, I was told I had to give the baby up?

What a cruel world we lived in.

I was wholly torn in so many directions. Before today, I hadn't been sure I wanted to be a mother, but I wasn't going to say *no*. The thought of getting an abortion churned my stomach. I wasn't against abortion—I believed women should have a right to choose what to do with their own bodies.

But that was the thing. If I was given a choice, I'd keep the baby, hands down. But could I do that if it meant neither of us would survive?

Holy shit, I was already thinking about *us*, as if this baby was already mine. Slowly, I sat up straighter and placed my hand on my belly. I couldn't believe there was a tiny little human growing inside of me. The thought of a baby felt more like an *idea* than anything. It didn't feel real.

But it was, and that terrified me, because now that there was an *us*, I didn't want to give it up. We had the chance to become a family… but that obviously wasn't going to happen. I couldn't bring a child into the world as it was today, not unless we fled the coven completely. Would that even help if this baby was destined to suffer its whole life?

It seemed no matter what I did, my family was destined to be torn apart. I'd lost my parents, and now Grammy, and it killed me to think they wouldn't be around to see our baby grow up. My parents could've been grandparents, and Grammy could've been a great-grandmother, but that was never going to happen now because they weren't here. Lucas's parents were abusive, and we couldn't rely on them for anything. This child wouldn't have a family to lean on, and I feared if we started a family of our own, it wouldn't last, and our baby would be taken from us, too. Maybe Lucas and I only needed each other.

This wasn't just about me, either. If I refused the procedure and it killed us, I'd be leaving Lucas behind. All of my friends would have to fight the priestesses without me. The coven would be left without a Curse Breaker, and there would be no one to use the Curse Breaker Wand to end the Waning.

I *didn't* have a choice.

Abortion was my only option. I had to go through with this, even if I didn't want to.

Somehow, I had to find a way to tell Lucas. I just knew this news would break his heart.

Tears streamed down my face, and I clutched my stomach as a sickness rose inside my gut. The next thing I knew, I was curling over the side of the bench and heaving into the nearest flower bed.

I heard a door, then footsteps approached quickly. "Are you okay? Do you need me to find a nurse?" a female voice asked in concern.

"No," I insisted. "It's just morning sickness."

I was almost certain it was a lie. The entire encounter with Doctor Malach had left me ill.

I groaned as I sat upright again. The girl who'd approached me was about my age, with long brown hair and deep brown eyes. She carried a baby on her hip. The baby couldn't be more than a year old, if that, and had a black tuft of hair on her head. The baby was dressed in a bright pink outfit, with a huge bow on her head. She looked so cute, and it made me want to die inside thinking about my own child.

"How far along are you?" the woman asked.

I cleared my throat. "I just found out, so that must make me four weeks."

"That's exciting!" She smiled brightly. "Congratulations."

I tried to force a smile, but all I could do was scoff.

"Oh, no." Her voice came out so small and caring, and she rushed over to sit beside me on the bench. She dropped her diaper bag at her feet and set her baby on her lap. "I'm Sophia, and this is my daughter, Ava-Marie."

I glanced down at the badge hanging off her diaper bag. "Do you work here?"

"I'm just a volunteer," she said. "I help with ASL interpretation when the clinic is short-staffed. I'm working on getting my certification."

She was talking like she was trying to distract me, which was nice.

"I'm not volunteering today, though," she added. "I just got out of a prenatal appointment."

I hadn't noticed before, but now I saw she had a small baby bump. She couldn't be more than four months along.

Ava-Marie squirmed, and Sophia tickled her belly. Ava-Marie giggled, and my heart broke all over again. According to my doctors, I'd never hear my baby giggle like that. I hadn't known how much I wanted to hear that sound until now, and in an instant, it'd been taken away from me.

Tears rose to my eyes, and I tried to choke them back, but I could feel my face heating.

Sophia's features fell. "Whatever's wrong, I'm sure the doctors can help you figure it out. They're very good at what they do."

I grimaced. "That's what the receptionist told me about Dr. Malach. *World-renowned*, she called him. That angel can go to hell."

I sure wouldn't feel bad about watching him burn in that lake of lava I saw when I was down there.

Sophia crinkled her nose. "Ugh. Dr. Malach's the worst. I'm sorry you had to deal with him. He's not great, but the clinic keeps him around because there are so many patients that need help."

I shrugged. "I'm sure he didn't tell me anything another doctor wouldn't. I'm too sick to have a baby. I have lupus, and the pregnancy would be too high risk, so I guess I can't go through with it."

My voice cracked. I didn't know why I was opening up to this girl. She was a complete stranger. But maybe that's why it was so easy, because I was never going to see her again.

"What does he mean you can't go through with it?" Sophia demanded. She sounded like she was ready to go to war for me, some witch girl she just met. I liked her already. "Women with lupus give birth to babies all the time—*Ava-Marie!*"

She cut off as she scolded her daughter, who was wiggling so much she nearly fell out of Sophia's arms. Ava-Marie reached out for me, and instinctually, I picked her up. The little girl crawled onto my lap, and Sophia watched curiously as her daughter leaned her head against my chest. I wrapped my arms around her, and for a brief moment, I felt what it'd be like to hold a child. It was so comforting and full of love, yet the most heartbreaking thing all at once.

Ava-Marie put her hand on my belly, as if she recognized the life growing inside of me. I nearly broke down all over again.

"That's interesting…" Sophia mused. "Ava-Marie doesn't usually like strangers."

"Maybe it's because I was crying," I offered. "I'm sure kids understand empathy better than adults do."

Sophia furrowed her brow, keeping her eyes on her daughter. "She certainly seems… concerned. Doctors don't always know what they're talking about. They told us my husband couldn't have kids, and they were sure he'd pass on his illness, but Ava-Marie is fine. Maybe you should get a second opinion. I know the woman who runs the clinic—in fact, we just came from her office. She doesn't have another appointment until this afternoon. I can take you to see her if you'd like."

I nodded. "I'd like that very much. Thank you."

Sophia slung her diaper bag over her shoulder. Ava-Marie wouldn't let go of me, so I stood with the child in my arms and followed Sophia inside. She led me down a long hall and stopped outside an open door. I peered inside and was shocked to find Luana sitting at a desk. Her luna moth Familiar fluttered its wings from her shoulder.

She was the chieftain's daughter who we'd met earlier this year when we came here for information on the Oaken Wands. I recalled that she said she worked at the clinic. She seemed so young to be running it, but maybe she was older than I originally thought.

Luana stepped out of her office and into the hall to greet us. Sophia signed something to her, and whatever it was must've alarmed Luana, because she got a look of concern on her face. She signed back quickly.

Sophia turned to me. "Luana has asked me to interpret. You may address each other directly, and I will interpret everything that is said. This conversation will remain confidential, and I may interrupt for clarification. Are you okay with that?"

"Yes," I told them both.

Luana signed, and Sophia interpreted. "What exactly did Dr. Malach tell you?"

I repeated what he'd said word-for-word, pausing to give Sophia time to communicate. It wasn't like I could ever forget the conversation we had.

Luana's nostrils flared, and her face turned red. She turned on her heel and rushed down the hall, and we quickly followed. Luana stopped in front of a closed door and pounded her fist on it.

The office door popped open, and Dr. Malach stood there. He narrowed his eyes on her. "Yes, *Dr. Cauac?*"

It didn't sound like they got along.

Luana's signs grew bigger and more aggressive than before. She was *pissed*, but Dr. Malach more or less looked amused.

"I don't know what *this* means," he said, waving his hands in a mocking manner.

What a fucking asshole.

Sophia turned to Dr. Malach, interpreting for Luana. "Your behavior with your last patient was completely unacceptable."

Dr. Malach's gaze landed on me. "You mean the sick pregnant girl? She's chronically ill. Do you *really* think she can carry a baby to term? What if she passes her illness down to her child?"

I instinctually placed a hand over my belly and took a step back. Ava-Marie gripped tighter to my side, like she could sense Dr. Malach was nothing but bad news. Even if I did pass down my disease, it wasn't a reason not to have this child.

"Is that why you told her she had to abort?" Sophia interpreted. "You should know better, you ableist prick."

Dr. Malach threw his head back and let out a laugh that chilled me to the bone.

"You think that's funny?" Sophia asked, interpreting.

Luana flipped him the bird, and the meaning was abundantly clear. Dr. Malach's face paled, and Luana whirled around without a second glance back at him.

Dr. Malach turned on Sophia. "Tell her she can't fire me!"

"You're welcome to tell her yourself, and I'll interpret," Sophia said. "But technically, she can, and she just did."

"How *dare* you—" Dr. Malach took a step to follow Luana, but Sophia cut in front of him.

A fireball formed in her palm, and he stopped dead in his tracks. Several people poked their heads out of offices to see what was going on, but they quickly scurried away when they saw Sophia's Fire.

"I suggest you do as she says," Sophia warned. "Have your office cleaned out by the end of the day, and leave… before I make you. You are no longer welcome to practice here, in this clinic or anywhere else in *Hok'evale*."

I didn't know what kind of authority Sophia had around here. After all, she said she was only a volunteer. But when Sophia spoke, she spoke like someone in charge.

"I don't have anywhere else to go!" Dr. Malach protested. "The Celestials kicked me out."

"That's your problem," Sophia said.

Dr. Malach took a step back toward his former office.

Luana gestured for me to follow her. I did so quickly, before Dr. Malach could say anything else.

Victory swelled in my chest as I followed Luana down the hall and into an exam room. I hadn't meant for Dr. Malach to lose his job, but I couldn't say I was upset about it. He was a horrible doctor.

Luana waited until Sophia and I were in the room before she shut the door behind us. I sat down, and Ava-Marie seemed content in my lap. Sophia sat beside me.

"Pretend I'm not in the room," Sophia said, before she began interpreting. "I'm sorry about Dr. Malach. We hired him because the angels no longer allowed him to practice in Celestial City since he was helping patients without insurance against the Deacons' orders. Originally, we supposed he had a kind heart, but lately I've started to wonder if he was helping those uninsured patients not because he cared, but because he wanted to charge what he wished and pocket the money under the table. We've had a few problems with him being rude to patients, but nothing at this scale. I must deeply apologize and insist that nothing like this will ever happen again at my clinic."

Luana looked at me with the kindest expression, and I knew there was nothing I could say or do to show how grateful I was for her right now. All I knew was that Dr. Malach made me squirm in my skin, but here in this exam room with these two women, I felt completely safe. I needed that more than anything right now.

Luana continued signing, and Sophia spoke for her. "Dr. Malach doesn't know what he's talking about. I delivered a baby a few months ago from a mom with lupus, and she was fine. In fact, I've delivered many babies from lupus patients. As long as your symptoms are under control, you'll be okay. We just have to monitor you, because you'll be high-risk. I'm going to look up your chart."

Luana typed a few things into the computer, then read over my info quickly.

When she turned back to me, I asked, "Is my lupus going to return?"

Sophia signed my question to Luana, then paused a beat before interpreting. "You have a seven to thirty-three-percent chance of a lupus flare, which is about the same for non-pregnant women with lupus. Your pregnancy doesn't increase your chance of having a lupus flare-up. Since your lupus was under control before getting pregnant, you're very likely to deliver a healthy baby."

"So I'm not high-risk?" I wondered.

"All lupus patients are high-risk, but all that means is that you'll visit more often to be monitored more closely. Don't let Dr. Malach scare you. This is up to you, and I'm going to be here with you the whole way. We have a whole team of medical doctors, including rheumatologists, who will help."

"Is my kidney going to be okay?" I asked.

"It's recommended you wait at least a year after a transplant to start trying for a baby, but you can still carry to term without waiting that long."

My tone began to even out. "What am I at risk of?"

"Preeclampsia—or high blood pressure during pregnancy—preterm labor, blood clots, miscarriage—"

"Miscarriage?" My hand immediately went to my belly. I was worried about my lupus and my transplant, but more than that, I worried about the baby. A healthy child was more important than my illness.

"You just need to take it as easy as possible. Since your lupus is under control, you'll be at lower risk of flares, but if they do happen, we have pregnancy-safe medication. If you choose to continue with this pregnancy, controlling your lupus is our safest option."

"What if the baby ends up with lupus?" I questioned.

"The chances are quite low—about a two-percent chance your child will ever develop lupus."

To say I was pissed at Dr. Malach was an understatement. He had spoken like passing on my illness was a sure thing, and it'd scared the hell out of me. Luana was so reassuring, though, that a huge weight lifted off my shoulders.

I braced myself for the hard question, but forced myself to spit it out anyway. "Am I going to die if I continue this pregnancy?"

"There is always a risk of death for any woman—abled or disabled—in pregnancy, but let me reassure you we are the best at what we do here, and even with lupus your chances of having a healthy pregnancy, birth, and baby are quite high. We will monitor you closely so that if anything looks to be going wrong, we can prepare and provide you care."

I breathed a sigh of relief. Luana had greatly eased my fears. "What's the next step?"

"I'm going to do a complete physical exam, including a blood test, which will measure kidney function. You'll come back for frequent check-ups. Around ten weeks, I'll order an antibody test that will help assess the risk of complications. If you feel the risk is too high—"

"No," I said automatically. I hadn't even talked to Lucas about this, and he deserved a say, but I'd already made up my mind. "I want to have the baby."

There was no question. There was a tiny little person growing inside of me. I didn't know how it happened, but something about it felt like fate. This baby wanted me to be their mother—they *chose* me. No matter what happened, I had to be the best mother for them for as long as I could be.

"We don't know what the future holds. No two lupus patients are the same. But if you want to go forward with this, we will do everything in our power to make sure you and baby both make it through this pregnancy. Your pregnancy is high-risk, but we prefer to use the term *high-support* pregnancy for our patients, because that's exactly what you'll receive when in our care."

Tears sprang to my eyes again, but this time for different reasons. Luana was so caring and empathetic, and I didn't know what I'd do if Sophia wasn't here to interpret. It felt like a miracle I'd found these women.

Luana kept her eyes on me as she signed. I didn't need Sophia to interpret to understand she was asking if she could touch me. I nodded, and Luana placed her hands over my belly. Warm Anichi healing magic filled my body, in stark contrast to Dr. Malach's invasive exam. A wide smile spread across Luana's face, and she signed something I could only interpret as good news.

"Congratulations!" Sophia interpreted. "You're having twins."

My breath caught in my throat. I couldn't believe it. "Are you serious?"

"Identical. Due July twenty-fourth."

Tears streamed down my face, and my shoulders began to shake. I couldn't contain the joy I felt knowing Lucas and I were going to be parents—not just to one child, but *two*. My heart felt like it was going to beat out of my chest. I couldn't wait to tell him.

Once I calmed down, Luana performed a full exam using her magic, since it was too early for an ultrasound. She promised the babies and I were all okay, though she'd know more when the blood tests came back. Luana prescribed me the proper meds to take for my lupus while pregnant, as well as prenatal vitamins.

By the end of the exam, I felt so fucking relieved. Dr. Malach had scared the ever-living crap out of me, but according to Luana, my babies and I were going to be fine.

Sophia left the exam room with me, bouncing Ava-Marie on her hip. "Luana is the best Anichi healer in all of *Hok'evale*. She's also certified as a midwife and doula. She took care of me when I had Ava-Marie. She's the best person to have on your birth team."

"Thank you," I told her. "For everything."

Sophia smiled. "Of course. Us moms have to stick together."

"I never thought much about being a mom, but I like the sound of it," I admitted.

"You're going to love it," Sophia promised.

I couldn't imagine the opposite, because I was already head over heels for these babies, and I hadn't even convinced myself yet that this was all real.

It was going to have to sink in pretty quickly, because it was time for me to go home.

Once I got there, I had to find a way to tell Lucas we were having twins.

# LUCAS
## FIFTEEN

Time got away from me while Grant and I were fixing the bathroom drain. I didn't realize how many hours had passed until we were cleaning up and I got Nadine's text. I went into the hall and focused on our meeting place. A portal bloomed at my command, and Nadine stepped through.

"Everything okay?" I asked. "You were gone for a while. Everyone else is already back."

"Everything's fine," she said, but there was a hint of something in her tone I couldn't quite read. "I just had to do some shopping."

She held several bags in her hand. I recognized one from the pharmacy, but the other was a small gift bag.

A smile touched my lips. "My birthday isn't until the end of the month."

Nadine beamed, and I knew she must be proud of whatever was in that bag. "Consider it an early birthday present."

My eyebrows shot up. "You want me to open it now?"

Nadine glanced to the bathroom, where Grant was shuffling around still cleaning up. She gestured to the door across the hall, which led to the library. "Let's go in here."

The library had become one of my most frequented rooms in the house. The books Hattie had given me lay in stacks on the desk, and the whiteboard we'd been gathering clues on stood in the corner. I'd cobbled it all back together after I'd practically torn the whole display apart a few months ago. It looked better now, but the clues weren't nearly as organized as before.

Nadine shut the door behind us. "You should sit down."

I followed her instructions and took the seat behind the desk, eyeing her curiously. Nadine set the gift bag in front of me. She knotted her hands together, but otherwise hid her expression. I had no idea what she had in store for me.

I pulled tissue paper out of the bag and set it aside. "You really didn't have to do this…"

My voice trailed off when I found what was inside. It was just a pen and a notepad—nothing special. I didn't understand what she was so excited about. I guess the pen *was* nice. It was a smooth black with silver accents.

"Oh," I realized. "For my journalism major. Makes sense. Thank you, Nad."

I hadn't finished my classes before we'd fled Octavia Falls, but one day when this was all over, I wanted to return to school and complete the required curriculum to get my journalism degree.

I started to stand to give her a hug, but she stopped me. "That's not all. You have to write with it."

I hesitated and sat back down. She wore a grin, like there was a lot more to this gift than she was telling me.

"Okay…" I placed the tip of the pen to the notepad. The pen moved beneath my fingers as if it had a mind of its own. I jumped back and dropped the pen, but it didn't fall to the table like I expected. It remained upright, scrawling a message across the paper as if a ghost were writing with it.

I glanced up to Nadine. "It's an enchanted pen."

Her smile widened. "I enchanted it myself. Watch."

I kept my eyes on the paper as the pen spelled out a message. I read it aloud. "Congratulations, you're going to be a…"

My heart stopped when the pen spelled out the final word. It made a stabbing motion on the exclamation point at the end of the sentence, then dropped to the table and rolled across it, as if it was never enchanted at all.

I barely noticed when the pen fell to the floor. All I could do was stare at the words on the notepad. The smooth lines blurred in front of me, and I blinked a few times before I read the words over again.

*Congratulations, you're going to be a dad!*

My thoughts became cloudy. This didn't seem real. Nadine and I had always used protection. I couldn't understand how this had happened.

By some miracle, it *was* happening.

Nadine and I hadn't talked much about having kids. It'd only come up a few times several years ago, when we thought the Reaper's Shadow curse would kill her. She'd said she wasn't sure she ever wanted kids, and she'd be happy without them. I'd agreed with her at the time.

But here we were in this moment, our future laid out in front of us, a future with children and a family of our own. In a single moment, everything had changed.

It was something we couldn't take back, and I didn't want to even if I could. This was the beginning of a brand new life together, and though our present was shrouded in darkness, our future was bright. I never realized how much I wanted it until now.

Excitement filled my bones at the thought of being a father. It was strange, because I always thought if I was going to be a dad, it'd be the scariest fucking thing in the whole world. And it was… but it came with an all-encompassing joy I hadn't expected.

We hadn't planned this, and this was the worst time to bring a child into this world, but none of that mattered. Nadine and I were going to be parents, and we'd figure out the rest together, no matter what happened.

"Lucas, say something," Nadine begged softly.

I finally managed to tear my gaze from the paper. "You're pregnant?"

Tears brimmed in her eyes, and she nodded eagerly. "Are you upset?"

"No! Not at all!" I shot out of my chair and wrapped her tightly in a hug. "This is great news!"

Nadine broke down in my arms, sobbing into my chest.

I gently stroked her hair. "Nad, what's wrong? You seemed so excited a moment ago."

"I am. That's why I'm crying. I'm so, *so* happy." She drew away and wiped her eyes. "That's not all, though. Lucas, it's twins!"

I willed myself to remain upright. *Two babies!* I could hardly believe my ears. I could've sworn time had stopped altogether. I had to pull her tighter into my arms to remind myself time was still moving forward.

"How did we…? We use protection every time…" I stammered.

"Condoms break, Lucas," she said gently. "We conceived the night of our wedding. It's funny, because Chloe blessed me with fertility in the bridal ceremony before the wedding."

It took several moments for me to process what she'd said. I could hardly believe this was happening. "How'd you find out? I want to know everything."

The sound of voices came from outside the door. Nadine shot a quick glance at it, and we heard footsteps shuffling down the hall.

"Maybe we should take a walk," Nadine suggested.

I took her hand, and we peered into the hallway. I didn't see anyone, but it definitely sounded like someone was snooping a moment ago. We went to the front door and pulled on our jackets, then headed outside.

It was chilly out, but I think we were both too overcome with emotion to care. I kept Nadine's hand in mine as we walked through the trees, following the same path to the stream where we had our wedding ceremony.

"How long have you known?" I asked.

"I found out this morning. I thought I was getting sick, so I went to the clinic in *Hok'evale*, and they did a pregnancy test."

I got worried then. "What did the doctors say about your health? Is a pregnancy going to harm you?"

"They called it a high-support pregnancy, which means they'll be monitoring me closely," she said. "But they believe I have a good chance of delivering the babies safely. I trust my body with this, and I want to go through with it."

I relaxed and raked my fingers through my hair. "Wow. I can't believe it's happening so soon. I thought it'd be years… that we'd have more time to prepare."

Nadine slowed and turned to me. "You don't seem scared. It's not the reaction I expected."

I hadn't expected this reaction from myself, either. There were tons of reasons to be scared of becoming a dad—scared of how pregnancy might affect Nadine's body, scared of becoming like my father, scared of bringing a child into the world in the midst of the Miriamic Conflict, scared of being able to provide for them…

But none of that could compare to the great joy I felt when Nadine said we were going to become parents.

I took her hands in mine. "Of course I'm scared, Nad. We're in the middle of a war with the priestesses, and I don't know what that could mean for our family. But that doesn't mean I don't want to have a family with you at all. It's certainly unexpected, but I've become very familiar with fear, and I know that the only way through it is to face it."

"You're not scared of what world we're bringing these babies into?" she wondered. "We don't know what having children could mean. I can't battle against the priestesses when I'm pregnant, and when the babies are born, someone will always have to stay behind to take care of them."

The last thing I wanted was to put my wife or children in danger, but there was nothing we could do to back out of this. This was happening to us now, and all we could do was see it through to the end.

I squeezed Nadine's hands. "Children are born every day to all types of circumstances. Whatever happens, we'll do *everything* to protect our family, even if that means using the Oaken Wands to keep our babies safe."

Nadine drew a deep, calming breath. "It means everything to hear you say that. I can't believe we're going to be a family!"

She threw her arms around my neck, and I inhaled the rosey scent of her hair. I didn't know what the future held, and that scared the living daylights out of me. But I knew from the moment I saw those words on that paper that I wanted to be a dad, even if it was the most frightening thing I ever did. I didn't know if I was going to be a good dad or not, but I could sure as hell try to be the best father I was capable of.

I drew Nadine closer, and she rose to her toes to place her lips on mine. I relaxed into the kiss, gently lifting my hand to the back of her neck as she kissed me harder. I had to pull away to catch my breath.

"We're going to be a family," I whispered.

Nadine laid her head on my chest. "I can't wait."

I took her hand again, and we continued walking. The forest was quiet, and it was really nice to be alone with her. "Have you thought of any names?"

She shook her head. "Not yet. Do you have any ideas?"

"I honestly never gave it much thought," I admitted. "I always figured one day I might be a dad, but I never stopped to think of what that might look like."

"It will be great," Nadine said dreamily. "I'll sing our babies to sleep at night, and you'll toss them in the air and tickle them to make them laugh. I'll bake cookies with them, and when they're old enough, you'll teach them how to ride a bike. We'll sit on our front porch and watch them play in the yard. You'll write them poems, and I'll read them books. We'll take them to school together, and we'll watch their powers awaken during their Evoking Ceremonies."

I smiled at the wonderful image she'd painted for us. "How many kids do you think we'll have in total?"

"Three," she answered automatically. "One more, after the twins."

Comfort settled in my chest. "Three is perfect."

Everything she said sounded so magical. I wanted to believe in our future so badly. But for that future to happen, we had to obtain the remaining Oaken Wands and bring an end to the Miriamic Conflict—and we had to do it before our babies were born. I wasn't going to let our babies be born into a world that could hurt them.

We had less than nine months to prepare, and I swore on my own soul everything would be different nine months from now.

"How do you want to tell everyone?" I asked.

"Let's just do it," Nadine said. "They're going to find out sooner than later. I don't know about you, but I'm not going to be able to keep this a secret."

"We'll get everyone together and tell them all at once," I suggested.

We turned and headed back toward the house. I opened the front door for Nadine, and she stopped in her tracks.

"CONGRATULATIONS!" A chorus of cheers broke out as we stepped inside.

Everyone was gathered in the living room. Streamers from Nadine's bridal shower had been haphazardly twisted around the room, like it'd been decorated in a hurry. Miles threw shredded pieces of paper in the air, and the confetti rained down on us.

"Uh… what's this?" I asked carefully. They couldn't know we were pregnant already, unless Nadine mentioned something to someone before coming to me. I shot her a quick glance, and she looked as confused as I was.

Before anyone could answer my question, Nadine narrowed her eyes at Talia. "You had a vision, didn't you?"

Talia shook her head and pointed her finger at Miles. "It wasn't me!"

"Miles, you were eavesdropping!" I accused. It must've been *his* footsteps we heard outside the library earlier.

"I didn't mean to!" he insisted. "I was just walking by. We heard the good news and had to throw you a celebration. Congratulations, you're going to be parents!"

Miles threw his arms around Nadine, and she hugged him back.

"I guess we don't have to tell them," she said to me when he finally drew away.

Verla approached Nadine. She wore a kind smile, until she pulled Nadine into a hug, and the smile disappeared from her face completely. She looked worried, though it was clear she didn't want Nadine to notice.

"Is this what you want?" I heard her whisper.

"Yes," Nadine replied.

Verla drew away, plastering on a smile again. "Then I'm very happy for you both. You'll make wonderful parents. We're all here to help you every step of the way."

"Thank you," I told her.

Professor Warren shook my hand firmly. "Congratulations, Lucas. This kid is going to have one hell of a dad."

"Kids," I corrected, and I couldn't help but smile. "We're having twins. I sure hope I can be the best dad possible for them."

"Can the babies call me Uncle Grant?" Grant asked.

"They won't have a choice," I teased. "You're already a brother to me."

Grant went to shake my hand, but I yanked on his arm and pulled him into a hug. He squeezed me tightly, then clapped me on the back while he choked back tears.

"That means I'm Auntie Tal," Talia said brightly as she squeezed Nadine into a hug, before practically jumping into my arms.

Onyx hugged Nadine next. "Congratulations to both of you."

Mandy jumped up and down as she came in to hug us both. "Congratulations!"

"Thank you, everyone," Nadine said with a big smile. "We really are excited."

The whole room seemed to glow a brighter color than ever before. It was really nice to have everyone's support. I wasn't sure how they'd take the news.

I noticed one person hadn't said anything. Chloe sat on the couch, staring into the fireplace. She looked deep in thought.

I approached her. "I guess we have you to thank. You blessed us with fertility on our wedding day."

Chloe lifted her gaze to mine, but her eyes weren't filled with the brightness of everyone else in the room. She looked worried—no, *terrified*.

"I didn't mean it like *this*," Chloe stated in a wavering tone.

The room went silent as all eyes turned to her. I couldn't figure out why she wasn't happy like the rest of us.

"I'm glad you're all happy, but I'm doing the math, and something isn't adding up," Chloe said. "Or rather, it adds up *too* well."

I furrowed my brow. "What are you talking about?"

Chloe stood and faced Nadine. "When you got married, you suffered a great loss. That's the second stage of the Reaper's Shadow curse, isn't it?"

All the blood drained from Nadine's face. I stumbled back a few steps, placing myself between Nadine and Chloe, as if I could shield my wife from this.

"You aren't saying what I think you are," I demanded.

Chloe swallowed audibly. "I think the Reaper's Shadow curse is still active. You didn't break it; you just thought you did. Which means if you have a baby…"

"It will kill me," Nadine finished in a whisper.

The room went dead silent. Nadine slowly sank onto the couch as she processed the realization.

The Reaper's Shadow curse had been cast over two-hundred years ago by the son of a Reaper's Apprentice named Samael Davis. He was an evil warlock who had killed his mother, which cast a curse upon all lovers of any future Reaper's Apprentices. Those lovers were known as the Reaper's Shadow. If a reaper fell in love and showed it physically through intimacy, the Reaper's Shadow would suffer a great illness. If the couple got married, the Reaper's Shadow would experience a great tragedy.

And if the couple reached the third and final stage and had children… that child was destined to kill its mother.

The Reaper's Shadow curse was over, though. I had discovered the names of all the women who had suffered the curse before. Nadine and I found their graves in the cemetery at Octavia Falls, and she had siphoned the curse from their bones and broken the spell. It was the only reason Nadine and I were able to get married. Otherwise, we'd have never gone forward with our marriage knowing Nadine would suffer a tragedy—

My thoughts cut off when I realized Chloe was right. Nadine *had* suffered a great tragedy the night we were married.

My head spun. *No fucking way* was this happening.

My hands balled into fists. "Helena dying on the night of our wedding was a coincidence. Nadine broke the Reaper's Shadow curse."

Nadine placed her hand over her belly protectively. "Maybe I didn't —not completely. You said it yourself before I broke the curse, Lucas. If I had tried to just break the curse on myself, it wouldn't work, only delay the consequences. I dissipated some of the curse's magic that night in the cemetery, but if we missed just *one* of the women affected by this curse, then I never broke it fully. All I did was weaken it for a while."

"Let's not rush to conclusions," Warren stated diplomatically. "We can't be *sure* this curse is still active."

Nadine's eyes glazed over with terror. "I think we can."

"No," I insisted. "We broke it."

She swallowed hard. "I thought we did, but I'm feeling with my magic just now… I'm so used to being cursed that I didn't *realize…*"

"What are you saying?" I demanded.

"Chloe's right." Nadine's voice cracked. "There's still a bit of the Reaper's Shadow curse left inside of me. If I carry the babies to term—"

"Don't say it," I interrupted. I began pacing around the room frantically. "I found all those women connected to Reaper's Apprentices. We found the graves of the Reaper's Shadows. You broke their curses. You ended up in the hospital by breaking this curse."

"I broke *some* of the magic, but that doesn't make the curse obsolete," Nadine replied. "Those other women are dead. I pulled the curse from their bodies. It's over for them. But I'm still living, which means if the curse is still active, it will always find me. I can delay it—I can transform the magic inside of me into something else over and over again, but as long as someone's body is still out there holding on to this curse, it's never going to end for me. We missed a Reaper's Shadow. If I'm going to make it through this, we have to find her grave and break the curse on her bones, so that this magic can't affect me ever again. It's not going to end until I end it for every Reaper's Shadow who ever lived."

I raked my fingers through my hair. "That brings up another issue. This curse was originally cast by a child of the Reaper's Apprentice. If the stories are true, Samael killed his mother because he was born with a darkness his father passed down."

"I don't believe that," Nadine argued. "Your magic isn't dark—there's no darkness for you to pass down. People aren't born with darkness inside of them. Darkness is something we create, and we can also create our own light to outshine it. We don't know what happened to Samael growing up, or why he killed his mother and cast this curse. But I know damn well that's not going to be our kid."

"The curse still poses a great risk," Verla insisted. She kept her voice calm, but the look in her eyes told me she was terrified for Nadine's safety. "We don't know the timeline in which a Reaper's Shadow child might kill their mother. This could happen during childbirth."

My insides felt like they were on fire. This couldn't be happening. "Talia, use the Seer Wand to look into our future. What's going to happen? How do we stop it?"

Talia hesitated. "I'm not a prophet. I can't foresee your destiny."

"Give us *something*." I begged.

"I can try..." she said warily. "Visions aren't for sure, though. Even with the Seer Wand, I can only get a *possible* future and see the path you've already chosen. You can still change it."

"Then let's see what our future holds, so that we can make the right decision," I insisted.

Talia looked to Nadine for permission. Everyone just stood there. Nobody was *doing* anything. It was driving me fucking mad.

Finally, Nadine nodded. "Let's see where we currently stand."

I sat beside Nadine and wrapped her in my arms. Talia withdrew the Seer Wand and knelt at Nadine's side. She took Nadine's hand in hers, and the end of the Oaken Wand began to glow.

Her eyes darted back and forth behind her lids. "I can sense a powerful curse. The details are fuzzy."

"So we *do* still have to break this curse. We never finished the job," Nadine said calmly.

I didn't know how she remained so calm. I was freaking out.

"What about the birth?" I demanded. "Is Nadine going to be all right?"

"Are the *babies* going to be okay?" Nadine added.

Talia furrowed her brow, like her visions were difficult to decipher. She remained steady, though, so the visions couldn't be too strong. We needed a clear answer. I feared we couldn't go forward with this if we weren't certain of the outcome.

"I see Nadine holding a baby," Talia started, but she paused, as if still deciphering the visions. "Lucas is holding the other."

A wave of relief washed over me, but almost immediately, my stomach clenched. "Is everyone okay?"

If Talia saw Nadine holding our babies, then that meant she would survive the birth… but we didn't know how long she'd have after.

Talia grimaced, like there were visions that weren't easy to swallow. "I can't be sure what's happening, because it's more of a feeling than anything. There are a lot of variables, and you can still change your path. What I do know is that whatever you do, you're not going to be able to avoid at least one horrible fate."

I felt as if a black hole had opened up in my stomach. It was obvious what Talia meant. If the babies were born, Nadine would die. The only way to prevent that was an equally horrible tragedy. It wasn't a decision anyone should ever be asked to make.

"You may need to consider termination," Verla practically choked out. It was clearly difficult for her to even suggest it, but someone had to. "It's a horrible fate for your children, but it may be the only way to save Nadine's life."

Less than an hour ago, I thought our lives were just beginning. Termination had never even crossed my mind. Now I was almost certain it was our only choice.

"That's the last thing I want," Nadine said bitterly, like she couldn't believe Verla would suggest it.

"Maybe I'm misinterpreting the vision," Talia said quickly. "You both looked very happy holding your sons."

The room shared a collective gasp. Tears beaded in the corners of my eyes, and Nadine reached out for me.

"We—we're going to have baby boys?" I stammered.

Talia threw her hand over her mouth. "Sorry. I didn't mean to ruin the surprise."

Tears fell down Nadine's cheeks. "You didn't ruin anything. Did you see anything else?"

Talia shook her head. "That was it. Just know, this wasn't a prophecy; Seer visions aren't written in stone. It's up to you guys to use this information wisely. One of the first rules in my Seer classes is that if we have the ability to look into the future, we use it sparingly. Don't ask me to keep looking, or things will change. I do know one thing. Whatever you decide, you need to stick with it, no matter what else comes up."

"Perhaps we should leave Nadine and Lucas to make that decision in private," Verla suggested, before turning to us. "Please consider what I said. We can't lose you, Nadine."

Nadine gaped at her and couldn't respond. I quickly said, "We'll talk about it."

Nobody else really knew what to say, and it made me really uncomfortable. I wanted to get out of there as soon as possible. I took Nadine's hand and led her upstairs. We sat on the bed, and neither of us said anything for a long time as we tried to process what we'd learned.

Finally, I spoke, though my throat closed up around my words. "We need to talk about what Verla said. If the babies live, that means you won't."

Nadine stared into the distance and shook her head, like she wasn't convinced. "We don't know that for sure. A *horrible fate* could mean anything, not necessarily death."

"But we know death is a part of the Reaper's Shadow curse," I pointed out. "I know you want to give life to these babies, but in doing so, you're asking me to raise these children on my own. I would do it in a heartbeat if I had to, but I don't want to make that choice willingly. It isn't right to raise the twins without their mother."

"There's a third option," Nadine insisted. "If we find the Reaper's Shadow we missed, I can break the curse for good. Then this tragedy Talia is seeing won't come to pass at all."

"Where are we going to find this information?" I asked hopelessly. "I dug through all the coven records to find the Reaper's Shadow women the first time. I've been through every document the coven has on Reaper's Apprentices. I searched marriage documents and birth certificates. If we missed someone, the information isn't there. We don't have much time to make this decision. We could run out of time."

"Talia has the Seer Wand," Nadine pointed out. "It might help us track down what we missed."

"And if the information is warded or magically guarded in some way, then what?" I asked. "The Wands are powerful, but if we don't know where we're looking, they could prove useless. The Reaper's Shadow women died because they loved men like me."

I'd come to terms with my gift, but being the Reaper's Apprentice really fucking sucked right now if it meant choosing between my wife and my children.

"It was their choice out of love, and my choice, too," Nadine said. "We have to at least try to break the curse, because I'm giving birth to these babies one way or another. I don't know the outcome, but I know intuitively that we have to go through with this. I already decided this morning at the clinic that I'm not giving up like they wanted me to."

"Excuse me?" I balked.

Nadine frowned. "The doctor I talked to was a jerk. He said I couldn't have a baby because I'm sick. He wanted me to schedule an abortion."

The word made my stomach clench. "You're not even willing to consider it?"

Truth be told, I didn't want to think about it either, but I feared we had no choice.

"Aborting our babies isn't going to break this curse," Nadine said. "The doctor I talked to was fired, and then I spoke with Luana. She said because my lupus is under control, my odds of delivering a healthy baby are good. I just need to be monitored closely."

"That doesn't change what Talia said. *Whatever you do, you're not going to be able to avoid at least one horrible fate,*" I repeated. "That sure sounds like we have to choose between you or the babies."

"Or we can break the curse, and the babies and I both survive," Nadine suggested. "We still face a horrible fate, even if we don't know what that is, but at least it gives us a chance."

"Is that a path we're willing to take, if we have to gamble on the outcome?"

She hesitated. "I'm not sure."

Tears welled in my eyes. "I don't want to lose you."

"Lucas..." she started.

"I know," I said quickly. "I *could* lose you. I'd survive. But I don't *want* to live a life without you. If we don't break this curse before the babies are born, there's no telling when the final stage completes. Ultimately, I know it's your choice."

"I don't want it to be just my choice," Nadine said softly. "I want to keep the babies, but I also want us to make this decision together."

I placed my hand on her belly, and the conflict warring inside of me grew. "I want these babies, too. But if we move forward with this pregnancy, there has to be conditions. We can give ourselves a few more weeks, but we have to make a decision before you're ten weeks along. The doctors won't agree to the procedure after that."

"That's right after Christmas," Nadine said.

I nodded. "If we haven't broken the curse by then, we need to terminate. We can't wait longer than that."

Nadine sniffled. "Okay. We'll give ourselves until Christmas, and if we don't break the curse by then, we'll have to face the alternative."

I wrapped Nadine in my arms and drew her close. My tears fell into her hair as I thought of the heartbreak that lay before us. Something occurred to me just then.

*"It is along this path that she will face her greatest joy and her greatest pain,"* I whispered.

Nadine drew away from me. "What did you say?"

I furrowed my brow as the pieces came falling into place. "It's something Santos said the night Hattie and I summoned him. He asked if I was sure I wanted to save you from the demon's spell, because as he put it, *It is along this path that she will face her greatest joy and her greatest pain.*"

"I already lost my grandmother, and that's the greatest pain I can imagine," Nadine said. "If at the end of this we have our baby boys, then they will be our greatest joy."

When she said that, it was like a huge weight had lifted off both our shoulders. These boys *would* be our greatest joy, no matter what happened.

"Why didn't you ever tell me what Santos said?" she asked.

"I didn't want you to expect suffering," I admitted. "I didn't want you to feel like you didn't have a choice, because your destiny wasn't written yet."

Nadine drew a deep breath and snuggled close to me again. "I don't know what our true destinies are, but I know we're supposed to be together, and I know we're meant to be a family—all of us. We're going to break the curse, and we're going to be a family, Lucas."

Nadine couldn't know the future, but when she said that, my fear began to subside. We'd fought greater odds before; we could do it again.

She touched her belly again, and I placed my hand on top of hers. Joy filled my heart. Nadine was right about that. Whatever we were meant to do, being parents was the most important destiny of all.

"I'm sorry I dragged you into all this," I whispered.

"You mean getting me pregnant? Lucas, that's not something to be sorry about."

"No, I mean the Reaper's Shadow curse. There's nothing that could stop me from being with you, but I'm sorry you were cursed to do it. I wish I could've found a way to break the curse before we ever got together."

"We can't change the past," Nadine said. "And there's nothing you could've done differently. No one can break this curse but me."

"I could've kept it in my pants," I teased. It felt good to joke with her, because the rest of this had felt so heavy. I didn't want that for us. This should be the happiest time of our lives.

Nadine chuckled. "*I'm* the one who gave you oral and ended up with kidney failure. We got intimate, so I got sick."

"Do you really think it happened that way?" I wondered.

"I don't know," she admitted. "I think I would've ended up with kidney failure whether I was cursed or not."

I stroked her hair. "I wish I could've given you a better experience. We spent so much time trying to rationalize what we were doing so that we wouldn't trigger the curse. I wish we hadn't had to worry so much."

"You gave me the best experience," Nadine argued. "We took things slow, and that's okay. What a fucking stupid curse anyway. Sex is just a concept, and we never should've had to rationalize any of it in the first place. I'm sick of feeling as if our love has brought destruction. I don't want to believe that anymore."

"This curse nearly broke us, and it never should've had a hold on us in the first place," I agreed. "No one else should get a say in our relationship, certainly not some guy who lived two-hundred years ago. I hate that this caused so much hurt and shame. I want to heal that part of us together and move forward without fear of hurting each other anymore."

Nadine offered a smile. "I'd love nothing more than that. That starts with acknowledging that we aren't at fault. We didn't do anything wrong."

My eyes scanned her beautiful features. "You're right. All we did was love each other deeply, and that shouldn't be a curse."

She shook her head. "Never."

Desperate wanting overcame me, and I placed my hand on the back of her neck as I pulled her close. Nadine grabbed my hip, drawing me into her. We melted together as passion surged through the kiss. Our hands roamed each other's bodies as our pulses quickened in sync.

"I can't believe I put two babies in you," I said between breaths. "It's so fucking sexy."

Nadine kissed me again, heaving breaths as she drew away. "So sexy. Maybe you could remind me how you did it."

I laughed playfully as I dipped my hand into her pants and squeezed her ass. "Is it safe? I don't want to hurt the babies."

Nadine patted her stomach. "They're safe in here. Everything else is free game."

I cocked an eyebrow. "Everything?"

A wide smile spread across her face. "Are you willing to try something new with me?"

She was going to be the mother of my children. Honestly, Nadine could do anything to me right now and I'd lay here and let her.

I nodded eagerly. "Anything."

# nadine

## SIXTEEN

My heart hammered in exhilaration as I rolled off the mattress to search through the box of sex toys we kept under the bed. I'd been nervous about them at first, but now I was excited to give them a try.

I withdrew the box and set it on the bed.

Lucas laid down, placing his hands behind his head as he beamed at me. "What did you have in mind?"

"I don't want to be scared of taking things further together. I want to try it all."

"Perhaps we should start slow." Lucas rolled over to peer into the box. He picked through it for a moment, then pulled out a vibrator and a few different types of lube. "Let's start with these."

As I was putting the box away, I spotted nipple clamps, and I pulled those out as well. "And these," I added, before sliding the box back under the bed.

He gazed up at me with a wanting look in his eyes. "Anything else?"

"I want to do a ritual with you." I turned to the bottom drawer of the nightstand and withdrew our wedding gifts—the candle Chloe had given me at my bridal shower; the Alchemy crystals, herbs, and spell book Onyx had gifted me; and our Wedding Wand.

"Will you brew a potion with me?" I asked as I set the items on the nightstand. "We're going to be a family. We have a lot to celebrate."

"Absolutely." Lucas sat up and came to the edge of the bed to sit beside me.

Onyx had said this potion was safe, even for pregnant women. I found a lighter in the drawer, and Lucas took my hand so we could light the candle together. I gave him the Wedding Wand, while I took the Alchemy crystals and began to crush the herbs in a small bowl they came with. I poured in a small amount of water and mixed it all together. It smelled *really* good, like roses and cinnamon.

"It came with an incantation," I told him. "Together?"

He nodded. "Together."

Lucas pointed the Wedding Wand into the bowl, and I placed my hand over his. The magic in the Alchemy crystals intensified as I withdrew it to perform the spell.

*We speak this prayer tonight*
*To celebrate our union*
*May our hearts be opened wide*
*And our souls come together as one*

Magic filled the bowl, leaving it glowing with a pretty pink light. I handed the potion to Lucas. He took a sip, before lifting the bowl to my lips and helping me drink the rest.

Almost immediately, my body began to buzz with a frequency that magnetized me to Lucas. His whole form seemed to have an ethereal glow to it that I wanted to be a part of, to literally melt into and become one with. His eyes shone brighter than ever before, and I noticed the deep crevices of his muscles in a way that I hadn't in the past. Heat pooled between my thighs at his mere proximity.

Lucas's infatuated gaze roamed over me, like he was desperate to touch my curves and feel my body on his. He reached out to place his hand on the side of my face. That simple touch did something to me. A spark ignited between us that made us both go wild.

His lips connected with mine, and passion ignited hotter as his hands roamed over me. I suddenly became very hot and couldn't handle these clothes between us anymore. I yanked his shirt up over his head, and he nearly tore mine getting it off of me. The rest of our clothes disappeared in moments, until the warmth of his skin was on mine.

I reached for his rock-hard cock the same time he dipped his fingers between my thighs. We both let out a blissful moan. I gave his dick a few good pumps. He must've liked it a lot, because he tossed me onto my back on the bed and kissed me harder. Heart hammering, I tangled my fingers in his hair and yanked on the strands, as if that might ground me back into my body. He moaned in response, and all it did was send a thrill of exhilaration between my legs. I was *so* ready for him.

"I guess we won't be needing that lube," Lucas joked.

"No, but there are other things we can try." I reached for the toys on the other side of the bed and grabbed a small tube of lip gloss. "This says it's activated by saliva. I'm supposed to put it on my lips and then kiss you with it. It's supposed to tingle wherever I touch you."

Lucas got a thrill in his eyes. I unscrewed the cap and rubbed the felt tip applicator over her lips. I licked the gloss, and my lips began to tingle. I kissed Lucas, and he shivered beneath my touch.

Lucas rolled over, and I climbed on top of him. I began trailing kisses down his body. Every time my lips touched his skin, he gave a shudder. I kissed him until I ran out, then rubbed more gloss on my lips to kiss him more.

"What do you think?" I asked as my lips dipped dangerously close to his erection. I didn't reach it just yet. I was teasing him, and I could tell it was driving him wild. He practically squirmed on the bed, begging for more.

"Very good," he said breathlessly. "It tingles everywhere."

Lucas closed his eyes to take in the sensations. My lips dipped downward, and I sucked him into my mouth. He filled me up completely, and he gasped as I rolled my tongue over him. Lucas plunged his fingers into my hair, unable to control himself. He seemed to be holding himself back, like all he wanted was to thrust his hips upward. I could tell he was really enjoying himself, and so was I. I moved over him until he was close to his peak, but Lucas pulled away too soon.

"I want it to last," he whispered. "It's your turn."

My heart lifted in my chest as Lucas flipped me onto my back. He knelt between my legs.

"What do you have in mind?" I asked.

"Close your eyes, and I'll show you," he whispered.

I did as I was told. I heard him grab something from the nightstand.

Then he slid two fingers inside of me, and I gasped as a new, sensitive feeling tingled across my body. Lucas massaged me inside and out, and I gripped the sheets as I let out tiny involuntary moans. I was completely lost in the moment, and my mind went entirely blank. All that existed right now were the two of us, our bodies moving together with the most pleasurable sensations.

"Does that feel good?" Lucas asked.

"Dear Goddess, it's so sensitive. What is that?"

"G-spot cream," he said.

I smiled. "I like it. Keep going."

Lucas continued massaging me until my moans grew louder and my breaths became shallower. I began to climb my peak, but before Lucas worked me to my release, he paused.

"Keep your eyes closed," he instructed. "It pleases me to see you so lost in the moment."

I sank deeper into the mattress. Slowly, he ran his hands over my breasts, then something cold pinched my nipples. The nerves in my body ignited, sending a wonderful sensation straight between my thighs. I opened my eyes to see he had placed the nipple clamps on.

"How does it feel?" he asked.

"I love them. Make them tighter."

Lucas twisted the screws on the sides of the clamps, and they tightened around my nipples. My back arched, and I let out a desperate moan.

Lucas smiled from above me. "I think we found your kink."

I snickered. "I can't imagine either of us are surprised. I've always enjoyed nipple play."

"Let's see what else you like to play with," he teased.

He grabbed the vibrator, which was several inches long, with a spherical shape on the end meant to stimulate my clit. Lucas turned it on and smiled when he saw it had a charge.

"What are you going to do with that—?" I started to tease, but my word halted on my tongue when he pressed it to my clit. Holy fuck, I could've sworn my spirit left my body in that moment.

I tensed for a beat, but as he held the vibrator to my clit, the most glorious sensations filled me. Every muscle in my body relaxed. Lucas slipped two fingers inside of me again, and he gently stimulated my g-spot while the vibrator worked my clit. My limbs seemed to turn to water, even as my face became hot and my heart rate increased. I'd never felt so *in* my body and present with Lucas than I did when he worked my pleasure centers like that.

Passion rose within me. Just as I thought I was going to reach my peak, the pleasure kept on building, until I hit a high I'd never felt before. My hands fisted in the sheets, and my back arched off the bed. My jaw dropped open, and my moans became louder. Lucas pressed the vibrator to my clit harder, and the orgasm just kept going.

"Lucas!" I cried. I grabbed him and yanked him on top of me. "I need you inside of me *now*."

We didn't bother with a condom, because we didn't need them anymore. Lucas turned off the vibrator and set it aside, then positioned himself above me. He gasped when he filled me up, like he'd never felt anything so incredible.

I felt *everything* as his cock moved in and out of me. There were ridges to his dick I'd never felt before, but it was smoother, too. His skin on mine was unlike anything we'd experienced together. The friction was better, and he glided into me easier. I'd never felt closer to him than at this moment.

My fingers tangled in his hair as I dragged him closer. He let out wavered breaths that drove me insane as he slammed into me harder. He had to grab the headboard to steady himself. I wrapped my arms and legs around him and tugged on his hair. He went as deep as he could, and I moaned with every thrust.

Color burst behind my lids, and wave after wave of pleasure swept through me. Lucas buried his cock deep inside of me as he reached his peak, and we spiraled into an incredible orgasm together.

We fell onto the bed side by side, both of us sweaty and breathing hard.

"Holy fuck," I breathed blissfully. The whole thing had happened so fast, but it was definitely the best sex we'd ever had.

He wrapped his arms around me and kissed the top of my head. "What do you think of your toy?"

I smiled as I cuddled close to him, my legs twisting around his. "I know it was a gag gift, but the joke's on them, because I like it."

I melted into him, letting the beat of his heart command my own pulse, slowing to match his. We lay there for a long time, taking in the blissful moment.

Talia had been right. Using toys had helped ground me to the moment with Lucas, and they'd brought us closer together. I felt something within me heal as I curled up next to my husband. The Reaper's Shadow curse had kept us apart for so long, but I refused to let it dictate our future. Lucas and I belonged together, and no curse could change that. I would surrender to my husband—mind, body, and soul.

That meant that no matter our fate, I was going to break this curse—and nothing could stop me.

☾

LUCAS and I woke the next morning curled in each other's arms. I could hear voices in a distant part of the house, and dread filled my gut at the thought of leaving this room. I sat up, but I didn't move to get out of bed. My hand instinctively went to settle on my belly.

"What is it?" Lucas asked. He sat up and wrapped his arms around me. He placed his hand over mine, and I felt so much more secure with him beside me.

I hesitated, unsure how to put my worry into words. "It's easy to celebrate becoming parents here in the privacy of our room, but once we step outside that door, there's a million things that need our attention—researching reapers so you can pass the Warlock's Trial, finding the Curse Breaker Wand, and now breaking the Reaper's Shadow curse all over again."

"I understand your worries, but we're going to get through this together, okay?" he promised.

When he said it, I had no choice but to believe him. I nodded. "Okay."

Lucas drew me into his arms. "We should talk to Talia and see if she can use the Seer Wand to learn more about the Reaper's Shadow."

"I think that might help," I agreed.

Lucas and I showered and dressed. We went downstairs and heard Talia's voice coming from the den. We didn't use it much, but it was a nice quiet spot to relax. It was a small cozy room with a couch and two chairs facing an electric fireplace. We entered the room to see Talia seated in a chair opposite Verla. Talia had bags under her eyes, and it looked like she'd been up all night.

"It doesn't make any sense," Talia was saying. She had her eyes closed and held the Seer Wand in her hand.

"I know it's difficult," Verla replied sympathetically. "That's why I'm here—to help you focus."

Both of them turned to look at us when they heard us enter.

"Are we interrupting?" I asked.

"No," Talia said, lowering the Wand. "We're just trying to make sense of my visions."

I took a seat on the couch, and Lucas sat beside me.

"Are you making any headway?" Lucas asked.

"I'm trying, but the Seer Wand is not all-knowing," Talia said. "It's still limited by my Cast's abilities—and my own. The Seer Wand increases my power, but I still have to learn how to utilize it. There's so many visions coming in at once that it's hard to make sense of any of it. Sometimes, I can hone in on one thing, but I'm still getting all these visions and feelings coming at me in all directions. It's difficult to decipher unless I know exactly what I'm looking for."

"Can you look into the Reaper's Shadow curse?" I wondered. "You might be able to see what we missed. We might still have a chance to break this curse for good before the babies arrive."

"I've tried," Talia assured us. "I've been looking for clues since last night, but the visions are hard to understand. From what I see, there are many paths that could potentially lead you toward answers, but I can't tell you which one is going to be *the one*. There are still things that have to happen yet, and even a Seer can't know everything about the future."

"There must be more powers that you can tap into aside from visions," I suggested.

"The empathic abilities I get from the Seer Wand are overwhelming," Talia said. "It's like I can feel all the emotions of the entire coven all at once, but I don't know *who* is feeling *what*. With my natural gift of psychometry, it's like I had one tab open on my browser. With the Seer Wand, it's as if the entirety of the Internet is hitting me all at once. The information is *there*, but I can't sort it out."

"You aren't able to focus on one problem at a time?" I asked.

"That's what we're working on," Verla said.

Talia twisted the Wand around in her hands. "There's areas I feel blocked in, too. I know I have all Seer magic at my fingertips, but there are things even I can't break through."

Lucas furrowed his brow. "Things like what? Counter magic of some sort?"

Talia shook her head. "I can't tell. It could be *me*. I tried to have Miles use the Seer Wand, and he found it too overwhelming. He didn't want anything to do with these visions. Maybe subconsciously I'm just trying to shield myself from that."

"Don't push yourself too hard," I told her. "Your visions won't help us if you aren't in a space to properly interpret them."

"I'm trying to use it sparingly. Every time I use the Seer Wand, I'm taking power from another Seer," Talia added. "I don't want to take more than is necessary."

"Is there anything else you've found that's useful?" Lucas wondered.

"I've tried to locate the Curse Breaker Wand, but it makes no sense," Talia said. "All I see is blackness. There's an emptiness to my visions that makes it feel so out of reach. I haven't figured out how to interpret that yet. I'm still watching the priestesses, and I can see them discussing the Wands, but that's about all I can get from them that makes any sense. Every future I look into seems to change."

"Thank you for trying," Lucas said, but I wasn't ready to give up yet.

"If we can't look into the future, maybe we could look into the past for answers," I theorized.

"I'll try," Talia promised. "But it's a lot of information to sift through. There's hundreds of years of history, and I don't know who or what I'm looking for."

Verla stood. "Perhaps you should take a break, Talia. Go back to your room, and when you're feeling well-rested, we can try some exercises to hone your focus."

"Thanks, Verla—I mean, Clarice." Talia placed the Seer Wand in the pocket of her sweatshirt and left the room.

Verla turned back to us. "I'm sorry we don't have the answers you're looking for, but maybe Nadine is on to something. We may not be able to decipher all the clues from the Wand just yet, but maybe we can still dig into the past."

"How?" Lucas furrowed his brow.

"A past-life regression," Verla suggested.

"Like getting visions of our past incarnations?" I asked. "How does that help us now?"

Verla sat down to explain. "Reincarnation is more than just about bringing your soul back to Earth one life after the next. It serves a purpose, and oftentimes as a fulfillment of that purpose, our destinies can be entwined, either with each other… or with future lifetimes."

"So I could have been a reaper in a past lifetime?" Lucas wondered. "In that lifetime, I might've known more about my powers than I do now."

"It's possible," Verla said. "But we won't know until we try. Even if we don't get clear answers about the issues that pertain to us today, past-life regressions can be very eye-opening regarding the journey that you're on. Through each incarnation, a piece of your soul returns to Earth to learn new lessons. Some of these lessons can be carried from one life to the next. Or in some cases—such as with identical twins in the Miriamic Coven—a soul may split to experience lessons alongside each other in the same lifetime."

"Twins must be really close, then," I said sadly, thinking of the sister she'd lost.

Verla nodded. "Yes. It's an unfortunate tragedy when one is lost. Within the Miriamic Coven, identical twins are a form of twin flame."

"Our babies will be twin flames, then," I realized, rubbing my belly. "Are they here with us already—their souls? Have they incarnated in these bodies already, even though they haven't been born?"

"It depends on the soul," Verla explained. "You can choose when to incarnate into your body. Some souls choose to do so in utero, and others wait until birth."

"I feel like they're here with us already," I said. "It's kind of nice to think our babies are each other's soulmates."

"Soulmates are those we are destined to be with due to soul contracts we made before this incarnation," Verla explained. "You and Lucas, for example, are likely soulmates. Twin flames, on the other hand, are much deeper, more intense bonds, and they aren't necessarily romantic—though in some cultures they can be. Not all twin flames are genetically related as they are in the coven."

"What makes a twin flame connection more intense?" I wondered.

"A twin flame refers to two halves of a soul who are meeting in the same lifetime. Soulmates, on the other hand, are separate souls," Verla said. "Twin flames are meant to live their lives together, in different bodies, but still supporting one another in their life's journey. Each half of the twin flame bond makes the other whole. This bond is meant to last a lifetime, although some twin flames find the bond so intense that they are not able to coexist with each other and are forced to go their separate ways. On the other hand, soulmate bonds may come and go when the lessons have been learned."

Lucas squeezed my hand, and I understood what he meant without having to say a word. *I don't want to lose you.*

Verla must've noticed, because she quickly added, "Of course, soulmates can stay together to support each other, even when the lessons they've agreed to teach one another have been learned."

"Why do we forget these lessons?" I questioned. "Each time we incarnate, we become these blank slates all over again."

"Consciously, you forget," Verla agreed. "But deep in your core, your soul remembers. The past versions of yourself still exist, but you become a new piece of the whole. Some lessons are only learned by viewing them through certain lenses. We must forget our past lives so that we can experience new things without old worldviews and beliefs holding us back. This is why sometimes souls choose to reincarnate in other religions, so they can see the world from a different point of view."

"So we could have been fae or Elementai in another life?" Lucas asked.

Verla nodded. "It's entirely possible. You could even be lovers with someone in one life, and parent and child in the next. You could even be your own grandchild."

I leaned forward, intrigued by the lesson. "How many lives have we lived?"

"That depends on the soul," Verla explained. "Gods have the power to create new souls, so some of us have been around longer than others. Would you like to return to your first life?"

Lucas and I nodded in unison.

Verla conjured a bowl and several vials of herbs. She set them on the coffee table in front of her. "I'm going to create an herb mixture and light it. The fumes will put you into a relaxed state that will assist with deep meditation. I will lead you through a guided meditation, and we'll see what answers we can find."

My hand instinctively went to my belly. "Is it safe?"

"Of course it's safe, Nadine," Verla said seriously. "I promise you that I will *never* do anything to harm your babies. And if anyone so dares to try, I will personally end them myself."

Her passion for the safety of my children soothed me. I couldn't think of anyone better to lead this ritual.

Verla spoke as she began mixing the herbs. "Lucas, take a seat on this empty chair. Nadine, you may lie down on the couch. I want you both to be able to completely relax."

Lucas settled into the chair across from Verla, and I lay flat on my back across the couch cushions. Verla infused her magic into the herbs, then lit the mixture with a match.

Smoke billowed out of the bowl, and the sweet scent filled my nostrils. My muscles began to relax.

"Close your eyes, and focus on the sound of my voice," Verla said softly. "Alone in this room, it is safe to let your guard down and explore memories outside this lifetime. Inhale a deep breath, and notice how your eyelids are beginning to get very heavy."

I sank deeper into the couch, feeling as if I could melt into it.

"Now imagine a white light above your head. This is a warm, welcoming light—the light of Mother Miriam herself," Verla continued. "Imagine that light entering the top of your head, then traveling down your body. With each cell it moves through, feel it filling you up with love, relaxing each muscle. Feel the tightness in your jaw release, and your shoulders fall away from your ears. Feel the light travel down your arms and into your fingertips, and swirling in your hips, relieving any worry and tension you may be holding on to."

I pictured the light permeating my body all the way down to my toes, until I felt more relaxed than ever before.

"Now I want you to picture yourself in this moment, as if you are floating above your body, looking down on the room," Verla instructed. "As you float higher above the room, you will find yourself looking down on this moment as if peering through a portal. You are now outside of time and space. Look around you. What colors do you see?"

In my imagination, I saw an endless navy-blue sky in all directions.

"As you gaze into the moment once more, you notice that a golden string extends from this moment in both directions," Verla said. "In one direction is the future, which has not yet been written. In the other is your past. Turn now to your past, and begin walking down the timeline. You may see moments of your past through portals, as if viewing them from above."

Memories flooded my mind—recent memories, like telling Lucas we were pregnant, then images from our wedding.

"See each memory as a snapshot as you pass by them," Verla continued. "Take yourself back to the moment you walked through the doors to Miriam College… now even further back, to your first day of high school. Keep going, further into your childhood. Find a memory that sticks out, view it for a moment, and continue on."

Memories of my time in the hospital before my lupus diagnosis passed through my mind. I wanted to stop at them, but I didn't. I let the memories pass by, then kept going.

"See yourself on the playground in elementary school," Verla said. "Now see yourself learning to take your first steps. See yourself as a baby, in the arms of your mother."

I'd never had memories that went this far back, but I could see my mother clear as day, sitting in a rocking chair in our old living room. She held a baby in her arms and sang her a lullaby.

"Turn your attention back to the golden thread," Verla instructed. "Notice that it goes far back in time, further even than your birth. Continue on down this timeline, stepping far back into the past, through as many lifetimes as you must to reach your first."

Images flickered across my vision, but I couldn't make sense of any of them.

Verla's calming voice continued to fill my ears. "Now take yourself back to your first incarnation, however far back that may be. In this life, there will be a pivotal moment, a moment so profound that you have carried it with you from one life to the next. Allow yourself to be drawn to this moment."

In my imagination, I found myself floating along the timeline, until I came to a portal that showed a small timber-framed cottage. The cottage was nestled between rolling hills beside a beautiful meadow.

"Now that you have found the memory, step into it," Verla said.

Verla's voice faded, until I found myself strolling through the meadow. The hem of my wool skirt danced around my ankles. I gave no thought to the couch I was lying on, because that seemed lifetimes removed from where I was now.

☾

*"MOTHER ISN'T GOING to be pleased when she learns how you killed that chicken," I said in an accent that wasn't mine, but felt entirely familiar.*

*I turned to my brother, who was carrying the dead chicken by its feet. His features were different—darker hair and more stubble—but my soul recognized him as Lucas. I was nineteen now, and my brother was only two years older. We were the youngest of five children and had been very close our whole lives, though we didn't always get along. Now was one of those times I didn't particularly approve of his actions.*

*"Mother will be proud," he insisted. "I didn't even have to touch it. It will make a wonderful stew."*

*"If you can kill a chicken without touching it, what else can you do?" I demanded. "Your powers are dangerous, Mortimer. You must be careful with how you use them, or the wrong person is going to end up dead."*

*"It's dinner, Alora," he shot back. "I'm not killing people."*

*"But you could," I insisted.*

*He kept his chin forward as he answered, "Then perhaps they deserve to die."*

*I frowned. "I'm not saying you can't use your powers. Only that you must be cautious."*

*"Sorry that I'm not a Curse Breaker like you," Mortimer shot back. "I can't make medicine potions like Maud, or control people's minds like Percival. I can't see the future like Cecilia. Gods know not a single one of us are as powerful as Mother and Father. Sorry that my magic scares you, but if I've got this power, then I'm going to use it for good, and that starts with bringing home dinner. Unless you're not hungry..."*

*Mortimer dangled the dead chicken in front of my face, and I turned up my nose.*

*"Get that thing away from me!" I shouted.*

*"Or what? You'll run to Father?" he teased.*

*"I don't need Father to save me," I sneered. "I've got magic of my own."*

*I formed a battle orb and aimed it at him.*

*He only laughed. "What are you going to do with that? I'm not the only one who can kill. Watch your magic, Alora. You might kill someone."*

*He was mocking me.*

*"Ugh!" I complained. "You're insufferable."*

*He dangled the chicken out in front of me again. I'd had enough, and I shoved his arm aside as I took off running across the meadow toward our cottage. Our cottage was bigger than most, as Mother and Father had built it themselves. We lived a quiet life here in the countryside, where our magic was concealed from those who wished to take it.*

*I burst through the door to the cottage. "Mother, you'll never believe what Mortimer did—"*

*I came to an abrupt halt when I spotted my mother and three of my siblings gathered around the table. Cecilia sat in the center chair, her skin ashen as if she's just received the worst news. My sister's name was Cecilia, but my soul knew her as Talia. My sister Maud—whom my soul recognized as a man named Grant—and my brother Percival—who I knew as Chloe—sat on either side of Cecilia, looking to be comforting her. They all shared a look of terror.*

*"Alora," my mother said hastily. "We must fortify the protection spell now. The fae have discovered our power, and they will kill us to keep another magical race from even the chance of opposing them."*

*"It's too late," Cecilia stated in a whisper. "They're already here."*

*"MOTHER!" Mortimer's scream came from outside.*

*We rushed out the door together. My mother stopped in her tracks when she looked to the sky to see hundreds of flying creatures descending upon us. There were all kinds of magical beings—wolves with wings, griffins carrying riders, alicorns with shimmering horns that were more threatening than beautiful, and dragons with razor-sharp teeth. Fae sorceresses had insect-like wings growing out of their backs, but even their graceful nature appeared deadly as they aimed their spells at our cottage.*

*"Gods dammit!" Mother yelled. "The Seelie fae have found us!"*

*Mother blasted a deadly spell at the sky. The magic crackled like lightning, knocking dozens of riders off their shifters all at once. Fae sorceresses fell out of the sky, and dragons and griffins dropped dead into the meadow. As impressive as Mother's spell was, it barely killed a fraction of them.*

*"How can we know what's real?" I demanded. "The fae have illusion magic that we do not!"*

*Percival waved his hand, and the scene above us changed. Percival used his magic to force the fae to drop their illusions. The amount of fae above us doubled, only they were coming at us from both directions. They'd intended to keep us focused on one army so the other could sneak up behind us.*

*Spells spun in our direction, and one hit Mother in the shoulder. She fell to the ground, screaming in pain.*

*Instinctually, I grabbed Maud's hand. "Together!"*

*She reached for the others, and we all grabbed hands. Their power surged through me, and a shield formed around my family, so powerful that the fae's spells couldn't break through.*

*A primal scream broke out of Mortimer's lungs. He aimed his hands at the air, and one by one, fae began to drop out of the sky. A darkness swirled in the clouds as his power of death stole the lives of the fae.*

*Spells continued to rain down on us, and my shield wavered.*

*"I do not know how long I can hold it!" I screamed.*

*Mother winced as she righted herself. "Believe that you will win this fight, and you will!"*

*"We can't!" I yelled. "There are too many."*

*She ran over to me and grabbed me by the shoulders. "Seelie fae cannot use magic that is not their own, but you can, Alora. Take their magic, and use it against them!"*

*I gritted my teeth and searched the sky for their magic. Their powers were different from mine, for I had demon blood running through my veins. But I was also the daughter of a god, and I had power even the oldest of the fae could not fathom.*

*I ordered their magic to become mine, and my protection spell grew larger. Dragons landed around us, shaking the earth. As much magic as I'd stolen, it was still a small amount compared to the hundreds of fae surrounding us.*

*My family continued to aim deadly spells at the fae shifters. Mortimer stole their lives straight from their bodies, but soon he fell to his knees. Fae continued to fall, while others clawed at my shield, trying their damndest to get through and kill us.*

*All for being different. All because they were afraid of what we could do.*

*"Mother!" I screamed. "There are too many."*

*Mother hit another dragon with her deadly spells, but I saw the horror on her face. She knew that we were strong, but there were only six of us and hundreds of them.*

*"We need your father!" Mother yelled.*

*"Where is he?" Cecilia screamed.*

"Call to him, and he will hear you," Mother promised.

"Father!" the five of us screamed together.

Like a beacon of light, a figure appeared in the sky—a tall being who stood like a man but had the face of a ram. A beastly roar erupted from his lungs, and my father flew through the sky as if he could control the air itself.

My father aimed himself at fae women. He grabbed them by the head before tearing their wings clean off their backs. The women fell to the ground one by one. Shifters noticed what was happening and turned their attention away from us, their sights set on my father.

A massive black dragon shifter went in for the kill, but my father smashed his foot into the dragon's face, and the power sent the creature reeling through the sky. The dragon landed hard on the ground, and I heard the snap of his neck.

My father lifted his hands, and dark smoke billowed from his palms. It swept through the fae army, killing each one the moment it touched them. A dragon roared, and shifters turned to flee. Any who stayed were immediately slaughtered by my father's wrath.

The meadow quieted. I fell to my knees, my breath ragged. My father landed softly in the grass, and his form shrank, revealing his human features once again.

"Father!" I cried, stumbling to my feet and throwing myself into his arms.

Mortimer did the same, and soon, we were all embracing Father.

"You came just in time," I cried.

My father stroked my hair. "Of course. I would never leave you alone. I have work in the other realms. Your mother and I are building an afterlife, a place for our souls to go that is away from the fae. But you are my children, and I will be here whenever you call."

"This was too close," Mother said. "We have already done so much to hide our magic from the fae. We have had protection spells in place for ages, and we've ensured they cannot translate our grimoires. Now that they have found us, they will most certainly attack again. We must move north, find a new place to settle."

"The fae will not find us," my father promised. "Miriam, take the children inside and begin packing our belongings."

My heart broke to think about abandoning the place we grew up in. It was the only home I'd ever known.

I turned to follow my mother, until my father called, "Mortimer, Alora, may I have a word?"

The others disappeared into the cottage. My father approached and took each of our hands in his.

*"All of my children have inherited incredible power," he said. "You all have your roles, but the power you two have inherited is exceptional. Mortimer, you have the power to protect this family from threats, to kill those who wish to kill you first. And Alora, you bring this family together. With your magic we can unite all our power as one. You two have the most important jobs when it comes to protecting our family. I do not make this request lightly, but it is up to both of you to protect us in times of conflict. Are you willing to take on that monumental task?"*

*Mortimer nodded firmly. "Yes, Father."*

*"In this life and the next," I agreed.*

*Father gave us a kind smile. "So shall it be."*

☾

THE VISION FADED, and the golden string that had been my timeline seemed to act as a rubber band, snapping me back to the present.

My eyes shot open, and my heart hammered. I pushed myself upright to see Lucas taking in ragged breaths.

"You were there," I whispered. "Talia, Grant, and Chloe were there, too. And Mother Miriam and Santos. I recognized them like I recognize my own parents."

"I was Mortimer," Lucas said breathlessly.

Verla's eyebrows shot up. "Mortimer? As in, Mother Miriam's son?"

"We were *all* their kids." Lucas sat up straighter, then dove into an explanation about what we'd seen in our vision.

Verla appeared shocked as she took this all in. "This makes sense. The five of you have become leaders in this rebellion, because you were meant to fight alongside each other from one life to the next. You must've chosen to come here at this time to heal the coven from this conflict. That's why Everly's prophecy is about *you*, because you made the choice to save us before you ever incarnated in this life."

"What about the others?" I asked. "Talia, Grant, and Chloe were there, too, but Everly's prophecy is just about Lucas and me."

"It's as Santos said," Verla reminded me. "In the midst of conflict, you two have the most important job—Lucas to defend, and Nadine to bring everyone together."

"The prophecy says our souls are bound, because we've already lived lives together," Lucas realized.

"Isn't it weird that we were brother and sister in one life, and now we're married?" I wondered.

"It is not strange to the soul, because we differentiate one life from the next," Verla explained.

"That was our first life," Lucas said. "We might've lived other lives between then and now, but it's clear to me that Mother Miriam and Santos created us."

A beat passed as I took this all in. "I never quite understood why I cared so much about the coven, because I didn't grow up here, and most of the coven doesn't want me around, anyway. But now I get it. It's because I've been here before. This will always be my home—my family."

"It also makes sense why you are both so talented with your magic," Verla added. "You were demigods in a past life. Your souls are very powerful."

"A demigod, as in, children of the gods?" I asked.

"That is one definition," Verla said. "But it is also a classification of supernatural power. There are average supernaturals, as most of the coven is. Then there are talented supernaturals—those who can handle magic beyond the average supernatural, such as the two of you. Beyond them are demigods, who are either born from the gods, or in rare cases, born from two talented supernatural parents. It's more about their power than their origin. Demigods have power beyond anything that we can imagine. They have the ability to create and destroy worlds. They need no energy source, because they themselves can create power. They have their own limits, but there are always exceptions to these rules when the circumstances are right."

"We can't do anything like that," Lucas remarked.

"No, because you aren't demigods in this lifetime, but you are still very powerful," Verla stated. "With enough practice, you may be capable of far more than you realize. With the two of your powers combined, there's no telling what you might be able to do."

We may not be demigods in this lifetime, but our souls had experienced it before. Demigod power could show up in our reality again, even if we weren't demigods in this current incarnation.

This past-life regression had given me hope. It felt like no matter what lay ahead of us, we were destined to win—whether in this life or the next. The only question was, what were we willing to lose along the way?

☽

WEEKS PASSED, and the Winter Solstice arrived on December twenty-first. Yuletide cheer filled the house that morning. I'd slept in, because the pregnancy made me tired all the time, but otherwise I was handling it really well. I'd only had morning sickness twice, which was nice because I thought I'd be throwing up on the daily. So far, I was really enjoying my pregnancy, and I couldn't wait to feel the babies kick for the first time. I hadn't started showing yet, so I had a few more weeks until I started feeling them.

I tried not to think about what might happen if we didn't make it that far. Lucas and I had given ourselves until Christmas to break the Reaper's Shadow curse, or we'd be forced to face the alternative. We were running out of time and hadn't found any leads, but we still had a few more days. I wasn't giving up yet.

Today, I chose not to worry; instead, I held on to the hope that through our ceremonies and rituals, we might call in a holiday miracle.

I'd never experienced a proper Yule celebration within the coven. My first semester at Miriam College, I'd left Octavia Falls over winter break. Last year, Yule had followed the Burning, and nobody had been in the spirit to celebrate. I was excited to finally partake in the traditions. Yule was a time of rebirth, to celebrate the longest night of the year and welcome the return of the sun. Today was supposed to mark the end of our descent into darkness, and new beginnings into the light.

The scent of spruce needles and baking apple pie filled the house. The hallways had been decorated with twinkling lights, and wreaths hung on each of our bedroom doors. We'd made them last night by twisting evergreen branches together and decorating them with pinecones and winterberries we'd found in the woods.

Meanwhile, Grant, Lucas, and Miles had chopped down a small spruce tree and dragged it inside, since evergreens were said to bring prosperity and protection. We'd decorated the tree with popcorn garlands and acorns we'd enchanted to sparkle like glitter. We didn't have a lot of deco-

330

rations on hand, but we worked with what we had. I thought our decorations turned out better using natural accents, anyway.

Verla and Onyx were already in the kitchen preparing the feast, and I still had to make a present for the gift exchange. Since we couldn't leave the safe house to go shopping as often as we'd like, we'd agreed that instead of getting everyone presents, we would pick names and exchange gifts that way, with the caveat that our gifts would all be hand-made.

I'd picked Talia's name, and I had this great idea to make a pendulum out of a crystal and an old necklace chain, but I couldn't figure out how to secure the two together. I needed to find a quick solution or come up with another idea before this evening.

I approached Mandy's room and knocked.

"Don't come in!" Mandy called. "I'm wrapping a present."

"When you're done, can I get your help?" I asked.

Her door swung open a second later. "Everything all right?"

"I'm all right. It's just this." I opened my hand to reveal the crystal and the chain. "I'm trying to make a pendulum for the gift exchange. Any chance you can fix it?"

"I can give it a shot," she offered, gesturing me into her room.

My shoulders fell with relief. "Thank you so much. I was hoping you'd still have your jewelry-making supplies, because that would make this so much easier. I tried wrapping the chain around the crystal and securing the end into one of the chain links, but it won't hold. I think I need wire, so I can twist it to hold the crystal inside—like your necklace, but not as fancy."

I gestured to the necklace she was wearing. A pretty red stone hung off the end of a chain, with an intricate metal design encasing it.

Mandy touched the necklace. "This is all my jewelry I managed to escape Octavia Falls with. I'm sorry to say I don't have any extra supplies."

I frowned. "Bummer. I'm going to have to think of something else before tonight. It wouldn't be fair to leave Talia without a present."

Mandy tapped her chin. "There *is* one thing we can brew up quickly, but I'll have to sneak some supplies from the kitchen. We can make Talia some loose-leaf tea that will make her see colors when she hears music. You can cast Alchemy magic with the right crystals, can't you?"

"Yes. Should I go get them?"

"Go get your crystals, and I'll meet you back here in five minutes," Mandy said.

I followed her instructions, and she returned to her room with a small draw-string bag and several bottles of herbs, which she spread out on the bed. I read the labels to see that she'd grabbed peppermint, ginger, cinnamon, and black pepper.

"All you have to do is mix a bit of each herb in the bag, and we'll infuse it with your Alchemy magic and it'll be good to go!" Mandy held the baggie open for me.

I popped off the top of the peppermint container and gave a few good shakes into the baggie. I sprinkled in ginger, then cinnamon. "Where'd you learn to make this?"

Mandy dropped her gaze, and her tone shifted like she was trying to hide her sadness. "Amy made it for me once."

Silence settled over the room, and I could tell Mandy didn't want to talk about her.

I tried to lighten the mood as I picked up the pepper shaker. "We're really putting black pepper in the tea?"

"It's a requirement. It doesn't taste the best, but it's effective."

I finished adding the ingredients, and Mandy sealed up the bag and shook it. She handed it over to me, and I funneled Alchemy magic into it from the crystals I'd brought.

"That's it!" Mandy said brightly. "What'd I tell you? Easy peasy!"

I smiled, because it was really nice to be getting along with her again. I'd never asked her about what the priestesses had done to her, and I thought she'd never forgive me for the torture they put her through. But that didn't seem to be the case. Mandy could've gone to *Hok'evale* with Tate, and she'd chosen to stay. I really appreciated her friendship, because it seemed no matter what had happened between us, we'd eventually find our way back home.

I clutched the baggie in my hands. "Thanks again, Mandy."

"You're welcome. Now go," she teased, pushing me toward the door. "You're not allowed to see me wrap your present!"

"Hey, you aren't supposed to tell me you have my name!" I protested playfully.

"Whoops!" Mandy placed her hand over her mouth. "I guess you're still going to have to wait for the surprise."

I left her room, then returned to mine so I could wrap Talia's gift. When I finished, I went downstairs to place the present under the tree.

All the others were gathered downstairs. Lucas and Professor Warren were in the hall, and I followed the sound of their voices to see what they were doing. Lucas held a box full of bells, flowers, and twigs, and Professor Warren was hanging them from above the front door.

"What are you doing?" I wondered. "Can I help?"

Lucas's eyes lit up when he saw me. "Sure! We're hanging bells, yarrow, and mistletoe in the doorway to keep the fae away."

"I think we have enough wards for that," I teased as he handed me a set of bells and tacks to hold them up.

"It's tradition," Warren explained. He was taller than Lucas, but he still stood on his toes to hang a sprig of mistletoe as high as he could reach. "Centuries ago, when the witches lived in Europe, we did all we could to stave off the fae. The Winter Solstice is their day for a celebration they call the Winter Hunt. Each year, the fae put on a grand festival, and their most accomplished hunters go into the forest in hunt of their dark god Droga. According to fae lore, the dark god Droga chased away the sun at the Fall Equinox. Today marks the day Tomir, king of the fae gods and lord of the Winter Hunt, brings it back. Witches don't want to be caught in the middle of a fae hunt, and therefore, it is tradition to stay inside. That is why we sing, drink, and feast in our homes until morning, once the sun returns and it is safe to venture outside once more."

"So what's with the bells?" I asked as I hung one up.

"The fae don't like bells," Lucas said. "If they were to come through the door into our home, the noise would annoy them, and make them go away. As extra protection, we hang yarrow, which the fae are allergic to, and mistletoe, which helps ward off evil of all kinds."

"The fae aren't getting past this," I said proudly. I lay yarrow in front of the doorway. It seemed silly that such a simple thing was so powerful, but that's how it was in the supernatural world. Some magic required effort and exceptional power, and others were as simple as a tiny flower that you didn't realize could kill you until it'd already done its damage.

We finished hanging all the bells, yarrow, and mistletoe and returned to the great room. Onyx and Verla were brewing something that smelled of cinnamon and nutmeg in the kitchen. Mandy was downstairs now, and she'd joined them to bake cookies. In the living room, Chloe and Miles were curled up under a blanket, sipping steaming cups of hot cocoa. Grant and Talia sat in front of the fireplace, dangling pine branches above the cats' heads.

The cats batted at the needles with their paws. Talia laughed as she tossed her pine branch across the room, and seven of the eight cats chased it all at once. Isa caught it first, but Oliver tackled her to the ground, and they went tumbling under the Christmas tree together. Talia's cat Gus snatched the end of the branch in his mouth and started running across the room. Grant's cat Bella and Miles's cat Kiki both chased after him. Onyx's cat gave up and started licking his paws. Marley, Chloe's cat, sprinted from out of nowhere and snatched the branch out of Gus's mouth. It was really funny to watch.

Odin didn't look amused. The black cat lazed on the back of the couch and merely blinked at the others, like he didn't understand what was so interesting about a pine branch.

"Lighten up, Scrooge," I teased Odin, scratching him behind the ears as I passed. He started purring but got a disgruntled look on his face when I stopped.

Chloe got up and went over to the fire, where she shifted around the coals with an iron poker. "The fire's ready to burn our Yule logs."

"What exactly is a Yule log?" I asked. I'd heard of it, but I hadn't burned one before. My parents and I had always celebrated Christmas, but the Yule log wasn't a tradition my mother brought with her when she left the coven.

"As you know, Yule is a time in which we reflect on the previous year and make oaths, promises, or goals for the year to come," Chloe explained. "Traditionally, the Yule log was a whole tree brought into the home and burned over twelve days, to beckon in the return of the sun. The traditions have evolved over time, and now we each take our own log and write or carve our wishes on it for the new year. You don't have to make it complicated; it can be a single word that holds your intention for the year. Then you'll burn the log to surrender those intentions to Mother Miriam."

"Are there any incantations or spells to cast?" I wondered.

Chloe shook her head. "The act of burning the log itself is a spell. You will start here at the Yule altar, to pray to Mother Miriam and leave your burdens of this year behind."

Chloe gestured to a small table set up near the tree. Beside it was a box of pinecones, acorns, and spruce branches left over from our wreaths and ornaments. "You will choose your offering from the box and place it upon the altar. Traditionally, our ancestors offered plants and food, because that's all they had to give centuries ago. This offering symbolizes what you are willing to let go of. Light a candle as you say a prayer to express your gratitude to Mother Miriam, and hand over what is no longer serving you. In return, she will shoulder your burdens and bless you with prosperity for the new year once the sun returns. Shall your intentions be pure, she will guide you to accomplishing the goals you carve into the Yule log."

She turned to a pile of small logs stacked beside the fireplace. "Once you have done that, you can choose a log and carve your intention into it, then place it in the fireplace to be burned. Who wants to go first?"

"I'll go!" Talia offered chipperly. She practically danced across the room and knelt in front of the altar. Nobody bothered her as she silently said a prayer to Mother Miriam and lit a tealight candle. She used her wand to carve the word *Abundance* into her Yule log, then placed it into the fire.

Once she finished, Grant went next. Lucas brought me a mug of apple cider from the kitchen, and we snuggled up on one of the couches. I could feel the warmth of the fire from here, and it was really cozy. We nibbled on gingerbread cookies, and Talia led us in Yuletide carols as each person took a turn at the altar.

As the others went, I tried to think of all the things I needed to let go of, and a horrible thought came to mind. I'd already lost so much this year when Grammy died, and I didn't want to lose anyone else. I could hear a voice in my head saying I had to let go of *her*. I wanted to kick that voice in the mouth, because it certainly wasn't my own.

I knew Grammy had moved on to Alora, but she couldn't truly enjoy where she was at if I was holding her back. Grammy was worrying about me; I was certain. I knew I needed to accept that she was gone, but I was never going to let her go. I *couldn't*.

I didn't consider letting go of the twins, because I wasn't going to let that happen. I wouldn't even entertain the idea unless absolutely necessary.

Hours passed as we sang carols and waited for the Yule logs in the fire to burn down so others could add their own. I'd had plenty of time to think about what I would let go of in this ceremony, but nothing felt right. All I could think about was Grammy. It was a joyous day, laced in melancholy that she wasn't here.

I knew my sadness wasn't serving me, nor anyone else. I could focus on the good and all the great Christmases we'd had in the past. Grammy had always come to visit, and she'd bring along her famous brisket and always gift handmade presents. She'd once given me the sweetest pine-scented candle she'd made herself, and I'd never burned it because I didn't want the scent to go away.

Then I thought about how I'd lost the candle in the move. It seemed I'd lost so much of her now. Focusing on the good didn't seem to help when it reminded me of what I'd lost.

Consciously, I understood that letting go of Grammy didn't mean forgetting her, but my heart wasn't convinced. I worried that if I let go of all this pain, I'd lose my connection to her. It'd be like I never cared at all. I couldn't do that.

I was the last to kneel beside the altar. Nine tealight candles burned, leaving only one that hadn't been lit. I hesitantly withdrew a pinecone from the box beside me. I caught sight of a cinnamon stick at the bottom, and I placed that on the altar as well. The others let me be while I silently reflected on my own. It was like they weren't even here.

My mind raced, because I knew what I had to do, but couldn't. My friends had made this look so easy. They'd each spent mere moments at the altar to whisper a prayer, but I'd completely frozen up.

I had to choose something else, because I certainly wasn't ready to let go of my grandmother. I tried to think about what she would say to me. I recalled a conversation we had months ago, where she encouraged me to let go of control. She said I feared letting go, because I wasn't sure I could handle the outcome. I wondered where in my life I was still holding on to control.

My hand instinctively went to my belly. I thought about how I hadn't been in control of this conception. Lucas and I hadn't planned it, but it was one of the best things that had ever happened. I hadn't even given birth yet, and I already knew I loved these babies so much. I couldn't tell what the future held, but I knew by this time next year, everything would be different.

*Mother Miriam,* I prayed silently. *I thank you for the children you have blessed me with, for I know this is my destiny. I let go of control over this pregnancy, and over the birth of my children. Whatever future may come, I trust that you will protect us. So shall it be.*

I struck a match and lit the final candle. I felt a little lighter as I went over to the fireplace to pick up a log. I conjured my wand and cast a spell to carve my intention into the log. The word *Family* scrawled across the bark, and I smiled as I placed the Yule log into the fire.

I felt much better when I stepped away from the fire, like a weight had been lifted off my shoulders. Verla, Onyx, and Mandy had joined us in the living room while the food finished cooking. It was at least an hour until dinnertime, and Grant suggested we do the gift exchange now.

He handed out our presents, until we were each holding one with our names on them. "To determine the order we open gifts in, we'll be playing Spin the Candy Cane," Grant announced, holding up a red and white striped candy cane. "Chloe, if you will."

Chloe waved her hand, and her telekinesis levitated the candy cane into the air. Grant gave it a tap, and it began spinning. It slowed, until it came to a stop, pointing at Talia.

She tore open the paper and opened the box to reveal the bag of tea Mandy and I had made earlier today. Talia opened it and inhaled the scent. "It smells wonderful. Who made this?"

I raised my hand. "I infused it with Alchemy magic. It's a tea blend that will make you see colors when you hear music."

"I love it!" Talia exclaimed.

Grant spun the candy cane again, and it landed on Lucas. He opened his gift to find an assortment of chocolates Grant had made himself. They looked really fancy, with colored chocolate drizzled over the top of each one. Lucas popped one in his mouth, and the end of his nose started to glow red.

"You look like Rudolph the Red-Nosed Reindeer!" I laughed.

Lucas crossed his eyes and wiggled the end of his nose to try to get a good look at it. "This better go away by Christmas Eve, or some guy in a red suit is going to be knocking on our door asking me to guide his sleigh."

"And you'd do it in a heartbeat," I teased. I grabbed his face in my hands and kissed the end of his nose. "You look adorable."

"For a reindeer," he joked with a laugh.

Onyx and Chloe had gotten each other. Onyx had gifted Chloe a collection of bath bombs she'd made herself, while Chloe gave Onyx a pair of origami doves she'd enchanted with Mentalist powers. The doves fluttered around the room and landed in Onyx's hair.

She snickered as they tickled the top of her head. "I love them!"

The candy cane continued to spin, and wrapping paper littered the floor. Everyone had been really creative with their gifts, and it was tons of fun seeing what everyone had made. Grant had received a hair gel potion Verla had brewed herself.

"It's temporary, so it holds during the day and disappears at night so you don't have to wash it out," Verla explained.

Talia had crafted a wreath made from clothespins for Miles, and she'd put a condom in each of the clothespins. He let out a deep belly laugh when he saw it.

"It's perfect!" Miles cried.

"Tal, I see you're living up to your promise to keep us all supplied," I laughed.

Professor Warren had gifted Verla wooden salt and pepper shakers he'd carved himself. They even had images of cats etched along the sides.

Miles had obviously struggled with coming up with an idea, because he'd gifted Warren an origami apple. He shot a nervous glance at Chloe, and it was clear she'd taught him how to make it.

Mandy and I were the only ones left, and the spinning candy cane landed on her first. She opened her present to find several sheets of paper. She flipped through the pages and furrowed her brow. "What are these?"

"They're incantations I wrote to aid with sleep," Lucas told her. "They should help you focus your powers to walk through others' dreams."

"Oh!" Mandy said brightly. "That's so thoughtful of you."

Everyone else had gone, which meant my present was from Mandy. I opened my present to find a jar filled with a gritty brown substance.

"It's a cinnamon sugar hand scrub," Mandy said before I could ask what it was. "It's made with brown sugar, cinnamon, vanilla extract, and coconut oil. It's a natural way to exfoliate and hydrate your hands!"

I opened the jar and inhaled the sweet scent. "That's so creative. I love it, Mandy."

We all exchanged hugs as we thanked each other for the gifts. While we were cleaning up the wrapping paper, the timer on the stove went off. Everyone worked together to finish up dinner and set the table.

We gathered in the dining room and feasted on ham, mashed potatoes, and stuffing. Canned green beans we'd preserved from Grammy's garden over the summer were passed around the table, along with pear slices and apple cider we'd made from the trees outside. Grant had made enchiladas, because that's what his mom always made at Christmas time, and Miles said it wouldn't be the holidays without it.

Grant started telling stories about his Christmases as a kid, and soon, everyone was chiming in and laughing about their holiday memories.

As our plates cleared, Lucas stood. "I'll get dessert."

"I'll help," Miles offered.

The two left the room, while the rest of us continued laughing and telling stories.

"My family caroled every year at Yule," Talia said. "The neighbors next door got sick of how often we came over, so they put a *No Caroling* sign on their door. My siblings and I would stand at the end of their lawn and sing at the top of our lungs."

"*Rawr!*" Miles called as he jumped into the room. He was wearing a terrifying goblin-like mask with curved horns coming out of the top. He'd draped a fuzzy white blanket around his shoulders like a cape—or was it meant to be fur?

Chloe shot out of her chair and screamed playfully. "It's Krampus! Everybody run!"

I'd heard of this tradition before, but I hadn't yet experienced it. Krampus was a monster of lore, known to emerge from the depths of hell in early December each year. Krampus would beat naughty children with sticks or toss them in his sack and take them back to hell. The monster hadn't appeared in our world since ancient times, but members of the coven still dressed up as him and chased people around in a tradition known as the Krampus Run. It was another way to ward off the fae and disperse the ghosts of winter.

We all leapt from our chairs and raced for the entrance to the room. Miles growled and hissed to block our exit, but then he caught sight of Chloe and went straight for her. She ran around the table, and he chased after her, until he'd cornered her on the other side of the room. He caught her, then nuzzled his face in her neck like he was going to eat her. We all slipped around him and ran out of the room.

Lucas was there in the hallway waiting for us in a second Krampus mask. "Run, little children!" he cried in a mystical voice.

"Don't eat me, Krampus! I've been a good boy!" Grant shouted as he took off down the hall. Talia followed him, and they ran into the library. Verla and Warren ducked into the den, their laughter echoing behind them.

Lucas grabbed Onyx and Mandy, but they both struggled away from him and made a break for the stairs. I was the last one out of the dining room, and Lucas jumped in front of me to block my path to the living room.

"You have nowhere to go, you naughty girl!" Lucas teased.

I got a thrill in my stomach. "Then I guess you're going to have to catch me."

I whirled down the hall, and Lucas gave chase. He caught me around the middle, and my heart lifted. I lifted my feet off the ground, putting all my weight on him. He wasn't expecting that, so I fell out of his grasp, then ducked under his arm to run to the other side of the house. He pursued me, and I skidded to a halt in the living room when he jumped over the couch and landed right in front of me.

"No, Krampus, no!" I teased playfully.

Lucas grabbed me, and we fell onto the couch together. He pulled me on top of him and pretended to eat my neck. I laughed as the mask tickled me. He tore the mask off and tossed it aside, taking a deep breath like it was hard to breathe under the mask. Then his lips touched my neck, and he started kissing me. My lips met his, and we began making out.

I snickered. "I've been a very naughty girl this year."

He kissed me again. "Very naughty. I'll have to take you to my lair."

Something lightweight landed on my head, and I grabbed it to find it was one of the condoms from the wreathe Talia had gifted Miles. I turned to see Grant and Talia had returned to the living room, and they'd witnessed our make-out session.

Grant was holding the wreathe and had tossed the condom at us. "Get a room!"

Lucas took the condom from my hand. "We have one, and we won't be needing this."

He tossed it back.

Everyone was still laughing as we cleaned up from dinner. We gathered around the fire, where the last of our Yule logs were burning down. Everyone took a seat, except for Chloe and Talia.

"Talia and I have one more gift to give," Chloe announced.

Everyone quieted down and focused on the girls.

"As you all know, we've been working on advancing our powers using the Oaken Wands," Chloe continued. "However, we're still limited by our own Casts' abilities and our skill levels. Utilizing the Wands isn't just about having power, but knowing how to use it. We've been looking for ways to read the priestesses' minds, so that we can get a step ahead of them. While some Mentalists and Seers can perceive others' thoughts, Talia and I have been struggling to do this on our own. Instead, we came up with the idea to combine our powers in a process we call teleinsight."

Verla sat up straighter, looking intrigued. "Mind-reading is advanced magic, even for those who possess such a skill naturally. Those who do are still limited in many ways, either by requiring consent or needing to be in close proximity to the person whose mind they are reading. How does this work between the two of you?"

"We can still only perform teleinsight if we're in the same room as someone," Talia said. "But the more we hone this power, the more useful we think it will be. The thing about mind reading is that most witches who have this gift can only interpret certain things. We don't know of anyone who can truly infiltrate another's mind and hear their thoughts clearly."

"Such a power would be difficult even for a demigod," Verla pointed out.

"Yes," Chloe agreed. "But we think we've found a way to focus our power to get much clearer with our readings. Most often, Mentalists either project their own mind to manipulate the world, which is how I perform telekinesis. Or they infiltrate the minds of others to place thoughts and ideas there. That's why Mandy can go into other people's dreams, and it's why some Mentalists can control others like puppets. *Extracting* information is another power entirely, because not only do you have to *find* those thoughts, but you have to know how to *read* them. Thoughts can be communicated in words, images, or concepts, and interpreting those ideas is very difficult without consent of the other party. That's where the Seer part comes in."

"Seers hold power of perception," Talia explained. "Members of my Cast can perceive future outcomes or witness past events through visions, but many Seers can also feel other people's emotions or perceive their trauma, even when the subject isn't aware of it themselves."

"Therefore, we discovered that if I use the Mentalist Wand to infiltrate the mind, and Talia uses the Seer Wand to perceive what's inside, together we can see what someone's thinking. Although like Talia said, we're still limited by distance, and we have to use the Wands together," Chloe explained.

"We even came up with an incantation!" Talia exclaimed.

"Are you girls sure about this?" Verla asked. "Power like this will be very draining."

"We're sure," Chloe stated confidently. "We've already tested it on Miles."

Talia scrunched up her nose. "His head is full of dick jokes and nothing else."

"Hey, that's not true!" Miles protested. "I also think about food."

"Does anyone else want to give it a shot?" Chloe asked. "The more practice we get, the better."

Grant raised his hand. "I'll try it."

Chloe and Talia locked hands and lifted the Oaken Wands. They spoke in unison. *"By the goddess' light and candle fire, illuminate the information I desire."*

The girls closed their eyes and swayed on their feet, like they were in some sort of a trance. I could feel their magic swelling over the room, and it was certainly one of the strongest spells they'd cast.

"We're in your head…" Chloe mused. "You're thinking—*Grant!*"

Chloe's eyes sprung open, and Talia blushed.

Chloe scowled. "Your thoughts are as dirty as your brother's."

Grant held his hands up in surrender. "Hey, you're the one who wanted to go poking around in there."

Chloe crossed her arms. "I didn't want to see a mental picture of Talia's ass, but thanks for that one."

"Hey, I have a great ass," Talia said with a laugh.

"True," Chloe agreed. "Let's try someone whose mind is *not* in the gutter."

Onyx volunteered, and the girls read her mind to find she was thinking of holiday candies and hot cocoa. She must've set a precedent for holiday cheer, because other people started thinking about the holidays, too. Professor Warren volunteered next, and the girls read images of him playing in the snow at Yuletide as a kid. They read Lucas, and found he was thinking about the times he went sledding with his brother down the hill behind their house.

They tried to read Mandy next, and Chloe's features fell. "I'm sorry, Mandy. I'm not announcing that. It's too personal."

"It's fine," Mandy said. "I want everyone to know your spell works, and it's not like nobody knows how I feel."

Chloe sighed. "I hear the same words over and over. *I wish Amy was here.*"

The room went silent. We were all really sad about the people who weren't here this holiday season, and talking about them put a somber tone over the room.

"How about you, Nadine?" Talia piped up. "Do you want to go next?"

"Sure," I said, but I already knew what they were going to read.

The ends of their Wands glowed. I couldn't feel them poking around in my head, but I knew what they must've seen. I was thinking about Grammy, and how much I missed her.

Chloe dropped her gaze. "Sorry, Nadine."

I gave her a reassuring smile, though it was forced.

Talia turned to Verla. "How about you, Clarice? Want to give it a go?"

Verla crossed her hands over her lap. "Yes, but I'd like to try something, too. I won't tell you what it is until you let me know what you see."

Talia and Chloe spoke their incantation, and the ends of their Wands glowed. They swayed from side to side in that trance-like state the spell put them in. Seconds turned into minutes as they poked and prodded inside Verla's mind, but Chloe's brow only continued to furrow. Talia looked like she was struggling to see anything.

Finally, the girls dropped their Wands. "I don't get it. We didn't see anything," Talia said.

"That is because I have placed mental wards up," Verla replied. "This power you call teleinsight is strong and may prove useful against our enemies, but if we can learn how to use it, the priestesses have the potential to learn teleinsight as well."

I didn't think Verla meant to spark a panic, but we all sat up a little straighter then.

"Within the coven, only something as powerful as the Wands can get into your head without consent, but there is magic in this world that is not confined by witch rules," Verla continued. "Vampires, for example, do not need consent to compel you, because their abilities are different from ours. What's to stop the priestesses from obtaining a vampire object that could read our minds? Alongside learning how to use this power, we must all learn how to defend against such a spell. If our enemies can get into our minds like this, they could easily find us and the Wands at any time."

"But how did you *do* that?" Chloe asked. "You aren't as powerful as two Oaken Wands combined."

Verla shook her head. "No. But I only have to be more skilled at warding my mind than you are at extracting information, and at utilizing the potential of the Wands. It's about skill, not power. I'm an experienced and powerful witch who has been practicing mind warding for quite some time now. I spent my summer with vampires, and I had to learn how to protect my mind from potential threats. Mind reading is difficult, even for a demigod to do, so if you're talented enough, you should be able to hold anyone off, even if they're using teleinsight."

"Can you teach us?" I asked.

"Certainly," Verla offered. "Let's begin with a meditation."

We all got in a comfortable position. Verla began breathing deeply so we could all follow along.

"To protect yourself, you will visualize two layers of magic," Verla instructed. "The first will encompass your body, to protect from physical threat. Imagine the second layer as an impenetrable shield around your mind. That way if the first protection spell is penetrated, you have a second that's even stronger."

I drew a deep breath and imagined protection magic wrapping around me. In my mind's eye, the protection spell glittered with gold.

"Project your aura outward, and expand beyond your physical body to create the first layer of protection," Verla said. "Lucas, you're already getting it!"

I opened my eyes to see Lucas's aura glowing beside me. His whole body was outlined in a purple glow. He looked down at himself and flipped his hands over several times, like he couldn't believe what he was seeing.

"It feels easy," he remarked.

"And yet we can still hear your thoughts clear as day," Chloe said as the end of the Oaken Wands glowed. "We're still connected to you, and you're wondering why you're glowing purple."

"Purple's the color of spirituality," Onyx offered. "People with a purple aura often go through deep spiritual journeys."

Lucas nodded. "Then I've got to utilize that somehow to force the girls out of my head. It's strange... I can't even feel you trying to read me."

"That's one of the things that makes teleinsight so powerful," Talia said. "You don't know it's there."

Verla drew another deep, calming breath. "You're doing great, Lucas. Now imagine another layer of protection expanding from your third eye. Visualize a wall being built between you and the girls, to force them to retreat."

Lucas closed his eyes again and got a deep look of concentration on his face. Minutes passed. I meditated alongside him, following Verla's instruction. I expanded my aura outward and created a second shield around my mind, but I couldn't tell if it worked.

"You're all doing great," Verla encouraged. "As you practice, you'll be able to extend this spell outward without exposing your aura, so no one will be able to tell you're doing it. Chloe, Talia, why don't you try reading Nadine?"

My focus faltered, and though I couldn't feel the girls in my mind, I was certain my spell wasn't strong enough to rival the Oaken Wands.

"She doesn't think she's strong enough," Talia said, reading my mind.

"You will be," Verla told me. "This is hard magic, so your skill to block out mind reading has to be better than the person casting the magic, even with the Wands. You're stronger than me, Nadine. If I can do it, so can you. It will just require practice."

We continued to meditate and learn from Verla, but over an hour passed, and no one had managed to protect their minds.

"You must practice this every day," Verla pressed. "We can't afford for the priestesses to get into your head."

"Even if we can't shield ourselves from power like this yet, this power is in our hands," I pointed out. "Teleinsight gives us hope, because we can use it against the priestesses."

"How can we utilize it?" Grant wondered. "We'd have to get close enough to them."

"We don't need to use it on them directly," Lucas suggested. "They've built a movement and a following, which means that when we go up against the priestesses, we're going to have to face all of Miriam's Chosen."

Chloe understood what he was saying. "We'll have to destabilize the cult before we can move in on the priestesses. We can't go in guns blazing and kill off these people's cult leaders, because they'll never listen to our side. Just because we kill the priestesses doesn't mean other people won't rise up. We need to understand the priestesses' motives and plans, as well as how these cult members think. Otherwise, it doesn't matter what kind of power we have, because they already have their hold on the coven."

Talia tapped her chin. "We'll have to figure out who the cult's major supporters are and get rid of them before we take out the priestesses. Which means Chloe and I will have to sneak around the outskirts of Octavia Falls and learn as much as we can using teleinsight."

"It's dangerous," Verla protested. "You could be caught."

"You're right, but it's a chance we have to take," Chloe insisted.

"If we're going to destabilize the cult, it's our only choice," Talia agreed.

This was powerful magic that the priestesses didn't know we could use against them.

We just had to get close enough to them to put it work.

# SEVENTEEN

Our Yuletide celebration had been a welcome reprieve to the worry that plagued us each passing day. Nadine and I had agreed to wait to make a final decision on our future until Christmas. December twenty-fifth arrived, and we weren't any closer to breaking the Reaper's Shadow curse for good. We had until the end of the day to solve this mystery, and at this point, it was going to take a miracle.

I'd become a mad man obsessed with obtaining the Mortana Wand. If we couldn't decipher visions from the Seer Wand, then I was certain the Mortana Wand was the answer to breaking the Reaper's Shadow curse. We had to locate the remains of all the Reaper's Shadows who came before Nadine, and remove the curse on their bones. All the other Reaper's Shadow women had to be dead by now, so surely a Wand with the power of death could track them down. It had to, because that Wand was our last hope.

To get it, I had to pass the Warlock's Trial. I still didn't know what that entailed, so I was researching as much as I could about the afterlife. Each supernatural society had a different way of crossing over. The Elementai were greeted by their ancestors to be welcomed into the Ancestral Lands, while the fae were escorted to the Great Hunting Grounds by their gods. Witches, of course, had reapers to lead them to Alora. Each method was so similar, yet the magic was entirely different.

I was poring over the books in the library Christmas morning when I heard the front door burst open. Heavy footsteps sprinted down the hall, and Grant burst in.

"Lucas," he called breathlessly, doubling over in the doorway.

I shot out of my chair. "Is someone hurt?"

"Executors," Grant said. "Two more of them."

I rushed out of the room and followed him down the hall as quickly as I could. I threw on my coat, but Grant had already raised alarm bells all throughout the house. Nadine and Talia had been in the kitchen making lunch, and they hurried to our side.

"What's going on?" Nadine demanded.

"I was patrolling the border," Grant explained. "There are two more bodies, just outside the wards."

"It might be soon enough we can still get some answers." Nadine reached for her coat, but I stopped her.

"You're not coming," I insisted.

Her jaw dropped. "The hell I am."

"Nad, we don't know if the killer's still hanging around," I pointed out. "You're pregnant with our children. It could be dangerous."

She yanked her coat off the hook anyway. "And what if you need me? I can't sit around for nine months doing nothing. Wherever you go, I go— until I can't anymore."

She wasn't going to take no for an answer.

"Stay close," I told her.

Talia threw on her jacket, and the four of us hurried outside. A thin layer of snow crunched beneath our feet as Grant led us to where he'd found the bodies.

Two Executors lay in the forest, their corpses empty and forgotten, just like the last ones. An eerie feeling traveled down my spine as I approached them. An emptiness I couldn't quite explain permeated the whole mountainside, just as I felt before. Something about this was very wrong, though I couldn't put my finger on it. Cautiously, I approached the bodies and knelt beside the closest one.

"Be careful," Grant warned.

"It's okay," I promised.

I placed two fingers to the side of the closest Executor's neck. No pulse, though I didn't know what I was expecting. I could already feel the hollowness of their bodies with my magic. There was no life force to be found, not a remnant whatsoever…

And yet his body was still warm.

It hit me then what was so strange about all of this.

"I've never seen magic like this before," I remarked. "Usually when people die, I can *feel* death. These bodies are fresh, yet I feel *nothing*."

"Like something's blocking your magic?" Nadine asked.

I shook my head. "My magic is working just fine. When people die, I feel a void, like their body has become this empty shell and something's missing. Eventually, the feeling fades the longer someone's been dead, but this emptiness is different. It's like there was never anything there to begin with."

"So you're saying… the priestesses are sending soulless Executors to find us?" Talia asked slowly.

"I'm not sure what I'm saying," I admitted.

A breeze swept through the trees, and a chilling realization hit me. "These bodies are still warm. They must've died in the last hour. Guys, I haven't heard a voice all day."

The woods went silent as the others exchanged a terrified glance. If these Executors died just now, I would've heard their last thoughts. I didn't know what it meant, but there was certainly sinister magic behind this. Anxiety built inside of me. I shot a glance around the forest, but I saw nothing.

"The only explanation is that these men aren't part of the coven," Nadine theorized.

"Then why would they be in Executor uniform and holding wands?" I asked as I pulled a wand from the Executor's pocket.

A chaotic buzz riveted through me when I touched his wand, like there was magic inside of it that resonated with my own. I inspected the wand to find a small black crystal embedded into the end of it. The magic inside the crystal seemed to ring in my ears. It was so familiar, yet I didn't understand how he'd gotten his hands on it.

"How can that be?" I whispered.

"What is it?" Grant asked, shooting another glance around the forest.

I barely heard him as I searched the Executor for his Cast mark. I yanked up his sleeves and found nothing, then pulled on the collar of his shirt. Just beneath the fabric on his neck was a tree with twisted branches —the mark of a Mentalist.

So why was this Executor carrying a wand embedded with a crystal that held reaper magic? The only explanation was that the crystal in the wand accidentally retained the power of a Mortana who'd cast a death spell. My cheeks grew cold as all the blood drained from my face.

"Lucas, say something!" Nadine begged. "You're scaring me."

I leaned back on my heels. "I think I understand what happened here, and why I didn't hear their last thoughts. It's because I'm not the only one collecting them anymore."

The pang in my gut felt strange. For the longest time, I wanted nothing to do with my reaper power. I wanted someone else to take it, so I could absolve myself of all reaper duties. But over the years, this power had become a part of me. I'd learned to work with it, rather than against it, and I was getting really fucking good at it. To think there was another reaper out there taking over *my* job felt like a piece of me had just been stolen.

"I don't know how they did it, but a reaper killed these people," I said. "When he did, the crystal embedded in the Mentalist's wand absorbed a piece of the reaper's magic."

Nadine began walking in an arc around me, surveying the area for clues. She kept her eyes on the ground as she spoke. "So there's a new Reaper's Apprentice running around. Probably some kid who hasn't learned how to contain his power."

"How can we be sure it isn't a reaper that's already passed on?" Grant asked. "What if it's Edgar? He could be protecting us."

"It can't be, because Edgar can't leave behind footprints." Nadine pointed to the snow. There wasn't much of it yet—just a light dusting. The footprints were difficult to spot, and I was surprised she'd noticed them at all. "There are three sets of footprints here. Two sets are from the victims, which means the third is the killer's."

Nadine returned to where she'd been standing beside Grant and Talia. "We can make assumptions and come up with theories all day, but none of it's going to give us answers. Tal, we need you to look back and see what happened here."

Talia conjured the Seer Wand. "I'll try, but like I've said, the visions can be confusing."

Nadine placed a gentle hand on Talia's wrist. "Don't use the Seer Wand. You need a clear head for this."

Talia lowered the Wand to her side, realizing what Nadine was saying. "Okay, I'll see what I can get with psychometry."

Talia subconjured the Seer Wand and closed her eyes. Slowly, she began pacing from one tree to the next, running her fingers along the bark. I held my breath, waiting in anticipation for some sort of answer.

"I see the cloaked man again," Talia said softly, carefully stepping around the next tree. "He's definitely alive. Something startled him. He's creating a portal!"

I stood so fast I got dizzy. "Where'd he cast it?"

Talia's eyes shot open, and she pointed between two trees. "Right there."

I planted my feet right where she had pointed. I closed my eyes and searched for an energy signature, but I couldn't find it.

"What are you doing?" Grant asked.

"I'm seeing if I can find out where the fucker portaled to," I growled. "He must've left an energy signature behind, right?"

"We're not going to follow him!" Talia cried.

"What else are we going to do?" I demanded. "Wait for him to break through our wards? I want to talk to this guy and get some damn answers."

I spotted the wand I'd left beside the Executor, the one with the crystal on the end that held the reaper's magic.

"Maybe using a bit of his own power will help us find him." I grabbed the wand, then went to stand back between the trees.

Nadine came up beside me. "Let me help."

I hesitated a moment. I didn't want her to come with me if things got out of hand, but I wasn't sure I could pull off this spell without her.

"You aren't going without me," she stated firmly. She wasn't giving me a choice.

Reluctantly, I took her hand. Nadine's power poured into me, amplifying my own. The power from the crystal filled me up, and I felt something tickling at the center of my chest.

"I've got it—" I started to say, but a portal bloomed right where I was standing before I could finish. The ground fell out from under us, and Nadine and I were sucked through the portal.

We landed on solid ground in a forest nearly identical to the one we'd just left. A light dusting of snow covered the ground, and the air felt the same. It was like we'd only traveled a couple of miles away. The portal slammed shut behind us.

Nadine held tight to me and glanced around the forest. "Is this where he went?"

"It's got to be," I answered.

My eyes caught sight of a small clearing not far from us, with a structure rising in the center of it. It was hard to make out what it was at this distance.

I squeezed Nadine's hand. "Stay close."

We crept through the forest, staying low as we came closer to the clearing. The structure came into view, and I saw that it was a small cottage. It must've been here for a long time, because the forest had grown up on all sides of it, except for at the front of the building.

The clearing wasn't very big, just enough to house a long table, a small garden that had already been harvested for the year, and a burning fire pit with a cauldron over it. Vegetables were laid out over the table, like someone was in the middle of preparing for a meal.

"What is this place?" Nadine whispered.

I shook my head. "I have no idea."

The front door of the cottage swung open so hard it slammed against the side of the building. A figure cloaked in black stomped outside. I grabbed Nadine's shoulder, and we ducked behind a set of trees. I peered around the tree trunk and watched the mysterious cloaked figure move around the clearing. He picked up a few sticks from a nearby pile and snapped them apart violently, before adding them to the fire. He was obviously pissed about something.

I couldn't take my eyes off the mysterious man. Something inside of me drew me to him, like my magic resonated with his. I didn't know why, but I felt like I had to go to him. I barely knew what I was doing when I stood and stepped out from behind the tree.

"Lucas," Nadine hissed, but I hardly heard her. I *had* to speak to this man. Something deep within me told me he held the answers I so desperately searched for.

The man bent to put more wood in the fire. Without turning, he spoke. "You don't have to sneak up on me. I already know you're there, Lucas."

I stopped dead at the edge of the clearing. The voice wasn't anything like I expected.

The figure turned and stood, then pushed the hood of their cloak back. Shock riveted through me as I witnessed a woman standing before me. She wasn't a young, new reaper as we suspected. She had wrinkles across her skin, and her dark curls were beginning to gray. The woman had to be in her sixties, at least. She knew my name, but I didn't recognize her.

"You're a reaper," I said breathlessly.

"A Reaper's Apprentice, technically," she replied as she crossed the clearing to grab another log from a stack against the house. "I'd be hard-pressed to join the Reaper Order. How did you find me?"

"I followed your portal," I replied.

She paused for a beat, eyeing me. "Hmph… you're a more talented reaper than I gave you credit for."

Nadine stepped up beside me. "I wouldn't underestimate him."

The woman placed her log next to the fire but didn't throw it in. She brushed her hands off on her cloak. "Relax, Nadine. I'm not going to hurt either one of you. I *am* going to ask you both to leave, though. You shouldn't be here."

I stepped further into the clearing. "I'm not going anywhere until you give us answers. You're a fucking Reaper's Apprentice?"

She pulled up her sleeve to show the skull mark on the inside of her arm. "Something like that. It's hard to be an apprentice without a master."

I scoffed. "Tell me about it. How do you know our names?"

"Everyone knows your names," she replied calmly. "I may have left the coven long ago, but I've been watching you, Lucas."

"What the hell does that mean?" I demanded.

She shook her head and turned to the table. She grabbed a carrot and began snapping pieces off and tossing them into the cauldron, like she needed something to do with her hands. "Like I said, you shouldn't be here."

Nadine spoke boldly, ignoring her last statement. "You know our names. Perhaps you'd be kind enough to provide yours."

The woman whirled back toward us. "I will give you no such thing.

You weren't supposed to find out I exist. Go home, before you start asking questions you don't want to know the answers to."

I planted my feet firmly in the dirt and crossed my arms. I wasn't going anywhere. "You killed those Executors in the woods."

She breathed a heavy sigh. "Yes. They were getting too close to discovering you. I had to do what was necessary to protect you."

"You left their bodies behind, like some sort of warning," I accused.

She smirked, like the notion was ridiculous. "No. I intended to get rid of them, but your friends showed up before I could."

"Why bother killing them at all?" I questioned.

She grabbed another carrot, but paused, as if contemplating how much to say. "I was meant to be your master, but the coven didn't want me. That doesn't mean I can't do my job to protect you."

"Protect me?" I balked. "If you are my master, then you should've been there for me!"

"I was!" she insisted. "How do you think you survived your skateboarding accident last year? My shield prevented deadly injuries. I didn't have to get directly involved to help you."

I couldn't believe it, but it made too much sense. I'd been skating boarding down the mountain when Nadine nearly hit me with her car, and I went careening off the road. I'd walked away without any major injuries. I'd blacked out, but the doctors said I didn't have a concussion. But if she wanted to help us, then why didn't she want us to know she existed? She'd left me alone, and that wasn't fair.

"That's a shit reason," I said. "I thought I was alone. You could've come to me and let me know you were there all along."

"So you could stop me from my work?" She turned back toward her stew and tossed a potato in, before stirring it. "I've watched you long enough to know that you would never approve of my methods. It would be futile to try teaching you."

I cocked an eyebrow. "And what method is that, exactly?"

"You wouldn't understand."

"Try me."

She narrowed her eyes. "You don't know what I've been through. Being exiled from the coven changes a person beyond anything you can imagine."

"You must've done something bad to be exiled," I figured. "Perhaps that's what changed you."

"As if the coven needs a viable reason to start a witch hunt," she scoffed. "All it takes is one person who doesn't like you, or someone who thinks you broke the mold. I thought I could do good with my reaper powers, but according to the coven, women shouldn't be reapers. They shunned me like they shunned all the women before me."

I reeled back. "You weren't the first female reaper, then?"

"No. There have been many female reapers, but the coven saw reaping as a *man's* job," she sneered. "They saw the mark of a Mortana and believed me to be nothing more than a common necromancer. They wouldn't let me live in my truth, so I left."

"I've researched all the reapers," I countered. "There's one per generation. Each time one dies, another receives his power."

She cocked an eyebrow. "True, but more than one generation can live at the same time."

Holy shit. A beat passed before I spoke again. "So… what? There's a female reaper for every male reaper, and they've just been erased from history?"

"Yes," she replied. "You say that as if it's so unbelievable."

"We live in a society that regards women as powerful," I pointed out. "Why would they ever question your power?"

"The coven is a matriarchal society built on patriarchal influences," she shot back. "It wasn't always this way, but the coven has become nothing more than a patriarchy in lipstick. You're ruled by misogyny."

"That's not true. We still have priestesses—women still rule," I insisted.

"Being a woman does not absolve a person of misogynist acts," she responded. "It is *precisely* because women hold power in the coven that other women are being hanged. Anyone different who breaks the status quo is taken out, so the priestesses can stop people from getting new ideas. Women hold power, and the priestesses don't like when other women speak up. Just look at your traditions—Miriamic women still take their husband's last name."

"Tradition isn't necessarily a flaw," I said.

"It is when it's used to reduce a person's power," she replied. "Think of what it takes to become a reaper—the *Warlock's* Trial. It's sexist language."

She turned her back to me. The woman kept her eyes down as she began snapping green beans to add to the stew. I sensed deep pain within her. My heart twisted, and I felt for her. Maybe it was the connection we shared with our magic, or the fact that she'd been protecting me all this time. I didn't really know *why* I felt the way I did, but I had a deep desire to get through to her.

"I understand that you've been hurt, and that may have driven you to do things you regret," I started softly.

She let out a light chuckle. "I don't regret dealing with the people no one else will."

"You mean by killing them?" Nadine asked in an even tone.

Something flashed in the woman's eyes, and the truth hit me.

"No," I realized. "Worse."

The emptiness I felt in the woods made all too much sense now. It's why I hadn't heard the Executors' last thoughts—because there was nothing left for me to hear.

"She destroyed their souls," I said hollowly. My stomach lurched, and I abhorred the idea that I felt any connection with her at all. "No wonder you were banished from the coven. You don't deserve this power. You *are* evil!"

"Is it evil to end evil itself, no matter the unconventional methods?" she challenged. "I told you that you would not understand."

"How's this even possible?" Nadine asked.

The woman tossed her beans into the stew. "Reaper magic can go wrong—so badly that it destroys the very soul you're trying to help. The first soul I reaped, I screwed up. I destroyed the woman I was meant to cross over. The guilt nearly broke me, until I learned that I could harness such a power and use it for good."

"There's nothing good about destroying people's souls!" I protested.

"Don't act as if you haven't had to make a tough call before," the woman said. "Sometimes, standing on moral ground is not an option."

"At least when I've killed people, I've given them a chance to move on," I insisted. "The people you've killed cease to exist."

"A *piece* of themselves is destroyed—not the entirety of their soul," she argued. "I'm destroying this incarnation, not everything they originate from. Their energy will be recycled by the greater forces of the universe."

"You can't know that, and it's not your call to make," I sneered.

"*Someone* has to make the call!" she yelled. "You act as if these choices are black and white, but they aren't. There is no good and evil. There are simply things that help and those that harm. Sometimes, it's not a choice between one or the other, but merely the decision to accept that one cannot exist without the other."

"That's the voice of someone who's given up," I accused.

"Giving up is the *last* thing I've done!" she shouted. "Don't you think if I'd given up I'd be long gone? I'd be far away from the coven. My master wasn't there for me when I needed him. I wasn't just going to *leave you.*"

"But you did!" I cried.

She placed her hands on her hips. "I didn't have to show my face to help you."

My hands balled into fists. "You could have helped more! I've been searching for answers on reapers since the day I got these powers, and there's been one right on my doorstep all along."

Her tone softened. "What good could come of that, Lucas? Now that you know who I am and what I can do, you'll only try to stop me from my work. You can't save my soul like you've tried to save so many others. I'll never become a part of the Reaper Order after what I've done. I'm not going to Alora. I'm just trying to do the best with my magic while I still have it. I'm not part of the coven anymore, but I still have this power, so I'm going to do something with it."

"That's not true," I argued. "You can still be redeemed."

She shrugged. "Maybe I don't want to. Tell me, Lucas. Do you really want to learn your powers from a woman whose greatest magic is that of destruction?"

My jaw clamped shut, and an answer refused to move past my lips. I didn't know what to say.

Apparently, that was answer enough, because she scoffed and turned back to her table, where she began peeling an onion. "The reaper men never listened to us women, anyway. Why would I think you'd be any different?"

"Maybe I am," I offered.

She simply shook her head but didn't answer. She kept her eyes down, and her hands shook as she tried frantically to pull the onion skin off. I noticed her eyes were watering, and I didn't think it was from the onion. After all she had done, it was obvious she still cared.

The sickness swelling in my gut eased. It made no sense, because after what this woman had just admitted to, I wanted nothing to do with her. But maybe there was more to her actions than I could understand. Whether I liked it or not, this woman and I shared a bond. She was meant to teach me, but maybe I was meant to teach her something, too.

I approached her and placed my hand on her shoulder. She stopped fidgeting, and her glistening eyes turned up to mine.

"Do you still hear their thoughts?" I asked in a near whisper.

Her voice cracked as she answered in a wavered tone. "Every day."

"Then you're still a part of this coven," I said. "The choices you've made in the past don't make you a bad person. You always have the power to make better choices in the moment. You cared enough to stay here on the outskirts of Octavia Falls, so that you could be there for me when the time came. The time is now. Nadine and I have to break the Reaper's Shadow curse, and I need to pass the Warlock's Trial. So… are you going to help me or not?"

She stared at me so long, I wasn't certain she was going to answer at all. Finally, she said, "Autumn. My name is Autumn Loren."

Nadine eyed her curiously. "You wouldn't happen to be related to Nina Loren, would you? She teaches Incantations, Moonology, and Astrology at Miriam College."

The corners of Autumn's lips twitched, like she was trying to hold back her emotions. "Nina Loren is my mother."

"Your mother is a very kind woman," Nadine remarked.

Autumn nodded. "Yes. She's the kindest."

Autumn contemplated us a moment longer, then said, "Come. There is something I want you to have."

She turned toward the cottage, and Nadine shot me a wary expression. I wasn't scared, though. Autumn had been protecting me all this time. I didn't think she would hurt us now. I took Nadine's hand, and we followed Autumn into the cottage. It was a small one-bedroom home, with a wood stove burning in the corner and a small kitchen open to the living room.

"Please, sit." Autumn gestured to the kitchen table.

Nadine and I sat beside each other. Autumn turned to a bookcase and pulled out an old leather-bound book.

"This book is called the Reaper Records," she said as she sat across from us. "I obtained it before Edgar died. It is meant to be passed down from one reaper to the next."

*That's why there weren't any records to be found inside the coven*, I realized. Because the records had been here with Autumn this whole time.

"I've been researching the reapers for years, validating and expanding on the records of all the women like me whose reaper powers were forgotten," Autumn said. "I have learned much about our powers along the way."

She placed the book on the table in front of me, and I flipped it open. Pages of handwritten notes detailed all the reapers who had ever lived, including information about their family lineage, their spouses and children—if they ever had them—and other significant details. She even had several pages dedicated to me.

Before I could read what she'd gathered on me, she flipped the pages to a passage near the end. "One of the most powerful lessons you will learn is right here on this page."

I stared down at a spell titled *Anima Destructor*. It detailed the process of how to use reaper energy to pull a soul out of a body. Autumn described it like wrapping a magical rope around someone's neck and yanking the noose tight. It sounded like hanging a soul—the metaphorical snap of their neck being the literal breaking of their spirit.

Disgust returned to my gut. "The title of this spell translates as *Soul Destroyer*. You really want to teach me how to destroy souls like you do?"

Autumn leaned back in her chair. "If you were truly scared of what I've done, you'd be long gone by now, back inside the safety of your wards. I don't scare either one of you. You're merely intrigued by me."

"You don't want to change, do you?" I asked.

"I've already made up my mind," she replied. "You can't stop me from doing what I need to do, but one day, you may understand."

"I understand that what you're doing is an abuse of your magic," I sneered. "Perhaps I should bring an end to it."

She narrowed her eyes. "You don't have it in you."

"Don't I?" I growled. "How many souls have you destroyed?"

"What do you care about a couple of Executors?" Autumn asked.

"They made bad choices, but they're still part of the coven." My answer faltered on my tongue. Why *did* I care about men who wanted nothing more than to see my family and me burn at the stake? Maybe because I believed they could still be saved, even if it wasn't in this lifetime.

"These situations are not so black and white," Autumn stated calmly.

"You keep saying that," I snarled. "How many more will suffer your wrath?"

I waved my hand through the air, and my magic curled around her neck. I felt the rope she talked about, and I squeezed, threatening to pull the noose at any moment. My magic curled around her neck several more times, squeezing so tightly I could feel the cold touch of death enter the room.

Autumn's spine straightened, but she didn't protest. It was like she wanted things to end this way. I didn't yank back just yet, but I could sense her soul edging out of her body ever so slightly. I felt it on the edge of destruction.

"Lucas," Nadine warned.

A smile spread across Autumn's face. "You and I are not so different, I see."

I felt the blood drain from my face, and I dropped my hand. My magic around her neck fell away. She didn't want to die. She only wanted to push me to see how far I'd go.

I leaned over the table and spoke firmly. "If you want to use this spell for good, then use it to end the priestesses."

"You think I haven't thought of that?" Autumn asked. "I'd have to get through layers of protection spells, let alone get close enough to do it. I've tried several times and can't get to them. Perhaps one day you'll get close enough to destroy them."

"I will never use this spell," I growled.

Autumn cocked an eyebrow. "What does it matter who does it? The result will be the same. Is it because you fear for your own soul, Lucas?"

My teeth clenched.

"Believe me, if you resist your power, there will come a day when the priestesses break you, and you will be begging to pull off this spell. You don't need to use it now, but take it with you." Autumn pushed the book closer to me.

I snatched it out of her hands. "The only thing I'm interested in seeing in this book is the genealogy records."

I flipped through the pages. "We went searching for the Reaper's

Shadow women to break the curse, but there were more, weren't there? Only some of them were men—husbands of Reaper's Apprentices like you."

Autumn scoffed. "Us reaper women aren't stupid enough to take a husband. We know what the Reaper's Shadow curse entails."

"How *dare* you stand here and tell me that you were trying to protect me," I snarled. "If you were watching me so closely, then you should've known we never broke the Reaper's Shadow curse. You could've helped us, and you didn't."

"I cannot be expected to know all the details of your personal life," Autumn insisted. "As long as you are careful, you have nothing to worry about."

Nadine's hand instinctively went to her belly. "You haven't been watching *very* closely, have you?"

Autumn glanced between the two of us, and her eyes went wide when she saw the rings on our fingers. "I didn't know."

"You've been watching me this whole time, and you didn't know we'd gotten married?" I raged.

"It's hard to keep track of much when you've spent months hidden behind those wards!" Autumn shouted. "At least she's not having children."

Horror filled Nadine's eyes.

"Yes, we are," I snapped. "And soon. So which of the Reaper's Shadows have you been hiding?"

I flipped through the book and found that Autumn was telling the truth. The other reaper women had never gotten married. They understood the fate of the curse and didn't dare to mess with it.

My heart stopped when I landed upon Autumn's section. "The last remaining Reaper's Shadow is your spouse," I realized. "The other reaper women didn't marry, but *you* did, which makes your spouse the last Reaper's Shadow we need to break the curse for good. You chose not to send us clues, because it would've exposed you. You selfish witch!"

I shot out of my chair. "You don't care about protecting me, because if you did, you'd know how much losing my family would destroy me. You would've done anything to protect Nadine, too."

"I did what I had to do—what my magic *bound* me to do," Autumn insisted.

I took a step back. I could tell our magic was connected the second I saw her, but I didn't understand the extent of it until now. Autumn was destined to be my master, and as such, it was her job to keep me alive.

She'd done only the bare minimum.

"You never actually cared," I accused. "As my master, you're bound to keep me alive, and that's it."

"I helped in the ways I could," Autumn said. "I didn't want to, but I didn't have a choice, either."

I shoved the book under my arm and grabbed Nadine's hand. I'd heard enough, and I wanted nothing to do with Autumn *ever*. "Come on, Nad. We're going."

"Lucas, wait!" Nadine cried. She yanked her hand out of my grasp and whirled back toward Autumn. "Where is your Reaper's Shadow?"

Autumn's eyes glistened with guilt, but I refused to believe for a moment she felt sorry about any of this.

"Did you ever have kids?" Nadine snarled.

Autumn shook her head. "We couldn't."

"Then you know what it's like to live without them," Nadine said through gritted teeth. "Give me a chance to watch my sons grow up. Give me the chance you never had."

"The curse didn't take my wife," Autumn said in a broken tone. "It was a stroke, six years ago. Her grave is behind the house."

Nadine pushed past me and ran outside.

I glared at Autumn. "This book is the only reason you kept me alive, isn't it? So you had someone to pass your knowledge down to."

Autumn didn't answer, and that told me all I needed to know. Our connection be damned. She was not my master.

"Then I guess your job is done," I stated flatly. "Don't bother trying to save me anymore. No amount of saving me will save you."

I stomped out of the cottage and followed Nadine into the forest behind the clearing. Nadine stopped at a gravestone marked *Summer Loren*.

"Summer took her wife's last name," Nadine remarked as she knelt beside her grave.

As Nadine ran her fingers over Summer's grave, I flipped through the Reaper Records, just to be sure. "She's the last one. We broke the curse on all the others. Once you break this piece of the curse, it will be gone forever."

Tears welled in Nadine's eyes. "Finally."

Nadine placed her hand in the dirt over Summer's grave. Tendrils of magic worked their way up her arm. I held my breath and remained on high alert, so I could respond quickly if anything went wrong. I expected Nadine to pass out, or for the ground to break like it had in the cemetery the night Nadine broke the curse on the other women's bones.

Instead, a black cloud of magic materialized from Nadine's chest, and another drifted up from the grave. The clouds merged together, swirling into one. A gust of wind breezed through the clearing, and the magic dissipated.

It was like I was taking a breath of air for the first time in twenty-two years. A massive weight came off my shoulders, and the colors around us seemed to brighten. I couldn't explain it, but I felt like a completely new man.

Tears sprang to my eyes, and I fell to my knees beside my wife. "You broke the curse; I can feel it."

Nadine curled into my arms, weeping. "I feel it, too. Our babies are saved!"

I held Nadine close as our tears fell into the dirt. Relief didn't begin to describe our feelings. I thought for sure we were going to have to make an impossible decision tomorrow morning, but a miracle had happened, and we'd been spared from the greatest heartbreak of our lives. Autumn said she didn't know what was going on behind our wards, but by the Goddess, she'd been an answer to our prayers, whether she knew it or not.

We'd been faced with two dark choices, neither of which we wanted to make. Now, we didn't have to, but I couldn't help but think of what might've happened if we hadn't found Autumn today. Would I have become like her, if I'd been forced down one of these roads? Perhaps there was more to what she'd said than I realized.

"I think Autumn may be right about all these choices being gray areas," I admitted.

Nadine wiped her eyes. "Yes, except some shades of gray are darker than others. In the priestesses' case, it's pitch black."

I chuckled. "We've had to make a lot of hard decisions, and I'm still trying to get used to the idea that we can't save everyone. I don't want to become like Autumn, but what if we're left with no choice?"

"Maybe making a difficult call doesn't make us bad people," Nadine said. "Perhaps it's like Autumn said, that every decision harms and hurts. The thing is, even if we win, someone's going to lose. We just have to do what we believe is the right thing, to save as many innocent lives as possible."

"I want to do the right thing," I told her. "I'm not used to the idea of war. Other cultures like the fae are practically born with a sword in their hands. They don't question what they have to do out of duty or loyalty to their country. I wasn't taught what to do when the coven divides. In my house growing up, if there was ever a fight, I was taught to keep my head down and stay out of the way. I can't do that anymore."

I ran my hand over her stomach. "Now we've got these kids on the way, and we have to figure out all over again who we're going to be, because as parents, we're not going to be the same people we were as college students. The choices are only going to get harder to make."

"Then we'll make them together," Nadine promised.

I didn't know if Autumn was right or not. All I knew for certain was that Nadine had broken the curse once and for all, and because of that, our family would survive.

"Can breaking this curse really be as simple as it was?" I asked. "There was no earthquake, no struggle."

"I'm getting stronger," Nadine said. "And now that this curse is broken, we're stronger than ever. I know you're scared of what kind of dad you're going to be, but no matter what happens or how long it takes, we're in this together."

I smiled as I squeezed her hand. "Together."

# EIGHTEEN

After Lucas and I returned from Autumn's cottage, we explained everything to the others. Everyone was as equally shocked as we were to learn there was another reaper out there, but Lucas wanted nothing to do with her. As far as he was concerned, he had her book of spells, and that was all she could offer him.

Professor Warren had used his necromancy powers to send the Executors' bodies far away, like he had last time. Chloe cast a spell with the Mentalist Wand to confuse any Executors who approached our wards, which would keep the priestesses from getting too close again.

As the weeks passed, Lucas dove into the Reaper Records, practicing the spells within it to grow his power. That was, when the Waning wasn't affecting his powers. The Waning was getting stronger, affecting us all at different times, and it often lasted up to a week or more. Edgar had yet to show up with the Mortana Wand, but Lucas was determined to learn everything he could from that book.

Chloe and Talia spent time sneaking around the borders of Octavia Falls to gather intel, while Grant and Miles went along to protect the girls. It came as no surprise that the cult's greatest supporters were among the Executors' ranks, including Sheriff Baker, who was as bad as the priestesses. It was difficult to get much more information than that, because Chloe and Talia had to get close enough to someone to use teleinsight on them, and we had to be careful we weren't spotted.

A heavy snowstorm passed through the mountains at the end of January and blanketed the safe house for months. We hadn't seen Autumn since that day at her cottage. I thought she might try to reach out, but she hadn't. Lucas didn't think she cared, but I thought there was a part of her that did, but she was too ashamed to show it.

Cold, chilly days curled up by the fire with Lucas warmed to spring mornings. Each week, my stomach grew bigger, until I was so big I was starting to waddle. Between weekly doctor's appointments with Luana and making plans with Lucas for our future, it was easy to forget we were still fighting a war. Discussing baby names and picking out colors for nursery blankets made the Miriamic Conflict feel like a distant dream. In our little corner of the forest, life seemed perfect.

Lucas found me reading in the den on the afternoon of May seventh. Chloe was lounging in the chair across the room, infusing crystals with magic while her cat, Marley, purred in her lap. Lucas had been practicing spells all morning, and he came running so fast he nearly tripped over the rug.

"You're never going to believe what I can do!" he cried.

I sat up straighter. "Whatever it is, it sounds like good news."

Lucas tugged on my arm. "You have to follow me to the library."

Chloe's interest piqued, and she set her crystals aside. "Can I see?"

"Come along," Lucas offered. "You don't want to miss this."

We entered the library. I sat in a chair near the window, stroking Isa's head in my lap. Chloe leaned against the side of the desk, and Marley and Oliver lay sprawled out on the floor where the sun shined in through the window.

Lucas stood in the center of the room. "There's a spell in the Reaper Records that talks about Death energy and transformation. We know I'm connected to Death energy because I feel it when someone dies. I used to think what I felt was a void—an absence of their spirit. According to the book, what I'm sensing is the *transformation* of their spirit."

"You've known this for months, though," I pointed out. "The records are pretty clear about it."

"Yes, but I've finally made sense of how to utilize it," Lucas said. "Look at this."

Lucas grabbed the Reaper Records from the desk and flipped through the pages. He held the book up to reveal a drawing of the Death card from the tarot deck. "As we know from tarot, the Death card doesn't always represent physical death, but death to all kinds of things—cycles, seasons of life, belief patterns. It means *change.* When something dies, it gives way for something new to exist in its place. It all comes back to transformation. All transformation creates energy."

Chloe crossed her arms. "You have my attention. Where are you going with this?"

Lucas wore a bright smile. I'd never seen him more proud of himself. "All these months, I've been trying to work with Death magic, in the sense of the energy that lingers when life ends. But transformation happens in all stages of life, not just at the end. I thought that to utilize this magic I had to pull that energy from a graveyard or a morgue, but as long as there's transformation happening around me, I can find Death magic anywhere."

Lucas grabbed a potted plant out of the window and set it on the desk. "Take this plant for example. Every day, leaves are growing, some are dying to make way for fresh leaves, it gets bigger—it *transforms.* There's Death energy right here at my fingertips! I just have to get perceptive enough to see what's transforming in my environment so I can use that energy."

"But you aren't an Earth Elementai, so you can't manipulate the plant," I pointed out.

"Doesn't matter," Lucas said. "I can manipulate its energy, as long as it's transforming."

"This is potentially really powerful magic," I remarked. "How can you utilize it?"

Lucas beamed. "That's what I wanted to show you."

He hurried across the room to where his scythe was leaning against one of the bookcases. "In this instance, I had to get a little creative. A simple houseplant doesn't have enough transformation energy within it to pull this off, but *I* do. I'm in the midst of becoming a father, and there are old pieces of myself dying to become a new man. I'm literally transforming. So I felt into that energy, and I realized I could take it and put it into the scythe."

"Like an enchantment?" I asked.

Lucas nodded. "Exactly."

"But the scythe's already enchanted," Chloe pointed out. "From the night you used to kill the sluagh. The creature's blood enchanted it."

"Yes, and I was able to break your enchanted restraints with it that night, but this is completely different, a whole new tier of magic." He held the scythe straight out in front of himself, and the entire weapon began to glow a purple hue. He opened his hand... and the scythe remained floating mid-air.

I sat up straighter, and Isa perked her ears. "How's it doing that?"

Lucas stepped back, smiling. "I infused it with Death magic, and because I control Death magic, I can control this! Watch."

Lucas flicked his wrist, and the scythe followed his command. The blade swung at a stack of books in the corner, slicing several of them clean in half. I jumped, and Chloe's spine straightened.

"Uh, that was a little frightening," Chloe said.

"Right?" Lucas replied proudly. "I can literally use it as a weapon in battle. And it doesn't just *physically* transform things. I can also bring death to ideas. Look."

Lucas held out his hand, and the scythe sped across the room straight into his fingers. He held the scythe out in front of himself and turned to the bookcases along the wall. "Let's see... I want to read a good mystery novel. Perhaps I'll look over here..."

Lucas started in one direction, but the scythe jerked the other way. Lucas nearly lost his footing as he followed the scythe to the other end of the bookcase. The scythe spun in his hand, until the tip touched the spine of one of the books.

Lucas pulled it down from the shelf. "Actually, this is a romance novel, but he's still learning. The point is, he can change my mind and lead me in a new direction."

Chloe's eyebrows shot up. "Impressive."

"It's like the scythe has a mind of its own," I added.

"Kind of?" Lucas sounded unsure. "It's like a companion, but also an extension of me."

"The potential for this is huge," I said.

Lucas subconjured his scythe. "I just wish it was enough. If it was, I'd have passed the Warlock's Trial by now."

"What exactly do the Reaper Records say about the Warlock's Trial?" Chloe asked. "Can I see it?"

Lucas shrugged. "Sure."

Chloe used telekinesis to float the book over to her. Pages flipped open mid-air, and the book gently fell into her open hands. She began reading. *"The Reaper Order is a society of reapers who have demonstrated a clear understanding of their roles and responsibilities within the Miriamic Coven, as well as their magical powers, through practical application and keen comprehension. This system was developed by the coven's first reaper, Mortimer Imperia."*

Chloe paused. "Huh… I've never heard any of Miriam's family referred to by last name."

"I've been researching our past lives historically," Lucas said. "Our family name was Imperia, which the Imperium Council is named after. According to the stories, the children came together and chose this name for themselves. Most of the records we have go back to the kids. We know little about Mother Miriam's past, because she wasn't keeping records until she started writing stuff down for her kids. Not everything survived the witch trials, though, so there are gaps in the coven's knowledge."

"Interesting…" Chloe mused. "Listen to this. *Mortimer believed that a reaper's power and responsibility required great care, and because of that, the master-apprentice system was put into place."*

Lucas scoffed. "You'd think I'd know what I was doing, considering I was the one who designed all this."

"In a past life," I reminded him. "That doesn't mean that you consciously have any of the answers here in this life. It's too much to expect of yourself."

Chloe continued reading. *"To become a member of the Reaper Order, an apprentice must pass the Warlock's Trial. The Warlock's Trial was named for Mortimer, who designed the trial to indicate when an apprentice has become a master. Once an apprentice has demonstrated they fully understand their powers of death, the reapers will grant the apprentice welcome into the Reaper Order, and he or she may take on their own apprentice."*

"See, that's the part I don't get," Lucas said. "Autumn isn't part of the Reaper Order, yet she was supposed to be my master. How can the system work if I'm not learning from a master?"

"Maybe that's one of the reasons you incarnated right now," I theorized. "If you developed this system in a prior life, maybe you came here to correct the ways in which the system has failed its reapers in the past.

Maybe you don't need Autumn, because the answers are already deep inside of you."

"Maybe," Lucas agreed thoughtfully. "But like you said, that doesn't mean I have any conscious understanding."

"Try this," Chloe suggested. "Take a deep breath."

Lucas rolled his eyes. "Yeah, that's the answer."

Chloe frowned. "Just try it, okay?"

Lucas kept his eyes on her a moment longer before finally giving in. He laced his fingers in front of himself, closed his eyes, and took a deep breath. "Now what?"

"Tap into your intuition," Chloe said. "Tell me the first answer that comes when I ask the following question. What is it that you need to pass the Warlock's Trial?"

Lucas hesitated.

"You need to be quick about it," Chloe encouraged. "You can't let your mind start talking over your intuition."

Lucas opened his eyes, and his shoulders fell. "I don't know. I didn't really *get* an answer. Or… maybe I already know what I need to do, but I'm afraid to do it."

I realized what he was saying. "You don't want to learn all the spells in the book."

"How can I?" Lucas asked. "I can't destroy a soul just to show I know what I'm doing. But how do I demonstrate the full capacity of my powers unless I pull off the most powerful spell in the book?"

Chloe flipped through the pages. "There's got to be more to it than that. I don't think you'd design a system that worked that way. Not in this life, not in any."

"It's not just that spell," Lucas said. "There's another one I don't quite understand. Maybe that's the last piece to passing the Warlock's Trial."

Chloe flipped through the book. "Which spell?"

Lucas looked over her shoulder. "Two more pages. That one. It's a grief spell of some sort, but I don't understand it. It says it's to manifest the grief of living people, which doesn't make any sense. Why would I want to *create* grief for people? I don't even wish that on my enemies. Besides, I don't have power over the living, so I don't understand where it fits in."

"Maybe it's not a spell at all," Chloe theorized. "Maybe it's more of... a metaphor? I'm not sure."

Lucas sighed and took the book back. "I don't know, either. I just need to think about it for a while. I'm sure it will make sense eventually."

Lucas glanced at the clock on the wall. "I think I've made enough progress for the day. I might go lie down."

"Let us know if you need any more help," I offered, though I didn't know how much more help we could be.

"I will," Lucas said, before leaving the room.

Chloe breathed a heavy sigh and turned to me. "I feel bad for him. I wish we could help more."

"You don't have to help... but I'm glad you're here," I said.

Chloe chuckled lightly. "Of all the things I never thought you'd say."

I shrugged. "People change."

"Absolutely," Chloe agreed. "Just look at the two of us. I never did get a chance to say thank you for what you did for me in the Abyss."

I waved a hand. "You don't need to thank me."

"No, I really do," Chloe argued. "This kind of thing might be normal to you, but it's not the way I was taught. Kindness wasn't expected, no matter how hard I tried. I guess you'd never believe I wasn't always a mean girl before you came to town."

"Really?" I asked curiously. "Who were you before I came to town?"

"Oh, I was an absolute bitch," she admitted with a laugh. She hopped up on the desk, sitting on the edge like she was settling in for a long chat. "But not always. I tried to be nice as a kid, but I learned at a young age that it was easier to get what I wanted when I treated people with cruelty rather than kindness. Obviously, I've realized that's bullshit, but for a while, it was the only way I operated. But all that cruelty just reflected on me, and I ended up hating myself. It wasn't worth it."

"What would make you feel that way in the first place?" I wondered.

"Nobody listened to me when I was nice," Chloe admitted. "The only time I ever got my point across was when I was being aggressive. Growing up, I wanted to do nice things, but if I was too soft spoken, my parents didn't think I was passionate enough. I remember in middle school I organized a fundraiser for the animal shelter. I thought I could place all the stray cats into homes. My parents are a bit like my grandma, if you haven't guessed. They believed hard work could get you anywhere, so they said if I wanted to do a fundraiser, I'd have to figure it out myself."

"Do you believe that?" I asked. "That hard work can get you anywhere?"

"I used to," Chloe replied. "But it only gets you so far. Hard work didn't get my dad the connections his father made before he was born. Those connections earned him his first job, then his first promotion. Hard work didn't earn my mom financial support from her parents that bought her first house. I think connections and support are important—that's why we have community—but I also think my parents didn't realize how much other people struggle to get somewhere. I don't think privilege makes them bad people, but I think my parents' inability to recognize it prevented them from lifting others up. That's what I wanted to do. Help others."

Chloe sighed. "I spent weeks planning this fundraiser—talking to the shelter, posting flyers around town, trying to get people involved. I even set up a bake sale and made cookies for days to raise money. Come the day of the fundraiser, nobody showed up."

My heart dropped. "I'm sorry, Chloe."

"You know me. I'm headstrong. I wasn't going to give up," she continued. "So I ran the fundraiser again, only this time, I decided that if people weren't going to take my invitation nicely, I was going to bully them into showing up. At fundraiser day round two, the shelter said it was the best turnout they'd ever seen. Those stray cats needed homes, shelter, and food, and without me, the winter would've come in and they would've froze. Nobody else cared, but I did. If I had been *nice* and accepted that I couldn't make people want to help, all those cats would be dead. But because I was an asshole, and I threatened and forced people to see things my way, I saved lives. I realized that sometimes, being cruel was the only way to make people care and get things done. Because no one *would* care unless their own skin was on the line. My hard work meant nothing compared to my ability to bully people into complying. I didn't want to be that way, but I couldn't deny that it produced results. People might've gotten their feelings hurt, but at least those cats didn't have to be in pain, and that's what mattered to me. I had to pick and choose what I wanted, and I wanted to help more than I wanted to be good. Because being good means nothing if you're plastering on a polite smile while watching something suffer."

"That must've really affected you," I said sadly.

"Yes, but that's only part of it," Chloe replied. "My parents always strived for the best. My dad works in finance, and my mom's in business management. They both had to be the best at what they did. It was an obsession. My parents were hardly home, and even though they're still married, I barely saw them together. So I thought that's what relationships were supposed to be, that you were supposed to find someone who could elevate your status. That's the only reason I dated Ryan. He commanded respect the way I did, and I thought together, we could be this power couple. But we didn't have anything in common, and we barely got along. I didn't understand what a relationship was supposed to be."

"Until you met Miles," I teased.

Chloe smiled. "Miles actually treated me like a person, not just some trophy to put on display. Sometimes I feel like my parents had me for their image, because having kids is what they were *supposed* to do, rather than because they wanted a kid. They pushed me to be my best. I had tutors growing up so I'd get the best grades. I even had private lessons with a dance instructor so I'd be at the top of the team. I didn't realize until later that the other girls weren't getting one-on-one time with the coach. But it wasn't enough. Everything in my life had order, whether it was my schedule or the shoes in my closet. But there was *so* much shame around all of it. If one thing was out of place, I felt like I'd failed my parents. Maybe that's why I got so angry when you came to town, because for the first time in my life, that order was thrown out of whack. My future was suddenly uncertain, and I couldn't predict what you'd do."

"You were right to be angry," I told her. "But I don't think that was either of our fault."

"No, it wasn't," she agreed. "We shouldn't be held responsible for what our grandparents did. Can you guess what my parents said when I told them about you? They said the curse was *my* problem, and that if I wanted something done about it, I'd have to deal with you myself. My dad acted like he was the one who forced your mom out of town, and that I should be able to do the same. But from what I've heard, it sounds like your mom went more willingly than he lets on."

"She was just protecting herself," I said.

Chloe rolled her eyes. "And yet my dad took all the credit. He taught me people only understand one way of communication and that's through force, but you taught me it doesn't have to be that way. I learned you don't need everyone to help you. You just want the *right* people helping you. All my life, I was pandering to the wrong crowd. I wanted respect, and I learned from watching my grandmother that I had to command it. But I learned from you that it's better to earn it. I think it's possible to be authoritative *and* kind."

I stroked the top of Isa's head as I listened to Chloe's story. "That's really kind of you to credit me, but you're the one who put in the work. You could've chosen to follow in your grandmother's footsteps, but you didn't."

Chloe chuckled. "Boy, am I glad. My grandmother taught me that I couldn't trust people to do the right thing. She told me that if you don't force people to do the right thing, they won't, because we're all inherently selfish."

My eyebrows shot up. "It sounds like your grandmother is insecure in her own empathy."

"For sure," Chloe agreed. "My grandmother believes that people are inherently lazy and that they won't do anything productive if they aren't suffering. She believes people will always make bad decisions and thinks we have to work extra hard to be righteous, as if you have to make an effort to be kind. Maybe this has to do with growing up cursed, but I thought it was normal to go around wanting to do bad things, and that people just *didn't* because they'd be punished for it."

I felt really bad for Chloe that she'd grown up this way. "It takes a lot of determination to change your belief system like that."

"Yeah, but that belief system has to be challenged to begin with," Chloe replied. "You did that for me. I hated you. Despised you, really. I've come to find it's hard to do good in the world when there's hate in your heart, and I had to hate you to learn that. I think suffering requires people to make big changes, but I also think people can do really good things when they aren't struggling for survival. If you and I can get along, there's hope for the coven."

I nodded. "Absolutely. I think you're here to change lives, Chloe. I know you've changed mine. You've taught me to be more assertive and made me realize I have to go after the things I want. You've taught me not to jump to conclusions and judge people so quickly. Most of all, you've taught me that we all want the same thing, but we look at it in different ways, and so we need to come together and work together, even if our methods differ."

"That means a lot to hear you say that." Chloe let out a deep breath, like confessing all this had lifted a huge weight off her shoulders.

I eyed her curiously. "Why are you telling me all this now?"

Chloe gazed down at her hands. "I've been doing a lot of thinking these last few months. Verla gave me a past-life regression, and since then, I started diving deeper than ever before. I've been meditating to uncover the old stories I've told myself. I've only started to realize the impact it had on me. I understand myself better now, and I guess I wanted you to understand me, too. I see now that I had to be born into my family to show me what I didn't want. I know how these people think, and I know I don't want to be like them."

"That's a really interesting take on it," I said. "I'm really glad you're discovering who you are."

Chloe offered a light smile. "Thanks. It's not always easy, but it's worth it."

Chloe hopped off the desk and stood. "Anyway, I'm hungry. Are you?"

I laughed. "With these pregnancy cravings? Always."

Isa hopped off my lap, and Chloe grabbed my hand to help me stand. I'd be twenty-nine weeks pregnant tomorrow, and with two little kiddos in there, I felt huge already. It was definitely getting harder to get around. A lot of my energy had returned in the second trimester, but we'd just hit the third trimester, which meant we were already in the home stretch.

Everything had been going really well so far. I visited Luana weekly, and I took Onyx along to every appointment so she knew what was going on with the babies if I ever needed her help at home. Everyone had been super accommodating, and I couldn't imagine a better pregnancy. I couldn't wait to meet our little boys.

"How are the pregnancy cravings today?" Chloe asked.

I crinkled my nose. "Is it weird that I want jalapeños dipped in ranch dressing?"

Chloe gave me a weird look. "Are we talking deep fried jalapeños or straight off the plant?"

I opened the door to the library. "Straight off the plant."

"That's gross," Chloe teased as we started down the hall. Marley followed us, but Isa and Oliver ran off to another part of the house. They'd been sneaking off together a lot lately, and I didn't know what they were up to. Lucas thought maybe they were grumpy that we were having babies and would have less time for them.

"It's a nice day. Why don't we eat in the sunroom?" Chloe suggested.

"That sounds like a good idea." I entered the kitchen and started toward the refrigerator, but Chloe got there first.

"Go sit down," she instructed. "I'll see if I can find any *jalapeños*."

I chuckled. "Thanks, but you don't have to dote on me. I'm only pregnant."

Chloe blocked my way to the fridge. "Enjoy the special treatment while it lasts. You only have a few more months of it."

Chloe insisted on cooking for me, so I had nothing else to do but sit around. The house was quiet, and I wondered where everyone else was, until I walked into the sunroom and was met with a collective, *"Surprise!"*

I jumped a little and quickly surveyed the room. Everyone was here, seated around a long table filled with snacks and baby decorations. On a buffet table along the wall sat a watermelon cut into the shape of a baby carriage with fruit inside, along with a cake that had a teddy bear on top. A table filled with presents sat in the corner.

"You guys!" I cried. "You didn't have to throw us a baby shower."

Chloe came up behind me. "Yes, we did. Here's your jalapeños."

Chloe handed me a jar from the fridge, and I teared up a little. Damn hormones.

Lucas immediately shot out of his chair. He'd obviously lied about going to lie down. He knew this was happening and had probably portaled the others to *Hok'evale* to gather supplies and buy gifts. "Sit down, Nad."

"Thank you, guys. This was really sweet of you." I sat down, and Lucas pulled up another chair beside me. I narrowed my eyes. "You didn't leave the library to lie down. You were setting up for the party, and you made Chloe stick behind to distract me."

Lucas smirked. "To be fair, the party was set up before I got here, and Chloe's been watching you all afternoon. You can't blame *me*. If it were up to me, I'd never have thrown you a surprise party. I know you don't like them."

Miles went around the table handing out small rectangular boxes. I didn't know what they were for. "Why don't you like surprises? I think surprise parties are great."

"I guess I like having answers and clarity," I said as I took one of the boxes from him.

"That's not true, Nadine," Talia pointed out. "You do like surprises, because you like mysteries, and that's just another way of figuring out a surprise."

"I enjoy mystery novels and puzzles because by the end of it you've solved something," I clarified. "Surprises are different, because you don't even know you're looking for answers."

I shook the box Miles had given me, and it made a rattling sound. "What are these anyway?"

Miles wore a goofy grin. "Open it and find out!"

I glanced around, but everyone was waiting for me to open my box first. I pulled the top off and found the box filled with over a hundred small puzzle pieces. Everyone else did the same. I saw that they too had puzzles, but their pieces were different from mine.

My heart warmed. "A puzzle party?"

"It was Talia's idea," Verla said. "When we're done, we can frame them all up and hang them wherever you want them."

"This is really cool!" I dumped my puzzle out in front of me. "How do I know what I'm building?"

"That's the mystery, isn't it?" Grant teased with a wink.

I smirked. "You know that's only going to motivate me."

"Good," Talia said proudly. "We have prizes for those who solve their puzzles first. And the timer starts… now!"

I rushed to start organizing my pieces, and my friends did the same. I found the four corner pieces and set them aside. I realized this was going to be harder than I thought, since I didn't know which corners they went in. As I was separating some of the middle pieces, I noticed a familiar smile.

I held up the pieces. "Lucas, is this you?"

He studied the piece for a few moments. "It does look like me, doesn't it?"

I spread the pieces out. I noticed Talia's eyes staring up at me from one piece, then the jeweled bodice of my wedding dress.

I gasped. "This is the photo from our wedding!"

"Oh, no!" Onyx joked, fitting two of her pieces together. "She's on to us."

The photo showed Lucas and me standing in the center of the group near the cake table, with all our guests surrounding us. I fitted a puzzle piece near the center, and Grammy's smiling face became clear. Tears welled in my eyes, and I couldn't help it when they spilled over the corners of my lids. I started to sob—full, body-shaking sobs.

"I was only joking," Onyx said softly.

"It's not that," I said between hiccups. "I just love this picture so much."

Lucas placed a hand on my back. "Hey, it's okay."

"I know, and that's why it's so perfect." I sniffled and wiped my eyes. With a chuckle, I added, "Pregnancy hormones are really weird, you guys."

Everyone laughed, and it sounded so magical. It nearly brought me to tears all over again.

Once I knew what picture I was creating, it was easy to place the corners in the right places, then follow the colors to put the edges together. I fitted all the pieces into place, until I realized I was missing one. I looked around my chair to see if it'd fallen on the ground, but I didn't see it anywhere.

"What are you looking for?" Mandy asked.

I furrowed my brow as I looked around. "I'm missing a piece. It must've fallen somewhere."

Lucas snickered under his breath, and I shot him a narrowed glance. A blush rose to his cheeks, which was so damn cute and irritating at the same time.

I nudged him playfully. "You cheater! Where's my piece?"

Lucas placed his fist behind his back. "I have no idea what you're talking about," he feigned.

"Not fair!" I reached for his hand, but he stretched it far away from me where I couldn't reach. I crawled into his lap to get closer, but his arms were longer than mine. I tickled him in the armpit.

He laughed loudly. "What puzzle piece could you mean?"

He tickled me back, and I giggled so hard I nearly peed myself. The next moment, a sharp pain entered my ribs, and I gasped.

A horrified look crossed Lucas's features. "What's wrong?"

I sat back down in my chair and placed my hand over my stomach. My belly tickled, and I felt one of the babies' feet run along one side, then I felt movement on the other side.

I smiled as my eyes landed on Lucas. "Nothing. The babies are kicking. Feel."

I grabbed Lucas's hand and splayed his palm over my belly. The babies kicked really hard, and Lucas's eyes lit up.

"They've never been this active before," he remarked.

"Maybe they're trying to start a fight with you," Grant joked. "Dad's being mean to Mom, and they're just standing up for her."

"Yeah," I agreed. "The babies get it."

Lucas sighed and leaned down to speak to my belly. "All right, boys. I'll give Mama her puzzle piece, but only because you said *please*."

Lucas kissed my belly, and my heart swooned. He placed my piece back on the table. It was the center piece—the one that completed both of our smiling faces. I placed it in its rightful spot, then smoothed my hands over the puzzle.

"All done!" I announced proudly.

Talia stood. "I'm sure it comes as a surprise to no one that Nadine completed her puzzle first, which means she gets the first prize. Which present do you want to open first?"

"Mm…" I eyed the present table, and my eyes fell upon a large, slim gift leaning against the wall. It was too big to fit on the table. "That one."

Lucas went to get it and carried it over. "*To Nadine and Lucas, from Clarice*," he read.

We tore off the wrapping paper together to find an image of a double bassinet on the front of the box.

My jaw dropped. "Oh, my Goddess. Thank you so much!"

I started to stand, but Verla was already out of her chair. "I'll come to you."

I sat back down, and Verla leaned down to give me a hug. "That was so thoughtful," I told her.

She shrugged like it was no big deal. "The babies need somewhere to sleep."

Chloe practically bounced in her chair. "Open my present next."

The race to finish our puzzles seemed forgotten as our attention turned to the gifts. Chloe handed us a gift bag, and Lucas and I each pulled out several pieces of tissue paper. Inside was a pair of adorable black onesies that read *Son of a Witch* with a cute cartoon of a witch hat on it.

We got all kinds of wonderful gifts to prepare us for when the babies arrived—toys, bottles, a breast pump, clothes, blankets, and tons of diapers. Grant gifted me a container of homemade chocolate chip cookies to satisfy my cravings. Professor Warren got us matching carriers that strapped to our fronts like a backpack to carry the babies around in.

Mandy left the room to grab her present, and she came back carrying a box that was almost as tall as she was. She could barely get her arms around it. Lucas quickly got out of her chair to help her, and we opened the gift to find a huge box with a rocking horse inside. It was so big and bulky it was almost ridiculous.

"Wow!" I exclaimed. "I don't even know where we're going to put this."

Mandy smiled brightly. "I know it will be a while before the babies are big enough to ride it, but I saw it and couldn't resist!"

"Thank you, everyone," I said after we'd opened all the presents. "It seems we have everything we were going to need when the babies arrive."

Talia stood. "There's one more gift I'd like to give you. I know that looking into the future isn't always precise and that things can change, but I want to give you a chance to ask me anything, and I'll see if the Seer Wand can answer your question."

I eyed her curiously. "You've already been looking at the babies' future, haven't you?"

Talia nodded. "I wanted my gift to you to be some sort of advice for their futures, but the visions I've received are confusing. Every time I look into the twins' future, I see them using different types of Cast magic. At first, I thought it was because they're going to be separate Casts, but I've seen them casting magic from all five."

Lucas and I exchanged a glance.

"It's like I'm seeing multiple futures," Talia added.

"Maybe because their magic's not determined until their Evoking Ceremonies," I theorized.

"I'm not sure," Talia said. "I thought touching your belly might help me get clearer visions."

"Let's look deeper," Lucas agreed. "If Talia can figure out what Casts they'll be, then maybe we can prepare them better for it."

I took his hand. "Is that the question we want to ask—which Casts will they be?"

"I think it's an innocent enough question, but it also helps us prepare them for their future," Lucas said.

"All right," I told Talia. "That's our question, then. What does the Wand say about the twins' Casts?"

Talia conjured the Seer Wand, then knelt beside me and placed her hand on my belly. Long, quiet moments passed as everyone watched on. Her eyelids fluttered like normal, until an intense vision took over. The blood drained from her face, and her features went stark white. My heart lurched, but Lucas caught her before she could fall over.

"Talia!" Lucas shook her until her eyelids fluttered open.

"What did you see?" I asked breathlessly. "Whatever it was looked intense."

Lucas helped Talia into the chair beside me.

Color began to return to Talia's cheeks. "Yeah, it was. It was the most vivid vision I've seen of them. I saw your son Marcus."

My hand immediately went over my belly. It was instinctual now. Hearing my son's name out loud felt entirely new. I was still getting used to the idea that we were going to have babies, but giving them names made it very real, even more so than feeling them kick inside of me. Lucas and I had been discussing names for months, and we'd only decided on names last week. We hadn't told anyone yet.

"You know the names we picked out," I said.

Talia's shoulders fell. "Shoot. I ruined the surprise again, didn't I?"

"It's okay," Lucas insisted. "I guess we can tell everyone now."

I turned to the others. "The twins are named Marcus and Dean."

Verla smiled. "Those are lovely names."

Lucas turned back to Talia. "What was Marcus doing in this vision?"

"I saw him in a battle," Talia admitted. "He climbed onto the back of a wolven shifter. I'm pretty sure it was his mate."

"Marcus is going to mate with a *fae*?" Lucas spat. "I didn't know shifters could mate outside their species, not to mention the shifters are all males and they always mate with female sorceresses."

"Not always," I reminded him. "Beau told us he mated with another dragon shifter."

"It's rare, but fae *can* mate with other supernaturals," Talia confirmed. "This shifter was different, though. It was a woman."

Lucas shook his head. "That's impossible. There's never been such a thing. The power to shift only lies with male fae."

"I don't know how it happens, but that's what I see," Talia said.

"Then your visions are unreliable. They must be wrong, because that's never happened in history. A sorceress can't be a shifter," Lucas replied. "Besides, our kid would never fall in love with a fae. A fae would sooner kill him than love him."

I had the thought that he was wrong, because Beau Blankard's parents had fallen in love. His father was a warlock, and his mother was a fae sorceress. Plus, there were fae who had been kind to us when we went to Malovia. Maybe by the time the twins grew up, things would be different between our people.

I was hardly worried about that, though. Talia had said she'd seen Marcus in battle. "You're saying our children are going to have to fight a war like us? That's what we're trying to prevent."

"That's what I saw, but it was different, too," Talia said. "Marcus was more powerful than any warlock I've ever seen… He had the mark of all five Casts on his arm."

Verla gasped, and Professor Warren exchanged a glance with her. The entire room went silent as we all absorbed this information.

"Do you know what that means?" Lucas asked them. They obviously knew something we didn't.

Professor Warren wore a shocked expression. "I've never heard of *anyone* with magic from more than one Cast. Even if you *could*, the magic would overwhelm you. No one should be able to yield that kind of power, unless…"

He looked to Verla again, and she seemed to be thinking the same thing.

"Unless he's a demigod," she finished for him.

I furrowed my brow. "How's that possible? The twins aren't children of gods."

"Demigods is a classification of power, and they can be born of two talented supernatural parents," Verla reminded me. "If everything's just right and the twins are born during a significant astrological event, it's entirely possible they could be born demigods."

"I wasn't seeing multiple futures," Talia realized. "I saw the boys casting *all* Cast magic, because they're born demigods."

"Dean, too?" Lucas asked. "Was he in your vision?"

"I felt him there, but I didn't see him," Talia said. "It stands to reason they'd both be demigods, since the boys will share a soul."

"If they're that strong, then whatever battle you saw them in, they're going to win it, right?" I demanded.

Talia hesitated. "I didn't see the outcome of the battle. I'm not sure if I could even if I tried. There are certain things set in stone, and others that aren't. It appears that it's your sons' destiny to use their demigod powers to fight in a supernatural war. Whether they win that war or not, I can't say."

"Is that what the Miriamic Conflict will become?" Lucas asked incredulously. "Another twenty years of fighting, until the coven breaks into full-on war?"

"No." I refused to believe it. "We choose our own destiny. We can end the Miriamic Conflict before our children come of age. Things can still change. Even if the conflict continues, Marcus and Dean don't have to fight unless they want to."

"How do you know they haven't already chosen to fight?" Talia asked. "You know from your past-life regression that you chose to come back now, to heal what's happening in the coven. There's no guarantee that we'll win, but one thing's for certain—you will continue to choose this path, until you've achieved what you came to do."

"Does that mean we're going to lose, and our sons came to clean up our mess?" I asked in a shaky tone.

Talia shook her head. "I'm not sure I saw them fighting *this* war. The Miriamic Conflict could be long over before the boys' powers ever awaken."

Lucas raked his hands through his hair. "How can we possibly prepare them for this?"

"You be honest with them," Verla said. "Tell them who they are, but give them space to learn it on their own, too."

The thought of this responsibility weighing on my sons' shoulders killed me. Lucas and I were chosen ones, and I didn't want my sons to go through that, too. It made me wonder why we were fighting the Miriamic Conflict at all, if our children were just going to grow up to fight another war.

Then I thought of their childhood. What would their childhood be if all they knew was war? Wasn't it better if we gave them the best childhood possible, in a loving environment where we could build their courage and confidence?

"We just have to be the best parents we can," I decided.

Lucas nodded. "If it's their destiny, something they already decided on, then that's all we can do."

Lucas knelt at my side and took my hand. "They chose *us* to be their parents, and there has to be a reason for that. We have so much love to give these boys, and I have to believe that they chose us to show them what true love really is. Our sons are going to know unconditional love, and they're going to understand the power of community. We're going to teach them how to use their emotions to empower change. Whatever path they're on, they chose us to guide them, and we have to do just that."

I agreed wholeheartedly.

Talia's vision put a damper on the party. Lucas brought me a plate of food, and a few people continued quietly working on their puzzles while we ate. We chatted for a while, and Lucas told the others what he could do with his scythe. Nobody really wanted to talk about our powers or the Miriamic Conflict, though.

The food was really good. Grant had made chili, and I added heaps of jalapeños to it. He also made delicious peppermint iced tea. I let out a moan of pleasure as the sweet taste flowed over my taste buds.

Grant leaned across the table and winked at me. "I added a bit of ginger. It's good for the babies."

"It tastes amazing," I told him.

The party had completely wound down a few hours later, and the sun had set. Mandy offered to carry some of the presents up to our room, and she looked really proud as she left the room carrying the rocking horse.

By now, everyone had finished their puzzles, and Talia and Verla had moved them into frames. Each one depicted a photo of the group in one way or another. There were photos of me surrounded by my girls while we got ready for the wedding, and pictures of us singing around the fire at Yule.

Mandy returned to the sunroom to help clean up the food. I started to stand and went over to help, but Mandy stopped me. "Don't worry about it, Nadine. It's your party. We've got this."

I hesitated because I *wanted* to help, but it also felt weird to help after being told not to. I sank back into my chair.

"Everything all right?" Chloe asked. She was helping Mandy clean up, but she paused to come sit beside me.

Mandy carried a pile of dishes out the door, and I turned to Chloe once we were alone. This wasn't just something I could admit to anyone, but I felt like I could talk to Chloe about this. She opened up to me earlier, and I figured she would understand if I opened up to her.

"Being pregnant is weird," I said. "People treat me differently."

"They should," Chloe replied. "You're bringing life into the world."

I frowned. "This isn't a good thing. I'm in some of the best health of my life—I can find my own chair and get my own food, but everyone wants to do it for me because I'm pregnant. People are even changing recipes because it's good for the babies. And… that's the kind of help I needed when I was sick, and I didn't get it. I know you guys are just trying to be nice, but it's a little disheartening that we're trained by society to make this huge effort to accommodate pregnant women, when I feel better than ever. Society didn't care when I was sick, and that's when I needed help the most. When I'm in a flare-up, I'm treated like I'm a nuisance to society because I need resources. But now that I'm pregnant it's like I have value. It's insulting."

Chloe's features fell. "I don't ever want you to feel like you don't have value. If you want us to treat you differently, we can."

"That's not really the point," I said. "I appreciate what you guys did for me when I was in the worst of my lupus, and I'm grateful for that, but I have to realize now that you guys help me out a lot more now that I'm pregnant. You're more willing—you're happy to do it, instead of reaching out to me out of pity. It's like me being pregnant is seen as this huge blessing, but me being sick made you guys uncomfortable. It's an issue so ingrained in society, you wouldn't have even realized you were doing it."

Chloe leaned forward on her elbows. "Tell me more. I want to learn."

I sighed. "When you're disabled, society treats you like you don't belong and that your accommodations are an inconvenience, but *everyone* wants to accommodate the pregnant lady. It just proves that providing accommodations isn't the problem. It's people's attitude about it. People welcome pregnant women into society because they have something to offer, when disabled people are treated like they should just go away. It's sexist, too, because as long as the pregnant woman is creating new life, she's basically offering a service to the world, so it's a privilege to accommodate her, but disabled people are seen as doing nothing but sucking up resources. Even though pregnancy is technically a short-term disability, it benefits everyone, so it's acceptable for people to be inconvenienced short-term. At the end of it, everyone gets the reward of holding the baby and being part of the baby's life. But no one wants to help the disabled person, because they're always going to be sick."

"That's unfair," Chloe said sadly. "Things shouldn't be this way. Once the Miriamic Conflict is over and we're back in coven, we're changing things. We're going to educate people and provide more accommodations."

I fidgeted with the corner of the tablecloth. "I don't know if I can keep advocating for disabled people, though."

Chloe furrowed her brow. "What do you mean?"

"I'm in remission, and things are going *so well*," I said. "I should be relieved, but I just feel cheated. I don't know if I have the right to call myself disabled anymore."

"Cheated how?" Chloe wondered.

"It feels like my doctors lied to me, working me up about all these possible complications," I said. "I feel like I'm holding my breath, waiting for a terrible symptom to arise, but nothing happens. It's hard to operate this way when so much of my life has been invested in taking care of myself. Is this what it's like to be healthy all the time? You guys just... don't have to worry about any of this stuff?"

Chloe appeared genuinely interested. "What kind of stuff do you worry about?"

"Everything," I replied simply. "When I was sick, my lupus ran my life. I had to plan every day around my symptoms and schedule in recovery time. I still take my meds every day and monitor my diet, but I have so much energy now that I can do whatever I want, whenever I want to. There are no restrictions, not like I had before. My lupus could knock me down for an entire day, or sometimes even weeks at a time, and now I don't have to worry about it at all. I used to have to monitor where I could go, what I could do, when I took my treatments, when I rested, ate, went to the bathroom… hell, sometimes it felt like I had to be careful with how I *breathed*, because there were a million ways to fuck up and make myself feel worse. Now, I can do it all, and there are no consequences. Sometimes, it's like I have *too much* time on my hands. There's this empty space in my life that I don't know how to deal with, because I don't think of myself as ill anymore. And if that part of me is gone, who am I?"

"But you still have lupus," Chloe said.

"I know I'm not cured, but the chances of symptoms returning are low," I told her. "I don't feel healthy enough to be considered an able-bodied person, but I also don't feel like I'm sick enough to be disabled. This label used to be a huge part of my identity, and I don't know where I fit in anymore."

"You're having an identity crisis," Chloe realized.

I lifted my gaze to meet hers. "Yeah, I guess you could call it that. It feels like I've lost something, which is silly to think, because all I wanted when I was sick was to feel better."

"That doesn't mean you aren't allowed to grieve," Chloe pointed out softly.

"I don't know if grieving is the right word…" I mused. "Maybe? I'm just thinking… am I worth *more* now that I'm in remission? Am I more helpful to people? Wasn't I good enough when I was sick? I felt like I knew who I was back then, and now I have to change my perception of myself again. That's scary, because what if someday I get sick again, and I have to shift my identity all over? None of this is for sure, so now I'm just stuck in the middle, not certain if I'm sick or healthy."

"Your worth doesn't come from what other people can get out of you," Chloe insisted. "Your value is inherent, and it doesn't change depending on how disabled or able-bodied you are. You don't need to prove anything or accomplish anything to earn your worth. Also, being disabled does not need to be validated depending on how sick you are or not. That's ableist shit doctors tell patients in order to disregard their symptoms. There's no prize for being more handicapped than someone else."

Mandy returned to the room, and Chloe and I both quieted.

"Did either of you want anything else before I clean it up?" Mandy asked.

"You can leave the iced tea," I offered.

Mandy grabbed a few more plates, then left again.

Chloe stood and brought the pitcher of iced tea over to us. She spoke as she poured me another glass. "I think all of this questioning is a part of the grieving process. You feel like you've lost a piece of yourself, and you're leaving that old identity behind. A new identity has to take its place, and maybe that new one has one foot on one end of the spectrum and one on the other. You're in remission now, but your lived experience isn't going anywhere. You still have insight and understanding that able-bodied people will never have."

I took a sip of tea. "I guess so. Being pregnant just made me realize what life could've been like if people treated me differently, and I didn't have to be sick by myself. Instead, I went through a lot of it alone. People want to wait on me hand and foot now because I'm making children for others to enjoy, but when I was desperate for someone to take care of *me*, the world kicked me to the curb. I love my babies, and I would do anything for them—die for them, even—but are they worth more than I am, because they're brand new and I'm already used up because I was sick?"

I didn't really expect us to reach a resolution on this issue. Saying it all out loud made me realize things I'd never even admitted to myself. I had a lot to think about.

"Anyway, thanks for talking," I said as I finished my tea.

"Anytime," Chloe replied with a smile. "Just know that you can still be an advocate for the disabled community because you understand the disabled experience. You remember what it was like to be treated poorly because you were sick, and you can take your lived experience and use it to make change for the people who still struggle with chronic illnesses. Your experience isn't wasted; it's made you who you are. Now you can use it to push society to do better, because we need people like you. And your babies are worth the world, Nadine, but so are you. All of us are important. I'm sorry you didn't get the help you needed before, but now that you have more energy to fight, you can make sure the coven gives that help to the people who need it now. If there's anything else I can do to help you talk this out, you let me know, okay?"

"I will," I promised.

I left the sunroom and passed by the kitchen. Talia and Verla were doing dishes, while Mandy and Onyx were packaging up the leftover food. The guys were down in the basement putting some of the gifts in storage since we wouldn't need them for several months.

I returned to my bedroom and slipped out of my clothes to put on my nightgown. It was nearly nine o'clock, and I was exhausted. I just wanted to lay in bed until Lucas finished cleaning up and could come cuddle me. Isa and Oliver were sleeping on the bed and woke up when I entered the room.

I slipped the white nightgown over my head, and my breath caught in my throat. I covered my mouth to cough, and the taste of copper swept over my tongue.

Horror filled me, and I looked down at my hands to see they were covered in a sticky red liquid. I glanced in the mirror, as if needing the confirmation that I wasn't imagining things. My nightgown was speckled with red dots. The room seemed to sway around me, and my whole body trembled as I took a step back.

Isa shot to her feet and meowed loudly.

"LUCAS—" I started to shout, but the bile in my throat cut me off. I doubled over, clutching my stomach. Nausea hit me out of nowhere, and I vomited across the carpet. Terror clenched in my belly when I saw the deep red color.

*I'm vomiting blood.*

I tried to call out for my husband again, but I never got his name out before another wave hit me. I fell to my knees and caught myself with my hands. Every inch of my body shook. All I could think to do was pray to the Goddess that the babies would be okay. Isa jumped down from the bed and nudged me, like she was trying to keep me upright. Oliver started meowing loudly and scratching at the door.

My heart hammered. I was panicking, and I didn't know what was happening. I had the horrible thought that someone must've cursed me.

I placed my hand over my belly, ready to draw the magic out of me, but nothing happened. I willed my magic to respond, but it was dead inside of me, immobile and silent.

*The Waning.*

I didn't have my powers, at the worst possible time. There was nothing I could do to stop this.

I couldn't really make sense of what to do, but I knew I had to go get help. I began crawling across the room, barely aware that I'd crawled straight through the puddle of blood. The sickness soaked into my nightgown. My limbs felt like jelly, but by some miracle, I reached the door. I touched the handle the same time my stomach clenched for a third time. Blood spewed from my lips, dripping all over my front.

I rolled away from the door, gasping for breath. It felt like the blood was seeping into my lungs. I couldn't open my mouth without vomiting, and I couldn't stand on two feet. I slumped against the wall, wheezing. The cats continued to yowl, but I didn't hear anyone coming for me. I couldn't make sense of what happened. Was this some sort of complication with the pregnancy? It certainly didn't seem normal. I had the thought that my body was rejecting my kidney and I was going to expel it by vomiting it up. It was the silliest thing in the world, but it was the first explanation I could think of.

*Please save the babies*, I thought.

Footsteps neared, and Lucas burst into the room. "Nadine!" he screamed.

Tears leaked from my eyes, and I could only manage a whisper. "I—I don't know what happened."

He knelt beside me and grabbed the side of my face. He quickly looked me over, like he was searching for a stab wound or something. I gagged again, and blood dribbled down the side of my face. I could barely keep my eyes on him.

"HELP!" Lucas shouted down the hall, before turning back to me. "We need to get you to the hospital right now."

A portal bloomed. He tried to pick me up, but the second he moved me, my stomach lurched. I couldn't stand the thought of going anywhere right now. It felt like my body might fall into pieces if I moved.

"I can't," I rasped, but it was more like just moving my lips than making any sound.

Several people raced down the hall and entered the room. I didn't know who it was, until I heard Onyx shouting at Lucas. "Go get Luana and bring her back. Now!"

I wanted Lucas to stay right here, but when I reached out for him, he was already gone. My hands met soft fingers, and I looked up to see Verla.

"Let's get you into bed," she said quickly.

Onyx and Verla carried me to the bed, and they laid me on my side with a trash can next to me. I coughed and wheezed, then doubled over and threw up again. Onyx tried to hide her concern, but I saw it clear as day.

I reached out and took her hand. "What's happening?" I whispered.

Verla was the one to answer. "We won't know until the doctor gets here."

Great, I was complaining to Chloe five minutes ago about not being sick enough to be disabled. Look at me now. Tears streamed down my cheeks, because all I could think was that this was going to hurt the babies.

I heard several other people in the doorway, but I was so focused on keeping myself from vomiting that I couldn't pay any attention to them. I closed my eyes as I repeated prayers over and over again in my mind. I didn't want to die, but if I had to, I just wanted the babies to be okay.

A warm hand touched my forehead, and tears fell from my eyes as I opened them. Luana stood above me, beside Lucas. I hadn't even heard her enter. Luana signed something to me. I'd been learning what I could of ASL so I could communicate with her better at my appointments, but I could only pick up fragments of conversation. One sign was very clear, though.

*Help you.*

Luana was going to save my life.

# LUCAS

## NINETEEN

y heart raced as I watched my wife writhe on the bed. Walking in here to see blood sprayed all over the floor had terrified me beyond anything I'd felt before. I thought the priestesses had made it past our wards and come to kill Nadine and the babies. When I saw she was vomiting blood, I knew we didn't have much time. I portaled straight into Luana's office, and she came the second she saw the worry on my face.

Luana placed her hand on Nadine's chest, and a white glow emanated from her palm. Nadine's shaking body steadied, and her wheezing breath sounded clearer. I couldn't believe how fast Luana's healing magic worked on her.

"Lucas," Nadine rasped, reaching out for me.

I took her hand, squeezing it desperately. Tears streamed down my face as I choked back sobs. I had to hold it together for her, because she needed me right now.

Nadine let out a sigh of relief. "I feel much better now."

The tears I'd been holding back spilled over my lids. I'd been so terrified for her and the babies. Thank the Goddess for Luana and her healing magic. I didn't know what we'd have done without her.

I turned to Luana to thank her, but my eyes caught the others lingering in the doorway. Chloe and Talia stood at the front of the group, and the others were gathered in the hall. Chloe clutched the Mentalist

Wand, and Talia held on to the Seer Wand. The ends were glowing. Chloe's features had turned ghost white.

"We can read her mind," Chloe said hollowly. "It's not word-for-word, but we can sense the message. I'm not going to speak or translate for her directly, because I'm not a skilled interpreter, but I can put the gist of what she's saying together and get it across to you, as long as Luana's fine with it."

Luana must've read her lips, because she nodded to Chloe, telling her it was okay.

Chloe swallowed hard. "She says the babies are okay, but Nadine was poisoned."

Time must've stopped, because I wasn't sure how much I processed after that. I was aware that Verla and Talia were both freaking out. Their voices grew harsh as they discussed how this could have happened, in case there was a cure, but that was about all I picked up on.

It didn't make sense that Nadine had been poisoned. We'd all been eating and drinking the same food all day, and none of us were sick besides my wife. It wasn't that I didn't think this could happen. The priestesses certainly wouldn't hesitate to kill Nadine the first chance they got; she wasn't useful to them anymore. I just didn't know how they could slip anything past us. Our wards were iron-tight, and we didn't source any supplies from the coven anymore. Besides, I trusted every person in this house, so I couldn't even fathom where the poison had come from. The only thing that made sense was that something she ate had interacted with her meds.

I mentioned this, but Luana didn't seem convinced of it. I insisted that we couldn't possibly have a traitor in our midst. Luana suggested perhaps the poison was accidental—that maybe we'd been sold some bad herbs.

"What kind of poison was it?" I demanded.

"She doesn't know for sure," Chloe said. "It's not a poison she's healed before, so she's not familiar with it. What Luana knows is that the poison targeted Nadine's stomach and lungs, and she was able to heal those with her magic by healing Nadine's organs. Unfortunately, she couldn't process the poison out completely, because she'd have to heal her whole body, and that could trigger early labor."

"That's ridiculous!" Verla protested. "She should be able to heal Nadine of all ailments."

Luana glanced between Verla and Chloe, then started signing an explanation.

"Healing magic can have poor effects on pregnant women," Chloe explained. "She can target specific areas, or use her magic to observe and diagnose, but technically, the babies are foreign to the body. If she heals too much, the body might try to abort, and we can't risk that."

"Absolutely not," Nadine agreed in a groggy tone. "I'm not going to do anything to harm the babies."

"So what do we do?" I demanded.

"With time, Nadine's body will process out the poison on its own," Chloe said.

"We must be able to do more than that," I begged.

Luana frowned, and Chloe said, "There comes a point where neither you nor the medical staff can do anything. We just need to give it time and hope it doesn't affect the babies. Luana wants Nadine to remain on bedrest for the rest of the pregnancy."

Nadine winced a little as she moved. "Believe me, I'm not leaving this bed until my due date. Then Lucas is portaling me straight to a hospital bed."

Nadine looked really uncomfortable, and I took her hand. She squeezed as tightly as she could, though she didn't appear very strong. She gave me a look I'd seen a thousand times before that said, *All I want to do is sleep.*

"Let's give her some space," I suggested.

"I'll brew a cleansing potion that will get the blood stains out of the carpet," Verla offered, before following the others out into the hall.

As everyone went their separate ways, I stopped Grant and pulled him aside. I lowered my voice so no one else could hear. "I want you to go through all the leftovers. Test everything Nadine ate today."

"I can do that, but I might not have the results until morning," he said.

"I don't care. Just find out what caused this. And don't let anyone in this house eat anything else until we know what we're dealing with."

Grant nodded. "On it."

Chloe and Talia stayed to help interpret for Luana. "Nadine was very lucky," Chloe said. "She could've died without an Anichi healer, but Luana got to her just in time. She says the rest of us have to be very careful. It could've been a mistake, but from her experience as a healer, she thinks someone might've tried to harm us."

"Is Nadine going to be okay?" I asked Luana.

"She'll be fine for now," Chloe said while Luana signed to me. "She needs to rest. Luana wants you to portal into her office in the morning so she can come and check on Nadine. She promises to be back every few days to monitor her. If we need anything else, she wants us to portal her here immediately."

"Thank you," I told Luana, before I portaled her back to her office.

Verla returned with her cleansing potion and helped clean up, then left the room.

Nadine and I were alone again. I lay on the bed next to her. She was on her side, and we were facing one another. She looked super tired, but also relieved. Isa lay curled up next to her belly.

I pushed the hair back from her face. Though I was still terrified, my voice remained steady. "It's going to be okay."

Tears welled in Nadine's eyes. "I want to believe you but... Lucas, I think I did this to myself."

I furrowed my brow. "You couldn't have possibly poisoned yourself."

"But what if I did, accidentally?" she insisted. "I think I manifested it."

I propped myself up on my elbow, more alert than ever. "Nad, what are you talking about?"

She sniffled. "Right before this happened, Chloe and I were talking. I told her this pregnancy was going so well that I don't feel disabled anymore, and it was like a piece of myself had died. It's hard to know who I am without my lupus, and that scares me, because I'm afraid I won't be able to advocate for the disabled anymore."

I wiped a tear from her eye. "That's not true."

"It doesn't matter, as long as I believe it," Nadine said. "What if I accidentally cast a curse over myself so I'd be sick again?"

I wanted to tell her she was wrong, that this was some accident or fluke, but I wondered if maybe she was right. I couldn't understand what was going on inside her head, so I couldn't be sure this was unrelated. I felt helpless to assist her, because I couldn't understand what she was going through.

"If that's the case, you can break the curse," I told her.

She shook her head. "I can't. The Waning is affecting me, and my magic won't be back for over a week. Besides, if Luana's magic can trigger labor, who's to say mine won't if I cast it on myself? I just… barely feel like myself anymore."

I stroked her cheek. "No matter what your health is doing, you'll always be Nadine."

She placed her hand over mine and closed her eyes, as if taking in my presence. "I think I need to remember that sometimes. Could you get me the box from under the bed?"

"Now's not the time," I stated.

Nadine frowned, like she thought I was making a joke. "Not *that* box. The other one."

*Oh.* I had forgotten about the other one.

I crawled off the bed and found the box she was talking about, then handed it to her. Nadine pulled off the top and began placing the items in front of her on the bed. It was her box of mementos—things like birthday cards from her parents, pictures she'd kept of her family, and a necklace that looked like one Helena had worn often. A silver star charm hung off another chain, and I noticed the ticket from our first date. The house key I'd found in the abandoned mansion behind the school sat there. It had been a symbol of our sanctuary while we attended Miriam College. There was so much in there now that the box was nearly overflowing.

Nadine ran her fingers over each item, like she was trying to memo-rize every piece. I didn't say anything, only watched on curiously. With every item that she touched, another tear fell down her cheek. It was heartbreaking seeing her like that. I wished I could help, but I sensed all she needed was a quiet moment.

"Do you remember this?" Nadine held up the gift certificate we'd received when we solved the mystery at the haunted house one Halloween.

"Yeah, I do," I replied fondly.

Nadine spoke softly. "It was a good time—a happy time."

Her fingers trailed to the ancient key Helena had given her. It was an antique skeleton key that hung from a chain. Nadine had gifted it to me before we started officially dating, but I'd given it back last Valentine's Day. We'd agreed to share it, and she'd worn it almost every day since, until Helena died. I never asked her about it, but now I could see it was because it reminded her too much of her grandmother. There was a longing in her eyes, like she wanted to wear it again, just to keep Helena close to her heart.

I took the chain it hung on and slipped it over her head. "For protection."

I knew the rumored protection charm inside it was bogus, but it seemed to bring Nadine comfort.

She spent a moment admiring the key dangling from her neck, before turning back to the other items. Her fingers stopped on Helena's necklace, and she picked it up. She studied it for several long seconds, before her voice cracked. "I miss her so much, Lucas. I just know if she were here, she'd be singing songs to the babies and making them blankets for their nursery. She'd be concocting tea blends to help with the pregnancy."

"We still have some of her herb blends," I offered. "I can make a pot."

Nadine shook her head. "It was never about her tea. It was *her*, just having her here with me, knowing she cared."

"She still cares," I promised. "Even if she can't be with us physically, I think she's still here with us."

Nadine reeled back. "No, she's not! If she were here, she would've known what caused this. She could've helped prevent it in the first place."

"Her memory lives on. Everything she taught us is still inside of us, and the memories we hold of her are inside that box."

"I don't give a fuck about what lessons she had to teach me! I care about her being here, not in a place where I can't talk to her—hell, even see her! All I have left of her is this stupid box!" Nadine grabbed the box and tossed it across the room, then buried her face in the pillow and sobbed. Contents scattered across the floor.

My stomach dropped. I never wanted to see her hurt like this. I placed a hand on her shoulder, but she shrugged me off. She was really hurting right now, and the last thing I wanted was to make it worse.

I got up and began placing the mementos back in the box. "She is here, Nadine, whether you believe it or not. Maybe she was the reason I got to you in time tonight."

Nadine didn't respond with anything but a sniffle. I didn't want to push it, because whatever I could say, I didn't think it would help. Grief had been a theme in her life many times over, and I worried what it might take to bring her grieving to an end.

If it were even possible.

Nadine fell asleep, and I finished cleaning up her things. I changed and got into bed next to her, but I could hardly sleep all night.

The little sleep I'd gotten was interrupted the next morning with a light knock on the door. I got out of bed slowly, as to not wake Nadine.

Grant stood on the other side of the door, holding a notepad. "I've got your results."

I quickly shot a look back at Nadine, then stepped into the hall. "What'd you find?"

Grant looked anything but happy. "Nothing. The fruit was fine, the meat was thoroughly cooked, and the cookies were perfect. There was nothing."

Maybe Nadine was right and this wasn't poison at all…

But Luana had sensed it in her.

"Was there anything Nadine ate yesterday that you didn't test?" I asked.

Grant thought about it. "The iced tea. It was all gone by the end of the night, and the pitcher was washed. But everyone else was drinking it, too."

"Maybe there was something in it that only affects pregnant women," I suggested.

Grant's eyes went wide. "Oh, Goddess. I must've mixed the ingredients wrong, or something was wrong with the ginger. I poisoned Nadine!"

"We don't know that," I assured him.

Grant threw his hand over his mouth. "I never meant to hurt her. It was supposed to be pregnancy safe."

I grabbed him by the shoulders. "This isn't your fault. It could have been any one of our theories. But the fact is it was an accident, and no one's to blame. Honestly, that makes me feel better than suspecting there's a traitor among us."

"I want to talk to her," Grant said.

He followed me into the bedroom, and Nadine stirred when I opened the door. I knelt beside her. "How are you feeling?"

"Better," she said, though she didn't look well. She tried to push herself upright, and I immediately grabbed her arms. I fluffed the pillows and put two behind her back to help her sit upright.

Tears streaked Grant's cheeks as he approached the bed. "I believe this is all my fault, and for that I am very sorry. I brewed the iced tea, and I mixed it wrong. It was meant to be pregnancy-safe, but I screwed up. I never meant to hurt you, Nadine."

"If this was truly an accident, then we have nothing to worry about," Nadine assured him. "Thank you for being honest with me, Grant."

"I will be sure not to let you eat or drink anything magical from now on—not until the babies are born, at least," Grant vowed. "Nothing touches your lips unless we've checked it for magic."

"Deal," Nadine said.

Nadine took Grant's confession very well, and he seemed to relax as he left the room.

I checked the time. "It's almost time for me to portal Luana in. Do you want someone to stay with you?"

Nadine settled into a more comfortable position. "I want Onyx here."

I hurried to get Onyx, then left the girls in the bedroom while I portaled to *Hok'evale*. I found Luana standing in her office next to her father.

"Luana has asked me to accompany her to interpret," Chief Cauac said. "But only if you're okay with it."

There were very few people I trusted to come into our safe house, but I trusted these two with our lives. Teleinsight had been useful in a pinch, but a skilled interpreter was always the better option.

"Yes, you're more than welcome," I told him.

Luana grabbed a medical cart beside her and followed me through the portal with all the equipment. Her father entered the portal behind her. Nadine lay propped against the pillows. Onyx sat on the bed beside her, holding her hand.

"Hello." Nadine greeted Luana with a smile and a gesture in American Sign Language. Luana signed back kindly.

Chief Cauac stood next to me, on the opposite side of the bed from Luana, so that she could easily see us all. "I will be interpreting everything said today, and all conversation will remain confidential. You may speak between one another as if I'm not here. I may ask you to slow down or pause, and I may need to ask for clarification. Do I have everyone's consent to do that?"

"Yes," we all agreed.

"How are you feeling today?" Chief Cauac interpreted for Luana.

"Better than last night," Nadine answered.

Luana made a questioning gesture, and Nadine nodded. Luana placed one hand on Nadine's head, and the other on her belly. A magical white glow filled the room. Luana tried to mask her disappointment as she drew away, but I saw it on her face clear as day. She signed to Nadine.

"Your blood pressure is high," Chief Cauac said. "I believe you have preeclampsia, but I will need to do a blood test and urinalysis to measure your protein levels."

"It's a good thing I really have to pee, then," Nadine joked. I could tell she was feeling at least a little better, or she wouldn't be joking right now.

"You're not worried?" I asked her.

"A little," she admitted. "But we've known for a long time I was high risk, so I guess I've already been preparing for this news. I'm not surprised."

I looked at Luana. "I thought Nadine was taking meds to reduce her risk."

Chief Cauac interpreted. "Nadine's medication only reduces the risk by about fifteen percent. The meds may have helped reduce the severity, as her case is mild at the moment."

"So it could get worse?" I asked.

Luana gave an affirming nod, and Chief Cauac added, "Yes, but we can keep her symptoms under control with close monitoring."

I shifted my weight between my feet uncomfortably. "You've been monitoring her weekly. How could this happen so fast?"

Luana signed quickly, and Chief Cauac said, "Preeclampsia can come on suddenly. Many women don't even know they have it until it shows up on tests. When you start feeling sick, you need to be admitted right away, and we may have to induce early."

"Is this why she threw up blood?" I asked Luana desperately.

"No, that was something else entirely, though it could have triggered preeclampsia," her father interpreted. "We've prepared for this. Nadine has lupus, she's undergone a kidney transplant, and she's carrying twins. These are all risk factors, and we're going to keep her symptoms under control."

"You can't heal it?" I wondered.

"Since preeclampsia is widespread, Anichi can't heal it without the risk of triggering labor. Pregnancy, in particular, is difficult for even the most experienced healers to manage with Spirit magic. We Anichi believe that pregnancy is the magic of creation itself, and therefore, it's not able to be easily influenced without causing something to go wrong. Keeping Nadine's symptoms under control is the best option. The only cure for preeclampsia is delivery."

"Cool." Nadine looked up to Luana. "Can I pee now?"

"I'd like to do an ultrasound before taking a urine sample. A full bladder helps with the imaging."

Luana started untangling cords from her cart, which I noticed for the first time had a laptop on top.

"Here, let me help," Onyx offered. She only knew one sign in ASL, which I guess was the word *help*.

The girls worked together to get the ultrasound machine plugged in. Nadine had two ultrasounds before—one right after we found out she was pregnant, and one at twenty weeks. Still, I couldn't get over how special it was to see our baby boys on the screen. I held Nadine's hand as Luana ran the wand over Nadine's belly. I couldn't take my eyes off the screen as I watched the boys wiggle. According to Luana, they appeared healthy and unaffected by last night's incident.

After Luana finished with the ultrasound, I helped Nadine to the bathroom. We got her urine sample, then returned to the bedroom, where Luana took Nadine's vitals, as well as a vial of blood.

Luana signed to Nadine, and the chief interpreted. "I want to continue seeing you once per week for urine tests. You'll have to do kick counts to make sure the babies are still moving. Once per day, count how long it takes each baby to kick ten times. If it takes more than two hours, alert me right away."

Luana turned to Onyx, and Cauac added, "I'm going to leave you with medical equipment so you can take Nadine's blood pressure and vitals daily. Nadine should stay on bed rest, only getting out of bed to shower and use the bathroom. Preeclampsia puts stress on the body, and we want to reduce that stress as much as possible."

"What other kinds of risks are we looking at?" I asked.

Luana turned to me and signed. "Preeclampsia, as well as being pregnant with multiples, increases the risk of preterm labor," her father said. "It's too early to deliver now, but waiting too long can be risky for the mother. We typically plan for women with preeclampsia to give birth at thirty-seven weeks, but since you're having twins, we may be looking at thirty-six weeks depending on how the pregnancy is progressing. However, in cases like this, delivery can happen much sooner and unexpectedly. I will have all the medical equipment ready to go in case Nadine goes into labor early."

"What do we do if that happens?" I asked.

"It's my philosophy that mothers should be as comfortable as possible throughout the delivery process," Chief Cauac interpreted for Luana. "I've assisted in many home births. However, due to Nadine's condition, I believe it best if Nadine labors and delivers in the hospital."

"How long will we have to stay?" Nadine asked. "It's not safe for us to leave the house for long periods of time."

Luana appeared sympathetic, and Cauac's tone reflected that. "Since the boys will most certainly be premature, they will require extra care and equipment after delivery. That said, since Onyx is here with you and you have a nurse in the house, I'm willing to provide all the equipment you'll need to keep the boys here. I'll be available on-call anytime you need me to portal back for assistance. Of course, plans may change if your preeclampsia worsens, but for now, you can stay home with close monitoring."

"That all sounds good," Nadine said. "Thank you so much for all your help. One more question. Can we still have sex?"

"Nadine…" I started, but Chief Cauac didn't even miss a beat interpreting.

"That depends on your typical reaction to it. If it's a relaxing activity for you, it can actually lower blood pressure."

Nadine gave a light smile. "Excellent."

Nadine didn't seem bothered by all of this information, as if all the new meds she'd been prescribed and the doctor's orders were more of a comfort to her than anything. I think she'd come to expect this kind of news and had become accustomed to dealing with it.

Her nonchalant nature helped ease my nerves over the next few days. I worried for her and the babies, but all Nadine could talk about was how excited she was to meet them. Since she couldn't get out of bed, we spent a lot of time making things for the babies. I'd found craft supplies in Helena's closet, and Nadine was learning to crochet. She'd already made several hats for the twins, and we'd worked together to make each of them their own fleece tie blanket.

Nadine was learning how to crochet baby socks the following week while I worked on hanging some of the pictures she'd drawn for the babies. Her drawings had the babies' names on them with cats crawling over the letters. They were really cute.

Our room had become crowded with medical equipment that Luana dropped off when she came to visit. I'd rearranged the furniture to make room for two incubators. We prayed we wouldn't need them, but we wanted to be prepared for anything. I'd had to move the bed to another wall, and everything that we usually stored beneath it was still piled out of the way in the bathroom.

I arranged Dean's sign over his incubator, then stepped back. "What do you think?"

Oliver meowed at my feet like he approved.

"Mm…" Nadine mused from the bed. "I think Marcus's sign is a little crooked."

I nudged the frame just a little. "Better?"

"Better." Nadine set her crochet project aside and began stroking Isa's head.

I didn't even have to think about it when I grabbed a bottle of lotion off the nightstand and sat on the bed beside her. I ran lotion over her hands and began massaging them. "How are you feeling?"

"It's hard to breathe sometimes, but I think that's just from the babies getting bigger."

"We can't know that for sure. We should mention it to Luana when she comes this week."

"I've told her everything," Nadine assured me. "I'm not vomiting, so that's a plus."

"If you start vomiting, I'm taking you to the hospital right away," I warned.

"Deal," she agreed, though she sounded certain it wasn't going to happen.

I finished massaging her hands. "We only have to make it a few more weeks. You three better behave yourselves."

Nadine snickered as she ran her hand over her large belly. "I have a feeling these boys are going to be nothing but trouble."

"The least they can do is wait until they're teenagers," I teased as I stood from the bed.

I didn't like the feeling of the lotion on my hands, so I went to the bathroom to wash it off. The counter in the bathroom was stacked with boxes we'd kept under the bed that I hadn't had a chance to return after rearranging the room. I ran the water, then looked around for the soap. I found it shoved in the corner behind one of the boxes and pulled it out.

Oliver chose that moment to jump up on the counter. There wasn't any room for him, and he could barely fit all four legs on the edge of the sink.

"Oliver, no!" I scolded.

I nudged him off the edge of the counter with my elbow. He clamored for a foothold, and it all happened so fast. Oliver's tail swished, and it smacked into the pile of boxes. The box on top teetered, and I rushed to catch it, but it was already too late. The box burst open, spilling its contents into the sink under the rushing water.

Panic swept through me when I saw the photographs and other mementos shrink under the water. It was Nadine's memento box.

*Fuck!* Oliver took off running out of the room. He knew damn well he was in trouble.

I hurried to shut the water off, but the damage was already done. Photographs were soaking wet, and the ticket from our first date was beyond repair.

"Lucas, are you hurt?" Nadine called.

"No, I—" I cut off. How did I even begin to explain to her what happened? I pulled the photographs out of the sink and laid them out on the floor, as if I could still save them. The corners were wrinkled, and some of the ink had smudged on a few of them. I couldn't even begin to express the sickness that rose in my gut. I felt horrible.

I heard footsteps, then the sound of Talia's and Grant's voices as they came into the bedroom.

"Is everything okay?" Talia asked.

"We heard a crash," Grant added.

"Lucas is in the bathroom," Nadine told them. "I'm not sure what happened."

"I'm okay," I called.

The bathroom door was open, though, and Talia came to investigate. She gasped when she saw what I'd done. I was on my knees on the floor, trying to separate everything so it could dry, but it was no use. It was already ruined.

I leaned back on my heels hopelessly. "Nadine's going to hate me," I whispered.

"No," Talia said gently. "Just… be honest with her."

I drew a deep breath, but my heart was pounding. "All right. Can you help me?"

Talia helped gather the things, and I placed a few items back in the box that hadn't been completely destroyed. There wasn't much.

I dropped my head and stepped out of the bathroom. "Nad, I'm sorry—"

Nadine's breath caught, and she threw her hands over her mouth. "Is that…?"

"Your memento box fell into the sink," I admitted. "Oliver accidentally knocked it over."

Tears sprang to Nadine's eyes. "Oh, Goddess, Lucas. All my pictures… they're ruined."

Grant quickly grabbed a towel and placed it on the bed, and Talia and I spread the mementos next to Nadine.

"I think some of them can be salvaged," I said hollowly.

Nadine stared down at the items I'd destroyed. A faraway look entered her eyes, like she couldn't believe what she was seeing. She looked wholly broken. "Some of these pictures don't have digital copies. These were all I had."

"Nadine, I am *so* sorry—" I started.

Tears streamed down her cheeks. "It isn't your fault. I manifested this because I called the box stupid. I didn't want this box to be all I had left of my family, and now I don't even have that."

She reached for the ticket from our first date, and it crumbled into two pieces in her hand. She went to pick up a photo of her and her parents, but drew away at the last second, as if afraid that too would fall apart.

"There are a few things that didn't get destroyed," I said desperately as I picked through the box. "Your dad's license plate is still good. Your mom's apron got some soap on it, but we can wash that—"

"*No!*" Nadine cried.

I went rigid.

"You don't understand! If we wash it, it's not going to smell like her anymore." Nadine brought the apron to her nose, and the dejected look on her face broke my heart.

"It got wet, and it's already lost her scent," Nadine cried. "All these photos, all my memories, they're destroyed…"

Talia knelt at Nadine's side and spoke gently. "I know this is really hard, but you have to remember, these are just things. It was the moments and the memories that mattered."

"No, these aren't just *things*," Nadine bit. "This is the last stuff I have to remember everyone by. My parents are gone. Grammy's gone. This is all that's left of them."

"Your memories will always be with you," Grant offered.

"Fuck my memories. I don't want to live in the past. I want these tangible things here in the moment with me right now." Nadine's shoulders began to heave with heavy sobs.

"I can't tell you how sorry I am," I told her softly.

She wiped her eyes. "Can I just… be alone for a while?"

I had the horrible thought that she was never going to forgive me for this. I knew it was an accident, but it still made me feel like the worst husband in the world. I should've been more careful. Those mementos meant everything to her.

I turned to follow Talia and Grant out the door, but Nadine stopped me. "Lucas? Where are you going?"

I paused. "I thought you wanted to be alone."

"Alone with my *husband*," she begged.

My heart lifted, and I hoped she would forgive me. I shut the door behind Talia and Grant, and Nadine moved over on the bed. I moved the mementos aside, then pulled back the covers to snuggle up beside her, taking her in my arms.

"I really am sorry," I whispered.

She sniffled. "I know it wasn't your fault. I'm just really sad. I need you to hold me."

I kissed the top of her head. "Darling, I can certainly do that."

Nadine shivered, and I quickly pulled off my sweatshirt and wrapped it around her shoulders. She pulled it close around her and inhaled the scent. For some reason, that made her cry harder.

Nadine's tears soaked into my shirt. "I'm glad you're here. You're the only person who can help me when I'm grieving."

It was really comforting to hear that. Her words repeated in my mind, and something hit me. I quickly conjured the Reaper Records and flipped the book open with one hand.

Nadine tilted her head. "What are you looking for?"

I pulled her tighter to my chest with the other arm. "What you just said… that I can help when you're grieving. It made me think of the grief spell I couldn't figure out. Maybe I can use my magic to help."

I found the page I was looking for and skimmed the spell again. "It says I need to feel into your grief and draw it out. Do you want to try it?"

Nadine looked over the spell. "What does it do exactly?"

I reread the spell. "I think it puts your grief into physical form, like you can talk to someone who's passed on—not in a literal, ghostly sense, but like an illusion. I think it will help if you can talk it out."

Nadine nodded. "I want to talk to Grammy."

"All right. Let's give it a shot," I said.

I wrapped my arms around Nadine, drawing her close to my chest. She kept her eyes closed and steadied her breathing. I reached out with my magic and let it flow into her. According to the records, I was supposed to be able to sense her grief deep in the pit of her stomach.

My power hit a wall, like there was a hollow emptiness that my magic brushed up against. I knew immediately that was the grief I was looking for. I twisted my magic around it and called it to the surface.

Dark energy swirled out of Nadine's body. She trembled in my arms. "Lucas, what's that?"

"It's okay," I assured her. "It's your grief. She wants to talk to you."

I guided the energy out of her, and a figure took shape in front of us. Only, it wasn't Helena.

It was Nadine.

She appeared as solid as the version of Nadine lying in my arms. Every inch of her body was the same, except this version of her wasn't pregnant. She looked so much like my Nadine that I could've easily been fooled into thinking they were one and the same. And maybe that was the point—she was a part of her.

"Why'd you make *me?*" Nadine sneered. "I thought I was going to get to talk to Grammy."

I shook my head. "I didn't do it intentionally. All I did was manifest your grief into physical form. I think she took the form you needed to talk to the most."

"What am I supposed to say to her?" Nadine asked bitterly. She eyed her grief up and down in a cold manner. "I mean, she's me."

"Speak from your heart," I told her.

She took a deep breath. "All right… How do I get rid of you?"

"Nad, I don't think that's—" I started.

"No, I'm serious," Nadine cut me off. "I keep thinking I'm better, yet she keeps coming back."

Nadine turned toward her grief. "I thought I dealt with you when my parents died, but you're still here. What do I have to do to get rid of you once and for all?"

"You don't," her grief answered. She sounded just like Nadine, but she spoke calmly, like she understood Nadine's feelings. "I'm a part of you now, and I'm here to stay."

Nadine shook her head, like she refused to accept that. "No. I got rid of my darkness. I can remove any curse. I can get rid of you, too."

"I can change, if that's what you want from me," Grief Nadine said. "But I'm not going away, because I can't."

"Well, you need to, because I'm sick of you hanging around," Nadine ordered. "You've been here for years, ever since my parents died. Then again when Amy died, and now Grammy. No matter what I do, you just keep getting stronger. I don't want to feel this way anymore. I don't want to end up like Beau, whose grief consumed him for decades. I refuse to let you become all that's left of me. I want to move on, which means you have to go."

Grief Nadine remained calm. "I'll always be with you, whether you wish me to be or not. You'll never be able to get rid of me. If I become all you are, that is a choice that you have made. You can choose to become nothing but grief, or you can choose another path."

"Tell me what I need to do, so I can move on," Nadine begged.

"There is no moving on," her grief responded. "Only moving through. Moving on means forgetting; moving through means continuing despite. You must feel this in order to reconcile yourself to it."

"You're lying," Nadine spat. "If I let myself feel it, there is no way out of this pain."

"Your heart hurts because you are resisting the process," Grief Nadine explained. "Your loss is not a failure, but a completion of a cycle. I know how you feel, Nadine, because I am you. Our grief reflects our desire to remain connected, and you're afraid that if you aren't hurting, you'll lose your connection to the people you love. But you can tap into that connection at any time and keep your loved ones in your life. You must accept that the connection is not gone, but merely changed into something else, and you must change with it."

Nadine sat a little straighter. "Why are you being so difficult? You're only a piece of me, which means I have power over you. I can choose to feel however I want. As time passes, I'm not going to feel this way anymore. One day, I'll get to a place where my parents' death and Grammy's death don't hurt anymore."

"It doesn't work that way," her grief stated. "Hundreds of years could pass, and it could still hurt just as much. The only way to make it hurt less is to love more."

Nadine recoiled. "Love is what broke my heart in the first place."

Grief Nadine crossed her hands in front of herself. "The only way to get rid of me is if you don't love at all. But if you were willing to let go of love, I wouldn't be here in the first place."

"That's ridiculous," Nadine sneered. "I'll never stop loving people."

Her grief appeared sympathetic. "Then you're going to have to continue to grieve, because that's the price you pay for love."

"You're not listening to me!" Nadine shouted.

My heart broke for her. I wanted to stop the spell, but I also thought maybe her grief could still help her.

"You *my* emotion, and I'm in control of you," Nadine added.

"You're acting like this is a choice, but I'm one of the few things you don't get to choose," Grief Nadine said softly. "The harder you suppress me, the stronger I'll become. Allow me to become a part of you, and we'll do this together."

Nadine turned her head into my chest, like she couldn't bear to look at her grief any longer. "Lucas, you need to stop this. This was a bad idea."

I looked back to her grief, begging desperately for one last piece of advice that would change Nadine's mind. But her grief only replied with a sad look. I realized her grief couldn't help if Nadine didn't want her to.

I waved my hand, and the image of Nadine standing next to our bedside became a mass of energy once again. Wisps of black magic returned to Nadine's body, and the spell ended.

I curled my arms tightly around Nadine. "I'm sorry it didn't work."

Nadine sniffled and drew away. "It will. We'll figure out this spell together. When I've figured out how to defeat my grief, then you can do the spell again. Then I'll vanquish her and make her go away."

I wanted to tell her I didn't think that was going to work, but when I looked into her desperate eyes, I knew my words would be anything but helpful. The only thing I could do was be here for her through it.

"We'll figure it out," I agreed. "I'm right here, Nad."

She relaxed into me. "I'm glad you're here, Lucas, but I wish that was enough to stop me from falling apart. I know you love me, and that all our friends are in my corner, but none of that helps to make this go away."

I stroked her hair. I wish I could tell her it would get better someday, but I understood grief all too well. Her grief was right, and I hadn't realized the truth of it until I heard it said out loud. This wasn't something that disappeared. It was just something that you learned to live with because it would always be a part of you.

I would never get over Eric's death. A thousand years could come and go, and I'd be just as sad over his suicide as I was the day that it happened. It didn't sting as much anymore, because the shock was over and so much time had passed, but I still missed my brother every day. I'd grieve for him until time itself ran out, and because I'd loved him so much, I was willing to accept that.

Nadine wasn't. She'd do anything to escape. I knew how she felt, because there'd been some dark days after Eric died when I'd pleaded to Mother Miriam to take my love for my brother away, just so my pain had somewhere to go. That didn't happen, though. It festered inside of me and made me sick until I realized the only way to cope with it would be to allow myself to accept that this was the way things had to be.

Nadine had a long way to go before she got to that point, if she did at all.

One day, she would understand, and I would be right there alongside her to help her through it. I understood the point of this spell now. It was clear I had more than one job as a reaper. I could help the dead cross over into Alora, but as long as I was living, I could also help the living cross over into a new life after they'd lost somebody.

Problem was, I was still learning how to do that myself.

# nadine
## TWENTY

Lucas and I didn't talk about that day after he performed the spell. There seemed to be no solution, and my grief was insistent she wasn't going to walk away. What a bitch.

The best I could do was ignore her, and maybe she'd disappear on her own.

I knew the best way to take my mind off all of it was to dive into fiction. On Sunday, I asked Lucas to bring me a book from the library. He'd brought a whole stack, but I'd already read most of them before. I found a few I hadn't read and binged them all day. I was already on my third book that evening, and it had to be my favorite so far—not because it was good, but because it was laughably silly.

The whole premise of the book was that this woman had mind-blowing sex with a ghost in her sleep, and she'd learned from a psychic that the ghost had since possessed a man but lost his memories. But it was okay, because the man he'd possessed was a bad guy who'd been shot and killed, and the ghost had possessed an empty vessel. To find the ghost—who was apparently the love of her life—she had to gather clues about him and then fuck the guys who fit the bill until she found the one who made her toes curl. Apparently once they made love, his memories would be restored, and they could live out their days happily fucking until they died. Or in his case, died again. The whole thing was ridiculous, and yet I couldn't put it down. I tried to stifle a laugh as I read the passage.

*The man from the bar brought her into the bedroom and tossed her onto the bed. Her skirt rode up around her thighs, tickling her sensual areas. She was already turned on. He realized with a thrill that she wasn't wearing any underwear. His trembling member turned hard so fast it broke the zipper on his jeans, and he tossed the pants aside. She took one look at his rod and knew it was going to be the best pleasure stick she'd ever ridden. She was certain the man from the bar was the erotic ghost she'd encountered two months ago. His Johnson was everything she'd dreamed it to be.*

*He leaned over her and whispered seductively, "Do you want me to make you come, sweetheart?"*

*"Yes," she begged. Her nipples became hard immediately. "I want you to fuck me hard."*

*He shoved four fingers inside of her, ravaging her with his vigorous touch—*

I burst into a fit of laughter. This had to be the silliest thing I'd ever read. If Lucas ever came at me with four fingers and a *vigorous touch*, he'd be waking up with a black eye.

Lucas sat beside me on the bed, reading one of the books I'd recommended to him. "What's so funny?"

"Paranormal erotica," I giggled. "It's hilarious. The author refers to his junk as a *trembling member* and *pleasure stick*."

"Oh?" Lucas cocked a curious eyebrow. "Would it be any better if the author referred to it as a *magic wand*?"

I nudged him playfully. We had a bit of an inside joke going about that one. "You're not going to get the full effect unless I read it to you. Listen."

I restarted the passage, reading it out loud. I stopped at the part where he shoved four fingers inside of her.

Lucas set his book aside. "Keep reading..."

Obviously, he wanted to see how much worse it could get.

*She tried not to scream, because the neighbors would hear. She bit down on the pillow, but the man from the bar ripped the item from her hands and threw it across the room.*

*"You don't have to hold back for me, baby," he said. "Scream for me. As loud as you can. Scream my name."*

*She didn't know his name. She only knew one thing about him, and that was that he was a god in bed.*

*"Oh, God!" she screamed, begging for mercy.*

*"You want my willy inside you?"*

*"Yes, God, yes!" she begged.*

*He laid down beside her, and she screamed because she thought his ten-inch meat sword was a one-eyed snake. She grabbed it to throw it off the bed, and he howled.*

*"Oh, sorry," she said, before settling down and opening her legs—*

"Oh, my Goddess!" I cried. Tears of laughter streamed down my face. "I didn't think it could get any worse, but it does."

Lucas chuckled and ran a hand down my leg. "Maybe we need to show these characters how it's done."

My eyes caught something further down the page. "Someone needs to, because it gets *even worse!*"

*He spread her labia and rammed his massive pecker inside of her. She gasped and moaned as his dong moved circles inside of her.*

*"John Thomas is the name," he whispered...*

I couldn't continue. I was gasping for breath now because I was laughing so hard. "Would it hurt... to just... say dick?"

Lucas's eyebrows shot up. "We're concerned with semantics when his cock is literally moving in *circles*? Is he part helicopter?"

I laughed even harder. "Wait, *cock* is a good word, too."

Lucas smirked as his hands inched up my legs. "His cock grew hard in wanting..."

"Oh?" I set my book aside. "She became *wet* at his touch."

Lucas's hand moved between my thighs. "He didn't care much for the paranormal erotica, but the excitement in his wife's eyes turned him on. He wanted to take her right here."

I bit my lip as I eyed him up and down. His white t-shirt stretched across his muscled torso, and heat pooled between my thighs. "She wanted him, too, but she was self-conscious because she hadn't bathed all day."

Lucas kissed the side of my face, his breath tickling my ear. I loved it when he did that. "He didn't mind, but rather suggested they take a bath *together.*"

My eyebrows shot up. "Really?"

Lucas smiled but didn't break character. "That is what he suggested, yes."

"Hold on." I picked up my novel again. "Did this scene *turn you on?*"

Lucas sucked a breath between his teeth. "That would be weird, wouldn't it?"

"You didn't want me to keep going to see how bad it got," I teased, swatting him playfully with the book. "You wanted to see how *good* it got."

Lucas kissed me again, so sensually I could easily forget what I'd been saying. "Well, I was obviously disappointed."

"What was it that did you in?" I snickered. "It was the word *willy*, wasn't it?"

Lucas smirked, and that was all the answer I needed.

"We can't have that," I said. "She gently set the book aside and asked him to help her out of bed."

Lucas stood and came around the side of the bed. "He did as she asked, for she was his queen."

I got a thrill in my stomach hearing him say that. It was so sweet.

Lucas helped me out of bed and into the bathroom. He flipped on the lights, then dimmed them as he led me to the jet tub. He poured some bubbles on the bottom of the bath, then twisted the faucet.

"He turned on the water, which reminded her of warm summer days," he narrated. "She thought back to the waterfall they never got the chance to make love in."

I laughed, loving every second of this. "But the waterfall quickly drifted from her mind when he dropped his pants. All she could think about was his massive *eggplant*."

Lucas practically ripped the button of his jeans as he pretended to recreate the scene from the novel. I was giggling so hard I had to sit on the side of the tub.

"She couldn't take her eyes off his bulging muscles," he teased as he pulled his shirt over his head. He flexed his biceps for me.

"Oh, yes," I agreed playfully. "He was so turned on by her breasts that had grown to the size of cabbages, due to her raging pregnancy hormones."

Lucas nearly choked on his own laughter. "He quickly reminded her she was supposed to be narrating *better* than the paranormal erotica nonsense that had turned her on only moments ago."

I covered my mouth as I snickered. "But in fact, it was *he* who was turned on by the man from the bar's *trouser snake*."

Lucas lifted my nightgown above my head and dropped it to the floor. "She was delusional."

My gaze darted down to his hard on. "And yet he was so ready for her."

Lucas shot me a charming smile as he took my hand. He stepped into the tub, then helped me in. Neither of us said anything as we sank into the warm water. Lucas leaned against the back of the tub, and I rested my back against his chest, letting my head fall against his shoulder. Bubbles surrounded us, and they smelled of lavender. I felt so relaxed.

"This tub is perfect," I said dreamily.

"Yeah, I'm sure we're not the first to fuck in it," he teased. Lucas found a bar of soap on the lip of the tub and rubbed it in his hands, then spread the suds over my neck and shoulders.

"Mm…" I relaxed deeper into the water.

Lucas ran his hands up and down my arms, before sliding them across my tender breasts. I'd grown over a cup size during my pregnancy, but he was so gentle with them that they didn't hurt at all. His cock grew even harder against my back.

Lucas ran shampoo through my hair, massaging it gently into my scalp. I hadn't realized how much of a tension headache I had until he started massaging me. The tub was large enough for me to lay down in, so that he could rinse the suds from my hair. I sighed blissfully as the tension eased out of every muscle in my body. He found the sugar scrub Mandy had made me and massaged it over my hands, until they were silky smooth.

Warm water dripped down my body as Lucas kissed the side of my neck. I tilted my head so he could run his lips over my skin. Tingles spread down to my toes, putting me more at ease. It was a perfect, intimate moment.

Soon, my wanting for him became too much, and I took his shaft in my hand and began pumping. Lucas got a hungry look in his eyes, and he placed his hands on my hips, then positioned me atop him, my back to his front. He thrust upward, taking me from behind. The first thrust made me gasp, and I grabbed the edge of the tub for support. Water sloshed around us, and we both gave a little giggle.

Lucas slowed, moving gently inside of me. His hand dipped between my legs, and I couldn't stop the moan that escaped my lips. I was loving every second of this.

Pleasure built up inside of me, and Lucas increased his speed. I reached my peak, and the most relaxing sensation burst inside of me, tingling down to my extremities. Lucas gasped as he thrust one more time, and he held me close as he came inside of me.

We sagged into the warm water together, letting out a collective sigh.

Lucas pushed my wet hair back and kissed the side of my face. "How do you feel, darling?"

I kept my eyes closed as I answered, "So, so relaxed."

We stayed in the water for a long time, until we started getting cold. Lucas helped me out of the tub and wrapped me in a warm bath robe. He fluffed the pillows on the bed and laid me on my left side, before running lotion over my arms and legs. My wedding ring felt tight on my hand, but when Lucas massaged my fingers, it felt better. Every touch was gentle, every caress sensual. I felt so at peace.

I closed my eyes and slowly drifted off to sleep.

I didn't know how long I was out, but I woke suddenly when Lucas gave a start. His breathing slowed quickly, like it was nothing more than a bad dream. He was still out cold.

Night had fallen, and the moonlight shone in through the windows. I rubbed my blurry eyes to get them to adjust to the darkness. I checked the clock to see it was already eleven o'clock.

A mild cramp deep in my belly prompted me to get out of bed. Slowly, I sat upright, giving myself a moment to breathe—which was becoming more difficult the bigger the twins got. One of the twins must've had a foot shoved under my right ribs, because it was really uncomfortable there. I got out of bed and waddled to the bathroom.

When I returned to the bed, Lucas stirred awake. "Everything okay?"

"I've got a stomach bug or something," I said.

He sat up straighter. "Vomiting?"

"No, I just have weird cramps," I told him. "It's nothing to worry about."

Lucas relaxed and moved closer to me, snuggling his frontside against my back. He draped his arm over me, holding my belly. I loved it when he did that. It made me feel so safe and protected.

Half an hour passed, and I couldn't find a comfortable position. I watched the clock and waited, but I couldn't fall back asleep. The moonlight seemed to darken, taking on a reddish hue. I placed my hands on my belly beside Lucas's and started counting kicks. The baby on my right was active and moving. The one on my left must've been sleeping, because I didn't feel any movement there.

My cramps worsened. I winced and shifted in bed. Lucas sat up straight in bed, never once moving his hand off my belly.

"Are you doing that?" he asked.

"Doing what?"

"That thing with your stomach. It's… hard. I think you're having a contraction!"

I scoffed. "It's just Braxton-Hicks contractions; they're normal. There's no way I'm in labor. We just hit thirty weeks. The babies can't be coming this soon…"

I trailed off as my eyes landed upon the incubators across the room. My stomach dropped. "Dear Goddess."

I went to sit up, but as I shifted, I heard a *pop*. Water gushed between my legs.

Tears of panic welled in my eyes. "It's too early!"

Lucas tossed the covers off himself so fast he was practically a blur. "I'll get the hospital bag and tell the others."

"Find Isa," I begged. "I need her."

It was unusual for Isa not to sleep by me. She must've gotten locked out of the room.

I didn't want Lucas to leave my side, but as the next contraction hit, the room seemed to disappear around me. I curled onto my side and squeezed my eyes shut tightly as the wave of tension washed over me. The pain was intense, and I couldn't believe I'd been lying in bed for thirty minutes in *labor* and hadn't realized it.

I couldn't wrap my head around how it was even possible to give birth this early. Luana had said the babies should be born closer to thirty-six weeks, unless complications arose. My preeclampsia was only mild—

I cut off mid-thought when I realized that I'd overlooked those symptoms as well. I was so used to being sick that something as simple as a headache or blurred vision didn't even register as out of the ordinary. Swollen hands were a normal part of pregnancy, so I hadn't thought that my ring being tight was anything unusual. The pain below my ribs had barely seemed like an inconvenience.

It was silly to think that all of this went over my head. I'd been showing symptoms of worsening preeclampsia all day, and now, I was going into labor. I had the thought that I couldn't trust myself to know what was happening with my own body. If I'd been more cautious, I'd have recognized something was wrong, and we might've been able to prevent this.

A horrifying thought hit, and I hoped to the Goddess I was wrong. The baby on the left wasn't moving. I thought he was asleep, but what if…?

The contractions were intensifying, and I couldn't organize my thoughts much beyond what my body was doing.

I heard clamoring all throughout the house. I was almost certain everyone must've awoken when they heard the commotion. Someone touched my shoulder, but I didn't know who it was. I shrugged them off. I wanted to tell them not to touch me, but I couldn't find my voice. Another contraction hit me, and it was like my whole body was being squeezed by an external, magical force.

"Nadine." Verla's kind voice brought me comfort. I opened my eyes to see her standing above me. "It's time to go to the hospital. We have to get you out of bed."

I couldn't fathom the thought of moving from where I lay. I feared if I did, I might collapse and never get back up. All I could manage to do was shake my head.

"If she can't talk already, she's pretty far along," I heard Onyx tell Lucas. "How long has she been contracting?"

"I—I don't know," Lucas stammered. "Less than an hour."

I heard shuffling near the medical equipment in the corner, then the snap of a glove.

Onyx appeared above me. "I'm going to check your cervix. Are you all right with that?"

I nodded.

Onyx pulled back the covers and gently moved the fabric of my bathrobe aside. She placed her fingers inside of me, which would normally be weird as fuck, but in the state I was in, I didn't mind at all. In fact, all I could think was that I was too hot and I just wanted to get rid of this bathrobe; I didn't care who was in the room. I stripped it off and tossed it to the floor.

"She's already at five centimeters," Onyx said calmly, though I was certain she was the only calm one in the whole room. "It looks like precipitous labor—meaning it's progressing quickly. In cases like this, mothers give birth within three hours after contractions begin, but it could be sooner. Lucas, you need to portal Luana back here *now*."

"It's almost midnight!" Lucas panicked. "Luana won't be at the clinic."

"Then find her at home," Onyx ordered. "I don't care where you look for her—just get her here. Go!"

"No!" I heard myself cry. I reached for Lucas and clung so tight to his arm that he couldn't go anywhere, even if he wanted to. I pulled him toward me, until he knelt at my side.

"Stay," I begged as tears beaded in my eyes. "One of the twins… he's not moving."

Lucas's features went stark white. It was all I could manage to tell him. I couldn't speak the truth out loud. Deep down, my intuition told me something was very wrong.

Lucas must've felt it, too. "But Talia saw us holding both babies in her vision. She felt Dean there with Marcus in the future."

"*Felt* him," I emphasized. The reality hit me harder than the contractions. Talia had felt Dean fighting alongside Marcus in her vision, but that didn't mean he was there in physical form. It could've been his spirit she recognized.

I knew without a shadow of a doubt that's exactly what it was. I was naturally intuitive, but the intuition I felt as a mother was beyond comprehension. I needed no one to confirm it.

There was nothing we could do. Dean was already gone.

"I felt him," Lucas realized, and his voice became hoarse. "In my dream. His last thoughts weren't words, but a feeling. I hadn't realized what I felt until now… He loved us both. So much."

"You have to bring him back," I begged.

"I can't," Lucas said hollowly.

"You brought me back," I reminded him.

"Under extraordinary circumstances," he said. "Even all the magic in the coven can't bring the dead back to life. You'd have to be god-like to do that."

I trembled as my grief began to take over. My grief was wrong to say I had a choice to let it consume me, because it already had.

"I have to get a doctor," Lucas told me desperately.

I didn't want Lucas to go. I reached out for him, but he was already gone. A soft hand met mine instead. My whole body shook as I squeezed Verla's hand.

*It's too soon,* I wanted to tell her, but I couldn't speak. I trembled as my body contracted, as if I could stop the labor and reverse it.

Verla knelt at my side and pushed my hair from my face. "I know you're scared, but I'm here for you. We all are."

Her words were so comforting that some of the tension in my body actually eased.

"You're about to meet your baby boys," Verla reminded me.

I tried to focus on that, because I couldn't think about alternative realities right now. If I lost myself in it, I didn't know if I'd make it out of this alive.

"You can do this," she encouraged. "Women give birth all the time. We're built for this."

Verla drew a deep breath, and I copied her. My breath wavered on the way out, but my panic began to subside. I had to compartmentalize my grief for now, because my babies needed me to focus.

*All right, boys,* I told them silently. *We're going to do this. Together.*

Verla squeezed my hand again, assuring me she wasn't going anywhere. "I remember when your mother gave birth to you."

I thought she was trying to distract me, which was nice.

"It was a beautiful birth—only six hours long," Verla continued. "You came out eight pounds, two ounces. Your parents were thrilled. I led your mother through a birthing meditation. Would you like me to do the same for you?"

I'd never known Verla had been at my birth. It was comforting to hear in my time of need. I wanted to ask her about it, but all I could do was nod.

"Close your eyes and listen to the sound of my voice," Verla instructed. "You're in the midst of a beautiful transformation. Your body is strong, and it's doing exactly what it's meant to. Release all tension in your shoulders, your arms, and your legs. There is nothing you have to do, because your uterus will do all the work for you."

As the next contraction came, I willed my body to remain relaxed. I was shocked at how much better it felt. It was still painful, but it was easier to detach myself from the fear.

"Your babies are coming at the perfect time," Verla said gently. "Recall that your boys are meant to become demigods—born of two talented supernatural parents beneath a significant astrological event. A full lunar eclipse has begun."

I could hardly believe it. I forced my eyes open and looked out the window. Verla was right. The red light from the moon I'd noticed before had been the beginning of the total eclipse. I could see the moon from where I lay, looming high in the sky. It had become a deep red color.

"Allow your boys to arrive, just as they planned," Verla said softly.

I had been terrified of the boys being born too early, but this was exactly as it was meant to be. It was comforting to hear Verla speak of the boys arriving together, as if this was all part of a cosmic plan. Even if Dean wasn't going to make it, I was still bringing him into the world tonight.

This was his time—what little he had—and he needed me right now.

I completely relaxed, and though the pain in my belly was intense, I welcomed it.

"Breathe," Verla reminded me, and she guided me through the next contraction.

A portal bloomed across the room, and Lucas and Luana raced through. "We're here!" Lucas cried. I didn't know how long it'd taken him to find Luana, but it seemed like forever. It was probably only fifteen minutes, but my contractions had grown even more intense in that time.

Lucas rushed to my side, while Luana hurried toward Onyx, who already had a pair of rubber gloves ready for her. The pair of them moved in sync. They didn't need to be able to speak the same language, because the medical staff in a birthing room seemed to have a language all their own.

"It's okay," Verla told Lucas. "It's exactly as it's meant to be."

She gestured out the window, and when Lucas saw the eclipse, his shoulders relaxed. Relief entered his eyes as he knelt by my side and took my hand. "Our demigod babies... We're about to become parents."

I nodded as pure joy filled my chest. A moment later, a pain deep in my abdomen overtook my joy, and I winced. I still lay on my side. Lucas quickly situated himself on the bed behind me to rub my back.

His touch was like magic. He pressed down firmly on my lower back, and so much of the pain eased. It was nothing like I expected. All I had to go by was what I'd seen in movies, and it usually depicted the mother screaming at the father for all the pain she was in. I couldn't imagine feeling any animosity toward Lucas. He was everything I needed right now, because this was the moment that our family grew from two to four, and I wouldn't have it any other way. This moment was so, so beautiful.

In fact, it was so beautiful I barely noticed Luana checking my cervix. She held up eight fingers, indicating I was almost fully dilated. I couldn't believe how fast I was progressing. Contractions had only started forty-five minutes ago. Onyx had said my labor was progressing faster than normal, and she hadn't been exaggerating.

"Go get Chloe and Talia," Lucas ordered someone. "We need them to interpret."

I heard worried voices across the house. At first, I thought they were terrified for me—that I'd gone into labor so soon. Then I heard the sound of the front door slamming, and the voices stopped. Everyone had rushed outside, though I didn't know why.

Moments later, the sound of shouting came from far in the distance, yet too close to the safe house for comfort. The blast of exploding battle orbs shook the house.

"What's… happening?" I managed to rasp out.

"Nothing to worry yourself with," Verla said as she rushed into the room. I hadn't even realized she'd left my side.

She dropped her voice as she spoke to someone, thinking I couldn't hear, but I honed in on her words. "Chloe and Talia aren't available right now. Executors are at our borders, but the others have gone to fight them off."

"Tonight of all nights?" Onyx asked incredulously.

It was obvious. The Executors were coming to take my babies. I didn't know how they knew to come tonight, but my intuition told me exactly why they were here.

And yet somehow, I believed Verla was right. I *didn't* have to worry myself with that right now. My friends had three of the Oaken Wands, and they would obliterate any Executors who came our way. Outside, there would be carnage and death, but right here in this room, I would give life.

The Executors fell from my mind. All that mattered was what was happening right here.

Another half an hour passed, and the contractions became even more intense and closer together.

I felt the urge to push. I rolled onto my back and Lucas was right there to hold me. He was sitting on the bed, and he wrapped his arms around me as I leaned against him. I squeezed his hand as an intense contraction rippled through my abdomen.

"That's it!" Onyx cried happily.

"He's crowning!" Verla added with excitement.

The whole atmosphere of the room shifted. Their celebration seemed infectious, and though this was one of the most difficult things I ever had to do, I felt incredible joy.

"Another push, Nadine," Onyx encouraged. "You're doing great. Five… four… three… two… one…"

I pushed until she reached the count of one, then paused to catch my breath. Tears sprang from my eyes. I couldn't believe I was about to meet my baby boys.

"One more push," Onyx said.

I looked up to see tears of joy streaming down Lucas's face. He was so *in* the moment, so focused. It was beautiful.

Lucas squeezed my shoulders. "You've got this."

Complete peace washed over me. I couldn't imagine anything that could bring me closer to my husband or to our babies. Another contraction squeezed my belly, and though I pushed, I was completely and utterly relaxed.

Relief swept through me as the baby emerged, the magic of the moment unmatched by any spell I'd ever cast before. I looked down to see Luana holding a very tiny, squirming little boy. I couldn't believe how small he was. He couldn't be more than four pounds. Lucas hugged me close, and my whole body shook as I cried tears of joy.

"Marcus," I whispered. "He's so little."

Verla looked at the clock. "May sixteenth, twelve-eleven a.m. Born at the peak of the eclipse."

"He's not crying," Lucas panicked. "Why isn't he crying?"

Luana placed two fingers on Marcus's chest, and a white glow filled his little body. Still, no sound came. I had the horrifying thought that he wasn't going to make it, either.

Luana came around the side of the bed and placed Marcus straight on my chest. Our skin connected, and Luana draped a tiny blanket over Marcus's back. The feeling of joy when I touched my son for the first time was unmatched. Marcus curled his tiny legs upward and snuggled close to me. I didn't want this moment to ever end.

Luana tried her healing magic again, placing her fingers on Marcus's back. A beautiful glow filled the room, only this time, it wasn't just her magic. The skeleton key I wore around my neck emanated a powerful white light, as if it too was working to heal him. I hadn't taken it off since Lucas put it around my neck the day I tossed my memento box across the room.

I was shocked. Grammy had said this key held a protection charm, but that never made sense, because it hadn't protected us before. It was clear in that moment that this was so much more. Grammy had said the key wasn't meant for me, and I realized now that's because it was meant for *Marcus.*

The most glorious sound broke from Marcus's lungs. It was so quiet, but that tiny little cry was everything.

"That's it, baby boy," Lucas said gently. "You're so strong."

I started to cry in relief, but gasped as another contraction hit me. Luana quickly handed Marcus off to Onyx, and Verla already had gloves on to help. Across the room, Onyx worked at the incubator, hooking Marcus up to all kinds of wires and tubes. I couldn't be more grateful for my birthing team. Because of them, Marcus had a fighting chance at life.

Sweat dripped down my brow as I gave another big push. Suddenly, our baby Dean came into the world. It was over so quickly. I couldn't believe how fast it all happened.

Everything seemed so quiet at that moment. My body sagged against Lucas, feeling so relieved. Small contractions continued, but nothing like it was before.

Luana must've known since the moment he arrived that Dean wasn't going to survive. I was certain she had felt it with her magic, because she didn't try to resuscitate him. She simply wrapped Dean up in a blanket and placed him on my chest. She let us cry over him as we held his little body close. Dean was even smaller than Marcus, and he was precious in every way. Lucas placed his hand on Dean's back, and together, we let the tears flow.

People poked and prodded at me, but I barely felt it. All that mattered was this tiny little boy in my arms. He was so perfect.

Lucas ran his fingers over Dean's tiny little arms. When I looked up at my husband, he had the most loving look in his eyes. He didn't even look sad; he looked so, *so* in love.

"I'm sorry," I whispered.

Lucas shook his head. "You have nothing to be sorry for. You did great."

"My body didn't do its job," I sobbed. "If I'd been healthier, then maybe we would've had more time with him. I didn't see the signs…"

"You can't blame yourself, Nad," Lucas insisted. "Sometimes babies die, and it's part of life. It's the worst part, but this is a process of death."

I stroked the little hairs on the top of Dean's perfect little head, and I realized that as much grief I felt from losing him, I felt so much more love. Nothing could have prepared me for how deeply I loved these boys.

"I'll always remember you, baby boy," I whispered.

I kissed the top of my baby boy's head, and that deep love I felt for him intensified. It was so overwhelming that I wasn't sure it was all my own, as if my love had quadrupled.

I realized then that it wasn't all mine. It was mine, it was Lucas's, it was Marcus's, *and* it was Dean's. Though Dean wasn't in this body, I could still feel him here in this room.

"He's not just a memory," I realized, looking up to Lucas. "He's an *energy*. Even though I know people live on after death, I always thought they moved on without us. It doesn't work that way, though. We can still have our loved ones with us at any time. We can spiritually reach out to them. It's not going to be the same, but they can still be here. Not just in memory, but in spirit."

Lucas seemed comforted by my realization, because he completely relaxed beside me. "You're right. We'll always be a family—not the three of us, but the *four* of us."

"No matter where he goes after this, he's a part of our life now," I agreed.

I shuddered to think of everything we had lost. We hadn't just lost an infant—we'd lost a toddler, a kid, a teenager. We lost birthdays and Halloweens. We lost all the hugs and kisses, and everything in between. We'd never get to see him fall in love, attend his wedding, or have children of his own. We'd never get to see him grow close to Marcus and be brothers, like they deserved to be.

But none of that made his existence meaningless. We'd had thirty wonderful weeks with him, and we would always be his parents. As much as this hurt, I would still go through it all over again… just to hold him in this moment, and to be with him for the short while we had.

"It was worth it," I told Lucas. "I want to honor him and throw him a celebration."

Lucas stroked Dean's cheek with the back of his hand. "We will. Our baby boy will get the proper sendoff he deserves."

Lucas and I snuggled with Dean for a long time while the others cleaned up. Blood soaked the sheets, but Verla worked around us to change the bedding and mattress liner. I barely noticed any of it as I took in these precious moments with our baby boy.

After Luana checked over Marcus and took his vitals, she wheeled his incubator to the side of the bed so the four of us could be together. I wanted to hold him so badly, and though he was close, he still seemed so far away. His incubator was merely a see-through box, with only holes for our hands to touch him. He was hooked up to all kinds of tubes and looked so fragile.

Onyx helped me into a clean robe and pulled a fresh blanket over us just before I heard multiple pairs of footsteps outside the room. I lay in Lucas's arms, with Dean wrapped against us both.

"Are you up for visitors?" Verla asked.

"Yes," I said. "They can come in."

Verla opened the door and welcomed the others inside. Everyone was here, except Miles.

"The perimeter is clear, and the Executors have all been eliminated," Professor Warren told Verla in a low voice.

"The reaper woman showed up and got rid of all the Executors, though she left before we could explain what was happening here," Mandy added. "She saved us, and we're safe now. Miles suffered an injury to his arm. He's out of it, but he's in bed resting."

The others remained quiet, and the atmosphere was melancholy. I was certain they'd all heard the news already.

Grant's eyes locked on Dean, and tears flowed down his cheeks. "I'm so sorry. It shouldn't have ended up like this."

Lucas sniffled, holding back tears. "It's okay, you guys. Dean's still here with us."

Chloe and Talia stood side-by-side, and the end of their Wands began to glow. Chloe shot Luana a questioning glance. It was obvious by her expression that Luana had much to tell us that she hadn't yet been able to communicate. Luana nodded kindly.

"Luana says there's nothing you could have done," Chloe said, conveying for the doctor. "Dean died in utero, and that's what triggered labor. After you were poisoned, it seems like your body was unable to filter all of it out naturally, and some of it went to your womb. Dean absorbed the poison in your body, so that Marcus could live—he saved his brother. You couldn't have detected this or known it was going to happen. This was beyond even Luana's power to fix."

Grant began to sob. "I can't believe this. I gave you that rotten ginger, and it caused all of this. I took your baby's life."

"No," Chloe said quickly, interpreting for Luana. "That can't have been it. Dean was a supernatural child, and for him to choose to take the poison in Marcus's place, it had to be a magical poison that he absorbed willingly. Otherwise, it would've affected both twins."

"Executors have been snooping around the safe house for months," Mandy pointed out. "Maybe they slipped past our wards somehow and poisoned Nadine."

"It's got to be," Chloe agreed. "They certainly know where we've been hiding, and they've been waiting for the right time to strike."

Grant wiped his eyes as his sadness was replaced by anger. He cracked his knuckles. "We're going to find whoever did this and kill them."

Talia placed a gentle hand on his arm. "That's not important right now. We can investigate later, but the damage is done, and Lucas and Nadine need support. We need to focus on them right now."

I didn't want them to focus on me, because right now, Marcus needed attention most. "We weren't sure Marcus was going to make it, either, but he's doing well in the incubator."

"Three pounds, six ounces," Lucas added.

"Luana says he's stronger than most," Chloe told us. "His demigod powers helped heal him. She can't usually heal a premature baby, because her powers are limited by the body's own systems. Most preemies don't have the strength to heal themselves. But demigods can generate their own energy, so their powers combined made him stronger. She estimates he'll be out of the incubator in just a few weeks."

"That's our boy," Lucas said proudly.

There was one thing I didn't understand, though, and I spoke up. "I'm so happy he's all right, but I don't understand how a baby can have this kind of power. His powers won't awaken until he's older."

"His full potential won't be unleashed until he's of age," Verla confirmed. "But a demigod child like this is overflowing with power. He may discover hints of power here and there before he comes into his full power."

I looked up to my friends. "Do you guys want to come and meet them?"

Warren and Mandy stood on one side of the bed, while Talia and Grant came around the other side, near the incubator. Talia couldn't take her eyes off Dean, and she was trying to hold back tears.

"It's okay," I told her. "You can cry."

She sniffled. "I'm just sad I never got to meet him."

"He's here with us," Lucas said. "If you want to say anything, I'm sure he'll feel it."

"Can I sing him a lullaby?" Talia asked.

I stroked Dean's head. "Of course."

Everyone gathered in close, and Talia began singing a traditional Miri-amic lullaby. After just a few notes, everyone else joined in.

*Sweet baby, sleep quiet*
*Sweet baby, don't cry*
*Sweet baby, just listen*
*To this lullaby*

*Sweet baby, you're so loved*
*Sweet baby, you're fine*
*I won't let you go*
*'Til morning light shines*

I couldn't explain the energy that filled the room when our voices came together. There were so many tears, but so much love. I kissed Dean's soft little head again, then shuddered. He was wrapped in a blanket, but still so cold.

"What's wrong?" Grant asked.

I pointed across the room to the top of the dresser. "Can you bring me Dean's hat?"

A chill traveled down my spine. The meaning of my words were clear, though nobody said anything. I was certain that we could all feel that it was time to say goodbye.

"And the onesie there," Lucas added.

Grant brought over the clothes, and he helped us dress our little boy for the first time.

Verla's voice cracked, and she held up a small gift bag. "I didn't think I'd be giving you this so soon. I got the boys something."

"You didn't have to," Lucas insisted as he took the gift bag. He pulled out the tissue paper and withdrew two leather-bound books. "Grimoires?"

"They can be whatever you want them to be," Verla said. "Grimoires, photo albums, journals—it's up to you."

I had the thought that whatever we put in Dean's book, he'd never get a chance to read it. But maybe he didn't have to read it to feel it.

I took one of the books from Lucas's hand and gave it back to Verla. "I want you all to write in it. Send Dean a message—tell him how loved he is. Then pass it on, and we can all fill the pages."

"That's a lovely idea," Professor Warren said kindly.

Chloe stepped forward. I noticed she was holding a camera, the same one Talia had used during our wedding. "If it's okay with you, Talia and I would like to take some pictures."

It was so nice of her to suggest, because these moments were all we had of Dean, until we met with him again. It was sad to think of all the things that could've been, but so beautiful to think of the things that would someday come to pass. One day, we would cross over to Alora, and we would be reunited with him again. For now, these pictures would be all we had of him on Earth. It would be the last time we'd get to see, hold, or touch our baby boy until our souls moved on, so we needed these photographs.

"Yes, please," I told Chloe.

Everyone left the room except for Chloe and Talia. Talia helped position the babies on our chests. She did her best to hide Marcus's tubes, while Chloe snapped photos of our family. It was a beautiful moment, one that I never wanted to end.

"I'd like to get a few of Dean and Marcus together, just them," Chloe suggested.

I didn't want to let Dean go. I felt like I'd lost a huge purpose in my life. I wanted to be a mother, but a mother to twins, not a singular child. I still loved Marcus, but I didn't understand how I was going to tell him that his twin was gone once the time came.

I wish I could've died in Dean's place, and that he could've lived, but Mother Miriam didn't see it to happen that way. We'd lost Dean, but he hadn't lost the fight… he'd taken that poison down with him, to protect his brother until the end.

I had told my grief that she needed to get out of my life, but she insisted she wasn't going anywhere. I understood now. This pain was never going to leave. The worst thing about this wasn't Dean's passing… it was that he was going to stay gone, and he wasn't coming back. I'd never get a chance to do all the things I'd dreamed of with my son. Every day for the rest of my life, I'd wake up and continually have to say goodbye.

This whole thing felt unbearable, and it was. I feared I was going to die from my grief, if not for the people around me. I felt isolated, because no one here knew exactly how I felt except for Lucas. My husband was the only person who would know exactly what it was like to say goodbye to our son when we should've been celebrating his life.

I couldn't bear to feel any longer, so I forced myself to go numb. I had to focus on Marcus now, because he was my reason to keep going.

I had to depend on my community now. They were all I had now. They wouldn't fill the void that Dean had left, but they'd make this burden easier to bear. Because Lucas and I would never lay this burden down, not until we died, and no one could carry it for us. But our community could help us, so some way or another, we would pull through.

There wasn't any way to make this better, and there wasn't any way to make this hurt less. But perhaps there was a way to keep existing through it, because grief hadn't given us any other choice.

I sobbed as I handed Dean over to Talia. The girls quickly took a few photos of the boys, then placed Dean back in my arms. Lucas put Marcus back in his incubator, where he was safest. My sobs grew quiet, but tears continued to leak out of my eyes.

Lucas ran his fingers over the tiny tuft of brown hair at the top of Dean's head. "We're so glad we got to be your parents."

"You're the sweetest little thing," I whispered to Dean. I knew wherever he was, he had to be able to feel me.

We sat there for a long time, until Lucas quietly whispered. "It's time to say goodbye, Nad."

I knew he was right, but I didn't know how to say goodbye. I didn't think I *could*.

I kissed the top of Dean's head and whispered, "We'll be with you again, baby boy."

Lucas took Dean in his arms, but I still couldn't bear to let him go. I knew that once I did, I was never going to hold him again. My hands lingered on him just a little longer, and then he was gone…

The moment was over far too soon. Lucas stood with Dean in his arms. He didn't have to tell me where he was going with him, because I already knew. Lucas held Dean close as he left the room.

Verla was waiting at the door, and she came back in when Lucas left. She helped me to the bathroom so I could clean up in the tub. I moved slowly because I was sore, but I wanted to get back to Marcus as soon as possible.

After washing up, I dressed in the nightgown Verla had set aside for me, then returned to the bed. I rolled over to watch Marcus in his incubator, and I couldn't get over how perfect he was. I was able to put my hand through one of the holes and touch his tiny fingers.

Verla pulled up a chair to sit beside my bed.

"I'm sorry you had to go through this," she said softly. "Losing a child is not something I wish upon anyone. I know all too well there's nothing I can say or do to make this better, but please know that I am here for you. Whatever you need—anything—you let me know. I mean it."

"It all just happened so fast," I said without taking my eyes off Marcus. "You're the only person I know who can understand what Lucas and I are going through."

"I do," Verla replied kindly. "When I lost my son, I had no one. At the time, I was so confused, and I didn't know what to think. I think I had to go through that to know what I was up against, because no one helped me, but now I can help you. I like to think it was meant to happen this way, because your baby Marcus is important, and so are you."

"Did you ever get clarity?" I asked.

"I don't know if anyone can provide us all the answers," Verla admitted. "What I've come to learn is that some of us have to die so others get to live. Dean loved his brother even in the womb. That's how powerful love is. We give ourselves up for the ones we care about."

"He really did love him," I agreed.

I paused a beat before adding, "What was your son's name?"

Verla hesitated, like she wasn't used to people asking the question. I wasn't sure she'd ever told anyone, to be honest. It was like his name was sacred, so special and loved. I wasn't sure she was going to answer.

"Allyn," she finally said. "He was named after my father."

"That's a beautiful name," I told her. "A beautiful name for a beautiful baby boy."

Verla turned to Marcus with a sad look in her eyes. I didn't mean to hurt her with the question, but I understood why it would bother her. One day, someone was going to ask me the same thing, and I could only imagine what it would do to me.

"I know you lost your child, and that's a devastating thing, but you still have Marcus and he's a great blessing," Verla said. "I know you'll tell him about his brother and never forget about him."

I was really sad Dean was gone, but at least I had Marcus. Verla didn't have anyone.

I stroked his fingers with my thumb, and Marcus's fingers curled around mine ever so slightly. My heart melted, and I knew there would never be a greater love than this. "He's the greatest blessing of all."

## TWENTY-ONE

The forest was cold and damp as I trudged back toward the house, weighed down by the calamitous gravity of having just buried my newborn son. Losing a child was not a misfortune I wished upon even my worst enemies. Nobody should have to go through something like this.

Our friends had already given Dean a proper goodbye by singing and writing messages in his notebook, but burying him was something I had to do alone. Nadine wasn't well enough to come with me, and intuitively, I knew she couldn't watch anyway. I'd snuck outside and hadn't told anyone what I was doing, because I didn't want them to follow.

I hadn't used any tools, but instead, dug my hands into the wet earth in order to make my son's grave, laying him gently beside Helena. Dean had been given a proper burial right next to her. I liked to think she was with him, watching over him. He deserved to be with family, and his great-grandmother would make sure he didn't rest alone in those woods.

Thinking like that was the only way to get through this.

An all-consuming numbness took over me somewhere on my way back to the house, because I couldn't remember walking inside. Brown water swirled down the kitchen drain as I washed the dirt from my hands. I couldn't process how quickly it had all happened. A few hours ago, Nadine and I were sleeping soundlessly in bed. Now, our whole world had flipped on end.

Talia had said she foresaw a tragic fate no matter what path we traveled. We'd broken the Reaper's Shadow curse, and Nadine and Marcus had both been saved. But we'd welcomed one baby boy into this world, at the cost of saying goodbye to another. It wasn't fair, and I cursed all the gods in all the pantheons for allowing such a tragedy to take place.

Nadine hadn't died, but there was a part of both of us that did when we lost Dean. I could already feel it. None of us would come out of this the same people we were before.

All we could do was keep moving forward, if only for Marcus's sake. We were parents now, and we had to learn how to be there for him, and not just ourselves.

I only bemoaned the fact that Dean wouldn't be here to share our new lives with. I didn't know when the pain was going to stop, when this heaviness in my iron heart was going to lift.

It wasn't until Dean was in the ground when I'd realized it never would.

Footsteps sounded behind me, and I realized I'd been standing over the kitchen sink for Goddess knew how long. The water ran clear, and yet I still felt the need to scrub every inch of my hands. There was no amount of cleansing in the world that could be done to erase the heartbreak of losing a child.

I glanced over my shoulder to see Professor Warren standing there. I didn't really want company, unless it was Oliver or Nadine, but I didn't know where Oliver had gone. He must've been off sleeping in another area of the house.

Warren shoved his hands into his pockets. "I'm deeply sorry for your loss."

I turned back to the sink. "Thanks, but you don't have to check up on me. I'll be okay."

He spoke gently. "We both know that's not true. Now's not the time to mask your emotions."

I grabbed the scrub brush from the counter and scrubbed under my nails vigorously. My skin was turning red, and to anyone else it may appear painful, but I felt nothing. "I need to get the dirt off," I stated flatly.

Warren stepped up beside me and placed a gentle hand on my arm. "It's okay to not be okay."

The tears beading in my eyes spilled over the lids. I'd already cried so much. I wasn't sure I had any tears left in me. Professor Warren wrapped me in a hug, and all I could do was sag against him. Water dripped from my hands onto the floor, but it barely registered.

The hug was strange, because Warren was like a father figure to me, and all I ever got from my own father was lectures on how to man up. I couldn't recall a time when my father and I had exchanged a hug, yet it was everything I needed right now. I needed someone to tell me it was okay to be vulnerable, before convincing me to compose myself so I could be there for my wife and child.

My shoulders shook in sobs. "I loved him so much."

"I know," Warren said softly. "There is no grief like that of losing a child. I can't imagine what you're going through."

"I don't want you to," I told him. "No one should ever have to go through this."

Warren drew away. His eyes were red with tears. "You don't have to do it alone, all right? We're all here for you."

People kept saying that. I just wished it was enough, but it wasn't. Nothing could replace losing my son. Platitudes and sympathy only went so far, and they did *nothing* to ease this pain.

"It's not fair," I told him. "Helena and Dean are gone. Everyone I love either dies or leaves, and I'm sick of people around me getting hurt. I love Dean so much, but it wasn't enough to save him. All the love in the world wasn't able to bring him back."

"Just because the love you experienced didn't last doesn't mean it wasn't real," Warren said gently.

"You don't get it," I said harshly. "I told you before, everyone I love abandons me. My son didn't get a chance to even choose—he was forced to go, and none of us got a chance to even know him. It's fucked up. It's *wrong*."

"It is wrong. It's cruel, and awful, and shouldn't ever happen," Warren stated. "But sometimes it does, and there's nothing we can do."

"I should've been stronger. If I was more powerful, I might've been able to do something."

"You're an incredible reaper, but though you have the powers of death, you don't have the ability to stop it," Warren replied quietly. "There aren't any words anyone can give that will take away this pain. But I want you to know that your community is here for you, and we aren't going anywhere."

I didn't quite believe him, but I knew he was being genuine, so I merely wiped my eyes and said, "I need to get back to my wife now."

"Of course." He stepped aside to let me pass.

Each room I passed felt like a blur, until I reached the bedroom. Nadine was asleep on the bed, and Marcus was breathing quietly inside his incubator. Nadine's hand rested inside the incubator, with one finger placed in Marcus's hand. It was so precious that all I could do was stare for several moments, taking it in.

The lamp on the nightstand was on, but I didn't bother turning it off when I crawled into bed. I didn't want to miss a moment watching my precious little boy if I didn't have to.

I snuggled up next to Nadine. She stirred slightly but didn't wake. I watched Marcus's tiny chest rise and fall, until I drifted off to sleep.

An odd sensation came over my body, like I was drifting upward. I opened my eyes to see the room bathed in the familiar rainbow colors of the astral plane. Nadine's ethereal form sat at the edge of the bed, looking down into Marcus's incubator. Our bodies lay soundlessly snuggled up together on the bed.

"I see we both had the same idea," I remarked.

Nadine's spirit turned to me. "My body was so tired, but I didn't want to miss a moment with him. I figured I wouldn't *have* to miss a second if I was astral traveling. This way, I can be with him while my body rests."

I sat on the edge of the bed beside her in spiritual form and took her hand in mine. I couldn't take my eyes off Marcus, though. "We've been through a lot tonight, but I could've lost all of you, and I'm really glad I didn't."

Nadine rested her head on my shoulder. "I just wish we had more time to say goodbye."

The sound of a baby's cry filled the room, and we both immediately became more alert. I shot to my feet and peered into Marcus's incubator. Marcus was sound asleep.

The cry came again, only I realized it was coming from the other side of the room. I turned, and my spirit nearly dropped straight back into my body. Lying in the second incubator was Dean. His form was ghost-like and transparent, but his cries were strong.

Nadine and I slowly approached his incubator, as if we were both afraid this was some sort of trick. His little arms and legs wiggled, and he reached out to us, like he was looking for someone to grab on to.

"Nad, you were right," I said breathlessly. "Dean's spirit was here this whole time. We can see him now because we're on the astral plane."

Tears of joy streamed down Nadine's cheeks. "Come here, baby boy."

She reached for him, and her hands went straight through the incubator. She lifted Dean's ethereal form and held him close to her chest. His cries halted, and he let out a blissful sigh.

Warmth filled my chest when I placed my hand on our son's back. I leaned down to kiss his head, then whispered, "This is it, Nad. We get a second chance to tell him goodbye."

She touched her nose to his head. "I never want to let you go. Not tonight, at least."

"You don't have to," I told her gently. "We can take all the time we need."

And we did. Hours passed as we comforted our baby boy. We told him stories about how we met and all the fun things we'd done together. We recounted details from Nadine's pregnancy and told him the story of his birth.

"Your mama was so strong," I said. "We got to hold you for just a little while, and it was the most beautiful thing in the world."

"You're going home very soon," Nadine told him. "There, you won't have to worry about anything. Your grandma and grandpa will be there, and they'll make sure you're always fed and you have as many blankets as you could ever need. You're going to be so cozy, and everyone will love you."

"We won't be there with you," I added. "But we'll see you again. We promise."

We took Dean's spirit over to Marcus's incubator and showed him his brother. Dean let out a tiny coo that I could only assume was the sound of joy.

The dark hours of the morning brightened as the sun began to rise. Nadine glanced at our sleeping bodies on the bed. "We're going to wake up soon."

I held out my hands. "Can I hold him again?"

"Of course." Nadine placed the tiny little boy into my arms, and I swore, I never felt so alive than in that moment. Losing Dean was one of the most difficult things we'd ever endured, but being his dad was the absolute greatest blessing ever. I was absolutely smitten with these boys.

I had a realization then. "I was angry at Talia. She said she saw us holding our babies, and back then I thought that meant things would be okay. I felt like she'd lied to us. Now that I'm holding him, I realize this must be the future she saw, and maybe it will still be okay."

Nadine's features softened. "I think it will be. I understand now what my grief was trying to tell me."

"Oh?" I asked curiously. "What was that?"

Nadine didn't get a chance to answer before we witnessed two dark clouds swirl above our bodies, taking the shape of our forms. Images of our own selves stood before us, as if we were looking into a mirror. I hadn't even tried to draw our grief out, but I must've been working my magic subconsciously, because we had manifested our grief into physical form together.

An image of myself stood across from me, his arm wrapped around the spitting image of Nadine. There was sadness in his eyes that I understood all too well, because he and I were one and the same. I didn't have to think about it. I knew exactly what the two of them needed.

I stepped forward and placed Dean's spirit into Grief Lucas's arms.

Grief Nadine smiled, and the sadness in my grief's eyes melted away. I stood back, holding my Nadine's hand. Across from us stood an image of what could've been—a future holding our son that we would never have. Somehow, it didn't tear me apart, but made me happy for these final moments we got to share with him.

"I don't want to fight you anymore," Nadine told her grief. "I understand now that you aren't going anywhere. But I also know that your existence is not something I can blame myself for, because I'll never be able to fix it."

Grief Nadine looked up from Dean, wearing a soft expression. "I'm with you now, but we can work together."

"I understand," Nadine said. "I know it will take time, but I need to process this in a healthy way. Blaming myself is only going to destroy me. There is no fix or cure, because I can't make you go away. But I can learn to live in harmony with you. You're a piece of me now, and you will remind me every day of those I love, but I can use that love for good. Grief cannot come to an end, because it's a process."

"It's okay to grieve," Grief Nadine told her. "You don't have to run from it out of shame."

"I just thought I could change it," Nadine replied. "But I see now what I need to change is *myself*. I was grieving for those I'd lost, including myself, because I didn't know who to be without those people, or without my disability. It's clear to me now that grief requires you to change. It isn't something you get over. It's something you grow through and learn to live with, and it's something that changes your identity. You have to come out on the other side a new person. I can either let my grief consume me, or let it drive me forward, but I can't move forward if I don't give it a chance to move through me. Holding it back is only going to hurt more."

Nadine drew a deep breath. "I tried to run from it because I didn't want to change. My identity didn't feel secure because I could lose someone I love or come out of remission at any time, but I can utilize these shifts to do good. I'm going to make our society accessible for everyone. People aren't going to have to have this identity crisis, because even if they are disabled, they aren't going to feel like they're different in our society. And when people lose someone they love, they're going to have the tools available to make these big shifts, and know their community will take care of them."

Grief Nadine looked proud of her. "In grief, there is love, and I know you and I will do great things together."

I turned to my grief. "I guess you and I have become well-acquainted these past few years."

He chuckled lightly. "Indeed, we have. I know you want me to tell you the pain is going to go away someday, but you and I both know this is always going to hurt. It may not hurt as much, but you're going to have to deal with it the rest of your life. But just because it hurts doesn't mean it's bad. Stand by Nadine, and work together to amplify your love and do good in the world."

"We will," I promised.

They handed back our baby boy, and immense relief washed over me as they faded. Something about letting our grief hold Dean's spirit healed a wound deep inside me, and I could tell Nadine felt the same way. She breathed a huge sigh of relief and leaned her head against my shoulder. It was so beautiful and peaceful.

"It's interesting," I stated. "It was your job to bring him into this world, and it's my job to let him go."

Nadine curled close to me, until Dean was wrapped in an embrace between our bodies. "Goodbye, sweetheart," Nadine whispered. "I didn't want to let you go before, because I thought I could protect you, but I see now that you're safe and all right. I can let go now… until we meet again."

I cuddled Dean close. "You have nothing to worry about, baby boy. Someone's coming to get you now, and they're going to take good care of you. We love you, now and forever."

Magic tingled through my spirit as a portal formed beside us. The glorious white glow of Alora filled the room. All the tears I'd been choking back before were gone now, because all I felt was pure happiness. Our baby boy was going someplace where no one could ever hurt him, and that was something to celebrate.

A shadow appeared in the center of the light. I wasn't scared, because I recognized that silhouette all too well.

"Grammy!?" Nadine cried. She sagged against me, nearly collapsing under the shock of seeing her grandmother again

Helena stood at the edge of the portal, smiling happily. "It's wonderful to see you again, my dear."

"I missed you so much," Nadine sobbed.

"I know you've blamed yourself for my death, but I went willingly," Helena told her gently. "I would've given myself up for you a million times over, because you are my granddaughter, and I love you. I have no regrets about how I left, only that I had to leave you. Alora is a place of peace, without suffering, and your grandfather and I are finally together again. We are happy here. There is nothing to forgive, and I'll wait for you in Mother Miriam's realm of love, so we can be together again."

A tear streaked my cheek. "It's so good to see you, Helena. We never got a chance to say goodbye that night."

"I know you wanted to help me cross over," she said sadly. "But I didn't want to make things harder on you, Lucas. I didn't realize the toll it would take on you. Can you ever forgive me?"

"Of course," I told her.

"I watched over you both," Helena said. "I can't come back physically, but all you need to do is connect with me in spirit, and I'll be here as I am now."

The way she said it was strange, like she wasn't quite sure what had brought her back.

"Helena… do you know why you're here?" I asked.

"Because you summoned me," she said simply.

"Yes, but under normal circumstances, we shouldn't be able to see you," I told her. "You're here to take Dean home to Alora."

Helena took a step back into the light, seemingly confused. "No, that can't be. He still has work here. Dean's spirit is supposed to be on Earth at this moment in time."

Nadine and I exchanged a glance.

"I don't get it," I said. "I thought this all happened for a reason. If Dean is supposed to be here, how can he be dead?"

"Perhaps your assumptions are not as they seem," Helena said mysteriously.

I didn't like the way she spoke without giving clear answers. He wasn't coming back, if that's what she meant. "Dean is gone. I buried him myself."

"We can't keep him with us in spirit form," Nadine insisted. "He'll be lost."

"His time here is over," I added. "He needs to move on to the next life. You'll take him, won't you?"

"Of course I will," Helena said. "If what you said is true, he must cross over."

Hesitantly, I stepped forward. I knew Dean had to go with Helena, and we were running out of time on the astral plane, but it killed me to let him go. My spirit shuddered as I placed Dean into Helena's arms.

"Even if this is not the way things were meant to be, your loved ones can come back in many ways," Helena reminded us. "We'll be here for you whenever you need us."

Nadine stepped up to the portal, so that she was face-to-face with Helena. "Before you go, I want to tell you I've missed you. I may never be able to make sense of why you were taken from us so soon, but I know you were here for me for the time we did have together, and I know you're here for me now. I'll take so much of you with me—not just in memory, but in who I am. So much of your love and your lessons shaped me, and your impact will always live on. I love you so much, Grammy, and I just want to finally tell you… goodbye."

Tears beaded in Helena's eyes. "Know that my impact is not the only thing that will live on. Having you as my granddaughter was one of the greatest blessings of my life, and you impacted me as well. Keep giving your love, Nadine, because I know you have so much of it to share."

"We'll miss you, Grammy," I told her.

"Grammy?" she questioned. "Lucas, you always call me Helena."

I realized then what I'd said. It felt so natural that I hadn't even realized it. "You *are* my grandmother. We may have only been family for one day on Earth, but you were always family to me. You taught me what family is because I didn't have that. I had people who gave birth to me, but I didn't have a family until I met you. Now thanks to you, Nadine and I have a chance to start a family of our own. Even though we don't get to share our time on Earth with Dean, he will always be a part of our family, as will you. We know he's in good hands."

Grammy smiled. "I love you both. Keep in touch, all right?"

I wrapped my arm around Nadine's waist and pulled her close. "We'll be in touch so often you'll get sick of us."

"That's impossible," Helena said with a smile. "After all, grief and death are ephemeral, but love lasts forever."

"Ephemeral?" Nadine asked.

"It's a word for something that lasts for only a short time," Grammy said kindly. "Your grief will be a part of you forever, but the hardest parts will ease, and the pain will fall off of you entirely when it is time for you to come home."

Then she lifted Dean's tiny hand and waved to us. "Goodbye, my loves. Perhaps it will seem like some time until we are reunited, but to Dean and me, it will not be long at all. Farewell."

"Goodbye," we said in unison.

The portal faded, and Helena and Dean were gone. Even so, I could still swear I felt them here with us, though we couldn't see them.

Helena was right. They weren't going anywhere.

The sound of rustling sheets met my ears, and I realized our bodies were stirring. We were waking up. The room around me began to fade.

My eyes opened moments later. I was back in my body, feeling well rested. Nadine rolled over to snuggle against my shoulder. I melted into her, feeling so at peace.

After several long beats, she spoke in a quiet voice. "I still don't get it. The boys were born under a lunar eclipse, at the exact time they needed to become demigods, as predicted. But Grammy made it seem like Dean's death wasn't supposed to happen. So what was it—destiny, or not?"

"Maybe we're thinking too black and white," I suggested. "There are multiple paths to a single outcome. Maybe Dean wasn't destined to die, and it's just something that happened that no one could've controlled. Maybe we don't need to make sense of it to know things are going to be okay. I know it's harder when we don't have answers. But maybe we can be content knowing not everything has a cosmic reason behind it."

"I think we can," Nadine agreed.

A knock came at the door.

"Come in," I called.

Talia opened the door. "Uh, Nadine… Are you able to get out of bed?"

I sat up straighter. Something in her tone worried me.

"Yeah, I can," Nadine said. "What's wrong?"

"Nothing's wrong," Talia insisted. "It's Isa… you're going to want to come see this."

Nadine *could* get out of bed, but it was obvious she was still very sore. I helped her up and stayed close as we followed Talia down the hall. She led us downstairs and into the den, where Grant, Chloe, and Onyx were on their knees in the corner. It looked like they were trying to coax Isa out from behind the couch. Their cats surrounded them, and I worried something was wrong.

"Aw, look at the little paws!" Onyx sang in a high-pitched voice.

They all turned to look at us when we entered the room. "Shh…" Chloe whispered, gesturing us forward. "You don't want to spook them."

Nadine looked as confused as I was when we both approached the corner. The others moved out of the way, and my heart skipped a beat when I saw what was hidden back there.

Isa and Oliver lay snuggled up on a blanket, licking a tiny wiggling creature between them. Its eyes were closed, but it lifted its head and let out the tiniest high-pitched meow. The kitten couldn't be more than a few minutes old, because it was still covered in goop. I could just barely make out its tortie color pattern—mostly black, mottled with brown splotches.

Nadine gasped. "So this is where you were all night."

"I guess now we know where these two have been running off to for the last few months," I chuckled.

"Yeah, they've been getting it on," Grant joked.

Nadine adjusted a corner of the blanket to get the cats more comfortable. "There's only one kitten. Isa looks perfectly comfortable, though. Where's the rest of the litter?"

"Maybe she only had one," I suggested. "That might be why no one realized she was pregnant."

"Can I see?" Talia squeezed in beside us, then pulled out the Seer Wand. She reached out to pet Isa's head, and the end of the Wand glowed. "Lucas is right. There's just the one."

Talia tickled the top of the kitten's head as her voice rose several pitches. "And he's *sooo* precious—"

She stopped dead in her tracks. "Oh, my Goddess."

"What is it?" Nadine demanded. "What's wrong?"

Talia's jaw hung open for several seconds, before she composed herself. "Everything is just right. You guys, I can feel him. I... I can feel Dean!"

"Dean... reincarnated?" I could hardly find the words; I was so stunned. I didn't know why I didn't consider the possibility before. Our loved ones reincarnated into cats all the time, but when we lost Dean, it seemed like he'd be gone forever. I never pictured him coming back to us like this.

Nadine grabbed my arm. "Grammy was right! She said Dean was *meant* to be here, and he is!"

Talia drew back. "He has a great destiny. I don't know all the details, but I can feel it. Whatever Marcus is meant to face when he grows up, Dean is meant to be right there alongside him."

A beat passed as we all stared down at the kitten, admiring him. Then Oliver lunged forward, grabbed the kitten by the back of his neck with his teeth, and took off running.

"Oliver!" I screamed.

We all went running after him. Oliver scurried up the stairs and raced down the hall. I followed him into our bedroom. He hopped up on the bed, then on the top of Marcus's incubator. Gently, he placed the kitten on the plastic top. Marcus moved ever so slightly.

"Wait," I told everyone. "I think Oliver is trying to tell us something."

Nadine slowly approached the incubator. The kitten lifted its head and let out a tiny mew. "I think he's trying to tell us they belong together. This is Marcus's cat."

I turned to Onyx. "Can we put the kitten inside with him?"

"I think it should be safe," she said.

Carefully, I lifted the kitten and opened the incubator. I placed the kitten next to Marcus, and the most beautiful thing happened. The kitten wiggled his way into the crook of Marcus's elbow, and Marcus's tiny arm curled around the kitten in an embrace.

Nadine sniffled. "Marcus and Dean are together again, like they were meant to be."

"Rishi," Talia corrected her. "I felt it when I touched him. His name in this life is *Rishi*."

My heart melted as I stared down at the babies. "Rishi," I repeated. "Welcome to the family, little kitten."

I went to stroke Rishi's head, and something hit me. "It's interesting that even though Dean died, he came back to be here, as if fate is correcting itself. I always figured each incarnation was separate from the next, but maybe I've been looking at it all wrong. I thought life and death were these two separate things… that death is final. It's why I've always been afraid of it, because I'm scared of all of this coming to an end, of not living my life to the fullest. But death doesn't have to be an ending or a permanent thing. It's not separate from life, but all part of the same journey. It's just a transformation from one chapter of the journey to the next. That's why I can harness Death magic through transformation, because they're one and the same. I thought as a reaper, I was guiding souls to their final destination, but really, I'm just helping them along their path. Life continues after death, because it's all one."

I placed my finger in Marcus's hand. "I see now it's not my job to save you. It's my job to be here for you and guide you, because this is hard and we're a community, and the community helps each other. I'm going to be there for you while your soul is growing and evolving. That, I can promise you both."

A darkness swelled over the room, blocking out the morning light. I whirled around to see a cloaked figure stepping toward me. He wasn't alone. Over a dozen other ethereal figures wearing identical black cloaks stood behind him.

"Lucas, what is it?" Nadine asked.

The cloaked figure lifted his head, and I peered into the empty eye sockets of a skeleton man. The others couldn't see them.

"It's Edgar," I told her breathlessly. "And the entire Reaper Order."

Chloe nudged me. "Well, go on. Talk to them."

I took a hesitant step toward Edgar. "I thought I wasn't going to see you again until I passed the Warlock's Trial."

"That is correct," Edgar said calmly.

"You mean… I'm ready? But I didn't do anything." I was so confused about what might've prompted this meeting.

"You didn't have to *do* anything," Edgar said. "You merely had to *become* the reaper you were meant to be. As I said before, power over death is more than a magical feat."

I realized now what he meant. "It's a mindset… a comfort of letting go of your fear. That's what *really* gives you power, isn't it?"

"Yes," Edgar confirmed. "Death is a transformation, and every reaper understands that. You weren't ready to join us until you realized that death isn't a permanent state, just one more stop on the path of a soul's journey. Now that you understand your role as a reaper, you are ready to join the Reaper Order."

Edgar held a dark cloak out to me, and I took it. I almost expected my hands to go straight through it, but there was powerful magic at work here. My fingers curled around soft fabric, and a wave of pride washed through me.

"Thank you," I told him.

"There's one more thing," Edgar added, reaching into his cloak. He lifted a wand painted white and carved with a rib cage at the end. "I believe you'll be needing this."

A euphoric feeling filled me from head to toe. After all this time, we were finally in possession of the Mortana Wand.

I grasped it firmly. The end of the Wand glowed, and a chord in a minor key rang throughout the room. Dark purple magic swirled up my arm, then settled into my skin, so deeply I felt it latch on to my spirit.

I heard the others gasp in unison. They couldn't see the reapers, but it was clear as day that they saw the Wand materialize in my hand.

"When will we see each other again?" I asked Edgar. "Perhaps Mother Miriam will assign you to guide me into the next life."

Edgar tilted his head. "Mother Miriam does not make reaper assignments. It is our choice which souls to reap. We choose our own assignments, Lucas."

"So... all those souls I've helped cross over... I wasn't given some magical order to help them," I realized. "I chose to help all on my own."

Edgar nodded. "Yes. It is a reason Mother Miriam chose you as a reaper. You have always wanted to help others, and you will continue to do so. Now go. Live your life. When one of us comes for you, it will be a welcome meeting."

Warmth filled my chest, and I truly felt like I understood then what it meant to be a reaper. The reapers disappeared, and I turned to the others.

"We have four Wands!" Chloe exclaimed. "We should move in on the priestesses as soon as we can. We have the power to take all their magic, so we can beat them."

"We can't," I insisted. "We aren't ready. Marcus is just a newborn, and Nadine needs time to recover. It's going to take at least six weeks until they're back to full strength, and they need to be healthy enough to be moved if something goes wrong. If something happens and we're forced to flee, we won't have time to bring Marcus's medical supplies with. He needs to be able to survive off of support. We'll be safe here for now, because if the priestesses want to come for us again, we'll be ready for them."

"My grandmother isn't going to wait around," Chloe argued. "We've almost been discovered multiple times. Six weeks is too long to wait."

"I want to go after the priestesses as much as anyone, but I agree with Lucas that we need more time," Grant said. "You said it yourself at Yule, Chloe. We can't go in guns blazing. We don't have enough intel to destabilize the cult, and that needs to be done before we face the priestesses. Otherwise, their supporters are going to rise up. We can't just walk in and kill them. If we do, others will take their place, and nothing will really get done, because we'll just have to kill even more people. We aren't the bad guys. We need to have the support of the coven before we move in—or at least, have enough people on our side that they're willing to think about changing their minds. If we take the priestesses out now, it's going to be a mistake, because there *will* be resistance from the public, and Miriam's Chosen, if we don't do this the right way."

Talia stepped forward. "I agree. Chloe and I haven't been able to get close enough to town to gain a firm understanding of the cult's mentality and learn how to destabilize them. If we're going to do this the right way, we'll have to go undercover so we can infiltrate the cult and retrieve solid intel, because what we've been doing hasn't been working."

Chloe backed down. "All right. We'll do this the right way, but we can't wait longer than a few weeks. You guys need to promise me we'll make our move, and soon."

"We'll give Nadine and Marcus six weeks to recover," I decided. "We'll move in when we're ready, but not a moment sooner."

☾

NADINE and I spent the next two weeks snuggled up in bed, watching Marcus wiggle or reading him stories. We finally got to hold him for longer than a few minutes, and it was amazing. He was getting stronger by the day and gaining weight rapidly. With Luana's healing treatments, he was stronger than any preemie she'd treated before.

Nadine was recovering quickly from labor, though Luana was still monitoring her closely. Onyx said they wanted to keep an eye on her up until at least six weeks after delivery, but her blood pressure had come down, and she was doing much better. Luana was finally able to work her healing magic on her, which Nadine said helped immensely.

Isa had recovered as well, and she spent most of her time in our room, usually nursing Rishi. The kitten was already growing so fast and had so much fur. He'd gotten so big because he was a glutton who had no siblings to compete with. Rishi often made gagging sounds while nursing, because he drank so fast. When he wasn't nursing, he was whining for more food. He was clumsy and always falling off of things, and he had a stupidly cute little face. Rishi always wore a bug-eyed expression, and his tongue was always sticking out. He was the most adorable kitten.

Slowly, Marcus was taken off his tubes and monitors, and he was transferred from the incubator to a heated cot.

After two weeks, we were able to take him out of the room. I sat in the living room, snuggling Marcus in my arms the first night he was able to leave his cot for more than a few minutes. We were celebrating his progress and all getting together for a big dinner. Nadine was in the kitchen with the girls, laughing while they cooked and snacked on appetizers. The guys were outside doing nightly patrol on the ward borders. I just sat there taking in the joyous sounds of the friendly banter filling the house.

"You're surrounded by good people," I told Marcus.

He wiggled a little, snuggling deeper into my arms. Each time he did that, my heart melted a little more.

"How's he doing?" Verla asked brightly as she came into the living room.

"Great," I told her. "He's made so much progress."

Verla sat across from me on the couch. "I can see that."

"Can you believe how small he is?" I sat up straighter to show him off.

She smiled softly. "No, I can't. He's so precious."

"Do you want to hold him?" I asked.

Verla looked touched. "Do you even have to ask? Come here, baby."

I chuckled as I gently placed Marcus into her arms. It was strange handing him over, because no matter how much I trusted the people close to me, I never wanted to let him go. It terrified me that someone was going to drop him or something. As a new dad, I was a bit overly cautious.

"Aren't you the sweetest thing on the planet?" Verla cooed at him. She stroked his cheek with her finger, and the room went silent.

We sat there for several beats, just staring down at Marcus, until Verla broke the silence. "Do you ever think about bringing him back?"

I reeled back a little, stunned. "What?"

"Dean," Verla clarified. "Do you ever wonder… what would happen if you could?"

I shot a glance across the room. Isa lounged in front of the fireplace, and Rishi kneaded her belly while he nursed. Dean was here with us in spirit, but he could never come back as the child he once was.

"I never gave it much thought, because it's impossible," I admitted.

Verla cocked an eyebrow. "Is it, though? You have the Mortana Wand. With it, you can access all the power of the coven's Death magic—all the power on Earth and in Alora."

"And yet it wouldn't be enough," I said. "Even the gods don't mess with bringing the dead back to life."

"What is it to them?" Verla wondered. "Life goes on after we die, yes. I'm sure it makes no difference to the gods. But to us, having our loved ones here, it's everything."

I realized why Verla was asking. She had lost a child of her own and was wondering if it was possible to bring her son back to her.

I choked up a little and cleared my throat before I spoke. "If I had a choice between Dean living and dying, I'd choose his life, every single time. But we can't go back and undo what's already done. Even Death magic isn't enough to bring the dead back to life."

"You brought Nadine back," Verla reminded me softly.

"Because she hadn't crossed over yet," I said. "The circumstances were perfect. If we brought Dean back now—or any spirit after they crossed over—we don't know what kind of consequences that could bring. It could damage his soul, which puts both him and Marcus at risk."

"Souls are far more complicated and nuanced than we understand. They can fracture and exist in multiple places at once. Marcus and Dean shared a soul, and now, a piece of that soul is within Rishi, which means Marcus and Rishi are parts of one soul, existing on Earth together. Why couldn't a third piece of that soul exist here as well?" Verla asked.

I opened my mouth to respond, but I realized then that her question was rhetorical. I understood now why she was bringing this up. She knew it couldn't work, but she wanted to make sure *I* understood it, too. I couldn't believe I thought she would ask me to do something like bring her son back. She knew better than I that it wasn't possible.

"You don't have to worry about how far I'll take things," I told her. "I know Death magic is dangerous, and to take it this far could be catastrophic. I won't risk it. Not with my son's soul."

Verla kept her eyes on me, but she didn't get a chance to respond before the front door opened. Professor Warren stepped inside, and I could instantly feel like something wasn't right.

I shot to my feet. "Where are Grant and Miles?"

Warren lifted his hand, as if to tell me to calm down. "They've got the perimeter secure, but you're going to want to come with me. There's someone here who wants to talk to you."

My mind immediately started racing through the possibilities, but anyone I could think of shouldn't have a clue where to find us. "Who?"

"Autumn," Professor Warren said.

Of course. My reaper master was the only person who knew we were here.

"Well, send her away," I bit. I didn't want to talk to her, not after how our last meeting ended.

"She's quite insistent," Warren pressed. "She knows where we are. She'll keep coming back."

I scoffed. "I'd like to see her try to get through our wards."

Warren sighed. "She wants to make things right with you. You might want to hear what she has to say."

"You should go," Nadine said from behind me.

I turned around, and it was the first time I realized that the laughter coming from the kitchen had died. Everyone had gathered to see what was going on.

"Autumn spent years protecting you," Nadine said. "She made some bad choices along the way, but there's a part of her that cares. You should hear her out."

"What am I supposed to say, Nad?" I asked hopelessly. *"You came back, so you're forgiven?"*

"You don't have to *say* anything," Nadine suggested. "If she's come to apologize, then just listen. Extend an olive branch and invite her in for dinner. We owe her one. She kept an eye on us even after we blew her off last December. She was here the night the twins were born, and she killed the Executors so they couldn't get to our babies. It's the least we can do after she killed those Executors to protect us."

I breathed a heavy sigh, but I was only doing this because Nadine wanted me to. "All right. I'll give it a shot."

Chloe conjured the Mentalist Wand. "I'm coming with you."

"So am I," Talia said as the Seer Wand appeared in her hand. "If Autumn has any ill intentions, she's not getting past four Oaken Wands."

We followed Warren outside, and he led us to the edge of our border. Grant and Miles stood there, their wands pointed at Autumn. She stood only feet away from them on the other side of the ward boundary. She wore a dark cloak and held her hands up in surrender.

"What do you want?" I asked, a bit too harshly.

Slowly, Autumn lowered her hands. "I came to make amends."

"Why come after all this time?" I demanded. "It's been months since we last spoke. You showed up the night our children were born, but you didn't bother to stay long enough to accept a simple *thank you*."

Autumn's features paled. "I did not know your children had been delivered. It's true I saw the Executors coming and killed them before they could get to you, but I assumed it was another group of scouts like the others."

"You could've stayed and let us explain," I growled. "Instead, you come only when it's convenient for you to tear Executors to shreds. Is there a group closing in on the safe house now? Is that why you're here?"

"No!" Autumn insisted. "I've not come to hurt anyone. Those months since we met that I spent in silence, I was trying to convince myself to come see you."

I crossed my arms over my chest. "What stopped you?"

"I was afraid you wouldn't want to see me," she admitted.

"Then you were right," I stated coldly.

"Please, Lucas," Autumn begged. "I'm here because I want to apologize. I never meant to cause you any harm. I should have come to you years ago. I should've told you the truth. I can't change what I did, but maybe I can do better in the future."

I took a long stride forward, until Autumn and I were face to face, with nothing but an invisible magical ward between us. "You left me alone. All the times you claim to have been there for me were only when it was convenient for you. If there was ever a risk of you being exposed, you never showed up for me. Your one job was to hand down the Reaper Records, and you did that. Now you show up after all this time wanting to make amends? It's too little too late. I didn't need you then, and I don't need you now."

I whirled around to head back up to the house, but Autumn shouted after me. "The Reaper Order failed me, too!"

I stopped in my tracks and slowly turned back around. I was aware the others' eyes were on me, but all I could focus on was Autumn. "The Order didn't fail me, so don't act like we have that in common. I passed the Warlock's Trial."

"You did?" Autumn appeared stunned.

I eyed her skeptically. "It's strange, you know. You don't speak to me for months, but just weeks after I join the Reaper Order and obtain the Mortana Wand, you want to come crawling back? Why are you really here?"

Autumn's brow furrowed. "You're not suggesting I came looking for the Mortana Wand. What use would I have of it? I didn't know you'd passed the trial, Lucas."

There were very few people I trusted in this world, and Autumn was certainly not one of them. I turned toward Chloe and Talia. "Read her mind. See if she's telling the truth."

The girls lifted their Wands in unison, and Autumn didn't even flinch. "Do what you must," she said. "I am telling the truth."

The ends of the girls' Wands glowed, and they spoke an incantation. They appeared in a trance-like state for only a moment before Talia opened her eyes and said, "Autumn is being honest with you. She didn't know about the Mortana Wand. She came to apologize."

"I came to tell you I was wrong," Autumn said softly. "My master may have found clarity in death, but when he was here, he left me to fend for myself. I had to find strength in myself, and there are times I find that I'm still searching. For so long, I blamed him for that, and I used my pain to convince myself that what I was doing to help you, or not help you, was justified. I thought that if I had to figure things out on my own, then you could, too. Now I see that the system failed us all. It was not Edgar's fault, but my choice alone to withdraw. I could have put an end to this cycle, and I chose to not only allow it to continue, but to participate in its process."

She sighed. "I came to say I'm sorry. I understand that you have moved on and there is nothing more I can teach you, but if there's one last thing I can *do* for you, I'd like to heal this wound I've caused."

The pain in her eyes was all too familiar. She may be older than me in years, but there was a part of her that was still a hurt child, the one who had been left behind. She was not the reaper master I thought was meant to teach me. She was still a Reaper's Apprentice, even though I—her successor—had become a master. Our roles had been reversed, which meant that perhaps I had something to teach her now.

I realized then that she hadn't come to ask for my forgiveness, but for my compassion.

"It means a lot to hear your apology," I said. "I owe you one as well. I could have reacted with more kindness when we met. There are clearly many layers to this story, and perhaps I haven't given you the space to tell it fully. I hope you can forgive me."

"You don't have to ask my forgiveness, because there is nothing to forgive you for," Autumn said kindly. "Your reaction was well warranted."

"Maybe we can start by mending things over dinner," I suggested.

Autumn smiled. "I'd like that very much."

I reached out my hand, and Autumn took it. With my invitation, she stepped through the ward. Miles and Grant pocketed their wands, as did Chloe and Talia. Professor Warren shot me an encouraging smile. It was clear he thought I was doing the right thing.

When we entered the house, Marcus was crying. Nadine sang him a song as she rocked him, but she quieted when she heard the door. Her eyes locked with Autumn's, and she nodded kindly. "Welcome to our home."

"Thank you all for inviting me in," Autumn replied.

"Dinner's almost ready." Nadine gestured toward the dining room. "Please, have a seat."

Marcus continued bawling, and Nadine's attempts to calm him weren't working.

"He probably has a dirty diaper. I can go change it," Mandy offered as we started gathering around the table.

"It's no trouble, really," Nadine insisted.

Mandy sighed. "You don't have to do this alone, Nadine. We're all here to help. You brought me in at my lowest point and showed me so much kindness. I've felt nothing but useless these last few months. You need to be here for Lucas tonight. Let me help with Marcus."

Nadine gently placed Marcus in Mandy's outstretched arms. "Thank you for the help."

We all gathered around the table, while Mandy went upstairs to change Marcus. I sat at the head of the table, with Nadine on one side of me and Autumn on the other. We started passing the food around and filling up our plates.

"Lucas, can I ask you something?" Autumn asked.

"Sure," I told her.

She passed me a basket of dinner rolls. "What was the Warlock's Trial exactly? How did you pass?"

I swallowed my bite of food before answering. "It's not a trial in the sense of a ceremony or some big display of magic. It's about learning what death means and the role you play in it as a reaper. I had to figure out that death wasn't just an end to create new beginnings, but part of the journey."

"That's quite insightful of you," Autumn remarked before taking a few bites of food.

I kept my eye on her. I could sense the wounded child I'd seen earlier, but she had wisdom in her eyes, too. It was like she'd figured that one out long ago.

"What do you think is holding you back?" I wondered as I scooped up a green bean.

Autumn pressed her lips together. "Honestly? I don't think the Reaper Order wants me."

"They do," I said automatically. "I'm part of the Reaper Order, and I want you there. I understand you feel discarded by what happened in this life, but if we keep learning and growing after we die, the Reaper Order must know the mistake they made. They may not be able to intervene now, but I think things will be different once we get to the other side."

Autumn's gaze dropped to her pate. "You really think they'd want me, after all I've done? I left the coven."

"And you can come back," I pressed. "That's the thing about the Warlock's Trial. I don't think it was ever meant for the Reaper Order to judge us. I think the reapers show up when we've decided we're ready. Don't forget that you're a reaper, Autumn. It is your birthright. To be accepted into the Reaper Order is to accept yourself and your power."

Autumn looked up at me, and a kind smile spread across her face. "Thank you, Lucas. I really needed to hear that."

Nadine set her fork aside. "Marcus is really quiet. Mandy must've gotten him back down for a nap. I'll go let her know she can leave him in his cot and come get something to eat."

Nadine left the table, and the room went silent. A full minute must've passed where no one said anything.

Finally, Verla wiped her mouth with her napkin. "So, Autumn, tell us a bit about yourself."

"I was born in Octavia Falls and lived there through my early twenties," Autumn explained. "You may have heard of my mother, Nina Loren."

"Nina's a lovely woman," Verla said. "We worked together at the college."

"She's a very good professor, but an even better mother," Autumn praised. "She raised me well, and I thought I would become a leader like her. Then I received the powers of a reaper in my Evoking Ceremony, and nothing was ever the same since. I was called a liar, and told I was seeking attention, as no one believed a female could possess the powers of a reaper. I left shortly after graduating from Miriam College of Witchcraft. I became a travel photographer and went all over the world. I'd have gone anywhere as long as I didn't have to live in Octavia Falls. It was on my journey that I met my wife while I was photographing national monuments in Arizona."

Her features brightened as she began talking about her wife. "Summer was a light in my life when I was going through the darkest of times. She was a skilled hypnotist; I'd never seen power like hers in any woman before. I didn't know my place in the world, but she showed me that my place could be anywhere, as long as it was with her. I never had to lie to her about what I was, because she always believed in my power. We traveled together for decades, even though she battled many health issues. Her health took a turn for the worst several years ago. She had always wanted to see where I grew up, so I brought her here. She died of a stroke before we could leave. I lost the will to travel after that, because I didn't wish to be separated from my wife. I now live in my father's old hunting cabin, and my mother and I still speak on occasion. She is the only one who knows where I went when I left…"

Autumn trailed off as Nadine came downstairs, looking worried.

"Where's Mandy?" Nadine asked in a shaky tone.

The look in her eyes worried me, and I immediately sat up straighter. "Isn't she in our room, putting Marcus down for a nap?"

"I just checked there," Nadine said. "And all the other rooms upstairs. I thought she must've come back down."

I felt the blood drain from my face, and I shot to my feet. "She didn't come downstairs. Nadine, what are you saying?"

Panic entered Nadine's tone. "I'm saying I don't know where Marcus is!"

Verla was at her side in an instant. "I'm sure they're here somewhere. It's a big house."

"Mandy!?" Nadine called, but no answer came.

I must've taken the stairs two at a time. My heart was beating so fast I hardly processed the next few minutes. Chairs squeaked against the floor as the others quickly stood and spread across the house to go looking for them. I thought Nadine followed me to the second level, but I was passing each room so quickly I wasn't sure.

"Mandy! Mandy!" Our voices overlapped, echoing throughout the house. I checked every room upstairs and heard doors open all the way down to the basement. We checked everywhere, then double-checked again. Every room I checked was as empty as the last.

From downstairs, Rishi began to cry. Each high-pitched mew was like a piercing dagger through my heart. Rishi was calling out for Marcus, too, but there was no answer that could calm the torment.

I stopped in the doorway to our bedroom, where Nadine had slumped to the bed. Her hands trembled as she lifted Marcus's baby blanket to her nose. Verla sat beside her, but no amount of comforting words were enough.

Tears broke from Nadine's eyes, and she began to wail. Footsteps sounded on the stairs as the others ran to check on her. A huge group formed in the hall.

"Where are they?" I demanded. "Did you find them?"

I was met only with silence. Then Professor Warren shook his head and said, "They aren't here, and there's no sign of a struggle."

The whole house seemed to flip on end. I had to brace myself against the doorway as the reality hit me.

Marcus was gone. Mandy had kidnapped our son.

## TWENTY-TWO

Horror permeated every cell of my being. At first, I didn't believe it. This had to be some sort of misunderstanding. I thought at any moment I'd hear the cry of my baby from across the house, but no matter how many people surrounded me, the house felt entirely empty.

I wanted to believe someone had gotten past our ward borders and taken them, but I knew our wards were strong. We'd brought Autumn past our borders, but she hadn't left Lucas's sight since she got here. My intuition told me Autumn had nothing to do with this—that her presence had merely distracted us, giving *someone else* the perfect opportunity to strike.

Mandy had betrayed us again.

I thought about the Executors that had come the night the twins were born. The priestesses had been planning this all along. Mandy must've been working with them and told them I was in labor, then took our son to break us.

"Where have they gone!?" I cried, as if someone might have the answer. "Where has she taken him!?"

Talia pushed past Lucas and grabbed my shoulders. "We're going to find him. I promise. Let me see what I can learn."

She withdrew the Seer Wand and clutched it tightly as she slowly walked around the room, touching various objects to trigger visions. She closed her eyes and tilted her head. "My visions are blurry. I don't know what I'm looking at. It's like something's blocking me."

"How's that possible?" Onyx asked. "You have the Seer Wand. It should be stronger than any ward or protection spell."

"I'm not sure," Talia said. "Give me more time."

My sadness quickly turned to anger, and I slammed Marcus's blanket onto the mattress beside me. "I can't *believe* this! We took Mandy in. We gave her a second chance. I believed that she never meant to hurt us, but she's been working with the priestesses the whole time! How could my intuition be so wrong?"

"We don't know that she meant to do this," Grant tried to assure me. "If the priestesses are manipulating her—"

"I don't give a shit what the priestesses have over her. I would never give up an infant for anything!" I yelled.

Miles looked confused. "I don't get how Talia didn't see this, or that the Wands couldn't read her mind and see her intentions."

"We didn't have a reason to suspect her, so we didn't know to look into it," Chloe said. "The priestesses tortured her. We never imagined she'd still be on their side."

I pressed my face into my hands as tears streamed down my cheeks. "I *hate* myself for putting my trust in her again."

"Nad," Lucas said gently. "This isn't your fault. She took advantage of your good intentions. We're not going to let anyone hurt Marcus. We'll find out where she's taken him, and then we're going after him."

I wiped my nose with the back of my hand. "Good intentions be damned. Our choices led to this, despite having the best intentions, and the outcome was still terrible. Good intentions aren't enough. Is it worth making choices at all and continuing to fight?"

"You're right," Lucas agreed. "It's not enough to be good people. All we can do is the best we can, and right now, our best means going after our son."

"You do realize it's a trap," Verla pointed out.

Autumn scoffed. "*Of course* it's a trap. The priestesses took your son to lure you in."

"We still have to go after him," Lucas insisted. "What are the priestesses going to do to us? We have four Oaken Wands. We're more powerful than they'll ever be."

"I'm certain that's precisely what they're after," Verla said. "They're going to want a trade."

"What point are you trying to make?" Lucas growled. "I don't give a damn about these Oaken Wands if my son's life is at stake! I've already lost one son. I'm not losing another."

"I'm merely stating the truth, so that you know what you're getting yourself into," Verla said calmly.

Lucas's hands curled into fists. "I've already walked through hell and back for these Wands. You think I wouldn't do the same for my son? I don't give a flying fuck what the priestesses want. We're getting him back, even if we have to exchange the Wands for him."

"How's it coming, Talia?" Professor Warren asked.

Talia furrowed her brow in concentration. "I can't seem to get a clear vision on Mandy, but maybe if I focus on Marcus, I'll get something."

Several moments passed, and then she gasped. "I see it! Marcus is being taken to the priestesses at Octavia Hall."

Lucas went over to the dresser and pulled out his reaper robe. It was made of black fabric with images of a skull embroidered along the hem—the mark of the Mortana Cast. When he put the robe on, it was scary how deadly he looked, and yet every part of me wanted to march into Octavia Falls at his side. The hood loosely framed his face, and the ends of the sleeves were tattered so that they swayed like a warning of death when he walked.

"If you don't want to fight, you can stay behind, but I'm going after my son," Lucas told the others. So much for not going in guns-blazing. The priestesses hadn't given us a choice.

I stood and took his hand in mine. The tears dried quickly as stone-cold resolve came over me. "I'm right there alongside you."

Autumn stepped forward. "As am I."

The others chimed in with agreement.

"Then let's get moving." Lucas lifted his hands, and a massive portal bloomed in front of us, big enough to fit all ten of us. The cats stayed behind to guard the house. Our sanctuary had been compromised, and we needed them to hold the wards so we had a safe house to come back to.

Lucas didn't bother with secrecy or the element of surprise. He portaled us straight onto Main Street and out in the open. He was so furious he *wanted* the priestesses to know we were coming for them.

The dark streets of Octavia Falls loomed in front of us, and Octavia Hall rose above the trees. Hundreds of Executors in dark uniforms stood in front of the doors to the council's headquarter building. Every soldier the priestesses had at their disposal must've been standing in the street waiting for us. They wore cocky grins, as if they thought they were strong enough to stop us. They'd been *planning* this.

Heat flared in my bones as pure rage overcame me. These bitches thought they could take *my son*? They had no idea what my friends and I were capable of.

"They're here!" an Executor shouted. "Kill them all, except the Curse Breaker! She's the only one they need!"

Lucas immediately threw up a shield. Magic slammed into it from all angles, and I could feel the edges of it cracking.

"Together!" I shouted.

The others let their magic pour into me, and I combined it with Lucas's. The shield grew stronger, until the hundreds of spells raining down on us simply bounced off. We marched down the street until we were face-to-face with over a hundred Executors.

Sheriff Baker stood at the front of the group, smirking like he'd find joy in watching us die. My stomach twisted at the sight of him. He'd been the one to arrest Professor Daniels over a year and a half ago, and she'd later been hanged. He'd dragged Professor Wykoff out of school after she wrote a letter to the editor at the *Miriamic Messenger*. He'd been vicious to the students whenever he was at the college, and he forced searches of our stashes. He'd arrested Lucas before our trial, and cruelly followed any orders the priestesses gave him. He'd been nothing but horrible to my friends and me since I became a priestess. He'd wanted to get rid of me then, and it was clear by the glimmer in his eye that he hoped to see my demise tonight.

*Wasn't going to happen.*

Lucas's reaper robes billowed in the wind. "I'll give you one chance to step aside. If you don't, you *will* die."

The Executors didn't even blink. For a brief moment, I felt my feet leave the ground, as if a Mentalist was trying to lift me with their telekinesis.

Beside me, Chloe's Wand glowed brighter as she siphoned their magic for her own. Talia and Grant stepped up beside her, and Lucas withdrew his Wand. Tendrils of magic swirled through the Oaken Wands, rendering the Executors powerless. Executors began looking around at one another in confusion when they realized their magic was no longer working. Whispers accusing the Waning spread through the crowd.

"What are you going to do?" Sheriff Baker mocked. "You're just a bunch of stupid kids with big guns. And ours are bigger."

Dozens of Executors withdrew pistols. I recognized them for what they were and knew they weren't typical guns. They were filled with noxite tranquilizer darts. Those darts were laced with the same type of metal the town's jail cells were made of. Lucas and I had been locked behind noxite bars before our trial, and our powers had been rendered useless. If one of those darts hit one of my friends, their magic would be drained by the noxite's power. They'd lose access to the Oaken Wands' magic.

"You don't have the guts to kill us," Sheriff Baker sneered. "We're going to break down your weak-ass shield, and then you and your little friends can enjoy a one-way ticket to the Abyss."

Baker lifted his hands, and with a quick flick of his wrist, the Executors raced forward, surrounding us at all angles. They dragged a heavy metal chain with them, and I could feel it draining our powers as it surrounded us at all angles. It was a noxite chain, and they were trying to box us in. It wasn't something that could keep us contained, but all it had to do was drain our powers for a moment to drop our shields. The Executors aimed to fire the darts.

But they never had the chance. Before the chain circle closed around us, Lucas blasted our shield outward. Executors went flying, and the chain dropped to the ground.

Lucas chuckled darkly. He lifted his hands, and small portals began opening up beneath the Executors' feet. One after another, Executors fell through the portals. I caught sight of gothic peaks surrounded by maple trees. He only portaled them to the other side of town, but their screams cut off completely when the portals closed behind them.

It was a warning—and it was clear by the way Lucas's lips curled back that it was the last warning they were going to get.

Rage marred Sheriff Baker's features. "Go to hell!"

Lucas smirked. "Been there. Survived that. Now give me back my son!"

I felt the moment Lucas snapped, because magic surged through him so strongly that it changed the air around us. Wind began swirling in the opposite direction, and dark clouds rushed in to drown out the stars. Lightning cracked overhead. Witches couldn't control the weather, but the power surging through the air was enough to shift its course.

Lucas lifted the Mortana Wand, and I was shocked to see bony fingers appear beneath the sleeve of his robe. The hood of the robes fell back, and I saw that the skin had disappeared from his face, leaving behind only a skull with dark, empty eye sockets.

He was summoning all his power and had become a living reaper.

Sheriff Baker's eyes widened in horror. He whirled around and disappeared into the crowd before Lucas could attack him.

Several Executors scurried backward, but Lucas aimed his magic at them. A dark fog whipped through the crowd. I witnessed the moment Lucas yanked the Executors' souls from their bodies, because their spirit left a brief ethereal imprint in the air, before fading away completely. Dozens of bodies slumped to the ground all at once, then crumbled to dust under the power of the Mortana Wand.

Lucas pulled his hands together, and a darkness swelled upward. He took control of the Death energy that came from the corpses, transforming it to his will. Executors began to flee, but Lucas twisted his hands, aiming the dark cloud at the scattering men. The magic pierced straight through their chests all at once, and dozens more Executors fell. Their bodies withered away to nothing, until they were mere piles of dust on the pavement.

Lucas had spared those Executors' souls, and they would be escorted to the afterlife by other reapers, but there was no reprieve for them here on Earth. Death swept through them all until over a hundred Executors' bodies were reduced to nothing but powder. It all happened so fast that none of us even had a chance to cast a spell of our own.

I expected Lucas to slow down. There was so much death, so much carnage. He must've been hearing their thoughts all at once, overlapping one another. But Lucas stepped forward confidently, as if the voices were nothing more than whispers in the background.

Several men lunged for him to stop him, but he merely conjured his scythe and swung it at them. He sliced six men in half in a matter of moments. Blood pooled across the pavement and began trickling down the street. Screams of terror echoed throughout the town.

I should have felt something sickly when I witnessed all those people die, but all I felt was the satisfaction of revenge. I felt no mercy for these people who had stolen our son and were terrorizing an infant. They deserved death.

Lucas released his scythe, and it began flying down the street as if it had a mind of its own. It chased down the few surviving Executors who were fleeing, then swung at them. They were dead in moments.

Sheriff Baker was the last man standing. He sprinted away from the approaching scythe, shooting terrified glances over his shoulder. He tried to shoot magic behind himself, but nothing worked. Sheriff Baker tripped, landing flat on his face. He quickly rolled over and held his hands up in front of himself, like he was trying to conjure a shield.

"Please, no!" he screamed. "It's the priestesses you want—"

His words halted on his tongue as the scythe sliced through the air, lopping his head off in a single swing. His bloody body slumped to the ground, and his head rolled several feet away.

Eerie silence filled the air. Lucas had single-handedly killed them all— hundreds of them. Dust scattered the street, along with the remains of broken noxite pistols. Only ten bloody bodies killed by the scythe remained.

Lucas's scythe flew back into his hand, and he subconjured it. He bent over, bracing his hands against his knees. I could hear his labored breathing from several paces away.

Slowly, I approached him and placed my hand on his back. "Lucas…?"

He stood upright and turned to me. The skeleton-like reaper I'd seen only moments ago was gone. He looked like himself again, though his features were ashen.

"Are you going to be okay?" I asked.

He let out a heavy breath. "I'm a bit worn, but I'll make it. Let's keep moving."

We stepped over unmoving bodies as we raced up the stairs to the entrance of Octavia Hall. I threw open the doors—and stopped dead in my tracks.

Ghostly moans filled the foyer, and dozens of ethereal forms floated inches off the ground, staring back at us. At first, I thought they were the spirits of the Executors Lucas had just killed, but they wore all different types of clothing. There wasn't an Executor uniform in sight.

Before any of us could react, the ghosts surrounded us, flying at us from all angles. Hands materialized into solid form and began attacking us. An icy cold finger curled around my ankle and yanked my feet out from under me. I fell to the floor with a heavy crash.

Blood pulsed in my ears. I quickly went to kick the ghost off of me, only I hesitated when my gaze met a familiar face.

It was Scott, Meredith's husband. We'd seen him at the Festival of Chosen when we'd snuck into town. The priestesses had forced him to stand on stage and disavow his marriage. It struck me that he'd done as the priestesses had asked, and he had still died for it.

"How are they doing this!?" Chloe screamed. "We shouldn't be able to see them, let alone feel them."

"I don't know!" Miles kicked one of the ghosts off of him. "Something about their magic doesn't feel right. They don't feel like ordinary ghosts!"

Another hand came down on me, but I grabbed it before it could reach my face. I felt into its magic and was surprised to feel a high frequency buzz. The taste of citrus filled my mouth. It was all too familiar.

Then I caught sight of Scott's brother, Simon, who the priestesses had poisoned on stage in front of us. It made perfect sense.

"It's Alchemy magic!" I told them. "These are the victims of the priestesses' poison. They were manufacturing it with the Alchemy Wand before Hector died. He told us it was designed to control their victims, even in death!"

Professor Warren rolled across the ground as he dodged a ghostly attack. "So they don't have a choice but to attack us? They're just following orders."

"Grant!" Lucas cried. "Use the Alchemy Wand to free them! We'll do it together."

Lucas ducked a fist as a ghost tried to attack him. He quickly made his way over to Grant, who was trying to fight off three ghosts, but his hands just kept going through them. They could touch us, but we couldn't touch them. The ghosts tried to pull the Alchemy Wand from Grant's grasp, but he struggled against them, refusing to let go.

The end of the Wand began to glow as it siphoned the Alchemy magic from them. A loud *snap* reverberated through the foyer when he broke the spell. The ghosts backed off.

Lucas whirled around, as if he could see something the rest of us couldn't. "Go!" he shouted to the ghosts. "Quickly!"

The ghosts rushed in the direction he was looking, then one by one, they faded away. I realized then what he'd been seeing. It was a reaper portal. He'd crossed them over the moment the hold the priestesses had over the ghosts had ended.

Lucas looked even paler now. I could tell this much magic was taking a toll on him. Even though he had the Mortana Wand now, he hadn't utilized it for every spell. He'd been drawing on his own magic this whole time, too. It was a lot of power for one person.

I quickly got to my feet. "Come on! Let's keep moving."

We hurried up several flights of stairs, keeping on high alert for another attack by the priestesses, but it never came. We reached the top floor and burst through the door to the Imperium headquarters, only to come face to face not with the priestesses, but with Mandy.

She raced around the room, gathering valuable artifacts that the priestesses had on display. One by one, she subconjured them, until she came to an immediate halt when we charged through the doorway.

The *nerve* she had! She'd been working with the priestesses this whole time and took our son for them. Now she was robbing them? It was like she was trying to get herself killed. If we didn't kill her, the priestesses would. It was so unlike her that I could hardly believe what I was seeing.

Mandy didn't get a chance to open her mouth and defend herself, because Lucas had crossed the room in an instant. He grabbed her with all his strength and slammed her back against the wall. One of his hands curled around her throat, while the other pointed the Mortana Wand straight between her eyes.

Mandy kicked her feet and tried to fight him off, but Lucas was a hell of a lot stronger than her. A blazing fire burned behind Lucas's eyes, and it was clear to everyone that if Mandy made one wrong move, he wouldn't hesitate to kill her.

"You kidnapped our son, you evil bitch!" Lucas seethed. "Where are the priestesses? Where have they taken him!?"

Mandy made a choking sound. Lucas loosened his grip on her throat, but he pinned his forearm across her chest so she couldn't get away. Mandy turned her face away from him without a word.

"ANSWER ME!" Lucas roared. He curled the Mortana Wand in his fist and smashed his knuckles into the wall beside her head. The wall cracked, and the sound echoed down the staircase. Mandy said nothing.

"Don't want to talk? Fine. We don't need you to talk." Lucas cocked his head. "Chloe, Talia, use teleinsight on her. Read her mind."

The girls lifted their Wands in unison, and the ends glowed. They spoke the incantation and entered a trace.

Chloe's brow furrowed. "We can't. It's like something's blocking us."

I narrowed my eyes on the traitor. "The Wands have power over all witch magic. There has to be a power greater than the Oaken Wands working on her. Or something the Wands can't influence."

I approached her, and tendrils of blue magic swirled out of my fingers.

"Don't you fucking touch me!" Mandy growled.

My powers crept over her skin. I felt nothing at first, not even an indication of her Cast, until my magic brushed up against something strange. It was similar to witch magic, but different, too. It vibrated at another frequency, a frequency far too reminiscent of our time in Malovia. It was dark, though—darker than any magic we'd encountered when we visited the fae.

It had to be Unseelie magic, the magic of the dark fae. My eyes fell upon the red gem hanging around her neck. I knew without a shadow of a doubt that was the object giving off the power. It hadn't ever registered as strange, because Mandy was always wearing jewelry.

"Fucking fae magic!" I sneered. I grabbed the fae amulet and tore it off of her, then tossed it aside. "I see you made a deal with the fae as well as the priestesses."

Mandy chuckled lightly. "I didn't have to make a deal with any fae. I found an Unseelie roaming Octavia Falls, trying to get away from the fae war. He wore this amulet to disguise his magic from being detected easily. One sip of tea was all it took to kill him."

Heat flared through my body. Mandy had never been a killer, so why was she speaking of murder so casually?

"Why would you ever work with the priestesses after what they did to you?" I demanded.

Mandy didn't answer.

"You can answer willingly, or we'll make you talk," I started, but it was at that moment that my magic sensed something else. Now that Mandy was no longer in possession of the fae amulet, I could feel her magic again.

Only… it wasn't hers.

I took a cautious step back. "I sense Alchemy magic. Mandy's a Mentalist. Which means…"

"This isn't Mandy," Lucas finished for me. His eyes went wide. "All this time, Mandy was never with us to begin with. It was an Alchemist with one hell of a transformation potion."

Lucas dug the tip of his Wand under Fake Mandy's jaw. "Tell us everything."

"Why? So you can just kill me?" the Alchemist said in Mandy's voice. "You're not going to let me go now that you know."

"Doesn't mean I can't get answers from you first," Lucas said darkly.

He cocked his head, and Chloe stepped forward with the Mentalist Wand raised. Lucas dropped his arm. Fake Mandy rose into the air, her back pressed firmly against the wall. Chloe used her telekinesis to pin her there, until her toes dangled off the ground.

"Who are you, really?" Chloe demanded, the end of her Wand glowing brighter than ever before. Now that the fae amulet wasn't blocking their magic, Talia and Chloe could use teleinsight to get inside Fake Mandy's head. Only this time, their spell was stronger, because they used their power to force Fake Mandy to utter her own confession.

She had no choice but to answer in a rasping voice, "Magnus Knight."

My heart should've stopped in my chest. I should've felt the world tilt on its axis and experienced it all come crumbling down. Instead, all I could think was that it made perfect sense.

If there was anyone in this coven as bad as the priestesses, it was this man. He was the Alchemist behind nightshade, the one who'd been working with Priestess Stella to try to obtain the Alchemy Wand from the Crock of Death. He'd killed so many innocent people to do it. The priestesses had discarded him after he'd failed, but clearly they'd found another use for him.

I recalled the last time we'd seen Magnus. He had been throwing up behind a dumpster in an alleyway. It was no surprise that he'd made some kind of deal with the priestesses.

I couldn't believe we'd let this man into our *home*! For months, he lived alongside us, attended our Yule celebration and baby shower, only for him to do the unthinkable and take our son when our guard was down.

It was all coming together. We'd gotten into Octavia Falls so easily the night we rescued Mandy and Tate. We'd written it off as a result of the Festival of Chosen, but all this time, the priestesses had actually *wanted* us to rescue them, so that they had a man on the inside. The only other option the priestesses had was to set the girls free, but by that point, Tate had already been captured, and they knew we'd come for her regardless. If they let Tate and Mandy escape, we'd have suspected something for sure.

The priestesses only came for us later that night when we'd broken into the school. They'd wanted us to rescue the girls, but they hadn't intended for us to find the Oaken Wands.

"Where's the real Mandy?" Lucas growled.

Magnus laughed in Mandy's voice. "In a holding cell somewhere."

His apathy for one of my friends' lives made me want to snap his neck. Tendrils of magic twisted out of my fingertips again, curling around Magnus's throat.

"Don't kill him yet," Lucas warned.

"I'm not going to kill him," I said. "I want to look into his real eyes before he dies."

The Alchemy magic pulsing through his veins was strong. I sensed traces of fae magic mixed in with the potion he'd taken to disguise himself as Mandy. The priestesses had obviously supplied him with rare herbs to keep up the charade. I curled my magic tightly around his, and I felt the spell snap.

His limbs elongated, and his hair shortened. The softness of his jaw morphed into sharper features, until it was not an image of Mandy hanging in front of us, but Magnus.

"We should've known it was you!" Chloe growled. "We read your mind at Yule. We should've been able to tell you were deceiving us."

"The amulet disguises me under all circumstances," Magnus sneered. "Even your little party trick couldn't expose me. All I had to do was come up with something you'd believe, so you didn't keep digging. I did my homework before I infiltrated your little safe house. I knew Mandy was close with that Amy girl who burned on the pyre. Every time I mentioned her, you all backed down."

I thought of the morning of Yule—how he had mentioned her when I'd come into his room for help with my gift. He'd said Amy had taught him the tea we'd made for Talia, but that wasn't true. Magnus knew the spell because he was an experienced Alchemist. I should've known something was up when he pretended as if Mandy had lost all her jewelry-making supplies when she left Octavia Falls. She wouldn't have let all that leave her stash.

"The amulet is why I struggled to gather intel on the priestesses," Talia realized. "Because *you* were involved, but my visions couldn't see past the fae spell."

Magnus gave a chilling laugh. "Of course. Not even the power of a Seer could expose me."

"You've been here all this time, haven't you?" I demanded. "You've been posing as Mandy since the night we found you in Lilian's basement last November."

Magnus strained against the wall, but he was weak compared to the Mentalist Wand. "Yes."

"This never should have happened," Onyx insisted. "How did he trick our wards?"

"He didn't have to," Professor Warren said hollowly. "We invited him in and led him through."

Lucas's face turned red in rage as he stared down Magnus. "What was your objective? Why hang around so fucking long?"

"The priestesses made me a deal," Magnus replied. "If I infiltrated your safe house and brought back the Oaken Wands, they would restore me to my former glory—get my businesses back up and running and put me in a position of power within the coven once again. I was meant to bide my time until you found all the Wands, then take them all, and return them to the priestesses."

"Then why bother taking a child?" Verla snapped.

"Priorities shifted," Magnus said. "When I found out the Curse Breaker was pregnant with demigods, I consulted with the priestesses."

He couldn't even bother to say my name—as if I was that unimportant. Ironic, since I was apparently central to his plans.

"That's where you disappeared to during the baby shower," I realized. "You weren't upstairs organizing our presents! You ran off to tell the priestesses what you learned."

"Yes, though I would've left sooner if I didn't have to keep up god-awful appearances," Magnus stated snidely. "I still can't believe I had to attend one second of your stupid puzzle party."

"What did the priestesses tell you to do?" I questioned.

"They told me to forget about the Oaken Wands… that a demigod child was more powerful than all the Oaken Wands combined. The priestesses intended to use you to cast a powerful spell, though they didn't tell me what it was. The poison was meant to remain dormant inside of you, until that spell was cast. Then once you performed the spell, the poison would take effect, and you would die instantly."

I scoffed. "Well, you screwed that up."

"How was I to know there was ginger in the iced tea?" Magnus demanded. "It changed the chemical make-up of my potion and turned it into something else. The poison took effect immediately, though the altered properties weren't enough to kill you."

"So my ginger didn't poison Nadine," Grant realized, sounding relieved. "*You* did! My ginger actually prevented her from dying."

"What about the sugar scrub you made me for Yule, or the tea we made for Talia?" I demanded. "Were those poisoned, too?"

"The tea we made was safe," Magnus scoffed. "It was merely a way to gain your trust. The sugar scrub was my own recipe. Each time you used it, it collected data that was sent back to the priestesses, in order to monitor your vitals and track your pregnancy."

Talia furrowed her brow. "But if you were working for the priestesses this whole time, why were they sending Executors to attack the safe house?"

"They didn't come to *attack* you," Magnus spat. "They came to exchange information. After you killed the first group of messengers, they sent groups of Executors to the next ridge to throw you off, to lure you into a false sense of security—as if your stupid plans would ever work. They knew you were watching them."

"You're the reason the Executors knew to come the night the babies were born," I realized. "You told them I was in labor."

"Of course," Magnus sneered. "But I knew the babies wouldn't be able to make it on their own if they were born that early. I told the priestesses to hold off, that we had to be strategic, but they didn't listen. They came that night to take the children. After your friends killed off the Executors, I convinced them we had to wait until the time was right, and to give me more time to obtain the child that survived."

"What are the priestesses planning now?" Lucas asked.

"A trap, of course," Magnus said. "I was to take the child to lure you here."

"For what?" I demanded. "That Executor outside said they needed me —a Curse Breaker. If they already have Marcus, what do they need me for? You were planning to kill me, anyway. Why bother keeping me alive now?"

Magnus curled his lips back. "They don't tell me everything. I simply follow orders."

"Well, we're here," Lucas said. "Where are the priestesses?"

Magnus let out a chilling laugh. "Oh, they're here... waiting for the rest of you to die. Do us all a favor and cork off so we can finally get this over with—"

A loud *snap* filled the room, and Magnus's head cranked so far in one direction that it looked like it was on backward. His body slumped to the floor lifelessly.

Slowly, we all turned to Chloe. "What?" she asked innocently. "He told us everything we needed to know. I was sick of listening to him talk. Always hated him, to be honest."

Lucas took one last look at Magnus, then turned away. "The priestesses must still be nearby with Marcus. Let's go find them."

Lucas hurried out the door and down the stairs.

"Wait, we need a plan—" Verla started as she followed behind him, but a distant sound gave her pause.

"Is that... someone screaming?" I stopped on the steps to listen again.

"*Help!*" a woman cried.

My stomach plummeted. I knew that voice far too well.

It was the real Mandy.

# lucas

## TWENTY-THREE

We sprinted down the stairs and through the hallway, hearts hammering to the beat of our racing footsteps. We turned several corners until we came upon a narrow dead-end hall at the back of the building. It was dark and looked like the kind of place you kept storage boxes—not people.

"Help!" Mandy's voice came again, much louder this time.

I hurried to the door the screaming was coming from and flung it open. We flooded inside to find ourselves in a darkened storage room. Beyond the crowded shelving stood a metal cage that stretched from the floor to the ceiling. It looked to be a kind of storage locker one would keep valuables in to prevent theft. Instead, the locker had been cleared out to make room for two women.

"Thank the Goddess," Mandy wept. It was *our* Mandy this time. The relief in her tear-filled eyes was undeniable. The priestesses hadn't been kind to her. She'd dropped a considerable amount of weight, and her dark hair was matted in a tangled bun. She had cuts and bruises all over her arms.

Mandy sniffled. "I've waited so long to see you guys."

"We're going to get you out," I promised.

I stepped up to the cage and laced my fingers through the metal fencing. Miles fidgeted with the lock, trying to set them free. My attention was captivated by the other woman inside the cell. She was in her thirties with caramel colored hair and wore a long skirt that had been ripped on the end. She looked so frail, with bruises mottling one side of her face.

"Professor Wykoff," I breathed. "What have the priestesses done to you?"

This hadn't been the first time the priestesses set out to hurt her. Last year, Professor Wykoff wrote a letter to the editor that was published in the *Miriamic Messenger*, in which she came out against what the priestesses were doing. The priestesses had made a big deal at school about making her answer for it, but we'd protested, and managed to save Professor Wykoff from being hanged.

She knotted her hands together. "I continued your work and kept your news column going. I published articles in secret to expose the priestesses' true intentions, and I gathered quite a following. There are people who will side with you. Unfortunately, despite my best efforts to conceal myself, the priestesses found out I was behind it. They brought me here with the intent to execute me publicly any day now."

"That's not going to happen," I assured her.

Miles kicked the cage. "This lock is protected by magic. I can't get through."

Nadine lifted her hands. "Everyone stand back."

We all took several steps back, and Mandy and Professor Wykoff huddled together in the corner. Nadine took control of the magic protecting the cage, then transformed it. Blue, electric power crackled across the metal like sparks of lightning, then a huge *boom* sounded as the door blasted inward. The heavy door clanged against the wall, then fell to the floor.

I reached my hand inside the cage. "Quickly."

Mandy took my hand and scrambled out of the holding cell. She was so weak that she practically sagged into my arms. "I'm so sorry!"

I stared down at her incredulously. "You have nothing to be sorry for."

Tears leaked from her eyes. "I do. The priestesses tortured me. They made me send you visions through dreams, to lure you to Octavia Falls. I didn't want to, but they forced me. I figure they got what they wanted, because they eventually dragged me here. That cage wasn't just enchanted to keep us in, but also to block our powers. I had no way of getting in touch with any of you..."

Mandy trailed off as she looked around. "But you're all still here. They didn't hurt you. Then what did they want from me?"

Dear Goddess. Mandy had no idea Magnus had been pretending to be her for months.

"We have a lot to tell you—" I started, but I was cut off by the sound of an animalistic wail coming down the hall. It was reminiscent of nails on a chalkboard, almost like the distorted tone of a horse's bray.

"There's no time to chat," Verla insisted. "We have to get moving."

We left the storage room and turned a few corners until we entered the wide expanse of the main hallway. My heart dropped to my stomach, and I skidded to a halt when I saw what awaited us.

On both ends of the hall stood half a dozen horse-like creatures. They had no skin—just red flesh coating their bodies. Each horse had only one eye, along with a rider attached to its back. Each rider had long, spindly arms that dragged on the ground.

We'd seen these creatures before, when we'd made the trek to hell. *Nuckelavee*, the Ferryman had called them.

"Everyone stay back!" I cried.

Professor Wykoff grabbed Mandy, who was shaking at the sight of the beasts. Slowly, she dragged Mandy back down the hall, out of sight of the *nuckelavee*. Mandy was in no condition to fight right now.

I took a few paces back, but the *nuckelavee* inched closer, as if stalking prey. I could see their chests rising and falling. I remembered what the Ferryman had said about them.

"They can kill cattle in a single breath," I told the others. "I'm certain that poison doesn't discriminate."

"Didn't he also say they're terrified of fresh water?" Grant asked.

"I don't see any freshwater streams around!" Miles's voice rose a few pitches.

"I've got this." Chloe stepped forward confidently, and the end of the Mentalist Wand glowed. "Turn around and go back to where you came from!"

Chloe was trying to get into their heads, but the herd kept creeping closer. The way behind us was only a dead end. To escape, we'd have to get to one of the stairwells on either side of the hall and down to the main level. The monsters were blocking off all exits.

"Uh, I don't think it's working!" Talia squeaked.

"Use the Oaken Wands," Verla encouraged. "There has to be a spell that can break them."

"What am I going to do?" Talia demanded. "The best I can do is feel their emotions, and it's obvious they were sent to kill us!"

Grant held up the Alchemy Wand. "I'll poison their blood. That should stop them."

The dark blood in the *nuckelavees'* veins glowed as Grant infused it with his magic. In moments, their muscles seemed to grow an extra twenty-five percent. It had the exact opposite effect he intended.

Grant chuckled nervously. "Uh… I see you all have been spending some time in the weight room."

"They're already poisonous," Onyx pointed out. "You've only made them stronger."

"Let me try," I offered, taking another step back as they stopped their hooves at us. I lifted the Mortana Wand and curled my magic around their throats. I tried to rip their souls apart one by one, the same way I'd dragged the Executors' souls from their bodies, but the darkness I felt within them didn't budge.

"It's not going to work," Autumn said in a shaky tone. "They're already dead."

"Autumn's right," I told the others. I felt into their energy, and I could tell something was off, the same way I had sensed that Professor Leto was a demon last year. "They're raw dark spiritual energy. They can't be influenced by personality, which means there's nothing for our power to manipulate."

The *nuckelavee* were getting too close now. They'd backed us into the wall, and any moment now they'd be close enough to breathe their deathly breath on us.

"Then we're going to have to turn to brute force." Professor Warren lifted his hands, and I quickly caught on to what he was doing. Footsteps sounded on the stairs—the heavy boots of dead Executors from downstairs, reanimated by Professor Warren's necromancy magic. Several *nuckelavee* turned their heads to see what was coming. In the moment they were distracted, I gestured to the others. We quickly slipped to the side and raced toward another stairwell at the other end of the hall.

We weren't fast enough, though. Two *nuckelavee* got to the stairwell before we did to block our path. They huffed and stomped their feet.

I shoved the others back. "Don't let them breathe on you!"

Chloe shrugged me off and stepped forward to face the *nuckelavee*. "For fuck's sake, get the hell out of our way."

She thrust her hand forward, and the two *nuckelavee* went flying backward in response to her telekinetic magic. They tumbled down the stairs, but immediately jumped to their feet on the landing. They narrowed their eyes at us and scraped their hooves on the ground. I threw up a shield to hold them back.

"All you did was piss them off!" Nadine cried.

She barely got the words out before a group of *nuckelavee* came charging down the hallway. I immediately conjured my scythe and swung it at the nearest monster. The horse's head rolled off its shoulders, and its rider screamed a high-pitched cry that reverberated through the walls.

I ordered my scythe to fly down the hall and swing at the second closest *nuckelavee*. All I had to do was think about it. But before the blade could make contact, the *nuckelavee* caught it in his spindly fingers and tossed it aside. My scythe clattered to the ground.

My shoulders slumped. I'd already performed so much magic, and it was wearing me out.

Nadine thrust her hand out, blasting the closest creatures back with battle orbs. It wasn't enough to get rid of them, though. How were we going to kill something that was already dead?

Down the hall, ten dead bodies had reached the top of the stairs. Professor Warren moved them like puppets, ordering them to attack the *nuckelavee*. Blood dripped out of slashed wounds in their abdomen, and they slumped over. My scythe had delivered so much damage that even in death they couldn't walk right. Two of the corpses had been sliced clean in half by my blade, and their bottom half marched up the stairs, while the top half dragged itself upward by its hands.

The dead tried to climb onto the monsters' backs, and the *nuckelavee* turned their heads to deliver their deadly breath. Naturally, it didn't work on the dead bodies. When the *nuckelavee* realized this, they began punching and scratching at the Executors. They tossed the bodies off their backs, then stomped them with their hooves. The crunch of bones echoed off the walls. It all happened so fast.

"Lucas, portal us out of here!" Verla cried.

I lifted my hands, but only sparks appeared. "I'm... drained," I admitted breathlessly. I couldn't perform much more magic. Not when I'd already done so much to kill the hundreds of Executors. Whatever power I could still do was up to the ability of the Mortana Wand.

"We're not leaving without Marcus," Autumn demanded. "If it's portals you want, then let's portal these creatures back to the hell they came from."

She stepped in front of me, but I wasn't about to let her do this spell alone. It was a powerful one, even for a reaper.

I grabbed Autumn's hand and lifted the Mortana Wand in the other. "Together."

Autumn looked up at me and nodded.

Magic swelled through me, filling me up from head to toe. A powerful gust of wind swept through the hallway, then the shimmering edges of a portal bloomed at the *nuckelavee's* feet. I could hear the snap of bubbling lava below us. The red glow of hell reflected off the walls. One by one, *nuckelavee* let out horrifying cries as they were sucked into the portal.

A single monster remained at the end of the hall. He set his sights on me, then began galloping in our direction. Autumn and I only funneled more magic into the spell. Our portal expanded, until it was so large it touched each wall. I could see the lake of boiling lava below us—even feel the heat of it on my face.

The *nuckelavee* jumped, soaring over top of the portal. I was certain he wasn't going to make it and would fall into the pit…

The monster's front hooves touched solid ground, but its backend dropped into the portal. His feet scraped at the floor, desperately searching for a handhold. When he didn't find one, the long arms of his humanoid half reached outward—and connected with my ankle.

I was swept off my feet in an instant and felt myself being dragged across the floor. My heart jumped into my throat.

"NO!" The word echoed around me, and I was certain multiple people had screamed it.

My legs slipped into the portal, being dragged down by the weight of the *nuckelavee*. I felt the heat of hell on my clothes as the monster attempted to drag me into the portal, down to hell with it. I thought for certain I was a goner, and that the fires of hell would consume me. But at the last second, my friends reached me. Multiple hands grabbed my arms, my clothes—anything they could reach. Autumn clung to me as she kicked at the *nuckelavee*, trying to force him off.

I felt his hand break free. It was at that same moment that Autumn's eyes filled with terror. A split second of panic hit, and then, her hands left my body. The *nuckelavee* had grabbed hold of *her* instead, and she'd lost her grip on me.

"Autumn!" I screamed. I reached out for her, but it was already too late. Her fingers slipped from mine, and she went tumbling into the lava below. I looked through the portal to hell. It all happened so fast that she was a mere flash of color, reduced to a splash...

And then, she was gone.

*I hope my sacrifice has redeemed me.* Autumn's voice rang through my mind.

My friends pulled me back to solid ground. Tears welled in my eyes. "I shall see you in Alora," I whispered, hoping that somewhere out there, Autumn could hear me.

The portal slammed shut. In front of us, the dead bodies Professor Warren had reanimated lay sprawled out on the ground. The *nuckelavee* were gone—they'd all been swallowed up by the portal.

Or so I thought. Hooves stomped up the staircase. Somewhere in the chaos, my shield had broken, and the two *nuckelavee* left in the stairwell came charging at us. They had their sights set on the nearest person —Nadine.

I wasn't close enough to stop them. I choked back my tears and immediately sprang into action. I lifted my hand to cast a shield, but I wasn't as quick as Verla. She threw herself in front of Nadine and lifted her palms. A crackle of magic made the hair on my arms stand on end a moment before battle magic unlike anything I'd ever seen burst from Verla's hands.

A thundering *boom* consumed the following moment. It was as if a bomb had detonated, sending a wave of magic blasting down the hall. The two charging *nuckelavee* were reduced to a pile of ash in the blink of an eye. Windows exploded outward, and the sound of glass filled Octavia Hall.

My friends and I were thrown backward. The wind knocked out of me when I hit the wall, and my ears rang. My friends lay scattered across the hallway.

I thought it'd be over in a second, but the building began to creak, and I realized the ground was shaking beneath me. A loud *crack* broke through the air, and building materials rained down from above us. Half the building gave way all at once, and a gaping fissure opened in the floor.

Professor Warren didn't get a chance to move as the rift split under him. His legs slipped into the opening.

"Professor!" Nadine and I screamed at the same time. We both lunged forward, but Professor Warren had already fallen.

I heard the hard *thud* of his landing on the level below us, along with the snap of what I assumed to be building material.

My heart hammered as I peered through the opening. I found relief when I saw Professor Warren lying on the floor below us, trying to catch his breath. His leg was twisted at an odd angle. I realized the snap I heard had been bone. He was hurt, but he was alive.

"Professor, are you okay!?" I called.

He sucked a breath between his teeth. "I'll live…"

I whirled around to assess the damage. The fissure was six feet wide at its largest spot and progressively got smaller, until it stopped halfway down the hall. My friends groaned and rubbed parts of themselves that had been hit in the blast.

"Everyone all right?" I asked.

Murmurs of *I'm okay* spread through the hall. Apart from a few bruises and Warren's broken leg, everyone looked to be fine. The *nuckelavee* were gone, and we were all still alive. Mandy clung to Professor Wykoff as they slowly inched out of the hall they'd been hiding in.

Nadine turned her gaze to Verla. "How did you do that? A blast that big should've killed you."

"I had to stop them…" Verla took a step forward, but it was shaky. All at once, the blood drained from her face, and she collapsed.

Nadine and I were at her side in an instant. I quickly flipped Verla over and rested her head in my lap.

"Stay with us," I demanded.

Verla winced as she tried to get up. "We need to keep moving. Marcus needs us."

"No, Clarice," Nadine pressed. "Your magic is completely drained. If you cast one more spell, even a small one, it could take the rest of your energy and kill you. You can't fight anymore. You and Warren need to get out of here. You need medical attention."

"But Marcus…" Verla rasped.

"We'll bring him home," I promised. "Onyx, can you help?"

Onyx stepped forward. "I'll take them to the hospital and make sure they get the medical care they need."

"You'll need help supporting Warren on the way out," Miles said. "I'll help."

"Take Mandy and Wykoff, too," I added.

"I'll stay," Professor Wykoff offered. "I'm prepared to fight."

She was still banged up from what the priestesses had done to her, but the confidence in her eyes told me she wouldn't leave even if I made her.

"All right," I agreed. "Onyx, Miles, get Mandy, Verla, and Warren out of here."

Verla slumped in my arms, and I realized she'd slipped into unconsciousness. Mandy hurried over to lift her up, and Onyx helped. They started carrying her toward the stairs, carefully maneuvering around the fissure.

Miles hurried in front of them. "Hold on, Professor Warren! I'm on my way."

I picked up my scythe and subconjured it, then turned back to those who had remained—Nadine, Grant, Talia, Chloe, and Professor Wykoff.

I gritted my teeth. "The priestesses are going to get sick of playing this game sooner or later. It's time we found them and put an end to this."

Grant smashed his fist into his opposite palm. "They're going to be sorry they ever messed with the Shield Squad."

Chloe eyed Grant. "You're not going to give that up, are you? I guess the Shield Squad it is."

Talia lifted her chin high and repeated what we'd said before we'd jumped into the hell pits. "To hell and back?"

"Even if it kills us," Nadine and I confirmed in unison.

The Shield Squad was getting our son back… *no matter what.*

My hands curled into fists, and I was ready to give the priestesses exactly what was coming to them. "Tal, now that Magnus's fae amulet isn't blocking your powers, can you see where the priestesses went?"

Talia closed her eyes and ran her fingers over the wall. "I see them coming down this hall before we arrived. Marcus is with them, and

Priestess Margaret is saying, *We'll go through the tunnel and wait out the* nuckelavee *where it's safe, until all but the Curse Breaker are destroyed."*

"What tunnel?" I demanded.

Talia shook her head. "I'm not sure, but I can use my visions to follow them. If we're fast, we might still be able to catch up with them before they realize we've killed all the *nuckelavee*. Follow me."

We raced behind her. Talia led us down the stairwell, until we reached the basement of the building. Verla's explosion hadn't reached this far down, and the ceiling appeared stable above us.

Talia ran her fingers along the walls and paused at the end of corridors to assess her visions. We turned a corner, and I figured we'd reached the front of the building by now. I thought for sure we were going to hit a dead end. But instead, a long, dark hall stretched in front of us. It looked like it traveled under the street and appeared long enough to reach the courthouse.

"They went this way!" Talia cried. "Let's keep moving!"

Nadine cast a witch light, because the hall was so dark. The six of us sprinted down the hall, until we came to a stairway at the end. It didn't appear to lead anywhere, until I looked upward to see a trap doorway. I took the stairs upward before anyone else could reach them, and I shoved the trap door open with my shoulder.

The dark walls of the coven's courtroom surrounded me, and sconces flickered with candlelight from the walls. I emerged from behind a long podium, and I realized the secret tunnel opened directly beneath where the judge sat during trials.

I stepped down from the podium and looked around the courtroom, but it was empty. Nadine climbed out of the trap door, and the others followed into the courtroom. Professor Wykoff came up beside me and spun around, looking confused.

"Where'd they go from here, Tal?" I asked desperately.

Talia placed her hand on the podium, but she didn't have a chance to speak before the front doors of the courtroom opened. Heels clicked against the marble floor. We whirled toward the sound to see three priestesses coming our way. Claudia's dark dress swirled around her ankles, and the Seer priestess was flanked by Mira—the false Curse Breaker—and Professor Hernandez—the new Mortana Priestess.

"You found our secret tunnel, I see," Claudia sneered. "We didn't expect you all to survive. Of course the idiots we planted to stop you didn't do their job."

"I'll take care of them," Mira stated, but her confidence was unfounded. She lifted her hands, and black tendrils of magic curled out of her fingers. It was all too reminiscent of what I'd seen her brother Leroy pull off the night we fled Octavia Falls a year ago. With just one touch of his magic, people would drop dead. It appeared she was gifted the same power.

I aimed the Mortana Wand at her, and her magic shriveled to nothing. Mira's features darkened, like she had thought she was impervious to the Wand's powers.

My friends already had their Wands out, which put the priestesses in the crosshairs of four Oaken Wands. I didn't know what the council thought they were going to do; the Oaken Wands were far more powerful than they were.

"The only reason you're still alive is because you're going to tell us where our son is," I growled.

"So you can kill us afterward?" Claudia gave a chilling laugh. "You're too scared to go through with it. I can feel it."

All our friends instinctually shrank closer to me, apart from Professor Wykoff, who'd been standing several paces away and closest to the priestesses. She didn't dare make a move, though.

"That's it?" Nadine demanded in a shaky tone. She inched even closer to me, until our arms were touching. "That's been your power all this time? A Seer who can feel fear? Of course we're afraid! You don't have to be a Seer to know that. What use are your powers?"

A sinister smile spread across Claudia's face. "It's certainly helped my business negotiations."

"We aren't here to negotiate," I seethed. "Tell us where our son is, or die."

"I wouldn't do that if I were you." A female voice came from the hall. Lilian and Margaret stepped out of their hiding place and into the courtroom.

Margaret held a bundle in her arms. My heart skipped a beat when I saw the tuft of hair on Marcus's head poking out of the end of the bundle. A moment of hesitation stopped me from ripping their souls straight from their bodies, because Lilian was standing alongside Margaret, pointing a wand at Marcus.

"Your child has been cursed," Lilian stated. "Hurt any one of the priestesses, and he will instantly die. Are you willing to risk that, reaper? Do you really want your son to meet his brother in the Abyss?"

I had the thought that she could be bluffing. Yet I realized if I truly believed that, I'd have killed them already.

The priestesses were playing a dangerous game. And they were holding the most valuable card in the deck.

"Name your price," I stated. I took Lucas's hand in mine, because it was the only way to keep from falling completely apart. I didn't really care what they wanted. They could take the Oaken Wands, or have my life. I'd give it to them, as long as they didn't hurt my son.

Lilian got right down to business. "You will help us create a Master Wand—an all-powerful wand that rivals the power of all the Oaken Wands combined. This wand I'm holding was carved from a branch of the Protection Tree. It is much like the Oaken Wands you possess, but it requires an enchantment to hold true power."

"Why not just take the Oaken Wands from us?" Lucas demanded. "Why go through all this trouble?"

"The Oaken Wands are five different Wands, and therefore must be in the hands of five different people, which requires trust," Lilian said. "Any one of its wielders can stab us in the back. It's better to have all that magic in one place."

I narrowed my eyes. "That's why you needed me alive. You need one person from all five Casts to complete the spell."

Lilian laughed, like she found me naive. "Even the making of the Oaken Wands required cooperation from the entire coven *and* proper alignment of the stars—one singular member of each Cast would not be enough for their power. But the Oaken Wands can only utilize magic that is already in existence. True power would be that which can create energy from nothing. What we need is a demigod such as your son."

"Demigod magic is not given up easily," Margaret added. "The child will only lend his power to someone he trusts—to his mother. It just so happens that his mother is a Curse Breaker, able to transfer magic from one place to another. Help us create the Master Wand, and your son will live. Refuse, and he will perish in the Abyss for all eternity."

I realized this was the spell Magnus had mentioned. The priestesses had been planning this ever since they found out I was giving birth to demigods.

"We have the power to control your son in death, so you don't have a choice," Margaret continued. "All it took was a small modification to our potion, which he's already taken. The potion's spell will activate if you refuse to do this for us."

A chill traveled down my spine. She was talking about the potion they'd forced Hector to make with the Alchemy Wand—the one that not only killed people, but controlled their spirits. I thought of the ghosts we'd encountered in Octavia Hall, and how they'd had no choice but to follow the priestesses' will. I couldn't subject Marcus to such a fate.

There had to be a way around this.

"Don't try anything clever," Lilian warned. "We've cast more than one spell upon your son, so that you cannot break the magic. The potion we gave him is to ensure your compliance. You *will* create the Master Wand, or your son will perish. The second is a curse to ensure our safety. If you cast another spell before completing the enchantment on the Master Wand, or if you try to harm us, your son will die. The only thing that will ensure he survives is if you complete this enchantment."

"There's no need for this," I insisted. "If it is power you want, the coven has already given it to you! You have complete control."

Lilian smirked. "Not entirely. But we will."

"We must be able to negotiate," I begged. "Your soldiers are gone. People are dead. What good is your power if there's no one left to rule over? No one else has to die for this—"

Lilian twisted her fingers, and an invisible force squeezed my wind-pipe. I gasped for breath. Her Mentalist powers curled around my neck like a noose.

Chloe must've made a motion behind me, because Lilian pointed an ugly finger at her. "If you dare try to siphon my powers with the Mentalist Wand, the child dies. The same goes for every one of you. Any use of the Oaken Wands will be treated as an act of aggression against us, and the curse we cast will kill him. I wouldn't risk it if I were you."

The priestesses had thought this through. They'd created two spells to work against one another, so that if we tried to break one, or we tried to use the Oaken Wands, the other spell would take my son's life. They'd completely backed us into a corner.

Margaret strolled forward, staring down her nose at me. "You're wrong, Nadine. People *will* continue to die, unless you do as you're told."

"How do you expect your plan to work?" I rasped. Lilian left my airways open just enough so I could talk. "He's just a baby."

"His full power won't awaken until he's older, but he still has traces of demigod magic inside of him," Margaret explained. "We can't put demigod power into *us*, so we must enchant an object with his power. You will draw his magic out and put it into this wand, so that we can utilize it for our own intentions. What will it be, Nadine? Will you do this to save your son's life?"

We couldn't lose another son. I was his mother, and it was my job to protect him. He incarnated at this time for a reason, and he had a destiny to fulfill. I wasn't letting the priestesses take him.

Lucas and I exchanged a glance. If we did this, the priestesses would be more powerful than ever before. They could use the Master Wand to create spells we couldn't even dream of.

And yet, the answer was obvious. We would do anything to save our son.

"You swear he'll live?" I choked out.

Lilian wore a triumphant smile. "Yes."

For how long, she didn't say. The priestesses wanted to play games, but all I saw was a puzzle worth solving. If they wanted to play, we could play.

"And if we do this, the spells you cast on him will be broken?" I added.

"The second you complete the enchantment, the potion we gave him will lose all power," Lilian confirmed.

She said nothing of the curse they'd cast. I couldn't break the curse before enchanting the Master Wand, and we couldn't harm the priestesses, either. We had to tread very carefully.

Lucas gave me a subtle nod.

"I will make your wand if you can promise my friends will walk out of here alive and unharmed," I offered.

Lilian exchanged a glance with Margaret. I saw the twitch of her eye that said they'd agree to my terms, but it didn't mean they wouldn't kill us the second we stepped foot out of the building.

It didn't matter, though. All we needed was those few moments of safety. We could get out of this. We just had to play the game.

Lilian released her hold on me, and I gasped a greedy breath of air. I took a step forward.

"Nadine, you can't give them this power," Chloe insisted.

Mira crossed her arms. "She's already made up her mind."

"Quiet, Mira," Professor Hernandez hissed. I took it the two of them didn't get along well.

I turned back to Chloe and gave her a desperate look. I hoped she understood what I was trying to say. "Please, Chloe. You have to let me save Marcus."

I shot her a look that said, *Get ready to fight*. Whether she picked up on it or not, I wasn't sure. Chloe was very good at masking her emotions when she needed to.

I turned back toward the priestesses and reached for Marcus.

Margaret pulled him away. "You do the spell first."

Steeling my nerves, I swallowed the lump in my throat. "All right. We'll play by your rules, but I need to touch him."

Margaret held tight to Marcus, but she let me put my hand on his head. His eyes fluttered open, and he looked up at me.

"It's okay, baby boy," I whispered. "Mama's here for you."

I wrapped my magic around him like a comforting hug. I could feel all different types of magic within him at once—so powerful that I stumbled back, even though I was only observing. I hadn't actually touched his magic yet.

"That's it," Lilian encouraged. "You can feel how powerful he is, can't you? Do the spell!"

I straightened and tried again. The magic within Marcus was both chaotic and ordered. It was different from anything I'd seen before, and difficult to make sense of. I dug deep, until I found the spells the priestesses had put on him.

One tasted of citrus, and I knew that was the potion they'd poisoned him with. The only way to eliminate it was to create the Master Wand like they asked. Then I felt the darkness of the curse they'd cast. If we hurt the priestesses before I enchanted the Master Wand, Marcus would die, too. Two different spells... both deadly.

I had to time this just right.

Then there was Marcus's demigod magic. It moved through his body like the motion of an infinity sign, twisting and pulsing through him in ways I'd felt with other witch magic, but different too—more powerful. If this was only a trace of demigod magic, I couldn't imagine what he'd be capable of when he came into his full power.

"Place the wand on top of him," I instructed.

Lilian laid the Master Wand over Marcus's chest, but she didn't dare let go of it. I placed my palm over top of the blade, so that I was touching both Marcus and the Master Wand at once.

I stroked his head with my other hand. "Marcus, sweetheart. I need you to share your power with me. Do you feel that warmth moving through your chest? That's your magic, and Mama needs a bit of it to keep you safe. It's okay, because I'm not going to let anything bad happen to you."

I knew Marcus couldn't understand my words, but we shared a connection that went far deeper than spoken language. I felt a small amount of his magic budge, but it wasn't enough.

Tears welled in my eyes. I hated that the priestesses were making me do this. I despised them for using my son—for making *me* use my son. I abhorred every moment that they were still breathing. I wanted to tear every ounce of magic from their bodies and use it against them, until they weren't just dead, but wiped from existence completely.

I leaned down and kissed the top of Marcus's head. A tear fell from my eye and soaked into his blanket. "Mama's here for you, baby. Do this for Mama, give me your magic, and then we can go home."

Something broke inside of Marcus then, as if a dam had ruptured. His magic swept through me so fast that I felt like I was floating several inches off the ground. My spine straightened, and I felt so lightweight that only my toes touched the ground. I gasped, and a bright golden glow passed between our bodies. His magic permeated every cell of my being, and for a brief moment, I felt it for what it was.

There was so much light, the power of creation... but for every particle of light that filled me up, there was a dark side—the power to destroy whole nations. The lightweight feeling transformed into a dense heaviness. My heels fell back to the floor, and I shrank under what felt like a two-hundred-pound weight on my shoulders.

If this was what demigod magic was, it was absolutely crushing. I couldn't take his power for more than a moment. I quickly funneled it into the Master Wand, and the wood glowed with that golden energy. The weight pushing me down upon me eased, and I felt the potion's magic within Marcus break. I'd completed the spell, and he was no longer bound by the priestesses' threat of control.

Before the priestesses could notice, I grabbed hold of the darkness swirling in Marcus's gut. They said I couldn't cast magic before I forged the Master Wand. They said nothing of breaking this spell after the enchantment was complete.

The curse snapped, then sank into me as I absorbed its power. My friends acted in sync and flicked their Wands at the same time...

But the Wands did not obey their commands.

Lilian threw her head back and let out a chilling laugh. She yanked the Master Wand from under my palm and shoved me backward. "Your Oaken Wands are of no use anymore! The Master Wand is stronger, and I have already cursed the Wands you're holding to fail. They are powerless!"

I stumbled backward in horror, realizing what I'd done. This was never going to end.

"And don't think that's the only curse I've already cast," Lilian seethed. "I have cursed your son to never be able to create another Master Wand, should you go getting any ideas. Furthermore, no witch or warlock will *ever* be able to tell him what kind of weapon he is. You will *never* be able to tell him of his magic, his powers, or that he is a demigod. Your son is going to hurt people one day because he won't know what he is or what he's capable of, and there's nothing you can do to prevent it!"

"Give Marcus back!" Lucas raged.

Margaret cackled. "We only promised he was going to *live*, not that you could have him. We're taking the boy and raising him on our own. He won't know what he is, but he'll certainly know how to use his power for whatever we desire him to do."

"You can't do that!" Chloe shouted.

"Oh, I think you'll find that we can." Lilian wore a sinister grin and tilted her nose up at her granddaughter. "At what point did I fail you, Chloe? I did everything I could to show you how cruel this world could be, and yet you still refuse to do whatever's necessary to get the job done."

"No one was as cruel to me as you," Chloe sneered.

"What about all those people who never showed up to your fundraiser?" Lilian asked innocently. "I recall those tears quite well."

Chloe stumbled back a step, and realization crossed her features. "It was *you*... Nobody came to my fundraiser because *you* sabotaged it!"

"You needed a breaking point," Lilian snapped. "So I gave you one."

"You bitch!" Chloe snarled.

A high-powered battle orb, fueled by Chloe's rage and sizzling with the intent to kill, erupted from her palm. Lilian barely flicked the Master Wand, and the battle orb fizzled into nothing.

"What kind of priestess would I be if I didn't follow through with my word?" Lilian asked. "I promised you'd live long enough to walk out of here. I suggest you start walking."

"All except Nadine," Margaret added with a laugh. "I don't believe we made any promises about her life."

A part of me always figured I'd die at the hands of the priestesses. The power they wanted from me could only keep me alive for so long. Now that they had the Master Wand, they had all the power they desired. I was of no use to them anymore.

Lilian aimed the Master Wand straight for me. I should've felt terrified to die, and yet for some reason, I felt totally calm. It was as if a loved one had reached around me to offer their comforting hug, like they were whispering in my ear that everything was going to be okay. I heard nothing, but I felt *everything*. It was the kind of feeling where you just *knew* you had to trust the person you loved. It didn't make any sense.

The following moment passed by in a mere second, but it was like it was happening in slow motion. A loud cry broke from Marcus's lungs the same time an ethereal shape formed between us. A ghostly creature over eight feet tall appeared, with dark fur covering his human-like body, long claws dangling at the end of spry arms, and curled ram horns growing out of his head. He was facing away from me, staring down at the priestesses with pupil-less, pitch black eyes.

It was Santos in spirit form. He'd come to save us.

A deep, animalistic roar shook the courtroom. The priestesses took a frightened step back, and Mira's high-pitched scream pierced the air. In their moment of hesitation, Professor Wykoff lunged forward and yanked Marcus straight out of Margaret's arms. Wykoff ran to the other side of the courtroom to protect our son.

Santos swiped his claws at the priestesses. His ghostly hands became solid for a moment, slicing through the bodies of three priestesses at once. Blood splattered across the walls at his claws. They didn't get a chance to cry out in pain before their bodies collapsed into a heap on the ground. Claudia, Mira, and Professor Hernandez were dead in the blink of an eye.

I witnessed the brief moment of utter terror enter the remaining two priestesses' eyes. They may have the power of a demigod in that Wand, but it couldn't rival the power of a god.

Santos lowered his horns to charge at them, but they had already made their move. Lilian flicked the Master Wand, and a portal bloomed beneath the two priestesses. They went falling through it. Santos leapt at them at the same moment, but his ghostly form landed on solid ground where the priestesses had been standing a moment ago.

The portal had disappeared, and the priestesses were gone. I didn't know where they had gone, but I hoped it was far away from here.

I took a step back, trembling. Lucas reached out for me, and he too was shaking. Santos turned to us, but he didn't speak. Slowly, we both got to our knees and bowed our heads before our god. Our friends followed our lead.

"Thank you," I told Santos. "You saved our son."

Santos bowed his head... and then he vanished. Just like that, he was gone, like he'd never appeared in the first place. The courtroom went completely silent.

Lucas sagged beside me in relief. "Our family is saved."

We got to our feet, and Professor Wykoff approached with Marcus bundled in her arms. I reached out to take him, but I paused when Marcus's little fingers extended out of his blanket. He touched Professor Wykoff's cheek, and a single tear rolled down her face.

"I do not have children of my own," Professor Wykoff said gently. "I cannot imagine what it's like to be a parent, but I know that I'll always be here to protect this child."

She gently placed Marcus in my arms. "If you ever need my help for *anything*, you only need to ask."

"That's very kind of you," I told her as I pulled Marcus close to my chest. He closed his eyes and snuggled in close. It was incredible how he seemed wholly unbothered by what just happened here, like to him it had all just been a dream.

Good. I didn't want Marcus to know the horrors that faced him here tonight. I wanted nothing more than to keep him safe.

Lucas wrapped an arm around my waist and stroked Marcus's cheek. He sniffled, like he couldn't believe it. "We got him back."

"What just happened, though?" Talia asked. "It was almost like Marcus's cry *summoned* Santos."

"Maybe he did," Lucas theorized. "Summoning the gods requires powerful spellwork, but *Marcus* is powerful. He's a demigod, so maybe he can reach out to our gods and bring them here. It's interesting, though… it's like Santos knew this was going to happen. The last time I saw him at Hattie's, when we banished the demon's spell from Nadine, he promised we'd meet again."

"I felt him," I admitted. "Right before he appeared, it was like he was *hugging* me. I felt his powerful love."

Grant eyed the spot in the hall where Margaret and Lilian had disappeared. "What do we do now? The priestesses are going to come back."

"Not if they know Santos is protecting this place," Chloe said. "They've probably figured the same thing we have—that Marcus summoned him—and they know he can do it again."

"They have his power now, though, in the Master Wand," Talia pointed out. "Can't they summon Santos—or even Mother Miriam for that matter?"

"Even if they could, they're not powerful enough to control him," Chloe pointed out. "Even a demigod like Marcus can't control him; he just brought him here, and Santos wanted to protect him. The gods are still more powerful than the priestesses are, and if they're on our side, it's the one thing holding the priestesses back. They're not going to come in guns blazing. They're going to bide their time and slowly infiltrate the coven all over again, until they can eliminate the threat."

"Eliminate us… and Marcus," I said hollowly. "They don't want a child to grow up that has the ability to summon a god."

"They'll try," Chloe confirmed. "But this time, we'll be ready for them."

"So what do we do in the meantime?" Grant asked.

"There are five openings on the Imperium Council," Professor Wykoff pointed out. "The coven will need leaders to fill them."

I shook my head. "The coven doesn't want us to lead."

Professor Wykoff peered out a window. "You'd be surprised. Why don't you ask them yourself?"

I followed her gaze to see a crowd had formed outside Octavia Hall across the street. Hundreds of people had come to see the damage.

Lucas looked out the window with heartbreak in his eyes. "The least we can do is tell them the truth about what happened here tonight."

I nodded. "The coven deserves to know."

"We have to be careful," Chloe warned. "The priestesses didn't always keep secrets just to manipulate their people. Sometimes, secrets are for the better. We can't tell them about the Master Wand. It'll create a panic. Others might get their own sinister ideas."

Lucas nodded in agreement. "We'll tell them what they need to know, and we'll figure out where to go from there."

We made our way outside. Across the street, Octavia Hall was in ruins. Windows had been blasted out, and debris littered the streets. The building was technically still standing, but it looked like it might come crumbling down at any moment.

The streets were eerily quiet when we stepped out the courthouse, despite the large crowd that had formed. People looked around, trying to figure out what had happened, but it was like they were waiting for someone to speak.

Lucas glanced around at the piles of dust that had once been Executors that were scattered over the street. I didn't think he'd quite processed how many people he'd slaughtered earlier. I thought I saw the pain of regret in his eyes, but it quickly turned into something else entirely.

"What is it?" I asked him, quietly so only he could hear.

"Maybe there *is* a part of me that deals in gray areas," he admitted. "But I know one thing for damn certain. We saved our son tonight—which makes me the best fucking dad out there."

Joy filled my chest as I stared down at Marcus sleeping in my arms.

We could've lost him tonight, but he was still here with us. It felt like a miracle.

I smiled up at Lucas. "It certainly does."

People began to notice us, and murmurs spread through the crowd. Someone shoved their way to the front—a younger man with long hair, suspenders, and mis-matched socks. It was Professor Clarke, my Miriamic Law professor. The last time I'd seen him, he'd been passing out flyers at the Festival of Chosen last November. He didn't look happy to see us.

"*You* did this!" he raged. "What happened here? Who's that child in your arms? Tell us, or—"

"There's no need for threats," Lucas insisted. "I intend to tell you exactly what happened. This child is our son."

Professor Clarke wore a look of disgust. "A bastard child! Born of two Casts."

"Half of us were born of two Casts!" someone in the crowd shouted, though I couldn't locate who had said it. "Let us hear them out!"

The crowd quieted, awaiting our response.

Lucas stood at the top of the stairs to the courthouse and raised his voice for all to hear. "I'm sure you're all wondering what occurred here tonight. The truth is, the priestesses kidnapped our son, to lure us here with the intent to kill us. What the priestesses have done to the coven is wrong, and we've been fighting to make it right. We have spent the last year searching for artifacts that can help end the Waning. The priestesses, however, were trying to stop us from restoring your magic. They've escalated to stealing infants. We tried to negotiate, but they refused to stop their nefarious plans. Many people died tonight, including Autumn Loren, a coven member who sacrificed herself to save us. But the priestesses' intentions went beyond killing people. They committed a terrible crime against the coven tonight, attempting to create a weapon to gain total control over every witch and warlock. We didn't want anyone to get hurt. We gave them a chance to run, but they insisted on defending their evil cause. We came here tonight to stop them."

"Where are the priestesses?" the crowd demanded.

"Three of the priestesses perished in the fight," Lucas admitted. "Priestesses Lilian and Margaret fled."

"How do we know you're telling the truth?" someone shouted.

"It's true!" Professor Wykoff insisted. "I was there. The priestesses locked me in a cage, with plans to kill me. They wanted me gone because I dared to question them. These witches standing before you saved my life."

"I understand it may be hard to trust us," Lucas said gently. "For years, the truth has been manipulated, and words and intentions have been twisted. The coven deserves to know what's going on, and that's why I'm sharing the truth with you right now. Give us a truth serum if you don't believe us, and let us show you what we know to be true."

"I believe them!" a man called. It sounded like the same person who suggested the crowd hear us out. People parted to make way for him. He approached the front of the crowd with a woman at his side.

It was Professor Richards, who taught my Miriamic History and Alchemy classes, and Professor Loren, who taught Incantations and Moonology.

Tears filled Professor Loren's eyes. "You met her? You met my Autumn."

Lucas nodded and lowered his voice. "I did."

She spoke in a trembling tone. "And my daughter's gone?"

"I'm sorry," Lucas told her.

"But is she in a better place?" she asked desperately.

"I believe she'll find her way to Alora," Lucas replied sincerely. He wasn't just saying it to make her feel better, either. He really believed it.

When we'd first met Autumn, she was certain she was going to end up in the Abyss, but she'd come back to speak with Lucas for a reason. I believed she'd found what she was looking for.

Professor Richards turned toward the crowd. "I am Professor Anthony Richards. I teach history at Miriam College of Witchcraft. I am an old man who's been around this coven a long time, and I have studied its past. If there's one thing that history has shown us fails every single time, it's the witch hunts that seek to silence our people. I say we hear them out!"

Several people booed, but the chorus of agreement drowned them out.

"And if we like what they have to say…" Professor Richards added. "I say we put *them* on the Imperium Council."

Several more people joined in the protests. They were willing to hear us out, but they weren't willing to go that far.

"Listen to me!" Professor Richards shouted. "Nadine was sanctioned as a priestess by Mother Miriam herself. She's the only one left. You've all seen what the Imperium Council has done this last year—they've sectioned Casts off to different areas of town, drove us all into debt, broken apart families, and raised an army against their own people. Which one of you can say their soldiers actually *protected* you? Or did they drag you out of your homes, raid your businesses, and take your children from your arms? Every intercast couple knows what I'm talking about! The priestesses did it all in the name of ending the Waning, and yet it only continues to worsen. The hangings have only increased in number. The council once convinced you that *these* young people were the reason for the Waning, but they've been gone for months, and things have only gotten worse. How can they be to blame?" Richards gestured to us, and several people murmured in agreement.

"We are living in unprecedented times, influenced by a council that has the power to shape our coven without our input or approval," Professor Richards continued. "I'm telling you that if there's ever been a time when we need the coven to change, that time is now. Nadine was voted onto the council by the other priestesses. They told you they kicked her out for trying to gain power. If that's the case, ask yourselves *why* she was found not guilty by Mother Miriam in her trial. Why would the priestesses still keep her off the council, after Mother Miriam gave her ruling? They unified against her because she knew what they were planning, and they took away her power because she stood up for the people."

"The priestesses said she deceived us!" someone shouted.

"The priestesses said a lot of things that turned out to be untrue," Professor Loren spoke up. "They also told us that when the healthcare system changed, people would still get care, but they didn't. They died waiting for it! The priestesses said the Waning would get better, but it's worse than ever. The priestesses promised we'd be strong and be able to defend ourselves against the fae, but if the fae came here right now, we'd be killed immediately. We did everything they said, *gave up* everything, and they never came through on their promises. They lied! Who's to say they didn't lie about Nadine?"

Whispers spread throughout the crowd.

"Mother Miriam would not choose this division!" Professor Richards pressed. "We have chosen ourselves to suffer under the doctrine of Miriam's Chosen, but we can choose differently."

He turned to Lucas and spoke lowly. "The priestesses have gone too far. You did the right thing getting rid of them. Now tell the people what you plan to do moving forward. Convince them that you're the right choice."

Lucas hesitated, like he wasn't sure what to say. Then someone in the crowd shouted, "They only came here to get power! Richards is working with them!"

The uncertainty fell from Lucas's face, and he stood straighter. "If power is all we seek, then we will fail, because no one can give power to the Imperium Council but its people. The priestesses could not remain in power because they were hurting the coven, but a new council must take their place. We want to prove to you we can be good leaders, but we don't want to lead you without your consent. It's always been our goal to reunite the coven and put the power back into the hands of the people. If you allow us to, we will rebuild. We'll bring an end to the Waning and bring magic back for good. We will forgive the predatory loans the priestesses gave out, give business back to the people, and restore your normal lives."

"You can't promise that," someone shouted. "We've lost people—people we *loved*! Things will never be the same."

"You're right," Lucas said without missing a beat. "Things won't go back to the way they were, because not a single one of us are the same people we were when this conflict began. But all your dreams and your goals can still be realized if we choose to lift each other up and become something new… together."

A chorus of cheers came from the crowd, but not everyone was so convinced. It was easy to see we still didn't have their full approval.

"Give us a chance," Lucas requested. "If we don't change things to your satisfaction in a year's time, we'll hold a general election, and you can vote someone else in. What the priestesses did to hurt you is going to take time to recover from, but we will do everything in our power to change things for the better."

"Why you?" a voice came from the crowd. "Why not hold a general election now?"

"The priestesses are gone, which leaves the council seats empty," Lucas said. "We need coven members sitting on that council now, to help smooth things over before an election can be held. It's too dangerous to organize an election when we need to be taking immediate action against this weapon that Margaret and Lilian have. All I'm suggesting is an interim council—nothing permanent. As for putting us on the council, we've been investigating the Waning since it started. We can help stop it, but we need more time. In the meantime, the priestesses possess a powerful weapon, but we have the power to protect you."

"You're trying to use fear to rule over us!" someone insisted.

Professor Richards climbed a few stairs and raised his voice. "If they're as powerful as they say they are, they're at risk to admit it. By being open with us, they're putting themselves at risk, something they'd only do if they're willing to risk it all for *you*."

Chloe stepped forward. "There are two sides in this war that have extreme power. Us, and them. I used to be on the priestesses' side. I was *raised* to believe in everything my grandmother stood for. But I know who she truly is now. If you want a full council, you need Nadine on it, because she's the only Curse Breaker we have. For that council to accomplish anything, you need her working with people who aren't going to stab her in the back, as the priestesses have done to each other so many times before. Everyone in this coven knows the beef Nadine and I had with each other, so if I can align myself with her, so can you."

I held my head high and spoke to the coven. "This isn't about me, but about us, together. It's about who will stick up for you in the face of danger. Lilian and Margaret wouldn't stand and fight against the gates of hell for you. They'd turn and run. I wouldn't, because I believe in this coven, and I believe in you! They'd sacrifice any one of you for a shot at power, but we will go up against them and give ourselves to this coven, even if it means giving up our lives."

Half the crowd looked ready to grab their pitchforks and march alongside us, while the other half looked like they wanted to just go home. They were sick of fighting, and I understood them far too well.

"I can't promise that no one will get hurt," I added. "But I *can* promise the coven will survive if you follow us. Let *us* go up against the priestesses, so you can live your lives in peace. We're not asking for power over you. We're asking for your help and cooperation. We'll get through this together, but we need to *come* together, because it's up to all of us now to do the right thing."

"*Come together!*" Professor Richards repeated.

Professor Loren shot him a glance. "Come together!" she called.

Slowly, more and more coven members began repeating my words. It was one by one at first, until voices overlapped one another. They soon became one, a massive crowd chanting as if they were one voice.

"COME TOGETHER! COME TOGETHER!"

There was no denying the coven's vote. They wanted us on the council —for now, at least. It was a tall order to fill, and we'd made a lot of promises, but I was wholly confident that one way or another, we would fulfill each and every one of them.

"Now go home," Lucas called out to the crowd. "Be with your families tonight. We will begin our work in the morning."

The crowd began to disperse.

Professors Richards and Loren approached Professor Wykoff. "Let us take you home," Richards offered.

"I'd like that very much," Professor Wykoff said weakly.

As they walked off, a small group of people from school approached. Samantha and Gregory were among them, both necromancers from Lucas's classes. Brayden held Gregory's hand, looking nervous, and Alex followed alongside them.

Gregory stepped forward. "We want to help."

Lucas furrowed his brow. "I thought you joined the priestesses. I figured you'd be an Executor by now. Why do you want to help us?"

"I did what I thought I had to do to survive," Gregory admitted. "I never wanted to be a part of their cult, but we knew we'd eventually hang if we didn't comply. I'd rather follow you—not because I think it will save me this time, but because your cause is something I'd actually die for."

Lucas looked toward Samantha, his eyes searching her arm for the mark of the Chosen. There was no mark to be found. "You never joined them?"

She shook her head. "I was going to, but then I thought of you and Nadine, and how much you fought against this. I just knew you'd be back, and I told myself once you came, I was going to fight on your side."

Lucas hesitated, like he wasn't sure he wanted to get more people involved. We weren't asking for soldiers, but we needed support. We couldn't do this alone.

"All right," Lucas finally said, keeping his voice low. "We need necromancers to help move bodies. There are ten Executors inside Octavia Hall, and three priestesses in the courtroom. Gregory and Samantha, you need to get rid of them so nobody tampers with the corpses. Move them to unmarked graves and don't tell anyone what you're doing."

Gregory gave a firm nod. "We're on it."

The two of them hurried inside the courthouse.

"Alex, Brayden, I have a special job for you," Lucas said. "I portaled a dozen Executors across town, which means they're still roaming around. They'll kill us the first chance they get. I need you to find as many people as you trust to work with you to hunt those Executors down. We'll lock them in the city jail tonight and decide what to do with them later."

"Professor Blackbird has military training. He'll help us, along with others," Brayden said.

He and Alex took off the same time a man and woman approached. I'd never seen them before, but the woman looked all too familiar, with dark hair and a straight nose identical to Chloe's. These had to be Chloe's parents.

"If you've come to stop me, save your breath," Chloe sneered. "I've already made up my mind, and the coven has spoken."

"Chloe, honey," her mother begged. "We aren't here to stop you. We're here to tell you how proud we are. We were out there in that crowd cheering for you."

"Do you really think we'd side with your grandmother?" her father added.

Chloe spoke slowly, appearing stunned. "Well... she *is* your mom. Aren't you on her side?"

Chloe's mother scoffed. "Your grandmother is a coward who ran from her own people. You always came first, Chloe. We always knew you were destined for greatness. We'd rather see you on the council."

Tears welled in Chloe's eyes. It had to be the first time I'd ever seen her cry. She'd told me stories about her parents—how they'd always pushed her to be the greatest. She never thought anything she did was good enough for them, and it was clear all she ever wanted was their approval.

"You really mean it?" Chloe whispered.

"Of course we did," her father said. "Does this mean you're coming home now?"

Chloe sniffled. "You mean... you want me to move back in with you?"

"I mean home to Octavia Falls," her father clarified. "You're an adult now. You should get your own place."

Chloe scoffed. "Yeah, let me just borrow a down payment."

"There's no need," her father said. "Your grandmother's house belongs to the family estate. I imagine it will be vacant for some time. If you want it, it technically belongs to you."

Chloe's jaw dropped. "Are you serious?"

"Your mother and I already have a lovely home," he said. "What would we do with that big empty house?"

"You're right…" Chloe mused. "It is a big empty house. I can't live there alone."

Slowly, she turned to the rest of us, looking hopeful. "What do you guys think about continuing our roommate arrangement?"

Something in her eyes told me that Chloe had really enjoyed our time together at the safe house. She wasn't ready to give that up.

"There's lots of room," she started.

Grant chuckled. "You don't have to convince me. The more time we spend together, the more we can get done."

"I'm on board," Talia agreed.

I looked down at Marcus. "Are you all sure you're okay having a baby in the house? He's going to make a lot of noise."

"Are you kidding!?" Chloe asked. "Marcus is part of the family now. *Of course* we want him there. There's a whole section of the house with a second kitchen and everything. You and Lucas can stay there. It will be like your own apartment. Plus, it will really piss off my grandmother, and I'll do anything at this point to put her in her place."

Lucas wrapped an arm around my shoulder. "It's a very kind offer. Of course we'll stay with you."

"Yay!" Chloe clapped in excitement. "Thank you so much for the offer, Daddy! We're going to be so happy there. I just know it."

She threw her arms around her father's neck, and he went completely still. Chloe quickly realized what she'd done and backed off. It seemed she'd only done it on instinct, but they didn't appear to be the hugging kind of family.

Chloe took a step back. "Sorry…"

Her father finally composed himself. "Don't be sorry, honey. Come here."

Her dad pulled her back into his arms, then grabbed her mom. The three of them embraced, and for the first time, I saw a tear roll down Chloe's cheek. It was everything she ever wanted from them.

"Oh, my Goddess!" Talia gasped. She tugged on Grant's sleeve and pointed down the street. I followed her gaze to see her parents and brother, along with Grant's dad.

Pure joy fell over Talia's and Grant's faces. The two of them took off running before they could say anything else, and they fell into the arms of their family members. It'd been so long since they'd seen them.

Talia's mother smoothed down Talia's hair. "It's so good to see you. Do you know anything about Tate? We haven't seen her in months."

"She's safe, Mom," Talia assured her. "I promise. She's been recovering in a refugee city. I'm sorry we couldn't get in touch with you."

"It's okay!" her dad insisted. "You're safe, and that's all that matters."

I turned back to Lucas, who was looking down at our son. He wrapped his arms around me and pressed his forehead against mine, until we were cradling Marcus between us.

"I'm so relieved you're both safe," he breathed.

"For now," I agreed.

Lucas sensed my hesitation. "Nad, we won tonight. That's something to celebrate."

"I know, and I'm happy we won," I replied. "I'm just thinking about what you said up there, about how things will never go back to the way they were, because we aren't the same people. I used to think that one day, life would be perfect. I thought we'd defeat the priestesses, we'd get married, I'd have my new kidney and my symptoms would go away, and we'd be given this brand-new life together. But we have so much of that already, and my life is better than ever, but it didn't fix everything. In some ways, it got worse. I went through the surgery and got my kidney, but I still couldn't have our babies on my own terms. I'll be better, but I'm never going to be cured. We got married, and then we lost people. One day, we're going to defeat the priestesses. But even when that happens, I'm not going to have that perfect life because I'm not the same person who dreamed it."

Lucas rubbed my shoulders. "You can still have the life you wanted, even if that girl you were before isn't there anymore."

"Maybe I can move on and become someone new. But I can never resurrect the girl I was before all this shit happened to us," I said. "After everything we've been through, there's no going back. Things are going to keep changing, and I don't know who this new person is. I have no idea who I'm going to become."

Lucas smiled. "That's exciting, though, because we get to meet her along the way. I'm not the same, either, which means we get to meet each other all over again."

I looked around at the coven. Dozens of people had stepped in to help with the clean-up, and I still could hardly believe they wanted to help us. For so long, the coven didn't want me here, and now, they wanted me to be their leader.

"If we're meeting each other all over again, that means we get to meet the coven again, too," I said. "I don't know who I'm going to become, or what I'm going to do as their leader, but I know this is a brand new beginning to figure it out—not just for us, but for the whole coven."

It may not be the beginning we hoped for. The priestesses were still out there, and we would face them again before all this was over. But it was the beginning of something new.

For all of us.

## TWENTY-FIVE

Our new beginning started with a sunrise the following morning. It was the most beautiful sunrise, with shades of pink and purple illuminating the sky. It reminded me of a rainbow, a signal of hope shining down on us after a devastating storm.

I woke in a guest room at the Olson estate. Nadine lay beside me, and Marcus was safely curled in her arms. Neither of us wanted to let him go, so we'd taken turns sleeping.

I expected to feel strange being in Lilian's house, but it didn't feel like the house of a priestess. If anything, it seemed more like Chloe's home than her grandmother's, and I felt welcome here.

It'd been a long night. The Executors I'd sucked through my portals had been discovered hiding in a warehouse across town. Ryan, James, Leroy, and Cody were among them. I'd hoped they'd perished with most of the others, but they had survived. We'd locked them up in jail, and they would stand trial for the part they played in the Miriamic Conflict at a later date.

We didn't know where the priestesses had gone. They had enough power now to create ironclad protection spells, so we couldn't track them even if we wanted to.

We all managed to make it back to the estate safely. We'd stopped by the hospital on our way and were able to bring our friends home to rest.

The doctors had given Verla a clean bill of health, and Professor Warren had to get a cast on his leg. Mandy was shaken up, but she was able to get her first decent meal in a long time. We'd filled Onyx, Miles, and the others in on everything that happened once we arrived at the estate.

My eyes landed upon Nadine, and I pushed a strand of hair out of her face. "How are you feeling?"

"I'll be all right," she replied.

She said so much in so few words, and I felt it deep in my core. Things were okay for now, and we were safe for the time being, but there was so much to face before our family was safe for good.

I heard footsteps across the house. "It sounds like the others are waking up. We should join them soon. There's a lot to do today."

Nadine and I were staying in a corner of the house that I could only assume was meant to house staff. We had a bedroom, a private bath, kitchen, and sitting area all to ourselves.

I'd gotten some of my strength back, so I portaled to the safe house after I woke up to gather a fresh change of clothes and bring the cats back to the estate. They circled around my feet and meowed happily when they saw me. They must've been so worried.

I hurried back to the estate and got dressed while Nadine fed Marcus, then held him while she got ready. He slept in my arms peacefully. I still couldn't get over how perfect he was. Isa purred happily on the bed while she nursed Rishi. The other cats hurried to find their respective owners.

Nadine and I wandered to the other side of the house. A huge kitchen was connected to a large dining room. Everyone else was already awake and sat around a long table eating breakfast. Pancakes, sausage, and eggs were laid out across the table.

"Nadine, Lucas," Verla greeted as she finished her food. "It's good to see you up and about. Here, let me hold Marcus while you eat."

I hesitated, because the last time we let someone care for him, he'd been taken from us. But my hesitation only lasted a split second. We trusted Verla with our lives, as well as our son's. I gently set Marcus into Verla's outstretched arms, then sat beside Nadine.

"Now that everyone's here, it's time to get to work," Verla said. "First things first. Nadine needs to decide on her council members."

Nadine poured syrup over her pancakes. "The coven voted us all in."

"Technically, they voted for you and whoever was going to support you best," Chloe pointed out. "There are other seats on the council that need to be filled, and several of us to fill them. It's up to you to decide who's going to serve best alongside you."

"I want us all on the council," Nadine decided. "We all have ideas and insight we can provide. I want us working together."

"We will," Verla promised. "But the coven is going to want a singular figure to look up to from each Cast. We need to be clear with them about who their council members are."

Nadine nodded. "All right. I want Lucas to be the Mortana priest."

I furrowed my brow. "The role typically goes to a woman. Are you sure?"

"Yes," Nadine stated without hesitation. "My grandfather served as a priest on the council. Why not you? I trust you completely, and you're a great leader."

"You have my vote," Professor Warren said. He sat at the head of the table, with his broken leg propped up on another chair.

I eyed him. "You're Mortana, too, and you have more experience than me. Why don't we make you a priest?"

"Because you showed last night how powerful your voice can be," Professor Warren pointed out. "You know how to rally the people, and a large portion of them want to follow you. Don't forget that you were found not guilty by Mother Miriam, too, and that's earned you quite a bit of respect. Besides, my place isn't on the council. If we're going to work together, we need people in specialized areas reporting back to the council. I'm better suited to helping get the school up and running again."

"As am I," Verla added. "The school is a cornerstone of the coven, where young witches and warlocks come to learn their power. They need the best education they can get—not just magical instruction. We need to restructure the entire curriculum with a holistic approach, or we're bound to repeat these mistakes in the future. I am not done with being headmistress yet."

"You're one of the most powerful Alchemists we know," Nadine argued. "You've always had respect from the people. You'd be a huge asset to the council."

"I understand that, but I do not desire to be in a place of such power. I need to be leading the school, not the whole coven," Verla insisted. "I will be here every step of the way to consult with you, but nobody else in the coven understands Miriam College of Witchcraft the way I do. Professor Warren and I have the experience and expertise to get the school up and running again, and so that's where our focus needs to be."

"I think Grant should serve as the Alchemy priest," Onyx suggested. "If it's not Verla, it's between him or me, and I think it should be him."

"That's kind of you, but I know you'd make a great leader, too," Grant said.

"Maybe someday I will," Onyx agreed. "But my place right now is in healthcare, helping as much as I can. You didn't see what it was like in the ER last night. People were being turned away. They didn't have enough help. The priestesses screwed up our healthcare system, and the coven needs nurses and doctors who really care about their patients to provide healthcare while we work on fixing it."

"Onyx is right," Nadine agreed. "She needs to be working in the medical field so that she can help us restructure the healthcare system. Having a strong ally in the medical field will help facilitate communication between the council, medical providers, and patients. She's a great nurse, and Grant will make a wonderful priest."

Grant smiled, looking proud to be a part of the council. "I'm honored, and I'm glad to help. We need Chloe on the council, too. She knows how to speak to people who oppose us, and we need a strong voice like hers. She trained for this since she was a kid. She knows what the fuck she's doing."

"Absolutely," Mandy agreed. "I'm the only other Mentalist in the room, and there's no way I'm sitting on any council. After everything the priestesses put me through, I'm not sure I'm going to stay in Octavia Falls at all. The position is all yours."

"I don't know if that's a good idea," Chloe admitted. "The last thing I want is to turn out like my grandmother."

"You won't," Nadine promised. "You've already made the choice not to be anything like her. Sitting on the council won't change that. It will only give you a chance to make an impact for good, the way your grandmother failed to do."

"I'm not sure the coven will want me on the council, though," Chloe added. "They won't believe I'm nothing like my grandmother. If they want her off the council, they certainly want someone who isn't her family to take her place."

"That's actually one of the reasons you need to be on the council," I said. "We received support from the coven last night, but there are many who will still oppose us. Lilian gained a lot of respect during her time on the council, and it's going to be hard to earn her followers' trust after we drove her out of town. You'll be able to win them over *because* you remind them of your grandma."

"You make a good point. All right, I'll take the position." Chloe glanced between Miles and Talia. "That just leaves the Seer position then."

"It should be Talia," Miles insisted. "She handled the Seer Wand well, and I could hardly take its visions. If it's a powerful Seer you want, she's it."

"Miles…" Talia sighed softly. "You're a powerful Seer, too."

"In a different way," he agreed. "I spent time undercover with the Executors. I know how they were taught to think. Let me work with law enforcement and come up with solutions on how to reverse the damage the Executors did."

"Law enforcement was all on the priestesses' side," I pointed out. "We're going to have to replace the entire police force."

"Then you need me there," Miles said. "Technically I'm a rookie, but I still completed my training course. There aren't a lot of people left who are qualified to serve as police officers, so I need to be on the force with the few who remain."

"Then we all have our jobs," I stated. "Nadine, Chloe, Grant, Talia, and I will serve on the Imperium Council for one year, while Verla and Warren restore the school, Onyx can restructure the healthcare system, and Miles can get our law enforcement back up and running. And Mandy…"

I turned to her. "I can't apologize enough for leaving you with the priestesses."

Mandy shook her head. "It's not your fault. Magnus played you all. I'm sure it was hard for any of you to trust me after your trial. I don't blame you for not seeing the truth."

"We should've known it wasn't you," I insisted.

"You don't have to apologize," Mandy pressed. "I broke your trust. I did what I thought was right for the coven, and it was a mistake. I should be the one apologizing. I never meant to hurt any of you, and even if you don't trust me anymore, I hope you can trust that I truly mean that."

"Of course," Nadine said. "I've always believed that. All we ever wanted was to mend our friendship. Bad things happened, but we know you always cared."

Mandy dropped her gaze. "I really did, and there isn't a day that goes by that I don't regret turning you in. I didn't understand the depth of the threat the priestesses posed, and I see now that you were doing the right thing. I hate that the priestesses used my powers to lure you to Octavia Falls, and I let them. I want to use my powers for good now. Maybe when I've recovered from all of this, I can study dream therapy. I don't want to keep making mistakes. I screwed up, and I can never change that, but I hope you can find it in your hearts to forgive me."

"Mandy, you're already forgiven," Nadine said softly.

Mandy sniffled. Nadine stood and rounded the table to give her a hug.

"Thank you so much," Mandy sobbed. "It means everything to hear you say that."

She wiped her eyes and drew away. "Thank you all for taking me in after what I did. I can't thank you enough, but I also can't stay here."

"There's a refugee city in California called *Hok'evale*," I told her. "Tate's there. I can portal you there as soon as you're ready."

Mandy stood. "I'm ready now."

"Is there no one you'd like to say goodbye to first?" I asked.

Mandy shook her head. "My family fled the coven over a year ago. You're the only people I have left to say goodbye to."

Talia stood, and the two exchanged a tearful farewell. I opened a portal to *Hok'evale*, and Mandy waved before stepping through. The portal closed behind her.

Moments later, the doorbell rang.

"Are we expecting someone?" Professor Warren asked.

"It's Hattie," I told him. "There's something Nadine and I need to do before we begin our work, and we asked her for help."

I went to answer the door. Hattie stood behind it, holding a polished square stone in her hands—a plaque with words carved on it.

"Are you ready?" Hattie asked.

"Yes," I told her. "Let me ask the others who'd like to join us."

I returned to the dining room and explained our idea. Verla said she wished she could come along, but she had to get to the school right away to begin her work. Onyx decided to stay at home in case Professor Warren needed anything, since he wasn't going to be up and about for a while. Miles must've not wanted to intrude, because he offered to clean up breakfast so we could leave right away.

Talia, Grant, and Chloe agreed to come, so I portaled us across town to the cemetery. Nadine held Marcus in her arms, and he slept soundlessly.

A small group of people gathered on the other side of the cemetery. I could swear they were shooting daggers our way the moment they noticed us.

"Pay them no attention," Hattie said. "They're family members of Executors who died last night. They're searching for their graves."

My stomach sank. It was easy to kill the people threatening my family, but harder to remember they had families of their own. Even though the coven voted us onto council, it was clear we weren't completely trusted. I'd reduced over a hundred Executors to ash, and none of their families had bodies to bury or graves to visit. After what I'd done, I didn't blame them, and I didn't know if I could ever make it better.

"Are they going to hurt us?" Talia asked warily.

"No," Hattie assured us. "The coven put you on the council. Hurting you would only make them a target. You're safe for now."

The group left the cemetery shortly after we arrived. We were alone.

Hattie guided us over to an empty corner of the graveyard. "This is where we will honor them."

She handed me the plaque, then reached into her pocket and placed an acorn in Nadine's hand. Hattie lifted her palms, and the dirt moved to her command, opening to create a small hole in the earth.

Nadine sniffled. "Thank you all for coming. Lucas and I wanted to put together an area of remembrance for Grammy and Dean. They deserve a proper resting place here with the coven, but we didn't want to move their bodies, so we decided to plant a tree in their honor. We know that to go forward with our work and start anew, we need Grammy and Dean here with us. So today, we plant this oak tree in their honor, to keep their spirits with us so they can continue to inspire us with their kindness, innocence, and love."

"Helena and Dean will be greatly missed." I tried to steady my tone, but my voice cracked.

Nadine knelt beside the hole and placed the acorn inside of it. I gently set the plaque next to it, then stepped back to read it.

*In loving memory of Helena Tucker and Dean Taylor.*
*Grief and death are ephemeral, but love lasts forever.*

Hattie waved her hands, and the dirt came together to close the hole. The plaque sank several inches into the ground, secured now in the earth. With her power of Earth magic, a sprout began to grow from the ground.

Nadine leaned into me, and tears streamed down her face. She reached for Talia. "I need you guys," Nadine sobbed.

For so long, she'd been trying to handle her grief alone. Now, we could all grieve together. We gathered close, until we were all circled in a group hug.

Tiny oak leaves grew bigger and bigger as the tree grew from the coaxing of Hattie's magic, reaching toward the sun. Twigs turned to branches, and the trunk thickened until it was as wide as my arm. A young oak tree filled with luscious green leaves stood before us.

I glanced down at my son's name, and it was like a dagger to the heart all over again. I'd wanted to protect my sons from all harm, but it was clear to me now that I couldn't shield them from everything. The world was going to hurt them. All I could do was teach them how to keep fighting.

We stood there a long time, taking in the memorial. My eyes scanned nearby graves, and my breath caught when I saw a fresh grave with a name I recognized. Nadine looked up at me in concern, then followed her gaze to the gravestone.

"Willa Poppy," I read aloud.

Professor Poppy had taught Crystal Studies and Astral Travel. She was one of the older professors, but couldn't have hit seventy yet. I was surprised to see her name here.

I turned to Hattie. "Do you know what happened to her?"

"It was a horrible viral respiratory infection," Hattie said sadly. "It's been going around human populations for years now, but it swept through the coven a few months back. Willa got it worse than others. She should've been put on a ventilator, but she died waiting for care."

My stomach twisted. "That's not right. The priestesses had plenty of money. If they were low on medical resources, they could've brought in more supplies. They could've set up a temporary clinic. They chose not to."

Hattie dropped her gaze. "There's more you should see. I shared what news I could with you while you were gone, but it's one thing to hear about it and another to see it first-hand. Follow me."

Hattie instructed me to portal us to the center of town, near the main shopping district. When I opened the portal, I didn't recognize where I was standing. The mom-and-pop shops were gone, completely bulldozed to the ground. Heavy machinery stood in their place, along with piles of rubble from what remained of the buildings.

"The priestesses bought up all these businesses," Hattie explained. "They tore them down to build a shopping complex. They were selling franchise licenses, so that small business owners had to operate under the priestesses' trademarks, earning them money for every sale."

Talia's features paled. "That's horrible. Not only would it earn the priestesses profit, but they'd get to decide what was sold in every store. They could control the whole flow of commerce."

Hattie nodded. "That was their intention, but there's more. We should visit the Catwalk."

I opened a portal to the Catwalk. At first, I thought that I'd portaled to the wrong place. Then I noticed the ruins of Pinewood Manor in the distance across Lake Santos, and I realized the location was right. Everything else was wrong.

The Catwalk was an iconic shopping area in town, the site of the original settlement. The original cabins had once been preserved and turned into shops. There used to be a trail twisting through the trees, but now it was all gone—the buildings, the trail, the trees… Everything had been completely cleared, until there was nothing but dirt that remained. All of our historical buildings, and everything that had lasted through the years since the 1600s, was no longer here. My heart ached for the neighborhood we'd lost.

Chloe's voice became hollow. "Why would they do this?"

"They claimed it was the best view on the lake," Hattie said. "They were going to build a luxury lakefront apartment complex."

"So they could control people's living situations, too!" Grant raged.

"They've wiped out our history," Nadine said in a horrified tone. "Those buildings stood for centuries, and now, they're gone."

I shook my head, unable to believe what I was seeing. "The coven is worse off than I thought, and it's been going on longer than I realized. All the dying thoughts I hear are so depressing. We shouldn't be treating our people like this. None of this should've happened."

The priestesses had gone too far. They obviously didn't care who they fucked over to gain power. It was clear that to them, anything out of their control had to go, but their quest for power had completely devastated the town. Now we had to rebuild from the ground up.

Grant looked around at the devastation. "This is horrific. We tried to save the coven and defeated the priestesses, but what if we came too late? We might not be able to save the coven now, because the priestesses destroyed so much of our world. We have a lot of work to do. Just because the priestesses are gone doesn't mean this is over. We got elected to this council, but we don't know if we're actually able to *help* the coven. What if we can't fix this?"

Chloe sighed hopelessly. "Grant's right. We made a lot of promises—promises I don't know if we'll be able to keep. It's not just buildings we need to rebuild; it's the whole town's infrastructure, economy, and healthcare system. Plus, we need to get the school back up and running, all while providing for our people. We have to completely rebuild from scratch. There's so much to do, and I don't know how we're going to do it all. We're going to have to pick and choose who we help, because we only have so many resources. We can't fix every problem as badly as we want to, so someone's going to be let down."

"We're not going to let that happen," Nadine insisted. "We can't."

"I don't know if you understand what this is going to take," Chloe said gently. "We're in a position of power now, but no matter how powerful we are, it doesn't fix these societal problems, because to do so takes everyone's cooperation. We're young and inexperienced, and there's enough people who aren't willing to work with us as it is. Besides that, we need power to go up against the priestesses. Having Santos on our side isn't enough, because gods don't like to meddle in human affairs. The fact that he showed up to save Marcus is a miracle. We can't count on him to show up every time."

"Perhaps the people are enough," Talia suggested. "Surely the whole power of the coven can rival the Master Wand."

I shook my head. "We can't ask these people to fight for us, and even if we did, we can't guarantee that these people will do that. They don't want to fight or be made into soldiers, and it isn't right to make them. The Waning is happening *because* we're fighting, and the more we ask them to fight, the worse it will get. We promised we'd fix it, and that means working together."

"Technically, yes, we have more power together," Nadine added. "But we'd have to get all these people to agree to fight, and we can hardly get ten people to agree on one thing at the same time. They voted us in, but we still have to earn their trust. We all know the Law of Love, one of the three laws of Miriamic magic. Through love, our magic is stronger, so our duty on this council is not to rule, but to guide through love. We need to support these people in healing first and foremost. The individual comes first, because there can be no community without each one of us working together."

"Where do we start?" Talia asked.

"We need to get this town working again, or no one's going to fight for our cause," Nadine said. "The coven needs access to education, medicine, and housing, and we must restore their sense of purpose. If we're going to change the coven and undo what the priestesses did, we need to care for these people's emotional and spiritual well-being first, because turning them into soldiers is going to take away their individuality and purpose."

Nadine took a breath and looked over the remnants of the Catwalk. "The coven's job needs to be rebuilding the town, because this is going to take a huge group effort, and that's something they'll be motivated to help with. Rebuilding these structures and implementing new programs are things we can delegate to the people, but we promised to go up against the priestesses for them. We need to follow through on our promises, all while giving them back the lives they deserve, and that starts now."

"The Oaken Wands pull power from the coven. All we can ask our people for is their cooperation, to use the Oaken Wands, and hope that it's enough," I said.

"The Oaken Wands don't work anymore," Grant pointed out.

"Perhaps we can restore their power," I replied. "Lilian said she cursed the Wands we were holding—four of them. She didn't curse the Curse Breaker Wand, because she doesn't know where it is, and therefore, can't focus her power on it. Nadine isn't strong enough to break a curse cast by the Master Wand on her own, but the Curse Breaker Wand may be enough to do it. If we find it, we can break this curse on the Oaken Wands, and gain enough power to stand against the priestesses one last time. We don't know if the Oaken Wands are as powerful as the Master Wand, but they're more powerful than anything else we've got, so they give us a fighting chance. It might just be enough to stop them."

"It doesn't matter if the cards are stacked against us," Nadine decided. "We have to beat the priestesses regardless."

"So, what do we do?" Grant asked.

Silence filled the air. It was obvious none of us had an easy answer.

"We just have to keep going, no matter what happens," I finally said. "You're right—we don't know if we can save the coven, because it might be too far gone, but we're going to try anyway."

"We can't keep existing with the priestesses around," Nadine added. "Either they have to die, or we're going to die fighting them. We can't let Marcus grow up in a society like this. If we die, then so be it, but we aren't going to give up until the coven heals or we're dead."

"It's our only choice, and the coven's only chance," I agreed. "The priestesses will be back. They'll use the Master Wand to try and regain control of the coven, but we have to fight until our last breath to prevent that. The priestesses are going to stay away for a while because they're afraid Santos will come back, but eventually they'll find a way in. We're going to find the Curse Breaker Wand, to break the curse on the rest of the Oaken Wands, so that when the priestesses come back we have the power to defeat them. When they're finally gone, we'll destroy the Master Wand, along with the Oaken Wands."

"Destroy them?" Grant asked. "But they were created to protect us against the fae. If we destroy them, we destroy the coven's greatest weapon."

"The Oaken Wands may be our greatest weapon, but they've become our greatest threat," I said. "These Wands were created out of fear. The coven made these Wands to take on our greatest enemy, but we became our *own* greatest enemy, because these Wands are a bigger threat to our people than the fae ever could be. The coven has proven they can't handle this kind of magic, and therefore, we need to get rid of it. If we don't get rid of it, this is just going to happen again. Magic shouldn't be in the hands of one person. This magic belongs to everybody."

Only one choice remained. We were going to use the Oaken Wands one last time—and then we were going to send them straight to the Abyss, right alongside the priestesses.

Nadine took my hand. "Then let's save the coven. Even if there isn't anything left to save."

**END OF BOOK FIVE**

Continue on to read a special excerpt from book six: *The Witch's Fate.*

# HIDDEN LEGENDS

Read more from the Hidden Legends universe! Each Hidden Legends series takes place within the same world, but in separate and unique societies. Every series stands on its own, and they can be read in any order.

☾

**ELEMENTALS, DRAGONS, & MORE**

Academy of Magical Creatures by Megan Linski & Alicia Rades

☾

**SHIFTERS, FAE, & SORCERESSES**

University of Sorcery by Megan Linski

☾

**SUPERNATURAL PRISON**

Prison for Supernatural Offenders by Megan Linski & Alicia Rades

☾

Never miss a new release! Join our newsletter at www.hiddenlegendsbooks.com/fanclub

# THE WITCH'S FATE
## CHAPTER ONE

*Lucas*

I'd been an interim priest for a week, and already it was apparent that our first order of business was to restore the coven's hope. I'd made a nice, fancy speech the night we drove the priestesses out of town, but it wasn't enough to get our people moving to rebuild the town. The coven had chosen my friends and me to lead them and restore what the previous Imperium Council had destroyed, but the priestesses had broken the coven far beyond its infrastructure.

These people were hopeless. It was up to us to show them that we could heal this community together.

Nadine and I approached the hospital doors at the clinic entrance. We'd spent the last week speaking with coven members and visiting public facilities to survey the damage and learn as much as we could about where we could help.

People needed us… everywhere. Buildings, businesses, and services all around town had been destroyed. It was already an overwhelming job, but I forced myself to stay positive. These people needed us, and I wasn't going to back down, no matter how desperate things seemed.

Nadine paused outside the hospital doors, and I stopped beside her. We were alone, because Talia and Grant were back at the house watching

Marcus, and Chloe was at Miriam College, working with Verla and Warren on plans to reopen enrollment so that classes could resume in the fall.

Nadine kept her voice low. "Before we go in, we need to be prepared. Not everyone is going to be happy to see us. Some of these patients were members of Miriam's Chosen, and they won't want to speak with us after we drove their leaders out of town."

I took her hands in mine to reassure her. "For every person who's angry, there will be someone who's grateful to see us. We just have to go in, listen to their concerns, and take them all to heart—the good and the bad. We need to show these people that we're listening, and that we're going to get them the help that they deserve."

"How are we going to promise that?" Nadine shot a glance toward the front doors, though we were alone. "The priestesses completely drained the council's funds before they left. There's no money left to run this town. We can't give these people promises we can't keep."

"We'll find a way," I vowed. "The priestesses may have stolen our resources, but we aren't giving up that easily. We'll find a solution. We *have* to."

Nadine nodded in agreement, then took a deep breath to steel her nerves. "You're right. The priestesses have taken so much from us before, and it hasn't stopped us yet. We just have to keep moving forward. Let's go see what assistance we can provide."

Nadine and I entered the hospital. The registration area was packed, but it was eerily quiet. The only voice that could be heard was the single receptionist behind the counter checking patients in. Other patients sat and waited their turn, but there weren't enough seats for everybody. Some patients were standing in line. It was obvious the clinic was severely understaffed.

A nurse hurried through the room, and an elderly man with a cane tried to stop her.

"Excuse me," he said weakly. "I'm looking for the radiology department."

"Ask reception," the nurse snapped. "I'm very busy."

Onyx entered the reception area in her nursing scrubs. We were supposed to be meeting with her so she could lead us around the hospital.

The elderly man approached her. "Excuse me, can you point me to radiology? I've checked in for my appointment, but I can't find where I'm going."

Onyx gave the man a kind smile and pointed. "Radiology is on the first floor down that hall. I can walk you there if you'd like."

"I don't want to trouble you," he insisted.

"It's no trouble at all," she replied. "Would you like a wheelchair?"

The man nodded, and his eyes brimmed with tears. He looked like he'd been ready to give up seeking help only a moment ago. I wondered how long he'd been wandering the halls looking for his appointment office.

"You stay right here. I'll be right back," Onyx assured the man. She approached the entrance, where Nadine and I were standing. She offered us a bright smile, though she looked exhausted, and her shift had only started an hour ago. "Good to see you both. If you want to follow me, I have a patient to help, and then I can show you around from there."

Onyx grabbed a wheelchair that was sitting by the door, and she helped the man into it. We followed her down the hall.

He looked up to me. "Are you a patient as well?"

"No," I told him. "My name is Lucas, and this is my wife, Nadine. We're from the Imperium Council, and we've come to see how we can help."

"Hmph," the man huffed. "Can't say I've heard of a man on the council for ages. What happened to the other council members?"

Nadine and I exchanged a glance. It'd been big news that the priestesses left town and we took over the council. I was surprised he didn't know.

"They left town," Nadine answered simply. "Coven members asked us to stand in their place."

The man frowned. "I don't keep up with politics. If you think you can help, then you can start by staffing this hospital. My hip has been bothering me for months, and I'm still waiting for a diagnosis."

"We'll see what shows up on imaging today, and hopefully you'll walk out of here with some answers," Onyx encouraged.

"I doubt it," he said flatly. There was no emotion behind it—no anger or anything. He merely expected that no one could help him, and he had already resolved himself to his fate. "It's time to accept that my last good years are over. My body's given up."

I wished I could offer him words of encouragement, but what could I say? So many people in the coven shared the same sentiment.

We reached the end of the hall, and Onyx led us into a small waiting room. There were several patients there, including a middle-aged man with a beard and a mother with her young child. Nadine recognized the elderly woman in the wheelchair closest to the door.

"Rose!" Nadine exclaimed. "I didn't expect to see you here."

I'd never met Rose, but I'd heard of her before. Nadine used to spend time with her at the nursing home, and they'd put puzzles together to pass the time.

Rose reached out for her, though her hands trembled weakly. "Priestess Nadine. It's so good to see you."

Nadine knelt at her side. "How have you been?"

"I've been better," Rose said. She spoke slowly, like finding the energy to talk was taxing. "I've been experiencing some knee pain, and the doctors at the resident facility were unable to help. They sent me here for more tests. How are you? Last I heard, you left town."

"I'm back," Nadine said.

The bearded man scoffed from across the room, though he didn't say anything. I noticed the mark of Miriam's Chosen on his wrist. He was most definitely a part of the cult and was among those who didn't want us here. The man crossed his arms and shifted in his seat until he was turned away from us. He certainly didn't want to speak with us.

The woman with the child kept her gaze on me. She too bore the mark of the Chosen, but she didn't appear afraid of us. "Why are you here?" she asked.

I sat two chairs down from her so that I was at her level, but not so close as to make her uncomfortable. "We're here to speak to people and address their concerns. Is there anything we can do to help?"

I looked at her child, who was holding his arm. It appeared to be injured, though there were no visible external injuries.

"My main concern is getting my child proper medical care," the woman said. "We believe he's dislocated his arm, though we're waiting for imaging to confirm. We've been sitting here for hours. The staffing and resources at this hospital are severely lacking. What are you going to do about it?"

She wasn't angry; she was merely curious. She'd been part of Miriam's

Chosen, but it didn't appear that she was going to write us off immediately. Her main priority was ensuring her family was safe and well cared for, and she was willing to wait and see if we could provide for them in ways the priestesses hadn't.

I wanted to give her specifics, but like Nadine said, we couldn't make promises we weren't able to keep. We were still trying to gather information to develop the best plan moving forward. I couldn't tell this woman we were going to fix everything when we didn't even know if that was possible.

"We're going to do our best to provide this hospital with more resources so that everyone is well taken care of," I answered. It was all I could promise. I only worried our best wouldn't be good enough.

"I truly hope you're right," she said, before dropping her head. "I've gotten that answer from the priestesses before, and they never came through."

It was disheartening to know that wasn't the answer I'd wanted to give her. I wished I could provide more, but I didn't know how we were going to do that right now.

"Lucas, Nadine." Onyx gestured us over, and we stepped out into the hall. "I ran into Dr. Tracey in the hall. She's willing to speak with you."

Down the hall, I saw a woman I recognized in a white lab coat. It was Dr. Anna Tracey, Nadine's nephrologist who we'd met during the kidney transplant. She reached out to shake our hands when we approached.

"Nadine, Lucas, it's nice to see you again," she said. "I only have a few minutes, but Onyx says you're here to listen to our concerns. I'd like to know what the Imperium Council plans to do to rectify the budget issues we've been facing."

"That's what we're here to figure out," I told her. "What would you say are your main concerns?"

Dr. Tracey pursed her lips. "My main concern is that this hospital won't be able to continue treating patients, and that it will completely shut down within the year. People are losing trust in us, and we aren't able to provide them with the level of care they deserve. They believe we don't care about our patients, but that couldn't be further from the truth. We want everyone to be taken care of, but we simply don't have enough resources to go around. We've already been forced to shut down several patient wards, because we don't have the staff or the medical supplies to keep them running. So many of our nurses and doctors left town to find work elsewhere, and we've used up everything trying to treat the patients here."

"What would be the most help to this hospital?" Nadine asked. "What if we sent volunteers?"

"We already have volunteers, but without proper medical training and licensing, they can only help so much," Dr. Tracey said. "What we need is money. In the last year, the priestesses diverted the bulk of our funding for themselves. We had to fire staff, as well as pick and choose which medications and supplies are a priority. Non-life-threatening illnesses have gone untreated, but we can't keep these people waiting around forever. We need you to restore our funding, so we can bring back our staff, purchase more medical supplies, and give these people the care they deserve."

"Thank you for the valuable insight," I told her. "We will do our best."

I heard the words come out of my mouth again, and I hated that it was the only thing I could say. I was a priest, and I was supposed to have power, but it was difficult to wield power without proper resources.

"What exactly do you plan to do?" Dr. Tracey cocked an eyebrow. We needed to give these people *specifics*, but we didn't have the money sitting around to simply hand over.

"We'll ask for resources and assistance from *Hok'evale*," I offered. "They've been willing to help us before, and I'm sure they will again."

It wasn't enough, and we all knew that. Assistance may help alleviate some of the burden, but it wasn't a long-term solution, and *Hok'evale* had their own people to provide for. Furthermore, they were on the other side of the country. I was the only person in the coven who could create portals to get our people to their healers quickly, and I could only transfer a few people at a time on days when my powers weren't affected by the Waning. We could ask for help with the worst of our injured, but *Hok'e-vale's* clinic was already full of refugees from supernatural nations across the world. They couldn't take care of themselves and a whole witch city on top of it.

Dr. Tracey left with a frown on her face. She'd obviously been hoping for a better answer.

I turned to Nadine and Onyx. "We need to come up with a real plan, because I can't keep promising these people our best and giving them jack shit in return."

"What can we possibly tell them?" Nadine asked desperately. "They're just so devastated. We thought people would react when we arrived, at least be angry or grateful—*something*. But it's like they've gone numb. They don't even *care* who's in power anymore, because it doesn't matter. They feel their lives are over. The priestesses sucked the life right out of them."

Onyx frowned. "It doesn't look good if you two are in the most powerful position in the coven and even *you* are completely helpless. If we can't change things in the coven, they'll throw you off the council."

"Worse than that," I muttered. "Things are still tense around here. It's a possibility people could get angry at the lack of progress and blame us for it. We could still hang."

"There have to be resources we can utilize that aren't reliant on money," Nadine insisted. "We can trade and barter with other supernatural societies to obtain resources. We can utilize volunteers, and we can provide incentives of some sort to get businesses back off the ground. Once our economy is going again, we can fund the hospital. We just have to move quickly."

"It sounds nice when you say it, but our best resource for trade is magical potions, and without access to ingredients, we aren't going to be able to trade anything," I pointed out. "Volunteers are nice, but people can't give their time when they're struggling to survive—"

*Kaboom!*

I was cut off by the sound of an explosion. My heart leapt as the ground shook beneath us. The blast sent us flying off our feet so fast that none of us managed to cast a shield in time. I landed hard against the floor as building materials rained down around us.

My ears rang, and it took me a moment to orient myself. Nadine and Onyx lay beside me, but the waiting room we'd just left had caved in. There was still some structure to the building, but the hall was covered in dangerous debris, and dust billowed into the air.

Nadine scrambled to her feet and shouted something, but I couldn't hear it. I shook my head, and the ringing in my ears began to subside. The sound of an alarm grew louder, and screams filled the air.

"We need to search for survivors!" I heard Nadine shout.

Onyx was already following her, and the girls climbed over rubble to get back to the radiology waiting room. I shook off the shock and quickly got to my feet. We'd been on the edge of the blast zone. If we'd been only a few more feet down the hallway, we'd have been crushed under the rubble.

"I'm right behind you!" I called over the sound of the alarm. I cast a shield around us, so that if any remaining debris fell, we wouldn't be injured by it.

The radiology department hadn't been far from where we'd been standing, but it seemed like a mile as we traversed the rubble. The alarm continued to blare, but the panicked screaming that we'd heard had faded. The hospital must've evacuated.

As we came closer to the worst of the blast, it became abundantly clear that we weren't going to find any survivors. There was too much rubble, and this waiting room had been too close to the explosion.

Then we heard it—a distant whimper. "Priestess Nadine?" an elderly female voice called out.

"It's Rose!" Nadine cried as she jumped over a pile of rubble to get to her.

I didn't see Rose anywhere. Then Nadine knelt next to a pile of debris, and I saw a wrinkled hand reaching out for her. Rose was pinned beneath pieces of concrete and building materials. I quickly came to her side to see there was a small hole in which we could see through. Rose was lying on her back, and a small but weak shield shimmered around her. She'd been quick enough to cast it so that she hadn't been crushed.

"I don't know how long I can hold it," Rose whimpered weakly.

"I'll hold the shield," I told her. "Onyx, go find as many Mentalists with telekinesis as you can. We need help moving the rubble! Call Chloe, too. We're going to need her."

Onyx took off immediately to go find help.

Nadine took Rose's hand in hers. "It's going to be all right. Lucas and I are here, and we aren't leaving."

I formed a shield around Rose. I tried expanding it outward to push the rubble aside, but it was so heavy that it required all my strength. The rubble shifted, and several pieces tumbled over each other, nearly knocking into Nadine and me.

"Lucas, stop," Nadine pressed. "Wait until the Mentalists arrive. We have to work together."

I'd be lying if I said I wasn't panicking. This was a deliberate attack, and unless we found out who did it, it was going to happen again.

Mere moments passed before Onyx returned with a team of doctors and other medical staff. They'd already been on their way when they heard the explosion, and they quickly surrounded Rose to help get her to safety. Mentalists used telekinesis to carefully remove the rubble, then they levitated Rose into the air and hurried off to another ward to provide immediate care. Other staff members looked for more survivors, but I wasn't sure we'd find any.

Onyx gestured us over, and Nadine and I went to her side. The worried look on her face scared me. "Did you get a hold of Chloe?" I asked.

"I did, and she's already on her way. There's something you're going to want to see," Onyx said hollowly. "You should both follow me."

Onyx led us back down the hall, and it seemed to take forever before we reached an area that wasn't covered by debris. Onyx took us outside into the parking lot, and she pointed upward. My stomach turned to stones, and Nadine grabbed on to me tightly. There in the sky was a message, written out in dark smoke—a spell obviously cast by whoever had caused this.

*Long live our rightful priestesses!*

I didn't know who was specifically responsible, but it was obviously someone within the priestesses' cult.

Tires squealed, and a black car with gold trim came screeching to a halt in front of us. It was Priestess Lilian's car, but Chloe had claimed it as her own once her grandmother left town. It was really fancy and belonged to the family trust, so Chloe technically had a rightful claim to it. Chloe jumped out of the car. She didn't even look up at the writing in the sky, as if she'd been watching it the whole ride here.

I still couldn't take my eyes off the smokey black words. "If they wanted to target Nadine and me, why take these other innocent people with them?"

"People like this don't care about the sick," Nadine said hollowly. "They think disabled people take up resources, and they surely believe the ill are the same people who put us in power."

Chloe marched up to us, looking ready to kick someone's ass. "Make no mistake, Lucas, this wasn't just an attack on you. It was an attack on us all, to destabilize the coven and create distrust in the new Imperium Council. I just received word from Miles. We know who did this."

"Miles has only been leading the police force for a week. He's already caught the guy?" Nadine asked.

"No, they've fled," Chloe replied. "The Executors that were locked up in jail are gone—every single one of them."

"What!?" I roared. "How could this happen?"

Chloe shook her head. "We don't know. Miles went on his lunch break, and when he came back to the station, the cell doors were unlocked, and the Executors had taken off. Miles is sheriff now, but other people stepped up to help him out with the police force. One of the volunteers must've helped the Executors escape."

It was the only explanation, because the Executors couldn't have gotten out by themselves. The jail cells were made of noxite bars.

"Miles received a call from a witness saying they saw the Executors heading toward the hospital. The witness watched them cast a spell to blow up the radiology wing," Chloe explained. "Miles and his team are patrolling the nearby streets, but the Executors are gone."

"Fuck!" I growled, kicking a rock so hard it skidded halfway across the parking lot. "We should've been more prepared! If someone on the police force betrayed the coven, that means there are more people inside the city *right now* willing to help the priestesses. Someone who was supposed to be on our side helped them escape. There are more people willing to turn their backs on us right now than those who are willing to help us!"

We knew we'd be met with backlash, but I didn't think the coven would continue the priestesses' torment of murdering innocent people. The reality was harrowing.

Anyone could turn on us at any time. We had no way of knowing who was already plotting their next move. Betrayal could come from anyone…

Even someone we trusted.

*Continue The Witch's Fate to defeat the priestesses and save the coven!*

# BONUS OFFERS

Find coloring pages, games, quizzes, and bonus content at hiddenlegendsbooks.com.

Join the *Orenda Academy: Hidden Legends Fan Group* on Facebook for all things Hidden Legends!

Check out the *College of Witchcraft Official Playlist* on Spotify!

Never miss a new release! Join Alicia's email list at aliciaradesauthor.com/newsletter.

# About the Author

Alicia Rades is a USA Today bestselling author of young adult and new adult paranormal fiction. When she's not dreaming up magical stories, she's either binge-watching Netflix, meditating, or spending time with her family. She has an unhealthy obsession with psychic characters and writes with a deck of tarot cards next to her computer.